THE ADVENTURES OF
GOODNIGHT & LOVING

THE ADVENTURES OF
GOODNIGHT
& LOVING

LESLIE THOMAS

PRICE STERN SLOAN

Los Angeles

Copyright © 1986 by Leslie Thomas
Published by Price Stern Sloan, Inc.
360 North La Cienega Boulevard
Los Angeles, California 90048
First published in Great Britain

10 9 8 7 6 5 4 3 2

Library of Congress Cataloging-in-Publication Data

Thomas Leslie, 1931-
   The adventures of Goodnight and Loving / by Leslie Thomas.
      p.   cm.
   ISBN 0-89586-844-X : $17.95
   I. Title.
PR6070.H647A67   1989
823'.914—dc19   89-3873
                                                          CIP

Dedicated to Paul Gauguin
and other men who have run away
– and discovered the consequences

There was some books . . .
One was *Pilgrim's Progress* about
a man that left his family,
it didn't say why.

Mark Twain, *Huckleberry Finn*

I

He had missed yet another day of summer. He had known it all along, of course; the sun segmenting the streets outside the office window and the bouncing Thames bearing its boats to God-knows-where, but he realised it again with familiar, almost programmed, certainty when the train had cleared London and he saw the man fishing beside the green river. His heart, his eyes and his mouth fell simultaneously. At 6.30 the man was unfailingly there and even when George was required to stay late and it was 8.30 or even 9, there he was with his rod, as if he had spitefully waited. Even when George looked down he could not resist looking up again. Staring from the train he would have given quite a lot to see that stranger topple into the weeds and water just as they travelled by. To see his tackle splash, to view his hat floating away. Damn him.

He was alone in the first-class compartment. His customary evening companion, a puce-skinned, globular man, a turnip in City clothes, invariably alighted at Hartsbourne with a disgruntled grunt, a sort of 'here we go again', as if he dreaded leaving the train and going home, a farewell George acknowledged by looking up from his paper. It was their only communication. They were like a pair of travelling Trappists. Once the man had departed there was no need for George to read the newspaper any longer. Two more stops, a few more acres of evening sun unrolled across fields, and the fisherman would appear and mercifully be gone, and then it was time for him to leave the train at Shillington. The compartment, the fellow traveller, the fisherman, Hartsbourne, Shillington, his office, the editor, the documents, the threatening letters, Fenner at the other desk, lunchtime, afternoon tea, home, Felicity, his stamps, dinner, television, and bed, all slotted into place, like patterned dots or holes or whatever they were, into a computer. Next week he was going to Cornwall.

George Goodnight was a man of forty-three who was half-used, in whom ambition, activity and even avarice had diminished to vanishing point, desire had become stilled; a man who had put on the habit of life. It was, he well knew, all too early.

At one time, not so long before, he had been truly alive. He had enjoyed books, listened to music and, on occasions, made love with his wife. In addition he had met a young woman in Pimlico and enjoyed the secrecy of that. But now it had all become too much trouble. The fat was on him. Everything else had dried or drained. He never went to concerts, he fumbled through both books and love-making.

Over only five years or so he had withdrawn, pulled away, from the *feel* of living, hiding himself behind the husk that was a company lawyer. In his working life as the legal adviser to a morning newspaper, he concealed himself behind a façade of pompous references and precedents, which he often quoted to frighten people away. 'Barnes versus Quilling,' he would mutter at some conversational advance. 'Venney versus Redbolt Properties' at another. It was enough to warn most people off. Sometimes he would walk in the Embankment Gardens for a few moments of solitary sunshine. His great solace was his intimate moments with his stamp collection.

George would have liked to blame his wife Felicity, and often he did. She spent much time at the hairdresser's, the Friends of the Cottage Hospital meetings or the conclaves of Conservative Women. She had mentioned standing for election to the local council. They were determined activities, programmed to prevent her running to intellectual and emotional fat as he had done. Neither, if asked, could have recalled the last time they ever laughed together. Tina, Felicity's daughter, who was like a window in his life, had gone away to school, a voice on the telephone. George Goodnight was an everyday desolate man, bored, routined, unhappy and lazy.

At Shillington the ticket collector discharged his joke as familiar as the evening star: 'Goodnight, Mr Goodnight.' George had lived with it, and similar, for years. At school they had called him Bye-Byes. He walked across the broken stones of the station yard to where Felicity would be, and was, waiting with the car. He opened the door, climbed in, threw his briefcase in the back and kissed her all in one movement, born of familiarity. The kiss almost missed her and he had a quick feeling that she had very nearly pulled away. Her face and neck were ruddy. She had been sunbathing in the garden. 'How was it?' she asked, meaning his day. She was fair-haired, forty and fed up.

'Claustrophobic not to say catastrophic,' he answered buckling the seatbelt, another confinement. He looked from the window at the older cottages, once part of the Hertfordshire hamlet, now merely an addendum to the modern houses, like elderly relatives hanging around their grown grandchildren. He tried to think of something to tell her. Eventually he said: 'Burtenshaw's got the paper in trouble again.'

'You don't like Mr Burtenshaw,' she commented without taking her eyes from the road. At one time she would probably have turned to him.

George shrugged in the seat. 'It's called jealousy,' he said honestly. 'He's an arrogant, uneducated bastard.' His voice dropped hopelessly. 'And he goes to Paris and Istanbul and places like that.'

'And you're going to Cornwall,' she replied so mockingly that he glanced sharply towards her.

He said: 'He costs the *News* thousands. All the damn time. His travelling, his high and mighty living, and then we have to clear up his mess after him. Usually settling out of court.'

They were approaching their house now, peering through its own trees, in the area curiously called Uplands Valley. George had never inquired why, although when they had first lived there he had intended to find out. Now even that ambition had diminished. She drove through the farm gate. Their dog had died six months before and George still missed the excitement of his welcome. They had hung back from having another, as some couples might have deferred having children because they were uncertain of the future. They had no children either, although they had Tina from Felicity's first marriage.

'We ought to get another dog,' he said as firmly as he could. 'I miss old Rex running up over the lawn.' Rex versus Rex, the famous dog-bite case, he thought. These days he kept his jokes inside.

'Not now,' she replied just as firmly. Then, as if feeling obliged to qualify it, 'After Cornwall.'

'I wouldn't begrudge it to Burtenshaw if he wasn't so flameproof,' he resumed, grumbling as he got from the car. The evening sun, positioned between the beeches, caught his face, at once a greeting and a taunt for what he had missed.

'The *News* must think he is worth it,' she said. 'His name's always on the front page.' She walked briskly a few paces ahead. She was quite tall, almost as tall as him; there was a heaviness around her waist. She was wearing a sun dress, white with dots, that he did not recall seeing before. Her breasts, too, were fuller than they had been. She bent still gracefully at the knees and rearranged the blooms in an ornamental tub, leaving them looking much the same. 'Don't forget tomorrow,' she said casually. 'The Webster-Martins.'

'How could I?' he muttered. 'The Webster-Martins are unforgettable.'

'There you go,' she complained. 'You're truculent before you even get there. You promised, didn't you?' she regarded him challengingly. 'After the last damn time.'

'How could I know their cat liked brandy?' he asked. A small smile of remembrance and pleasure touched his solid face. 'Climbed right up her legs, didn't it?' He looked at her but she was not reflecting his smile. 'All right,' he sighed. 'I promise.'

Burtenshaw came in to George's office twenty minutes late and sat familiarly on the corner of his desk. George was glad that Fenner, the other company lawyer who shared the room, was out jogging. Clemmie, the secretary, was typing swiftly in the adjacent room. One day, thought George, it would be expected that *he* should go to Burtenshaw. Burtenshaw was smoking. He knocked the ash into the ashtray on a low middle table and then scattered it with his sleeve as he put the cigarette back to his mouth. He was portly and tanned, fair thinning hair and spiky blue eyes. There was a smirk adhering to the corner of his mouth; there usually was. Burtenshaw nodded towards the tapping of the typewriter. 'Glad to hear there's some activity up here,' he observed. 'Can't imagine how you stand all this silence.'

'Daily newspapers,' remarked George, 'are not all people in shirtsleeves shouting "Hold the front page".' George added, but then wished he had not: 'And where have you been this time?'

'Honkers, Rangers, Bangers and Sinkapops, old chap. Don't you read the paper?'

'Yes, yes, of course,' answered George abashed. 'I was simply wondering if you could remember. You get to so many places. How was it?'

'Honkers is awaiting 1997 with a fixed smile. So am I for that matter. I'll be sixty-two, for Christ's sake. Rangoon is miserable. Bangkok is its usual onomatopoeic self, and Singapore is like Croydon but not so sinful. Not a wicked woman in sight.'

'There is here,' put in George picking up a letter from the desk. 'To whit, one Mrs Teresa Cowler – or rather Ms, however you say that – who is going to sue you and us for everything we've got. According to her solicitors, Brown, Folly and Brown. Apparently she was not in the bed you alleged she was in. She was not even in the country you alleged she was in.' He added thoughtfully: 'Greaves versus Watcanil Newspapers.'

'Anyone can make a mistake,' answered Burtenshaw affably. He took the letter and, sniffing, glanced at it. 'She's another one,' he said. 'She goes to so many places. I've given that particular informant the shove. Takes too many chances. And he's too expensive.'

'You don't know how expensive,' murmured George. 'Seems like we're going to have to settle. Unless you have any other ideas.'

'One or two,' answered Burtenshaw. George knew he had too. The reporter stood up from the desk. 'Leave it for a few days. There's no desperate hurry, is there?'

'We're never in a hurry to be sued,' said George. He replaced the letter in its file. 'You'll let me know then.'

Burtenshaw smiled. 'Of course. I have a few things I can suggest to Teresa Cowler, and her old man for that matter. I don't think he wants to be seen in print again all that quickly. I expect she'll climb down. Don't worry, George.'

George winced inside.

'Been on your hols yet?' asked Burtenshaw scattering ash as he made for the door. He put his head into the smaller room and called: 'Get on with your work, Clemmie!' The frantically typing secretary laughed.

'Next week,' answered George before Burtenshaw had a chance to forget he had asked. 'Cornwall,' he said defiantly.

'Love it,' said Burtenshaw. 'Love it. Rio you can keep, mate. St Ives for me every time.'

'We go abroad in the winter,' added George defensively. 'Skiing usually. Zermatt. My wife skis, I drink.'

'Don't try both at once,' laughed Burtenshaw. He looked as though he really cared. 'Anyway, old boy, have a good time.' He went out of the door then put his head back into the room, catching George scowling. 'Have a wish with the Cornish piskies for me,' he said.

When he was sure Burtenshaw would not return a second time, George sat down at his desk. He fitted the desk well, it was large and he was a big man. His face was set, his forehead lined, his hair dark. Recently he had been invited to play in a veterans rugby team called 'Eventide' but he had declined. The room around him was oak-panelled with bookshelves occupying one wall and windows the other. To pull himself out of his own stare he picked up *Carter-Ruck on Libel and Slander*, a familiar volume, and replaced it on the shelves with *Chitty on Contracts, Clerk and Lindsell on Torts* and *Bullen & Leake and Jacob's Precedents of Pleadings*. At one time, when he was young, he once had a fantasy about writing a definitive law book or being the senior partner in a law firm. He would pick his under-partners carefully, so that they sounded appropriate and memorable. Goodnight, Dorn and Noone had been his favourite. It had never happened and he had never met anyone of those other names, apart from a man called Bert Noone who was now in prison. Nor would the definitive volume be composed unless, he thought fancifully, it might be *Goodnight on Lassitude*.

Fortunately the day was dull so he could afford to look out of the window without excessive envy. He stood at the casement. The Thames was proceeding eastwards almost below his nose, its surface like the skin of an elephant. A sewage disposal barge went heavily downriver and he played a game in which it was going to Rangoon. If the greyness was some comfort to him in his confinement then its continuance (the long-range weather forecast smugly predicted rain and below-average temperatures for July) offered an unpleasing prospect. A vision of Cornish teas, jam on cream like some dreadful wound, floated before his eyes. Teas taken in hunched little cottages with the rain slashing the windows, restless children demanding ice cream and chips,

14

and water dribbling from mackintoshes. Come on, come on, he said to himself. After all it was *he* who agreed to go to Cornwall year after year. It was less trouble than going abroad and they got the house, Felicity's brother's, for nothing in return but mowing the lawn and feeding the parrot. And there were good days when the grinning sea rushed, wide and white, to the shore. There were big blowy beaches, wet and full though they were with screaming kids, and places of interest to see when the traffic allowed. And there were pubs, of course. Sometimes it was quite reasonable.

It *was* him. There was no getting away from it. It was *him*. He sat down irritably and heavily. Clemmie continued typing briskly off-stage; something she wanted to finish before lunch for Fenner when he returned from his jog. Everyone was occupied. He had to be fair. It was *not* Felicity. Sulky she might be, but it was *his* fault. It was, after all, Felicity who had insisted that they went skiing, or in his case drinking, in Switzerland in January. He thought of her daughter Tina, fourteen now, wearing a red ski suit, coming down the white like a swift ladybird and he felt a smile wrinkle his face.

He heard the telephone sound in the other room. Clemmie answered it and called: 'It's for you, Mr Goodnight, the editor.'

George picked up his phone. It was not the editor but his secretary. 'He did want to speak to you,' she said. He could hear she was searching around the office suite. 'But he's gone now. He had to rush to the Connaught for lunch.'

'That's hard luck,' sighed George without sincerity. She missed it because she was still only half on the phone, still looking around. 'No, he's definitely gone,' she announced. 'It was a last-minute rush I'm afraid, Mr Goodnight. Anyway, it was because of that he was ringing you. He's supposed to be entertaining an American to lunch and he wanted you to take his place. Can you manage it?'

George sighed: 'Well, I was going out with Bo Derek, and straight back to her place afterwards, since there's not much happening this afternoon.'

He heard her giggle. 'You're quite funny, Mr Goodnight,' she said. 'At times.' He could hear her sorting through papers. 'I've got his name,' she said. 'John Honeystone. He's a newspaper editor and proprietor from somewhere ... Texas ... yes, Texas, somewhere in Texas. Here it is, Bartholdy. Quite a small place, I think.' She laughed. 'Can't be Dallas, can it? Anyway, he'll be at the Dorchester at one if you can manage it.'

'I'd ditch Bo any time for Mr Honeystone,' muttered George. 'What am I supposed to say to him? Anything in particular?'

She had the answer. 'More or less anything you can think of,' she told him brightly. 'It wasn't important. Just social. That's why Mr Moncur went to the other lunch. He'd more or less forgotten about this man.'

George replaced the receiver. That was one of his functions in this office, a stand-in for expendable lunches. He glanced at his watch. Twenty minutes. 'Clemmie,' he called. 'I'm going out to lunch.'

'All right, Mr Goodnight.'

Fenner came through the door in his blue tracksuit, sweating, pink-faced. George wished he would arrive elsewhere after his run. He could feel the warmth. The man was as thin as a stick anyway.

'Off are you, George?' said Fenner who was twenty-seven.

'Going to lunch,' said George. 'With a cowboy.'

'This town,' said John C. Honeystone, 'is some place for girls.' George glanced at him in surprise and liking. The Texan was neat, short and gingery. His marbly bright eyes gleamed across the restaurant, not salaciously but with the real interest of a collector. 'See those two,' he suggested. George did not need to look again since he had already observed them. They sat a few tables away, poised, painted, pecking young women gossiping with no glance for those around or the food before them. They drank like birds.

'We could,' suggested Honeystone, as if all that was needed was careful planning, 'just take off with them. Go some place where we could have fun.' He glanced guiltily at George. 'I mean all of us have fun,' he added. 'The girls as well.'

George twirled his soup. 'I'm afraid,' he said, 'that much of middle age is taken up with seeing unattainable girls across restaurants.'

'You're married,' said Honeystone giving the impression that he had made a difficult guess. 'Me too. Mrs Honeystone is right now patrolling your Bond Street trying to buy some trinket or some garment which will enhance her. She does it

16

every place we travel, and we just about always travel together. Sometimes I get to Austin from Bartholdy without her. But that's all. One time she used to warn me – about women – you know, 'just behave, honey'. Now she just says to be careful crossing the street, so I guess she figures I'm past it.' He sighed confidently. 'She'll return with the dress or the trinket and she'll be pleased with it, and she'll display it to me, and I'll say it's fine. But she'll still *look* like, and she'll still *be*, Grace Honeystone. That's her fate. And mine.'

George nodded, an admission tinged with admiration. He had ordered sole and the American beef.

'In Texas,' Honeystone said regarding the meat as it was served, 'they'd serve this on a bun.' He meant no criticism of his home place, indeed there was a suggestion that he would have liked a bun now. 'And naturally, there would be three times as much.' Without pausing he said: 'You have a famous name, Mr Goodnight.'

George, mishearing it as a question, shook his head. 'No, not really. It's a bit unusual though. There are no Goodnights in the London telephone directory.'

'It's a famous name in Texas,' shrugged the American. 'You never heard that?'

'No, I can't say I have. I'm surprised. We originally came from Devon. I think some of us might have gone over there.'

'Charles Goodnight,' continued John Honeystone, 'was a great, great cowboy. A drover in the days of the old trails. There's even a trail called after him in New Mexico, running into Texas. Named after him and his partner Oliver Loving. The Goodnight and Loving Trail.'

George was genuinely pleased. 'I'm glad one of us succeeded,' he said.

'He certainly did. He and Oliver Loving drove cattle where they'd never been driven before. Back in the eighteen seventies, over the desert where the herd would go wild for the smell of water. They were great partners. Oliver got himself shot by an Indian arrow and died of blood poisoning at Fort Sumner. He was the daredevil, the romantic one. Charles Goodnight was the kind of Gary Cooper type, I guess you could say. Strong, steady, not saying much that wasn't worth saying. He lived on until the nineteen thirties.'

'I've never heard that before,' said George. 'Not that I've ever taken much interest in cowboys and Indians.'

The American looked thoughtful, almost dreamy. 'When Oliver Loving died,' he related quietly, 'Goodnight strapped his coffin to a mule and took it back seven hundred miles to his home town.' His reflection deepened. 'You don't get people doing that sort of thing these days.'

'Not often,' agreed George.

Honeystone went on, almost hurt: 'All the glory now goes to politicians or goddamn people in soap operas. There is no room for ordinary men of destiny.'

George grinned across the table. He said: 'I've been to New York a couple of times when there's no one else to go, but I've never set foot in Texas. If I ever get that far I must get to the Goodnight and Loving Trail.'

'You can do better than that,' said John Honeystone. 'There's a place called Goodnight, named after the great man, and there are plenty of folks there of your name. There's also a town called Loving, in New Mexico, named after Oliver. You should see them some time. Give me a call in Bartholdy and I'd be glad to take you.'

'At the moment,' said George sombrely, 'I'm due to explore Cornwall.'

George returned to the newspaper office feeling heavy. It had been a good lunch and he had enjoyed Honeystone's company. They had parted with warm and unlikely promises that one day they would explore the Goodnight and Loving Trail intrepidly together.

'A cowboy,' he muttered to a motorcycle messenger as he left the lift on the top floor. 'Imagine that, a cowboy.' The youth put on his helmet and slammed down the visor.

Along the corridor, outside his open door, was a frieze of people silently peering in. On their fringe the tea lady rocked her trolley nervously, her expression indicating that she judged her services might be required at any moment. George hurried his steps and firmly pushed through the group who were mostly from the accounts department on the same level. Clemmie, candle-faced, was looking down at something on the floor. Elbowing through, George saw Fenner being lifted onto a stretcher by the two men from the post room who doubled as medical orderlies. They had put Red Cross armbands on their sleeves for the occasion.

When she saw him Clemmie said: 'It's poor Mr Fenner.'

Fenner opened his eyes as though answering his name. One of the orderlies said: 'Steady, steady,' not making it clear whether it was to the patient or his colleague who was lifting the legs.

Fenner smiled, a smile as thin as cotton, at George: 'You should run, George,' he whispered. 'Try running.'

They carried him out feet first. George and Clemmie went as far as the lift with him but there was no room for them inside. Other employees turned on the tea lady. As the doors closed on Fenner, for ever as far as they were concerned, the editor ran up the stairs, laden with lunch and ruby-faced enough to suggest that the next stretcher might be bearing him. 'Is he gone?' he asked; then like the reporter he once was: 'What happened?'

Clemmie was smearing her eyes. They all had a cup of tea from the loitering tea lady who had done the brisk business customarily associated with emergencies. During the Falklands war her trade had trebled.

The editor paid for all three teas, muttering oddly that it was the least he could do. They went with the steaming plastic cups into George's office.

'He just fell down,' sniffed Clemmie. 'One minute he was standing there quite normal, the next he was on the floor.'

'Heart,' decided the editor. 'Poor chap. All that jogging. Never did anyone any good.' He lapsed into the past tense. 'How old was he?'

'I'm not sure,' said George. 'Late twenties.' Clemmie nodded then offered to look it up. George patted her hand not to bother.

'I've told my secretary to call his wife,' said the editor indicating that he had thought of everything. 'We'll get a car to take her to the hospital. Where's he gone, by the way?'

'St Thomas's I think they said,' Clemmie informed him lugubriously. 'That's where they usually take them from here.'

'I'll get one of the newsroom people to check,' said the editor. He regarded George. 'Sorry I had to push that lunch on you,' he said as if it had been on his conscience. 'Couldn't be helped.'

George found himself only a little surprised at the turn of the conversation. 'That's perfectly all right,' he replied. 'It was quite educational.' He returned to the present. 'Poor old Fenner.'

'Indeed. Poor chap. It's the jogging, I tell you. We ought to run a campaign against jogging.' He looked thoughtful. 'Might lose readers, though. Perhaps I'll get a medical authority to write a feature pointing out the dangers, but carefully.' There was a pause and he added: 'Have a glance through his papers, will you, George. In case there's something important pending.' He had the grace to look embarrassed.

When the editor had gone Clemmie began to cry and George patted her on the back awkwardly as if it were indigestion. 'It's that jogging,' she confirmed. 'I knew he shouldn't do it. Sweating like that. There wasn't anything of him to start with.'

George said slowly, 'He told me I ought to start running.'

That evening it was raining but the fisherman was still on duty by his tantalising stream; George could have sworn he was grinning towards the train from below his hat. 'Hope you get pneumonia, you bastard,' he muttered.

Now, however, he had a distraction, a distraction which also helped to keep his mind from the gloomy and looming prospect of the Webster-Martins' dinner party. He would *not* become irresponsible. He had promised Felicity that and now he also made the vow to himself. *No* irresponsibility. The distraction was a sere newspaper cutting he had filched from a file in the *News* reference library, a single-column article from a journal now long defunct. 'Last Link with the Old Wild West' said the headline, and below it a dozen aged paragraphs about Charles Goodnight, the trail blazer, who had recently died in his nineties. 'Goodnight,' he read again, 'and his partner Oliver Loving drove two thousand head of cattle across the waterless New Mexico desert to Fort Sumner, where the United States Army had to feed seven thousand Navaho Indians held as prisoners in stockades. It was one of the greatest adventures in Western history and the Goodnight and Loving Trail is still marked today . . .'

There was more. The two partners, starving in the desert, were obliged to boil their cowhide gloves for food, like Charlie Chaplin had boiled his boots. After that, Charles Goodnight devised the chuck wagon, the first mobile kitchen, drawn by a team of oxen, which rattled along cattle trails throughout the West from then on.

George's train ran on through the soaked suburban land. Rain streamers, themselves like trails, wriggled across the window beside his face. In the motion of the commuter train he could almost feel the movement of the rangy horse between his thighs. He had never been on horseback in his life; he had scarcely been on anything apart from a few trembling childhood rides on a beach donkey at Bognor Regis.

His face became set and anxious as he read again about Oliver Loving struck by an Indian arrow while shooting it out from a dried riverbed. They carried him to Fort Sumner but he died of blood poisoning and Goodnight transported him across the desert by mule, seven hundred perilous, hard miles, to his home. Seven hundred miles. George's jaw stuck out. Seven hundred. Somehow it seemed more real than Fenner being carried from the office on a stretcher. They had said from the hospital that Fenner was in intensive care, but that his condition was stable. Stable. George found himself wondering if it was too late to start riding lessons.

By the time he reached Shillington the rain had diminished to widespread damp. Tentative birds sounded in the sodden countryside and concerned men emerged from houses to wipe down their rained-on cars. Felicity was not meeting him that evening because she had a hairdressing appointment at Jacques La Tour (Watford and Paris), a ritual preparation before any dinner party. He groaned at the reality. He was not sorry she was not there with the car. It was only fifteen minutes' walk. The careful gardens were scented after the rain, roses shone with drops, fuchsias dripped onto geraniums and African marigolds, the nearest Shillington ever got to the tropics. George began to walk home. Seven hundred miles across the desert. Eyes this way, eyes that, sliding side to side, watch for Indians. When would they reach water? When would this burning sun go down?

As he climbed the evening hill from the station George saw his neighbour walking ahead. Freddy Birch was a rounded, shiny man and he turned cheerfully as George called. Red-cheeked he waited for George to catch up. He was wearing a large pair of jeans and a blue and white striped shirt. 'Took the day off,' he said. 'I thought I deserved it.'

George was frankly envious. 'God, I wish I could,' he said fervently. 'Here am I, forty-three years old, and if I want a day off I have to blame the dentist, a sudden colic or the recurring death of my grandfather, just like any office boy.'

Freddy's cheeks puffed when he laughed. They walked up the long shadows of the suburb together. 'My day off only resulted in the mower expiring when I'd done half the lawn,' he grumbled. 'Mowers drive me mad. I had to take it to Waite's garage and you know how long that's going to take.'

'That's why they're called Waites,' said George. As he walked he opened his briefcase so that it hung like a slack jaw, fumbled and found the old newspaper cutting. 'I've discovered a sort of ancestor, Fred,' he announced. 'Take a peep at that. Charles Goodnight, cowboy.'

His neighbour read it on the move. George sighed: 'What a life, eh?' He surveyed the roses and rooftops around them. 'Goodnight and Loving, riding the range.'

'Don't think much of the idea of eating your own gloves,' remarked Freddy wryly.

'But think of driving all those cows across the desert. No grass to cut there.' He patted Freddy's substantial shoulder. 'How about it? You and me. We'll do a bunk and ride the West. Doesn't that appeal to you?'

'Couldn't until Friday,' responded his neighbour affably. 'Cricket club committee meeting. And then our Lizzie is taking her exams.'

'And the lawn's half cut,' George reminded him.

'The lawn's half cut,' agreed Freddy. 'And, of course, there's Cynthia. She'd be bound to notice I'd gone.'

George paused and sighed. They were almost at the brow of the hill. Swollen red, the sun was hanging at the back of a line of regular poplars. Even the sun was behind bars.

'Felicity would notice eventually,' George nodded. He remembered the coming evening. 'Talking about being half cut,' he said, 'we're going to the diabolical bloody Webster-Martins tonight and I've been direly warned about my behaviour.' He made a drinking motion.

'Put the cat up a woman's leg there last time, didn't you?' mentioned Freddy.

'Ran up of its own volition, mate. I merely fed it a saucer of brandy.'

Freddy smiled happily. 'Christ, yes, I remember. You told me.' They were at George's gate. They parted laughing about the cat. Freddy called over the hedge. 'Look at my lawn at the back, George. Half cut, half not. It looks like a fixed grin.'

George let himself into his house. It was cool after the walk up the hill. Felicity had been sunning herself in the garden. She must have returned early from the Library Circle or the Stray Cats League or whatever it was today. The lounger and the table, with the various glasses and cups set upon it like chessmen, were still on the back lawn.

He made a substantial gin and tonic on the grounds that his intake would need to be severely rationed later. Sitting on the terrace he consumed it swiftly and poured another. Holding that, he walked into the study where he kept his stamps. It was shaded in there. A low rosy light drifted quietly through the pleasing window. With the affection of familiarity he touched each of the bound albums before taking one from the shelf and rolling open the smooth pages. The simple action never failed to give him a sense of anticipation. At Bermuda he paused, as he always did, smiling to himself, and looked once more at his most treasured possessions. The three stamps, appropriately occupying an island on the creamy page, were overwritten in the pen of a long-ago postmaster. Felicity said she could never understand how he could merely *look* at them; once you had seen them, surely you had *seen* them. But she was pleased they were valuable. He turned the pages slowly. They always seemed fresh to him, adventure trapped in the pages of a book. Men had been known to die for a stamp. He heard Felicity's car on the gravel outside. He closed the album and quickly drank his gin.

The Webster-Martins lived in a new house built to appear old. Henry Webster-Martin liked to walk around prodding the timbers and saying: 'That's very old wood, that is.' Barbara Webster-Martin, with a face that might have been turned on a lathe, always fell short of resisting the temptation to tell her guests how much everything cost. Sometimes she disguised her weakness by relating what a bargain something had been at only hundreds or thousands of pounds. They had shelves of untouched leather-bound books and they played safe ethereal music, the Beatles or James Last, over their dinner parties.

'I don't see why we *have* to go,' grumbled George as they got into the car. It was still raining, thinly, smearing the houses, the streets and the garden trees. 'Even you don't like them.'

'Don't *start*,' warned Felicity. 'Not as soon as we leave the house. Please.' She arranged her dress like packaging around her in the car. 'They've invited us because we invited them to our last dinner party.'

He lunged into the driving seat. 'And why did we invite them?' He answered his own question, squeaking up his voice to imitate hers. 'Because they invited us the time before, and they invited us before because . . . Christ, it's like some ghastly game of shuttlecock.'

Her face when she turned was stony. 'Now listen,' she muttered, switching off the ignition which he had just switched on. 'Stop this *now*. Understand, George? Stop it *now*. If you start your nonsense tonight I won't forgive you in a hurry. I'm tired of leaving people's houses to stares.'

'All right, all right,' he conceded wearily. 'No rebellion. I'll keep quiet.' He started the car and they moved from the drive, the windscreen wipers making grimaces to match their own.

'You don't have to stay silent,' she said. 'For God's sake, why can't you converse like other people? You don't have to act in the way you do.' Her voice became decisive. 'It's the red wine that does it.'

'I like red wine,' he answered like a boy. 'And all the wine in this world is no balm for the inanities that pass for conversation around the Webster-bloody-Martin table.' He sighed. 'But I'll watch it. I promise.'

'Good,' she said more softly. 'I'm sure you'll find someone interesting there. Perhaps there'll be a nice young woman.' He could feel her glancing sideways in the dark.

'Anyone interesting,' he answered, not committing himself on her final observation, 'is bound to be at the distant end of that damned great show-off table, made of *old* wood, you'll remember, and costing four thousand eight hundred quid, which was a tremendous bargain considering it seats sixteen.' He became thoughtful in the dark. The headlights searched down wet and vacant roads. Television sets glowed like navigation lights in the rooms, revealed through picture windows. Lamps, bookshelves and prints fixed like the set of a domestic stage play.

24

'Has it occurred to you that nothing ever actually *happens* around here?' he said looking from side to side as if searching. 'In an age of violence nothing *happens*.'

'What do you want to happen?'

'There's bombs and robberies and rapes everywhere else. You just have to read the papers. God, there was a dead man found in a dustbin in Watford.'

He heard her sniff. 'I can always arrange for you to be found dead in a dustbin,' she said. He laughed like someone shovelling stones.

'Four thousand, eight hundred pounds for a table,' he ruminated. 'Sixteen around it. That makes three hundred quid per person. Reminds me of Venables versus Clinton, or was it the other way round?

She glanced at him oddly, as she often did now, but did not provoke further exploration of the thought. He would not leave her alone, however, and she began to fear for the night. 'What do you bet they have the Beatles Instrumental Hits, wafting over the prawn cocktail,' he pursued. 'Strawberry Fields Forever and for ever amen. Or the Last of James Last, over the pudding.'

'*Please*,' she pleaded. It was half a plea, half a threat. They were approaching the house now. 'Please behave.'

They left the Jaguar among the Mercedes and BMWs on the drive and crushed across the few yards of wet gravel. Strategic areas of the garden were illuminated by slyly concealed floodlights which extracted an added wetness from the rained-on shrubs and flowers. The bell warbled three mellow notes, like the opening of an out-of-season carol. A smirking pseudo-butler answered the call and bowingly took their coats. It was a charade because he was undisguisedly the local newsagent, who hired himself out for such occasions (and with his chubby wife did the waiting at the table). Everyone in Shillington knew them because they bought their *Times* and *Telegraph* from them each day, but at evening everyone pretended that they were different people as newsagent and customers became servant and guests and shifted from house to social house in the neighbourhood. George was one of the few who did not subscribe to the subterfuge.

'Hello, Boggins, old chap,' he said affably as his coat was taken.

'Bollins, sir,' corrected the newsagent whom everyone knew as Mr Catling. 'It's Bollins.'

'Sorry, Bollins,' said George. He was aware of Felicity's warning hand on his sleeve. 'What's the company like tonight? Any nobility?'

'Stacked with it, sir,' responded the newsagent sportingly. 'Stacked with it. Taken half a dozen tiaras so far.'

Further exploration of the theme was forestalled by the appearance of both Henry and Barbara Webster-Martin, who approached ominously to greet them. Their movements were contrasting. Henry was an oozer, sliding towards them as though on oiled skates, while she progressed in little bounces, springing like the bird she so sharply resembled.

'So glad, so glad,' bounced Mrs Webster-Martin, contriving to make each syllable a separate jump. She was doing it on the spot now like someone on a pogo stick. Her husband wobbled oilily, a genie flowing from a lamp. They exchanged meaningless small talk, walking into the room where the other guests were engaged likewise. There the hostess came to earth and teetered. She waggled a brittle finger. 'We've hidden our pussy cat,' she said archly. '*Someone* naughtily gave her brandy last time.'

'Good brandy too,' added Mr Webster-Martin. 'Seventeen quid a bottle.' His face lightened briefly. 'And she ran right up Mrs Burlington's legs, didn't she?' George thought he detected a smoulder of humour in his host's right eye and decided that he wasn't so bad after all. A man approached, his glass held before him like a begging bowl, and greeted George heavily. Felicity was telling a jagged old woman that they were going to Cornwall for two weeks on Saturday. '*Know* Cornwall!' uttered the old lady triumphantly. 'Know it very well!'

The man looming over George was called Henderson, a ponderous insurance executive. 'What sort of wheels have you got these days, old boy?' he boomed.

George looked down deliberately at his own legs. Webster-Martin poured him a second gin. At least they were not mean with the stuff. That was two doubles and two trebles so far, counting the ones at home. He thought he could smell red wine in the distance. 'Wheels?' he inquired. 'I have legs. Look, there they are. One, two. Want to insure them?'

Henderson was too dense to take offence. 'The car, old chap. The vehicle. What are you running. Not still that old thing?'

'Still the same old XJ thing,' confirmed George.

'You should get yourself sharpish into the Porsche club,' enthused the man, dropping his voice as one imparting secret information. 'Just taken the new one. My God, when that tool gets on the motorway it leaves everybody else white-faced.'

'Rex versus Jehu,' murmured George. 'I should look it up if I were you.'

Mrs Webster-Martin, her invisible strings jolting more gently now, had propelled the old lady who knew Cornwall towards George. 'I think Mrs Findlayson is the only person you don't know,' she said. 'She'll be sitting next to you at dinner.'

'Oh good,' said George.

There was a youngish blonde across the room, the wife of a stockbroker, who George had hoped would be alongside him at the table. They had touched thighs before. He shook the hand like a bunch of twigs that belonged to Mrs Findlayson, and said again: 'Oh good.'

'*What* shall we talk about?' demanded the old lady briskly. 'I do like to get the subjects for conversation clear in my mind, don't you?' She regarded George doubtfully. 'Cornwall,' she suggested firmly. 'We could talk about Cornwall.'

'Cowboys,' said George. He finished the gin and guiltily caught his host's eye. 'The Wild West.'

She looked rather shocked. 'Oh, now that's a subject I know nothing about,' she said.

'I'll tell you all about it,' said George as they moved to the table.

They sat down and Mrs Findlayson said: 'Cowboys?'

Moodily George surveyed the other side of the table. Felicity was sitting facing him but two places to the right. Alongside her was a bald man who was, so he said, chairman of the golf club greens committee, a woman who burst from her dress like puff pastry, and another man who had forgotten his glasses and blinked around distrustfully. The attractive wife of the stockbroker was at the far end of the table, as he had known she would be, half a dozen sets of thighs between them and where old Webster-Martin could get a good look down her opened bosom. George had managed to get the gin into his glass and some of it down his throat before they were ushered to the table. At his elbow was the opaque wife of the car bore. She smiled at him grimly because she had been in houses with him before. She made an immediate patrol into conversation. 'What sort of wheels do you have now?' she inquired.

He answered her civilly with some difficulty and then listened to the old lady's reminiscences of a Cornish tea she had once scoffed. Mrs Webster-Martin whispered to the man now known as Bollins, the butler, to increase the volume of the taped music while people excavated their prawn cocktails. Obediently, the Beatles tunes drifted through the room. Mrs Findlayson began to la-la to the music between mouthfuls of prawn and sauce-soaked lettuce.

'Fucking hell,' muttered George. He had not meant to say it. The words just came out. They were not very loud and the old lady sitting next to him did not react. Perhaps she did not understand. Cautiously George looked up to see Felicity's eyes spearing him from across the table. Some people, sitting near, stopped their eating and their conversation. George shook his head in silent panic towards his wife, indicating some devilish ventriloquist had been at work. He pushed his glass of white wine determinedly away and wondered if he should call for water. He *should* be able to handle a situation like this. God, all he had to do was to sit quietly and drink carefully. Red wine was being poured. He waited several tenuous minutes before turning concisely to the woman on his other side. 'I do think there are such a lot of twats in this neighbourhood,' he mentioned, 'don't you?'

'Yes, I suppose so,' she said unsurely. 'We don't get the blacks though, do we?'

Cowboys, he decided. He would have to talk about cowboys. He decided to address his thoughts to the old lady. A glass of red wine, which appeared to be his, had diminished and it was with mixed feelings that he was aware of Bollins leaning over to refill it. The trouble was there was so much bloody time between courses. How could they expect anyone to keep sober? Particularly in his state.

Felicity was fixing him like a sniper. The beef arrived and he quickly ate a slice to soak up some of the internal wine, choking heartily as he did so. He looked up apologetically and realised everyone else was waiting for vegetables. He began to feel unhappy as well as drunk. Carefully rehearsing the words beforehand he turned to Mrs Findlayson. 'A man with my name, Goodnight, Charles not George, was a very famous

28

cowboy,' he said successfully. 'He had a partner called Oliver
. . . Oliver Loving . . .'

She was still being unaccommodating. 'Cowboys,' she complained. 'I know not a thing about cowboys.'

'Stamp collecting,' suggested George hazily. 'Stamps?'

'I know nothing of stamps either. Let's discuss the sea. After
all, you *are* going to Cornwall. I had an uncle who was a
sea captain. Most illustrious, too. White Star Line. Captain
Hillberry Carter.'

Spookily, again as if the voice was not his, George heard
himself reciting to her:

> The Captain's name was Carter,
> He was a stupendous farter,
> When the wind wouldn't blow,
> And the ship wouldn't go,
> Then Carter the farter would start 'er.

He said it quite softly but he was aware of Felicity's amazed
and blazing eyes lifting from across the table. Desperately he
swallowed a whole glass of red wine. Throwing everything to
the winds he revolved on his other neighbour who, turning
defensively, regarded him as she would a wild man.

'There was a young man from the Cape,' he uttered, 'Had it
off with a Barbary ape.'

Felicity was trying to reach across the table to stop him, like
someone gasping and drowning, trying to grasp a bank.

'The Cape? The Cape?' exclaimed Mrs Findlayson desperately, knowing something was going amiss but unsure what it
was. 'Would that be the Cape of Good Hope?'

His head was flying like a flag. The table had become a
roundabout. Horrified faces swept by. He was conscious of
Felicity staggering to her feet and heard her voice coming to
him over miles. 'George, we're going. Right now. Everyone has
heard enough.'

'Oh, no, they haven't,' he rejoined extravagantly. 'What
about this one?' She stood up and he knew she was crying.
Madly, like a man who has killed once and cares not how
many more times he kills, he bawled:

> There was a young girl of Pitlochry,
> Had sex with a chap on a rockery.

Felicity was coming round the table after him. He thought she might even have a knife in her hand. Mrs Findlayson was howling: 'Pitlochry – I know Pitlochry!' He staggered round in the opposite direction knocking shoulders and the food from forks. When he was behind Mrs Webster-Martin he held onto her like a a hostage.

> She said to her chum,
> These stones hurt my bum,
> This isn't a fuck, it's a mockery!

His wife howled like a stricken wolf and after making another hapless rush at him, swerved off and ran out of the room. Webster-Martin was on his feet, his face like a white balloon. 'Time and place for everything . . .' he was mouthing. 'Rugby club and suchlike . . .'

'Just going,' assured George cheerfully. He staggered around and was caught by the hands that daily and unerringly sorted *The Times* and the *Telegraph*.

'This way, sir,' annunciated Bollins.

'Right,' said George agreeably. 'Better cancel my papers, old mate.' He fell out into the hall and then seeing the front door open fell out of that. Felicity was standing on the wet gravel drive.

'Can you manage, madam?' called Bollins from the door.

'Manage! Manage!' cried Felicity towards her husband. 'I don't *want* to manage. Never! Ever! Oh, you *bastard*!' She came at him with her handbag. He dodged away and staggered off down the gravel. She did not pursue him but stood weeping in the middle of the drive, trying to wipe her eyes with her handbag. He turned and shouted back at her.

'I want . . .' he began. 'I want . . .'

She strode towards him, the crying stemmed for a moment, her face like metal. 'You want. *You* want,' she grated. 'What do you want? Go on, tell me.'

He stared at her in amazement. She was remote and still. He took a deep breath as though that would sober him. 'I want,' he said brokenly. 'I want to *do* something, see. I've got to *do* something. Before it's all too late. I want to run away.' He gazed at her manically and asked: 'Don't you understand? *Sometimes men want to scream too.*' He made off up the drive again, his legs sagging this way and that. Even in his state he was aware of the silhouetted heads at the door and the illuminated windows of the house. He shouted back, for her and for them too:

'I WANT AN ADVENTURE!'

Even in the distance and in his condition he could see the shimmering of her tears. She walked quite firmly towards him. When she was alongside him she thrust her smeared face very close to his. She began to beat his chest with her clenched hand but softly, impotently. He despised himself for not reaching out and touching her cheek.

'I want an adventure,' he muttered lamely. 'Any adventure. I'm trapped.'

'Go,' she told him bitterly. 'Piss off.'

II

In the Bailiff Club he sat under one of the glowering picture lights which illuminated the pink cheeks and unremitting eyes of some far-gone counsel and, lower down, his own pale countenance. He had deeply and privately vowed never again to touch gin so he had a double Scotch instead. There were only four or five men at the bar because it was the time of day when the shifts changed over. The evening men would soon be in, mostly daily newspaper journalists, whereas the daytime clientele were predominantly from the law courts. Moodily George sat with his Scotch then, thoughtfully, opened his briefcase.

It was as though he were taking stock, surveying his resources, like Robinson Crusoe on his beleaguered island; planning something unknown although he realised it was merely a pretence, a game. His passport was there, always carried in case, as decreasingly happened these days, he was sent overseas on behalf of the paper. There had been one exotic rush to Rio to try and negotiate the serial rights of an absentee criminal's life story. It had failed but he had enjoyed his three hot days and had met a woman on the beach. In the briefcase was also his cheque book and he knew there was just under £1,000 in the current account. Another month's salary was due next week. There was a deposit account with a credit balance approaching £10,000, and he and Felicity had shares in their names. The house was worth £150,000 and had the tax-free, low-interest mortgage, through the company, of £50,000. The cars were paid for. His stamp collection was worth several thousand pounds. They were financially, if not emotionally, comfortable.

Also in the case were some papers, some contracts for his perusal, the annual report of the pension fund and the documents so far relating to Burtenshaw and his latest libel, and his old school magazine. As George moved his fingers along the

32

paper edges, Burtenshaw himself, also a member at the Bailiff, came in and stood loitering at the distant end of the bar. George made out he had not seen him but when he ventured half a look there was the reporter with his glass raised, even at that distance mockingly, in his direction. George raised his without verve and, to make a shield, he took from the case the copy of his old school magazine which had arrived a few mornings earlier. He had not opened it until now but with Burtenshaw still distantly fixing him he became engrossed. It opened at the Old Boys' Roundup.

'Richard Fearnley-Banks writes from Simla, Himachal Pradesh State, India, with greetings to all Old Surrians. Fearnley-Banks would be glad to receive news. If any OS happens to be in Himachal Pradesh State he would welcome a visit. His full address is: P.O. Box 4, Simla, Himachal Pradesh, India.'

George sensed Burtenshaw approaching. He was not the type to keep his distance. That was what made him a reporter. He wandered genially through the gloom, glass in hand, and sat down, legs spread out, on a chair opposite George.

'When are you off to Cornwall?' he asked deliberately.

'Oh, soon. Tomorrow actually.'

'Morning or afternoon?'

George bridled and regarded him with frank dislike. But Burtenshaw appeared genuinely interested and said: 'All-day drive at this time of the year.'

'Yes, well, we'll start earlyish. We usually do. Get down there about tea time.'

Burtenshaw peeped into his drink. 'Would you like one?' he asked half rising. He nodded towards George's glass which was empty. George accepted uncertainly. He watched the journalist stroll to the bar. He was served at once and returned with two Scotches.

'Grouse,' said Burtenshaw. 'That was yours, too, wasn't it? So Harry said. Is it all right?'

'Yes, of course. I only switched to Scotch because I had rather a lot of gin last night.'

Burtenshaw smiled as though he had learned something of value. 'Did you now? Somehow I can't picture it. And did you behave improperly?'

'I can't tell you how much,' muttered George. He began to wonder why they were talking.

Burtenshaw said: 'We're going to be without legal advice next week, then. Pity about the other chap. Fenner, wasn't it?'

'It was,' nodded George. 'Yes, a shame. There's always legal cover, of course. They have someone on tap if needed. You were going to sort out that spot of libel trouble weren't you?'

He thought Burtenshaw would have done nothing and he was illogically annoyed when the reporter said: 'Oh, that's all squared. You can take that completely off the file. I had a quiet word with the parties.' He took a drink from his glass and said: 'I wish *I* were going to Cornwall.'

'You're just taking the piss out of me, aren't you?' snapped George.

Burtenshaw looked sharply concerned. 'Not at all, old chap,' he said. George saw he meant it. 'I'd give a lot just to go down there with my bucket and spade like everybody else. Walk along the sands with my missus.'

'Why don't you then?'

'Because she's gone off with some other bugger, that's why,' Burtenshaw told him with quiet bitterness. 'You think that it's wonderful traipsing around the world at somebody else's expense, don't you? But it isn't. Not all the time. They only send me because I'm available and expendable. If I'm shot in Beirut nobody's going to cry for all that long. And when I go home I open the door and there's nobody there. I can't even tell anyone how dangerous it was or how boring, or how hot. When I've been away for a few weeks you can smell the disuse. It's like walking into your own bloody tomb.'

He finished his drink and accepted George's offer of another. While he was going to the bar Burtenshaw picked up the school magazine and was smiling over it when George returned. 'Old Boys' Roundup,' he said. 'Sounds like something to do with elderly cowboys.'

'Really,' said George. 'I'd never thought of that.'

'I think in headlines,' shrugged Burtenshaw. He appeared now to regret he had revealed so much and they drank their third Scotches almost in silence. Eventually Burtenshaw stood up and said: 'I've got to be going. I'm supposed to be pursuing inquiries, as the saying goes. Cheers.'

They nodded to each other. Then Burtenshaw went from the bar, the light in the door showing through his fair wispy hair.

George picked up the magazine and wrote down in his diary the address of Richard Fearnley-Banks in Himachal Pradesh.

Confronted with the truth, he had to admit to himself that he really did not *want* to go home. He was not afraid. No, it was not that. Why should he be afraid? The deed was done and he would have to brazen it out. It was not the first occasion. He could stand up to Felicity any time, even at her most belligerent. It was not that at all. He simply did not feel like going home.

It was still light when he emerged from the Bailiff Club, an ashen sort of evening, quiescent and empty. The Scotches, and the wine he had consumed with a shepherd's pie, were rolling about, low like ballast inside him. It was only nine o'clock and he knew there was a train at 11.30. That would be quite early enough to go home. He decided to walk, drift really, he told himself, meander on a generally northerly course which would bring him to the station in easy time for the last train. He went along the London pavements, almost deserted in the office areas, under the big dumb trees, looking mostly at his feet. He spent a few moments trying to step in the squares and not on the lines but it was hardly an adventure. There were some travel agents and airline offices along his haphazard route and he paused and studied their windows, his briefcase like a coalman's weight in his hand. Enticements and prices were displayed colourfully. He gazed at sunlit seas and youths and girls consuming cool drinks and each other under languid palm fronds; Spain and Portugal, France, Italy and the West Indies were represented; a photograph of Sydney Opera House, its roofs like the upended skirts of old women sharing a secret. He regarded the posters without excitement. That was not it. It was something more; something different. He could not fix it himself. How could a travel agent know? A mere assessor of fares, a surveyor and purveyor of amenities.

He journeyed on to Covent Garden, the pubs and restaurants amber-lit in the dusk, buskers playing in blind alleys, and watched, with sympathy, a man encompassed by chains trying to wriggle out of them. An old woman encouraged him with foreign cries and a small crowd on the cobbles looked on without fascination. George paused by the open door of a French café, alongside a waiter who had come out to watch, patently with real interest. The escapologist, who was old and worn, grappled from within the chains. His ancient assistant limped to a tandem bicycle nearby, a machine hung with brown paper bags and damaged suitcases, and took a collecting bowl from a bag. She dropped a few specimen coins into it and began to make the rounds of the spectators, rattling the bowl challengingly under their noses while, with an achieving and somewhat surprised grunt, the man slid off one of the chain loops. His partner shared his triumph and apparently his surprise but eyed him as if to caution against a too-quick escape as she rattled along the remaining spectators. Some put a few coins in the bowl, others stared resolutely, perhaps requiring evidence that the man could really do it before committing themselves to giving a reward. The lady hovered adjacently, bowl at the tilt, admiring her partner and uttering short encouraging phrases until he discarded the last chains and with a 'hoop-la!' shout rattled them aside and leapt to his aged feet. He stumbled as he did so and fell back onto the cobbles, an action which brought the first disorganised clatter of applause from the watchers. Seizing the moment the lady hurriedly retraced her steps with the bowl and nodded approval towards the star as if saying she thought they ought to keep that bit in the act. She made a quick swoop towards George and the waiter. The waiter had his contribution ready but George had to fumble for some change. '*Merci, madame,*' said the waiter as he put his money into the bowl. His tone indicated that he had waited a long time for this. The escapologist was metallically gathering up the chains. George said: 'I know how he feels.'

'*Monsieur,*' observed the waiter very seriously. 'They are different. They travel the world. They are artistes.'

Storing the chains away in one of their many bags the ancient couple mounted the tandem and pedalled away with continuing teamwork, the man, in the front, giving an elaborate hand signal as they turned right into the next street. Watching them George murmured: 'Next stop Marrakesh.' The waiter had gone back into the café and the other spectators faded into the dusk. George recommenced his trek. It was still only 9.30. How content and trusting the old couple had been, working together, travelling together, pedalling together. He *had* to trust her, after all, for she was in a position of power; she could shackle him up so that he found escape impossible and then she could *abscond with the money and the machine.* An echo of a precedent sounded,

36

as so often, in his mind. Was it Hogsnorth Christmas Fund versus Clancy'? He had a walking reverie of himself and Felicity pedalling the world like that, stopping at corners, doing their show, collecting the cash, and wheeling on to who-knows-where. That *was* adventure. But it would be no use. He knew that. He would get drunk and Felicity would keep wanting to go to the hairdresser's.

Singing was issuing from a yellow-windowed pub and, after a moment's consideration, he went into a bar that appeared to be equally crammed with people and smoke. Ordering yet another double Scotch he put his briefcase on a bar stool. He realised how soberly-suited he was compared with the rest of the customers, when a girl, sitting with a young man wearing a sweat shirt and earring, squawked: 'Come to do some abortions, mate?'

She squealed with laughter at her joke and the youth nodded first at the bulky briefcase and then shook his head at George as if to say: 'She's a one, she is.'

They were singing a raucous version of 'Goodnight Irene' and he listened for a while, leaning his back on the bar, but with the sudden worry that he should not attend too closely to the words lest he remember them and they emerged unbidden at some dinner time.

'Goodnight Irene, Irene Goodnight . . .'

Irene Goodnight. He liked the sound of it. Finishing his Scotch, he went out into the street.

The one double appeared to render him far more unsteady than the previous Scotches and the red wine. He sat for a moment on a· doorstep and immediately a lupine man approached and said: 'You waiting to go in, Squire?'

George remotely heard himself saying that indeed he was.

'Righto,' said the man. 'Auntie Gloria's there now. Give me the money and you can go in.'

'How much?' George's other voice inquired. 'For Auntie Gloria,' he added. It was like a far-away echo.

'Usual,' replied the man. He looked closely at George as if he had a plan. He had opened the door and they were in a grossly perfumed passage, painted a nightmare purple. A child's pedal car was parked against the wall and they had to climb around it. 'Twenty quid basic,' said the man. 'And then if you want any extras it's up to Gloria.'

Dumbly, scarcely able to believe it, George found himself handing over two ten pound notes and allowed himself to be ushered upstairs. Gloria, a damp woman in her thirties wearing a fat lace dress and pink bedroom slippers, greeted him without emotion. 'What do you want today?' she yawned.

'What have you got today?' he said bravely like someone opening negotiations with a costermonger. There was underwear hanging on a clotheshorse.

'Spare me the cheeries, mate,' she pleaded. 'I've been on all day. Do you want the rub-down, rub-down with oils, rub-down with pictures? Then if you want any extras we can talk about it!' She paused as if disposed to give him some friendly advice. 'Don't 'ave the oils if you're going 'ome,' she confided, apparently deciding he looked decent enough. 'Not if you got a missus at 'ome. They niff something 'orrible.'

'Oh, thanks,' said George genuinely. 'That's worth knowing.'

'And the bleedin' projector's gone up the spout,' she went on. 'So if you want pictures you'll 'ave to wait until 'Arry boy fixes it.' She leaned closer to him. She looked very worn, the sort of woman who would have been better off at home watching television. 'Why not just have a rub?' she suggested. 'Then I'll get you a cup of tea.'

'All right,' said George. He could not believe he was there. How could you just walk through a *door* and this happen to you? It obviously occurred all the time, you just did not see it. If all the walls in London were to fall down at one moment hundreds of men being rubbed down by hundreds of Glorias would be revealed. 'I'd love a cup of tea,' he said.

Gratefully she said: 'You're a good sort, I can tell. Just take your clothes off and lie on the table and I'll put the kettle on.' She turned to a stove in the corner. 'I just get fed up, like everybody else,' she called over her shoulder. 'Put your trousers over the chair, will you? This is not all fun and games, believe me, no matter what they reckon. If I 'ave to rub another bloke's bum today I reckon I'll scream.'

To his continuing dreamlike astonishment George had taken his clothes off and was about to lie down on the table when she interrupted.

''Old on a mo',' she said, leaving the kettle. 'I'll put a clean sheet on.' She took a sheet from a pile and spread it across the table with a housewifely flourish. 'I'll do your back while the

38

water's boiling,' she suggested. 'Put your bum face up, will you?' Obediently he turned over. She began to massage him offhandedly. A rub here, a squeeze there. Her hands were heavy despite the lack of effort. 'Been on your holidays yet?' she inquired.

Before he had a chance to answer she had gone away to deal with the kettle. He heard her pouring the water into the pot. 'I'll let it stand a minute,' she said returning.

'I'm going tomorrow,' he said, his face against the sheet.

'Oh, on your holidays. That's nice. I can tell you 'aven't been yet. Your skin's too white. Somewhere nice?'

'America,' he told her deliberately. 'Texas and New Mexico.'

'Very nice,' she said as though he had told her Cornwall. "Ave a good rest. You probably deserve it. 'Ang on, I'll get the tea. Sugar?'

'Two,' said George. 'Thanks.'

She went away and he heard the friendly sound of pouring tea. He turned and sat up on the table as she came back with two large enamel cups, shining with cleanness. She put a towel over his lower parts. 'In case you splash,' she explained solicitously. She drew at her tea. George thought his was very good. Absently she undid her front and released a pair of large, damp breasts. They seemed to breathe with relief. 'You're entitled to them,' she explained. 'It's all in.'

George was sitting on the edge of the table and she was sitting beside him.

'I wanted to get into show business,' she confessed suddenly as if she had to sell someone. She looked down at her bosom and giggled sadly: 'I s'pose I am in a way.' She brought her cup up to her face like a mask. Her words echoed from it. 'Go there much, do you? America?'

'All the time,' George replied calmly. 'The West, you know. The prairies, the deserts, it's great.'

'Where there's cowboys?' she said.

'Where there's cowboys,' he confirmed.

'I 'ad a chicken strangler in the other day,' she reminisced. 'We get all sorts. What's your name? Or don't you want to tell me? It's probably not convenient.'

'I don't mind,' said George finishing his tea with a gulp. 'It's Oliver. Oliver Loving.'

*

Before he left she called him a decent cove and told him to come back whenever he felt like it. Outside in the street the youth who had let him in grinned raffishly and said: 'Orl right now, mate?' as if he had previously been ill or injured and was the recipient of a miracle.

'Magic, thank you,' George replied in the distant voice he had found it necessary to believe was his own. 'I'll come back for more.'

Although it was late a small child appeared, its bandy legs thrust through what appeared to be a cloth bag which was tied round its neck. The youth reopened the door and lifted the pedal car from the passage. While George watched he placed the child in the machine. 'Can't get orf to sleep,' he said. ''Ave to take him for a ride.' He smiled wolfishly at the baby. 'Don't I, mate?' The baby beamed agreement and the youth pushed him along the pavement in the lights of the pub.

George turned north, oddly feeling that he had achieved something, some minor exploration of another country, a contact with foreign people. Seeking to take a short cut down a tiled alley between two streets he almost tumbled over the escapologist and his partner. He realised at once it was them because their tandem was leaning against the dark wall. The pair were stretched out on the paving stones, sharing a ragged blanket and their heads encased in a big cardboard box marked 'Fragile'. Snores came from within.

He arrived still half an hour early for the train and loitered on the station among the late night denizens, people lolling on benches, dozy pigeons, a woman selling plastic beakers of tea from a trolley. He bought one and stood sipping it, observing those around. 'Gets quiet around 'ere about this time,' commented the tea woman, deciding he was worth some conversation. 'Settles down quite early really, compared wiv Waterloo. At Waterloo for years, I was. On the go, that was, all the time. But it tends to settle down 'ere. This travelling lark is funny altogevver.'

The train was chill and empty, and he sat hunched into a doze. At least, he thought, the fisherman would not be there to taunt him. He looked anyway after they had passed Hartsbourne station and caught his breath angrily as he saw a light, a single eye, on the bank of the river. Did that bastard never go to bed?

The porter at Shillington was surprised, even shocked, to see him so late, as though to be on the last train was a misdemeanour. He almost forgot his joke and failed to say 'Goodnight, Mr Goodnight' until George was outside in the station yard. 'Good morning,' George called back.

He did not feel drunk any longer, only weary. The summer night was damp, the houses dark with people properly abed, the compatible and the incompatible under their joint blankets. He thought of the tandem couple in their box; they were undoubtedly used to that now, a bed would be uncomfortably strange. They were adventurers. Artistes.

Slightly surprised he found that his key opened the door without trouble. He avoided their bedroom, however, and went into one of the guest rooms. Wearing his shirt he climbed into bed. He thought he could detect a suspicion of Auntie Gloria's scented room on his body. What was it she had called him? A decent cove. It made him remember that tomorrow, today, they were going to Cornwall.

Saturday mornings at Shillington saw shopping done and lawns cut. When George went carefully down to the kitchen, where he could hear Felicity moving about, there was no opportunity for an opening exchange before Freddy Birch looked cheerily round the door.

'Morning friends, sorry to barge in, I know you're off today.' He looked towards George. 'George, could I borrow the mower? My blighter still isn't back and if I leave it any longer the house will vanish.' He looked abruptly uncomfortable, detecting an atmosphere. 'If it's convenient,' he added lamely. It was Felicity who answered.

'Yes, take it,' she told him. They would not be needing it.

'Right,' confirmed George firmly. 'Help yourself, Fred. As you say, we're off.'

Freddy backed from the kitchen door. 'Have good hols, then,' he wished forlornly. His expression was frankly worried and he looked as if he wanted to ask them if there was anything he could do. But he closed the door and went across the garden towards the summerhouse where they kept the mower. Silently George poured himself some coffee from the maker and sat down with it. The morning letters were piled tidily on the kitchen table, a neatness that struck him as slightly odd, but only slightly. Felicity said nothing and went from the room.

'What time are we going?' he called once she had gone. He heard her walking upstairs without answering. In five minutes that morning she had not offered a word to him. 'We *are* going to Cornwall, aren't we?' he shouted challengingly out of the door. 'Good old, jolly old Cornwall,' he muttered to himself as he opened the top letter. Felicity reappeared at once, hurriedly, as if taking her place at the last minute at some performance. He saw her watching him with a sort of eagerness, the expectant expression of one who has a half-share in a prize and wants to learn how much it is. He opened the envelope and she pulled a chair out and sat opposite, strangely, and at last, intimate, her hands together in a roof under her chin.

He did not understand. Then he did. He opened the letter and saw it was from a firm of solicitors, Peck, Peach and Pilbeam, of Watford. Even Watford solicitors had solicitors' names. He read it. She was going to divorce him.

He lowered his head towards the notepaper and checked it again. 'Your wife, Felicity Margaret Goodnight, has this day instructed us to apply for a decree of divorce.'

A whoosh of anger engulfed him. He ogled across at her, trying to frame some words. She had made her face up, unusual for her so early in the morning, perhaps especially for the occasion, and she looked rigidly, but with a trace of triumph, over the top of her white knuckles.

'Divorce!' he suddenly found the word that had been staring him in the face. 'Di-bloody-vorce. Whatever are you doing, woman!'

'Applying for a divorce,' she replied coolly. 'As you might put it, Goodnight versus Goodnight.' She blatantly tapped the letter.

'Absolute nonsense!' he said dismissively. He stood but she remained seated, although it looked as if she might be ready to spring. 'You . . . you . . .' he blustered. 'You can't! Not now. Not today! WE'RE GOING TO CORNWALL!'

That did it. As though the spark of a fuse had reached her at last she jumped up in front of him. Her face was abruptly disarranged. *'WE'RE* NOT GOING ANYWHERE!' she shouted almost up his nose. He backed away and knocked over his coffee cup. For an instant it looked as if she might let it run

42

but she turned and got a cloth from the kitchen sink. She started to wipe up the coffee then thrust the cloth at him for him to finish the job.

'*Anywhere,*' she repeated. 'Never again. Not together, George Goodnight. Because I've had you up to my ears.' He found himself obediently wiping up the coffee. It was giving him time to think. He bent to wipe it from the floor. 'Not with that!' she snarled. She swung round as if turning to face an attacker and marched to the broom cupboard. She took a mop and rubbed the tiled floor furiously.

'But . . . a divorce,' he said. He looked about him seeking some nonexistent arbitrator.

'Divorce,' she confirmed. 'Divorce. Divorce. Divorce. And the sooner the better.'

'We're not going to Cornwall, then?'

'For Christ's sake! *I'm* not going to Cornwall. *Me – I'm* not.'

'You can stuff Cornwall,' he agreed with her. 'I don't want to go. Every bloody summer we go to . . .'

'Cornwall!' she finished the complaint for him and started for herself. 'I don't even want to talk about it. *You* go. Go and tell your dirty limericks to the piskies.'

'I'm not going by myself,' he answered, angry again. She was backing towards the door but she stopped and pushed her head truculently towards him once more. 'You *wouldn't,*' she said bitterly. Then: 'You'd be *afraid* to go by yourself!'

Afraid! Afraid! Him? Of going to Cornwall? What rubbish! What affrontery! Arrogant bloody woman. How could she be a friend of anyone, even the Cottage Hospital? He dashed about the empty house like a large wasp trying to escape from a room, his anger resurging. He went into every room and swore in every one as if each had personally insulted him. He swore twice in the bedroom, once at each set of pillows. But then he sat on the bed and made himself calm. *Now,* he realised. Now of all times was the time to go.

When he had regained control, still angry but calm, and he had overcome the shock, he saw that she had packed his suitcases for him. Hers were still empty. Cursing to himself he opened one and added his pinstriped suit in case he landed up anywhere official or was in some place where that sort of British

43

look might attract women. An adventurer simply could not tell . . .

From the window he saw that Freddy Birch had taken the mower and was obediently following it down the first swathe of lawn. George watched him, apparently content, even happy in his servitude like a ploughman of old. The snores of other lawn mowers dragging their masters sounded across the trees and fences. Automatically George glanced at his own lawn. It would need a trim within a few days. Who would do it?

Undeterred, however, he threw the cases in the back of Felicity's Ford. She had thoughtlessly, or thoughtfully, driven off in the Jaguar when she left for the shops or the hairdresser's or wherever she had so determinedly gone. Then, as a final thought, he took his best stamp albums and carried them tentatively, like a priest with an offering, across to Freddy through the trees. His collection of British Empires and Colonials to 1914. As Freddy steered the mower, swinging out behind it with some verve, like a suburban Roman on a chariot, he saw George approaching with the books and halted the machine.

'Freddy,' said George. 'Freddy . . .'

'Yes, George?'

'I thought you did that very well, with a bit of *élan*, you know,' said George procrastinating. 'Turning the corner.'

Freddy smiled. 'So did I actually. Cracking the whip over the horses, you know. Nearest to a bit of excitement I get these days.'

'Oddly enough, that is what I've come to see you about,' said George sombrely now. They had known and liked and partially understood each other ever since Freddy and Cynthia had moved next door.

'The mower?'

'No. Excitement.'

Freddy said quizzically: 'Really?'

'Yes, excitement. I'm . . . I'm going off for a while.'

'Going off?'

George said it. 'For an adventure. The wife suggested it actually. We're going to spend some time apart.' He glanced at his neighbour. 'Probably the rest of our lives.'

Freddy was distressed. 'Oh, it's like that,' he said but without surprise. 'I'm sorry, old chap. I knew things were a bit ribby.

44

Your dinner table recitations are the talk of the town.' He laughed silently and shook his head. 'Christ, that must have been wonderful. I'd have given anything to be there.'

'It's not been all that wonderful since, Fred. That's why I'm going off for a while.'

'How long? Where?'

George considered. 'I don't know how long,' he said, adding uneasily: 'Cornwall. I'll start off in Cornwall and see how I go.'

'So we can expect you back in a fortnight as usual,' smiled Freddy with relief. 'It'll have all blown over by then. Go and sow a few late wild oats in Penzance, mate. Get it out of your system. You want me to look after the stamps, I take it.'

George held out the albums. 'Would you mind? They're the only things I really value.' Freddy read the letters on the top album. 'British Empire, Colonies and Protectorates to 1914,' he recited. 'Sounds like *Mastermind*.'

Freddy left the mower and patted George on the shoulder. 'That's not *all* you care about, old son,' he said kindly. He took the albums. 'I'll keep an eye on these for you. I'll put them in my safe. And I won't tell anyone – not even Cynthia . . .'

'Especially not Cynthia,' pleaded George. 'She'll tell Felicity. You know women.'

'Right,' the other man agreed. He smiled. 'Your secret is safe with me.'

'I don't want Felicity doing anything to my stamps, that's all.'

'I'll guard them.'

'I'll be off then.'

He put out a hand and Freddy grasped it genuinely. 'Have a good adventure, old chap.' He paused thoughtfully. 'Have one for me as well, will you?'

George smiled but walked away with sadness. He liked Freddy. As he went through the trees he heard the telephone ringing and hurried forward. Freddy watched him go. 'See you in a fortnight,' the neighbour said quietly to himself.

Going into the kitchen George thought that it might be Felicity calling to tell him to wait for her; forgiving him once more in her specially weighty way. He hesitated before picking up the receiver. It was Tina.

'Aren't you off yet, George?' she asked. 'I thought I'd missed you.' At school they had a coin box and she knew how to tailor

45

her conversations. Her mother had forbidden her to reverse the charges.

'Just off,' he said. He knew the rules of phoning also. 'Your mother's not actually coming. I'm going by myself.'

'By yourself! Ace, George! What are you going to do?'

'Have an adventure,' he replied steadily.

'How wonderful! Wish I could come.'

'I'm going alone,' he said dramatically for her. 'Who knows where I may end up.'

'That's brill!' she squealed. 'Oh, George, you *must* telephone me. Tell me how it's happening. Promise?'

The time-up warning began to sound. 'Promise,' he promised.

'Mind you do. 'Bye, George. Take great . . .'

The call was cut off. Sadly he put down the receiver. He did care about more than his stamps. Oh shit, he said regretfully to himself. He surveyed the kitchen and then walked into the sitting room and the dining room. In the dining room he looked around and muttered to the empty chairs: 'There was a young girl of Pitlochry . . .'

He sighed once then turned and went hurriedly from the front door, closing it with an unintentional bang behind him. The Fiesta stood red as an apple in the sun. He got in and with no further glances back he drove from the gate. Only Freddy Birch saw him go. Freddy watched the car turn the corner and then went back to the mower. On the next bend he became reckless and almost turned it over.

George crouched like a hunchback behind the wheel as he drove down the everyday hill and into the shopping street of the village suburb. People crowded the pavements; children, husbands and wives and dogs, the Saturday sun on their faces. He felt guilty and alone. Once he had gained the main road, however, he straightened up and purposefully turned the car's nose south towards London. Suburban fields and painted houses rolled by brightly. Convoys of cars, all loaded with luggage and families, were on the road also. Many of them were joining the motorway and, as he intended to do, eventually turning West for Devon and Cornwall and their holidays. He tried not to look at the contents of the other vehicles. God, if Marco Polo could do it, if Mr Polly could do it, if Phineas Fogg went round the world in eighty days, if Gauguin ran away to the South Seas, if Captain Ahab pursued the Great White Whale, if

46

Livingstone, if Hoffman (of the Tales) and Don Quixote followed their visions, their dreams, their quests, if Oliver Loving and Charles Goodnight dared forth, why not George Goodnight? He was joining the long convoy of men who had risked adventure, or simply run away.

He arrived at the roundabout where the traffic was queuing to enter the motorway. It was one of the busiest weekends of the year. He chaffed as they crawled timidly with their suitcases piled above and their children bouncing about in back seats. 'Family fools,' he growled. Eventually he got to the junction. There it was, a signpost saying simply: 'To the West.'

'To the West!' shouted George defiantly and urged the car forward. Passengers stared at him from other cars. 'To the West!'

III

If the motorway had been clear his suddenly elevated mood
might have remained; he would have put his foot on the
accelerator and driven swiftly towards possible adventure,
perhaps even singing as he went. But the holiday traffic was
thick and there were the customary roadworks, festooned with
gay cones, cheerful lights and celebratory flags or bunting
which brought the westward moving convoys to slow and then
to stop. George crouched cursing to himself. In the old days the
adventurer would have galloped gallantly over an untrammelled
horizon without a multitude of morons carting their moronic
kids to the bastarding seaside. There was a cassette in the car
stereo, its nose poking out suggestively. He gave it a push. He
failed to share Felicity's taste in music either, and he groaned
unsurprised when a lachrymose lady began to lament lost love.

When would Felicity hear that favourite regret again? When
would she next be in this car? When would *he* be in *his* car
again? What was to happen to them? The people surely, but
the cars as well. An inventory of personal possessions paraded
through his mind as he waited in the unmoving traffic. His
thoughts progressed like the conveyor belt of prizes in a
television quiz game. Furniture, lamps, books, the beds, the
pictures on the walls, the television set, the things that had
been accumulated over the ten years of their marriage. *His lawn
mower*. Who would be using his lawn mower, pressing the
button for that easy electric start of which he had been both
proud and proprietorial? The domestic appliances, the very
nuts and bolts of his and Felicity's life; where would *they* go?
Who would adopt them?

Even in his original mood that morning, of deep hurt followed
by bravado, there had floated around within him, like a small
white cloud in a thunderstorm, the thought that it would all be
all right in the end, that this was all temporary; it would pass
away and they would relapse into their old life again, the

48

solicitor's letter discarded in exchange for promises he would fully mean to keep. They would cagily kiss and make up and he would go back to the office and she to the hairdresser's, or wherever, and each evening he would see the man fishing by the stream and return to his dinner and his stamps, strengthening all the time his resolve and guard against drink, despondency, and the rebellion of unruly rhymes. Two weeks of freedom lay before him, extending out in front of the now slowly progressing bonnet of the car. He would take that. He had never been away so long by himself and, after all, he had been *ordered* to go. There could hardly be complaint if he met some sweet and lusty fishgirl, or a secretary from Sheffield ripe for holiday romance. That in itself would be countable as an adventure. Modest, but perhaps all he really required.

Such possible compromises were working through his mind when the car gave an almost imperceptible nudge to the left, jolted along a few yards and settled down with a list like a holed trawler. 'Oh bugger it!' snorted George. 'Damn and bugger it.'

The puncture had occurred in the single lane forced upon the travellers by the roadworks, an avenue stretching to the very horizon of the motorway, lined by red and white cones as shoulder to shoulder as guardsmen. He stopped and got out. As he did so he heard the anguish rise behind him. Howling heads poked from cars. Children began to cry and wives chide. 'That's lovely, that is!' bellowed a face thrust from an old Cortina immediately to the rear. 'That's bleeding lovely!'

Taking a heavy hold on himself George glanced at the tire pressed down into a toothless grin, and then made his way back to the following vehicle. The road before him was now as clear as a country lane. Behind, the traffic seethed as far back as he could see.

'I appear to have a puncture,' he said calmly to the driver of the Cortina, an aghast man in a flowered shirt bearing the legend 'Honolulu'.

'Lovely,' said the man again but lower, appearing to ponder his lines. 'Bloody lovely, that is.'

George glanced around at the scenery as if he were missing some beauty he should appreciate. There were eight children and one staggered-looking woman in the car. Five of the children were crying and two hitting each other. The third, apparently placid, picked her nose and piled the harvest on the seat-back in front of her.

'We've got to get to Dawlish!' bellowed the anguished driver in George's face.

'Dawlish,' confirmed the woman. '*Devon*.' She nudged the man. 'Go on, tell him,' she said.

George examined the wailing children. The nose-picker smote the stock of bogies sideways. 'And you're in a hurry,' he suggested.

'Course we're in a bleedin' hurry,' responded the driver. Other idiot cars were tooting behind. 'We got the caravan from three o'clock, mate,' he added boastfully. Then as if contemplating a lawsuit: 'We're not going to make it now, are we?'

'You won't like Dawlish,' ventured George. He became aware that other angry men and several women of bitchy demeanour were approaching, in two Indian files, along both sides of the cars. Shouts and gesticulations came from them as they rocked alongside an excavation in the closed section of the road. Eventually they formed two long, narrow but threatening crowds, like queuing enthusiasts who have been refused admission to a show. The people at the front scowled and spoke angrily about him; bare elbows were waving in the distant sunlight.

'Dawlish,' reiterated the man in the scarred Cortina. 'I've got to get the kids to Dawlish.'

Everyone now began shouting their destinations like bids at a noisy auction. One man claimed to be going as far as Land's End. George faced them.

'How can *I* damned well help it?' he bellowed. Several of those near him appeared taken aback by his force and possibly his accent, as if a man with an accent like that had no right to have a flat tire. 'A puncture is a puncture.'

''E's stopping me getting my kids to Dawlish,' put in the Cortina man stubbornly. 'On their 'olidays.'

Angrily George rounded on him. 'You'll get your orphans' outing to Dawlish!' he shouted.

''Ey, wait a minute,' snarled the man trying to get from the car. 'Orphans? Who's orphans?' He could not open the door because of the other people. When he tried to force it he knocked a frail woman backwards so that she sat down felling half a dozen of the red and white cones. A man, apparently her son, pushed the door forcibly back again jamming the Cortina owner's leg in the door. He shouted with pain. The cones rolled from side to side. There was increased shouting now. Children bawled anew. A mêlée seemed possible. Horns were sounding all along the motorway as if some gigantic hunt were moving across the countryside.

'Listen! Listen!' Everybody stopped and listened. A big leaderlike man bundled his way along the line of protestors. 'Listen. Why doesn't everybody stop squabbling and let's get his wretched car off the road?'

George tried to comment but his words were lost in a universal approval of the suggestion. Men moved forward and in a moment a posse was pushing the injured vehicle down the single available lane of the motorway, with the authoritative man summarily inside at the wheel. At the point where the long trench ceased and the cones corralled firm tarmac, the big man turned the wheel and others pushed the barrier aside. Sounding a relieved cheer the drivers, wiping their hands, went back to their vehicles leaving George standing hopelessly by his car, marooned among the silent Saturday steamrollers and piles of gravel. As the Cortina went by, the driver upped a calloused two fingers, several of the tear-ravaged children followed suit, and the woman poked out her tongue.

'I hope it pisses down!' bellowed George after them. He turned and began to walk along the middle, between the roadworks. The cars streamed by. No one stopped and offered him a lift. Like pioneers their eyes were fixed on the West. On the other side of the roadworks, cars were going by in the opposite direction, away from holidays, back to reality. He thought perhaps he ought to ask for a lift that way.

It was the oasis towers of the motorway service area on the skyline ahead that deterred him. He tramped across the sand, gravel and cement as if he were navigating a desert. The sun was growing and it burned on his head. He took off his sports jacket. Getting to the service area took a long time. So long he began to think it might be a mirage. Eventually the roadworks ended, leaving him in the cleft of the traffic. He waited for a gap and ran across to the hard shoulder, continuing his tramp from there. Cars went by as if by conveyor belt, faces looking askance from their windows. He felt hot and dispirited. But

51

there, on the edge of the road, he detected a scent of mown grass and what he thought might be elderberry.

Eventually he trudged up the incline towards the shops, the restaurant and the toilet facilities of the service area. The fuel pump section was beyond. In the central kiosk, sitting behind glass like the pilot of a plane, was a youth with orange hair.

'Only take the cash and give out the games,' he said dismissively after George had stood in the queue of people waiting to pay. 'Nuffin' else.' With a quick change of heart, however, he gave George a plastic card which promised a fortune if it concealed certain numbers. George thanked him and dropped it on the ground where it was recovered by the next customer in the line who began scratching its surface expectantly.

'Is there a manager?' asked George.

'Benny,' smirked the youth behind the glass. 'There. 'Im 'obblin'. A Suzuki went over 'is toes.'

George turned and walked towards the bent Benny. He was helpful despite his injury. The breakdown truck had lived up to its name and broken down but he knew a man in a neighbouring village who might be persuaded to come out, but at some cost. 'I've got two broken toes,' he explained as they went together towards his office. 'Why don't you change the wheel yourself?'

'I'm not sure how,' admitted George shamefacedly, realising his limitations as an adventurer. 'And it's stuck right in the middle of the motorway. In the past I've always managed to get somebody else to change it.'

'You're the sort who helps to keep garages going,' philosophised the manager gratefully. He had picked up the telephone and was dialling. There was no reply. 'I'd come and help you myself,' he said decently. 'But I can't leave here, not weekends. And there's my toes. I can't put pressure on, see.' He demonstrated, leaning onto his left foot and emitting a little yelp of pain.

He suggested that George should go to the restaurant, have a cup of tea and return later. George thanked him and walked across the hot tarmac. The riot of the motorway filled his ears and nose, the rushing engines, fumes in the gritty air. His shoes were rimed with dust and he thought he could feel it drifting up his trouser legs. The sun struck the ground and flashed harshly in the windscreens of the endless belt of vehicles. Every moment they were reeling off and driving to the service area like racing cars going to the pits. He went into the restaurant and sat down unhappily. It was one o'clock. His shirt was damp. A waitress, a clean and rosy girl, arrived at his elbow almost soundlessly because she was wearing pumps and said: 'I saw you walking over with Benny, poor man.'

'A Suzuki ran over his foot,' said George looking up and oddly flattered by the intimacy. Her hair was fair as straw.

'Toes. Only his toes. But it must've hurt.' She looked over his shoulder at the menu. 'Have something cold,' she confided. 'The chef's been throwing stuff around the kitchen all the morning. He's a Pole.'

'Thank you for telling me,' acknowledged George. He ordered a ham salad with which the waitress returned, peeling off the transparent paper as she walked. 'At least you know *that's* not been on the wall,' she winked. He was only fifty miles from London and already the accent was rural.

Benny stumbled in as he was eating and said flatly: 'I got him and he went up to where you said you'd left the car. It's gone.'

'Gone!' George let a segment of tomato drop onto his shirt. 'How do you mean – gone?'

'Not there,' explained the manager unruffled. 'Half a mile you said, didn't you? By the steamrollers. He's been right along there and it's gone. He just telephoned. He's gone back home now. He charged a tenner.'

'But . . . I can't believe . . .'

Benny was standing on one leg, like a stork, shaking his head.

There must have been some mistake. 'I left it there,' George said rising. The waitress was coming towards him anxiously. 'I'll be back later,' he said to her.

'Right you are,' said the girl picking up the salad plate. 'I'll keep this clean.'

At the door Benny offered to drive him along the motorway so that he could see for himself. 'I can go slow,' he said. 'As long as I don't have to press too hard.' Gratefully George accepted and they got into the manager's blue car and limped out onto the motorway. They had to drive to the next exit and then transverse the bridge and return. Soon the steamrollers hove into view like ships at sea. Even from that distance George could see his car was not there. Opposite the spot where he had left it Benny pulled over to the hard shoulder and George stood outside and looked up and down the sunlit road. He got back into the car again.

'Call the police,' suggested Benny. 'They might know.'

They returned once again to the service area and Benny used the telephone. 'Won't be long,' he forecast putting down the receiver. 'Generally they're not long if they haven't got a pile-up or anything.' He looked down reflectively. 'Mind you, they never caught the swine who ran over my toes on his bloody Honda.'

'I thought it was a Suzuki,' suggested George sitting down in the corner of the office. The two o'clock sun glared through the window. Benny looked at him narrowly.

'How do you know?' he asked.

'People told me,' said George as if he had lived there for years. 'They all said it was.' Buggins versus Grand Parade Garages, he thought to himself, pleased that he recalled it so easily.

Benny looked thoughtful. 'Maybe it was,' he reflected. 'In that case I told the police all wrong. No wonder they didn't catch him. I could have sworn it was a Honda. It still hurt, whatever it was.'

The police arrived and appeared oddly shy at entering the office. George watched them through the window, two officers stiffly arguing in their patrol car. Eventually they both shuffled in. 'It's been stolen,' blurted out one of them before George had said a word.

'That's quick,' said George glancing towards Benny. 'How do you know?'

'Two officers,' recited one policeman carefully. 'Two officers ...' Removing his hat he ran his hand above his eyes. He glanced at his colleague and, as if accepting a cue, that policeman continued.

'Yes, these officers observed two men changing the wheel. Being mindful of the courtesy expected of this county's force they stopped and assisted. When they had changed the wheel ...'

'The two men drove away,' George finished for them.

'Yes, sir, that just about sums it up.' The policeman bowed like someone acknowledging a difficult deduction. '*You* left the keys in the ignition, I take it, sir.'

George nodded miserably. 'You,' he nodded to either side, 'were the two officers, I suppose.'

'Winners of the courtesy prize last month,' said the first policeman smugly.

'There are a few more obvious signs of courtesy than helping somebody nick a car,' put in George. 'Everything . . . my suitcases, everything was in the back.'

He turned and stared out of the window at the white afternoon, the bright sky, the streaming hot sunshine, the cars belting by, the pumps and the tarmac. The fumes filtered through the glass. He had only been an adventurer for one morning, he had journeyed less than fifty miles, and already he was marooned on a concrete island and had lost everything. He felt perhaps he ought to go home.

There was a basic motel like a large coal bunker at the rear of the service area and, at the thoughtful Benny's suggestion, he took a room there. Life on the concrete island was, at least, almost self-sufficient and he was able to buy a toothbrush and razor at the shop together with *The Times*, the *Mid-Wiltshire Chronicle*, a beach shirt (the only article of clothing they sold) and a bottle of lemonade. The amenities fell short of a bar although he felt a perverse satisfaction in this. He would not get drunk in his despair.

It was still warm at seven o'clock. The motel was little more than a prefabricated box but adjoined by a small courtyard with an ambitious pair of potted trees and some cowering geraniums. He had a shower, donned his Palm Beach shirt, and took the canvas chair from his room to sit in the sun's evening beams. He felt much calmer now, fatalistic. In a detached way, as if he were no part of its world, he read *The Times*. In the absence of gin and tonic he made the best of the lemonade. At eight o'clock he walked across to the restaurant, stopping on the way to telephone the police for any news of his car. There was none, but they had some clues, they said reassuringly. He was to try again in the morning.

The straw-haired girl whom he thought of as his waitress had gone and he felt a mild annoyance at this as a man might whose wife was absent when he returned home to dinner. Her replacement was a solid and sympathetic lady with a fruity Wessex accent. 'That chef's gone 'ome, sir,' she confided before he had even inquired. His story had obviously circulated the community. 'The night chef is all right. Can't cook much, mind, but 'e don't go on behavin' like that Pole. He's done a nice toad-in-the-'ole.'

George accepted her recommendation and had some heavy Wiltshire pâté to start.

'Gone and lost your car, I 'ear,' said the waitress as she bought the main dish. 'Bad luck. I bet you was off on your holidays.' She regarded him as if she was uncertain whether to proceed. She decided favourably. 'All your cases gone as well, Benny says. If you want some pyjamas I'll bring some up of my husband's.' She measured him with her eye. 'They'll fit all right.'

Astonished at her concern and kindness he thanked her but refused the offer saying he intended to buy another beach shirt for bed.

'Very cool they are,' the lady approved. 'And they *look* nice and cool, don't they, with all them trees and flowers and things on them.' She went away and he returned to wondering what he was going to do. When she came back she seemed to have been occupied in the same manner. 'What will you do, sir?' she asked. 'You can't stay 'ere the rest of your life, can you now? You could get a taxi to Trowbridge station and go from there.' She added thoughtfully: 'But then you haven't got any luggage, you poor soul.'

'And I haven't got anywhere to go, either,' thought George. At least the car had been a protection, a moving base, a cocoon, a safe house. Now he felt vulnerable, unattached even to a Ford Fiesta. He finished his meal, drank some coffee and went to the telephone. It was the right time of the evening to call Tina. One of the other girls brought her to the phone.

'George!' she exclaimed with delight. 'Where *are* you? Have you had any adventures?'

'Some,' he admitted.

'Ace! What sort? Where are you, anyway? I was playing table tennis. I'm all puffed.'

'I'm on the motorway. Well, at the service area. I'm staying here.'

'Staying? On the motorway?'

'Yes, my car's been stolen – with the assistance of the police,

56

I should add. I've lost all my belongings except for my passport and some money.'

He heard her draw breath. 'George, how exciting! What will you do next, do you think?'

Soberly he said: 'I'm seriously thinking of going home.'

'Don't!' It was nearly a shout. Her voice subsided. '*Don't*, whatever you do. Mother's been on to me. Oh, darling George, she *hates* you. She said you've done terrible, awful things. I should stay away for a long time, if I were you. At least a year.' The tone became confiding. 'What did you do, anyway?'

'The terrible, awful things, you mean? Your mother didn't tell you?'

'No. She *wouldn't*. Was it other women?'

'No, not at all. It was limericks, as a matter of fact.'

'Limericks? Like amusing rhymes, you mean?'

'That's correct. Dirty amusing rhymes to be exact. At somebody else's dinner party.'

He heard her young laugh. 'Oh George, how wonderful. Can you tell me one?'

'On no account. Anyway I'm trying to give them up.'

'Well, you won't be welcome if you go home,' she said, then, thoughtfully: 'At least you're travelling *really* light now.'

When he replaced the phone he felt encouraged. He *was* travelling light. Surely he was not going to turn tail at the first setback. When Goodnight and Loving lost their horses, they walked. The shop was still open and he went in and bought another beach shirt, this time with ice cream cones on a blue background, to wear in bed. He was starting to get a wardrobe together. When he walked out into the evening the sun had slipped behind the land, the air was grey and warm. Several cars were filling with petrol but fewer were driving west on the motorway. A group of crows sat at the side of the hard shoulder awaiting the opportunity to approach some tidbit in the fast lane. In the nearest car on the forecourt he could see a man and a woman quarrelling. The man got out to the pump and swore at the woman. He pointed the petrol nozzle at her like a gun. A child in the back seat burst into tears. George experienced a sudden feeling of independence and peace.

There seemed nothing more to do but to go to his motel room. From its window he looked out on the drifting light of his first day's quest for romance and adventure. Sighing, he acknowledged that on this opening day of his bravado it was nine o'clock and he was going to bed. He drew the curtains to obscure the evening and donning the shirt with the ice cream cones he got into bed, turned on the fringed light on the locker and opened the *Mid-Wiltshire Chronicle*. There had been a carnival at Trowbridge and its sensations occupied much of the front page, both in words and pictures. An abashed girl, carrying buckets on a yoke, topped a wagon of hay as carnival queen, maypole dancers were shown and a surprised and delighted man who had correctly guessed the weight of a cake. Other headlines caught his eye. 'Melksham Man was Drunk.' George found himself turning up his nose as he sat in the bed. After all, *he* had been drunk and yet he had never found fame in a newspaper. He pictured the words: 'Shillington Man was Drunk,' or even less of note: 'Fleet Street Man was Drunk.' At Salisbury there had been a successful Sale of Effects. He wondered if his effects now stolen would meet a fate like that. A man had been fined for urinating in the street at Westbury. Ah, the truth was coming out now. The skeletons. And what was this? 'Devizes Man Wins Prizes.' It touched a chord:

> There was an old man of Devizes,
> Had balls of two different sizes,
> One was so small, it was no ball at all,
> One was so large it won prizes.

He fell to sleep still reading the paper, awaking in the early hours of a wan summer morning. From his window he could see the pale light in the forecourt pay kiosk, and a figure sitting in solitary. He returned to lie in bed, staring at ephemeral shadows on the ceiling, made by some noisily journeying vehicle. He would have to go *somewhere*, do *something*. The few options revolved in his mind. After an hour awake he got up and put on his trousers then wandered like a daybreak ghost out into the forecourt of the service area. Corners of dawn were just showing, the pumps stood in silhouette like patient men waiting for work. He walked over to where the insipid light hovered behind the pay kiosk. The man who had been on duty all night was an Indian. He crouched like someone at prayer, speaking through the grille.

'Most pleased,' he said. He pushed a card through the slot

and George was able to read: 'H. V. B. Patel. B.A. (Econ.) Entrepreneur.'

'I would be happy to shake hands,' hissed Mr Patel through the gap. 'Unfortunately, however, I am locked in. It is to prevent robbery. I am sorry about your vehicle.'

'Ah, you know about that.'

'Of course. This service area is like a village. Everybody knows everything. Benny had his toes run over by a Suzuki.'

'It was a Honda,' answered George.

'Ah, see, you are becoming part of it too. Once you have been here a few days you quickly settle in. Benny has also lost his wife. After almost losing his toes. She went away with a man from Basingstoke. Very bad luck.'

'Yes, it is. Where do you come from, Mr Patel?'

'Trowbridge,' replied the man sounding surprised at the inquiry. 'Previously from India.'

He pushed his face nearer the grille and George said: 'Ah, yes.'

'Bombay,' said the man. 'I came here with nothing. Now I am in charge of this pay kiosk and handling hundreds of pounds. That is why it is necessary to lock me in.'

George nodded sagely. He looked at the card again. 'What sort of entrepreneur would you be?' he asked. 'What line of business?'

It may have been the growing dawn but he thought he saw a new light come to the side of the man's face that he could see through the grille.

'All nature of businesses,' said Mr Patel. 'Buying and selling or exchange even.' He reached behind him and lifted a plastic carrier bag to the aperture. 'For example. Already I know earlier that you had the unhappy experience of losing your car and your luggage. Nothing is to be done about the car but I have already ascertained your sizes and I have brought a set of clothing. Trousers, grey worsted, thirty-six waist, thirty-three inside leg.' He produced the folded trousers from the bag and held them close to the opening, encouraging George to feel the texture. George did so with one finger.

'Very nice,' he said.

Mr Patel looked relieved. 'Excellent shirt. Bond Street quality but coming from Salisbury Market,' he said, producing a blue shirt and then another in cream. 'Also a second shirt,' he added. 'Fifteen collar. Double cuffs. Easy to wash.' He was looking increasingly pleased and fumbled into the bag like a conjurer. 'Underpants, best cotton. Three pairs.' He produced them. 'Also socks, variety of colours, four pairs, and one pair of shoes. Best from Bata, size eight and a half, give or take a little.' He crouched further and regarded George seriously through the partition. 'It is, I suppose, not suitable weather to sell you a sweater? Although it might turn chilly. England is changeable, is it not?' The sweater, blue ribbed with red around the neck, was produced. 'St Michael,' announced Mr Patel. 'As from Marks and Sparks. An unwanted Christmas present.'

George stood grinning. It was the first time he had felt amused for weeks. 'What about a tie?' he asked jokingly.

'Also I have a tie. I did not like to mention it so I am glad you did. Tootal. Smart stripes. Could be Old School.' He peered earnestly through the window like a prisoner seeking parole. 'The entire outfit, forty-five pounds, fifty pence, sir. A bargain.'

George now, to his own surprise, found himself laughing and as he did so agreeing to purchase. 'How do I get these things?' he asked, 'When do they let you out?'

Mr Patel fumbled with some keys below the counter and in a moment the door had swung open. 'It is possible to get out, but not in,' he explained, adding vaguely: 'Unless you have already come out.' He handed George the parcel of clothing. 'Nothing must get in the way of commerce,' he said like a proverb.

Taking his wallet from his back pocket George counted out the notes.

'Forget the fifty pence,' said Mr Patel expansively. 'Forty-five pounds for cash. You only get big by thinking big. The transaction complete he returned to his kiosk and locked himself in.

George wandered back to the motel with his plastic bag of clothes. In his room he lay on his bed observing the second day of his freedom grow across the window. He dropped into sleep while watching its progress from left to right and awoke at ten o'clock with machinery roaring by once more on the motorway. Startled, he looked at his watch then stumbled drowsily to the window. It was another brilliant day, the sun already reflecting from the concrete and tarmac and bouncing from the roofs of cars streaming by. The pumps were fully occupied and children were being dragged off to the lavatories. He washed and shaved, put on his new shirt and trousers, which fitted well, and went to the restaurant for breakfast. On the way he telephoned the police, who seemed to have some difficulty in recalling his case. No, there had been no developments. All sorts of strange things happened on the motorway. Please ring later. The straw-haired waitress was working and they smiled at each other.

'Still awaitin'?' she said showing him to a corner table. 'No news yet?'

'Not a thing,' he confirmed. 'I've just telephoned them, the police. All they could do by way of reassurance was to tell me that all sorts of strange things happen on the motorway.' He ordered his breakfast. He felt much better today.

'They're right about the strange things,' she confirmed. 'There was a funeral came in one day, coffin, mourners, everything, and filled up with self-service four star. Never seen anything like it. Some people eating their lunch started crying.'

She poured his coffee. She was a big girl, not fat but full with a fine large bust under her apron. It hung close to his nose while she bent over with the coffee jug. He could smell the stiff cleanness of the cloth. Her arms were fawn and decorated with bangles. While she fetched his bacon and eggs he went to the shop, where he was greeted familiarly, and bought a newspaper. He had scarcely returned to his table when Benny limped in. 'What do you think you'll do?' he asked.

'I don't really know. I'll probably get a taxi to Trowbridge station and go on by train. Or I could hire a car, I suppose; that would be the sensible thing.' He smiled at the manager. 'On the other hand I might just stay here.'

'We could keep you busy,' said Benny straight-faced. 'We thought of making a bit of a garden behind the workshops, grow vegetables and that and a few flowers. Have a go at clearing that, if you like. What do you do for a living? If you don't mind me asking.'

'I'm a lawyer,' George told him. 'I work for a newspaper.'

Benny grinned grimly. 'You could help me with my divorce then, if you like. The missus went off with a chap from Basingstoke. And I thought she loved me.' He looked suddenly abashed. 'What with the toes and everything,' he said sadly. Then: 'Better be off. Things never stand still around here.'

The waitress came back. He asked her name and she told

him it was Molly. After he had eaten the breakfast she returned and, since there were a few customers now, they discussed what he should do next.

'Cars,' Molly shrugged. 'Can't abide them. More trouble than they're worth.'

'How do you get to work?' he asked. 'You must come on the motorway.'

'Not me,' she said. 'I comes on across the fields. There's a hole in the hedge.'

When he had finished she said it was time for her break. 'I'll show you if you like,' she offered. They walked together from the buildings of the service area, the sun now striking fiercely, the noise unremitting and the smell of oil thick on the air. She led him behind the workshops where there was a vacant piece of tangled ground.

'That Benny wants to start a garden there,' she mentioned. In front of them was a high hedge of hawthorn and hazel, blocking the view as effectively as a wall. She went ahead, her big body swaying gracefully in her frilled apron. She turned by a tree and pulled aside a rough door of wood and corrugated iron. ''Tain't very posh,' she laughed.

She stepped through first and George followed immediately. He stumbled, stood, and then saw. Astonished, he looked out on a dappled countryside of green and yellow meadows, hills tumbling from below his very feet and rising smoothly into the middle distance. The sun spread over it all, lost only in small clutches of trees and in the great hanging wood on the farthest rise. It glinted on distant water. Red and grey roofs slotted together in the valley and there was a single cuticle of the palest blue smoke rising into the morning summer sky. No sound of the traffic could be heard. A dog barked clearly from the valley and then he realised he could hear a stream running noisily across stones. Molly turned and smiled at him encouragingly and began to walk down the slope, through the buttercups. George followed, walking with wonder. Towards a new country, a changed world.

IV

As they descended through the buttercupped fields, so he felt the warmth and peace of the valley close around him. Somewhere among the rosy roofs below he could hear milk churns being moved. The stream's clatter became louder. Molly turned and smiled her cornfield smile at him. She held her large hand back invitingly. ''Tis called Somerbourne Magna,' she said.

George cast a single glance backwards. Only the tops of the service area buildings were now visible above the hill's crest, as innocent as cow sheds. He turned to look down the valley again as a man moved from the houses and dipped a bucket into a pond formed by a brief weir in the stream which, in George's next few steps, had shown itself. Molly stopped, grass and flowers forming a hem around her skirt, and holding George's arm aloft like a boxing referee proclaiming a winner, she called down to the man: 'Bert, I got 'un!' The man put his hand to his eyes and peered up, setting the full bucket cautiously on the ground. The girl called again: ''Ere'ee be!'

Bert waved uncertainly, picked up the bucket and went round a stone corner. Molly propelled her smile to George once more. Her neck flowing down to her pinafored breasts was glistening. 'That's good,' she breathed deeply. 'Bert likes you.'

Less certainly, George allowed himself to be led into the lower slopes of the vale. 'Bert is *who*?' he inquired.

Their path was now interrupted by the stream, silver clear in its shallow places, bottle green in its depths, with stepping stones the size of men's heads.

''Tis a bugger in winter,' Molly told him going ahead and balancing with a rounded grace across the bridge. George followed, and, observing her fine backside sway under her cotton dress, missed a slope on one of the stones and fell sideways, his foot in the cool sliding water. Molly turned, uproariously laughing, and helped him up. Her hands were

63

wide but soft. 'Strangers always be doin' that,' she said. 'Should 'ave told you, shouldn't I? Sit you down there.'

He sat on a stone platform alongside a milk churn and to his surprise and pleasure she at once knelt and took off his wet shoe, draining it carefully into the stream and shaking it afterwards. He retrieved his eyes from the open front of her dress, where her neck spread to rich shoulders and the foothills of her bosom. Her free hand held his wet socked foot as if reserving it. To this she turned, pulling away the sock and wringing it with one hand.

'Bert?' she answered, again squeezing the sock mightily. 'He's my dad. He keeps the Red Cow.' She looked suspiciously at the sock which she had untwisted and laid out like a fish on the pale palm of her hand. ''As that darkie bugger been selling you socks?' she inquired seriously. Her huge blue eyes, clouded with concern, turned up at him.

'Yes . . . Mr Patel,' he said. 'Why? Shouldn't he?'

'I know him of old,' she muttered. 'Trying to get rich quick, he is.' Carefully she laid the sock out on the stone beside him. 'Won't take long,' she forecast glancing like an explorer at the sun. She made to straighten up and, with a quick stab of guilt, he had a furtive look down her front. She smiled to show she had seen and put her big hands on his knee to lever herself to her feet. In a moment, however, tutting to herself as if annoyed at her own neglect, she was back on her haunches and wiping fragments of wet reed from his foot.

George put his hands on her warm shoulders and said gently: 'It's almost dry.'

She rose. 'You got a nice strong foot,' she announced like someone about to award a prize. 'Nice and strong.'

Bert appeared round the edge of the building, the bucket now again empty in his hand. He was almost a third smaller than his daughter, a bent, brief, brushy man, stiff hairs on his chin and cheeks, hanging in clusters from above his eyes. The rest of his head was brown and bare. Distantly he considered George's bare foot. 'Your gentleman in some kind of trouble, Moll?' he inquired.

'Fell in the bourne,' said the girl. Her cheeks became suddenly scarlet.

'And wearing that darkie bugger's socks,' observed Bert, staring at the sock on the stone. 'Better dip the other one in.

64

Never know where they been.' His continuing study of George's foot apparently provoked a further thought: "'Ow be Benny's hurt?' he asked. His swampy eyes lifted. 'Got 'isself run over,' he said to George.

'By a Suzuki,' agreed George. 'Or a Honda. He's hobbling.'

Molly was regarding him in a pleased way. 'You're getting quite at 'ome,' she said.

'I be real sorry for 'im,' confirmed Bert, swinging the bucket like a bellringer. 'That Benny. Wife gone off with a man from Andover.'

'Basingstoke,' corrected George seriously. 'I understood it was Basingstoke.'

'Works in Basingstoke. Lives in Andover,' Bert said. As though that had finally decided matters he moved to the stream and filled the bucket. Carefully examining the contents first, he was apparently satisfied and, turning, walked away from the water bank and towards the tree-enclosed buildings of the village. George put on his wet shoe and he and the girl followed.

The air was heavy, tranquil, and deeply smelling of dung. A loaded cart had progressed down the single street dropping small gobs and occasional complete cowpats every few yards as if fertilising the small thoroughfare itself. A dog investigated the debris and a woman wearing a straw hat and bearing a basket rolled round a leaning corner. 'Going to the shop!' she bawled with what might have been triumph. Molly waved towards her and Bert snorted down his matted nostrils. He turned into the dark door above which was a sign depicting a rust-coloured cow. Molly pushed George encouragingly ahead and they entered a passage hung with the smell of old beer, went through a frosted glass door and into the bar, a place of plastic and pink with a fruit machine and a jukebox standing shoulder to chrome shoulder. On the bar was a tall mound of silver coins, an ant-hill construction of ten pence pieces.

'For charity,' pointed Molly proudly. She rolled her country eyes to him. 'We got a room as it 'appens,' she said. 'We could lodge you.'

'Just 'ad the place done up,' announced Bert also with pride. 'Gone and done it a real treat, 'aven't they?'

Molly smiled supportively and taking a coin from the charity pile dropped it into the fruit machine which, on a pull of the handle, obediently deposited several further coins into the metal mouth agape below the screen of coloured fruits. This was apparently no surprise and after repaying the coin to charity she took another coin and pressed it into the jukebox. An arm swung within and a disc was placed in a slot. 'Frankie Goes to Hollywood,' announced Molly turning her lovely eyes on him.

'Does he?' mumbled George. 'Perhaps I could take your room for a few days.'

Bert had drawn him a half pint of beer in which sediment revolved balefully. Without enthusiasm, George picked this up while Molly placed a further coin in the fruit machine. 'It's an old room,' she said. 'But it's a nice bed.' She began singing, badly, with the record, tossing her straw-coloured hair away from her pink cheeks. Her bosom heaved with happiness. Bert began to bawl at someone upstairs. Tentatively George sipped at the murky beer. Molly turned towards him. 'I reckon you'll really like it 'ere,' she forecast.

He allowed her to lead him upstairs, a place of beams and passages, so confined he had to crouch. 'We're going to 'ave it all done,' Molly promised leading the way and trailing her hand behind like a coupling. 'Modernised.' She paused. 'This is the room,' she announced huskily. She opened the rough door and George looked into a beautiful beamed bedroom; a fine-paned window filled with sunshine which fell in patterns across the girth of the counterpane covering a powerful four-poster bed. 'Don't bang your head when you sit up 'cos you be hearing the ghosts,' laughed Molly. She moved to the window as if to check that the view was still available, before turning, her dress spinning. 'What do you reckon, then?' she asked.

'I reckon I'll really like it here,' echoed George.

For two hours in the July afternoon he slept, crumpled in a faded deckchair under the apple and plum trees at the bottom of the Red Cow's unkempt garden. The stream curled through the orchard and it was its introspection which eventually awoke him. Bees were moving, there were birds among the branches, and a close, sweet and rotten smell everywhere.

George uncurled and lay back, his eyes half open, realising where he was. His watch had stopped at four. What day was it? Sunday. Without knowing why, he wondered what Freddy Birch was doing. Had he mowed his lawn completely? How did the cricket club committee meeting fare? Would his daughter pass her exams?

There came a call and he saw Molly approaching through the distant screening green trees of the overgrown garden. She had changed into a pale blue dress which gave her some resemblance to a large butterfly. He was gratified by the vision and the fact that she was balancing a tray which carried a white tea cup.

'Just woke, have you?' she called heartily.

He waved and called back: 'I think so. In fact I'm really wondering whether I'm still asleep.'

'You have yourself a good rest,' she encouraged. She gave him the cup and saucer and put a spoonful of sugar into the tea. There was a plate displaying a pattern of biscuits on the tray. 'I expect you have to work hard, don't you? And what with your car and everything you need a rest . . . Mr Goodnight.'

He realised she had learned his name from the bill at the motel which she now held out to him. There had been no proper introductions. There had seemed to be no need for them. He thanked her.

'Mr Goodnight,' she repeated.

'Charles,' George heard himself saying. He could scarcely believe it. He was lying to her. His name was George.

The girl's broad fresh face above him opened into a smile. 'I reckoned it would be something like that,' she said.

He was regarding her seriously, ashamed now of his fiction.

'I brought your things down,' she said. 'I didn't think you'd want to go climbing the hill again, and there wasn't much to fetch anyway. I've washed your shirt and put it on the line and I've put an iron over your trousers and coat.' She regarded him with abrupt anxiety. 'You don't mind, do you?'

Smiling he shook his head and patted her hand. A feeling of enjoyment had come over him like a spreading warmth. He felt that, had he wished, she would have stirred his tea. She nodded towards the motel bill. 'Benny's coming down tonight and you can settle it then.'

'How're his toes?'

'No better. Hardly hobble poor man, what with his wife and all. He says there's no news of your car, either, but he'll phone the police for you before he comes on down.'

When she had gone, tripping with large grace across the

orchard, George finished his tea, sensuously broke the biscuits with his teeth, a small piece at a bite, and then lay back and considered what was happening to him. Here he was, lounging on a dilapidated canvas chair, in an aromatic orchard full of bees and weeds and the thoughtful sounds of a summer stream. A big, but fresh, beautiful and young girl had washed his shirt, ironed his trousers and transported tea to him. It was Sunday and he had not even seen a newspaper, nor wanted to. He stretched in the chair, took his feet from his shoes, and pushed out his socks. It was not what he had envisaged, but it *was* an adventure.

A bee and a butterfly briefly contested the same clump of fluffing weeds. George watched them both fly away and then looked up through the apple branches fragmenting the blue sky. There were no clouds but a lofty airliner drew a creamy rope of vapour. He watched and wondered where it was going but with no envy.

Eventually he yawned, replaced his shoes, and stood up. Picking up the tray he first walked across to the stream which unrolled like a bale of satin below its overgrown banks, and then turned back towards the inn. As he passed the open kitchen window, Molly's face appeared, framed, and he handed the tea tray through to her. "Et all the biscuits, that's good,' she enthused as if encouraging a convalescent. 'We've got some tasty roast pork for tonight, after I get back from church.' She pushed her face some way through the frame. 'I don't suppose you'd like to come to church?'

George smiled, surprised, but he said: 'Yes, why not? I haven't been for years.'

Pleasure flushed her face. 'Good job I ironed your trousers and jacket,' she said. 'Your shirt's dry in this sun. Soon run an iron over that.' She looked a trifle apologetic. 'I always go when I can,' she said. 'It shows willing, don't it?'

At a quarter to six a single bell began to knell through the vale and a few people walked through the small houses towards the church, their footfalls sounding distinctly in the enclosed street of the village.

Feeling self-conscious, his suit still warm from the pressing, George set out with Molly through the pale sunlight.

'Not many go,' she said in a Sabbath whisper. 'That's why I

68

shows willing. I gives a hand with the flowers sometimes too. Mr Timms wanted me to take Sunday School but I didn't feel up to that. I got no real learning about the Bible and some of the kids about these parts are real little buggers.' His smile gave her further confidence. They were walking along the brief village pavement, a few inches apart, when she said: 'Mind if I just hold your arm?'

'Please, Molly,' he said crooking his elbow.

'Little buggers,' she went on. 'Alfie Barnes went right up on the bell rope once, larkin' about, and one of the other kids got locked in all night and drank all the wine for Communion. Wonder he didn't get struck stone dead.'

She sniffed appreciatively as they neared the church. There was a small crowd at the lych-gate, progressing slowly through it up the churchyard path between the graves and into the porch door. 'More worshippers tonight,' she observed almost professionally ecclesiastical. 'Probably want to have a look at you.'

George was shocked. 'But how . . . ? I mean . . .'

'Word soon gets around here,' she winked greatly. 'And they like to be a bit nosey. Afore long they'll know more about you than Mrs Goodnight.'

He did not reply. They were at the lych gate and strangers were smiling at him. He felt a small fragment of anxiety. Here he was in an unknown village, going to church, and with a strange young woman. He swallowed noisily. There was no turning back. The vicar, a face white and creased as his cassock, appeared gratified as they shook hands at the porch door. 'I wonder, Mr Goodnight, if you would mind collecting the offertory?' His face contracted to even tighter lines as if someone had pulled a string behind his neck. 'They like to have a good look at you and they'll give more if a stranger pushes the plate under their noses.'

Mumbling that he would be pleased, George walked in with Molly. The evening coolness of the church fell over them. The building was twelfth century and half full. Heads turned as the pair took a few paces down the aisle. He sensed that Molly would have relished walking to the front pews but he discouraged her with a firm touch of his hand on her elbow. She compensated once they were in their seats by collapsing resoundingly to her knees in prayer, a crash like a felled tree.

Further heads peered round. One of them belonged to Henry Wintle, partner in the city firm of Wintle, Webb and Wintle, solicitors, who knew George quite well. A smile like a crack in his lower face appeared and he touched his brow in salute. George felt as though dry debris was falling down a chute inside his body. He acknowledged the greeting with disconsolate slowness.

Now he closed his eyes, his mind filling with apprehension. Not only was he standing among strangers in a strange church, with the noisiest young woman ever to descend upon a harmless hassock at his side, and one still praying with evangelical vigour, but five yards away was a man who not only knew him but, he now realised, had met Felicity.

'Let Jesus Christ be praised,' invoked the vicar from the front. 'Our opening hymn on this beautiful summer evening when I would like to welcome you all – especially our visiting worshippers.' There were squeaks, scrapes and clatters and two people dropped their hymn books as heads screwed once more towards George. Glancing guiltily sideways to Molly he saw she was scarlet with pleasure. She saw his glance and, leaning bustily towards him, giggled.

George was grateful when the service began and the congregation was required to look towards the altar, although there were still those who turned periodically and smiled as if to make sure he was still there. He remembered the words of the ancient service sufficiently to mumble as it unwound, all the time trying to fix in his memory how many times Henry Wintle might have met Felicity.

The vicar was reading the first lesson, intoning: 'Cast your bread upon the waters; for thou shalt find it after many days.'

Two-thirds of the way through the service the vicar cocked his eye in George's direction and made a milking movement with his hand. A bulbous church warden, as if his stardom were being usurped, sulkily pushed an offertory bag with a wooden handle towards George who rose uncertainly. Further heads turned, some nodding encouragement.

'You take the North, I'll take the South,' whispered the church warden as if plotting an ambush.

Waiting until the man had indicated the South by moving to that side, George walked unhappily down the aisle with his collecting bag. The burnished cross on the altar seemed to be

70

admonishing him and the brass eagle poised on the lectern fixed him with a glinting eye. The words of 'The Young Girl of Pitlochry' drifted with terrible mocking through his mind. Oh God, what had he done? He turned left and began mumbling along the front worshippers as they put their pieces of money in the bag, all too conscious that four pews back, pound coin poised, like a crumb in the beak of a blackbird, was Henry Wintle. A lady with lips which seemed to have been indiscriminately squashing blackberries was standing with a further rigid contribution beside him. Now that *was* serious. The organ blurted the offertory hymn: 'Now Thank We All Our God.'

He was conscious of the congregation singing variously in his ear as he progressed along the pews. 'Who wondrous things have done.' More hands thrusting into the bag; baritones, monotones, flats and falsettos sounded. 'In whom this world rejoices.' Now he was on the fourth pew. Wintle, he perceived, was a precise performer whose mouth formed neat ovals and circles of varying circumferences as he sang. 'Who from our mother's arms.' He continued in tune but lower: 'See you later, outside.' The words of Mrs Wintle's praise, squeezed through those blue lips, were scarcely audible. She turned two deadened eyes onto George as he offered her the bag, appeared to be in two minds whether to trust him with the hovering coin but finally dropped it in. Miserably George passed along the pews until he finally reached Molly who sang blissfully as she pushed a concealed gift into the bag. 'With countless gifts of love, That still is ours today.' Molly dropped her hand and felt underneath the bag, testing its contents with a sensual smile.

George joined the church warden at the chancel steps. The man was no more benevolent. 'Inserted yours, 'ave you, sir?' he inquired.

'No, sorry, forgot,' George flustered and in taking the hurried money from his pocket scattered small change which ran ringingly over the stone floor. Worshippers in the foremost rows bent over and searched around, and with enthusiasm but difficulty picked up the coins and returned them to him. A choirboy spotted a ten pence piece and, still warbling, left his stall to retrieve it and honestly hand it back.

The vicar collected the two bags and tested their weight appreciatively. 'Splendid job, Mr Goodnight,' he whispered before turning to bless the collection at the altar. A slighted

71

look settled on the church warden's face. 'Huh,' he said and, 'Huh.'

Eventually the congregation trooped two by two from the church, through the porch into an amber evening with rooks cackling in the hamlet trees. Warmly the vicar shook George's hand and thanked Molly for bringing her friend. 'We have the Men's Christian Club on Thursdays,' he mentioned in an almost sinister aside.

At the lych gate the ominous Wintles loitered. There was no avoiding them. Nor any way to abandon Molly. With her he went towards them.

'Good evening, Goodnight. Whatever are you doing in Somerbourne Magna?' began Henry at once. 'You remember my wife?'

Mrs Wintle nodded a grisly nod, transferring her attention only for a moment from the blushing Molly. 'How is Mrs Goodnight?' she scrutinised.

'Very well, very well indeed, thank you.'

'She's not with you?' inquired Henry, also examining Molly as if some transformation might have occurred.

'Er . . . no, actually not,' answered George. He realised he did not know Molly's surname. 'This is . . . this is Molly.'

'From the Red Cow,' confirmed Henry firmly and in the manner of one scoring a point before a judge and jury.

'Evening, sir,' said Molly. 'Nice singin' tonight, wa'n't it?'

'I'm staying there,' explained George. They were brazenly awaiting explanations. 'The Red Cow.'

'Taking a few days off, are you?' continued Henry.

'Yes. I have some difficult work to get through so I came down here.'

A question was visibly forming on Mrs Wintle's blackberry lips.

'Felicity is at home,' he forestalled. 'Busy. I needed some peace and quiet.'

'Absolutely,' agreed Henry. His wife looked irritated with him. 'And there's nowhere more peaceful. We're down most weekends. We've got a cottage. Pity we can't stay for a drink but it's off to London now, I'm afraid.'

Relief oozed through George. 'Pity,' he said.

'Our deepest regards to your dear wife,' sighed Mrs Wintle

turning her eyes on Molly. 'Please give her our best wishes. Whenever you next see her.'

George watched them go. 'Rex versus Bannimail,' he thought. 'The case of the garrotted wife.'

When they returned to the Red Cow the bar was already beginning to fill. George stood conspicuously awkward and alone among the villagers of Somerbourne Magna until Molly, wearing a white frilled pinafore, touched his arm and announced loudly enough to halt the general conversation, if not the tune on the jukebox: 'This way please, Mr Goodnight. Dinner is served.'

Smirking with embarrassment he followed her through a door with a smoked glass panel into a close and quiet room mostly taken up by a broad rough-grained table. There was an iron fire grate, its mouth stuffed with newspapers as if to silence some secret, a dresser bearing some odd plates and a sagging rank of paperbacks, and a wall clock that ticked to fill the silence. The table was laid with a single dinner plate, a cork mat with a design of faded flowers and a small mouse-like nibble at one corner, a recently polished knife, fork and spoon, a chequered napkin, a saltcellar in the shape of the Great Pyramid of Cheops and a pepper pot fashioned after the Leaning Tower of Pisa which proved awkward to use. There was also a glass of water with replenishments available in the Pyrex jug standing a little way off.

'I expect you'd like something else as well,' said Molly as he eyed the water with doubt. It was still moving in the jug like a slightly troubled sea. 'A bottle of ale, perhaps?'

He touched her round arm. 'Do you have any wine, Molly?' he asked. 'Anything will do. Red or white.'

She looked perplexed but brightened quickly. 'Now, we *did* have some wine,' she said. 'If I can lay my hands on it.'

George thanked her and she said: 'It's no trouble. You're the only one eating. We don't generally.' As she moved from the room she called back in her fruity voice: 'The pork looks a treat. And I've made a bit of nice soup.'

He sat in solitary. The tag end of the day's sun was in the street outside the small window. As he watched it the faces of two boys appeared above the sill like spies, crouching and staring in at him. They seemed oblivious of his returned stare

73

and examined him comprehensively before withdrawing in their own time. Molly saw the last of them as she returned with the soup and exclaimed, 'Nosey!' but without real annoyance. She placed the bowl before him. 'Everybody wants to have a good look at you,' she said. 'There's a rumour going around the village that you're a Cabinet Minister who's gone mad. Come down here to get your brains sorted out. People are swearing they seen you on the television.' She sat down as if she were prepared to hear his confession. She leaned earnestly. 'You're not . . . are you?'

He gurgled in his soup. 'What?' he asked laughing as his head went up. 'A Cabinet Minister gone off his trolley?'

'I didn't say it,' she assured him worriedly. ''Twas the others.'

'I'm not, I'm afraid. Not a Cabinet Minister, I mean. It's possible I may be a trifle bonkers.'

Molly, her round and lively face pink in the steam from his soup, bent even closer. Her fine bosom, scarcely pinioned by the pinafore, hung like a prospective avalanche over the table. Dramatically she breathed, taking in a column of steam as she did so. 'Are you on the run, Mr Goodnight?' she asked throatily.

'In a way,' he confessed. His soup dish was empty. Not taking her cornflower eyes from his she reached for it. 'Wait a minute,' she implored. 'I'll get your pork dinner.' She rose, lifted the dish with graphic slowness and held it before her like a worshipper carrying a libation. 'I'll be back in a minute,' she whispered. 'Don't move. Please.'

She returned with a ponderous plate of pork and vegetables, a dusty bottle of red wine and a cork opener. 'I found the wine,' she said breathlessly. 'I hope it's fresh enough.'

It was a bottle of Chianti. He pulled the cork and sniffed at it for her benefit while she gazed admiringly.

'Is it all right?' she inquired, closing one eye and attempting to peer down the neck. He poured a glass and sipped at it. 'Hope no dust got inside.'

'It's fine,' he said. 'Would you like a glass?'

'Oh no, thanks,' she flustered. 'Not much for wine, I'm not.' Anxiously she again leaned forward and one pinafored breast crept like an inquisitive child across the table. She moved sideways and its twin followed. 'So . . . you were saying . . .' she prompted. He was cutting into the tender pork.

'Lovely,' he said tasting it.

'Please talk while you're eating,' she encouraged. 'I don't mind one little bit, I don't.'

'What about the crackling?' he teased her, picking up a ruddy husk with his fork. 'It might be a little noisy.'

'Oh stop it,' she begged. 'You're pulling my leg. Tell me the story. You said you was on the run. What from?'

'I'm not sure. Life. My wife. Myself perhaps.'

She looked mystified. 'Oh. Just domestic,' she said disappointed. 'Nothing serious.'

'I haven't done a bank job or stolen state secrets if that's what you expected,' he said. 'Sorry about that.'

'It's all right,' she said accepting the apology genuinely. 'We're used to domestic around here. Benny's wife is in the bar with that boy of 'ers who's a funny colour.' Intently she watched him eating a carrot, following it up on the fork from the plate to his mouth. 'What are you going to do?' she asked. 'That man and his wife in church recognised you.'

'Oh, I'm not really concerned about them. It was just a bit of a surprise seeing them, that's all. When I thought I was away from everything.'

'You never are,' she observed wisely. She paused. 'You'll be staying a bit then?'

Nodding he said: 'I'll have to get my car back. And my luggage. I was just heading in a sort of careless way for Cornwall. I'm not even sure why I was going there. A compromise I suppose. If I'd been really brave I would have headed for Rio de Janeiro.'

'Cornwall's nice,' she confirmed as if she were one of the few who had been there. 'Too many people this time of the year, though.' She looked at him frankly. 'You'll probably be staying for a while, a day or two, then?'

He smiled fondly at her. 'I expect so,' he said.

'I'll let you finish,' she said with a quick sadness. 'There's apple pie or treacle tart.'

'Apple pie, please,' he answered.

'Have some of each,' she offered. 'I made them both.'

'You're spoiling me,' he said, accepting. She went and he contemplatively poured himself another glass of wine.

*

75

While he had been eating, the shadows on the frosted glass to the bar had become more dense, less moving, and the voices increased. Eventually Molly returned to the room, went to the bar door, opened it a fraction, peered through and said: 'Ben's wife is over there. With that boy. She wants to talk to you.' She regarded him with frank esteem.

'Me?' asked the astonished George. 'Why me?'

Molly widened the crack in the door and signalled him with her head. 'She reckons you can 'elp,' she whispered over her shoulder. 'She knows you've talked to Benny. She's 'oping he'll be down too, but she wants to see you first.'

'God help me,' breathed George. 'Here I am, running away from my own problems and getting other people's.'

'Other people's woes are easier,' she announced firmly but sweetly, still looking through the door. She widened the gap enough for him to see into the crowded bar. 'She's just over there, see. With the brown-looking boy.'

Without waiting for his further comment she strode out of the door and, forcibly pushing some loungers away, flung it open wide. Tentatively George walked out. A silence fell across the bar but was followed at once by fragments of comment. He attempted to appear casual as he walked to the bar where several men made room for him. He reached into his pocket and taking a ten pence piece he added it to the charity mound. There was a general murmur of approval. Molly's father pushed across the Scotch which he ordered and whispered heavily: 'She's over there. With the darkie.'

Benny's wife was pinched and pale with rings below her eyes. Few men would have taken her away. She watched him approach with scant hope in her face. ''Twas really because of the boy here,' she began without any introduction and hardly giving him time to sit down. It was obviously something she wanted off her chest. The youth looked at George with moony eyes and looked away again as if he quickly lost interest in things. She faced George doggedly. 'It was a mistake,' she said bluntly. 'I only knowed his father three days.'

'What has happened to the gentleman from Basingstoke?' said George at last. 'Or Andover?'

'Works in Basingstoke, lives in Andover,' she recited. 'Got his own bungalow.' Her eyes fluttered down. 'That's what I mean. I only did it for the boy. I thought he might get him a job, what with the unemployment.' Her doleful expression lifted again. The circles below her eyes were like reflections of her thick eyebrows. 'Not that he did,' she said sullenly. 'He only wanted me for one thing.' A hand like a chicken's claw clenched against the wood of the table. She had not finished. 'And 'im,' she nodded sharply sideways at the youth sucking his Coca-Cola. 'Running over Ben's toes. Well, that was the end. I just went.'

Leaning towards her, George said cautiously: 'He . . . ran over Ben's toes?'

'On my Honda,' said the youth speaking for the first time but with a sort of pride. 'Right over them.'

'But . . .' began George. 'The police . . .'

'It weren't Ben what told them,' the woman sniffed. 'Somebody else up there reported it after they'd gone and taken Ben to the hospital. Ben wouldn't let on. It was an accident.'

The dark youth sent his straw probing the bottom of his glass for the last dregs of Coca-Cola. 'I meant to just miss them,' he confirmed, lifting only his alien eyes. 'But Ben moved. And I'm not insured.'

'He'd have got into bother with the police,' put in his mother. She looked at him forlornly. 'And he's not as bad as he looks.'

'What,' asked George, 'do you want me to do?'

'Get us together again,' she said bluntly as though he should have realised. 'You're a solicitor. And you're sort of nobody around here. When he comes in bring him over.' She paused. Her face became a plea. 'Will you?'

Molly's father· edged through the crowd of drinkers. 'Ben's outside,' he announced. ''E won't come in.'

George sighed, patted the woman on the tight hand and followed the innkeeper through the crowd. Everyone knew why and watched him go. Outside the light was almost gone, the little street was musky, the air was grey and warm. Ben was sulking against a wall of the pub, half leaning on his stick.

'I saw you,' he said accusingly. 'Talking to 'er. What's she got to say for 'erself?'

With a shrug George said: 'It was all a mistake, Ben.'

'How could it be? How could 'er going off be a mistake?'

'She wanted to get employment for the boy.'

'I bet she got some for 'erself.' He had been looking solidly to the front, but now he turned and George saw a cobweb of tears across his eyes. He patted Ben on the arm.

'She wants to come back,' he said quietly. 'She's sorry.'

'She usually is,' returned Ben. He almost glared at George. 'It's not the first time, you know. How do you think she came by *him*?' He nodded towards the door. 'Not that he's a bad lad.' His voice and his face dropped again. 'That was two weeks after our honeymoon, that was. I went off on a course.'

'He went over your toes, didn't he?' said George.

Ben's face came up quickly. 'They told you?' George told him they had and Ben said: 'It was an accident. I didn't want the police involved. He's not insured. Somebody else called them and it was too late then. That's why I said it was a Suzuki.'

There was silence between them. Ben showed no inclination to move and George took a pace forward with the aim of encouraging him into the bar. In doing so he stepped on Ben's toes.

'Aaaaah!' Ben howled wildly. He pushed George away and began hopping about like a mad stork, bellowing and holding his foot in his hand. The door of the Red Cow was thrown open and people began to pour out. George, still trying to explain and apologise, was pushed even further into the street. Ben's wife and the boy came out almost at the rear of the mob. The thin woman elbowed her way through and the villagers respectfully hung back while she held Ben's foot and tried to embrace him at the same time. The youth had his arms looped round Ben's sparse head and was shouting endearments in his ear.

George slowly returned to the empty bar. He was leaning against it, surveying the bottles, trying not to listen to the tumult outside, when the door clattered and sprang open and the angry head of Ben's wife was thrust in. 'Clumsy bugger!' she bawled.

He slept well that night in the copious bed below the beams and only woke when there was sunlight outside the window and the garden was bright with the sound of birds. Someone was tugging at his sleeve and he opened his eyes to see Molly holding a large flowered cup of tea. She had obtained a long pair of striped pyjamas which he had worn to bed.

78

'You look nice in them pyjamas,' she said. He pushed his leg from the bedclothes. That made her laugh and she put down the cup and boisterously hoisted the limb back into the bed.

'Where did you borrow them?' he asked.

'I'm not telling,' she said primly. She smoothed down her fresh dress. Suddenly her eyes were bright. 'I'm off to work,' she murmured.

'What am I going to do without you?' asked George.

'You'll 'ave to get along as best as you can,' she answered. He saw she was blushing a deep rhubarb colour. 'You could have a bath,' she suggested in a slow voice. 'Water's nice and hot now.' She turned away. 'I'll be getting you some towels.'

Noisily, she went out. Calling back from the corridor, she said: 'Lance's pyjamas look fabulous on you.' He sat in the great bed feeling like a nabob. Across the passage in the bathroom water gushed and echoed. 'Lovely and hot,' she called, her voice dampened by the steam. 'We be going up to Willington, s'afternoon. The Old Rectory, that was. There's a sale. Effects and everything, you know, after the Reverend Mister Welham went and died.'

Steam was curling out into the passage. She padded through it like someone floating through the sky and put her damp face round his door again. Her blue eyes glittered through the vapour. 'We only go to be nosey,' she confessed. 'See what they got.' A fraction of sadness touched her. 'Or 'ad got, more like it. Bert thinks there be some good kitchen pots, saucepans and suchlike, we could use here.' She regarded him with intense hope. 'Come if you like.' There was a cautious pause. 'Lance 'as gone off.'

George laughed at her diffident eagerness. 'I'll come,' he said. 'Of course. I might be able to buy some old clothes.'

She went then after saying, 'Get on with you,' and he heard her strong steps on the stairs. She called back. 'Don't get in the water too hot, Mr Goodnight. We don't want you bein' boiled.'

He walked across the corridor to the bathroom. The pair of large blue towels she had set out for him were new. He rubbed them and fluff came off on his fingers. After testing the water, he ran some cold and stopped the taps. He climbed luxuriously into the old clanging bath and lay back. Outside he heard Molly's footfalls as she left for work, calling to someone in the street as she did. Yes, it was a nice morning, yes, their gentleman was still with them. Yes, they would be going to the sale.

For ten minutes he lay in the water moving his feet against the bath bottom, sounding it like a muffled bell. Things seemed far away, even recent things like his lost car and the belligerent eye of Mrs Henry Wintle.

After he had shaved and dressed he went down to the morning pallor of the dining room. Bert appeared, leaning at an acute forward angle and carrying a tray like a juggler.

'Moll said you was to have brown eggs,' he said. 'Two. Is that all right? And she cut the bread and butter 'erself. She don't trust me.' Doubtfully he handed George *The Sun*. 'Ben rang to say 'e's sorry you got blamed. It was you accidentally standing on 'is bad toes what did it.' He sniffed. 'Anyway, 'e's taken 'er back. For 'ow long I don't know. She's no good, never was, never will be. There's no news about your car either.' He glanced at George with a fragment of concern. 'What will you do?'

George decapitated both eggs which were sitting up expectantly in a double eggcup.

'Four minutes,' said Bert bending closer to peer in at the contents. 'Most particular about that she was.'

'I'll just stay for a couple of days, if that's all right,' said George. 'There's no hurry is there?'

'Not for us,' shrugged Bert. 'Don't make no difference.' He became thoughtful then decided to say: 'Lance is back today, that's all.'

'Lance? I think I've been wearing his pyjamas.'

'More 'n' likely. He's Molly's, like, boyfriend.' Bert became embarrassed. 'Well, not exactly boyfriend.' He giggled and his broken teeth appeared like pennants. ''E certainly ain't no boy. But you know . . . he's a funny bugger and 'e might just take jealous.' His expression crinkled as if he had said too much. 'Molly payin' a lot of attention to you, see.'

Smiling, George thanked him. 'You should walk up Somerbourne 'ill,' suggested Bert. 'Nice on a nice morning.' He nodded towards the window. 'Other side of the vale from where you came down,' he directed. 'You can see Salisbury spire from there, they reckon, on a clear day. Not that I've looked for it myself. Ain't been up there for years. When I was a boy with the girls.' Regret appeared in his eyes. 'There don't seem any point now.'

After his breakfast George went out of the inn door into the street. The sun had not topped the roofs. A woman sweeping the pavement outside her house waved her broom familiarly at him.

'Up there,' she called as if she possessed second sight. She now used the broom as a pointer. 'Through the alley. Then up the hill. See Salisbury spire from up there today.'

Wondering at the telepathy, George entered the alley, rough-walled and wriggling through clumps of sunflowers, cow parsley and exploding rhubarb. A green smell closed around him; bees and other insects nuzzled flowers. From behind this jungle, slowly at first, appeared a man with a narrow face and pale rural eyes. George was startled and stopped. The head rose, like that of a giraffe, until a tall, thin, anxious-looking man was revealed to the waist.

'Morning,' he said to George briskly. ''Ow long do you reckon on staying in Somerbourne Magna?'

George could not remember seeing him before. He wavered.

'I 'ear 'tis for a few days,' pursued the inquirer. His black hair was thick over the back and sides of his head with a semi-circle of freckled baldness at the front, so symmetrical it might have been especially fashioned.

'Yes,' said George. 'I imagine so.' He was now becoming unsurprised.

'You would be in your forties going on fifty,' said the man among the sunflowers. 'That's my reckoning.'

'And how old are you?' demanded George testily.

'Not as old as that,' replied the man. 'Ask Molly.'

'Ah,' said George. 'You're Lance.'

'That's right. Lance Onions. I been away. Drivin' a Heavy Goods.'

'Well, she's a nice girl,' George assured him. 'You look after her.'

Lance appeared relieved but not entirely placated. 'Oh, I do. And when I'm not 'ere, when I'm driving my HGV, there's others what keep an eye on 'er for me.'

'Splendid,' enthused George without warmth. 'That's what friends are for.' He nodded to the slope ahead. 'I was just going for a walk up the hill.'

'Somerbourne 'ill,' identified Lance. 'You can see Salisbury spire from the top.' He waited and examined George further. 'At least I can.'

'I'll look very carefully,' promised George. He moved off along the lane.

Lance poked his head round the sunflowers. 'Take it steady,' he advised. ''Tis a steep climb, for somebody your age.'

George grunted but to his dismay found that the forecast was accurate. He was aware that somewhere below, the head of Lance would be extended like a periscope to observe him. He would not allow himself to pause or stumble, and he arrived with breathless gratitude at the first ridge with lungs creaking, legs uncertain and sweat rolling down his backbone. His eyes were misted as he straightened up on the path that ran along the ridge and viewed the way he had come. At his back was a second steep ascent. Down he looked onto the roofs of the village, red and askew as if they had all collided long ago and nobody had bothered to untangle them. The far slope of the vale was lush green, clouded with the yellow of buttercups and dandelions. On its top he could see the crouching roofs of the motorway service area where Molly was doubtless serving the first of that day's cottage pie and chips. His thought of her made him succumb to the temptation to peer down towards the garden by the lane and he at once regretted it. Lance was protruding from the foliage and, observing George's surveillance, he cupped his hands and bawled: 'You can see Salisbury spire from up the *top*! Up the *top*! Get up the *top*!'

'All right! All right!' shouted George, likewise cupping his hands. 'I've seen it before.' He relaxed his arms and added softly: 'Prat.'

Angry at himself for rising to the challenge he turned inwards on the hill and began the second half of the climb. His pause had helped him regain breath but shouting had dispelled most of it again. Now he panted and pawed, pulling himself up through the tussocks of spiky grass and painfully grasping unseen nettles.

He gained the top with a wracked triumph and straightened up unsteadily to scrutinise the landscape. Salisbury spire was nowhere to be seen, lost apparently in July morning mist. He breathed deeply again and again to fill his lungs. He was much out of condition. But at least he was there; at the top.

82

'Somerbourne 'ill,' he recited to himself. When he was breathing naturally again and his knees were stilled, he once more looked down towards the garden where Lance had been. At first there was no sight of him. George clamped his jaw with annoyance. He had wanted to show him.

Lance, however, almost at once reappeared, this time in the lane. He stared up at the outlined man on the hill, cupped his hands and bellowed mightily: 'Telephone! Telephone call for you. Urgent!'

'Christ!' swore George. He glared towards the shouter, aware of the glee in his voice. He started down the slope, through the knolls and nettles, muttering and cursing, half falling, recovering, half falling again.

The descent left him almost as breathless as the climb. The sweat trembled from his face. As he reached the lane, Lance's ostrich head appeared now from the greenery. 'Telephone from London for you. Might be the missus.'

George gave him surly thanks and stumbled across the hamlet street to where Bert was holding open the door of the Red Cow. 'London on the line,' he announced.

It was Henry Wintle, drinking tea. The clatter of the cup sounded distinctly over the telephone.

'Ah, Goodnight. At last.'

'Sorry,' said George. 'I was up the mountain.'

'Somerbourne Hill,' acknowledged Wintle. 'Wonderful view of Salisbury Cathedral from the top isn't there?'

'I couldn't see it.' George was impatient.

'Really. Perhaps you were facing the wrong way. Now, to the point. Goodnight, I'm sorry about all this, but I thought I'd better telephone you. Just in case.'

'In case of what?'

'Your wife calls.'

'Felicity! Whatever do you . . . ?'

'Mrs Wintle, I'm afraid, committed an indiscretion. She is inclined to do so. She telephoned Mrs Goodnight just to tell her . . . well, that we had run into you, so to speak, in church at Somerbourne Magna . . .'

George felt his mouth dry. 'She told *Felicity* that I'm . . .'

'Staying at the Red Cow,' murmured Wintle. 'Women don't realise, Goodnight, do they? Being myself a man of the world I thought I had better call and tell you what had occurred.'

83

'Fucking hell,' said George.

'I beg your pardon, Goodnight.'

'You heard. *Fucking hell,*' repeated George angrily. 'Next time you come down here, why don't you buy a large turnip and stick it in Mrs Wintle's bloody great mouth.'

He only heard a moment of Henry Wintle's gasp before he rammed the telephone headpiece back so fiercely on its hook that the entire fitting fell from the wall and hung groaning like some strangled creature. Bert came along the passage and picked it up philosophically.

'Bad news?' he inquired.

'People not minding their own damned business,' muttered George. 'Sorry about the phone.' In the back of his mind he could hear Henry Wintle telling the story throughout Fleet Street and the Law Courts. 'Goodnight's gone mad, you know. Absolutely mad.' Perhaps he had.

Bert had replaced the telephone on its wall hook and almost tenderly lifted the headpiece to test that it remained operative. Like a doctor with a stethoscope he listened. His features lightened as it purred. He put it back on the wall and it jangled immediately. The two men stood staring at it before Bert made the decision and picked it up.

'The Red Cow,' he announced carefully. He listened for a moment, then eyes swivelling sombrely he inched it towards George. 'It's a lady,' he said.

George was tempted to run out of the door but, hypnotically, he accepted the offered instrument. 'Hello?'

'You haven't got very far then,' Felicity began tartly.

'I've mislaid the car,' he replied with care, making a firm effort. 'So I'm down here in Merrie England, striding about, smelling the fresh air and the pretty flowers, attempting to view Salisbury spire which, believe it or not, you can see from Somerbourne Hill, restoring my soul, communing with the simple things.'

'Including the local milkmaid, from what I hear.'

'Anything you hear from Mrs Wintle must be treated with the gravest suspicion,' he warned. 'I thought even you might realise that.'

She had hoped to shock him. Disappointedly she said: 'Well, she simply happened to telephone me.'

'She wanted you to add the Parrot Club to your list of

84

activities, I suppose,' he responded. 'You have naught to worry about, Felicity. I am merely progressing to Cornwall by the scenic route.'

Her thin snort came snaking across the line: 'I really don't give a two-penny damn,' she said. 'But I was glad to know where you are because I have to inform you that, on the advice of my lawyer, I have withdrawn all the cash from our joint current account. You must understand that I have to live, debts have to be paid.'

'Don't they just,' murmured George. 'Well, that's all right. I had no intention of leaving you penniless, no matter if you leave me penniless.'

'You've got your credit cards,' said Felicity. There was an edge of guilt.

'To their limit,' he agreed. 'But I should be able to afford a few ice creams, mystery tours and Cornish cream teas on that. So don't worry about me, please.'

'I'm not worried about you. I only thought it right that I should tell you about the bank.'

'Well, thank you. It certainly saves me the embarrassment of bouncing cheques everywhere.'

'Good,' she said, he was glad to hear lamely. 'That's just about all.'

'Yes, it is,' he agreed. 'I'll be in touch sometime. I have to go now. It's milking time.'

V

They travelled to the sale at Willington by horse and trap brought to the door of the Red Cow by a challenging woman called Mavis, shawled and hatted, who was apparently someone to do with Bert. When the conveyance arrived outside the inn little Bert became agitated and hurried out to mount the step of the trap and, almost boy-like, one short leg hung out romantically behind him, placed a kiss on the rouged cheek of the driver. Mavis made no sign that she had received it, merely staring straight ahead at the flies between the horse's ears.

Giggling fruitily, Molly rammed her elbow into George as they spied through the window at the meeting.

'Fancies 'er, 'e does,' she whispered resoundingly. 'Ever since All Souls' Eve last year. They 'ad a fancy dress disco out the parish hall and some'ow they must have got together then.'

'What was Bert?' inquired George.

'What did 'e go done up as? Well,' she said, ''e was reckoned to be a monk but 'e was more like a sack of potatoes. She went as a witch. Very lifelike too she looked.'

They went outside into the sunshine thrown in columns across the street. The horse moved a pace forward so that he could stand in the shade. George was introduced to Mavis who smiled with false teeth like egg cups. 'I've heard a packet about you,' she said wolfishly. 'Jump on the cart.'

As each one clambered into the trap the horse fidgeted more irritably. When they were all seated the animal turned to them with a hurt expression.

'Baggins won't go down Willington Hill,' forecast Mavis with confidence. 'The brakes on this claptrap are no bloody good and he knows it.' Her voice was countryfied but with a certain tone.

Bert opened a ravaged smile to George. 'Talks nice, don't she?' he whispered.

'And he won't go up coming home because of the weight,'
86

added Mavis. 'By and large we might as well have left the bastard thing at home.'

'But we might be buying something,' pointed out Molly.

'Yes, we might be that,' agreed Bert, adding softly, 'dear.'

Mavis snorted and the horse oddly repeated it. 'What they had in that dump won't be worth carrying home,' she said. 'When the old mad rector was alive I went in there once and it was like a rag and bone shop then. And that was years ago.'

She flipped the reins and the horse tugged once or twice, failed to move the cart and drifted back to immobility. Mavis released the handbrake, jerked the reins, and the horse almost fell on its face at the next pull. It glared over its shoulder before clattering forward with an ill grace. 'Handbrake works sometimes,' commented Mavis, 'and sometimes not.' She examined George. Despite the warmth of the day, Molly had placed a plaid rug across her knees and those of George. 'Know anything about these rigs?' asked Mavis.

He shrugged and said: 'First time I've ever been in one.'

'They're no good at all,' sniffed Mavis. They were moving out of the short hamlet now, among the moulded fields, the slanting shoulders of the vale on either side. 'Once this swine is dead I won't have another. The trap's too rickety. It's a toss-up which will go first.'

The horse snorted again like a comment and increased its pace. As they jogged through the July green and yellow landscape, the sun warming the rippling air, the smells and sights of the season crowding about, George found a smile growing across his face. Molly's thigh lay with warm friendship and familiarity, abutting his, deep below the folds of the unnecessary rug. Bert was sitting beside Mavis, smiling at the side of her head. 'Watch the road,' she warned him eventually and impatiently. 'You'll be wearing out that silly grin.'

As she had predicted, the horse refused to go down the hill. It stopped and stood. 'Baggins, get on with it,' threatened Mavis but without reaction from the animal. 'He knows,' she sighed. 'He knows about the brakes. Everybody off.' They dismounted and walked down the hill to where a grey bridge looped over a gurgling river. Mavis took the horse's bridle and Bert walked alongside her, small but patently proud. At the bridge the horse was led to the side where a path descended and shown the rapid water. Agreeably he moved forward and drank with noisy dignity.

'He's quite a quiet drinker,' apologised Mavis. 'Bert here makes more noise.' Bert smiled idiotically.

Together George and Molly stood on the bridge, looking over. There were grey stones in the water, dividing the stream into shimmering tails. It was ten minutes to two on a Monday afternoon. As he looked at his watch he found himself smiling again.

'A good guzzle might put Baggins in the mood to go up the next hill,' offered Mavis without much hope. The doubt was justified. As soon as they got the animal on the road again and had all remounted the trap, it surveyed the steady incline ahead and shook its head.

'Shanks's pony,' said Mavis. 'Disembark.' They all obediently climbed down and began on the rising walk. It was heavy in the sun. George took off his jacket and hung it across his shoulder. At first Mavis took the horse's head but halfway up the hill she called for Bert who trotted obediently to replace her. Molly moved from George's side and picked a fleshy yellow flower from the hedge. Her nose wrinkled as she smelled it. 'They call that a smelly helly,' she said. ''Tis dead poison.' She threw it away.

'He wants me to marry him,' mentioned Mavis to George, nodding in the direction of the tiny Bert. 'Funny little bugger, isn't he?'

'What will you do?' asked George politely.

'Oh, I really don't know. I met him at the Hallowe'en Ball last year. It was fancy dress, you know. Very pagan. A lot of things are around here. I went as a princess, a sort of Senior Snow White I suppose you could say, and he was one of the Seven Dwarfs I think. He had a sort of robe on and it trailed on the floor behind him, like Dopey. It was all very romantic. We walked out below the moon in our costumes. But, of course, next day you're back in reality. He hasn't stopped bothering me since. I mean, look at him.' She nodded ahead to where the brief and bandy Bert was leading the horse. 'He'll always be Dopey to me,' she sighed.

Molly took her place, walking beside George. They were almost at the crest of the gradual hill now, an elevation that changed the shapes and angles of the landscape with each few steps. At the summit, Baggins paused, it appeared to admire the view, and his passengers climbed once more into the trap. There was a modest descent to a clutch of houses half a mile away, their red tiles threaded among elms and oaks, the church tower alone with enough tallness to overlook the trees.

'Willington,' announced Molly for George's benefit. 'The Old Rectory is right along by the church.' With a brief leap and a shake of his mane, Baggins, in a sudden surge of good humour, trotted down the slope with the carriage and the passengers jolting and jangling. George began to think he had never been so free, so happy.

What had once been the sitting room at the Old Rectory was arranged with chairs, cushioned seats, and puffed-out sofas, each place taken by 2.30 when the auctioneer took the rostrum and struck a blow with his gavel that startled the room, an amazingly fierce strike for a man who looked both under-nourished and studious. An old lady fell sideways from a stool and had to be helped from the floor.

'Please,' said the auctioneer in a pained fashion. 'Be careful with the furniture. It has to be sold.' The old lady, on the stool again, mumbled a toothless apology. Olde Antiques versus Butcher, remembered George.

'Mr Pinchbeck from Warminster,' Molly said in George's ear. ''E does nearly all the sales in these parts. He's pally with all the undertakers, bailiffs and furniture removers so 'e's got a good idea what's likely to come up next.' The information was delivered in an elongated whisper that nevertheless sounded throughout the buzzing room. Mr Pinchbeck gazed over his spectacles towards Molly who blushed and put her hand across her mouth. The air was very close in the room; every window was open and each framed a portrait of a green garden. Bees and other browsing creatures moved in and out of the windows and through the open door at the end of the room. People sat or stood around the walls, among the chattels of what had once been a home.

Mr Pinchbeck's spectacles signalled in a sunbeam. He adjusted them and in an ecclesiastical voice announced: 'I'm very pleased to see you here in such numbers. It is comforting to know that most of the possessions, those that remain here today, will find new homes in this locality. You all knew the rector and his family.'

'Afore he went mad,' added a man's voice from the back of the room. There were murmurs and heads moved in agreement.

'Lot one,' frowned Mr Pinchbeck. 'A mahogany washstand.'

'Went proper mad 'e did,' whispered Molly to George. 'I mean not just quiet mad, like peculiar, but proper ravin'. Shouting from the top of the church tower, 'e was, and that. Thought the moon was God.'

'A natural mistake,' whispered George.

'Maybe. But when 'e dropped little Susie Martindale on 'er head at the Christening he started to laugh and they couldn't stop 'un. That's when they reckoned he ought to be certified mad. Reckoned the chemist in Somerbourne was the devil incarnate and 'course there was some around 'ere that believed 'im. Started taking their prescriptions to Westbury.'

The bidding was unenthusiastic for the mahogany washstand. A dealer from Salisbury paid twenty pounds for it and left at once, nodding to himself.

'Lot two. Four dining chairs. As seen. One with a loose leg.' Mr Pinchbeck nodded towards the front row. 'That is the lot.' He nodded again towards the front row. 'You're sitting on them. Joe, just lift up yours, will you? So's people can view it.' A ruby-faced man stood sheepishly and lifted his chair with one great hand. A leg fell off. He picked the leg up and held it in his other hand like a rioter frozen in action.

'Two pounds,' came a morose bid from a dusty man standing at the wall. 'Soon mend the leg,' he added looking around in case anyone argued.

Looking in the dusty man's direction George's eye was caught by three large and faded books almost concealed by a collection of vases and topped by a flowered chamberpot. 'Could I have a look at those?' he whispered to Mavis who was sitting on the opposite side to Molly. Mavis stood up, put the chamberpot into Bert's hands, and blew cobwebs like veils from the books. She lifted them across to George. As he took them he saw that the dusty man had lost interest in bidding for the chairs after ten pounds, and was regarding him narrowly.

Two of the volumes were family photographs, well bound and filled with sere faces staring apprehensively and unsmiling. The other was a stamp album.

90

'Stamps,' whispered Molly her chin on his shoulder. 'I might just buy that for Ronnie, my nephew. 'Tis 'is birthday next. 'E likes stamps,' she said resolutely.

Mr Pinchbeck's drone, five pounds, seven, eight, ten, twelve, sounded through the room in chorus with the loud ticking of the clock whose future he was deciding. George turned the pages of the stamp album. At once he could see that it was a haphazard conglomeration, mostly worthless squares, oblongs and triangles of paper, stuck onto the pages with little care or cohesion. Some of the stamps were under the wrong countries, many were damaged, others stuck fast with adhesive, the rulers defaced; kings, queens, emperors and tyrants transfixed by an excess of glue. Others had been fixed with adhesive hinges but nearly all were dull and commonplace. Except two.

The three albums were Lot twenty-eight. Throughout the drowsy afternoon the bidding went on like a Buddhist prayer in the dim room, the garden sounds outside. Eventually a tinkling bell came to punctuate the bird and bee song and, as if a summons had been called, several people left the room. Mavis leaned Bertwards and issued instructions. He obediently stood and made to go out. 'Perhaps you'd be so kind as to get one for me,' mentioned the auctioneer looking up. Bert, unsurprised, nodded. 'A cornet, please,' Mr Pinchbeck added. 'Now, where were we?'

Consignments of ice cream were borne into the room, cornets, wafers and coloured tubs. Bert returned like an Olympic marathon man bearing many torches. Cornets were distributed along the row and the final one, the ice cream already wriggling down the biscuit, was carried to the rostrum.

'Splendid, thank you, Bert,' beamed Mr Pinchbeck. 'Next lot. Three albums. Two photographic. One philatelic. Who will start at five pounds?'

Disbelief hung in the hot room. There was a crack as someone bit into a cornet.

'Three pounds then,' amended the auctioneer.

There was still no response.

'Goodness me. All right. What am I bid?'

'Ten shillings,' said the grey man by the wall who had boasted that he could mend the chair. As he raised his arm a small but distinct cloud of dust puffed out to join the sunlit particles already dancing about the room.

'Fifty pence,' converted the auctioneer determinedly.

'One pound,' offered Molly throwing up her pink arm, the ice cream brandished aloft like a goddess.

'One pound, five shillings,' pursued the old man. His eyes were small and bright as he looked first to the auctioneer and then to Molly. 'I want they albuns,' he added threateningly.

'So do I,' returned Molly briskly. 'One pound fifty.'

'One pound, fifteen shillings. I goin' to 'ave they, too.'

'Two pounds.'

'Two pounds . . . ten shillings.'

Molly glanced at George. 'What you think then?'

'Keep going,' nodded George.

'Three pounds.'

'Three pounds, two and sixpence.'

'Three pounds, twenty-five.'

'Three pounds, ten shillings.' Suddenly the dusty man shouted angrily across to Molly. 'Drat you, girl, I want they photos! There's photos of me when I were a lad in that albun, like when I worked in the garden 'ere.'

'I don't want your old photos,' returned Molly stoutly. 'It's the stamps I want.'

'Drat the stamps. I want they pictures.'

Enjoyably the audience moved their heads from one belligerent party to the other. Mr Pinchbeck peered impatiently over the nibbled cone of his ice cream. 'Call it three pounds and split it,' he suggested with a weary sigh.

'Done,' said the grey man.

'Done, too,' exclaimed Molly. 'A pound for me. Two for 'im. 'E be getting two books for my one!'

''Arf each!' spluttered the man. To make his emphasis he had ceased to lean against the wall and now stood swaying with the force of his own argument. 'Settle for 'arf or nothing.'

'Not likely!' returned Molly. George's eyebrows went up at the rasp of her voice. 'Two for you. One for me.'

George leaned near her. As he whispered, the curls of her hair touched his nose giving him a whiff of meadow sweetness. 'Don't fight with him,' he said. 'It's worth it.'

'Halves it is then,' said Molly to the patent surprise and disappointment of everyone in the room. Her rival himself looked a trifle cheated at the abrupt surrender.

92

'There,' he said mildly, leaning back against the wall and coughing into a cloud of his own dust.

The lots droned on through the summer minutes. At four o'clock Mr Pinchbeck announced that there would be a twenty-minute interval for tea, provided at a modest cost by the ladies of the church. They walked out into the overgrown garden, clouds of zizzing insects rising from choking plants and riotous flowers as the humans invaded their country. The neglected lawn grass was almost knee high and the tea servers had found it necessary to trample it down before they could set up their trestles. One squat and square-legged woman had burrs sticking to her stockings. Others scratched.

'Just look at 'un,' said the man who had bought the photo albums. He approached George as if he recognised in him a man with whom he could converse on level terms. His hands swept around the dissolute garden. 'Makes me cry to see it.' He carried the two photo albums under his arm. Molly, seeing them, returned quickly into the house to retrieve the stamps from the auctioneer. 'Look like it was,' said the man opening one of the books and displaying a page of pictures as brown as a desert. 'Look at they herbaceous beds, sir. Real beauties.'

George narrowed his eyes and bent close to the photographs. The borders of fifty years before had become as dead and dry as pressed flowers. 'Beautiful,' he murmured. 'I'm glad you got it.'

'So's I,' agreed the man. Eagerly he turned a page. 'There's me at sixteen, with Mrs Welham, the lady. And there is me again when I took her to Wincanton races one day. Long time ago that was now. War hadn't even started up then. Took her in the motor, I did. The rector never could drive. And he didn't like 'er going to Wincanton races neither. But she was one for life, Mrs Welham was, sir. Hinjoying 'erself. See, there she's got her hand on my shoulder. I 'member that to this day.' His voice softened as if he were speaking only to himself. 'Seems like I can still feel it there.' He put his hand, as brown and dying as the photographs, onto his own shoulder as if he expected an answering touch.

Molly came blinking from the interior of the house carrying the stamp album. 'They're *ever* so pretty,' she exclaimed, ruffling through the pages. 'I didn't know there was so many stamps on earth!' Her enthusiasm melted when she saw her rival bidder.

The man accepted the look. 'I'll be on my way, sir,' he said. He tucked the books under his arm and murmured, 'I got *my* albums anyway,' before moving off and making a solitary path, like an explorer, through the long grass leading to the far end of the lawn.

'Him,' sniffed Molly using the aspirate for emphasis. 'There's a lot said about 'im too.' Gently, George smiled and took the stamp album from her. She brightened at once. 'Good, i'n't they?' she said breathlessly leaning closer.

'Especially this pair,' said George finding the page. He peered closely at the two heads.

'Now look at that,' said Molly vaguely. 'Blessed if they didn't look like Siamese twins, joined up together like that.'

'That's what makes them interesting,' said George. 'Sarawak imperfects. Very nice.' He closed the album secretively. Molly was impressed. Her mouth ajar, her eyes excited. 'I'll tell you about them later,' he said. Someone was hitting a Benares brass gong to summon the bidders in from the garden.

'We'll have to be goin' on soon,' said Molly. She looked at the catalogue. 'Bert's pots and pans are next, so's it shouldn't be long. We could wait out here.' She sniffed and looked about the decrepit garden. 'In this paddock.'

'So the rector went mad,' commented George.

'Mad as mad. Mad enough to kill hisself,' she confirmed with a gush of satisfaction. 'Jumped off the church tower there. Right bang into the middle of a new-dug grave.'

Women were clearing away the tea cloths from the trestle tables. George and Molly had sat on a bench but now one of the cleaners moved near, rattling the empty cups and plates like a warning. She was wearing a brightly flowered pinafore but her expression was barren.

'Better move,' warned Molly loudly. 'They got no time for you 'round these parts.'

They walked from the garden and out onto the dry road. Rooks sounded coarsely in the trees about the church. Molly looked up at the parapet of the church tower. 'Right off there he went,' she said.

Mavis was already on the trap. 'Where *is* he?' she complained. 'The horse is getting tired of waiting.'

Obediently Bert appeared, bearing a pile of dull grey saucepans, each slotted into the one below. He clanked as he hurried, like a knight in armour. When they were all mounted on the trap, Mavis flipped the reins and Baggins turned reluctantly across the hamlet street.

'I was tellin' Mr Goodnight about the rector jumping from the tower,' mentioned Molly.

A small breeze had arrived, cooling the afternoon, and it was pleasant going beneath the moving trees.

'Into an open grave,' added Mavis.

'Aye,' nodded Bert. Then conspiratorially: 'But nobody was being *buried*. There was nobody *dead*. They reckon he dug it 'isself and aimed for it. He always had a good eye. I've heard said he was a good darts player.'

Molly served his dinner again that evening, a steak and kidney pie steaming like a volcano, a tureen of bright vegetables, and a boat of gravy.

'I had a conversation with Lance today,' George mentioned.

'Lance Onions,' she said haughtily. '*Him.*' Abruptly and noisily she dragged a chair to the opposite side of the table. Her bosom overhanging the cloth, she began to spoon the pie and then the vegetables onto his plate, followed by a libation of gravy almost as thick as treacle. She leaned further forward, regarding him seriously through the aromatic steam. 'He says 'e wants to wed me,' she confided. 'It's not that 'e's told me but 'e's told near everybody else.'

George began eating the pie. It was delicious. There was a glass of clouded wine. 'How do you feel about that?' he asked at last.

She looked worried. 'Well, I don't rightly know,' she answered. 'I got to marry somebody sometime, I s'pose. But 'e's a funny one. For a start I don't reckon 'is real name is Lance. He comes from down Somerset and some man who comes from the same place told us that really 'is name is Cyril. Cyril Onions. It's only since 'e came to Somerbourne and started driving that lorry that 'e's called 'isself Lance.'

Just as abruptly as she had sat she stood up and went from the room. George found himself smiling through the dinner steam. This was most certainly a different world. How many more different worlds there must be. He felt fed and comfortable. The sun that day had browned his face. The fresh air had relaxed him. Now he did not care any more about Henry

Wintle and his gossip wife; he had scarcely given a thought to Felicity since their telephone conversation; his work, his life, the life that seemed increasingly former, had not occupied his mind. Instead he wondered how the rector could have leapt from the church tower into an open grave, some feat surely, even for a man with a steady eye.

Evening customers began to assemble in the bar, their amoebic shapes moving across the smoked glass door. Molly came in to clear his plate and the dishes and replace them with a wedge of apple pie and a jug of custard. Under her arm was the stamp album. 'Will you show me they stamps again?' she asked. 'The pie's very hot.'

As she leaned to put the tattered album on the table the soft skin of her ample upper arm brushed against his face.

'Pardon,' she said blushing.

'Don't mention it,' said George. He took the album and opened it, finding the page quickly. 'There,' he said. 'As nice a little pair as you'd ever see.'

'Worth money, you say?'

'Oh yes. You notice they are not perforated.' He glanced at her. 'No holes,' he explained.

''Ow much though? Ten pounds? Or not so much.'

'A little more, Molly. If you would like me to do so, I'll send them to a friend of mine who's a stamp dealer. I'm not sure *exactly* how much he would value them at, or how much he would want to pay if you wanted to sell them . . .'

He glanced up to see her face and eyes shining. Fiercely she pushed back her heavy hair. The steam from the custard had moistened her brow. 'Oh yes,' she murmured. ''Course I'd sell them, Mr Goodnight. They're no good to me. And I wouldn't give them to that Ronnie, my nephew, because 'e's too daft to appreciate them. I'll give him the rest for his birthday, unless there's any others that's worth something . . . How much do you reckon?'

'Two or three hundred pounds,' said George calmly. 'At least two.'

Molly emitted a thick squeak. She stopped herself by putting her own hand over her mouth. 'Two *hundred*!' she gurgled through her fingers. Her voice choked. 'Or three . . .'

An alarm sprang in her eyes. Her hand was still over her mouth. 'Don't please tell anyone 'round 'ere, will you?' she

96

pleaded. She lifted the fingers a fraction. 'Not Bert especially. They'll all want some.'

Surprised, he looked more closely at her. Under the full hair and set in the open rural face, her eyes held a small iron glint.

She stood hurriedly and clumsily. 'Better be getting on,' she said as if embarrassed at what she had revealed. 'They're coming in.' With a short glance back, she added: 'That Lance will be in tonight. Lance Onions.'

Thoughtfully George finished the meal. He went to the window and studied the sky. The evening had greyed but it was very still. He went quickly into the bar and turned out of the street door before there was even a pause in the conversation. On the pavement the air remained warm. He was not sure why he had come out and now he was undecided which way to walk. There was only the choice of two and he turned left, along the closed and empty street towards the church. Rooks were about their noisy housekeeping around the tower and trees, relatives of those he had seen at the neighbouring village that afternoon. Until his arrival they had enjoyed the place to themselves and they set up a louder chant as he opened the gate. He strolled among the careless flowers and the tombstones. The grass had been cut that afternoon and the scent was vivid on the late air. On the stones the family names of the village were repeated – Ostley, Turner, Hailsworth, Borner. He said the names over to himself and realised that here was an unended serial. On some stones there were sensibly left spaces for the future use of members of the same family. Nothing was so certain as death. Roll up, roll up, reserve your place.

Deep in the sombre reverie he was startled to hear the door of the church open. Out came the vicar, wearing an apron and carrying a tin of Brasso and a polishing cloth. They wished each other a good evening. 'I've been polishing up the altar cross and the eagle on the lectern,' explained the vicar. 'The ladies who clean the church won't touch either. It's traditionally left to the vicar.'

To George's surprise he sat comfortably on a table-topped tombstone and invited George to do likewise. 'They won't mind,' he smiled affectionately, patting the stone.

'I've been looking at the names,' said George, glancing

around the churchyard. The rooks had subdued into a cackle. 'All the same families.'

'They go back to the sixteenth century,' nodded the vicar. 'Right through the church registers. There was a fat man living here in the seventeen hundreds, George Borner. He weighed thirty-two stone. It took ten men to carry his coffin. The Borners are still in the village and they're still overweight.'

'It's a wonderful continuity,' murmured George. 'Generation after generation.'

'It doesn't mean a damn thing,' said the vicar surprisingly. 'No one ever asks or wants to know.' He paused and then embarked on what George recognised as a suppressed sermon. 'It's not difficult for a stranger to come here and think this is *Far From the Madding Crowd* country. It looks quiet and lovely and pastoral. But like Hardy, it's only another soap opera, I'm afraid. The people here have all the usual bad habits, greed, lust, intrigue, especially intrigue, as people do everywhere. I see it all, Mr Goodnight. They cheat horribly. Somebody put Monopoly money in the collection bag last Sunday. Only ten pounds too.'

George grinned.

The vicar's smile was sorrowful. 'But they do,' he said. 'And prejudices rankle and there're jealousies and enmities that go on for years, generations. In a city most of them would be forgotten in a while, lost in the general rush of life, but not here. Country people love plastic, tinsel things, you know. Anything they think is modern or up to date. The reason the village streets are vacated at this time on a summer evening is that they're watching *Dallas*.' He began to scrape green moss from the incised letters on the tombstone. 'Josiah Abraham Hailsworth,' he recited. 'Who'd have a name like that today?' He tapped the tomb. 'The ancestor of a gentleman who went down for eighteen months at Winchester Assizes the other day – gross sexual assault.'

George said: 'I went to the sale at Willington Rectory today.'

'Ah, I suppose they told you the rector jumped from the tower.'

'Yes. Into an open grave.'

'Preposterous. They love their legends, you know. That's another thing. He was certainly found in the grave but he didn't drop from the tower. That was just a fanciful story that

98

went around. At the inquest it was clearly stated by the pathologist that he tumbled into the grave and drowned in nine inches of rainwater. The tower bit is bunkum. True, he used to go up there and bellow at the moon but he didn't jump. Quite mad, of course, poor chap. His wife sent him mad. She was a bit of a flirt, even before the war, even with the servants. Drink got him in the end. That's how he fell in the hole.'

George nodded understandingly. 'The tower is a better story,' he said.

'Oh, they won't let that go. In another few years it will be embroidered even more. They'll say he was trying to fly like an angel.'

The evening trees were becoming dark, their great roundels of leaves resembling heavy clouds. The rooks had lapsed to drowsiness. The two men rose and shook hands.

'Home to the crossword,' said the vicar. 'It keeps me going. Are you intending to stay in Somerbourne Magna for any length of time?' He sounded as if he were issuing a friendly warning.

George shook his head. 'I think I'll be moving on soon,' he said.

The clergyman smiled approvingly. 'You could come back for Molly's wedding,' he invited enigmatically.

George was astonished. 'Yes,' was all he could say. 'Perhaps I will.'

Wishing him goodnight the vicar turned away and walked like a swishing ghost through the churchyard, humming the tune of *The Sound of Music*. George shrugged and went out of the lych gate which squeaked violently as he opened and shut it. He glanced at the dark graves. 'Goodnight all,' he murmured moodily.

The street was still in half-light. Windows were yellow and, where the curtains were not drawn, the steely light from a television set was framed by the casement. As he neared the Red Cow he heard the shout of a single, loaded voice from within. He could see through the window that the bar was crowded, shoulders and heads near the panes blocking his view. Cautiously he opened the door and went in. Lance Onions was standing, large feet planted belligerently in the middle of the floor, next to the bar. Beer from his awry tankard was slopping over its edge.

'Me!' he roared. 'I been everywhere, I 'ave. Leicester, Brummingham . . .' He appeared lost for a moment. Then an explosion of inspiration made him tremble. 'Wick!' He glared around. Bert and Molly, looking frightened, were behind the bar. He had not seen George's entry and George remained behind the crowd at the door. 'Yes!' bawled Lance turning on Bert. 'Wick, I've been!' He saw that he was jettisoning beer and hurriedly lifted the tankard to his lips, sucking an inch from the surface.

Trying to appear unperturbed, George moved forward through the crowd and said pleasantly: 'Evening, Lance. Evening everyone.' He was sure Lance was about to attack him. The high and heavy man crouched. Hatred deepened the flush of his face.

'You!' he shouted. His voice descended: 'You . . .'

'You touch Mr Goodnight and I'll never speak a single word to you again, Lance Onions.' Molly was standing with wide arms folded behind the bar.

'Mr Goodnight's a solicitor,' added Bert menacingly.

The threats unsettled Lance for a moment.

'Mr Onions has no reason to be annoyed with me,' said George moving a step closer and putting out a pacifying hand.

'Coming 'ere to Somerbourne,' growled Lance. 'Spoilin' people's lives.' His glare became maniacal. 'I've travelled, I 'ave, mister. I've seen the likes of you. I've travelled . . .'

'Yes, I know,' said George foolishly taunting. 'To Wick.'

'Aaah!' The roar filled the bar and sent the villagers staggering back. White-faced, Lance put his trembling pint down first and then pushed at George with both hands, sending him staggering backwards into the crowd about the fireplace, spilling drinks and customers. A woman standing at the back sat down in the bowl of flowers that decorated the chimney in summer. She sat staring out from the plastic chrysanthemums. As George attempted to right himself he fell in comic supplication forward onto his knees.

'Lance Onions!' shouted Molly. 'You get out of this pub!'

'You!' bellowed Lance across the bar. 'You!' Molly's face went pale but she stood her ground. Picking up Lance's own beer she flung it over his head. That made him cry. He wiped his face with his hands like a huge child, and then with a howl of vengeance and anguish demolished at one blow of his fist the tower of silver coins that the Red Cow had collected so long and so patiently for charity. Tenpenny pieces flew like shrapnel, clinking and jingling all over the room, rolling among the tables and chairs. Several people were quickly on their haunches, almost as quickly as Lance delivered a second blow at the base of the column still remaining. Then, howling and sobbing through beer-and-tear-soaked eyes, he made for the door and banged out into the street. A stark moment later his crazed face appeared at the street window. 'Lance Onions 'as 'ad this place!' he bawled through the glass. The figure vanished. Everyone looked at the coins.

'We'd better start picking them up,' muttered Bert.

'Benson versus Barclays Bank,' muttered George as he bent to help.

The moon, sifting through the dormer, drifted across his room. It illuminated the gnarled door which made a sound like a low cough as it opened. George, who was falling to sleep, opened one eye followed by the other.

Molly was standing like a large and beautiful ghost in the moonbeams. She was wearing a long pale muslin nightdress that fell into a great open gulch below her neck, the skin of her bosom shining softly. 'I expect you'll be going on soon, Mr Goodnight,' she said quietly.

'Yes,' he replied from the bed. He had difficulty in saying even the simple word, but he rallied. 'I think I must, Molly.'

She stepped one pace into the room and pushed the door closed behind her. 'I just came to thank you for them stamps,' she muttered.

As it was Tuesday there was a bus going to Warminster. Molly did not wish him goodbye. She had gone to work while he still slept. Bert was silent and anxious at breakfast as if he had heard news of a crisis in some remote place. He agreed, however, that George could leave his suit hanging in the wardrobe until such time as he could return and claim it. George set out to continue his journey West, clad in the clothes that Mr Patel had provided and with the rest of his brief belongings comfortably contained in a plastic carrier bag.

There was no sun as he left the Red Cow; a low-slung sky and a drifting wind promised rain before long. It began to fall just as the bus pulled up at the stop outside the church. George had waited there for ten minutes with five villagers – a ruminating man and four basket-bearing women – who, strangely, now took no heed of him, their curiosity perhaps spent. In the trees the rooks were muffled. The vicar came from his house and began to brush down the front door of his church. 'Doin' 'is housekeeping work,' muttered a woman to another. 'Gets extra for that, 'e does. Keepin' the money from the workin' women what need it.'

'Funny bugger altogether,' sniffed the other. 'Saw 'im reading off the gravestones once. What can you read off gravestones? Only names.'

'Dead names,' said the other woman without compassion. 'I still reckon it was funny about 'is wife and the rector at Willington, don't matter what they say. 'Er dying so close too. Odd it was, I reckon.'

As the other said, 'Odd, it were,' the plum-coloured bus arrived along the street, 'Warminster' displayed in large, almost arrogant letters above the driver's window. As the rain deepened so the bonnet of the vehicle shivered. George waited until the villagers had mounted the steps then, following them, paid seventy-five pence to the driver who crouched over his big horizontal wheel like a wizard looking into a pot. George took a place in the rear of the bus on the long back seat of hard shiny plastic, torn into wide rifts. The other man who had mounted the bus by the church was sitting, gums still revolving, at the extreme end of the same seat.

The driver made sure everyone was seated and then he himself ran the bell for the conveyance to proceed. He obeyed his own signal and the bus moved forward. Rain began streaking backwards on the window. Through the channels it made in the coating country dust, George looked out at the dulled hills of Wessex, clods of trees, bent fields and houses cowering in the wet. He resisted a final look through the rear window at the village where, in such a few days, so much had befallen him.

Now he began to consider Molly again. She had lain in his mind for most of that morning; her full, clean, warmth, the widespread exploration of her body under the sheets, and the genial accommodation it eventually provided. Her big busy hands, her expansive mouth and the dizzy smell of blossom on her breasts. After that there had been no other course but for

102

him to leave Somerbourne Magna. She had made it easier by leaving early before he awoke. One day, when he went back for his suit perhaps, or even to claim his car, they would meet again. But there would never be another night as voluptuous, as tender. He closed his eyes and tried to regain some morsel of her fullness, her sweetness, below the eiderdown. He was glad he had known about the stamps.

As if comprehending a little of his dreaming the man at the far end of the seat, round-faced, small-eyed and wearing a stained cap and a robust suit, half turned and said, still chewing: 'You're goin' on then?'

Unsurprised now by the immediacy of rural inquiry, George agreed that he was going on. Within himself he felt oddly annoyed that, even as the village grew more distant, he was still travelling with some remnant of it.

'Good thing you are,' pursued the man tonelessly. 'That Lance Onions ain't one to be mucked with.'

'I've never mucked with him,' retorted George, but mildly. 'I had planned to move on anyway. I have to go places.'

'Warminster?' inquired the other man.

'Paris,' retorted George blatantly. 'I'm on my way to France.'

'Lance Onions 'as caused injuries afore now,' returned his fellow passenger. 'In Wick 'e did, wherever that may be.'

'Caithness, I believe,' George told him coolly. 'Or Highland as they call it now. He told you himself, I imagine.'

'For certain. I wouldn't know anybody in Wick or Hireland, now would I?'

A silence closed between them. The man turned away and looked unerringly out of the window as though not wanting to miss a yard of the damp landscape. The ruminant movements of his jaws could be seen from the back of his head. Gratefully, George turned just as solidly the other way. Eventually, at a village crossroads, his fellow passenger rose and with an apparently genuine wish that George should ''ave a nice time in that Paris', clumped from the bus on his country boots and descended to the rain-running street. 'Good riddance,' muttered George.

Now he was truly alone for the first time in days. The departure of the chewing man had completed his isolation from Somerbourne Magna and former and uncertain thoughts began to clock through his mind. The self-question, 'Where am I going?' was re-asked; the difference now being that he was heading West carrying only a plastic bag whereas before he had been surrounded, protected, housed even, by his car and his luggage. He took out his wallet and counted his money for both reassurance and stocktaking. That morning he had paid Bert a most modest thirty pounds and there now remained one hundred and ten pounds in cash, plus some loose change. As a man might do under siege he counted even these smaller resources pedantically and reached a total of two pounds, eighteen pence. There were his two credit cards each with a limit of one thousand pounds, although how much of this was already exhausted he did not know. Felicity had always looked after paying the accounts.

Felicity. What was she doing now? Probably having coffee with someone or flicking around the house in places where the bad-backed daily could not reach. Later she would probably meet a girlfriend for lunch, attend a committee and at some time would either be planning a visit to the hairdresser's or actually be enthroned there. Why did she go to the hairdresser's so often? Was it shelter or companionship or the attention of a young man? Her hair had never looked any different to him. It had taken three days for him to notice she had turned blonde.

Then there was Tina; at her lessons, waiting for the bell and for the end of term. When she was younger, and they were happier, they had usually taken her for a week at Whitstable where the smell of the whelks hit you as soon as you stepped from the train. He found himself smiling reflectively; the shelly beach, the tide sneaking towards Belgium, the roughly-singing gulls, the oozing sand. One day an onrush of wind from the sea had blown Felicity's hair out from her head like a shredded flag, the first time he had ever seen it flowing like that, and she had been furious, but then had laughed when she saw they were laughing. What had happened to those days? The wind and the tide, the gulls and the whelks were undoubtedly still there. Only the three of them had gone.

His introspection faded and the Wiltshire landscape appeared once more. Porous sheep staggered up the soaked hillsides, a farmhand carrying buckets sheltered in a barn door, his eyes lifted to the drips falling from the transom, and a woman, hooded in a coat like a suspect, scurried along a village street.

The bus's arrival in Warminster went unheralded. George

alighted to a gushing gutter and trudged towards the railway station. He had no plan but there was a signpost pointing to the station. There he discovered that a train to Exeter was due in an hour. He bought a newspaper and sat in the mute waiting room. Moodily he unfolded it. It was the next issue of the same local journal as he had read on the first night of his absconding. He found himself comfortingly familiar with some of the characters. The carnival queen had resigned because, she said, travelling on the lorry made her sick and her crown did not fit. George nodded understandingly. There was also a hint of romance with a man from Devizes. Ah, the man of Devizes again. George wondered how his various-sized balls were faring. Had he won any more prizes? Melksham man had been drunk again, this time with the embellishment of being disorderly and, what is more, indecent. He tried to recall the famous precedent – an acquittal for lack of a precise charge. Rex versus Tozer, he decided. There was to be yet another sale of effects.

An announcement caught his eye: a blatant enticement by the railways to the populace of Warminster to visit Plymouth – 'This historic city of Drake and Raleigh – the gateway to the Spanish Main!' George decided to make for Plymouth.

Before the western train arrived, its opposite number travelling for London rolled heavily in at the far platform. Its windows were lit in the dim day and there was a tempting flash of tables in the restaurant car. It was time for lunch. George regarded it with a spasm of longing. All he had to do was to cross the footbridge, open a door and climb in. In minutes he would be returning towards his starting place. Familiarity, ease, security beckoned him but then, like a cloud, came the truth that none of those comforts were actually now available. The starting place was no longer present. He stood, tall and solitary as a wet street lamp, and watched the London train pull out.

In a few minutes the yellow-faced express came in from the opposite direction. It sighed impatiently into the small station as its destinations were promulgated over the loudspeaker by a fruity Wessex voice. Doors fell open and a few country people alighted. An old lady was hugged by a child who had been waiting on the platform. 'Let's be getting home!' he heard the woman cry. The child led her with tender eagerness by the hand.

Heavily George boarded the train and sat down. His clothes felt clammy on his back. Adventure which had beckoned so boldly now seemed a figure of doubtful substance. Perhaps he ought to have gone home and asked Fred and Cynthia if he could stay with them for a while. That would have been a good ploy. Felicity's pride would hardly allow him to lodge next door for long. He almost smiled at the vision: each morning he would set out with his briefcase and wave cheerily as he went by his own window, and wave again, but in a more subdued manner, as he returned at the close of the day. There he would be hoeing or mowing in Fred's garden while hired help tended his or Felicity tried to do it herself. ('I say, would you like to borrow our rake?') And she would certainly never be able to start the mower. Surely she wouldn't be able to endure that set-up for very long. He might even join the cricket club.

He felt hungry but, proceeding West towards the rest of the world as he was still, he was aware of the need to conserve his funds. He was going in the wrong direction to patronise the restaurant car. Instead he left his seat and stood in the queue at the buffet. There were half a dozen others swaying like drunks in unison with the train, balancing plastic cups and bacon sandwiches as they moved away from the counter. Behind George stood a young man with over-burdened eyes and a thick lip. 'You wouldn't be a goalkeeper by any chance, would you?' he inquired.

'Actually, no,' replied George.

'Right you are. I just thought you looked about the stamp for a goalkeeper, that's all.'

'No, I've never been a goalkeeper.'

'Right you are,' said the young man again.

After they had been served he followed George back to his seat and sat strategically opposite. His ravaged eyes regarded the cheese roll that George was lifting towards his teeth. 'It's just that I've got a goalkeeper's jersey spare, that's all.'

Through the crust and cheese George said: 'Rugger man myself.'

'Bloody shame,' said the young man. 'It would fit you, just about.' He began to fumble in a commodious holdall and brought out a blue jersey with a high neck. He held it up, apologetically, by the arms. 'It's a navy one,' he confessed. 'Really.'

106

'Goalies wear green,' pointed out George.

'I know. In general. But in the navy, see, they wear navy.'

'Most appropriate. Are you in the navy?'

'That's the trouble,' said the youth, immediately confessional. He leaned forward. 'I'm adrift, see. Up in London. Women and drink, and that.' A guilty smile bulged on the thick lip. 'And a couple of fights. You know how it goes.'

'Oh yes,' George said as if it were a weekly occurrence. 'Too well.'

'Well, I'm in enough trouble *now*. Adrift and that. But if the ship sails without me I'm in dead bother – in the brig and no arguments. What I need is a couple of quid for a taxi to the ship. I'll just get there by the skin of my teeth and it won't be so bad.'

'Just clearing out the bilges,' offered George. 'No rum ration.'

The sailor appeared puzzled. 'Pay docked,' he corrected. 'No bingo. No privileges at all. But I can stand that. The brig's different.' He squeezed his damaged face into a plea. The lip rolled like a slug. 'A couple of quid for the jersey?' he asked.

'All right,' agreed George. He heard himself say: 'I'm thinking of going to sea myself. It might come in useful.' He felt in his back pocket. 'I'll give you three pounds for it. Then you can give the taxi a tip.'

Relief rumbled across the sailor's face. The money and the jersey were exchanged. The train rattled West. A spate of unexpected sunshine rushed over the Devon fields. 'I've got some spare socks too,' ventured the young man.

Plymouth stretched itself splendidly. The Sound was corrugated by bright wind; Drake's Island stood stoutly, with ships lying off and flags and pennants streaking from masts. The air that rushed up George's nostrils was laden with salt. Somewhere a bugle sounded.

He had boarded for the night in a house near the Hoe, a solid, comfortable berth, as he even now liked to consider it, kept by a stoker's widow. During darkness the wind had blown gustily and he was roused at daybreak by the coarse demands of gulls. There were maps and charts on the walls of the room where he breakfasted alone, the contours of Mauritius, and the Amazon as far as Manaus. There were seasonal tide tables for Accra and useful instructions on the navigable waters of the

Irrawady and the Humber. There was also a photograph of a black-faced man with a shovel, whom George took to be the late stoker.

The morning had been stirring and encouraging. Urgent jingles came from the taut rigging of miniature boats in an enclosed dock and at noon, wearing his sailor jersey, he squatted in the sun at a table outside a maritime public house, a pint of beer in his fist, his face to the tanning breeze.

'Just signed off?' ventured a nervous voice behind him. George turned to see a mild-looking couple, a middle-aged man and a wife, visibly uncomfortable in matching boating array, crackling yellow oilskins, short yellow wellingtons and red woollen caps with white bobbles.

It was the man who had made the inquiry. Now the woman added: 'You look like you just have.' Together they sat down. She had red bumps on her face like baby tomatoes.

'No . . . not just,' answered George.

'Oh, you haven't. Been ashore some time then?' The tomatoes wobbled as she spoke.

'Yes, quite some time,' agreed George truthfully. He fingered the collar of the blue jersey. Then he said it. 'On the beach.'

'We've watched you,' she confided. 'All morning, haven't we, Cess? Walking up and down, sniffing.'

'Like you couldn't wait to get back to sea,' confirmed Cess.

'The call is pretty strong,' George heard himself saying modestly. He was surprised, but less so now, at the facility with which he entered into these fantasies. 'Once you've got it, you never lose it.'

'Have a drink,' suggested the man hurriedly as if fearing the conversation might be terminated by George casting off and sailing out of sight. He looked at the empty tankard. 'Have another pint. Or would you prefer rum?'

'Rum afloat. Beer ashore,' George philosophised blatantly. He held out what he hoped might be taken for a horny hand. 'Loving is the name,' he said. 'Oliver Loving.'

'Meredith,' said the man gratefully. 'Cecil. And this is Annie, my wife. We're worried. Very worried indeed.'

The husband went into the bar, his short wellingtons dabbing the stone yard. 'You tell him, Annie,' he said over his shoulder.

Annie prepared herself to do so. The red knobs on her face became agitated as if they were jostling each other.

108

'We've hired a boat,' she began. 'A sailing boat. With a crew. My husband's got a grocery business, wholesale that is, in Wolverhampton, and we'd always promised ourselves we would sail away somewhere when we could manage it, with the time and the money. So we answered an advertisement, Boxing Day it was, for this boat with a crew and we've paid the deposit, naturally, and we came down yesterday.' She paused. 'And then we saw it.'

'No good?' suggested George. 'You didn't like it?'

'Not the boat. That's all right. It's the crew.'

'What's wrong with them?'

'I think Cess had better explain. It's more a thing for a man.'

'I'll explain,' agreed Cess appearing on cue with a tray of drinks, a pint for George, a half of shandy for himself and a lemonade for Annie. He sorted the glasses, putting them carefully before each person, and stored the tray under the table. He sat behind his shandy and fixed his face on George. 'Pansies,' he said darkly. 'Queer as moonbeams.'

'How many?' asked George, obviously to their surprise.

'Well, three,' answered Cess.

'Really terrible,' put in Annie. 'It's not natural.'

'We couldn't put to sea with them,' said Cess heavily.

'We'd be uncomfortable,' supported Annie.

George took an initial draw of his beer. 'But can they sail?' he asked.

'This lot could fly,' answered Cess bitterly.

'We didn't know,' sniffed Annie. 'We asked about everything else but we didn't think to ask about *that*. It's not something you cater for, is it?'

'Or insure against,' added her husband dolefully. 'But I just can't see us going across to France with a load of yo-yoes as a crew.'

The lawyer in George said: 'Have you complained to the owners of the vessel?'

'We did. Right away. But he was fruity as a cake himself. Said they were an experienced crew. Two of them had been around the Horn.'

Annie swallowed her lemonade with a decisive gulp, like someone drinking a desperate whisky. 'What we're saying, Mr Darling . . .'

'Loving,' murmured George.

'Pardon. My mistake. What we're saying . . . asking . . . is would you come with us?'

'Extra crew,' confirmed Cess. 'You look the experienced, dependable sort. I can tell a good sailor a mile away, even if I do live in Wolverhampton. We need somebody we can . . .'

'Rely on,' supplied Annie. 'Trust. And we'll pay you, of course.'

'Hundred pounds for a week,' said Cess leaning forward. 'Fifty in advance.'

'Otherwise we won't go,' sniffed Annie. 'It will all be spoilt.' Her face was fixed, the tomatoes scarcely quivering.

George, once more to his astonishment, heard a voice he recognised as his agreeing. He had truly intended to do the proper thing, put them right, correct their assumptions. But suddenly, unbidden, there were the words issuing from his mouth. 'Sure,' he said gruffly. 'I'll sail with you.'

Brief squeaks of appreciation came from Annie Meredith. Her bumps bounced. 'Don't squeak, Annie,' said Cess. He thrust his grocer's hand across and shook George's so firmly it hurt.

'This afternoon, then,' he said. 'Three o'clock tide. We'll expect you at two.' He pointed. 'She's just below the steps there. She is called . . .' His hesitation was lengthy. 'She's called *Sally-by-the-Shore*.'

Doubts and shame were already simmering in George. He stood up and as he did so Cess pressed five ten-pound notes into his hand.

'I know we can trust you,' he enthused deeply.

'Oh yes,' said Annie. 'With our lives.'

'Thank you,' answered George. He was mesmerised. *Now* what had he done? How did these things happen? 'I'll be there. I'll pick up my sea gear and be aboard at two.'

'Good afternoon. Brent and Raney.' It was the real world speaking. George pressed the coins into the slot.

'Hello. Could I speak to Mr Freddy Birch, please. Long distance.'

'I'll put you through.'

Freddy came on the line.

110

'Fred,' said George urgently. 'Fred . . . how are you? It's George.'

'George! How are *you* more like it? *Where* are you?'

'In a phone box. In Plymouth. I think I'm going to sea, Fred.'

'Good God!'

'Fred, it's no use me coming back, is it?'

'You could try. But I don't think it will work. She's pretty grim about it. She told the wife that the longer you're away the better. She hopes it's years.'

'Oh God. There's nothing for it then. I'll have to go.'

To his concern Fred did not seem to share his anxiety. 'Wish I were going to sea,' the voice said, George thought without much conviction. 'Instead of being stuck in here. Have you had . . . you know . . . adventures?'

'Some. But this is *it*, Fred. The moment of truth. I'm leaving England. It's the point of no return . . .' The warning pips sounded. 'Keep my stamps safe, Fred.'

'They're safe. Goodbye, sailor.'

'Goodbye, Fred.'

He replaced the phone and left the box. The afternoon had greyed and the wind remained brisk. Along the Hoe it was so strong that he abandoned his course and went down into the town among the afternoon shoppers. People seemed to be so busy, they had so much to occupy them, hurrying, going somewhere, doing things. His loneliness increased to melancholy. He had a sad cup of tea in a café crowded with women and then sought out another telephone box. It was Wednesday. Sometimes it was possible to ring Tina on Wednesday afternoons. He was lucky. She came to the phone quickly.

'George! I've been so worried. What are you doing?'

'I'm going to sea, Tina,' he said.

'George! That's really ace! Where? Where are you sailing?'

'Whichever way the wind blows,' he replied sombrely.

'How fab! George, I love you. How fab! Mummy says she never wants to see you again.'

'I understood it was only for a few years.'

'No. It's for ever. She's livid. She knows about your milkmaid. Oh, George, I can't believe it!'

'I must go,' he said sadly. 'I'll be sailing soon. And the money's about to give out. When's school finish?'

'Friday. Thank goodness. Oh George, goodbye darling. I'll pray for you. I'll restart my prayers again specially.'

Again the warning pips came. There seemed nothing more to say anyway.

'Goodbye, Tina.'

'Goodbye, George. God bl . . .'

VI

A sea fret was moving in from the Channel as they cleared
Rame Head. The yacht began to lift uneasily. The sky had
become thick. John, the skipper, began to sing deeply, while his
companions, Joe and Donald, scurried about maritime tasks.
They were under only light sail. Below George's feet he could
feel the engine breathing confidently. Mr and Mrs Meredith,
standing one each side in the cockpit of the boat, glanced at
him as though in response to some psychic signal.

'Well,' said George. He could feel the boards rising and
falling uncomfortably beneath his soles. 'They seem to know
what they're about.'

John had refused authoritatively to allow George to become
an extra member of the crew. 'Contract,' he said in his north
country voice. 'Contract says that I'm captain and these two
are crew. Mister Loving,' he added 'Can be extra passenger, of
course. There's nowt we can say to that. But *we're* the crew.'

'We would like him to do *something*,' put in Annie desperately.
'He's *very* experienced.'

The trio regarded George with scepticism.

'In what, may I be so bold as to ask?' inquired John.

'The sea,' returned Annie firmly.

'The seven seas,' confirmed Cess.

George, wishing they would turn back so that he could
disembark, gave a semi-nod.

'He's been to Venezuela,' Annie tossed in blatantly.

George blinked at this news, then pretended he had salt in
his eye and wiped it away. To his astonishment John began to
sing.

> . . . to pass away the time
> In Venezuela.

When he stopped he smiled in a conciliatory fashion. 'We
don't want to fall out amongst ourselves right at start, now do

we?' he said. Everyone shook their heads. 'So we'll consider Mr Loving an auxiliary. A help where help's needed.'

Nodding agreement, George said unhappily: 'I don't want to interfere with anybody.'

'You can help,' promised the skipper again. He appeared thoughtful, then encouraging. 'I tell you what . . .' He stepped forward and patted George on the chest. 'I tell you what you can do. You can stare at the sea for us. See if there's anything coming.'

His companions nodded eagerly. They were small men, Joe lithe but with big hanging hands, Donald rounded with sparse fair hair. John was a dark, sharp-cornered man. He had pale, almost liquid eyes. They each wore a blue and white sailor's jersey of horizontal stripes. The rounded Donald looked like a buoy. He and Joe wore earrings. They were from Barnsley and John from Oldham. All three had left their homes when they were boys and had begun walking towards the sea.

'We didn't actually *know* where the sea was,' confided Joe to George while they were peeling the potatoes for the evening meal. John had suggested this further duty for the extra man. 'I mean, we were only lads, and we decided to run away together, and in the end we walked in a straight line. We could have ended up anywhere. Scotland even, where the weather, as you might know, can be jolly inclement. But even then John had a feeling for navigation and we arrived safe and sound in New Brighton. A nice businessman took a fancy to us . . .' His voice dropped prudently. 'Well, *me* actually, but he let them come too. Off we went in his forty-footer to Ireland, which is a terribly rough place, and that's how we started off.' He sighed. 'It was years ago, simply years.' He cut the potato peel into a large smile and imitated it. 'And hardly a cross word between us since.'

The vessel was still moving in a worried way. They were sitting each side of the galley hatch. The shudder of the hull and the growing cooking smells from within were causing George discomfort. He swallowed heavily and Joe looked up from his potato and saw the swallow. 'Never been to sea in your life, have you?' observed the striped man.

George shook his head miserably. 'It shows, doesn't it?' he said.

'You wouldn't know a carbuncle from a barnacle,' said Joe,

114

again studying the potato. He sliced a long peninsula of peel and looked up from below his eyelashes. 'On the run, are you?'

'In a way,' confessed George. 'Not from the police or anything like that. From my wife and my life.'

'Both can be well worth fleeing,' said Joe philosophically. 'Not that I would know about a wife.' He sighed, an action in time with the heave of the hull. 'It's unlikely now, too,' he said with a sort of regret. 'It's too much of an adjustment. But we all sussed you were no sailor. It takes a bit of practice to even walk properly, you know. It was ages before I got the hang of it, or anything else. My navigation is a bit weak even now. Very hit and miss it is and, it goes without saying, in navigation it's generally better to miss than hit. John's clever like that. He's got all the certificates, but Donald's worse than me. He could get lost on the Manchester Ship Canal.' He laughed pleasantly. 'When we were all lads this chap tried to tell us the cardboard method.'

George looked up from his potato. He was feeling happier with the company now. 'What's that entail?' he asked. 'The cardboard method?'

'You get a square of cardboard and poke a hole in it with a pencil so that the stars show through. One hole one star, see. And then to find out if you're sailing on the right course you fit it around the stars every night.' He smiled and shook his head. 'The man who showed us that was a wicked old devil,' he remembered. 'And we were only lads, eager to learn, and trying to concentrate. He was also the worst navigator in the world. Silk he called himself. Captain Silk.'

They had finished the peeling. Joe took the pot of potatoes and dipped them over the side on a short line. 'Washing and salting at the same time,' he explained. 'We always boil them in sea water.' Retrieving the pot he ducked into the galley. 'There's only one speck of land in the very middle of the Indian Ocean,' he called back. 'St Paul's Island, no more than a rock really. There's thousands of miles of water on every side of it. India one way, Africa another. Australia straight on. And silly old Captain Silk collided with it. He did! With all that leeway he struck it fair and square. She went down in minutes, so the tale goes. And it wasn't the first time either. I've often wondered what happened to Captain Silk. Where he is today. Sitting in rags on some lonely shore, I expect. Waiting to be rescued.'

That night the sea rose and rolled. George clung to his bunk or staggered along on hinged legs to the latrine at short intervals. 'Lie the other way around,' suggested Donald, the duty man, helpfully as George returned from one of these journeys. 'Feet where your head was, see.' George muttered his thanks and took the advice. The hull continued to pitch and sway but he quite suddenly slept. He awoke at seven in the morning aware that the boat had calmed and slowed. Going on deck he discovered that they were creeping through an English Channel fog.

'Sailor,' called John from the wheel. George looked about then realised the call was for him. Cess and Annie appeared in the cockpit. Both wore dressing gowns, their woolly sea hats, and anxious expressions. 'Go for'ard,' ordered John. 'An extra pair of eyes on the bow we need.'

'Aye,' muttered George. 'Aye, sir.'

'Does he know where we are?' Mrs Meredith asked George diffidently.

'Does he?' asked her husband. 'Has he got a clue?'

'More or less,' whispered George reassuringly. He moved forward to the narrow bow. The sea had become quiescent, slopping balefully against the hull. Foghorns, at first hooting distantly and then disquietingly close, haunted the mist that lay around the small boat like a dirty drape. George set his eyes ahead, fixed to the fog. He heard music coming through the web. He even recognised the tune. 'Hang a Yellow Ribbon on the Old Oak Tree.' It was a long title and he had hardly identified it when through the murk directly ahead and coming right at them was a great shape, tall and spreading, like a moving wall. 'Ship ahoy!' he croaked. His shout was directed backwards towards John on the wheel. 'A big one,' he whispered pathetically to himself. John was already throwing the wheel over when their craft heeled violently, veering in fright it seemed, its bow curling to starboard, its mast waving like a baton, its occupants flung sideways. The bow of the big vessel soared above them, a shadowy look-out man even then hopelessly waving them out of the way. But there was no time.

There came a crunching blow and the small vessel heaved violently. George was flung with the others to the deck, but even as he was he saw John fighting to hold onto the wheel. Then with a high scream Annie Meredith, trying illogically to

116

get to her feet, was sent staggering by another lurch of the boat. George, from his prone position on the deck, tried to grab her leg but she fell against the rail and, with a look of surprise and terror, toppled into the sea.

'Man overboard!' spluttered George. The lawyer in him corrected the call. 'Woman overboard!'

It was Joe who first went in after her, quickly followed by Donald. With swift and decisive actions they clipped lifelines to their belts, threw in three lifebelts and followed them over the side. Annie Meredith's stark, soaked face appeared once, then again, in the foggy water. Cess began shouting unnecessary advice. 'Keep still, Annie!' he bawled. 'Keep your mouth shut!'

All George could do was to stumble to his feet, only to tip forward again, in an appropriate attitude of prayer. He crawled to the rail. Annie surfaced again and this time Joe caught her and held her up while Donald got a lifejacket over her head. Then Joe dived below the exhausted woman and pulled off her yellow wellington boots. They bobbed cheerfully to the surface just as he did.

But now they had secured her. George and Cess caught hold of the lines. John appeared muscularly beside them and shouldered George aside. 'Take the wheel,' he ordered briskly. 'Keep her head as she is.'

George heard himself answering 'Aye, aye, sir.' He was on his knees and he had difficulty in getting upright, so he went towards the wheelhouse at a sort of moving kneel, pulling himself to a stand with the rail as he got there. He levered himself behind the wheel and caught hold of its rim. His arms ached and his knees were raw but a previously unknown excitement was surging within him. John and Cess were heaving Mrs Meredith aboard. She was barely conscious. The skipper stretched her on the deck and began to apply mouth to mouth resuscitation. Cess, all consternation, made a move to restrain him, as if indicating he would rather perform the act himself, but John elbowed him so firmly aside that he sat back heavily on the deck. Joe and Donald were climbing aboard, waiting for the tip of the vessel and forcing themselves onto the deck with athletic heaves. Joe was first and he turned and helped Donald with the final tug that brought him to safety. They sprawled exhausted on the deck boards.

Annie Meredith opened her eyes and gazed up at the kneeling John in a startled way.

'You're all right, Annie,' howled her tearful husband. 'You're all right, girl. We got you out!'

Annie realised. A broken smile crossed her face. Her arms went about John's neck and she kissed him thoroughly.

Cherbourg's Chez les Marins, Sailors' Home, charitably operated by the Logements d'Accueil pour Marins en Détresse and called 'La Maison M'Aidez', overlooks the brisk Channel harbour on one side and the mazed port streets on the other. George's room, which he shared with an archaic one-armed Frenchman, a resident of years, and an Algerian who cooked couscous in the corridor, overlooked the streets.

The crew of the *Sally-by-the-Shore* had returned to England by cross-Channel ferry, the dearest of friends with Cess and Annie Meredith. They had come into port towed by a trawler, their stricken little vessel only submerging with a sigh after they had all gained the shore. They stood on the quay and watched her go down. John had doffed his cap and Joe and Donald sniffed, although it may only have been colds coming on as a result of their submersion. They boarded the ferry for home the same day, insurance and compensation being discussed. They waved cheerily to the solitary George standing on the quayside. Joe called out: 'Sally-by-the-Shore!' and George smiled wanly because the joke was on him.

Now he had done it, now he had crossed to a separate country, George was sharply conscious of the remoteness of strangers and of being alone among them. He had been directed to the Maison M'Aidez by the port authorities. The Sailors' Home was an insecure structure held up by so many wooden buttresses and cross-stays that it appeared, not inappropriately, like a ship the builder had failed to finish. It was run by a surly custodian with a wilderness of beard, which blew outwards when he spoke. His wife wore a flat cap and her sabots echoed like castanets through the wooden corridors. They had once attempted to run weekly dances in the place but these had not been a success. George did not like it there. On the first night the Algerian capsized his pot of couscous over the floor and it ran between the cracks of the boards before he could scrape most of it up. He wept because it was his

118

dinner. The Frenchman, a garrulous romancer, had the disconcerting habit of gesticulating with his missing arm. The house was hung with cobwebs which shuddered in the draughts and the beds sagged. George found a store of cigarette butts in his. He decided to move on.

His belongings, his passport and his money were still contained in the plastic carrier bag from Somerbourne Magna. He counted out his money on the bed. The surly custodian approached as he was doing this and when he saw the drying money became at once more amenable. He counted it loudly over George's shoulder, pointing to each note and inquiring how much it might be worth in francs, and what the total might be. George said about two thousand. It was the opportunity to inform the man that he would be departing. This evoked only an unsurprised shrug from the Frenchman who apologised that the place was not all it might have been. He had recognised a better class of lodger. When he and his wife had arrived there they had ambitions but all had been frustrated. After the failure of the weekly dances their interest had finally died.

Not knowing where he was going or what he was to do, George went along the quay. The tide was out and the fettered boats had descended deeply into the harbour, their masts hardly level with his walking knees. Gulls and smells occupied the air. It was a blank day with only a flimsy wind. No one noticed him. He scarcely looked the part of an adventurer; a wanderer perhaps, or somebody lost.

He walked aimlessly below the flying wings of the gulls, eventually turning away from the port.

The streets of Cherbourg near the quays and jetties grew close against each other, as if they were jostling to get a slight view of the sea. George took a random corner and found himself looking into low windows of food and hardware, seagoing clothes and shoes, a tobacconist, a place selling hued ice creams, and, soberly amid the others, a stamp dealer's. It was a cleft of a shop, a single window and a door. At once George felt a reassurance. He looked in the window for a few minutes, approving the wares, mostly French Colonials, Indo-Chino, Cameroons and Nouvelle Caledonie, one goodish set of Trinidad and Tobago, 1913, the first year 'Tobago' appeared on the stamps. He went confidently into the shop.

*

'Hello, Brent and Raney.'

'Hello. Could I speak to Mr Birch, please?'

'Yes, one moment.'

'It's an international call. From overseas.'

'Yes, I see. Putting you through.'

'Hello, Birch here.'

'Fred, it's George.'

'Good God, George! You again. Where are you now?'

'France, old boy. Cherbourg. Been shipwrecked and everything.'

'Wonderful. So things are happening.'

'They certainly are. Listen, Fred, I can't talk for long because I'm using Monsieur Julien's phone.'

'Oh, Monsieur Julien, I see.'

'He's a stamp dealer. Fred, you've still got the stamps safe?'

'As houses.'

'Turn up British Honduras, will you . . .'

'I haven't got them here.'

'When you get home, I mean. But don't let Cynthia see you.'

'She won't. She doesn't know I've got them. I'm a sly bugger when necessary. British Honduras.'

'There's a set of used Queen Victorias. Top of the page. Ten, including a green and black, five dollar.'

'Right. I'm writing it down. Green and black, five dollar. Got you.'

'Take the whole set off the page. Be careful, won't you, Fred. Send them to me here. Care of Monsieur Julien, 24 Avenue Racine, Cherbourg, Manche, Normandie, France. Express them or whatever, will you, Fred? And put some protection around them.'

'All right, George. I've got all that. Are you going to flog them?'

'Something's got to finance all this excitement, Fred. Seen anything of Felicity?'

'She went off for a couple of days somewhere. She never said where.'

'Oh, did she? By herself?'

'Don't know. Never mind. You have a good time.'

'I will,' George promised flatly. 'Send the stamps as soon as you can.' Slowly he replaced the phone.

'*Oui, monsieur?*' said Monsieur Julien. 'It is arranged?'

'The stamps. Yes, all fixed. They should be here in a few days.'

'*Bon, bon.* What will you now do?'

'Go somewhere more amenable than La Maison M'Aidez,' said George.

Monsieur Julien nodded with slow but certain understanding. His pale blue eyes, set in a bald face, seemed like little windows in the dimness of the narrow shop. 'That place,' he agreed, 'is not good. Once, it was good, there was much life. When the Germans were here, the hated Boche you know, they used to have some very good times there. It was their club, their canteen, singing and drinking and dancing every night. It was very popular. Then the Americans arrived, after the landings, and liberated it from the Boche and it was even better. Different music, different drinking, the same girls.'

'The fortunes of war,' muttered George.

'Indeed, *monsieur.* But since then it has gone below. They tried to start the dances again but it was no good.'

'All the magic gone,' suggested George.

'*Exactement.* Now you must have somewhere. There is a small, good *auberge* at the end of this street. Monsieur and Madame Müller. Wolfgang and Marie. He was one of the hated Boche. They will make you comfortable until the stamps arrive and we can do business. Tonight I will be there also, at the Villa Bismarck. Twice a week I dine there, for I am alone, and this is Friday.'

George said he would be delighted. Friday? It was Friday? Of course, it was. He had been away almost a week. They parted jovially and George went to the extreme of the street where he found the Villa Bismarck, a hunched house but with a bright green garden. The sun had come out again and Madame Müller was bending plumply, plucking weeds, and she sounded a brief squeal of surprise when he spoke to her over the gate. She calmed and smiled at the name of Monsieur Julien, the sort of friend, she intimated, who was beyond price, and she agreed that they had a room, in fact they had several.

Still clutching the trowel fork, points up like a sea god, she stamped up the stairs, yammering away in French so swift that George could not keep up with it. He gathered, however, as she panted onto the landing and opened a door, that they were not busy now. Their clients were mainly from her husband's

German homeland, coming back to view again their familiar wartime places.

'The room,' said Marie as though introducing a person. '*La chambre. Das Zimmer.*' She pointed at a tatty window. '*Regardez la mer,*' she said. '*Schau das Wasser an.*'

When Marie was gone, George walked to the window and saw that it squinted over various triangles of roofs, red and grey, with an indent at the distant end displaying a slice of sea. He lifted the sash and at once the breeze blew in and with it the sounds of the town and the gulls.

He stared through the window. Out there, across that sea, was his life-so-far, his familiars. Freddy Birch was preparing to go home from Brent and Raney. The stamps would shortly be on their way. Cynthia Birch would be thinking about dinner, Lizzie Birch about her exams.

Tina would be on that exuberant train heading for home, for today was the start of the summer holidays. He dearly wished he could see her. Felicity would be waiting at the station, so well-groomed that she would hardly allow herself a smile in case it might spoil the effect. She always stood out at railway stations. He had seen men, busy men, hurrying men, stop and gaze at her. He thought of Clemmie at the *News* office and Moncur the editor, and Burtenshaw. He wondered where in the world Burtenshaw might be. Most likely somewhere in a foreign land. Well, so was *he* now. Perhaps Burtenshaw was snooping in one of the streets below among the fishermen and the housewives. George withdrew from the window and, sitting on the bed, burned the last of his boats. He wrote a letter to Mr Moncur resigning from his position, for private reasons ('of a nature that require my long absence from the country') and asking that his personal effects be forwarded to his home. He also signed a separate letter giving authority for the money accrued in his pension fund to be sent to his wife. 'With my compliments,' he muttered grimly.

Going down the stairs he found a fatigued-faced man sitting behind the reception window, so still and staring that he appeared like a portrait in a frame. 'Herr Goodnight . . . monsieur, sir,' the man said partly coming to life. 'Welcome to the Villa Bismarck. Have you before visited Cherbourg?'

George said that he had not.

122

'It is all changed now,' said Wolfgang sadly. 'From the old days. Now everybody is a foreigner.'

'The world is full of them,' commiserated George.

They ate salt mutton, a speciality of the area, said Monsieur Julien, the sheep having grazed on the seashore meadows. At ten o'clock the old one-armed sailor from the Maison M'Aidez materialised outside the window and began to wave his stump. He stopped after a while and moved closer to the glass, grimacing, apparently to ascertain that he had captured their attention. Having confirmed that he had he retreated a pace or so and wagged the empty sleeve with new belligerence.

'For some the war is never over,' sighed Monsieur Julien. He poured some more wine. 'Every night he does this. Except when the weather is bad. Bad weather hurts his arm.'

'What exactly is he doing?'

'Making a Hitler salute with his arm that is no longer present,' shrugged the Frenchman. 'It has no meaning now. It is as empty as his coat.'

'It's because of Wolfgang and Marie being married, is it?' guessed George. 'He doesn't approve.'

'Marie, she is this man's daughter,' answered Monsieur Julien prodding a loaded fork towards the window with its antic figure. 'But now they never speak. If he sees her, or Wolfgang, in the street or at the market he shouts and raises a Nazi salute. But it is not so . . . not so noticeable if you have no arm.'

'When did it happen?'

'His arm fell off in the war,' said Monsieur Julien simply. He looked more closely towards the window. He sighed and raised his glass. 'He is gone,' he said. 'He does not stay for a great time – just for someone to see him. It is a gesture.'

'He was in the Resistance?' asked George. 'I heard him saying something about it at the Maison M'Aidez.'

'Everyone,' said Monsieur Julien. He pushed his plate away, changed his mind and brought it back to spear an overlooked shred of salt mutton. 'Everyone was in the Resistance. Everyone. Sometimes I think even the Germans. They will all tell you some story. As for the armless one, well he perhaps is telling a *soupçon* of the truth because he was always stealing from the hated Boche. The arm fell off when he was stealing from the Americans after the invasion. Something went bang.'

Enjoying the old man's company, George ordered a Calvados. Monsieur Julien had a glass of claret. 'Near this place,' the Frenchman said, as if he had been awaiting the proper moment to tell, 'there is an excellent stamp collection. Highly excellent. Not so much a collection, you might say. More a mass. Stamps and stamps and stamps. But in such a state, monsieur, that it would make you weep.' He drank his wine and shook the glass and his head at the same time.

'They belonged once to a man I knew, he was very famous in this town. Monsieur Joby, Robert Joby, the late. His daughter Janine is in the house with all these stamps and she does not know what to do with them. I could go tomorrow and buy them for I know she would take what I offered without questions. But I have told her that they must be catalogued and valued before they are sold. I would try it myself but I'm too old, too slow, and I make mistakes. They would fetch a big sum of money at auction.'

'Didn't the owner, didn't Monsieur Joby, have them in order?'

The Frenchman shrugged. 'He was not an orderly man.'

'Strange for a stamp collector,' commented George.

'He said he liked them in that way, all over and over, because that way they always would give him surprises. They would be new each time. I think some he got from his father and they were in order, catalogued, collated, but he scattered those also. He was a strange man. When he was dying he crept from the bed and tried to set fire to his own house. But somebody telephoned the firemen and they outed the flames. He was most angry. They say he dropped dead with it. Some of the stamps were burned but most were saved.' He paused, then drank the last of the claret. 'Another is called for,' he commented, studying the glass. 'And another Calvados perhaps, Monsieur Goodnight?'

George said he would.

'Tomorrow I am going to visit Mademoiselle Joby,' continued the Frenchman. 'If you would be pleased I will telephone and ask if it is possible for you to be with me. I am sure she would agree. It is a fine house, against the sea.' He paused. 'And Monsieur Joby, he *was* of the Resistance. There is no doubt.'

*

The 'Villa La Manche' stood solitary above the coast, its chimneys frequented by wind, gulls poised on its dark roof, its seaward face chaffed by years of maritime weather. The southerly aspect was sheltered and there an enclosed courtyard and garden with green creepers and climbers softened its walls.

It was early evening when they drove there in Monsieur Julien's pottering Peugeot. The day's weather had been squally but the rain and pointed winds had travelled away leaving the indented coast calmed with late, apologetic, sunshine. On the leeward side of the house there were doves in a cote, flowers filling boxes and tubs, and a carefully trimmed lawn upon which a great, white-painted ship's anchor was spreadeagled. Janine Joby came to the door to meet them. George asked her about the anchor and they walked across the grass to it. 'It is from the first vessel my father owned,' Janine said. 'And the first that was lost. In the cellar of this house is the anchor chain. Kilometres of it.'

Her English was next to perfect. She was slim and neat, her face and hair careful. Her hands moved as she spoke. She had green eyes and, George thought, was about forty years of age.

'My mother was English,' she said. They went into the house and walked to a room overlooking the sea, blue now but uneasy from the day's weather. She had poured some wine for them. 'She was from Sussex. In fact, I have been in London for almost four months. I have only just returned.' Turning towards the window, she said: 'My grandfather bought this house so that he could count his ships coming home.' They stood beside her, watching the Channel. She was quite small, only to George's shoulder. 'Sometimes he would pace about this room for days. Wondering if he had made money or lost it. People from the town, the wives and families of the crews of his ships, were permitted to stand in the garden for the news that their husbands, sons and fathers were safe. Or perhaps not safe.'

Monsieur Julien said: 'I told Monsieur Goodnight that it was your grandfather who began the great stamp collection. As I told you on the telephone, Monsieur Goodnight is a collector also.'

She smiled. There were shadows below her eyes. Around her pale throat was a velvet band with a single miniature brooch at its centre.

'Grandfather collected,' she agreed. 'Father scattered. There are stamps all over the house, Mr Goodnight, in every room. I have stuffed them away in drawers, cupboards and boxes. I am afraid I fail to find them fascinating.'

'I have advised that they should be properly catalogued and valued before there is any proposal of selling them,' added Monsieur Julien primly. 'Anything else would be crazy.'

'You would like to see some of the stamps?' suggested Janine.

'Please,' answered George. 'If it's not too inconvenient.'

'Not at all. It is amazing the interest.' She stood. 'I think the annexe.' She glanced towards Monsieur Julien and led the way through the rooms and corridors.

Despite its robust outward appearance, the interior of the house was delicate. Shadows and streaks of sunshine embroidered the floors, sidling in through lightly curtained windows. The furniture was elegant and the decoration and fabrics subdued. There were paintings of ships on quiet waters. They walked through three rooms like this and the corridors between before Janine opened an arched door which, despite its obvious bulk, swung at her fingertips. Her hand was slight and pale against the dark wood.

'My father's things are all in here,' she said. 'I must confess that I found it difficult to live with some of his belongings.'

They entered a long stone room, almost like a vaulted tunnel, daylight coming through deeply incised windows. The room was stacked with sombre furniture, massive tables supporting thick-legged chairs; cabinets and bookcases heavy against the walls.

'The sea is just outside,' mentioned Janine. Gracefully, she leaned forward and her fragile face was at once lit with a stab of sun from the window. It added strands of light to her fair hair and whitened her bare arm as she extended it. Monsieur Julien, smiling as though at some realised thought, moved aside and George stepped a pace forward, beside her, to look through the window.

'It's amazing,' he said truthfully. 'Almost alarming.' The twilight sea was moving up in belts, wide and smooth, to be split on a rampart of rocks directly below the house. Spray, flung from the rhythmic collisions, jumped almost to the ledge of the window.

'It is a good place to observe a Channel storm,' said Janine. 'Sometimes I come down here to watch.' She placed her hand on the powerful stone wall. 'The sea can be so wild and so massive that you believe it may even break through these.'

There was a sadness about her. The words about the storm were said on the verge of a reverie, something she realised herself because a quick apologetic smile replaced the melancholy as she said: 'But you were wanting to see some of the stamps.' She moved to one of the two frowning cabinets and slid open a drawer. 'As I say, they are not in good order. My father preferred them to be like that. They are valuable, I understand. But they are, to me, only small pieces of coloured paper.'

She had taken a ragged and bulky album from the drawer. George relieved her of its weight. She turned and pressed a button switch upon the wall. From the ceiling a spotlight beamed, making a pool of illumination. George placed the album on a table, crowded against the cabinet, and opened the heavy cover. It was like turning a hinged box. He blinked at the disorder of the page. He bent close and studied them. Austro-Hungarian Empire; faded blues, yellows and a fine rose, with the heads of emperors and their consorts long gone. Monsieur Julien moved closer and George stood slightly aside. The Frenchman had a glass fixed to his eye. He made small hummings of approval. 'These I have not seen,' he sighed. 'Every time I look I see something I have not seen.' He glanced reprovingly at Janine, the eyeglass still oddly fixed to his eye. 'Mademoiselle, you must have some action taken . . . something . . .'

'Done,' she finished for him. 'I know. You are right. When I return from Paris I will see to it.'

George turned the page and was astonished to see a fine set of Falkland Islands Edward VII. They were scattered on the page also, with an incongruously ordered rank of mundane Belgian Congo across the foot. Quickly, George's eye picked out each denomination of the Edwardian stamps. Two were missing. Instinctively, he turned the page. They were there, the twopenny purple and the twopenny-halfpenny blue, in mint condition, the King's head sitting royally among a poor selection of Peruvians.

'Splendid,' murmured George. 'Really excellent, mademoiselle.'

Monsieur Julien said: 'He is an expert of British Possessions, you understand.'

'I see,' acknowledged Janine vaguely.

'A collector,' muttered George gazing at a Tasmania Queen Victoria which he had never before set eyes upon. 'Not really an expert. But these are marvellous.'

'I will get some tea,' said Janine politely but decisively. 'Please carry on for a few minutes.' She turned quickly and threaded her way between the piled furniture.

'She doesn't mind, does she?' asked George anxiously. He turned the album pages, unwilling to waste time.

'Not at all, I am sure,' said Monsieur Julien. 'It is difficult to make enthusiasm out of the air.'

'These are astonishing, aren't they?' commented George. 'Some real gems among a lot of rubbish.'

The Frenchman turned and went to the second cabinet. 'Here, if I recall, is something that you would find of interest. Let me see.' He selected a small tattered album. 'This one.' He opened the cover. 'Ah yes.'

George found himself looking at a page of plain coloured stamps each showing the head of the young Queen Victoria. He moved it towards the light. 'Christ,' he muttered. He looked up guiltily. 'I'm sorry. But look . . .'

'Christ, *exactement*,' agreed Monsieur Julien sagely. 'Someone has laid a wine glass on them. A perfect circle of claret.'

'What a disaster.'

'He would have laughed,' said the Frenchman. 'Monsieur Joby. Probably he would have said it was the postmark.'

George turned two more pages and shut the album with finality. 'I daren't look at any more.'

'Perhaps we should go for the tea.'

'I think we had better.'

They extinguished the spotlight, walked among random furniture, and reached the door. Monsieur Julien paused and smiled in the dimness. 'Perhaps Mademoiselle Joby has locked us away with all the stamps,' he said. 'We would have plenty to enthral us before we starved to death. We could be down here for ever and no one would know.' He opened the door.

'No one would notice *my* absence,' corrected George. 'But they'd soon miss you. The shop would be shut.' They walked along the corridor.

'The way of trade at this time,' sighed the Frenchman. 'It would take a long time also.'

'Perhaps Herr and Madame Müller would miss us,' suggested George.

The other man laughed. 'When your rent was not paid,' he agreed.

Janine had come to meet them. 'Good,' she said. 'You are ready for tea.' They followed her into the drawing room. An elderly woman was setting out a table. Her hands shook with some palsy and she rattled the spoons violently against the china. This continued until she had arranged the table, whereupon she turned, making a suggestion of a curtsy as she did so, and went from the room. 'Poor Marie-Noëlle,' explained Janine. 'She is the last of the old servants. My father used to give jobs to widows and other dependants of his employees who were lost at sea. It was my mother insisted on it and he kept faith with it after she died.'

As they were drinking the tea she invited them to lunch on the following day. 'You can then see something else of the old stamps.'

Monsieur Julien excused himself. He had to go to St Malo. Janine looked hopefully at George. 'Perhaps Mr Goodnight, you could come. Are you here for some time?'

'Yes,' said George. 'For a few days, at least. I would be delighted.' He found himself looking into her pale face and green eyes. 'I have never in my life seen a collection like that,' he said.

He walked up from the town to her house in the morning. It was a blue day, the sun firm, the sea unwrinkled. Even in that calmness, La Manche stood formidably, squared-up against the sea as if unconvinced by its benignity, as half expecting a sudden gale or a rush of waves. From a spindly mast a pennant hung, something he had not noticed on the previous day. It was not entirely languid but occasionally stretched itself with a breeze, displaying a red and blue device. As he approached up the grass hill he could hear the taut wires, holding the mast, singing with a soft monotony.

Within the walled courtyard, George saw that a table had been set on the terrace at the sheltered side of the house, part in sun, part in shadow. Janine was walking a little further off. She had been cutting flowers and after she had seen him she approached, smiling, with the flowers across her arm. The stiff

129

old lady, wearing the same dress and the same grimace, brought them pale apéritifs. They sat at the table.

'Monsieur Julien mentioned that you were in Cherbourg because of some misfortune with your boat,' said Janine. 'Is the trouble serious?'

'Very serious,' smiled George. 'It sank.'

She looked startled. 'Oh, I see. How terrible.'

'It was not my boat. I was merely on board. A large vessel collided with us in a fog. We managed to reach Cherbourg, but she sank in the harbour.'

'My goodness, I didn't realise it was as dramatic as that. What happened to your friends, the others?'

'They've gone home. Back to England.'

'And you are here shipwrecked.'

'Indeed.' He paused, then said carefully: 'In my middle age I have been seeking adventure.'

She regarded him with mild astonishment and amusement. 'Seeking adventure? That's wonderful.' She backed away in her chair and studied him quizzically. 'You mean . . . you just set out. As people once did . . .'

'I ran away,' he shrugged. 'Bunked off. It sounds slightly implausible, I know, but I did. I left job and home and wife.' He grimaced apologetically. 'I've been away over a week now.'

Janine burst into a soft laughter. 'Excuse me, please,' she said. 'But it is quite extraordinary.' She looked thoughtful. The old woman arrived with a tray and served the hors d'oeuvre. 'It is a *crevette au cidre*,' said Janine when he said it looked delicious. 'Cider is a drink of Normandy.' The woman essayed her stiff half-curtsy and stalked away. Janine continued to regard George. 'I wish I could run away,' she breathed. 'It is such a marvellous idea.'

'Why would *you* want to do that?'

'That is the problem. There is no reason. It is necessary to *have* a reason, I suppose.'

'It helps to keep me running,' he agreed. 'It seems more like a year than a week to me, so much has happened. I'm not very brave, I suppose. Bravery seems to falter with age.'

'Or foolhardiness,' she suggested. 'Perhaps it is that.'

'Whatever it is, there's less of it available,' said George. 'If I thought I would have been made welcome I would have been back home by now.' A small bleak look touched his eyes. 'I've

130

had one boat sunk under me,' he said. 'And I've burned the others.'

Her smile dispersed his mood. 'But tell me, tell me, some of the things,' she pleaded. As she spoke more quickly so she appeared more French. 'From the moment you escaped.'

Through the long meal he told her of some of his early adventures. 'And the girl Molly,' she said intuitively. 'She was very kind to you?'

'Yes. Very kind. It was so odd, meeting strangers like that after your life has been so patterned, so ordered. Sometimes, with me, nothing special seemed to occur for weeks on end.'

The sun had moved round the enclosed space while they ate and talked. She suggested that they should walk to the warm part of the garden where some seats were set out against a wide and muscular vine. The old lady saw they had moved and made another face as she brought coffee for them.

'And *you* touch *other people's* lives as you go,' said Janine thoughtfully. 'You are a catalyst. You arrive and something happens to change everything. Just as if they were waiting for you.'

'An intrusion, really,' he said. 'But there's no doubt that the wanderer has an effect on people, even if he only intends to travel innocently, minding his own business.'

'His eyes on the horizon.' She smiled, then sighed. 'Ah, but it is wonderful. Just think of all the people that live ahead of you in your journey. Not knowing you or that you are coming, but still awaiting you.'

George looked worried. 'Don't,' he said. 'I hadn't thought of it like that.'

'You must not. You must travel accidentally.'

'That's how it's been so far. Like the boat sinking.'

'Would you like a cognac?' she inquired earnestly. He was about to refuse when she added. 'Perhaps we could have a little more wine. I have not enjoyed myself for so long. Please tell me about the boat.'

George entered into the saga of Cess and Annie Meredith and the fancy crew of the *Sally-by-the-Shore*. Janine began to laugh, quietly at first, her hands going to her mouth. The creaking woman returned, her expression more miserable at the laughter. She muttered as she went for the wine. When she

131

returned Janine's laughter burst out loudly in the garden. The servant closed her eyes as she limped.

'She does not like to see me happy,' explained Janine as the woman irregularly retreated. 'She does not believe in laughter.'

'Do you always live here?' he inquired. 'Alone?'

'Here and in Paris, although I have been travelling recently in America and in England, seeing my mother's family. Strangely I feel more at home there than here although I have always lived in France. And it is necessary I am here, at La Manche. I am the eldest, and my sisters and brother are married. They come for vacations only.'

'Vance versus Vance,' muttered George absently.

'What was that?'

'Oh, a case. A law case. A precedent in these circumstances. I quite often mumble like that.' He felt embarrassed. 'You're the one who has to hold the fort,' he said.

'Yes. And for a long time. And except for some weeks in the summer, alone.'

'There is always someone.'

'Indeed. I do not mind I have not married and I enjoy it here. I am the natural one for fort-holding. We are not exactly a close family, not in the way of the French, possibly because of having an English mother. Next week there is a wedding, in Paris, and I must go and see them all again. My niece is marrying a rich young man so it will be very society. But it's always a trial for me. And it is very tiring.'

It was almost four o'clock. The sun had edged completely from the garden but it remained warm.

'You have not had one glance at the stamps,' she said apologetically.

'It matters nothing,' he replied genuinely. 'It has been a wonderful lunch. Thank you.'

'Long and wonderful,' she said in a pleased way. 'Thank you for coming and telling me of your adventures. Tomorrow I shall be out all day but if you would like to come and spend the day in that dark place with those dusty books and the stamps then please do.'

'That would be splendid,' he said. 'As long as it is convenient.'

'Of course. I will tell Marie-Noëlle. Don't try and cheer her up. It is no use. How long will you be here in Cherbourg?'

132

George rose. 'A few more days,' he said. 'I am waiting for some stamps to come from England. I think I shall do some business with Monsieur Julien.'

'Ah, I see. This is how you finance your travels?'

'It's all I can do.'

'It is a very good idea.' They walked towards the gate in the stone wall and shook hands formally. 'Please come tomorrow,' she said. 'If you wish.'

'I would like to. I hope I shall see you again.'

'Perhaps we will meet again before you leave on your travels and your adventures.' She regarded him quizzically. 'Appearing in people's lives.'

Wolfgang, who had a heavy tread, brought the package to George's door. The morning window was lit with sunshine and a thread of sea breeze rippled the curtains. George, who had purchased further pyjamas, together with underwear, socks and two shirts (never, he reflected, had he bought so many clothes), sat up in bed wearing his new stripes and regarded the envelope. He was opening it when Marie appeared with a small jug of coffee, and two tiny biscuits. George poured himself some coffee before continuing with the opening. He did so with both anticipation and hesitation. It was, after all, a letter from home. Or from next door.

The stamps were there – British Honduras, Queen Victoria, including the pride of his collection, the green and black five dollar, all well protected by cardboard. Stamps he had last seen in his own house. He inspected them minutely. They had not suffered in their journey. Well done, Fred Birch; good old Freddy. There was a note: 'Dear Adventurer, Here are the stamps. Hope I've got the right ones. Everything is the same here. The grass keeps growing. Tina is home from school. Do you want me to tell her we are in touch? Let me know next time we speak, you from wherever, me from my boring office. Have a nice time. Fred.'

George broke one of the tiny biscuits noisily in his teeth and crunched it as he thought. Tina at home for two months. They had become friends and confidants almost from the moment he had become her substitute father when she was a very small girl. Her real father had gone, vanished, never even to try a contact. He could never know what he had given up. Now,

George reflected unhappily, he had given her up also. Sitting in bed in Cherbourg he remembered, for some unreasonable reason, a rainy summer in Cornwall when they had gone to a village cinema. Felicity had not been with them. The place was hardly more than a barn with a foyer. It was crowded because of the bad evening and heavy with the smell of wet clothes. They sat, holding hands, through *Abbott and Costello Meet The Mummy*, the little girl jumping up and down like a fish in excitement and laughter. When the mummy materialised she had buried her head in George's arm, her small body quaking, not daring to look while the cinema was filled with squeals and laughter in the dark. When the film was over they had gone out into the clearing night with the moon flaring between elephant clouds and the street damp and dripping.

Around their car were grouped six wet cows which had wandered from a field. He had ponderously ushered them away, watched by the admiring child. There was no reason why he should think of it now in Cherbourg, except that it was all past.

He took the stamps into the town after breakfast. Monsieur Julien did not open his shop before ten so George sat on a public seat on the harbour front. Among the small boats a big car ferry pushed its way towards the mouth of the port. It was sailing for England. It passed close by the quay where he sat. He was distanced from any other watchers and, as if they recognised him and fully expected him to be there, some homebound passengers waved and called in English from the deck. After waiting, George waved back.

When the clock over the town sounded ten he walked along the waterfront and then turned towards the edgewise street where Monsieur Julien kept his shop. The dealer was awaiting him, his face bright. 'I came to my shop early,' he said, 'because I could not wait. Even in the night I have a dream of these little matters.'

Opening the package, George smiled at his anticipation. 'I hope you will not be disappointed,' he said, knowing that he would not be. 'They seem to have travelled well.' He took the folder from the envelope and spread it open. 'There,' he said.

Monsieur Julien jammed his eyeglass so fiercely into his eye that he gave a little squeak of pain. George grinned. The dealer

134

was already leaning over the stamps. He blew out his cheeks. 'So fine,' he muttered. 'So very fine, monsieur.'

'I am glad you like them,' said George.

'Like them? Ah, I would be so happy to keep them for me.' He was still low over the stamps, eyeglass agitating. 'But that will not be possible.' He looked up briskly. 'I have informed the client which I have in Monte Carlo,' he said. 'And he trusts me to make the purchase for him.' He regarded George, the eyeglass still projecting from his face. 'Ten thousand francs,' he said firmly. 'Five thousand for each set.'

Close on a thousand pounds. It was a little more than fair. 'Yes,' George said.

'*Merci, monsieur.* It is good.' He smiled in his wise way and the men shook hands. 'Already I have the money for you. Yesterday I went to the bank.' He handed across an envelope, picked up the stamps and put them in his safe, set like an oven in the wall. On a tray, standing to the side of the counter, was a bottle of white wine and two glasses. 'We must drink to our exchange,' said Monsieur Julien.

They had two glasses each, toasting each other across the glass counter. Then, feeling pleased, George went out into the street.

At the junction an elderly Citroën came sedately to the curb and the driver, worn peaked cap over worn face, leaned from the window and said, 'Monsieur Goodnight,' in a hushed voice. Surprised, George stopped and saw at once a movement in the back of the car. Smoothly the window descended and he smiled. It was Janine Joby.

'*Bonjour, mademoiselle,*' said George.

'Good morning,' she returned. Seeing it framed in the window he realised that her face was not only delicate but sometimes, perhaps at certain times of the day, it was beautiful.

'You did not go to La Manche yesterday after all,' she said.

'No. No, I'm sorry,' said George. 'I spent the day walking around Cherbourg. I thought it would be better if I came at some other time – when you were at home.'

'I see.' Her face, with a sort of expectancy, projected further from the window. 'Have your stamps arrived from England?'

'Yes. Today. I have just taken them to Monsieur Julien's.'

'To finance your further adventures,' she smiled.

George was aware of his embarrassment. 'Yes.' He hesitated.

'More or less.' He was not certain that she was not quietly laughing at him. 'Further travel anyway.'

'You go to Paris next, you said?'

'I thought so. It would be the logical place. I've only been there a couple of times and that was years ago.'

'Before you go, will you visit me?'

For a reason he did not himself understand he was surprised by her tone. He merely said: 'Well, yes, of course.'

'When will you go?'

'Paris? Oh, I don't know. In a day or two I expect.'

'I am going tomorrow,' she said decisively. 'I believe I already told you. Perhaps we could travel together. Henri is driving me.' She looked towards the peaked old man at the front.

George felt abruptly pleased. 'But yes. Of course. That is very kind.' Again he hesitated. 'Are you sure?'

'Of course.' She smiled mischievously, all at once fully French. 'I have a plan. I have an adventure to suggest to you.'

VII

After he had paid his bill and taken a carrier bag with his few belongings from his room, George found Wolfgang and Marie standing in the tiled hall of the Villa Bismarck waiting to see him off. Wolfgang came to attention with a click and Marie glared at her husband as if she always wished he would not always do it. They bade him farewell with many hopes that he would return. 'When the times are better,' lamented Marie.

'There are too much foreigners,' repeated Wolfgang. He bent forward, still stiff but confiding. 'It is possible we go to Germany for ever and ever.' Uncertainly he added, 'Amen.'

Marie put down the suggestion with a glance. It had clearly been projected many times. 'Germany,' she said, 'is full of Turks.'

George shook hands with them and left the *auberge*. It was another good Channel day, bright with breezes wheeling around the stone corners of the town. He walked up the rising ground towards La Manche outlined against the wide sky, its pennant standing out like tin. An uncertain anticipation was in his stomach. She had said she had an adventure for him. He felt exhilarated at that; that she, who was so cool, should believe he was not only available, but qualified, for adventures. He swung the plastic shopping bag as he walked.

Entering the stone arch of the courtyard he saw that the bulky old Citroën was standing before the open front door. Henri, his nose sharp under the point of his cap, was loading luggage into the back. There were several suitcases and a brass-bound portmanteau. George smiled and wished the chauffeur good morning. The man's reply was only to touch his cap. Then he held out his hand for George's plastic bag. It was handed over solemnly. He took it and chose a place for it among the cases. He then indicated with a brief dip of his hand that George should enter the house.

Janine was standing in the overcast hall. Stripes of sun from the windows on each side formed a flag on the floor. She was ready to travel, her slight blue coat over a silk dress. She wore narrow blue shoes and held a pair of gloves. She walked a pace or two towards him smiling.

'It's a lovely day to travel to Paris,' George said when he had greeted her. They shook hands.

'Just beautiful,' she said. 'Have you given Henri your luggage?'

'Yes,' admitted George. 'It won't take up much room. Us adventurers tend to travel light.'

'Especially after being shipwrecked,' she agreed laughing. She moved towards the door. 'Come. We can go.' As she went out she glanced around the shaded hall. 'I never go, even if it is only for a little time, a few days, without feeling I am saying goodbye to this house for ever,' she said. 'I never know whether to be glad or sorry.'

Gravely, Henri was waiting to open the car door. He offered a faded travelling rug with some muttered phrase but Janine refused. She settled herself in the deep soft back seat and George sat beside her, the ancient leather giving like velvet. There was a worn leather arm between them. Henri was walking in a circle round the car, viewing it with suspicion, as if expecting some parts to be missing. He then went to the front and, bending at the knees, squinted along the bonnet.

'He likes to make sure it is straight,' smiled Janine. 'It is a very old car. It was my father's. So was Henri. They both came with the house. Like Marie-Noëlle.'

When Henri started the engine the vehicle began to move with scarcely a shrug. They slid below the stone arch and the port and the sea were at once displayed before them. Some clouds of light mist loitered in the Channel. A few boats were coming or going. The town clock resoundingly struck eleven.

'We will be there by five o'clock without hurry,' said Janine. 'That gives us time for a little lunch *en route*. We have a picnic basket.'

'Wonderful,' said George, meaning it. 'I haven't been on a picnic for years.'

She laughed lightly. 'My father was always taking us in this car. My brother and my sisters. The place where we will picnic is the same place as we always stopped on the way to Paris. This car almost knows its own way there, like an old horse.'

138

'How long,' he asked, 'have you lived at La Manche?'

'Oh, all my life. I was born in Paris but this was always our house. My father met my mother in the same week that Paris was taken back from the Germans. Nineteen forty-four, wasn't it? I saw a newsreel film of the liberation, they were showing it because it was the anniversary, and there were lots of soldiers and Parisian girls kissing and embracing. It was a good time for that sort of behaviour. The difference with my parents was that it was *she* who was the soldier. She was with the French army as a translator for the Americans and the British, and he was the liberated civilian. He was here in Cherbourg for most of the war.'

'He was in the Resistance, I hear,' said George.

'So I have heard,' she said noncommittally and to his surprise. 'But I do not know for sure. I am not very interested now. It is all so long ago. I cannot imagine it.'

The car had descended the seaward hill and skirted the town. Now it was on a flat narrow road, a parade of poplars on each flank, heading south-east. Normandy orchards and meadows with deeply set farms filled the land. Grey stones like rainclouds stood on gentle hills.

'It is like the West Country in England,' said George.

'Yes, it is prettier than the flat part of Normandy.'

'Have you never wanted to leave the area?'

'Well, someone had to be with my father and then the house.'

'And you are the one.'

'*Oui*, indeed. The others married quickly. So quickly, I suspect they plotted against me. The house cannot be sold in our lifetimes. My father was often dogmatic to the point of arrogance.' She regarded the spread of landscape. They had still not reached the main route and there was little traffic. Henri sounded the ancient horn as they overtook a man with a mule and a cart piled with hay. 'He was nearly always kind, and sometimes even jolly, with us,' continued Janine. She appeared to have thought carefully before saying it. 'But there was something dark about him. Something that not even I, nor any of the others, has ever understood. He had terrible passions and furious moods, especially after my mother died ten years ago. He was not an easy man to live with. He tried to burn the house down.'

'I heard there was a fire,' George said cautiously.

'He did it. There is no doubt. I caught him at it. He was dashing about with a flaming brand in each hand, setting alight to things in the middle of the night.' An inappropriate smile touched her face. 'The flaming brands were pages from his stamp albums,' she said. She watched his face for reaction.

'I am sorry to hear that,' he said lamely.

They reached the main road and joined the summer traffic heading towards Paris and the south-east. The old Citroën proceeded sedately along the middle lane while vehicles on either flank hooted with annoyance. The peaked cap of Henri, which was all that was visible of him above the partition, did not move a millimetre in either direction. Janine nodded towards the chauffeur 'He is also deaf,' she mentioned. 'As a stone.'

After an hour George sensed the car slowing. 'We are almost at the place,' said Janine looking out. 'A few more kilometres.'

From the right-hand side of the car a huge indicator, like an orange sword, clanked out. The big old vehicle moved into the next lane with no noticeable hesitation, causing a further furious howling of horns from the rear. George closed his eyes. Janine smiled calmly. 'He always does that,' she said. 'I don't think he realises there is a lot more traffic on the roads these days.'

As they left the main road the car was at once canopied with a deep shade of trees. Light, like a magic lantern, flickered through. 'Ah,' breathed Janine. 'We are at the place. It is still here. I am always afraid it will vanish one day, that somebody will build a house or a gas station on it.'

The car jolted like a horse and made another right-hand turn, again accompanied by the clank of the indicator, this time the manoeuvre completed without protests. They came to a bumping halt and Henri immediately switched off the engine and, it seemed in the same spry movement, opened his door, jumped to the ground, took off his cap and opened theirs. 'St Laurent l'Eglise, *mademoiselle*,' he announced sombrely.

They alighted in a glade beside a small river. There was a bank of grass and some reeds at the water's edge. Two swans patrolled near the further bank, now peering towards them in haughty curiosity. The two people walked around in a small area as if testing the ground below their feet. Henri was already unloading a table and two canvas chairs from the car.

'What do you think of it?' smiled Janine turning to him. She

140

was standing in a sunlit area and he was in the neighbouring shade. Her hair was shining.

'It's like the French painting of the picnic,' he said.

'Like Manet,' she agreed. 'But the people are gone.'

'It's strange,' he said. 'It's not far from the road and there were some houses not far back. You would think that people would know about it.'

With some difficulty Henri had carried the table from the car and set it up. George felt almost inclined to help but thought that it would not be appreciated. His glance was rightly interpreted by Janine. She put her hand on his arm, the first time that she had touched him, and said, 'He would be offended.' She looked around again. 'The place is private,' she told him. 'That is why there are no people. There is a gateman and he and Henri have known each other by sight for many years. The man who owned the estate was an acquaintance of my father's. He too is dead now. But the custom continues.' She smiled again but with some sadness in it. 'Today,' she said, 'is part of a continuing story.'

Together they walked to the edge of the water. Although the river was not wide it appeared very deep and flowed swiftly as if a short distance further upstream it was much broader. Looking down was like looking into a dark green room.

'Aren't you curious about the adventure I promised you?' she asked, still looking into the water.

'Of course,' he answered. 'But I thought you would get around to telling me in your own good time.'

'It is very obvious you are English,' she remarked with a silent laugh. 'A Frenchman would have been unable to contain his curiosity.'

George looked at the river again. 'Just as long as it doesn't involve any hair-raising exploits,' he said with a grin. 'I mean I hope you're not planning on swimming the river or anything like that.'

She half turned to face him. Henri was laying plates on the portable table. 'It is, I think, a little hair-raising, as you put it. But not like swimming the river.' He had also half turned towards her and now she took his arm and began to walk up the bank towards the car.

'I would like you,' she said slowly, in time with their walk, 'to be my husband. Just for a little while.'

*

141

They sat at the table below the tree shade. Henri had set up his own table on the track at the side of the car, like a groom with a horse, and proceeded to eat bread and a large portion of cheese with a miniature glass of red wine.

'It would give me much satisfaction,' said Janine, 'to introduce you as my husband to my family. We met and married in England.' She looked quizzically at him. 'Is there a precedent, a law case, for this?'

Their picnic was pâté and chicken, cold vegetables and salad. George was gazing at her. His first shocked answer to her proposal had been that he was already married, falling back at once, he realised, on something from which he was running. She had stilled his remarks with a firm smile. 'Just for a while. It will only be a pretence,' she said. 'Please let me explain further. The wedding in Paris will be a fine affair at St Philippe du Roule, followed by a reception at the Crillon, the very best. It is my niece, Delia, the daughter of my second sister. She is beautiful and she is marrying a rich man. She, like the others, has always regarded me as a bit of a joke, you know, the old maid aunt remaining on the shelf, really just a convenient housekeeper. I know that my sisters have always thought how amusing it was that I was left holding the baby — especially when the baby was our father and his house. I suppose the young people in the family have thought the same. They see me, a woman of forty, and they feel a little sorry and a little amused.'

She looked at him directly over the table. 'There would, of course, monsieur, be no further obligation for you, or for me. We would only be friends. It would just be a little play-acting.' He nodded and smiled at her. The swans had apparently detected Henri's cheese because they pushed against the bank, only their heads and necks, crooked towards him, showing above the reeds. He stood, tottered to the water's edge and slowly finished munching the cheese in front of them, throwing them only the newspaper in which it had been wrapped. They at once fought over that but dropped it disconsolately when they realised it was empty.

George said: 'How could we get away with that? Surely they'll suspect . . .'

She laughed outright. The swans looked up at her. 'Oh, I can just see their faces. Enter Janine Joby with a tall distinguished

Englishman. She quietly reveals that he is her husband. They met, fell in love and married all in a few weeks. And Mademoiselle Joby told no one.'

George could feel the wine glass growing warm in his hands. 'I simply . . . I simply don't know what to say,' he mumbled. 'I'm flattered, honestly, very flattered but . . . well, I don't know what to say.'

'Say yes, then,' she suggested calmly. 'It will be what you seek – an adventure. I will pay you to do it. I will hire you. I will pay you ten thousand francs – as much as you got for your stamps.'

The Joby apartment was in the Avenue Mozart, a shaded street in the Massenet district of the Sixteenth Arrondissement, between the Seine and the lakes of the Bois de Boulogne. It was a quiet place just away from the shops and restaurants. Pigeons walked under the trees scarcely disturbed. The buildings were mellow and high with the high summer sky framed by their eaves.

Henri brought the old car to the curb with a morsel of a flourish. From across the street a concierge spied from amongst her curtains. The apartment was on the top floor of the building and although there was a clanking lift George was concerned for the elderly chauffeur and the baggage.

'Do not worry,' Janine assured him. 'He has been doing it for years. If he needs some help he will get a boy from the street.'

They were in the lift. 'How will you explain it, afterwards?' he asked. 'Being married. I mean, when I've moved on.'

'When your contract has run out,' she smiled.

'How are you going to account for a new husband one moment and none the next?'

The lift reached the fifth floor, which was the top, but they remained facing each other within its narrow cage. Janine said: 'I am not concerned with that. With the distant future. Only the few days ahead.' She smiled again, almost slyly. 'It will be such fun for me, you must believe me. Just to see their faces.'

He opened the grille. They were on a small carpeted landing with a single polished door facing them. She produced a brass key and handed it to him. 'If you please,' she said. He opened the door and it swung with a plush movement to reveal a wide

143

entrance hall, like an antechamber, which opened into a broad and finely furnished drawing room. 'Do not worry,' Janine assured him with a small laugh. 'I will not expect to be lifted over the threshold.'

They walked in. The blinds were down and she went to each of the windows and released them. Tall sunlight fell into the big room. There was a misty view of the Eiffel Tower between the neighbouring buildings.

'It's very nice,' said George.

'Yes,' she said, looking about pleasurably. 'I have always liked it. Being the old maid aunt has had its advantages.' She looked at him quickly, a little slyly again. 'What will our name be?' she inquired, still with the inverted smile. 'It would not be wise to use Goodnight, don't you think? It is very unusual and, since you are running away, so to speak, there is always a danger. There are bound to be society writers at the wedding. We will have to lie low from them. We will tell the family that it is a secret. In any case I would not like to upstage the bride. That would not do at all. But we must think of a name.' Suddenly formal she said: 'Please sit down.'

They sat, he on the damask sofa, she on a slight chair. 'Have you any suggestions?' she asked. 'It must be your choice.'

'Perhaps,' he said thoughtfully, 'we could be called Mr and Mrs Oliver Loving.'

Her face lit a little. 'How wonderful,' she smiled. 'You seemed to have it prepared.'

'In a way I did,' he admitted. He told her of Goodnight and Loving and she listened, her hands clasped over her slim knee.

'That is very romantic,' she said when he had finished. 'Mrs Loving. I like that very much.'

Henri arrived outside with the luggage. He had found a youth in the street who carried the heavy cases and who now looked wide-eyed around the apartment. The chauffeur himself bore only George's plastic bag which he handed over with eloquent silence before departing, closing the door with a soft thump behind him.

Feeling a little foolish, George sat on the rich sofa with his shopping bag. Janine had gone to another room and she returned after a while with a tray upon which was arranged a small tea set.

144

'It is a matinée set,' she said. 'Just enough for two.' She poured thin tea. 'I hope you like it thin,' she said.

George mumbled that he did.

'There is a small apartment above this,' she said conversationally. 'But that is traditionally Henri's. I am afraid we will have to find a hotel for you.' She looked at him closely. 'There is a small but pleasant hotel quite close. It overlooks the ponds in the Bois de Boulogne. The Hôtel des Deux Lacs. I am sure they will have a room. Monsieur Le Clerc is a friend. I will telephone for you.'

'Oh, yes, thank you,' he said.

'Perhaps you would like an advance on the fee.'

He felt hurt. 'No. That is not necessary. I have some money.' He looked at her firmly, and formally. 'I will collect the fee when I have finished the . . . assignment.'

'The adventure,' she corrected.

'Yes. All right. The adventure.'

'You must get some clothes, also,' she said. 'It will be very formal. Tailed coats and finery. Tomorrow perhaps we can attend to that.'

George's doubts crowded in on him as he mentally saw himself disguised in a tailed coat pretending to be the husband of a woman he hardly knew. 'Are you sure about all this, Janine?' he said. 'Don't you think it's perhaps all a bit fantastic?'

'Fantastic,' she said, changing the meaning. 'That it will be. We must both be brave. There will never be another chance of such a thing. Tomorrow we will rehearse our parts. I will tell you things you must know about the family. If you get confused then it will be understandable. A stranger cannot know everything about strangers. But certain things we must be sure about.'

'Like where we met and where we married,' he nodded. 'It wouldn't do to get those things wrong.'

'And we must tell them we are leaving for England after the wedding. They will not follow us there.' She gave a slender laugh. 'I cannot wait for it to happen.'

Soberly George said: 'I wish I felt as confident. So many things could go wrong. You have to admit it's mad.'

She bowed her head, still laughing. 'Absolutely,' she acknowledged. 'That is all part of the pleasure. Trust me. Everything will be fine . . . Mr Loving.'

145

Putting down her cup she went to a white upright telephone, which stood like a stork, its reflection in a mirrored table. The dial turned silently. She spoke briefly and then returned. 'The Hôtel des Deux Lacs has a room for you,' she said.

'Not the bridal suite, I hope.' His face was solemn.

She laughed at him. He had called her Janine. Now she called him George, laying her light hands on his arm. 'You must not back out, George,' she said. 'To an adventurer an adventure is an adventure, a contract.'

'All right. Of course.' He leaned forward and kissed her gently on the cheek. 'I hope there's no law against impersonation in France, that's all.'

'It is impersonating someone who does not exist,' she shrugged. 'There can be no law for that.' They stepped apart. 'This evening,' she said, 'I must have dinner with my brother. I do not think it would be a good idea to expose you to an intimate examination such as that.'

'No, please don't,' George answered hurriedly. 'Give me time to learn my lines.'

'On the other hand, I will inform him I have a secret. And then, after a while, what the secret is. It will be good for the word to get around in the family. The thought of the intrigue! I can hear all the telephones ringing now.'

George asked: 'How will you explain that I am not with you?'

'I will tell my brother that you are flying from London tomorrow.'

Picking up his plastic carrier, George said: 'I must go. I think I'm going to need a good night's sleep.'

'Yes, please rest.' She stood back and regarded him smilingly. 'I want you to look beautiful at the wedding.'

'Stop it,' he admonished. He looked pleadingly at her. 'How do I get involved in things like this?'

A swift anxiety shaded her face. 'Please do not change your mind – not now.'

'Of course not,' he said.

Again she smiled and said: 'It is because you are here, because you are available.'

They left the room and stood by the lift.

'One more question,' he said. 'What about Henri? Won't he say anything? I mean, he *knows* we're not married.'

146

'Henri,' she smiled confidently, '*never* says anything. Goodbye, Mr Loving.'

'Goodbye,' muttered George. He regarded her smile and answered it. 'Mrs Loving,' he said.

The church of St Philippe du Roule in the Rue du Faubourg St Honoré is one of the most fashionable in Paris. People crowded its steps to witness the wedding and the invited guests queued beneath its thick columns, as though waiting under the legs of a huge and unmoving elephant. Bells echoed through amplifiers on the church roof.

As Henri drove them through the calm Saturday streets in the rolling Citroën, George was trying to still a trembling stomach. His hands were hot and every few moments he swallowed heavily causing his grey top hat to rock a little. He reflected with a sort of removed horror that only two weeks before he had been abused by drivers on an English motorway. Janine pressed his hand with her glove. 'Do not be afraid, husband,' she whispered. 'What can they do if they find out? Throw us into the street?'

She looked frail and beautiful in a blue, pale silk dress and a wide-brimmed hat that seemed to float above her composed face. Henri, peak forward like the nose of a crow, drove the car with miserly majesty through the streets, causing the people on the pavement and in the cafés to stop, stare and bend to see who were the passengers in the back. Easily excited Americans attempted to take photographs on the run.

At the church the car came to rest as smoothly as a boat to a familiar mooring. There were a hundred or more sightseers on the steps now and as many guests waiting to enter the doors. Henri left the car to open the door. George remained bettered. 'Can't we wait until the queue's gone down a bit?' he suggested.

She quietly kissed his cheek. 'Let us go now,' she encouraged. 'Let the world see us.'

Henri, deaf-faced, opened the door and they stepped out. At the top of the steps photographs were being taken, spasms of light flashing on the curves of the columns. People were making appreciative noises from the crowd, pointing at Janine's dress. George's clamped teeth formed an oblong smile; there was sweat on his Adam's apple. Suppose somebody saw him. Suppose somebody from *London* was there and recognised him.

Worse, much worse, suppose it was somebody from *Shillington*! People from Shillington visited Paris. Quite frequently, some of them. He knew *several* who had been. From beneath his topper brim he spied out like a soldier from a blockhouse. There! That face! Surely *there* was one! Surely that was Catling the newsagent who was also Bollins the butler. Surely that was him trying to creep behind that camera. No. No, no it was not. His mistake. Relief whistled through him. The man had been crouching, a guileless tourist taking a photograph. When he stood upright he was taller than either Catling or Bollins, who, although they were one and the same person, appeared in George's memory as of differing heights, Catling, bending and tending his counter of newspapers, and Bollins, stationed within a front door, straight and servile.

Janine's gloved touch steadied him.

'This is where we begin,' she whispered. A group of people were outside the door of the church and George, realising they were members of the family, swallowed so violently that his Adam's apple caught on his collar.

Janine moved forward with a smile and outstretched hands and kissed two younger but less beautiful women. She turned to George, who was blinking nervously below his hat, which he now removed. 'These are my sisters Antoinette and Gabrielle,' said Janine happily. 'Sisters, this is my husband, Oliver.'

Strangling his anxiety, George performed a semi-French bow and shook their hands. They both blushed. Their brother André, a slight and fair young man, next came forward to be introduced.

'I am very happy,' he said gravely. 'For Janine, my sister, and for you, Monsieur Loving.'

They were required to pose for the photographers at the top of the steps and George shuffled minutely sideways trying to lose his face in the shadows of the church and the brim of his hat. A girl assistant stepped forward and asked for their names. George's mouth opened but only a small hoot, like that of a remote owl, came out. It was Janine who announced sweetly: 'Monsieur et Madame Oliver Loving.'

Gracefully she turned and George, doffing his hat early in a further attempt at shielding his face, turned also and walked with her on his arm into the copious church. It was already crowded. An usher whispered the location of their seats and

148

they walked down the aisle towards the families gathered at the front. George was gratefully aware that the couple stepping before them, and those behind, formed at least temporary cover. There were only mildly curious looks from the congregation in the back and middle pews but then the couple before them stepped aside and took their seats and as George and Janine reached the front the faces of Janine's relatives revolved as though operated by a single lever. George felt the paleness creep over his face. He smiled like a piece of wire.

They were being ushered into a pew four from the front. Faces remained frankly turned, some trying to get a view of him between the heads of others. Their smiles he answered with a shaky simper. Somerbourne Magna came back to him as he knelt to pray. Here he was again, in church with a strange woman.

Organ music floated below the vast roof. George stayed on his knees as long as he properly could. Awkwardly he rose. Again the faces revolved to regard him as if he had surfaced from diving. Janine began to whisper their names to him and he smiled in the direction of each visage in turn, trying to home onto the appropriate stare. Eventually she whispered: 'And this gentleman is Monsieur Benoit, our family lawyer.'

The man was sitting beyond Janine but he turned as George looked towards him. The eyes pinned him. He knew that look. A dagger sharpened in the courts of law. 'I am pleased to make your acquaintance, *monsieur*,' whispered the man. 'And many congratulations.'

'God,' thought George miserably. 'He thinks I've married her for her money.'

Now he sat, topper on his knees, feeling both obvious and small in the grandiose church. All the guests were now expectantly seated and for the first time the precarious Englishman noticed the bridegroom standing at the front like a bit player in a major drama.

There was a pause, a silence, as if the organ were clearing its throat. Then it burst into the strident notes of a wedding march. The bride had arrived. Faces again were turned, still holding on him until the procession arrived.

They were all standing and George realised he was taller than everyone around. Janine came from a short family. The bride, as she passed, looked small and suffused. The groom revolved and nodded encouragingly but without conviction. The priest arranged them side by side and, spreading his robes, called upon the people to pray. As they knelt George slid a glance towards Janine. Her profile was set as she genuinely prayed and from below her closed eyelid squeezed a single tear.

The Hôtel de Crillon in the Place de la Concorde is a magnificence of marble and gilt. Golden furniture, so fragile it appears to hover an inch above the sienna floors, is distributed tastefully and the droplets of chandeliers reflect like stars in the same shimmering surfaces. Flowers spread themselves tropically and alcoves are peopled by moulded gods, nymphs and fauns peering out, naked and lost for words, onto a scene of unbridled luxury. Columns fly up through the grandest of grand staircases and the hotel's cool courtyard is classified as a place not only of summer teas but of historic interest. Diners use polished silver which will occasionally flash in the mirror of the walls while being used on the finest dishes Paris can offer. It is an expensive place.

'Very impressive, yes,' agreed Monsieur Benoit the lawyer, 'but it is named after a coward.' He took George's arm and led him like a conspirator towards the glassy bar. '*Voilà*, Monsieur Loving,' he said pointing to an inscription above them. 'It is, as you see, a letter from King Henry the Fourth to the Duc de Crillon in 1589. "Hang yourself, brave Crillon. We have fought at Arques and you were not with us!"'

Uneasily George studied the words. 'Odd place,' he ventured, 'to suggest that somebody puts a noose around their neck.'

Benoit agreed gravely. 'He did not even run away from the battle,' he smiled. 'He never arrived at all. He was *not* an adventurer perhaps.' The word was only lightly underlined. With hardly a pause, but glancing to the foyer where Janine was talking with her two sisters among the crowding guests, he added: 'Your wife looks very happy.'

George tried to smile and clear his throat at the same time. His *wife*. God, what would Felicity say? Nervously he flapped the tails of his coat.

As if it might have been an unknowing signal a waiter approached with a salver, levitating upon which were glasses of champagne. They each took one and raised an inch-high toast to each other. Their eyes clicked over the rims. 'You will be taking her away to England?' suggested the Frenchman.

'Oh, at first,' said George with imitation calm. Now was the moment to be sure of his lines. 'But we will spend part of the time in France, at La Manche and here in Paris.'

Monsieur Benoit smiled agreeably. 'The business of philately is good then?' he said.

'Like most things,' George answered carefully. Now he was certain. The man really believed he was after her money, or her stamp collection! 'If you know what you are doing,' he added. 'If you are an expert in one particular field.'

'Until now,' said Benoit, 'Janine has been less than fascinated by stamps. If she had not been restrained I believe she would have thrown her father's collection from the house at Cherbourg.'

They had been strolling slowly and had now almost reached Janine and her sisters. 'I shall try not to inflict it upon her,' promised George.

'Perhaps you may be the one to bring some order to that collection,' said Benoit, adding firmly: 'Then it could be sold.'

Janine's face, pink with pleasure, turned to them. 'You have been talking,' she said. 'I am pleased that you have met.'

The sisters were smiling. 'It is an amazement!' enthused Antoinette. 'That our sister should be here with a *husband*. It is so . . . so impossible!'

'It is a wedding,' corrected Gabrielle, the elder. 'What is better than to materialise with a husband at a wedding? Today our family is growing suddenly.'

They laughed and George regarded Gabrielle gratefully. Antoinette appeared abashed and drank too much champagne to cover it. She backed away with a little choke. 'I must bring André,' she said. Quickly she turned and went into the crowd.

Her sisters laughed. 'Antoinette was never very good at surprises,' said Janine.

'Not very big surprises like today,' agreed Gabrielle. She turned to George with only slightly suppressed enthusiasm. 'It is so romantic. How you met. At the opera in London.' She moved closer. 'What was the opera?' she asked excitedly.

Stemming the immediate temptation to catch Janine's eye, he said: 'What was it?' Now he turned to her. 'Blessed if I haven't forgotten.'

'*Tales of Hoffman*,' she supplied immediately. 'Remember it was our first conversation.'

'Of course. I've got a terrible memory for some things.'

'About a man who travels,' reflected Benoit. 'Seeking the love of women.'

André appeared through the crowd and George was relieved by the interruption. He shook hands again with the same gravity. 'I am so happy that my sister is now married,' he said haltingly. 'Now I shall not be concerned about her and the ghosts at La Manche.'

'The ghosts at La Manche are my friends,' Janine assured him, touching him with an admonishing finger. 'They are quite harmless if you understand them.'

'To you,' said André raising his glass. 'A toast to *another* bride and groom today.' After they had responded he said: 'I have explained to the bride, Delia, and the bridegroom, about your marriage. They are so happy for you also. They look towards meeting you. Please will you come now with me.'

The bride was still flushed, her pink face made pinker by the confection of her veil. She sat dumpily beside her groom in chairs placed side by side like thrones. A crocodile of well-wishers waited to speak, kiss and shake hands. Delia saw Janine and George being ushered across the floor by André. 'It is them!' she said leaning excitedly towards her husband. 'Clovis, remember. Be careful of your words.'

The bridegroom smiled, a smile like two wings briefly flapped, and said: 'Of course.'

Stepping lightly forward and before the others who were waiting, Janine kissed the bride on one cheek and the groom on two. Hesitating to move forward in front of those still waiting to congratulate the couple, George was quietly pushed by André. 'Please,' he said, 'Today you are a piece of the family.'

George was introduced to the new couple and attempted to assemble some phrases in his remote French. Their English was better.

'You have seen our wedding,' said the bride leaning forward as though it were a secret. 'Now we must know of yours.'

Janine laughed and held George's hand. 'Another time, my dear,' she said. 'Today is for you.' She extricated them from the crowd and for a moment they were alone.

'How am I doing?' whispered George. He looked directly at her and immediately knew how glad he was to be with her.

'You are wonderful,' she said quietly. 'It has been a success. You have made me a good husband.' A waiter drifted by and handed to each a new glass of champagne. They lifted the stems briefly to each other. Over her shoulder George saw Benoit, the family lawyer, watching. It was Saturday. The day he should have been returning from Cornwall.

They remained for two hours. George began to enjoy himself. A string quartet was playing over the talk. There was a sumptuous buffet and unending champagne. He was frugal in his drinking. He saw Janine smiling at him as he refused yet another glass.

Benoit approached and said: 'You have examined the stamps at La Manche?'

George made up his mind quickly. 'Yes, of course. But only in a perfunctory way. We were there last week but I had to fly back to London. Business.'

'What did you think about the stamps?'

'A terrible mess,' said George. 'But there's no doubt there are some valuable items. I'm not familiar with many of them. I specialise in British Colonials, you see. But they're crying out to be put in some order.'

'You know about the fire?'

'Yes. Janine told me about it.'

'The old man was crazy. He did some terrible deeds, *monsieur*. Perhaps some day you will learn of others.'

'I see. Then I will be prepared.'

Janine touched his elbow. 'I think it is time to leave now, *chéri*,' she said. They said goodbye to Benoit and then went to the bride and groom and other members of the family to make their farewells. Then they left. Every eye of every Joby was on them as they went out.

Outside, the traffic of the Place de la Concorde filled the wide thoroughfare. Henri had parked the old car directly outside the hotel and people were standing admiring it when George and Janine emerged. At once the precise and unsmiling chauffeur moved stiffly to open the rear door and a strange smatter of applause drifted from the watchers on the pavement. Janine smiled and waved a glove. George climbed into the car quickly.

They sat awkwardly together when they were alone. 'I'm glad I didn't fluff my lines,' said George eventually. 'I think they all believed it, didn't they?'

She smiled reflectively. 'I think so.' She turned away from him, looking out of the window at the Paris buildings and traffic. 'I am so sorry it is over,' she said. 'It was an adventure for me also.'

The silence came between them once more. They reached the Avenue Mozart and Henri drove the car away.

'Please,' she said hurriedly. 'I must settle my debt with you.' They were in the foyer of the building, at the lift.

He laid his hand upon her wrist. 'Janine,' he said. 'It was enough. I really don't want the money. It would be ridiculous.'

Her eyes dropped. 'But you must,' she whispered firmly. 'That was the arrangement.'

'I cannot,' he answered.

'You will need it to finance you. On your travels.'

'Please,' he said genuinely. 'I would prefer you did not.'

The lift was descending noisily and irrevocably as a guillotine. The moment had arrived. 'And I think I must go,' he said.

He moved close and kissed her on her pale cheek. Slowly her eyes closed. 'Yes, you must,' she agreed. 'There are things you have to do.'

The lift was there. He opened the clattery gates and she stepped in. She did not look at him again until the cage began to ascend. Her calm face, beyond the bars, remained with him for a few moments. Then he turned sharply, filled with regret, and went out into the evening street. There was a grey and silent warmth over it. Traffic was distant. The notes of a piano, quietly played, came through an upper window. George took a heavy breath and turned towards La Muette. He wandered along the windows of the shops and small restaurants. The street was becoming busy. Faces looked from windows. He went into a bar and drank a double cognac. Then he walked through the streets back to the Hôtel des Deux Lacs. Turning the final corner he saw the Citroën with Henri standing like a black watchman beside it. George caught his breath. He hurried his paces. The old chauffeur was facing the other way and did not turn towards him until he was a few steps away. Then, cap descending like a hatchet, he bowed and offered a small envelope.

'*Merci*, Henri,' muttered George. He took the note and held it, making no move to open it. Henri moved several metres away and stood, still at attention in his breeches, apparently intent upon something at the distant end of the street.

George opened the envelope and unfolded the note. 'Monsieur Goodnight,' he read. 'If you have no further adventures planned for the present, would you please accept a contract concerning the classification of the stamps at La Manche, Cherbourg? I await your reply as soon as possible. Janine Joby.'

They returned to Cherbourg late that night, deep in the back of the old car, she lying against him, sleeping as a child, Henri driving stoically through fierce rain. And for the next two months, through the best days of the ending summer and the coming of autumn, George remained at La Manche. Never in his life – not in childhood, or youth, or in the first good times of his marriage – had he ever been so constantly aware of such happiness. There were days of bright and blue, sunshine spreading itself extravagantly over the coast and shifting the tones of the sea. The good weather was punctuated by grandiose storms, watched from the vantage of the rampart house on the cliff. Each day George worked at a table set by the turret window where he had first looked out at the sudden drop to the sea. In the fine weather the sun would probe into the vault-like room and he managed to persuade one of the old iron windows to open so that the airy scent of the Channel came through also. When the swaggering storms or fog or maritime rain occurred, he would sit, arms folded at his table, and view the weather with the enjoyment of one safe indoors.

At the start of his task he spent a week merely sifting through the astonishing collection of random stamps, marking the location of British issues. 'I think it is best that I concentrate at first on the items I'm familiar with,' he said to Monsieur Julien. The stamp dealer had quickly obtained a catalogue of British Colonials and their French values. At the start of the second week George settled with great contentment at the window and began to match, annotate and value, taking the stamps with tweezers from the haphazard pages and collating them in a new album. After only a few hours he was certain, as he had always known, that the collection was exceptional and of great value.

He was also in love with Janine Joby and she with him. Conscientiously he worked fixed hours but at meal times and late in the afternoons he would finish and find her in the house or garden. They spent fine evenings walking along the sea fringe, over the shingle and sand when most people had gone for the day and the sky was diminishing to the west. Sometimes it was nearly dark when they returned with the final gulls sounding and lights flashing at sea. The lights of La Manche would be yellow at the top of the cliff and dinner prepared. On a few Fridays they went to a jovial fish restaurant in the town and sometimes George would walk in the middle of the day to a bar on the harbour where he would drink with Monsieur Julien and Herr Müller from the Villa Bismarck.

One evening, towards the end of his time there, after dinner, they were sitting together and Janine said, suddenly, as if she had abruptly made up her mind: 'When I was seventeen, you know, I had a child.'

He was drinking cognac. 'And what happened?' he asked eventually.

She smiled at him. 'You hide your astonishment very well,' she said.

'Behind my glass,' he told her.

'It was a baby girl,' she said. 'I do not know where she is now. I have never known.'

'You don't? That's very sad for you,' he said, touching her. 'Your father arranged things, I suppose.'

She sighed. 'Yes, he arranged things. The father of the child does not matter now. God, I can hardly remember him. But I wanted the baby. Very much I wanted her. But I was only seventeen and I was not strong enough to resist. She was taken away and I don't know where. She would be twenty-three now, wherever she is. Sometimes I imagine I have seen her in the street in Paris, but I know it is only fancy.'

George said: 'Doesn't Monsieur Benoit know? Surely the family lawyer would have some notion of . . .'

'He was not then the family lawyer. The man who was the attorney then always denied he was consulted in the matter. He said that the business was dealt with by some other man. Now he is dead in any case.' She looked at him strangely. 'They came and took the baby and promised I would see her the next day. But they were lying. I never did. My father was a very brutal man at times.'

'I don't know how you could ever have forgiven him,' said George.

'Indeed I did not. I remained here but I never forgave. When he went off his head I counted that as his punishment and I think he did. In his lucid moments. I hope he did.'

In the darkness of their room that night she said to him, when he was almost asleep: 'How long do you think your work on the stamps will take?'

He roused and turned to her in the bed. Wind was heavily blowing against the windows. 'Another week or so, I imagine. Say, ten days.'

'And then they will all be correct?'

'The British Colonials, yes. It should not be any longer than that.'

'Darling,' she said after a pause. 'Will you take them to Paris for me? Take them to Monsieur Benoit.'

'Of course. Won't you come too?'

'No. It is not possible. I have to go to the United States at the end of this month. Before that I must go to London. I will go straight from here. It is just business that is my responsibility.' He felt her smiling as he kissed her in the dark. 'To go to Paris will occupy you when I am away,' she whispered.

'Yes,' he returned. 'Of course I will. I'll take them.'

Even as he said it he knew that they would not now be very long together.

From the moment he passed through the door of Monsieur Benoit's office, George was aware that there were many things he did not know. The lawyer sitting leanly behind his desk rose and greeted him quietly. He took the case containing the three albums and offered George a chair.

Returning behind the desk he said: 'Were you happy with your task, Monsieur Goodnight?'

George began to reply and then halted. The Frenchman had used his real name. He was now regarding him amiably. 'Almost, if I may say, *monsieur*,' he added, 'a name as interesting as Loving.' He reached to a shelf at his back and brought out a book. George saw at once it was the Bar List of the United Kingdom. A page was singled out with a bookmark. He opened the book. 'Goodnight, George Algernon,' he read. He glanced up as if seeking agreement.

George said: 'I try to forget the Algernon.'

Monsieur Benoit smiled. 'Qualified 1966, Inner Temple, B.A. LL.B., *Daily News*, Tudor Place, London EC4.'

George nodded. 'That's about right,' he sighed. 'Who told you? Not Janine?'

The Frenchman blew out his cheeks. 'Not at all, *monsieur*. But the Jobys are a family, you understand, who require that things be known about new arrivals, especially those who come so unexpectedly as you. Out of the blue, as you say.'

'I see. They had me investigated.'

'It took only a few days.'

'But they didn't . . .' His voice was slowed by the thought. 'They didn't know before the niece's wedding . . . did they?'

'*Mais oui!* All the close members of the family knew. Information from Cherbourg.'

'Monsieur Julien, the stamp dealer?'

'No. Not from him. He does not know the relatives. No, it was from an unmysterious source. From the servants. From Marie-Noëlle and, of course, from Henri.'

George sighed. 'I thought Henri never heard or said anything.'

'Only when it is necessary to hear or to see and then to speak.'

Steadily George said: 'I was not on the make, you understand. It was not for gain.'

The lawyer smiled sympathetically. He rose and patted George's arm. 'Not at all, *monsieur*. We made sure of that. If you had been "on the make" then you would have said "*au revoir*" very quickly indeed.'

'The Joby family must be splendid actors,' ruminated George. 'Not to mention yourself.'

The lawyer smiled briefly and said: 'Janine wrote to me. This I received yesterday.' He picked up a letter on delicate notepaper. George was tempted to ask to see it but he desisted. Monsieur Benoit continued. 'She requested that I ask you to perform another task for her.' He smiled a little wryly. 'She explained that you are . . . shall we say . . . wandering. Looking for adventure.'

Faced with the statement from a man of his own age and his

158

own profession, George looked embarrassed. 'It is . . . just that . . .' he hesitated.

The Frenchman held up both hands. 'Please. Please do not apologise.' He looked towards the ceiling. 'I can only envy you. Would that I could do it also.' He went back behind the desk. 'Perhaps all men who reach our age should be entitled to a year of running away. From family, work and all responsibilities. Unfortunately, to speak for myself, I cannot leave my business and . . . I would miss the comforts of my home.'

'What did Janine ask?' said George.

The lawyer regarded the letter again. 'She has requested that you take the stamps you have collated to a person in Rome.'

'Why Rome? There are dealers here in Paris.'

'Don't worry. She is not merely providing you with employment, a chance to go further on your . . . er . . . adventures. So do not be concerned about that. Her father always wished the British Possessions stamps to go to an English friend, Sir Bernard Holmes, who now lives in Rome. He always wanted to purchase them. I know this is true because I have the request in his own writing.'

'Yes. Yes, of course,' George agreed quietly.

'Good. That is excellent. I must provide you with funds for the journey and accommodation. Also a fee for the assignment and there is payment for your expert and patient work at La Manche.'

George said sadly: 'I am being paid off. Somehow I didn't think it would be like this. It's all very . . . sudden.'

'*Monsieur*, this is *family* money. And the Joby family is glad to pay it. Outside any personal matters, you have fulfilled an important task.' He held out an envelope. 'You must accept it. Those are my instructions. You understand that.' Slowly George took the envelope. 'It contains enough money for the air fare to Rome and for an hotel for four nights. These are on my calculations, not from anyone else. The two fees suggested by Janine are also there. I believe they are correct, proper that is, in the amounts. Would you wish to regard them?'

'Thank you, no,' said George. 'I'm sure it will be more than satisfactory.'

'Janine has insisted upon this. So do the Joby family. I agree with them. So there is no more to discuss. The English gentleman, Sir Bernard Holmes, will be expecting you. His address in Rome is in the envelope. Also a covering letter.'

George rose to go. 'Somehow,' he said, 'something is wrong. I feel it is wrong.'

'The Joby family have gratitude to you, *monsieur*,' responded the lawyer. 'That is all I can say.' They reached the door.

Suddenly George said: 'Janine told me that she once had a baby. When she was only seventeen. It was taken away on her father's instructions.'

'Yes. That is the case as I understand it. We have been unable to trace that child. We have even had a private investigator searching. But with no success.' He looked thoughtfully at George. 'Perhaps, *monsieur*, that would be another task for you. Maybe you could find this girl.'

The suggestion startled George. 'How? I would not know where to begin . . .' Then he said: 'But, of course, I would try.'

Benoit nodded. 'Naturally I must consult with the family first. But if you can remain in Paris a day or two days then I am sure that will give me enough time. The papers, such as they are, are in this office. They were made available to the detective so I am certain that you can see them also.'

'I would be glad,' said George. They were still at the door. He added: 'He must have been a terrible man.'

'Joby. Yes, he was. He disposed of the baby during the 1963 International Philatelic Congress in Paris. Possibly the secret arrangement was with one of the other delegates.'

George said: 'Do you think so?'

'I do,' said the lawyer. 'It would seem the sort of thing that would have happened. How would you say it? Swapped, is it? Yes, perhaps. The baby was swapped for a set of stamps.'

Deeply unhappy, George walked through the dull Paris day back to the Hôtel des Deux Lacs which, at Janine's laughing insistence, he had reserved from La Manche. The feeling that there was something amiss, something he had not been told, remained heavily upon him. How could she send him away? Like this, so dismissively, so abruptly?

As he entered the hotel the reception clerk held out an envelope to him. 'Special delivery, *monsieur*,' he said. 'It arrived one hour ago.'

George recognised her handwriting. With an apprehensive

heart he took it to his room and sat on the bed, staring at the envelope, afraid to open it. Was she merely explaining that it was necessary to pay him off, that for some reason, her family perhaps, or something within herself, she wished him to leave? Falteringly he opened the letter. It was only one paragraph.

'*Chéri*, You are wondering why I have sent you away. I must tell you. I am ill from leukemia and it is necessary for me to leave La Manche and take some treatment, as I have done in the past. My time with you was the happiest of all my life.'

It was signed, 'With my love and my thanks' although he could not see it through his tears. They fell in great drops onto the notepaper and, unthinkingly, he wiped them off, leaving smudges in the ink. He put the letter on the bed and cried into his hands. His throat was full, his heart bursting. He picked up the telephone and dialled the code for Cherbourg and the house number. He could hear the phone ringing emptily. There was no reply.

Immediately he dialled Monsieur Benoit's number. The lawyer's secretary said he was out and would not be back for the rest of the day. George washed his face and left the hotel. He took a taxi to the Gare St Lazare. There was a train for Cherbourg within the hour.

He knew all the time it would be hopeless. At Cherbourg he took a taxi directly to La Manche but even as they climbed the wind-riven hill he sensed that she would be gone. He walked slowly, fearfully, into the walled courtyard and to the door. The bell sounded hollowly. Henri answered it. He stood as expressionless as ever.

'Mademoiselle Joby?' asked George.

'*Mademoiselle est partie*,' replied the man. '*Ce matin.*'

'Oh, I see.' George backed a few steps away from the door. What, he thought, had happened to the man's deafness? Henri, still unmoving, prepared to close it.

'Thank you,' said George. '*Merci.*' He looked pleadingly at the manservant. 'You don't know when she will return?'

Henri shrugged. '*Non, monsieur.*'

There was nothing more to say or to do. He turned from the door, from the house, and walked down the hill towards the town and the station, his heart full.

VIII

The man who sat next to George on the plane, Alitalia Flight 335 from Paris to Rome, was short, compact, had a long but dexterously combed moustache, and a gun. The man was against the window and George on the aisle; the seat in the middle was vacant.

Until the drinks came round they did not speak. Both ordered in English and then the stranger launched into a tale, hardly drawing breath.

'Coming out of Leonardo di Vinci last week Alitalia somehow got everything fouled up. Six of us found ourselves shovelled into the wrong flight. There we were taxiing, actually taxiing, when they welcomed us onto the flight to Milan. Milan! Now, I didn't want to go to Milan, I hate the place, I wanted to get to London — and on time. The other five felt the same but the Eyties were still going to take off with us. Said we could get the flight from Milan to London, which wasn't the point at all. I mean, for Christ's sake, what about our luggage, just for starters. Anyway, there was this old biddy among the six and she wasn't going to have any of it. She was all done up in tight tweeds, thin as a rake, with that sort of hat the late Queen Mary, God rest her dear old soul, used to wear. She kicked up bloody mayhem. She had a stick and she banged it on the floor like fury. That started the rest of us off, stamping our feet and chanting "England! England!" like football bloody hooligans. They had to stop the plane at the beginning of the runway and take it out of the queue. Then they sent a bus and we all trooped off cheering. The old lady was having a great time, waving her stick at the Eyties. So they took us back to the terminal and all through the back doubles, through the warehouses and God-knows-where-else until we eventually got to the right flight. There was a steward at the top of the gangway looking thoroughly pissed off, telling us to hurry because we were holding up the flight — as if it was our bloody

162

fault. We all got aboard smartish, except the old duck. She took her time up the steps – just like a Queen, I tell you – and then when she got into the plane she turned left instead of right and banged on the pilot's door with her walking stick. The steward was dumbfounded, he couldn't move. Then the door opened and this startled sort of face came out, the pilot. The old lady glared at him and sort of barked: "London?" '

George laughed dutifully.

The man had not finished. He began to talk comparative airlines. Alitalia was usually all right to and from Leonardo de Vinci, but to Cairo it was best to take British Airways from London if MEA were having trouble getting their planes out of Beirut, which not infrequently happened. Going south-east, Singapore Airlines served excellent food. On Qantas the girls were healthy, great big teeth, and on Japan Airlines they smiled when they hadn't a clue what you were talking about. Getting to some of the smaller Pacific islands could still be difficult even in 1986 but quite a lot, Truk for example, now had an adequate runway and the Air France service to Tahiti and back the other way round, through New Caledonia and what they used to call the New Hebrides, was dependable. Air France or UTA were also all right down through Africa, and British Airways too, but if you were going straight to Cape Town, of course, it would have to be SAA, despite the fact that they travelled round the long coast. Never travel Aeroflot if there was anybody else flying and don't go by Iran Air because there was no way you could get a drink.

'Of course not,' agreed George. He found difficulty in not staring at the man.

When they reached Rome the man had a car waiting for him and offered George a lift into the city. 'Sorry I talked so much on the plane,' he said in a more measured manner. They were sitting in the car. 'I was trying to stop someone killing you.'

'Me?' George asked unbelievingly. The man had to be mad. 'Kill *me?*'

His companion, first touching his lips with his finger, leaned forward and tapped, but only with his fingertips, the glass partition between themselves and the driver. Apparently satisfied it was sealed he took the black gun from his inside pocket and laid it across his knee. 'It would have been an accident, of course,' he said. 'But that would have been no consolation to you.'

A hollow feeling grew within George. 'Are you serious?' he said.

'Very. I am in the service of His Highness Sheik Abdul Mohamed Al Sakah. I am head of his personal security. My name is Robin Lowndes. What is yours?'

'George Goodnight,' muttered George. 'But I don't understand all this.'

'His Highness, so the Baruni thought . . .'

'The Baruni?'

'The opposition. Terrorist thugs. Remember the name.'

'I'm unlikely to forget it. But, for God's sake . . .'

'Allah,' mentioned Lowndes. 'Allah is God. Remember the name.'

'Why, for God's sake . . . all right, for Allah's sake . . . what have *I* got to do with it?'

'Well, this sort of operation *is* unusual. Certainly in Economy Class. We were merely testing out the system. We made a secret plan, which of course we knew would soon be common knowledge among our various enemies . . .'

George was staring at him. 'It would, wouldn't it,' he said.

'Exactly. I am glad you have some appreciation of the situation and the risks involved. It will stand you in good stead, perhaps.'

'But I *haven't* got any appreciation of it!' protested George vehemently. 'I'm here to sell some stamps. Why should it stand *me* in good stead. I'm having nothing more to do with it.' Quickly and anxiously he looked from the car window. 'I think I'll get a taxi.'

Lowndes laid a suprisingly hard hand on his arm. 'Don't. Please. It does not pay to jump from cars without warning. Not in this business. There is my escort car following immediately behind. If you jump they will most likely shoot you.'

'Christ,' moaned George sitting back in his seat. He turned and looked through the rear window.

'The grey Mercedes,' mentioned Lowndes. 'Don't worry, we will safely drop you outside your hotel.'

'I haven't booked a hotel,' protested George. He had another look at the Mercedes.

'The Grand Opera is very good. I am staying there.'

'Well, I'll go somewhere else, thank you.'

'That would not be wise. Whatever you may feel, Mr Goodnight, you are now embroiled in this situation. They saw you on the plane and without doubt they saw you get into this car. Didn't you see the Levantine-looking chap outside the airport pretending he was rolling a cigarette. He never finished rolling it. And once you start rolling a cigarette it is difficult to stop. The tobacco, you must have noticed, goes everywhere. So why did he stop? He stopped because he was observing us and he went to make his report to his control.' He looked at George sagely and sideways. 'I think it will be as well if you stay under our protection for a while.'

Fiercely, George turned in his seat. 'You've got a bloody nerve! How dare you get me involved in this hocus-pocus! I'll go to the British Embassy.'

'The British Embassy – British Embassies in general, and I speak from experience – spend much of their time trying to keep *out* of this sort of business. It would only compound the error.'

'But I'm a British subject.' Angrily George grasped for his passport and thrust it open under Lowndes' face. 'Look, I am entitled to the protection of Her Majesty's Government.'

Lowndes smiled as though at some distant memory. 'Those were the days,' he sighed. 'Please believe me, it would only, as I say, compound the error.'

'Error? What error? Whose error?'

'Yours, I fear, George. The error of sitting in that seat.'

'What the hell has the seat . . . ?'

'. . . got to do with it? Everything, old chap. Absolutely everything. If you had sat in Row G instead of F you would now be blamelessly on your way to sell your stamps. Sheik Abdul Mohamed Al Sakah is a great stamp enthusiast, incidentally. He will be pleased to see them.'

'Well, he's not going to,' answered George petulantly. He clutched the case containing the albums to his bosom like a baby. 'These are private.'

'We shall see,' intoned Lowndes. He leaned forward and opened the partition, speaking in sharp Arabic to the driver. Closing the window he reassumed his smile.

'Your seat F3,' he said, 'was supposed to contain the person of Sheik Abdul Mohamed Al Sakar himself.'

'*What*? In Economy?'

'Ah, that was the plan, the subterfuge. You are quick at grasping the weaknesses, George. You could be very good. Very good indeed.'

'Please,' pleaded George weakly. 'Let me get out of this bleeding car.'

'Not yet. We are almost there. And, as I have warned you, old boy, it would be both foolish and final.' As George, perspiring despite the air conditioning, collapsed back into the seat, the man continued: 'Our plan was to test their capability for assassination.'

'The Baruni,' said George weakly. He had closed his eyes.

'Who else? Although there may well be others. We made a clever and secret plan to transport the Sheik to Rome with the best of all disguises – Economy Class. It was a touch of genius. My idea, of course. Then we performed a double trick by not sending him at all.'

George opened his eyes. 'You're losing me,' he muttered. He glanced out of the window. They were in the noisy streets. 'Are we nearly there?'

'Less than five minutes. We have to make a few necessary diversions. We never go anywhere direct. Not in this business.'

The realisation made George crouch lower in the seat. Lowndes said: 'At least you are taking it seriously. Do you want to know the rest?'

'I might as well,' said George miserably. 'Jesus,' he muttered to himself.

'Their agents were on board. They had, of course, heard of the plan.'

'Of course,' muttered George.

'But not the *real* plan. We exposed them. We know now that our security has been breached.' He became sinister. 'And we know *how* and by *whom*. He is being dealt with. And it was all for *nothing*. It was merely a dummy run. If there had been an attempted assassination, you would have got it and our beloved Sheik would be alive.'

George was aware of a strange green feeling. 'I'm so pleased,' he breathed.

So was Lowndes. His smile formed a concave bow complimentary to his moustache. 'But,' he said as one who has a last triumphant card to lay, 'the joy, the beauty of the whole matter

166

is this. His Highness Sheik Abdul Mohamed Al Sakah *was never in Paris at all*. He was here in Rome the whole time, safe while the drama was going on in the sky.'

George scrutinised him acidly. 'As I said, I'm really pleased.' He looked out of the window as the car slowed. 'Is this it? Good.'

Lowndes laid a hand on his arm. 'Please, no rushing. As I've tried to explain, rushing in our business is often an error, sometimes a fatal error.'

'Don't keep calling it *our* business,' said George bitterly. 'It's *your* bloody business, not mine.'

The man shrugged. 'Please yourself, Mr Goodnight. But, as I have attempted to explain, whether or not you like it, you *are* involved. My suggestion is that you check into the Grand Opera Hotel, lie low for a couple of days and, when I give you the word, quietly slip away and deliver your stamps.'

The driver had left his seat and was outside the car. His face, dark and creased, appeared at the window. He turned sharply each way, surveying the street.

'I don't want to stay at the Grand Opera,' muttered George angrily. He looked out at the gilded doors of the hotel. 'For a start, I can't afford it.'

'There will be nothing to afford,' replied Lowndes calmly. 'Everything will be taken care of.'

Backing off with suspicion, George said: 'Are you setting me up for something else? If so, you can . . .'

'. . . forget it. Take a running jump . . . in the lake. Etcetera,' smiled Lowndes. 'No, dear chap, you've served your purpose. Now, as one Englishman to another, I'm trying to help you escape.'

'Escape!' George exploded. The driver opened the door. 'Escape?' His voice plummeted.

There was nothing for it. He followed Lowndes onto the pavement and realised he was crouching like a hunchback. 'Good, good,' said Lowndes. 'You're learning.' He looked left and looked right and then reversed the process.

The Mercedes had drawn up at the curb behind them but the dark faces remained inside. Still at a crouch, George hurried into the cover of the hotel and felt its shadow fall over him like a pall. Furtively he threw glances all around the extravagant lobby. Lowndes was already approaching the reception desk.

He spoke a quick sentence and the girl smiled and handed over two keys. He returned to George. 'Three forty-one,' he whispered. 'I am in the next room. In case you need me.'

Behind them the main door was opened by two porters to admit a wealthy looking couple and George thought of making a run for it, now, before it was too late. Lowndes was watching him, shaking his head and tutting. 'No, no. That would be too foolish for words. Take my advice and go to ground.' Miserably George accepted the key from him.

'That is all your luggage?' Lowndes asked, nodding at his plastic bag and the case containing the albums.

George returned the nod. 'Us sitting ducks have to travel light,' he grunted.

A brief bark of laughter hardly louder than a hiccough came from the other Englishman. 'Good for you,' he said. 'Why don't you go to your room and put your feet up. There is no need for you to register. It is all taken care of.'

Without saying a further word, George glanced at the room number on the key, turned and trudged towards the lifts. Briskly, Lowndes followed him. They got into the lift.

'First floor,' said Lowndes to the lift boy.

'It's three hundred and forty-one,' said George checking the key.

'First floor,' repeated Lowndes.

They alighted at the first floor. 'Now what?' said George.

'This is correct,' said Lowndes. 'You are in room one-four-three. The key numbers are reversed, you see. Basic security. The room is here.'

They walked a few paces. 'While you are involved,' said Lowndes like a final piece of advice, 'it would be advisable not to use your correct name. Everyone in this business has an alias, of course.'

'What else?' shrugged George unhappily.

'And yours?'

George Goodnight was beginning to hate Oliver Loving. 'Loving,' he said tightly. 'Oliver Loving.'

He lay on the bed in his braces, hands behind head, listening for warning noises above the muffled traffic outside, his eyes searching the ceiling for bugging devices. The sprinkler and the

168

light fitting remained the main objects of his suspicion. He had checked them three times and everything else twice.

The bathroom door was open offering a view of the washbasin and toilet cabinet above it. A creak, no louder than that of a mouse, came from that direction, and George's startled head darted around to see the mirrored door of the cabinet begin to swing open. With a suppressed howl he threw himself sideways off the bed on the opposite side. As he lay clutching the bedside rug there came a hollow voice.

'Excellent, Mr Loving. You move quickly for a big man.'

'Shit,' said George. With caution he levered himself up. 'Lowndes you prat. Thanks very much.'

'You're welcome,' returned Lowndes, his face framed in the cabinet.

Rising from behind the bed George went into the bathroom and spoke to the enclosed face. 'I thought I'd checked that,' he said grumpily.

Lowndes tapped the sides and the collapsible back of the cabinet. 'Very well made,' he said. 'From Moscow. The Russians put together really good stuff like this. We bought a whole lot very reasonably in a surplus sale in Leningrad. I would like to come in and talk to you.'

'Just come on in,' invited George resignedly. 'I expect there's some gadget that opens up the entire wall.'

'I like the idea,' nodded the framed face. 'Good thinking. But I shall have to come round by the door. I wanted to make sure you were alone.'

'The chief of the KGB's just gone out of the window,' said George.

Lowndes' face vanished and with a snap the cabinet became a cabinet again. George regarded it blankly and then with a sigh closed the mirror on his side. At once there was a secret type of knocking on his door. He walked over and let Lowndes into the room.

'You should never, never ever, make jokes like that,' warned Lowndes lighting a cigarette. 'About the chief of the KGB or that category. It's the very thing that's likely to cost you dearly.'

George sat down heavily on the bed. 'Now look . . .' he began.

'Now look,' intervened Lowndes. 'You have to realise that there are people in this business who would grab that like a barracuda grabbing your privates. Believe me, there are agents all over the place who never get a smell of *anything* authentic. They couldn't get the time right. And passing on a remark like that, in all innocence, gives them great kudos. Otherwise they have to make everything up and . . .'

'Now look,' insisted George. He leaned forward on the bed and wagged his finger. 'I don't want another word, another moment, of this mumbo-bloody-jumbo. I've had enough. If I helped you out, all right, fair enough, even though nobody actually informed me. But enough . . .'

'Is enough,' agreed Lowndes. 'But is it? I was just about to make you a lucrative offer.'

'I'm not interested. The next time they may get me.'

'Five million lire for a week's work,' said Lowndes dropping his eyes. He lifted them slowly. 'That is two thousand pounds.'

'Who is going to kill me?'

'That is not the point. There are some risks, of course, but it is quite good money.'

'Not if you're dead.'

Lowndes spread his hands in a gesture of honesty. 'I am going to tell you something now that is, to say the least, highly confidential.'

George's eyes went to the ceiling rose and the sprinkler. Lowndes smiled tiredly.

'They are disconnected,' Lowndes said. 'Elementary.'

'I'm not sure,' said George, 'that I want to hear this highly confidential stuff. It could land me right . . .'

'. . . in it,' finished Lowndes. 'Not just you. Both of us. But since you are already "in it", as you say, I think that you ought to hear what I've got to say.'

'All right,' sighed George. 'All right.'

'My function, as I have already said, is to provide security for His Highness Sheik Abdul Mohamed Al Sakah.' He looked moonily at George. 'It is a job for life.'

'*His* life,' suggested George.

'Obviously. Or mine. Or both.'

'You don't make it sound all that permanent.'

Lowndes eased forward. His mouth had acquired a small twitch. It was the first time that he had seemed anything less than sure of himself. 'For the next seven days,' he said, 'while he is here in Rome, he is at great risk. He is aware of this and

170

as far as possible he is keeping his head down. But he can't hide all the time. He would lose face with the other Arab rulers. He has to put on a front for them. And he has a meeting – an important meeting – right here in this hotel. His security, as far as I can arrange it, is good. But, this week particularly, I have found it necessary to make extra precautions. This is where you come in.'

'I thought it might be,' said George lugubriously.

'His Highness puts great trust in Englishmen. I am former SAS and so are three of my top men. You were never . . . I suppose . . . ?'

'In the SAS? God, no. The only thing I've ever joined was the Ancient Order of Buffaloes and I didn't like that.'

Lowndes said: 'Well, you *look* as if you might have been. You're pretty fit, I imagine.'

'I mow the lawn occasionally.'

'You *look* right. That is half the battle. What I'm proposing is that you join the security squad for this week only, while we're in Rome. Five million lire for the week.'

'Two thousand pounds,' ruminated George. 'It sounds much more in lire.'

'That's correct. Half now. Half at the conclusion of the contract.' He paused ominously. 'The successful conclusion.'

'If you don't mind,' said George. 'I would like to deliver the stamps first.'

From the moment he left the Grand Opera Hotel for the house on the Via Claudia, George was tailed by a solitary man in a black car. He had insisted on making the journey by taxi despite Lowndes' offer of one of the Mercedes at their disposal. The man in the black car, who had been reading the English football results in a day-old newspaper, spotted George as soon as he left the hotel and had little difficulty, since he was expert in Roman traffic, in tailing the taxi on its journey to the house near San Stefano Rotondo. It was early evening.

Sir Bernard Holmes lived in a substantial, faded mansion fronted by a fine courtyard. From the top windows there were views down the Via Claudia to the cheese-like slice of the Coliseum and in another direction over the trees and gardens to the Villa Elementana. It was in this top room, a study of considered comfort, that the two Englishmen sat. Sir Bernard

171

was a rounded man with two startled tufts of grey hair sprouting from behind his ears, between which curved a ruddy bald head. It was like the sun going down in clouds. He took the albums from George and studied them with unconcealed pleasure.

'Delightful. Quite delightful,' he murmured turning the pages. He looked up. George was sitting in a leather armchair with a gin and tonic held in both hands. He had a growing sensation of homesickness. 'You must have had an enjoyable time collating this little treasure trove.'

'It was a labour of love,' said George sincerely.

'Nothing like British issues,' sighed Sir Bernard. 'At least, former British issues. I loved the old GBs. Plain, no nonsense beauty, don't you think? Now they've become like something from the Balkans, everything on them. Film stars, for God's sake.'

'I have to say I agree,' nodded George.

'They'll be putting the *name* of the blessed country on them next. That's if we've got a country.' He looked up as if anxious not to offend. George was drinking his gin. 'Never could settle at home,' Sir Bernard confessed. 'Feel a bit ashamed of it really, I suppose. But after living everywhere else in the world I simply couldn't. Great Britain was just a country which employed me. Sad really.'

'How long have you lived in Rome, sir?' asked George.

'Seven years since retirement. I was at the Embassy here for five years before that. I suppose I'm here for good now.'

Anxiously, George leaned forward. 'Sir Bernard,' he said while the older man was still letting the pages drift through his fingers. 'I wonder if I might ask you a . . . well, a private question, I suppose?'

It seemed that the grey tufts behind the old man's ears stood up a little, like thistles opening. 'Yes, of course, old chap. As long as it's private, not secret.'

'No, private.'

'Good. Fire away.' He closed the album and laid it carefully on top of the others on the lamplit desk. 'Sounds intriguing.'

'Were you at the International Philatelic Congress in Paris in 1963?'

'Most certainly. Haven't missed one since the war.'

'You saw Monsieur Robert Joby there, I take it.'

'Of course. Doubt if he missed one either. His collection may

172

have been unorthodox, as you well know, but he was a great stamp man.'

There seemed no diplomatic way of posing the next question. 'Do you have any knowledge of him giving away a baby at the congress?' asked George.

Blatant disbelief filled Sir Bernard's eyes. 'A baby?' he asked astounded. 'Give away a baby!' He exploded with genuine laughter and picked up his whisky. 'My dear fellow, what an extraordinary question.'

George nodded unhappily. 'Yes, it certainly is,' he agreed. 'Unfortunately it appears that he may have done. The Joby family lawyer, Monsieur Benoit, whom I believe you know, has given me permission to go into this matter.' He reached and produced a letter from his inside pocket. 'On behalf of Mademoiselle Janine Joby, Robert Joby's daughter.' He handed the letter across. Sir Bernard's years in the Diplomatic Service had given him the facility to quickly overcome even the deepest doubt. He took the letter and read it.

'What then,' he asked looking up at George, 'is the story?'

'Simply that Janine Joby, who was unmarried, in fact was only seventeen, had a baby girl and the old man, who was, although you might think of him differently, something of a despot . . .'

'A swine,' nodded Sir Bernard. 'An undoubted swine, despite his fine collection.'

'Yes. So I hear. Well, Monsieur Benoit believes, and apparently so do other members of the family, that the baby was . . . well, fostered, shall we say, by someone who was a delegate at the Stamp Congress. Without the permission or knowledge of the young mother.'

'Good gracious. What a terrible thing to do.' He drank from his glass and then said convincingly: 'But I can see him doing it.'

'All records, if there were any of the matter, have vanished. This girl, who would now be twenty-three, is somewhere in the world and nobody knows where, least of all the mother who, regrettably, is seriously, perhaps terminally, ill.'

'Oh, I see. How sad.'

'Yes, sir, indeed. I thought you might remember having heard something of this matter.'

'Not a thing.' He laughed shortly. 'He didn't give her to me,

173

that's certain. I've got enough daughters of my own. I wish I could help. But this is the first I've heard of it.'

George thanked him. 'I imagine that there was great secrecy about it,' he said. 'Only the immediate parties would know.' He hesitated. 'Would you by any chance have any records of that congress, lists of delegates or that sort of thing?'

The elderly man brightened at once. 'There I *can* help you!' he exclaimed. 'We don't even have to leave this room.' He rose and turned to a cabinet at the far end, adjacent to the window. George stood up tentatively and laid his glass on the table beside his chair. Outside it had begun to rain, the spots making a pebble pattern on the big windows. Sir Bernard looked sideways as if someone were tapping to come in. 'Here we are,' he said. 'I may have been a diplomat but I would have made a hell of a fine filing clerk.' Taking a folder from the cabinet, he turned back into the room. 'Paris, sixty-three,' he said. Opening it as he sat down he immediately selected a folded sheet of paper. 'List of leading delegates,' he said. 'Prospective foster fathers.'

Thanking him, George took the list. 'Oh dear,' he said mildly. 'There must be a couple of hundred.'

'Easily,' agreed Sir Bernard. 'And from all over the show. And by now some of them will have departed the show altogether.'

'I thought it would be difficult,' said George. He looked up. 'Would it be possible, Sir Bernard, to have a copy of this list?'

'No trouble whatever,' said the other man. 'In fact there's probably a duplicate in the file. What use it is to me now, I don't know. But I'm a bit of a hoarder. I always like to know that I haven't thrown anything away.' He had risen and gone back to the cabinet. 'Let's see . . . a list of guests from the banquet . . . Yes, here we are, another copy of the delegate list. The same as the other one. You can keep it with pleasure.'

George thanked him and put the list into the inside pocket of his jacket. He declined another drink and rose to leave. The rain had been brief and he said he would get a taxi in the street.

'Where are you staying?' asked Sir Bernard.

'The Grand Opera Hotel,' answered George.

'Yes, yes, it's very decent, isn't it? Somehow these flashy

174

modern hotels haven't quite managed to get the knack. Giuseppe Verdi always stayed there, you know. There is a secret door from the hotel into the Opera House next door and he would dodge through there and be in the front of the orchestra like a rabbit coming out of a hole. People were always mystified by that one, and by all accounts it pleased him no end.' Together they had descended the fine staircase. A manservant appeared and opened the bulky front door. 'Giuseppe Verdi,' mused Sir Bernard. 'Just think if he had been English his name would have been Joe Green. Somehow it doesn't sound the same, does it?'

Still smiling, George went out of the arch. The man who had been reading the English football results but had now turned to the crossword put away his pencil and leaned from the window of his car. 'Can I offer you a lift somewhere, Mr Goodnight?'

George stopped and was at first tempted to run. But the Englishness of the accent reassured him. Carefully he walked towards the face. The car had been there some time because the road beneath was clearly dry in the light of the street lamps. 'Where?' asked George.

'To the Grand Opera,' replied the man. He was wearing a trilby. His face was lean and lined with shadows. 'But perhaps we could have a little talk on the way. There's a bar I know which is so loud that nobody can overhear you. Would you mind?'

Bending towards the window, George said: 'Would you mind telling me who you are.'

'Sweeting,' replied the man. 'Bill Sweeting.'

'Representing?'

'Her Majesty's Government. I'm counter-intelligence.' He picked up the newspaper. 'See, I'm doing *The Times* crossword in the dark.' He opened the door and George stepped in. He sat beside Sweeting. 'I'd rather see your warrant card, or whatever you carry. Anybody can buy *The Times*.'

'True. But can they do the crossword?'

George picked up the newspaper. Even in the dimness he could see that the crossword was almost complete. 'All by the light of a street lamp,' said Sweeting. He produced a document in a cellophane case and switched on the interior light so that George could peruse it.

'This is not something we counter-intelligence chaps do all

175

the time,' he said amiably. He put the document away and started the engine. 'What do you make of: "Quip about a girl, one cold and very strict"?'

'Don't know,' said George. 'How many letters?'

'Nine letters.'

'Don't know.'

'Did you find Sir Bernard in good form?'

'Excellent. I suppose you want to know why I went there.'

'You were delivering some stamps,' said Sweeting. He moved the car surely through the late-night traffic. They reached the Piazza Vittorio Emanuele and turned into a side street. They stopped beside a yellow-lit bar. It was silent.

'Nothing I ever plan works out,' complained Sweeting. 'This place is usually in uproar.' He left the car and went through the entrance. He returned and said: 'There was a football match and the television's broken so they've all gone to another bar, even the boss. There's just a girl left. It should be all right.'

'It's all right with me,' said George. 'I always thought secret agents went to quiet places but I can see that a lot of noise is just as good.'

'Better,' said Sweeting.

They walked into the bar, the tables and chairs thrown about as if they had been vacated hurriedly, the television set sitting in dumb insolence on its shelf. The girl behind the counter regarded them with resignation as if she had been looking forward to closing up. Sweeting ordered two beers. The girl served him and picked up a magazine. George had sat in a distant corner. 'All right,' he said when Sweeting had sat down. 'What is it?'

'Puritanic,' muttered Sweeting. He took the newspaper from his pocket and filled in the clue. 'That's more like it,' he smiled. They each sipped the beer. 'It's the company you've been keeping,' said Sweeting. 'Mr Lowndes in particular.'

'You've been keeping an eye on me.'

'Since you arrived at the airport. We had someone watching there.'

'Rolling a cigarette,' said George.

Sweeting looked genuinely shocked, then sighed. 'Everybody's a bloody James Bond,' he complained. 'Yes, that was

176

him. We know how they set you up on the airplane. This is by way of being a friendly warning.'

'They set me up?'

'The whole thing is a fraud,' said Sweeting. 'Lowndes has established this so-called security to protect a man who needs no protection whatever. Take it from me, Sheik Abdul Mohamed Al Sakah is not threatened by *anybody*. His kingdom is the size of Hyde Park, less the lake. It has no oil, no political significance, no nothing. It is a joke among the other Arab leaders. They only let the Sheik pretend he's powerful and important because Sakah has the best camel racing track in the Gulf and there is a special dispensation of the law which allows the dancing of the can-can. But that is its only significance.'

'The Baruni are not after him then?'

'Nobody is. There *is* no Baruni. All that charade on the plane was another set-up by Lowndes. He's created a whole fantasy where the poor little Sheik is scared out of his wits but at the same time he's flattered as hell because he likes to think he's important. We are watching it closely, but frankly as both parties are subscribing so enthusiastically to the fantasy there's nothing to be done about it. On the other hand I thought it would be the decent thing to let you know what's going on.'

Slowly George thanked him and shook his head. He looked around narrowly and realised it was becoming a habit. 'You mean to say that all this following by car through the streets, the guns, the secret cubbyholes and the rest of the cloak-and-dagger is just a pantomime?'

'Absolutely. Lowndes is raking in a nice monthly bundle just for providing the bogus security. He has no qualifications whatever.'

'He claims he is ex-SAS,' said George.

'Oh yes, Salvation Army Sergeant,' grunted Sweeting. 'He's done two lots of time in England.'

'What are you going to do about him?' asked George. 'It's like All-round Security versus Weaver.'

'Is it?' said Sweeting. 'I'm doing nothing for the moment. If we went to the Sheik he wouldn't believe us and he'd be offended. He's convinced he's important. And he thinks he needs protection. He'd be bloody upset if we said he didn't. It's only if Lowndes – the fifth of his names by the way, his real name is Stanley Arthur Perkins – if he tries to do a major diddle on the poor chap, then we'll move in.' He drank the rest of his beer. 'I thought you ought to be warned, that's all.'

'Yes, thanks. Christ, I've been scared out of my wits by all this skulduggery. What should I do now? Just vanish? He's enrolled me as a bodyguard. I'm on a weekly contract.'

'How much is it worth?'

'Five million lire.'

Sweeting whistled and the girl behind the counter looked up and, believing it was an order, poured two more drinks.

'That's not bad,' said Sweeting. 'If he pays up.'

'He's paid half,' said George. 'And I get the rest after the week. But you think I ought to get out?'

'No, no,' said Sweeting thoughtfully. 'It sounds like a nice number. In any case, it might be a good idea if you carried on. Perhaps you wouldn't mind keeping me, that is us, informed of what is going on.'

The girl arrived with the two unordered beers. '*Ma lei mi ha fischiato*,' she said when Sweeting said they did not require them. She put her fingers in her mouth and whistled violently.

George paid. 'I'll put it on expenses,' he said.

The door through which in the nineteenth century Giuseppe Verdi would frequently enter the Rome Opera House, to the surprise of many, was at the end of a marble corridor with a windowed garden on one side and racks of folded chairs and tables on the other. 'Today, signore,' said the assistant manager, performing a brief bow which caused the tails of his coat to jump like the behind of a bird, 'nobody goes through the door. This passage is no longer used.'

George put his hand on the door handle.

'It is locked, *signore*,' said the man.

'Is there a key?' asked George. He was enjoying being a security man.

'Of course. But it must be found.'

'Then perhaps you could find it. It is very important.'

'*Si, signore*. I understand well.'

He left hurriedly. George unfolded one of the racked chairs and sat down. The unaccustomed weight of the gun in its shoulder holster was bothering him. The straps of the holster were also rubbing uncomfortably. He took the gun and put it in his pocket to give his armpit a rest. Outside, a garden blazed

178

in an oblong of Roman sunshine that fell obligingly between the enclosing walls. An agreeable fountain splashed and gurgled. The assistant manager returned, briskly, his tails bobbing, still flat-faced but with a sliver of triumph in his eye. In his hand he held a large key. 'Giuseppe Verdi's own,' he said reverently.

George held out his hand and the Italian, after a fraction of reluctance, handed the key to him.

'I'll try it,' said George. The key was heavy. 'It will be good practice.'

'*Signore?*'

'I may have to use it again,' answered George. He moved towards the door and with some manoeuvring inserted the key.

'Ah, so I understand,' said the assistant manager. 'It is always kept in the *casella* – the pigeonhole you say – for Room 103. It has been there for many years.' He flushed with a little pleasure. 'Signor Verdi's own room,' he added.

George turned the key, with difficulty at first, but then firmly. 'I think I may have to keep it,' he said as he pulled the door towards him. It creaked open. A dark corridor was revealed. A mouse emerged from the tunnel, realised its mistake, and scampered back again.

'Keep it?' queried the Italian. He stared into the void before them before returning to George. 'You must hold the key?'

'Temporarily,' answered George with casual authority and not looking at the man. 'Until Sunday at least. I'll sign for it.'

The assistant manager shrugged with his face and his shoulders. An answering shrug came from his tails. '*Si, si.* If it is for the Security. Signor Verdi is not going to require it.' He went away. George took his gun from his pocket and replaced it in the holster. He could only withdraw it with difficulty and he preferred it in his coat. But Lowndes had said that security men always wore shoulder holsters.

The Italian returned with a typed receipt for '*La chiave di Signor Giuseppe Verdi*' and George signed. He practised opening the door several times and when he could do it in one he locked it, patted it and put the bulky key into his pocket. Then he went to seek out Lowndes.

He found him drinking coffee, almost enveloped in one of the commodious palms in the hotel lounge. Lowndes peered through the fronds like a tribesman in ambush. He was silent and his eyes seemed to protrude from the greenery. As George loitered they swivelled to the left, indicating he should sit down. George slid into a chair, the palm touching his shoulder like solicitous fingers. He realised that the legs of both Lowndes and himself were partly exposed below the hanging leaves and thought that, far from concealment, the effect was one of drawing curiosity and attention.

'Done it?' inquired Lowndes. He was always looking elsewhere when he spoke. 'Checked?'

'I've checked the ground floor,' answered George. A lounge waiter hovered and, appearing not to have noticed their camouflage, politely asked if either of the gentlemen would like more coffee. George declined for both. He was not going to tell Lowndes about Verdi's door.

'Thoroughly?' asked Lowndes, eyes still searching. He was scrutinising the waiter who had inquired about coffee. 'It's important that you should know every inch of this hotel, and the ground floor particularly. His Highness will be spending most of the hour he is here on this floor. He must be covered and his escape routes kept screened.' For once his eyes turned inwards. He peered at George through the greenery. 'Worry, worry, worry,' he complained. 'This job is nothing but worry.'

There did not seem to be a great deal of His Highness Sheik Abdul Mohamed Al Sakah to protect. A man the stature of a medium-sized boy, heavily upholstered with robes, stepped from his car outside the Grand Opera Hotel. His escort cars blocked the Via Nazionale and the pavement in the vicinity of the main door was walled by set-faced guards, uniformed in identical, easily recognisable, grey civilian suits.

George was standing in the lobby which had been roped off. The reception staff and the hotel's own portly chief of security formed a small phalanx at the centre of the hall. There were bows and greetings. The tension was visible. When the manager's shoes squeaked on the marble floor the security men's eyes fluttered with alarm. One of the desk clerks, leaning forward, knocked over his own propped-up nameplate. It fell from the counter and hit the floor with a sharp crack. In an amazing split second the Sheik had thrown himself flat and his followers had fallen on top of him like a robed rugby scrum. To his surprise George found himself behind a gilt table, the heavy

180

key in his hand, his eyes swivelling. He put the key away and took out his gun.

'*Scusi!*' called the reception clerk across the lobby. '*Scusi!*' Ashen-faced, the young man retrieved his nameplate from the floor and shakily set it up once more on his desk. The manager's face, like that of a baleful tiger, revolved to the youth as everyone picked themselves from the marble slabs. The Sheik was the last to be helped to his feet. Amid consternation, commiseration and cleaning down, he stood, a miniature hurt expression on his nutty countenance. His eyes flicked right and left as if he wanted to make sure for himself.

'Christ, that was nasty.' It was Lowndes' voice. George straightened with the rest and now found his chief, hovering near, half hidden by an Oriental vase.

'All's well that ends well,' mentioned George casually. The shaken Sheik was being escorted to an anteroom. The door closed behind him.

'Let's hope that's the last fright,' said Lowndes deeply. He looked at his watch. 'He'll be leaving in forty-two and a half minutes,' he said. 'After the meeting. It can't go quickly enough for me.' He emerged from the side of the vase and sat down. 'The SAS was baby play to this,' he breathed. 'Just keep moving. Move about the lobby area, watch everybody and everything.' He looked challengingly at George.

George nodded and set off on his security man's perambulation, around the ornate lobby, up the stairs and down again, in every public room. As he patrolled he passed other stone-faced security men walking the other way or investigating nooks that he had only just investigated himself. It was clearly a crowded profession. At the first washroom he lingered by relieving himself but in visiting the others, and the hotel was well provided, he had necessarily to act out the function. At one line of troughs he found another security man, also pretending to urinate. George and he stood side by side, staring ahead and doing nothing. Eventually the man zipped up and moved towards the washbasins. 'Another dry run,' he said laconically as he went to the door.

George returned to the lounge and then to the writing room. In the latter, cunningly concealed by a copy of *The Times*, was Sweeting. 'It's about to happen,' mentioned Sweeting from the corner of his mouth.

'Is it?' said George from his opposite corner. He felt his chest tighten. 'What do you think I should do?'

'Duck,' offered Sweeting. 'When the shit starts flying, duck.'

'Thanks.'

'Don't mention it. I'll be keeping an eye on you.'

'Thanks again.'

He went out, now scrutinising every person. Lowndes was still sitting next to the huge vase at the far end of the lobby, like a man beside a woman in a flowered dress. The business of the hotel was continuing now. A jovial party of businessmen were checking in, French it appeared, making jokes between themselves and rolling their eyes at the girl behind the reception desk. George saw Lowndes make a small movement, noticeable because he had been so still, and then the Sheik and his party appeared round a corner from the anteroom. Security men converged from each side like participants in some sort of formation dance.

Two men moved in front of the French businessmen who were walking away from the reception desk. The Frenchmen's jollity evaporated quickly and they were pushed aside to make way for the Sheik and his procession. There were protestations and some waving of arms. The Sheik strutted on purposefully, having apparently not even noticed the growing disturbance. George found himself taking a pace, then another, towards the incident.

Abruptly and alarmingly it blazed into a genuine fight. Shouts and curses, blows and struggles. One of the security men was sent sprawling among an array of gilt chairs. Then came a shot, then another. A ceiling chandelier was shattered, scattering glass; more shots and a great confusion of shouts and bodies. The Oriental vase disintegrated. The girl behind the desk began having hysterics. George moved forward just as a smoke canister exploded gushing black fumes everywhere and provoking more and louder cries. Below the smoke the Sheik's white entourage had flung themselves flat in their rehearsed protective scrum, lying like sheets in a blazing laundry. But, George saw with astonishment as he still moved forward, the Sheik was lying on his face well clear of the others. *They had missed him.* George collided with other people as he rushed through the enveloping smoke, the shouts, the cries and further pistol shots. Sheik Abdul Mohamed Al Sakah was sprawled at

George's feet, an unusual situation for him. George leaned down quickly. 'Your Highness,' he bawled. The Sheik's chin came up like someone awakened from a nap.

'What?' he asked.

'Come,' said George. 'I'm one of Lowndes' men.'

'Lowndes is an imbecile,' snarled the small Sheik. He nevertheless scrambled to his small feet and George, as though he were leading a boy, took his hand and hurried him through the smoke across the littered floor.

'Come, come, hurry, Your Highness,' encouraged George. The ruler's robes were impeding him and George had the urgent temptation to pick him up and carry him. The Sheik, however, realising this himself, hitched up his hems and ran faster than George.

'This way, sir,' snapped George. They turned from the lobby into the passage piled with chairs.

'Where is this?' demanded the Sheik in alarm. 'Where are we going?'

'To the Opera,' answered George.

'Ah, Verdi's door,' replied the Arab immediately. 'Very good thinking.'

George strode forward and taking the composer's key from his pocket he inserted it and turned it briskly. The door swung open and a great swell of music greeted them.

'Aida!' exclaimed the Sheik scurrying through the door. They were trotting through the dim corridor. 'Commissioned for the opening of the Suez Canal, you know.'

'Really,' panted George. There was another door and a curtain. 'Please, this way.'

The Sheik was now almost casual, moving as though on a short, conducted tour. George pulled aside the curtain and opened the door. The music blared around them. He stood stock still. Before him was the complete orchestra of the Opera di Roma busily playing in their pit.

'It is very good,' said the Sheik easily. 'A matinée.' Several of the nearest players began looking over their shoulders as they played. The timpanist paused above his kettle drums and only just caught his cue. George stood impotently but the Sheik knew what to do. In one corner of the orchestra were three spare collapsible seats. The Arab took one and motioned George to do the same. Slowly George sat down. Over the wall of the orchestra pit he could see the pebbled heads of the audience. The music swayed and swathed. The Sheik smiled from his robes. From their folds he produced a small gold notecase and a golden pen. 'Mister,' he whispered to George. 'You will please to write your name.'

IX

As His Highness's airliner banked over the brown of the desert and the blue of the sea, the Sheikdom of Sakah could be seen through one window. 'That's the race track,' said Lowndes who was sitting next to George. 'Camel racing of course.'

'Where are the can-can dancers?' asked George peering down.

Lowndes looked at him oddly and observed: 'You've been doing your homework.'

'I firmly believe in it,' replied George not looking at him.

The other Englishman looked worried. 'Very wise,' he agreed quietly. 'Time spent in recce is never wasted. If you are going to have any time here at all, then it's best to know your way round every corner and especially the exits. No information is useless.' He paused thoughtfully. 'Like the door. Fancy you knowing there was a door into the Opera.'

'I've always been an admirer of Verdi,' replied George.

They were sitting in the rear of the plane with other members of the Sheik's household. His Highness was in the front cabin strapped into an appropriately high seat, like a man on a camel. No one, even the pilot, was permitted to sit directly in front of the ruler.

Sakah's white airport, shimmering among its green trees, bordered the sea, the three colours, white, green and blue, echoing the ruler's personal standard. The aircraft banked over the blue and fishermen rose in their boats to wave their shirts as a salute to their returning ruler.

The pilot brought the airliner easily in to land. A uniformed band played, apparently mutely, until the engines died, when it transpired they had been rendering 'Celeste Aida'. The royal household staff left the aircraft first and formed two lines, one on each side of the main door, to cheer the ruler from the plane. 'He's always guaranteed a welcome,' muttered Lowndes.

Anxiously George glanced around in case the remark had

been overheard and was at once horrified to see what was obviously a senior Arab policeman, silver bars and badges blinking in the sun, striding towards them with four lesser policemen close behind. Involuntarily, George found himself edging away from Lowndes. Lowndes himself turned at the discreet withdrawal and paled as he saw the men moving towards him. The inspector was busily jangling a pair of handcuffs. Lowndes pleaded in a rasping whisper to George, measuring his message to the time he judged he had available: 'Get me out.'

'Mr Lowndes,' said the Arab inspector. He glanced at a document he carried with the handcuffs. 'Mr Robin Jeremy Chase Lowndes?'

'Yes, yes, Aziz,' said Lowndes impatiently. 'You know bloody well it is.' He held out his wrists for the handcuffs. Out of the corner of his mouth he said to George: 'I didn't do it. Just remember. I didn't. Get me out.'

The Arab inspector smiled warmly at George. 'Please, sir, if you could come also.' He looked abashed. 'After you have cheered His Highness Sheik Abdul Mohamed Al Sakah. May Allah protect him.'

'May Allah protect him,' echoed the accompanying constables and, more loudly, Lowndes.

Prudently George said: 'Yes, of course. May Allah protect him.' He looked at the inspector. 'I'll be right along after I've cheered.'

The Sheik's procession now descended from the airliner. The crew lined up at the bottom of the steps, the pilot being the first to greet the ruler, profusely, as if he had not been travelling with him and was overjoyed at his safe arrival. Along the twin lines of cheerers the small ruler progressed. As he drew level with George, one of his entourage, a man who had been waiting at the airport, bent gently, whispering against his headdress, and the Sheik paused, examined George, and proceeded on his way.

The official, a man like a tall eagle, waited behind. His eyes glistened so much above his hooked nose that George was uncertain whether his intentions were good or ill. The voice, however, was soft. 'Please,' he said. 'You must come to my office after sundown today. I will send a person for you.'

*

186

They drove George to a hotel on the waterfront. His room overlooked the hot, busy quays, where bulky dhows loaded cargoes. Below, the road streamed with traffic. Brown buildings, lost in a heat haze, crowded the far side of the harbour; the dome of a mosque glowed in the Arabian sun.

No sooner had the sun gone down in an explosion of orange and dust than the telephone rang and a voice told him that his car was waiting. George went to the lobby and saw a black limousine, as long as a truck, its shining flanks reflecting the lights of the town, standing at the curb. The hotel staff were impressed and bowed him out with the young man in a pale grey suit and an Arab headdress who had come to meet him.

'Abdul Hafeez is the personal assistant to the Deputy Chief Adviser to His Royal Highness,' the young man explained. 'He is a good man. He has formed a cricket team here. Do you play cricket?'

George confessed that he had not played for many years and had never been much good at the game even at school. He made the confession again when sitting in the large neon-lit room which was the office of Abdul Hafeez.

'That is a pity,' said the Arab. 'We are trying to encourage the game.' He smiled with unfortunate teeth at George. 'But you are good at music.'

'Music? Well, yes. I am fond of good music.'

'Verdi, for example,' put in the man.

'Oh, the business at the Opera. I see.'

'His Royal Highness is anxious to encourage culture,' said the Arab profoundly. 'Everything from cricket to cantata.' He appeared pleased with the phrase and studied George minutely, apparently seeking approval.

George smiled diffidently. 'I see,' he said again.

'Camel racing and French type of dancing. That is what Sakah is known for now. Our Sheik wants to change that. He was very impressed with you and with your musical knowledge.' He leaned closer. 'Do you happen to know who owns the London Symphony Orchestra?'

George admitted he did not.

Abdul Hafeez seemed disappointed. 'His Royal Highness wishes to invite them here,' he said. 'But they are always busy.'

'I think you have to book well in advance,' suggested George.

187

'Our Sheik is impatient,' sighed the Arab. He seemed suddenly to grow tired of the conversation. 'I hoped you might know someone, have a contact. It is a pity.'

He rose and several men appeared, all bowing George towards the door. Before he got there he paused and said, 'Would it be possible for me to visit Colonel Lowndes?'

'Lowndes? Why would you want to do that?'

'Well, he's my countryman and I think he may be glad to see me.'

Abdul Hafeez seemed mystified. 'If you wish,' he shrugged. 'I will arrange it.'

Lowndes was busily sorting out his references when George entered the cell. 'You never know what might be of help in this sort of country,' he said. He held up the wad of papers. 'Impressive, eh? Some of them very nearly genuine.'

George had sat down on a wooden stool. He sniffed around the cell. 'Not much of a place,' he said. 'Can't you ask to be moved?'

Alarm filled Lowndes' face. He nodded towards the barred window. 'They might put me outside.'

Moving towards the window George stood on tiptoe and peered through the bars. Outside, the hard and violent sun filled a stone-walled yard, bouncing from the stones, from the white walls, from the searing surface. There were no shadows apart from those thrown by a line of men who stood, almost hanging, motionless, with a second group crouched in the shade provided by their bodies.

Horrified, George muttered: 'I see what you mean.'

'They change places every five minutes,' Lowndes informed him dolefully. 'It's the only way they can get some shade.' He patted the wall like a friend. 'I'm happier in here, thanks.' He regarded George, who had sat heavily back on the stool, with some amusement. 'The ups and downs of this sort of life are astonishing,' he said. '*You* might be in here next.'

Lugubriously George looked up. 'Don't,' he muttered. 'The sooner I'm out of this country the better I'll like it.'

'It's not much of a place,' admitted the other Englishman, it seemed reluctantly. 'Have they told you why they wanted you here?'

'It seems they thought I might have some pull with the

188

London Symphony Orchestra. The Sheik was impressed with my musical knowledge.'

'Ah, Verdi and his door,' nodded Lowndes. 'That figures. They tend to adopt people they think might be useful in a cultural way. I remember they brought some poor soul here once, mystified as hell, because they thought he had written about Mahler, the composer, and it turned out to be Mailer, you know, the novelist. They do try though.'

'What will they try you for?' asked George pointedly.

'Nothing, old man,' replied Lowndes breezily. 'All this is just a bit of show. They go through the motions.'

'Because you loused up the security in Rome?' suggested George. 'Have you ever thought they might try to nail you for being behind it?'

'No hope of that,' said Lowndes in his previous tone. 'They *know* who was behind it, and so do I. And they know I know.'

George was admiring the aplomb. 'Who was?' he asked.

Lowndes laughed. 'You're not as sharp as I thought,' he said. 'The Sheik himself was behind it, of course. Who else?'

Astonished, George exclaimed: 'The Sheik!'

'Naturally. That was no genuine attempt at assassination. Anybody with eyes could see that. Seventeen shots went into the ceiling. It was just a phoney, stage-managed.'

'But why? . . . Oh, I see.'

'Do you? Not before time. He had it arranged just to show his Arab brothers how important he is. Nobody in their right mind would want to knock him off. He's insignificant. Messages of congratulation have been pouring in. He's as chuffed as hell.'

Slowly George shook his head. 'I'm miles behind,' he said. 'What will happen now?'

'Oh, in a couple of days I'll be whisked out of here and put on a plane to somewhere. That's the usual form. Our conversation in this cell has been bugged. See, it's up there in the light fitting, so you'll probably get your marching orders soon too. It's the way things work in these places.'

That evening George attempted to telephone Janine at Cherbourg but after a variety of rude noises had interrupted his efforts an operator came on the line and said all lines to France were closed. An increasing uncertainty came over him. A tray of food had appeared, unasked for, and when he ventured out in the corridor he was confronted by a uniformed man who said that he must stay at home that night.

In multiplying anxiety he asked the hotel telephone operator for the number of the British Consul only .to be told that the number was unobtainable. The line had broken down. Then, in a desperate throw, he tried to call Freddy Birch in England. He heard the number ringing but the moment the call was picked up the line went dead.

He lay on his bed and worried. At midnight, when he had begun to doze, there was a tap at the door and while he was still in the process of waking, it opened and in came a furtive man with his fingers to his lips.

'Please,' he said. 'There is not much time. It is necessary you leave here. I can arrange it. My name is Juma.'

He was a thin man with flickering eyes. He sat confidingly on the bed. 'It can be done. But it must be tonight. How much money do you have?'

'How much will it cost?' asked George defensively.

'Very much. There are bribes. There is my fee.'

'Is it safe? I want to get out of here. But I don't want to be shot doing it.'

'It can be safe,' said Juma. 'With me.'

'And where will I be going?' asked George doubtfully.

'It depends,' shrugged Juma. 'Where the dhow is sailing.'

The car stopped on gravel and Juma left the front seat. Crouched in the rear seat, George heard a whistle followed by an answering whistle. Despite the apparent need for secrecy, the driver lit a cigarette, the lighter flaring in the car. Juma returned and George, pointing at the driver, said: 'Is it a good idea for him to smoke?'

Juma said: 'It is bad for the health. But that is his funeral.'

The Arab looked surprised that George was still bent in the seat. 'It is okay,' he said. 'You do not have to stay here.' Gratefully George straightened. Juma opened the door and George got out to see the bulky hull of a ship, the size of a small building, lying fifty yards away.

'Behold your dhow,' whispered Juma. 'Come.'

They climbed the gangplank to a lamplit deck piled high

190

with cargo, crates and bales, a rack of bicycles and two cars wedged between other merchandise.

'She is five thousand tons,' said Juma with a sort of pride. 'You can escape to anywhere in this dhow.' He paused apologetically. 'Wherever she is going.'

They reached the raised bridge, like a veranda of a bungalow, at the stern of the wooden vessel. An Arab was squatting smoking a hookah, which bubbled with a mutual contentment. 'Everybody smokes,' tutted Juma. He spoke in Arabic to the man, who, taking a final puff at the pipe, stood and motioned George to a grim hatch under the bridge.

'You must go down there,' Juma said. He looked concerned. 'It will not be for too long.' The Arab watchman spoke to him and his mood lightened. 'There is another stowaway. Someone else escaping on the cheap. You will have some person so you can talk.' A guilty hand faltered forward. 'Good trip, mister, sir.' His mouth cracked villainously. 'Don't come back too quick.'

'I'm not likely to,' said George fervently. 'Ever.'

'It will all blow away,' said Juma. His hand was like a chicken's foot. George shook it and the escape negotiator whirled and swiftly padded down the gangplank to the quay. George turned back to find that the watchman had re-attached himself to his hookah. The man's eyes rolled reproachfully as he once more had to sever himself from the pipe. He indicated with a sort of sneer that the Englishman should follow him. In the half-light George stumbled on ropes and bags lying on the deck before they reached the hatch.

Fetid air came up into the warm night. Involuntarily George backed away but the watchman, indicating that he was not going below himself, not if he could avoid it, urged George into the hole and down a straight flight of shadowy wooden stairs.

The hot, stale atmosphere, spiced with prickly aromas, thickened as he descended. As his eyes grew used to the dark he made out that he was in a long low chamber, a hold, piled with sweet-smelling boxes. Cagily, head bent, he felt forward, navigating a passage between the cargo. Then he was in a brief open space with his feet entangled in some kind of loose cloth.

A match flared and made him jump. Someone was lying on the floor near the bulkhead a few feet away. The match went out.

'Sorry,' said George peering towards where the flame had been. 'I must have startled you.'

'Don't worry. I was expecting you.' It was a young woman; a harsh Welsh voice. George was astonished.

'Oh, I'm sorry,' he faltered.

'For Christ's sake, don't keep apologising,' said the girl briskly. 'There's not a lot of room for saying sorry in here. Lie down or you'll get a crick in your neck.'

He stumbled to his knees onto what he now realised was a rough mattress. At a crawl he moved along it until he was quite close to her. Now she struck another match at the level of his nose. She was sitting, her face round and rosy in the light, grinning rather than smiling. Dark hair swept back from her forehead fell and vanished into the deep shadow behind her.

'I'm Fanny,' she announced. 'Myfanwy Jones from South Wales. Blackwood, Mon.'

Remaining on his knees, George took one supportive hand away and held it out. She was very close and he did not have to extend it far. 'George Goodnight,' he said. 'From just outside London. Hertfordshire.' The match had gone out.

'Better not light another,' she said. 'These boats probably burn like mad.'

'Do you mind if I lie down?' asked George awkwardly. 'I'm getting uncomfortable.'

'Help yourself,' she said. 'You can't crouch like a tom cat all night.'

'Thanks.' Revolving, he stretched gratefully onto his back. He was conscious of her lying only a few dark feet away.

'Bloody hell,' she ruminated. 'One of them fortune-tellers at Barry Island told me I was going to run away with a dark man one day. I never thought it was going to be like this.'

Considering they had only just met, they fell asleep swiftly. George awoke when the sounds of chains and shouts indicated that the dhow was sailing. The girl was motionless apart from her brief breathing. He realised it was day because there were slivers of light fingering through cracks and holes in the wooden hull, bringing a dim illumination to the hold. The engine began to move, hardly more than a heartbeat at first but before long increasing thickly. The dhow was rolling. He lay staring at the tight ceiling, wondering where they were bound. After half an hour the hull began to seesaw easily and he guessed they had left the creek and were touching the open sea.

Once more he descended into a heavy sleep. When he awoke the girl was sitting cross-legged eating fruit from a bowl in front of her. He saw how hard her face was. 'Breakfast,' she said. 'Want a bit?'

George thanked her and took some dates. A hatch had been opened and daylight dropped into the distant part of the low hold. Sea air, cool and salted, came below. Fanny looked strained, dark below the eyes, but remained jaunty.

'Well, we got out,' she said triumphantly, an orange piece hanging from her mouth like a swollen lip. 'That's the main thing.'

'I wonder where we're going,' said George.

'Away. That's all I care. Away from bloody Sakah.'

'What happened to you?' he asked.

'Plotting,' she shrugged.

His eyebrows went up over the wedge of dates. 'What did you plot?' he asked.

'Oh, you don't have to actually plot anything,' she told him. Her face was of commonplace prettiness, but her eyes were round and deep. 'It can mean anything, plotting. Common as parking.'

George rubbed his stale face. 'What were you doing in Sakah?' he asked her.

'Dancing,' she sniffed. 'Can-can troupe. Been in the Gulf for two years. What about you?'

'Well, believe it or not I was a sort of cultural adviser. Very briefly. I think they wanted to get rid of me.'

She seemed both unsurprised and unimpressed. 'One of those,' she said. 'Well, naturally, you *would* be done for plotting, wouldn't you? They ship people in and they ship them out. They're bastards. I know.'

'What did they say you plotted?'

She shrugged. 'It's called "falling foul". Two brothers fell out over me and their old man decided it was time I got the elbow. It's all right having *one*, in fact you've more or less got to do that or you don't last. But *two* is trouble. And brothers – *that* was dangerous.' She scratched her head like an urchin. Then, to his surprise, she asked, 'Got your passport?'

193

'Yes,' he said feeling it in his pocket. 'That's about all I have got.'

'It's the main thing, George,' she said. 'As long as you've got that you can always start again.'

'You've not got any notion where we're going, have you?' inquired George. A vivid smell came suddenly from the hatch and an Arab crewman appeared with a pot of food. The bringer mumbled something and held out a dried hand.

'It's four dirhams,' said Fanny. 'Have you got it? You can take me to lunch.'

George paid.

She grimaced and said, 'Our first date.'

The Arab crawled back towards the hatch.

'God knows where we'll end up,' Fanny said, beginning to eat. 'Maybe Cardiff docks.'

George said: 'It's amazing . . . people like you. A young girl drifting around the world.'

'It's amazed me,' she confessed. 'My idea of a good time was Saturday night in Porthcawl and I got frightened by it. Mind you, I've been a bloody sight more frightened since.' She stretched and lay down, crooking a round knee. 'Porthcawl don't seem too bad just now,' she philosophised.

He lay back also. They were about two feet apart. He told her how he had run away. It was like telling an attentive child a story.

'What did you do for a job?' she asked eventually.

'I am a lawyer.'

'Christ!' She looked scornful. 'Fancy running off from *that*. What about your wife?'

'The faults, I fear, in retrospect, were largely mine.'

She sniffed. 'Clearing off's not all you think,' she agreed. 'Many a night I've had a quiet cry. Lying there alongside somebody foreign who has to get up and go to prayers.' Decisively she sat up and said she was going to look outside.

George did likewise. 'We must be well clear of the coast now,' he said. He went first, manoeuvring among the boxes. Mounting the short set of steps to the hatch he pushed his head out into brilliant daylight. A breeze rubbed around the ungainly ship. Blinking, he stepped out onto the deck. An almost purple sky was fragmented by the rigging. He turned to help the girl but she was already out, sniffing the air, blinking into the

194

blazing sun, pushing her hands through her dark and untidy hair. 'Bloody good,' she breathed. She put her arm round his waist.

The abrupt familiarity should not have surprised him, since they had slept alongside each other, but for some reason, a vestige of his past life perhaps, it did. They stood astride the heavy boards of the deck, the dhow dipping in the Gulf swell. The only Arab visible was the robed man on the wheel at the stern, a ghost swaying against sunlight. He waved wildly to them. All at once, George felt like a genuine adventurer. It was like Cornel Wilde in those films, or Errol Flynn flashing his teeth before the mast. They walked around, and sometimes scrambled over, the incredibly piled deck cargo, towards the bridge. It seemed fitting to hold out his hand to the girl, and she took it. He had meant it as a courtesy because of the sway of the vessel. Sitting below the ungainly bridge, under a wind-ruffled awning, was an Arab reading a newspaper. He looked up and smiled, the smile diabolical. Under his chin, hanging like a line of laundry, was a shortish white beard. 'Good day,' he said squinting.

They returned the greeting and Fanny said: 'It's safe for us to come out, is it?'

The man stood without hurry. 'I am the captain,' he said shaking hands and bowing. 'Madassar is my name.' He made a joke of peering to port and then starboard. 'I see no enemies,' he beamed. 'It is safe.'

'Is it possible, captain,' asked George politely, 'to know where we are sailing?'

The man regarded the dhow's sail and tugged at his chin beard in three separate places. 'We sail south-east,' he said, pointing to make it clear. 'We go that way.'

'Towards?'

'India,' he said.

In the middle of the next night, down in the deep of the low hold, he awoke from sleep and found that she had rolled against him. One of her youthful breasts was nudging his chest and the other pushed against his arm. Her left leg came up, as if on a rope, to straddle his middle. Believing she had rolled unknowingly in her slumber, he lay enjoying the stolen intimacy. Then she muttered: 'Awake?'

'Yes. I am.'

'Is this all right with you?'

He manoeuvred so that he could embrace her. 'It's all right,' he said hoarsely. 'If you don't mind.'

'Bloody hell,' she admonished in a whisper. 'There's no sense in lying down here together, a couple of feet apart like some old married couple.'

Drowsily she eased away from him, a movement, despite it being a withdrawal, filled with sensual promise. She undid the buttons of her shirt with one hand, right to the bottom, and opened it. Underneath, as he had been unable to avoid noticing during the day, she was naked. George's hands went to the shadowy whiteness and he caressed her bosom and moved to kiss it.

'I'll light a match if you like,' she offered. 'Then you can see them proper. They're quite developed, for a dancer.'

He refused the offer of the match but with his mouth still lying against her skin, he mumbled: 'You're the first dancer I've ever known. I'm no expert.'

'Look,' she said like someone making a special offer. 'You can take a decko at the rest of me. If you can see me proper.' Drawing again a little away from him, she worked her jeans over her thighs while still lying on her back. 'I've had to undress in some funny little places,' she said.

Almost impatiently she pushed her clothes aside and lay back, her arms above her head. He studied her spectral shape in the dimness.

'Have a look,' she urged, whispering. 'Here's the matches.'

Fumblingly he took the box of matches in the dark and struck one. The amber light glowed and in its brief globe she lay displayed, stretched out, naked and pale.

'Bit white, aren't I?' she said as if anticipating criticism. 'Sun's too hot this time of year. Fizzles you up.'

The match died, singeing the end of his fingers. He said 'Ouch,' then bent forward and kissed her stomach.

'Oh, that's nice,' she said genuinely. 'I don't generally get kissed there.' She was expertly unbuttoning his shirt, pulling it open, before levering herself up and rubbing her lips on his chest and over his nipples. 'Strike another light,' she offered, 'and I'll show you my tattoo.' She located the matches and handed them to him. 'It's three feathers,' she explained. As he struck one she rolled three-quarters over and the light falteringly

196

illuminated her backside. 'They're the Prince of Wales feathers,' she announced with pride. 'Not many people have got that on their bum.'

'I doubt if they have,' muttered George. Her casual eroticism aroused him further. He could scarcely say the words. 'Not that many, anyway.' He cried a small cry as another match died against his fingers. As if in response she rolled back towards him.

'This Arab did the Prince of Wales feathers,' she resumed chattily. 'A tattooist bloke. But he wasn't sure how to spell "*Ich dien*", you know, the motto, and it's not something you'd want to get wrong, is it? There was me, not certain. And you can't rub it out and start again because it's so painful, alterations, so I told him to leave it. It looks all right though, don't you reckon?'

'Yes,' he said in an entranced whisper. 'It's lovely, Fann.'

'Take yours off,' she suggested like a child enthusing about a game. 'Your things.' Helpfully she got to her knees, her breasts rocking with the ship. 'You do the zip,' she told him firmly. 'I'm accident prone with zips.' He tugged down his fly. 'But I'll pull them off for you.' She tugged his trousers away and then peeled his shirt from his shoulders. 'Not bad for an old 'un,' she approved. 'Not that you're all that old. My Uncle Dilwyn was as old as you, and that was years ago.'

He leaned across her and kissed her, first with consideration then fiercely as she returned the kiss. Cupping his hands under her breasts he eased her back. Her hands took him, pulling at him, guiding him to her.

'Want the matches?' she suggested breathlessly.

'No,' he said dreamily. 'We might start a blaze. It wouldn't do to . . .'

'. . . set the ship on fire,' she finished.

'No. It could be . . .'

'. . . very nasty.'

They were against each other, skin to skin, lip to lip. He eased himself onto her and felt her stir within. 'Fancy not being able to spell "*Ich dien*",' muttered George.

'He was a Lebanese,' she gasped. 'What . . . could . . . you . . . bloody expect?'

They lay and enjoyed each other in the close, aromatic hold, with the dhow obligingly swaying as they moved.

X

The small Indian port of Jeli lies one hundred miles north of Bombay near Surat on the Gulf of Khambhat. It is only small as such places in India are small, cramming a valley with its tumbled buildings, overflowing two peninsulas, one each side of the harbour, with oil tanks and ragged industry, and with terraced slums like disordered shelves. Apart from a single, white-domed building at its very centre and a pair of square business blocks on the harbour front, its highest construction was a mountainous refuse dump, lorded over by slow wide-winged kites.

'You can niff it from here,' said Fann, her nose wrinkling. They stood together on the dhow's wooden deck. It was early morning but the heat was already coming out from the town. Smoke and steam oozed through the thick atmosphere. Honking sounds were beginning to reach them over the dead water and they could see cars and crowds moving along the waterfront.

The dhow's captain, Madassar, shouted to them from the bridge.

'India!' He pointed with a sort of triumph as if he had been unsure of his navigation.

'I see it!' George called back. 'Nice.'

'What d'you reckon on doing now?' the girl suddenly asked George.

'Well, I keep thinking I ought to turn around and go home,' he confessed. 'But home is now getting so far away that it's probably easier to go on. How about you?'

'I'm hanging on to you,' she said decisively. Her hardened face confronted him. 'I'm not leaving you now. Not yet anyway.'

He put his arm gently about her waist and the Arab steersman called: 'Ah! Ah! Ah!' The captain joined him. 'Ah! Ah!' George took his arm away. It appeared, however, that they were communicating with a small, grubby boat which had

198

come out from the harbour and was now jogging towards them. A man with a once-white cap was in the bow.

'The pilot,' suggested George knowledgeably. He looked around at the boats creaking, jowl to jowl, in the harbour, forming their own floating town. 'You'd really *need* a pilot to get into here too.'

The small craft curved alongside and lost way, flopping in the oily, purple water. 'Welcome to Jeli!' shouted the Indian in the bow. Thinking he was calling to Madassar, George merely watched. 'Welcome to Jeli!' the man bawled again.

'Another place, another wog,' said Fann. She waved uncertainly.

George after looking about him to make sure, called back authoritatively: 'Thank you! Looks a nice place!'

The boat was directly below them. The man shouted again. 'You *are* the prisoners, I am imagining?'

'Prisoners?' said George aghast. 'Prisoners!'

'Prisoners? Bugger them,' said Fann abruptly. She backed off the rail. 'They're not putting me in their stinking nick.'

The man was scaling a rope ladder at the side of the dhow. He appeared on deck, a skinny brown face emerging from a suit of blue dungarees. He saluted happily. 'Ah, yes,' he said. 'Now I am perceiving you are the prisoners.'

Madassar and the steersman began to chorus. 'Ah! Ah! Ah!' as if in confirmation.

'Prisoners?' inquired George stepping forward with what he hoped was Englishness. 'Why should we be prisoners, may I inquire?'

'Ah, the British,' intoned the man as if he had been looking forward to this for a long time. 'The British.' He shook his head musingly. 'Everybody in the world is qualified to be a prisoner. Only excepting the British. The British are on this earth to send others to prison. But not *them*. They cannot be the prisoners.'

'The British rather like to know *why* they are prisoners,' suggested George forcefully.

'Now *that* is quite different,' agreed the Indian briskly. He produced a small oily book. 'Let me ascertain. Ah, yes. The reason is here, written in this almanac. You see . . .' He held the book forward convincingly. 'Penal Code for the State of Gujerat. Section four, sub-section five, paragraph three, amended June 1973. Illegal entry. Entry without permit. Entry without sufficient reason. Entry lacking sufficient funds.'

'We haven't entered the place yet,' argued George.

'Territorial waters,' smiled the man pointing over the side.

'Are you a policeman?'

'No. I am of the harbour pilots. But the policeman, he is overcome with vomiting once he leaves the dryness of land. Constant vomiting is not good.' He smiled acutely as if he had thought of a good joke. 'Not even for a policeman.'

'How did you know we were aboard?' asked George.

A sort of wailing: 'Ah, Ah, . . . Ah,' came from the bridge. It answered the question.

'He told them on the bloody radio,' muttered George.

'The skipper, he calls me,' said the Indian beaming confidentially. 'He cannot take this tub into Jeli without my intricacies, you understand, my intricacies.' He waved towards the captain peering anxiously from his bridge like a pigeon from its loft. 'I am coming,' called the pilot. He muttered for the benefit of George and Fann, 'You incompetent fool.'

'Welcome to India,' sighed George looking at the girl.

'I'm not looking forward to this,' she said. 'I don't like the look of that bugger for a start.' George put his arm round her again.

The dhow, under the pilot's loudly theatrical direction, was now edging towards the harbour, moving among the outer litter of boats. Smells intensified and the sun flashed from windows and windscreens on the shore. A faint noise, the hum of humanity, drifted to them.

The harbour water became glutinous and skinned with debris. Two boys swam amongst it. As the dhow came into a vacant berth at the jetty George saw the policeman awaiting him, his little white car, with a red light like a huge carbuncle on its roof, standing close. One leg of his shorts hung longer than the other.

'You!' he shouted, unequivocally pointing at George. 'Mister and Miss.' The finger triumphantly transferred to Fann. 'Both under arrest!'

'Come and get us, copper,' mimicked George below his breath. Fann laughed coarsely.

The dhow, with much fuss, was secured to the quay. Down

200

from the bridge the pilot hurried. 'Behold, the policeman,' he said nodding at the shore. 'Not vomiting.'

'We've already met,' said George. 'I hope he's got a warrant.'

'There is no doubt,' the pilot assured him. 'If it is a foreigner then you can get a warrant for almost anything in Jeli.' He jumped dexterously ashore and said to the policeman, 'They are all yours.'

The robed captain came along the deck to wail them goodbye. His echoing 'Ah ... ah ... aaah' followed them down the gangplank and onto the soil of India. Fann went first, carrying a small canvas bag, and George followed. The policeman, more diffidently now, moved towards them, came to attention, and said: 'Mister and Miss, good morning. Welcome to India. You are under arrest.'

'So you mentioned,' said George. 'Why didn't you come out to the boat?'

'That dog of a pilot went without me,' the policeman told him bitterly. 'Please come with me.'

He walked towards the car with the red lamp above it. Onlookers had gathered swiftly and there was now a congregation pushing and squabbling for the best view of the prisoners. One man fell from a bicycle. It toppled sideways and the rider, pushed by other onlookers, stepped through the spokes of his own wheel. It held him like a mantrap. Nobody cared. Behind the crowd was the jumbled noise of the Jeli traffic.

In the car was a police driver, staring ahead as if spellbound. The policeman who had met them took Fann's canvas bag and put it politely in the boot of the car which creaked rheumatically as he lifted it. 'This vehicle not our best car,' he said emphatically. 'All best cars are busy.' He glanced towards George. 'Mister, no luggage?'

'None,' answered George spreading his hands. 'I was planning to acquire some here.'

The Indian took out a notebook and recited 'No luggage' as he wrote it down. He motioned George to get into the front seat of the car and after putting Fann in the back sat beside her, very upright, knees nervously together, uncertainty gripping his face. The journey was short. They stopped outside the white-domed building that had been visible from the harbour entrance and got out to face a garrulous crowd on the pavement. Two inky nuns began to howl prayer. The inhabitants ignored them, pushing at their robes to move them along the front of the mob. The sun burned the top of George's head. They went into the dusty wooden interior of the building.

'The court is sitting,' instructed the policeman. 'You must appear and be charged. You will be remanded in custody for further investigations.' He now looked pleased and confident. 'The chief magistrate has already informed me,' he whispered. An apology clouded his face. 'There is one thing, before we enter the court,' he said.

'You want us to plead guilty.'

'Oh no, Mister, I could not ask you for that.' He had produced a short length of rope. 'I must tie your wrists,' he said with embarrassment. 'We are a poor police force and we do not have handcuffs. That also was our only car.'

'You're doing nothing of the sort!' retorted George angrily. Fann nudged him.

'Don't upset them,' she suggested. 'Rule number one when you're in trouble.' She seemed less apprehensive, as though the situation was one she understood.

Doubtfully, George offered his right wrist and Fann, smirking, her left. The police officer tied the knots like a keen boy scout, leaving a short length of rope between the two loops about the wrists. He was concerned that the bonds should not be too tight.

'I feel like pulling my blouse off one shoulder,' simpered Fann. She now seemed quite at home.

'It's not a film we're making,' warned George primly. 'We could be slammed in the Black Bleeding Hole of Calcutta for God knows how long.'

'Not Calcutta,' corrected the adjacent policeman. 'We have most good prison in Jeli.' He checked the rope on their wrists and encouraged them forward through fascinated onlookers in the foyer of the court. 'It is the first time many of these people have seen white prisoners,' explained the policeman.

The foyer narrowed and became a passage lit by a pallid electric bulb with benches down either side upon which sat two lines of limp and listless humanity. After the blatant sunlight it was difficult to see. The air was stagnant. Under his feet George could feel dust and dirt moving on the bare boards.

'Goodnight and Jones,' called a voice from an abruptly opened door.

202

They were persuaded forward. The courtroom was grim and grimy but, to George, it had an undoubted familiarity. Three magistrates sat behind a raised rail at one end, a clerk with his huge book open at their side. Before them were the benches for the legal contingent, sitting like random ravens in their coats and cloaks, each with its sheen of dust, and one with a badly-balanced wig. The man who wore this clung to the end of his bench and George saw that his striped trousers terminated in tennis shoes. The box-like dock was elevated among these seats and George and Fann were led to it. From there they could see a man sitting at expectant attention behind a massive cash till, curved and shining like a hurdy-gurdy. As they entered the dock the cashier appeared to size them up professionally. At his side, jammed onto a bench meant for two, were three reporters, notebooks hovering. George's heart dropped. He had forgotten about the press.

'George Goodnight and Myfanwy Jones.' The clerk's Indian lilt suited the Welsh although he mispronounced it. He took up two sheets of paper and closed his ledger with a bang, provoking a cloud of dust which for a while almost obliterated him. 'You are charged at the Port of Jeli on this day with entering India without proper means, guarantees or documents.'

The magistrates regarded the prisoners and the prisoners regarded them.

The Chairman was a sleepy, creamy-coloured man with a flurry of grey hair. He smiled benignly. On each side of him were two small men peering from identically tight blue suits.

'I would like to peruse the charge sheets,' intoned the Chairman. The clerk leaned forward, disturbing further dust, and handed the papers to him.

'What is your age, Mr Goodnight?' asked the magistrate. 'The charge sheets are lacking in information.'

'I'm forty-three,' answered George, adding, 'Your Honour.' He was conscious of a concerted stab of note-taking on the part of the reporters.

'And Miss Jones?'

'Twenty-three.'

'Ah, that's good,' said the Chairman as if approving of the balance. He took a fountain pen. 'I must do all the work in this court,' he said, writing the ages into the charge sheet. There was a mumble of laughter of the sort George recognised as being accorded to magistrates the world over. The Chairman looked up again.

'And your profession, young lady?'

'A dancer,' answered Fann. She sniffed and looked disdainfully at him.

'Ah, now what sort of dancer would that be, I ask myself?' The Chairman's expression was paternal.

'Classic ballet, tap, can-can.'

A moan of appreciation circled the courtroom. The reporters wrote madly. The Chairman leaned a little further forward, as if hoping for a demonstration, an interest interrupted by an explosion from the clerk's desk as he re-opened his book, provoking an eruption of further dust.

The Chairman, it seemed unwillingly, removed his eyes from Fann and settled them on George.

'Mr Goodnight. It seems that your profession is also absent from the charge sheet. Do you dance the can-can as well?'

Another smattering of duty laughter went around the court. Smiling sportingly, George replied: 'No, I'm afraid not, Your Honour. I'm a member of the legal profession. I am a lawyer.'

Another, but different, sound of appreciation occurred. The press noted feverishly.

'I see,' said the Chairman. His searching glance pinned itself to the policeman who had arrested them and who now moved his boots uncomfortably as though unable to get his feet aligned with his legs. 'And where, sir,' continued the Chairman returning to George, 'do you practise?'

'In London, Your Honour.'

'London.'

'London.'

'London.'

'In London.' The whispers went around the room. The reporters wrote avidly.

'I think,' said the Chairman, only consulting his colleagues by a half glance at each, 'that a brief coffee adjournment is called for.'

'Stand, please!' shouted the clerk, causing panic among the flying dust specks. Everyone stood and the three magistrates made their exit.

'Please, please, this way,' muttered the policeman miserably. George and Fann left the dock, the rope still between their wrists. 'Another day like this and they can have my resignation,' the officer confided.

Everyone in the court remained upright as they left through the door that led to the corridor and the foyer. As they reached the foyer they were confronted by a crush of anticipatory watchers. At the front of these stood a man with a camera who briskly fired off three flashlight shots. George blinked and threw up his tied hand bringing Fann's hand up with it.

'Good, good!' enthused the photographer.

'Stop him! Can't you stop him? Get the film,' George pleaded with the policeman. The photographer was already pushing through the spectators towards the door.

'In India,' answered the policeman piously, 'we are having freedom of the press. I cannot stop him.'

'Oh God,' muttered George. 'That's bloody well done it, that has. They'll contact the news agencies. The story will be everywhere in a couple of hours.' He looked at Fann distraughtly. 'Even back home.'

'Hard luck you,' she said.

'Brent and Raney. Good morning.'

'Hello. Mr Birch, please. This call is from India.'

'India? Oh, hello, Mr *Goodnight*! I'll put you through immediately. Is it hot there?'

'Very.'

'Thought it might be. Putting you through.'

'Hello, Birch here.'

'Freddy, it's George.'

'George! Are you still in prison?'

'Prison? No. I'm in India. What makes you . . . ?' He realised. 'Oh . . . it's been in the papers there, has it?'

'In the papers! All over them, mate. Front page of the *Mirror*, the *Sun* and all the rags. Your old paper went to town. Even the *Telegraph*. Pictures of you tied up to that dishy dancer. Runaway Lawyer and the Can-Can Girl . . . headlines and everything.'

'Oh Jesus, no.'

'Oh Jesus, yes,' confirmed Freddy exuberantly. There was a swelling admiration in his voice. 'I say, George, you really seem like you're having a hell of a good time. Especially if you're not in gaol. The papers didn't say what the result of the case was.'

George sighed. 'It's adjourned,' he said. 'It could take years, I gather. It's completely mad, Fred. I've been *sitting on the bench. On the bench!* They've made me a *magistrate*, for God's sake, in the same court where I'm accused. Fann has been behind the till, collecting fines.'

'Fann? That's the girl.'

'Myfanwy. She's Welsh.'

'I know. The *Mirror* interviewed her mother. What was the headline? "Fann the Dancer". Something like that. According to her mother she pillaged the gas meter before she left home.' A sharp worry entered his tone. 'You haven't reversed the charges have you, George?'

'No, don't worry. The Chairman of the magistrates is a decent sort and he's letting us stay in his house and use his telephone until I can get some money out here. Fann is teaching his son to sing in Welsh. Anyway, will you send some more stamps, Fred? There's a whole page of Queen Victoria and Edward the Seventh Indian States. Send them airmail, care of the Magistrates Court, Jeli, J-E-L-I, Gujarat State, India.'

'Right. Of course. I'll send them today. Jeli, Gujarat State. Can't say I've ever heard of Jeli. I'll look it up in the atlas when I get home.'

'Seen Felicity much?'

'Until the stuff appeared in the papers she was about as usual. But when the reporters started ringing her and knocking on the door she went off somewhere, to lie low I expect. She told Cynthia where she was going but Cynthia won't tell me. Anyway, she was bloody livid about the whole thing and now she's cleared off.'

'I'll never be able to come home now,' lamented George. He said it to himself.

'Doesn't look like it. Shouldn't think you'd want to yet, anyway. Not lashed up to a can-can girl.'

'That was temporary,' said George a little testily. 'They don't have handcuffs. Anyway, send the stamps quickly, will you, Fred?'

'They'll go tonight.'

'Thanks. Cheers, Fred.'

'Cheers, George. I bet it's hot there, isn't it?'

'Yes. Baking. Cheers.'

Sighing, he replaced the phone. He turned to find Fann

206

sitting in a basket chair, its high rounded back framing her beautifully.

'It's all been in the papers at home,' he related ominously. 'Pictures and everything. Missing Lawyer Tied Up to Can-Can Girl.'

Her face lit. 'Oh, that's good,' she said. 'Marvellous how they can spread the news. Always fancied a bit of publicity.'

'Well, I don't,' he replied sulkily. 'You can't even run away in private these days.' He glanced at her. 'Your mother gave an interview.'

'Get away! Fancy! What did she say?'

'You'd looted the gas meter.'

Her expression became offhand. 'Is that all?' she sniffed. 'Couldn't the old cow find anything better to say than that?'

'Apparently not.'

'Listen,' she said, her tone still hard. 'I've got something to tell you.' She took his arm and guided him onto the green terrace outside.

'It sounds serious,' he said.

'Depends how you look at it. I've decided to stay.'

George was astounded. 'Here? You're staying *here*?'

'For a bit. I quite like it.' She shrugged casually. 'You don't want me hanging around you.'

'But . . . well, it's up to you . . . What . . . ?'

'. . . will I do? Oh, I'll manage. I usually do. I'm fed up with wandering, George, honest. Trying to work out the next move, trying to keep out of trouble, trying to get money. I want to settle down.'

'Here?' he demanded.

'Why not? It's as good as anywhere.'

'But you can't earn a living teaching a little boy to sing in Welsh.'

She eyed him. 'He's twenty-five,' she said. 'He's got a video company and three cars.' Her eyes remained steady. 'He's going to show me his jewelled dagger.'

The train for the north ran between the Great Rann of Kutch and the Little Rann of Kutch towards Jaipur. All the land about the track was burned with the sun. Villages crouched under the shading smoke of their cooking fires. People washed in brown ponds along with their oxen. The oxen worked the fields, gave transport, turned water wheels, and provided dung to build walls and houses. People moved slowly or not at all, as if only too certain of their place in the landscape. Only children playing in dust or up to their necks in slimy water seemed truly alive.

Morosely George regarded the scene. It was as though he were moving deeper and deeper into an unwelcome yet uncontrollable dream. Thirty-six fans, whirling along the length of the caked and crowded carriage like a frenzied fairground, added to the fantasy. The train had started its journey at six in the morning, when most journeys start in India, and now two hours later many of the passengers were dozing against each other.

The man sitting at the window next to George had placed a bulging and broken suitcase on the rack. One of the hasps had fractured and the lid was half open. When the train jerked, a shower of brown particles of newspaper drifted down from the aperture. The owner had been half sleeping but now he awoke and considerately brushed the fine bits of paper from George's shoulder. He was dusty and thin. There was a hole in the toe of his shoe. Brokenly he smiled. 'I am a poet, you see. All of my poems are contained in the suitcase above our heads. The fragments have been descending on us.' His smile softened as if at a lyric thought: 'Like summer rain.'

The train jolted round a bend by a great grimy river and there was a further precipitation of brown newsprint.

'Poet is my profession,' confirmed the man. 'But my work is for the Income Tax Department. Now I am returning from leave.' A new smile, shining of revelation, occupied his lower face. 'To my posting,' he said profoundly.

A Sikh family squatted opposite, large parents and a large baby which now began to cry volubly. The mother gave it a red fruit, coated with a sticky substance, which was soon spread across most of the child's visible surfaces.

'Always,' said George's neighbour staring at the infant, 'I travel first class.'

George, who had seen people hanging like garlands from the windows of the third-class coaches, agreed it was more comfortable.

'Not only is third class very crowded,' muttered the man. His voice became even softer. The baby had thrown the sticky fruit at his father. 'There is the inconvenience of constant regurgitation.'

Small hills appeared on the left of the train and soon developed into uplands that filled the whole of the far window. On the ledges there were trees and white houses, lifted clear of the brown heat of the plain.

'The hills of India,' recited George's neighbour. 'I have for many years been composing a poem about the hills of India. It is taking a long time.' He appeared disgruntled. 'It is difficult to find a word to rhyme with India,' he said. 'Many poems I have composed about Delhi. It is much easier.'

The train eased into a vast, unkempt station. Leaden-eyed cows wandered the platform, passengers anxiously skirting out of their path. People lay in deathlike rows on the ground and vendors appeared at the windows with steaming food in doubtful containers. A fly-hung boy with no eyes and one arm begged. The fans stopped and the interior began to heat like a quick oven.

George was not sure where he was going. Only that it was with the train and that it had left the coast and was bearing him into the depths of India. The poet alighted at the next station, showering the Sikh family with dried newspaper as he struggled to pull his suitcase from the rack. The particles made a rash on the baby's sticky face but the occurrence was greeted with only a brief pursing of the lips by the mother and an adjustment to his turban by the father. After shaking hands profusely with George, the man left, bowed below the case. He gained the platform and waved.

After briefly waving in return, George moved into the vacant seat by the window and immediately attracted the attention of the beggars and vendors on the platform. He gave the eyeless boy a few rupees and at once further invalids crushed against the aperture, their hands thrust out beseeching, demanding. They were pushed away by an impressive man wearing a turban and a brass badge on his arm. He saluted George in an upright military fashion and called out: 'God save the King.' Uncertainly, George returned the compliment. People were crawling aboard the train. Everyone in India seemed to carry more than their own weight in baggage. The man who came to sit beside George was bearing a huge cardboard box, which he stood beside him in the gangway between the seats. 'I am transporting a Japanese miniature organ,' he informed George swiftly. 'In all India I am the sole distributor of this organ.' He backed a little away and examined George apparently in detail. 'Here,' he said eventually as the train began to roll, 'they still cherish the true word of an Englishman. We could sell many of these organs.' He leaned closer, his eyes sparking: 'Together we could conquer the world.'

His name was Chander Lal and he kept his organs in a shed behind a carpet emporium in Delhi. The entire stock amounted to three, including the one in the carton which he had been escorting on the train. 'Are you possessing a safari suit?' he asked George with Indian urgency. They were drinking coagulated coffee outside the carpet shop while the traffic of Delhi, rattling cars, heavy cabs, disintegrated lorries, a million bicycles and swarms of three-wheel mosquito taxis crashed by. George admitted that he did not have a safari suit.

'Then one must be possessed,' announced Chander. 'An Englishman should always possess a safari suit. People believe what they see. If we are selling a quality organ then we must appear to be quality also. In our business dealings, you understand, you will be the Managing Director, Suzihama Organs, India – in parenthesis – and I will be your humble clerk and demonstrator. In this way we will sell many organs.'

'I haven't seen many people who look as if they could afford an organ,' disagreed George. A beggar was crawling along the pavement on his knees. A woman with a baby was sitting dumbly in the gutter.

Chander touched his nose. 'Do not let India blind you,' he advised. 'There is much demand for the unnecessary.' He smiled as if some inner wisdom had just surfaced. 'We have a space programme, you know.' he said. He leaned forward and tapped George's arm. 'Twenty per cent commission will make you rich,' he promised. 'But you must be first purchasing a safari suit. Two shirts, because of sweating. There is loss of prestige when sweating.' He rose and said: 'I have business here in Delhi. Tomorrow we leave.' He had only gone three paces before he was engulfed by the pavement crowds.

An adventure, another adventure. Dolefully, George sat under the café awning, the compressed heat of the city bearing down on him. Sweat seeped across his face. The waiter asked if he wanted another cup of coffee or if he would like to attend a discreet afternoon discotheque. He agreed to coffee.

He realised the joke was getting beyond itself. Somerbourne Magna, yes, and Plymouth, even Cherbourg and Paris, and, yes, even Rome, but it was wearing thin by Sakah and now, *now* look where he was. The beggar crawled by again, a return journey, apparently having given up all hope. The clamour of the street a few yards away never diminished for a moment. A woman was knocked down by a mosquito taxi but the incident scarcely caused a pause in the traffic. A serious boy dressed in filthy rags approached and tried to interest him in buying a fly-strewn cake. Yes, look where he was. George Goodnight in India, about to become a salesman of Suzihama Organs. He felt hot and coarse. His socks were heavy and his hair was shagged. If Felicity could see him now.

Fann was far behind. As far, really, as cheery Molly and dear Janine. Fred in remote England had loyally despatched the stamps and the hospitable Chairman of the Jeli magistrates had purchased them at once without barter, for his son, who already possessed Fann and, by all accounts, a jewelled dagger. George reflected sourly that his collection was achieving world-wide distribution. As soon as the transaction had been achieved he was told pointedly that a train left for the interior in an hour. The hour was also all that was needed for the court charges against him to be dismissed. His passport was restored, a visa having been stamped into it, and he departed. At the moment he had reached the station at Jeli, Fann had driven by as a passenger in a big, shaded, car. Her wave had been brief, not unlike a dismissal, as if she had spotted him and was surprised he was still about. He held up his hand desolately, realising his envy of her adaptability.

He had finished his coffee, and was contemplating the purchase of a safari suit, when the serious, ragged boy returned, fly-hung cake still on offer and now balancing a large, still, glassy-green-eyed lizard on his stick of a forearm. He pushed the lizard towards George. Neither the boy nor the lizard blinked. George muttered something complimentary and, as though encouraged by the approval, the creature leapt in a swift slithering arc and landed on his sleeve. He let out a stunted cry that tailed off and then erupted as a full howl. The reptile had jumped inside his shirt.

It was done in a moment of a flash and wriggle. Down his chest and around the perspiring skin of his waist it scampered, its claws like blunt toothpicks. George erupted from the table, bellowing and grasping at his shirt, trying to capture the thin tubular thing that jerked, stopped and ran again around his horrified flesh. The boy was squawking and grabbing at the shirt also and two men abruptly appeared to assist. With enthusiasm they joined in the shouting and handling and one performed the vital act by pulling George's shirt out of his trousers, causing the lizard to fall to the ground, pause apparently to regain its breath, its eyes bright with excitement, its tongue forking, and then flick away. George recoiled. Sweat cascaded from him. 'Thanks, thanks,' he said. 'Can't stand them. Never liked newts or anything . . .'

But the men and the boy had gone, swallowed by the unending and ever-altering crowd that now pressed towards him to see what was occurring. George collapsed onto the chair. The waiter appeared to be paid for the coffee. 'It was the lizard trick,' he revealed.

'I'll say it was,' rasped George. He reached for his money in his back pocket. The waiter's expression disturbed him. 'What?' he asked. 'What trick?'

There was no money in the pocket. 'Christ,' George muttered then shouted: 'The robbing bastards!' He sprang up, made a few quick, vengeful steps only to be confronted by the packed faces of the people. The crawling beggar appeared through the many legs and held out his hand hopefully. George thought that for the first time in his adult life he was going to cry. He felt in his other pocket. His passport was still there. He sat heavily back at the table.

'The lizard trick, they played,' confirmed the waiter soberly. 'Also they rob me. Now you have no money for paying me for the coffee.'

'No, I fucking well haven't,' confirmed George, regarding him bitterly.

'I will call the police.'

'Call the bastarding police,' challenged the angry George. 'I can't bloody well pay, so there.'

'*Not* for my complaint but for *yours*,' corrected the waiter, taking offence.

212

'Oh, I see. I'm sorry.' George patted the man's tray, making a sound like a muffled gong. 'I'm upset, that's all.'

'The lizard trick,' philosophised the waiter, 'is upsetting. It is done all over Delhi. It was most quick, was it not? Over in two shakes of a hen's tail.'

Astonished, George glared at him but his glare collapsed. He put his head in his hands. 'Jesus wept,' he sighed. 'Now what am I going to do?'

'Every road has a silver lining,' recited the waiter. 'Is that correct?'

'Very nearly,' sighed George. The crowds and the traffic had resumed their joint bedlam. He stared towards the unending street.

'A stitch in time is worth two in a bush,' suggested the waiter.

George rose. 'There's no place like home,' he said to the waiter.

'Where there is life there is home,' returned the man in a pleased way. Politely he asked: 'Where is home for you?'

There were only the two of them now. Indifferent India whirled around their conversation. 'Hertfordshire,' muttered George sadly. He looked up with a sort of defiance. 'England.'

The man nodded. 'Hertfordshire I am knowing,' he assured. 'My brother is living in Watford. You are knowing Watford?'

George nodded that he did.

The man began to brush the table. 'My brother is making a lot of money in Watford. All-night long Tandoori. Soon he is moving house to some other place. In a greenbelt, he says, although I do not know what is a greenbelt.'

'It's . . . it's sort of green . . . countryside,' answered George nostalgically. He had paused as if the conversation might help him to return there. A sudden concern seized him: 'Not . . . Shillington . . . he's not moving to Shillington, is he?'

'I don't know. His letter is a puzzle. But perhaps . . . it is possible . . . If it is a nice green place he would like it.'

George thanked the man for his kindness and, making a forlorn feel of his empty back pocket, walked away. Every step he took he was waylaid by vendors and vagrants. He walked moodily by them, almost *through* them, stepping over the bowls, buckets and baskets, ignoring the beseeching hands, the begging expressions, the ingratiating grins. Now he was penniless also. All he had was his passport.

They had loaded the Suzihama onto the truck and now he and Chander Lal set out for the north. 'Meerut, Chandigarh, Simla, we are coming!' chanted the cheerful Indian as he started the engine. 'It is all the same,' he assured George who was sitting dumbly in his stiff safari suit. Chander Lal had lent him the money. Even in the first few yards the truck had begun to vibrate dreadfully. 'You wish to see the wonders of Himachal Pradesh, then that is where we shall proceed,' continued the Indian. 'When you are selling organs, anywhere is as good as anywhere. It is wide open. There are many schools in Simla. Perhaps the army at Chadigarh will purchase one or more for the entertainment of its soldiers. Also, there are many Tibetan refugees who will never have seen such a miracle. Their money is as good as anybody's.'

He drove airily through the careering traffic of Delhi, one hand on the wheel, curving in and out of the swarms of mosquito taxis, ponderous cars, and fleets of ill-ridden bicycles, blatantly taking to the wrong side of the road in a futile attempt at overtaking until confronted with an oncoming bus as bulky and uncompromising as a charging bull. George closed his eyes and clung to his rolling seat. 'Organs are good, very good,' shouted Chander, swerving inwards. 'There is a need for organs in India.' The small truck squealed sideways to avoid a brightly-clothed group of old women cowering and wailing in the middle of the road. A dog lay there also, peacefully dead, ignored as it had been in life.

It was hours before they were rid of the city. Street succeeded street, each one crammed and clamouring. Boys threw stones at the truck as they entered a crowded square and Chander said that this was a sign they were nearing the countryside. It was so and before long the truck was chugging away from the urban slums and into the slums of the fields. The land was flat and dusty brown. People squatted about every patch, hole and stretch of water as if guarding it. Villages were made of rough wood, corrugated iron and cakes of dung with little igloos of scrap material at their outskirts.

Peasants and oxen, every head bowed in submission to the hardness of the land and the life, worked the fields, on and on into the distance until they became clouds of dust. Among the paltry houses, beggars begged where there was nothing to give. Black kites circled with the same bare optimism.

Even Chander Lal became temporarily less sure. 'Poverty,' he recited. 'The curse of India.' He brightened. 'But there are those who have many riches also.' His voice became firm. 'There is,' he affirmed, 'an organ-buying public.'

That night they stopped at a large village and Chander deftly arranged to give a demonstration of the Suzihama in the cinema before the evening's performance. 'It is not the place to sell,' he confided to the already convinced George. 'But the word may reach others. Someone from here may strike rich, some boy, some man, who knows. It is for the future. Also for practice.'

The cinema, the Monte Carlo Galaxy, was the centrepiece of the village, its only building of any size or any hope, its kernal of fantasy, of dreams.

Every wooden seat was occupied, some it appeared by more than one patron, piled thin one against thin one, brown faces, berry-bright eyes turned to the platform. The manager, a bulbous man oozing out of a once-white waistcoat and cricket trousers, surveyed the audience with visibly mixed feelings. 'They are attending for the fil-lum,' he asserted to George who was nervously in the wings wearing his safari suit. 'This organ is only small matter. It is *Passion and Fruit* with Robin Sengupta and Mamata Shankar, also plus Gene Autry in *Pecos Kid* they have come to see. *Every* Monday it is a good house.'

The Suzihama was in its place under a canvas pall on the stage. Some patrons had crept forward to stare at it as they might at a catafalque, their chins resting on the boards. A thought that had not previously occurred to George suddenly and uncomfortably introduced itself. 'I hope you can play the thing,' he whispered to Chander Lal.

'Not greatly,' admitted the Indian affably. 'But these are simple people. They know little music. I can play anything and they will think it is a masterpiece. You are ready with your oration?'

'Ready,' muttered George, 'as I'll ever be.'

With military strides he launched himself onto the dust-strewn stage to be greeted by awed applause. It died of politeness but before he could begin to speak his introduction, rehearsed word by word that day on the truck journey, a youthful but authoritative person wearing a black suit and white spats, and sitting at the front, asked: 'Can you play a Barbra Streisand number?' He regarded George with undiluted challenge. '"The Way We Were",' he added.

George glanced over his shoulder. Chander Lal was fiddling with the canvas shroud that covered the organ. All the audience leaned forward in expectation except for the man with the spats. 'I want "The Way We Were,"' he repeated threateningly. 'By Barbra Streisand.'

'Of course, of course,' George placated. He caught Chander's eye. The Indian organ seller stepped towards him and he tiptoed to meet him halfway across the dusty stage. 'He wants "The Way We Were",' muttered George.

Chander's eye took in the man. 'The village troublemaker,' he decided. 'A mobster. I don't know it. Not for playing it.'

He retreated towards the organ. George blinkingly confronted the front row again. 'It will be included in the recital,' he announced brazenly.

'And "Evergreen",' returned the troublemaker defiantly. 'Also as sung by Miss Barbra Streisand.'

'He always plays "Evergreen",' said George. 'Always.'

'I am knowing them, believe me,' said the man wagging his finger at George. He turned in his seat to discuss his demands with his immediate neighbours who regarded him with admiration. Their attention, however, and that of the crowd, was immediately diverted by Chander who, like a magician unveiling a trick, took hold of one corner of the canvas organ cover. George, recognising his cue, stood stiffly to attention and announced: 'Ladies and gentlemen, I have great honour in presenting "The Silver Tiger" – the wondrous Suzihama Organ!'

There he was, far from home, in a safari suit, in a tin cinema of a slum Indian village, announcing the unveiling of an organ which no one could play. A small, mad smile surfaced on his lips.

Theatrically Chander pulled the cover away and the audience reacted with a hiss of acclaim, collectively pressing forward, eyes as bright as mirrors, to see the gleaming red and silver instrument.

George extended a flamboyant hand and then retrieved it professionally to lead and encourage widespread applause. It

216

was thunderous and made more so by those patrons on the flanks of the building banging the corrugated walls with their fists, a violent and vibrant tattoo lasting several minutes. In the wings the waistcoated manager lurked, looking none too pleased. He crooked his finger at George and George shuffled to the side of the stage. 'Do not be forgetting,' said the man wagging the same finger, 'that tonight's big attraction is *Passion and Fruit* with Robin Sengupta and Mamata Shankar, also plus Gene Autry in *Pecos Kid.*'

'Black and white,' said George. The applause was continuing. 'Gene Autry is in black and white.'

'There is enough colour in India,' responded the manager. 'They like black and white.' Again the finger wagged. 'Your organ is *not* the main feature.'

At last the applause was wavering. One of the tin sheets had fallen out of the wall under the bombardment of fists. The aperture was at once filled with the grateful faces of those who had wanted to see the wonderful organ but had not possessed the money to enter. Expectancy gathered in the thick air. The very breathing of the Indian villagers could be heard and their eyes danced in the dark. Only the man who wanted Barbra Streisand remained unmoved. He crossed one spatted leg over the other and waited, sniffing with doubt.

Chander had seated himself at the keyboard and was staring at the keys. Slowly his eyes rose to the valves. To George, his expression appeared one of deep mystification, like a novice peering into the working parts of a sophisticated engine. A small rumble came from the hub of the audience, a mutter of doubt and discontent. The manager lurked in the wings and Spats waited in the front row.

'Ladies and gentlemen,' announced George with what he recognised as a squeak of desperation. 'Before tonight's performance, may I remind you that the feature films to be shown, after the recital . . . demonstration . . . are *Passion and Fruit* . . .'

'With Robin Sengupta and Mamata Shankar,' bawled the manager from the side.

George called out a version of the names and added: 'And the ever-popular Gene Autry, the singing cowboy . . .'

Chander had lifted a flap and was looking inside the organ like someone opening the bonnet of a car. He rolled his eyes towards George.

'. . . Gene Autry in *Pecos Kid*,' continued George loudly. He looked towards Chander again and, buying time desperately now, called out: 'In glamorous black and white!'

At the front the troublemaker stood up with threatening slowness. There was a murmur as more distant members of the audience recognised him. 'I am wanting to hear "Don't Rain on My Parade" by Barbra Streisand,' he announced nastily.

'"Don't Rain on My Parade",' parroted others who could manage the words. 'By Barbra Streisand.'

Chander banged his hands down on the keys of the organ, at random; it emitted a strangled groan like something attacked when asleep. He stood up and made a tentative bow. The audience grumbled. George began to move, an inch at a time, towards the wings. He caught Chander's eye and was not encouraged. Chander sat down again and, in panic, smashed his hands on the opposite end of the organ which emitted a second wounded cry. With a sickly smile Chander turned and performed a seated bow. Members of the audience were rising, muttering in their seats, moving towards the front. George moved further sideways.

'Hurry, hurry,' ordered the troublemaker. 'Give us Barbra Streisand!'

Chander went berserk at the keyboard, crashing up and down the notes with hideous abandon, his eyes wild, his mouth open. All the villagers were now on their feet and advancing towards the stage. 'Jesus Christ,' muttered George. He was almost off-stage now. The manager gripped his arm violently.

'See!' he gasped. 'See what is occurring!' As if George had not noticed. 'What about *Passion and Fruit* with Sengupta and Shankar?'

'And Gene Autry,' muttered George as if hypnotised. He was not all that surprised to see a patrol of Indian soldiers standing in the wings behind the manager, eagerly, in the manner of troops about to subdue unarmed civilians. Another great discord came from the organ, this one louder and even more hideous. At its height the crowd began to rush the stage and at the same moment there was a flash and an explosion within and around the organ, and all the lights in the building went out.

George was only conscious of a crush of on-rushing humanity, shouts and possible profanities. He sensed that the hidden

218

soldiers were charging, buffeting him in the darkness. Then a torch was shone directly upon his safari-suited midriff. Orders were shouted and he found himself lifted bodily by a dozen pairs of bony hands and carried, stretched out, above the heads and out through a door into the widespread Indian night. He was not sorry.

'The organ,' said Colonel Ganga, 'was a write-off.' He sat, sharply military but urbane, at his desk at Chandigarh Garrison. Soldiers drilled outside under the hard sun. Two fans, out of time, swathed around the ceiling. The mounted head of an idiotically grinning jackal stared from the wall. A hockey stick was propped in a corner.

'I'm not surprised,' said George.

'It was difficult to save it from the mob, especially in the dark, you understand. The cancellation of *Passion and Fruit* with whatever they are called was a terrible inflammation of the audience.' He picked up a report from the desk. 'We made twenty-three arrests, seventeen with some sort of malfunction – broken arms and suchlike. Five of my soldiers were also injured.' His voice dropped. 'Unfortunately by each other. It was very dark.'

'And Chander Lal?'

'Oh, Chander Lal is gone. Very quickly. By now he is in some other place trying to sell something else. India has many like him. We call them spivs.'

George was sitting opposite. He could still feel the bruises where the soldiers had dropped him. Outside the cinema someone had shouted an order and they had obediently let him fall. 'The chap with the spats seemed to be the rabble-rouser,' he said. 'In the front.'

'Colin Ramsoon,' murmured the colonel. 'He is our village informer. We have to look after him. It was he who gave us the tip, you see, of there being some upheaval.'

'I see,' muttered George. Outside the sun and a drill sergeant's voice were bouncing from the barrack square. A fatigue party tramped by the open window, the eyes swivelling in awe towards the occupants of the office.

Colonel Ganga smiled: 'Fine boys. In India it is a great thing to be a soldier. There are plenty of recruits.'

'I imagine.'

'It was the British who gave us our feelings to be soldiers. It was one of the good things they left us. I myself was in the Indian army under the British. They made me what I am today.' He smiled a little slyly. 'I am a fan of the British.' His dark fingers touched on the desk. 'That is why I am only too eager to help.'

'Thank you,' said George. 'I thought I was going to be arrested again. As soon as I set foot in India I was arrested.'

The officer laughed almost a giggle: 'Oh, no, no. There is no arrest. This was just an incident, a fracas, as we say.' He paused and added: 'You do not appear to have any money.'

'I haven't. I was robbed in Delhi. A boy, two men and a lizard.'

'Ah, the lizard trick. They still do that?'

'They did to me. I have means of getting funds from England, but it takes time.'

'Getting funds always takes time,' said Colonel Ganga. Picking up his cane, he slapped his khaki thigh. 'My God how it does!'

George waited for him to finish. 'I need a base for a week or so. A hotel.'

'It may have to be here,' said the colonel. He put the cane on the desk and became thoughtful. 'Before I can allow you to go I must be having a sponsor for you.' He almost giggled again and spread his hands. 'It is a crazy regulation, but most regulations are. There must be written agreement from someone resident in India who will assume responsibility for you. You have no means of support, you see, not a rupee. It is the regulation.'

Disconsolately George regarded him. 'That's going to be difficult,' he admitted. He thought of Jeli and the magistrate but put the idea behind him. The press would soon get to know. He imagined the headlines at home: 'Wanderlust Lawyer in New Drama. Arrest after Cinema Riot!' Then he remembered.

'There is a chap who went to the same school as me,' he ventured. 'I have an address in Simla. His name is Fearnley-Banks.'

The colonel seemed delighted. 'The old school tie!' he exclaimed. 'Here is the evidence before our eyes!' Eagerly he picked up a pen. 'Tell me, please.'

220

George took his passport out of his back pocket and from that a piece of folded paper. He handed it doubtfully to the officer. 'It's only a post office box number,' he said.

The colonel examined the address. 'No problem, I believe,' he said. 'There are only a few British left at Simla. It was their place, their summer capital, you know, in the hills.'

'You think you can contact him then?'

'All foreigners are registered.' He pursed his lips. 'We will find him. I will see that the message goes at once. Now it is time for tiffin. Please to be my guest.'

It was a curious thing to be walking with the Indian officer through the camp. Along paths adorned with fire buckets, where every stone was white as salt, where hedges were trimmed to the ultimate leaf. Salutes flew up on all sides as they walked and George had to restrain a compulsion to acknowledge them personally. He compromised with a semi-civilian wave. Soldiers were in small groups, marching in various directions, lying in simulated ambush, taking weapons to pieces below flowering trees, stamping in the sun; sweating, brown, wide-eyed soldiers. Outside the officers' mess, recruits were on their hands and knees scrubbing a concrete path.

'When an army has no fighting it must be kept busy,' said Colonel Ganga, a shade apologetic for the men scrubbing. 'There is nothing worse than an idle soldier.' He giggled. 'He begins to think,' he said.

As if he were retelling secret information, he waited until they had walked out of earshot of the men and added: 'We have to be ready. China is only a few miles away over the mountains. And there is always our friendly neighbour Pakistan. We have unrest within our borders also.'

The colonel strode through the door of the mess and doffed his cap and belt which were taken by a white-coated steward who appeared nonplussed that George had nothing to hand him.

'I would like to offer you a drink,' said the colonel. 'Unfortunately, there is none. We are a dry army.'

He led the way into the main room of the mess and twenty officers, sitting at one long table, awaiting their arrival, stood to attention.

'Please, gentlemen, be seated,' said Colonel Ganga amiably. 'This is Mr Goodnight from England. He is our guest.'

XI

The great northern plain of India, after rolling unstopped for many miles, ceases abruptly beyond Chandigarh. Modest hills, little more than mounds, like bumps in an endless brown carpet, begin there and grow into more ambitious risings which fold and curl, up and up, hundreds, thousands, of feet, until they lie against the very flanks of the mighty Himalayas. The hot earth of the plain softens to green valleys, whorled with terraces as the altitude increases. There are farms, plantations, flowers and eventually pine trees, bare, vertical rock and then the snows. At Simla there is also the highest roller-skating rink in India. It is housed in a frail, near-derelict building, on the third floor, the efforts of the skaters causing the walls and windows to shake. From vibrating windows, however, there is a fine panoramic scene of Simla itself from one side and the snow escarpment of the distant Himalayas from the other. Clouds frequently close in on the view, also on the town and on the roller-skating rink itself.

It was here, in two rooms directly over the rink, and with exceptional outlooks on miles of great beauty, that Richard Fearnley-Banks, the Old Surrian, lived. He had left the school at the end of George's first term and they sat down to tea trying vainly to recognise or even vaguely recall each other. As they did so a small cloud, about the size of a dog, entered by the open door and after proceeding ghostily across the room exited from the opposite window. 'It often occurs,' commented Fearnley-Banks seeing George's eyes follow the vapour. 'Clouds drop in. Quite often they're my only visitors. We are rather high up here, you know.'

He told George he was fifty but he looked seventy, a face cut with dissipation and lack of interest, hands that shook, eyes rimmed with red, clothes hanging over his uncared-for body. 'I'm so glad you got here,' he coughed. 'I'm bloody well dying.'

He stood and limped to the window as if to see where the

small cloud had gone. The room was as unkempt as its owner, pink plaster holding desperately to the walls in the places where it had not actually fallen because of damp or the shaking caused by the skating sessions below. The rumbling of the rollers came through vibrantly, accompanied by snatches of an everlasting accompaniment – 'The Skaters' Waltz.' Fearnley-Banks said it was worse in the evenings. 'Sometimes I've gone down in my shirt-tails to tell them to shut up but the bastards won't. They just laugh at you,' he said brokenly. 'India's gone to pieces . . . like me.'

He continued to stare after the cloud. Another, slightly larger, came in through the door and took its course across the meagre room followed by George's still scarcely-believing eyes. It headed for the window. 'Here's another cloud,' said George like a warning. Fearnley-Banks stepped aside to let it pass through the aperture.

'Sometimes,' he said, 'they're thick as hell. You can't see a thing in the bloody place. Even when you shut all the doors and windows the swines find a way through. The only good thing is that it stops that ghastly racket downstairs.' He gave a bleak laugh. 'They have accidents, people colliding in the fog. Just like England really.' He took on a faintly quizzical expression. 'Perhaps that was one of the things the British brought to India, the fog.'

The thought seemed to cause him to turn inquisitively. 'What's it like now, England?' he asked sombrely. 'I can't afford the newspapers any more, not the English papers.'

For some reason George was taken aback by the sudden inquiry. It seemed a long time since he had been in England himself. 'Well,' he hesitated. 'It's still there. By the skin of its teeth, you think sometimes. Still beset by numberless crises.'

'Always was,' said Fearnley-Banks. He returned and sat in his chair. 'Terrible place for trouble, unrest and the rest of it. But I dream of it, strangely enough. Especially after I've had a skinful. The other night I dreamed of Peckham Rye. I used to live in Peckham Rye, you know.'

He looked bleak and ill, fixing George with a red-rimmed eye, not saying anything further as if no words could do justice to his sorrow.

'How long since you've been back?' asked George to break the silence.

'Years. Ten years. And that's the final time. There won't be any more. It's too late, even if I had the money, which I haven't. In my state I wouldn't get there anyway. It would be a waste of the bloody fare. I've had TB, pleurisy and phlebitis, and that's just this year. I've still got the TB of course. It's like living with somebody unpleasant.' He sniffed fiercely. 'It's all I do live with now, mind you. The opportunities are sparse. The odd half-daft lad from the skating rink or a pay-up job when I get my pension through. God, I'm so helpless, so hopeless, nobody could even blackmail me now. I'm not worth it.'

George regarded him sadly. 'You rescued me,' he pointed out. 'I'd have been in army custody if you'd denied any knowledge of me.'

'Old Surrians stick together,' recited Fearnley-Banks. 'What are you going to do?'

Shaking his head, George said: 'I'll write home. That's all I can do, write. A friend sends me stamps, collectors' items, from my own collection, and I sell them. That's how I've kept going so far. But it will take a while. Perhaps I can get some sort of job for a few weeks. I'll have to eat.'

Thoughtfully, Fearnley-Banks said: 'You could telephone, you don't have to write. It might take months.'

'But who would . . . ?'

'Let you? Well, nobody.' He put his finger beside his nose. 'But there is a way. There is a girl in the town who has the key to her boyfriend's place. He is a nasty sort, businessman, brash, show-offy, you know the type. He has gone off somewhere on holiday, Kashmir or somewhere, taking his girlfriend's sister with him and the girlfriend is very cheesed off.'

'So?'

'So she is letting people into the flat and allowing them to use the telephone. Anywhere they like. Half the town have been calling Bradford.' He shook his head. 'Women can be so shifty,' he said.

George only half laughed. 'He'll be broke,' he said.

'I know,' shrugged Fearnley-Banks. 'She knows. And the apartment is full up with people waiting for their calls. It takes hours sometimes. Even people who don't have anybody to ring are using it, just for the novelty. Some have been calling the speaking clock in London and some children have been listening to that telephone pop music for fifteen minutes at a time. The bill is going to be a fortune. I myself made a call. I tried to ring my brother in Oxford, but I found he'd died four years ago. That was a waste.'

George was groping with the possibilities. 'It's criminal . . .' He hesitated. 'I couldn't just . . .'

'Everybody else can,' pointed out the other man. 'You could always pay when your stamps come.'

'Hello, Brent and Raney.'

'Hello. Freddy Birch, please.'

'You're very faint. Mr Birch was it?'

'Yes. Urgently please. This call is from India.'

'Oh, hello, Mr Goodnight! Still in India then. Is it still sunny? You looked nice in the papers.'

'Thank you. Put me through, will you.'

'He's engaged. I'll send Stephanie in to get him off the phone.' Her words became muffled. George looked around at the rapt faces of a dozen Indians who were grouped about the room waiting for calls. The girl in England came back on the line. 'Hold on, will you,' she said blithely.

George said: 'I'm holding on,' only to hear the phrase repeated around the room at his back. 'He is holding on . . .' 'He is holding on . . .' 'Holding on . . .'

'I bet the weather's nice,' ventured the Brent and Raney operator. 'It looked nice in the picture where you were shackled up to that girl. Lucky her, I thought.'

'Quite pleasant,' said George through gritted teeth. 'Is Freddy coming?'

'Freddy is here,' interrupted the voice of his neighbour. 'George, how are you? Where are you?'

'I'm fine but broke. I was robbed. I'm in Simla.'

'Simla? Ah yes. Right. In the north. We're keeping a map in the office with little Union Jacks showing your progress. There's a sweepstake on where you'll end up next. We're not paying for this call, are we?'

'No. The chap who's paying doesn't know it yet. Fred, send some more stamps, will you?'

'Of course, old boy. You're getting through them a bit swiftish though, aren't you? How's the belly dancer?'

'She was *not* a belly dancer. I don't know. She's not with me.'

225

'Jesus, George, I bet you're having a great time.' The voice deepened with sincerity.

'I'm broke. I can't even eat without borrowing. Get the stamps to me, please, Fred. Two pages, three you'd better make it. Canadian provinces. Got it? Canadian provinces. Soon as you can, Fred.'

'Where to? What address this time?'

'Flat 3, Skating Rink Building, P.O. Box 4, Simla, Himachal Pradesh . . . look on the map for the spelling . . . India. How's Felicity?'

'Fine. Absolutely fine. She never mentions you. Not after the stuff in the papers. Skating Rink Building . . . George, you get some places.'

'Don't I bloody just.'

'Hello, *Monsieur Benoit, s'il vous plaît.*'

'*Un moment.*'

'*Oui? Moi, je suis Monsieur Benoit.*'

'Hello. It's George Goodnight. I am in India.'

'Ah, *monsieur*, you are indeed adventuring!'

'Sort of. Please, how is Janine?'

'Mademoiselle Joby died on the third of the month.'

'Oh God.'

'Yes, *monsieur*. It is sad that I must tell you.'

'Thank you. Well, that is all. I can't think of anything else to say.'

'I am sorry, Monsieur Goodnight.'

'So am I. Very sorry. She was . . . wonderful.'

'There is one thing. Something came up, as a result of her death as a matter of fact, someone read the notice in the newspapers. It appears that we have solved the mystery.'

'Her little girl?'

'We have not located her. But the man who took her was called Vaughan. Stuart Vaughan, a stamp dealer as we have thought. At that time he lived in Sydney, in Australia. But he is not there now. I've checked. He was mixed up in some scandal and he vanished. Perhaps if you find yourself in that direction sometime . . . in your travels . . .'

Sometimes the calls took hours to come through. There were always people waiting in the room. A boy came running to

226

fetch him one morning and he ran all the way to the telephone apartment, pushing through people waiting on the stairs. The call came through just as he reached the room.

'Hello. Is that St Margaret's School?'

A woman's sharp voice replied: 'It is.'

'Can I speak to Tina Carter, please?'

'Is it urgent?'

'Well, no.'

'In that case you cannot. It is the middle of the night.'

The town of Simla clings to the sides of the hills that lead up to the great white shoulders of the Himalayas. Its streets follow the line of mountain ridges and the top of the town is an airy square set on a plateau. This had been called Scandal Point by the British of former days because it was here that people promenaded and gathered to exchange gossip. The English-towered church was at one extreme of the plateau, now fronted by a statue of Mahatma Gandhi, its porch liberally pasted with hammer-and-sickle posters of the Indian Communist Party.

From the top of the town it was possible to look over long valleys and green mountains, which in winter would be laden with snow. The other side of the plateau hung over the misty corrugated iron roofs of what had once been the summer residences of the Raj, still entwined with eglantine, still with their faded names 'Coppice Corner', 'Weybridge Villa'. The Mall, the fashionable shopping street of the old times, where no Indian had been permitted to tread, was now a bazaar. Monkeys gibbered about the trees and the rooftops. Tiny hillmen carried gargantuan burdens. Small businesses were rife. A man had a shop devoted to the cutting of toenails. There were several photographers, each with its window displaying sun-whitened enlargements of English ladies of the 1940s and 1950s and even a few before, some probably well dead by now, their features preserved in these dusty windows of a forgotten outpost. It was here also that the Tibetan refugees mutely sold their weaving, that many boot and shoe shops vied for the feet of the populace, at least those who were cognisant with shoes; there were doctors' surgeries, the names embroidered with myriad qualifying initials, a dark dentistry, an egg-seller who also wrote letters and was an adviser on income tax, a wooden grammar school, a shed where 'Gil Khan – the ex-service man' sat with decreasing hope of attracting custom for the town's final work-ing rickshaw, a police station, and several cafés.

Above the skating rink Fearnley-Banks tentatively shaved. 'There's another bloody cut,' he complained. 'And these Indian newspapers can turn you septic, you know.' Doubtfully he stemmed the blood with yet another pinch of newsprint. His lower face appeared to be decorated with prayer flags. 'The restaurant used to be owned by an albino chap,' he called towards George who was trying to rub the damp from his shoes. It had become increasingly foggy in a few hours. 'But he died and this other fellow came along, from Goa, half Portu-guese, but quite a decent sort.'

'He must be since he allows people to eat for nothing,' said George.

'On credit,' corrected Fearnley-Banks. He started to cough, setting his chest rattling; the paper pieces fluttered on his chin, and one dropped away. He glared in the mirror at the cut it had staunched, willing it not to re-bleed. It desisted and he gave a grateful nod. 'Sometimes,' he called to George, 'I feel like one of those pathetic Catholics, Irish or Italian or whatever, watching for the statue of Christ to bleed.' He was almost sure it had stopped. 'Most of the British, such as they are, go there to dine at least once a week, and Periera waits for his money until their pensions come. He has a certain stature because the restaurant is still almost exclusively British. The Indians didn't like the look of the albino.'

'I've never been to an albino restaurant,' said George. He was now ready. He would have savoured a gin and tonic but there was none. The room felt clammy. Fearnley-Banks had edged across to the only cupboard, a space shared equally between his sparse food and his sparse wardrobe, and from the clothes section selected a collar, stiff as a trap, and a tie that George at once recognised as their old school.

'It's all that's left,' the older man said, seeing his glance. '*Festina lente* – Hasten slowly, remember?' He began to knot the tie with unusual briskness, for he was often tardy, as if he had been conserving energy and enthusiasm for the task. 'I thought I might eventually hang myself with it.'

George swallowed uncomfortably.

Fearnley-Banks said: 'The albino did himself in, you know. In the end. Fed up with being neither one thing nor the other,

228

I suppose. All the Indians came to have a squint at him. His body. Waited for hours, some of them, because the rumour went around that he would change colour. But he didn't and they lost interest.'

They went down to the misty street. There was little activity at the skating rink as they passed down the stairs, although it was not shut by the weather because the head and shoulders of a white-locked Indian with drooping eyes protruded above the counter of the paybox. He reminded George of a Tell-Your-Fortune machine. The eyes began to flutter as they came by on the stairs; it was possible he had been sitting asleep. But when he heard their English voices he apparently thought the effort was not worth it.

Although it was foggy, it was not yet dark and some Indian boys were playing cricket using the plinth of Mahatma Gandhi's statue as a wicket. One bowled a hard ball furiously. Others hopped and shouted. The batsman missed the ball and it struck his leg, the bowler claiming jubilantly that he was out. The batsman and bowler advanced on each other and began to struggle over the possession of the bat. The fielders joined in, making a rolling pile in the path of the two walking men.

'Out!' shouted Fearnley-Banks. He began to cough but stemmed it. 'Out. Leg before wicket!'

At once the struggle ceased. Seven pairs of small deep eyes turned to them. Silently the batsman handed the bat to the bowler and, head drooped, went to field. A new bowler took the ball and the misty game recommenced. The Englishmen moved on.

'They still trust our word, you know,' said Fearnley-Banks. Again he coughed nastily and cursed the mist. 'It means something even now. More than the word of a Russian or a Chinese or another Indian. Especially another Indian.'

The name of the Albino Restaurant had been changed to the Alpino Restaurant merely by the reversal of the letter 'b' in the sign. George said: 'Are you sure he'll let me have a meal on tick, until the stamps get here?'

'Oh, no doubt at all, old chap. He'll be pleased as hell to see you. A real Englishman, just out from England, not the potted variety like me. Anyway, I mentioned you would be coming.'

'Oh, you did?'

'Yes, when the army contacted me and said they were holding

on to you it was my weekly night here, so I told Periera and he was very chuffed.' He opened the panel door and they went into a room like an imitation Swiss chalet. There were only two other diners, a couple at a table in the corner, so crouched over their food they seemed to be examining it minutely. Periera appeared and led the two men to the opposite end of the room. 'Major and Mrs Firmidge,' he whispered confidentially, 'are not speaking to anyone tonight.'

'Thank God for that,' said Fearnley-Banks sincerely. 'They're both batty.'

They took their seats at the table for four indicated by Periera.

'When the British left,' Fearnley-Banks continued moodily to George, 'it was like a great warehouse being emptied. Like one of those at Southampton or Calcutta docks. Those of us who were left behind must have looked like a few forgotten packing cases. And we've been gathering dust ever since.'

The door opened and a florid man wearing a shabby ginger-checked suit came in, stamping his feet as if he felt cold.

'Here's another,' mentioned Fearnley-Banks. 'Another forgotten packing case.'

He was a heavy man and the rubber end of his thick walking stick thudded on the floor like the regular firing of a dull gun. 'Good God, Fearnley-Banks,' he said like an oath. 'You still here? Thought you'd gone to Delhi. To a boy's school, wasn't it?'

'I'm still considering it,' answered Fearnley-Banks defensively. He turned his hand towards George. 'Colonel, this is George Goodnight. From England.' He said the location distinctly as if the colonel might have forgotten. Demonstrating that he had not, the former officer, shaking hands fiercely, said: 'The old trolley buses.'

In the way of one observing an acknowledged ritual, he sat two tables away to their right and spasmodically shouted at them. The shouts disturbed the crouched couple at the far end of the restaurant who turned cracked, ashen faces like revolving plaster masks, noted who it was, and revolved again.

Periera brought the day's menu and turned up the volume of the music playing over a crackling loudspeaker jammed distantly in a corner. It was a samba. Major and Mrs Firmidge began to move, a motion hardly discernible at first. Then

230

shakily the frail husband rose, steadied himself against his chair and took her old-boned arm. After several failures, she became upright, staring ahead and clutching a spoon. The couple fell slowly together and there on the spot began to rock to and fro to the rhythm of the exotic dance, the spoon still held in the hand that held his. George witnessed the samba with amazement and pity. Fearnley-Banks and the colonel looked on like stones. Periera benignly clapped his hand to the beat and, as the ancient pair swayed, the Goanese sang softly:

> It's the laughing samba,
> Something like the rumba
> It's the laughing samba,
> Ha, ha, ha, ha, ha.

Major and Mrs Firmidge made no acknowledgement of either the song or the audience. When the tune had finished the old man tortuously helped his wife regain her seat, taking charge of her spoon as he did so. Periera changed his clap to light applause as soon as the major had lowered himself to the table.

'They still think it's Saturday evening at the club,' the ginger-suited colonel bawled across the intervening tables. 'Place fell down years-a-bloody-go.'

Major and Mrs Firmidge continued to spoon their desserts.

'That's the cabaret over,' said Fearnley-Banks feelingly. 'Silly old buggers.'

Periera, coming for their orders, smiled: 'It is their little moment. Now, sirs, what would you like?'

Unsurely George glanced at Fearnley-Banks, who was deep in the menu, before returning to Periera. 'Would it be possible to start . . . an account?' he whispered. 'I'm temporarily embarrassed. But next week it will be all right. I can give you IOUs.' He paused and then said hopefully: 'I am a member of the legal profession.'

The Goanese waved away the doubts with the menu he held. 'Everybody in Simla,' he announced, 'is temporarily embarrassed, Mr Goodnight. I live on temporary embarrassment.'

When they were halfway through the meal, an excellent lamb curry, Periera returned and said: 'There is an idea whizzing about in my brain.'

There was no wine. 'Too expensive,' Fearnley-Banks explained. 'Anything even nearly drinkable.'

The colonel heard and threw himself sideways in fierce agreement. 'Indian wine,' he confided loudly. 'Prune juice. Like the last emission of a dying donkey.'

Once more Major and Mrs Firmidge rose suspensefully at the distant end of the room. They swayed as they stood, each trying to hold the other up. Eventually, as if an unseen turbulence about them had subsided, they remained upright. Periera helped the old lady with her silk shawl. They turned carefully and began to totter towards the door, apparently not spotting anyone they knew on the way. Out into the Himalayan night they went, Mrs Firmidge yet again absently holding her spoon.

'Never are they restored,' sighed Periera. 'They must have one hundred of my spoons.'

At the neighbouring table, the colonel rose ponderously and said he had better make his way, intimating that there was much he had to do the following day.

'Yes, the dear old trolley buses,' he said to George as he was about to go. 'Sizzling.'

Periera, who had, as far as George had seen, taken no money that evening, asked if he might join them at the table. Fearnley-Banks, having glanced around, agreed and the Goanese sat beside them, a moodiness replacing his professional politeness. 'It is like serving ghosts,' he moaned. His dark eyes rolled up apologetically. 'Always excepting the present company, of course.'

'It certainly gets a bit spectral in here at times,' agreed Fearnley-Banks.

'Those two. The old Major and Mrs. They eat nothing,' continued the Goanese. 'They spill most of it. I could scrape it up and serve it again. It is untouched.' He looked hopelessly at Fearnley-Banks. 'I can no longer continue. I must have more native customers.'

'More Indians,' said Fearnley-Banks thoughtfully. 'Or even Tibetans.'

'Indians,' said Periera decisively. 'The indigenous population.'

Fearnley-Banks, who had forgotten his cough for the evening, now was seized by a stormy spasm which forced a cessation of

232

the conversation until it was past. 'How?' he eventually inquired. 'The buggers have never come in here. Why should they suddenly start now?'

The rounded Goanese face turned upon George with a rubber smile replacing the worry. 'This,' said Periera with pedantic drama, 'is where our Mr Goodnight comes into the plot.'

'What,' George asked, equally ponderous, 'does *our* Mr Goodnight have to do?'

Ominously Periera told him. 'It is only for a while, you understand. For a limited season only.' He had inspiration. 'In fact, that is how we will advertise it – "For a Limited Season Only!" '

'And what do I do for this limited season?' asked George. He was no longer surprised by the suggestions of strangers.

'You will like it,' assured the Goanese. 'It is a first-class plan.'

Standing just within the door, the tailed suit hot and tight, George had only a little time to reflect on the variety of opportunities afforded to the available adventurer. News of the new head waiter had spread quickly throughout the town and the mountain villages. There had been extravagant announcements in the newspapers. The Englishman was back, waiting to show you to your table and to take your order. The response was immediate and impressive.

Reservations on the opening night far outran the available tables. The cream of Simla society descended on the restaurant. As soon as the doors opened there was a rush for the tables and squabbles ensued. To his own surprise George found that British firmness still paid, and, indeed, was expected. Several elderly Indians addressed him as 'Sahib' and bowed at his approach. He began to enjoy taking the orders and despatching two expressionless Tibetan waiters to the kitchen for the food.

'They like it,' announced Fearnley-Banks when they returned to the room above the skating rink after the gala opening. 'Being told what to do, ordered about, and then not doing it. It's their nature. Once we got out of India the Indians started furiously ordering each other about and they've gone on doing it ever since. That's why it takes you two hours to buy a railway ticket or pay for your electric light here. Twenty people have to sign every form.'

There was only one bed in the room and they shared it, lying chastely stretched out in the dimness with the high cool wind and sometimes a moon seeping through the shutters.

'Mind you,' said George stretching out gratefully. His feet were sore and so were his armpits where the tight tailed coat had rubbed. 'They weren't exactly forthcoming with the tips.'

'You can hardly expect them to give gratuities to *you*,' pointed out Fearnley-Banks. 'And a hundred rupees a night isn't bad.'

'I've told Periera I'll stay until my stamps arrive. Then I must leave.' He had a sudden thought. 'Maybe you could take on the job.'

Fearnley-Banks appeared shocked. 'Oh, I couldn't. Not someone in my position. They don't *know* you, you see. They've seen me tottering around for years. Anyway, I'd start coughing.' He paused in the darkness. 'Where are you going to sell your stamps?' he asked. 'There's no one up here. Not for what they'll be worth.'

'I suppose not,' agreed George. 'I'll have to take them to Delhi I expect.'

'And you won't come back here, will you? Not ever?'

Slowly George said: 'No, I don't expect I will. I'll have to be moving on.'

'That's what I thought. I mean there's nowhere to go from here except back in the direction you came. There's only the bloody Himalayas the other way.'

George nodded although it was lost in the gloom. A street dog began howling. George said, 'Why don't you come down to Delhi? You ought to have somebody look at that cough.'

'Delhi? Oh no, it's too late for Delhi. I've got a rail warrant actually. I applied for this job in a boy's school. In a weak moment. I told a terrible pack of lies about my qualifications. I even said I'd played some first-class cricket in England. So they sent me the rail warrant to go for an interview but I won't go. I knew I wouldn't. Where will you go after Delhi?'

'East, I suppose. I've come so far now I might as well carry on. The world is round after all, so I'm told. There's someone I'd like to look for in Australia.'

'Australia,' muttered Fearnley-Banks hopelessly. 'I can't even imagine it.' He began to cough and George feared it might be one of the onsets where he would have to batter him on the back. Before George arrived, so Fearnley-Banks had told him, he had occasionally found it a matter of urgency to stagger coughing down the stairs so that the man at the paybox could bang him on the back. This time the cough quietened and he merely said 'Australia?' again.

'It's too late really to go anywhere now,' he continued. 'Even Peckham Rye. Even if I got there I know I'd hate it like hell. I might as well stay here. At least I know where I am.' Decently he touched the back of George's hand in the dark. 'But I'll be sorry when you go,' he said. 'Really sorry. When you go I'll just be left again with the bloody clouds that wander through.'

As the painted train began its descent from Simla, George knew a certain sadness and he was relieved when finally the old jumbled town, clinging so desperately above its chasms, went from his view. The scene was replaced by pine trees and a sky patched by ominous and silent kites.

The slender railway joined the Hills to the Plains. It had been painstakingly laid by the Royal Engineers a century before so that the British could travel to and from the cool uplands. It switched and turned, threaded through one hundred and three tunnels, and finally emerged after several hours on to the hot flatlands of Northern India.

He left Fearnley-Banks back in Simla, talking to his visiting clouds. Periera had pledged that the exile could eat three times a week without payment at the restaurant until not his pension but his fate arrived. George thought of the others, Major and Mrs Firmidge of samba fame, the colonel and his dreams of trolley-bus England. George had recognised the danger. It was unwise to linger anywhere too long for the uncaring world would journey on until it was far beyond reach. The traveller must travel. He had to keep moving if ever he was to attain his destination. Wherever that was. Perhaps home.

He still had the stamps. They had arrived in ten days but, as Fearnley-Banks had said, in Simla there was no one who could buy them. Delhi, they told him, was the only place. There were men in Delhi who habitually paid good money for such things.

At Barog the train was held up for forty minutes so that the driver could take his lunch. George left the carriage and stood below the trees out of the heavy sun. Several cows shared the platform with the passengers. A tea vendor, staggering under his urn and bleating because he was late, began to sell hurried,

235

hot tea. George bought a cup. From the rewards of his work at the restaurant he had bought a train ticket, left conscience money for his purloined telephone calls and paid Fearnley-Banks for his accommodation, a gesture which touched the Englishman so deeply that he became engulfed in a spasm of tears and coughing.

Then George had resolutely left, gone, made his exit; a last handshake, theatrically firm on his part, limp and regretful on the other hand; some thanks and a ridiculous promise not merely to return to Simla one day but to make a pilgrimage to Peckham Rye as well. He had left the room, throat lumpy, and gone quickly down the stairs, past the echoing skating rink. There was a solitary skater making circles, rather like himself, George ruefully thought. The old Indian clamped in the kiosk half lifted his eyes, decided the effort unjustified, and dropped them again.

Carrying his latest plastic shopping bag, adorned with message 'Simla Supermarket', he walked down the slope towards the station. He was still wearing the safari suit, crumpled as if it had really been on the exploration of some wilderness. At the foot of the hill he looked back and wished he had not because from a high window waved a white arm. He waved a return, turned resolutely and walked on.

At the station the train, its engine like a big motor car, stood waiting. Also waiting was Periera who said he had come to say goodbye, to thank him, and with the promise to feed Fearnley-Banks thrice a week until death. George told him that the exile had mentioned that one day he might hang himself by his school tie. Periera laughed. 'He will never do that now,' he said, patting George on the shoulder. 'Now he is dining free it will give him something to live for.'

When the mountain train reached the flat country at Kalka, George had to change to the Delhi express. People no longer looked at him with curiosity, and going into the waiting room, out of the heat, he was abruptly confronted with the reason. The first full-length mirror he had seen in many weeks was before him. Among its cracks was distributed a body he scarcely recognised. It had lost pounds, the skin was harsh, the hair dangled in shanks and the eyes stared fiercely dark from a burned face. He almost frightened himself. Stubble thickened on his chin; much of it was grey. His bones had adopted the

236

slipshod shape of his safari suit. Only the plastic bag, clenched in the coarse hand, looked spruce. 'Good God,' said George to himself. 'A pedlar.'

From Kalka the express took six hours to Delhi. Two and a half hours and a hundred and sixty miles before the city, George was speared by a pain in his lower gut and by blubberings through his pipes. Jammed among the hot humanity of the carriage he looked around in panic. There were no knowing looks from the other passengers, slumped on plastic seats on two sides of the aisle. Some of the fans had broken down and a baby was crying bitterly. Its mother cawed over it. No one paid heed. To live in India was to live with inconveniences. Outside, darkness, pierced only by village fires, had pulled across the country. Inside, light filtered from greasy lamp bulbs.

George attempted to relax his stomach but it began to heave like a geyser. He tried thinking of something else. Another gripe followed a further gurgle. Feeling his face go pale George stood and made for the aisle, tumbling over dozing knees. Faintness and nausea flew through him. He reached the aisle and stumbled along it to the lavatory. It was occupied and a swaying woman with a bleating child were waiting. 'Emergency,' George panted at her. 'Sudden illness.' He leered his thanks as she backed away tugging the child with her. The train shuddered and George's stomach vibrated with it. He banged on the lavatory door. It was opened speedily and a startled-faced man leapt out. 'Curry,' spluttered George pushing him aside. 'Curry, you see. Curry . . .'

He bolted himself into the fetid enclosure, pulled his trousers down and squatted over the waiting hole, feet clamped, faintness, sweat and flushes of nausea breaking over him. He tried to force his head down to his knees, but then he was looking down the hole and that was worse. The train swerved and he swayed, half standing to restore his balance, holding onto a wall that seemed to be circling the cubicle. His foot went down the hole. Onslaught upon onslaught seized him now. He squatted again. Demanding bangs sounded on the door and he cursed them, the effort provoking another convulsion.

How long he was there he did not know. He was almost comatose, leaning against the wall, trying to capture a snatch of outside air from a crack in the window, when there came an

237

official hammering at the door. Blindly he tugged up his trousers. 'Coming,' he responded weakly. 'Just coming.' He pulled open the door and was confronted by a shocked railway guard and half a dozen prospective lavatory users.

'What *is* this?' demanded the guard. 'What, I am asking, is *this*?'

'Diarrhoea,' slobbered George. He pushed his way through the small crowd and made for the half-open window in the corridor where he stood trying to draw in mouthfuls of baked air. When he felt a little calmer he returned as steadily as possible to his seat only to rise at once and charge back to the lavatory. He came out after ten minutes but was back in less than five, a process repeated through the rest of the terrible journey to Delhi. Passengers, recognising familiar symptoms, now willingly made way for him. The toilet was left to his lonely use and eventually he remained there, locked and rocking, until the train lurched into the city and he lurched out onto the platform.

It was late evening and many Indians were going to bed on the station. Others walked over and around them. George, white and weak, stumbled with the crowd. A refined, English, lady's voice recited over the loudspeakers. 'Please spit in the spittoons provided.'

Hugging his stomach George let the throng carry him along. Eventually he was outside the station where further multitudes were readying for bed. In the swirling city, night fires were glistening and people were moving in every direction as though fleeing some centralised calamity; shops and markets clamoured and traffic fought its unending fight. The air was hot and gritty. George felt light-headed.

There were hundreds of taxis, many the homes as well as the livings of their owners, and from these ran desperate drivers, each one begging him to hire his cab. One man, like a bouncing skeleton, grabbed George's only luggage, his plastic bag, and pulled him towards a pink saloon. George leaned against the dented roof to let his fainting recede. 'Hotel,' he gasped to the driver as he fell into the back.

'There are many hotels. Many.'

'The nearest.'

'Nearest not good.'

238

'Hurry,' begged George. 'I'm going to crap myself in one minute.'

The man leaned from his window and said to another driver: 'He is going to crap himself in one minute.'

The other man glanced at George and said to his friend: 'One minute is not a great length of time.'

The taxi jumped off and proceeded to wriggle through the hideously hooting traffic. The driver kept glancing at George's ashen face in his mirror. 'Please sir, legs tight. Nearest hotel is most near.'

It took a further seven minutes. George stumbled from the vehicle, paid without argument and staggered into the hotel foyer, the driver staring after him as a person interested in the outcome of a drama in which he has played some small part.

The foyer was crowded. Wildly George looked about for what might be a lavatory door. He ran and opened one fiercely to find it was a cupboard; another opened into a room where a beautiful girl in a sari sat serenely typing. Turning, George made for the reception desk, pushing people aside in his urgency. A grave young man stood behind the desk.

'Toilet,' demanded George hoarsely.

'One moment, sir. I will be able to attend to . . .'

'Toilet!' begged George. He began to scamper about. 'It's urgent.' He leaned forward gibberingly confiding. 'Very, very urgent.'

'Stand still, please, sir,' suggested the clerk pragmatically. He picked up some keys. 'Excuse me,' he smiled at the couple with whom he had been dealing. To George's huge relief he went round the counter and strode towards a door in one corner. He opened it with what George regarded as exaggerated ceremony. George rushed in.

When he emerged ten minutes later the clerk, smiling tersely and holding out George's carrier bag, said: 'Was there anything else, sir?'

'Yes,' replied George sullenly. 'I need a room, a lavatory, and I need a doctor.'

For several hours he lay in the dim room, his groans mixing with the uneasy creaking of the fan on the discoloured ceiling. There were shameless dashes to the toilet in the corridor which he had claimed for his own by hanging outside an 'Out of Order' sign sportingly provided by the receptionist.

The eventual doctor, a small Indian with a waistcoat and watch chain, was unsympathetic.

'What is the matter?'

'I'm dying,' George complained.

'We all die from the moment we are born. It is the way of things.'

George transformed a grimace of pain into a personal comment. 'I've got a dose of Indian tummy,' he amended grimly.

'Oh no, no,' corrected the doctor. 'You have *English* tummy.' He slapped in the vicinity of his watch chain. '*This* is Indian tummy. There is nothing wrong with it. It works perfectly well. It is the English tummy that is not working.'

'All right,' sighed George. 'To hell with its nationality.'

Apparently finding this more reasonable, the doctor produced a vial of yellow pills. 'Plug a burst dam, these little fellows,' he forecast heartily. 'Take one every two hours and that will be fifty-three rupees.'

George reached for his plastic bag. 'It's the latest craze from Europe,' he said. He paid the man, who left, laughing, and then groaned back onto the bed. Gathering his strength he went once more to the bathroom where he swallowed two of the yellow pills with a swift gulp of water from the tap.

He returned to the room bent like Groucho Marx, reached for the bed, sprawled out under the grunting fan and collapsed to sleep. He awoke six hours later, his stomach feeling as solid as an anvil. Sweat had dried on his face and chest but he felt a new lightness and great relief. He was even aware of feeling a touch peckish. He took another of the tablets and once more he slept, without knowing, and awoke in the middle of the night feeling wan but restored.

Lying there he thought he really *ought* to go home. It was only sense. Stop this *now* and go home. He was too old. He ought to get up from here and go straight back without even thinking. And not stop until he reached Shillington and . . . what? With a despairful grunt he lay in the foreign darkness and farted to answer the question. What indeed?

Once more he drifted to sleep and into a dream where his wife and Periera of the Alpino Restaurant were driving him at high speed in a taxi down the mountain railway descent from

240

Simla, pursued by a clanging train with Fearnley-Banks leaning from the driver's cab and puffing clouds from his mouth. Felicity and Periera fought for the driving wheel as the train began to catch up with them.

He woke once more, feeling calm, and turned his head to see bright daylight through the shuttered window. He went, composedly now, to the bathroom. Calmly he sat on the lavatory, washed his face and hands, took another pill and went down the stairs into the hotel foyer. The same receptionist was behind the desk.

'Ah, so you have not died,' he observed pleasantly. 'This is good. It is expensive to die in this hotel.'

'No, I'm still in the vicinity,' George assured him. He thanked him for his previous help. 'Can I get some tea?' he asked. 'And I would like to know the whereabouts of a decent stamp dealer.'

The receptionist seemed as unsurprised by the second request as the first. He suggested that George should sit to await his tea in the small rattan lounge that led off the lobby and promised that he would endeavour to trace a stamp dealer while the tea was being brewed.

George sat on the wooden couch in the lounge. On the low table before him was a pile of newspapers. One was whiter than the others and he pulled it out and saw with a sort of shock that it was the London *News*. As if he had met an acquaintance at an awkward moment, George gingerly picked it up. Burtenshaw's name was on the front page below a report about a battle in Beirut. Nothing changed; Beirut nor Burtenshaw. Carefully George turned the page. Association Football was in mid-season; unemployment was stable; there were new fashions and several fresh murders. The weather was reliably bad. The date of the paper was 4 December and it was two weeks old. It was almost Christmas. He had been away five months.

A waiter brought the tea and was swiftly followed by the young man from the reception desk. 'There is a street in Delhi,' he announced soberly, 'which is famous for its men buying and selling stamps, so I am informed, although I have never myself been there.' His voice rose jovially: 'I have no interest in stamps!' He had written the street name down and he handed it to George before saying: 'I suggest you take an omelette before you depart.'

George thanked him for his kindness and, as if to multiply this, the receptionist himself returned with the omelette decorated with a half-moon of mango. 'I am having further thoughts and ideas are coming fast,' he announced blithely. 'Will you be buying stamps or will you be selling stamps?'

'Selling, I hope,' George told him. He could feel a pendant of omelette dangling from his lower lip. The Indian half-leaned forward and for a moment George feared he planned to assist it back into his mouth. Hurriedly he did so himself.

The receptionist said: 'But I am thinking there is a better man for you. He is a buyer and born in England. He has a soft spot for the English. His name is Ravi Mackintosh.'

In the yard outside was an old railway engine, mottled with rust, and with a startling dent in the front fender. It stood beside a line of silent refrigerators, a pile of old tricycles, tangled together like dead spiders, cracked and yellow baths, a bullock cart crowned with cooking pots, and many random items of furniture. Above this dump flew both the flag of India and the Union Jack. Within the office, behind a desk so ornate it might have passed for an altar, Ravi Mackintosh rose and offered his hand. 'Well, mate,' he said hoarsely, 'I'm bleedin' pleased you've come.'

If the accent was accentuated London, the owner was visually Indian. He was about thirty-five years old, with a stout face and expanding eyes. They grew as he spoke and then retracted only to expand again, each one like the mouth of a fish. He was wearing a Burton's suit with a waistcoat.

'I understand you buy and sell things,' suggested George.

'I'll say I do, squire. Anything I'll buy. Anything I'll sell. That's 'ow I got where I am today, innit.' His smile enlarged horizontally as his eyes did likewise vertically. 'Bit of a shock 'earing the old London sound from a wog, I 'spect,' he said. 'Born in Southall, I was. Never set foot in bleedin' India till last year. I'll buy anything, like what I said just now.' He half revolved towards the window, his nose and his stomach projecting. 'See that railway engine, 'it a bloody elephant, that did. You can see the elephant's whatsit, 'is skull, in the Delhi Railway Museum, but this is what done it. I'm trying to sell them the engine to go wiv the skull. Makes sense, dunnit? Or asking them to sell the skull to me. Make a pair, like. But every bugger's so slow in this country. Before they've done somefink they're dead or nigh-on.' He sat down bulkily and, abruptly businesslike, said: 'What you got for me?'

'Stamps,' George told him, wishing he had gone to a proper dealer.

'Oh, philately, is it?' said Ravi, leaning slightly forward. 'Well, it's not my line exactly, but I don't mind having a butcher's. Maybe we can do some business. Might do an exchange, eh?'

George said soberly: 'I'm really only interested in money.'

'Like everybody, mate,' agreed Ravi enthusiastically. 'It makes the world go around, that's what. This lot – ' he took in India with one swirl of the eyes, 'they 'aven't realised that yet. They're so perishin' slow off the mark.'

He nodded at George's plastic bag. 'Like supermarkets,' he said. 'Used to work in Tesco's. Filling the shelves all night long.' George was still holding the stamps. 'Work, work, work, that's all I did. My mum and dad went over to Southall and sweated it out in the rubber factory. Making French letters mostly. I wasn't 'aving any of that. Not for me, son. I started out on my own, right away, even when I was still at school. And I wasn't just going to 'ave a corner shop or be a doctor, no bloody fear. I was going to be *rich*. Sometimes I'd go out to work at five in the morning, when there was no bugger on the streets 'cept black people. Work, work, work. Made a fortune, I did. Then I came 'ere, never been in India before, to make a bit more.' He drew breath. 'Now let's have a look at the stamps.'

George handed the page across the desk. Ravi Mackintosh studied them, narrow-eyed, and said: 'A mackintosh was the first thing my old man ever bought with his wages in Southall, and 'e 'ad to wait 'cos they kept a week in 'and. 'E still shivered but at least the poor sod was dry.' He glanced up, the eyes wobbling 'Want to leave these wiv me till later on?'

'How much later?' asked George doubtfully.

'Only s'afternoon. I won't piss off. Not wiv an 'istoric railway engine in the yard.'

'It would be difficult,' agreed George. 'All right.'

'Good for you, son,' said Ravi, decisively taking a folder which had apparently been lurking in the desk for the very purpose. 'It would have taken an Indian three days to make up his mind about that. Come back about two and I'll give you a price.'

George walked out into the street. The midday sun scarcely diminished the mayhem of Delhi. He found a place with red metal tables which had just been washed. The proprietor requested he wait a few moments until the steam had cleared, and then led him ceremoniously to a table, taking away three chairs. 'For privacy,' he explained. George ordered his second omelette that day. A gnarled man came to try to sell him a chutney plant but apart from that there was no interruption. Catching sight of himself in the window of the eating place he realised again how much he was merging with the landscape. He had an unruly beard, he could see his hanging hair by looking over his shoulder and the safari suit was reduced to sacking.

He ate the omelette and had a cup of tea, then remained under the shade of the canopy for a further hour. At ten minutes to two he walked slowly back to the yard where the railway engine was parked. He went up the dusty stairs. Ravi Mackintosh was already behind the ornate desk.

'They're not 'ot, these stamps, are they?' he asked at once. 'Nicked?'

'Good God, no. They're from my own collection.'

'There's collections and there's collections,' Ravi pointed out. 'Some people collect things *by* nicking them.'

'Well, *I* don't. They belong to me.'

Ravi sniffed. 'I believe you,' he said. He looked up with confidence bordering on ferocity and added: 'On my muvver's life I believe you.'

'Thanks. Now, do you want to buy them?'

'There was a reason for my askin',' pursued Ravi. His eyes had clouded with a sulk. 'There's some valuable stamps been nicked, see. Down at Jeli on the coast. Not far away, and all the dealer blokes reckon they're heading this way.'

'At Jeli?' said George.

'Nicked by a Brit, too. But it was a bird. Lifted them from some house where she was shacked up with some local big nob. Serves 'im right, I 'spect.'

'And the police are looking out for her . . . them, the stamps?'

244

'Very likely, old son. The coppers might well be on the look-out for 'er, the bird. But the dealers are all wanting to get their 'ands on the stamps, ain't they? You don't get bargains like dodgy stamps every day.'

George said: 'Well, these aren't dodgy. Are you going to buy them?'

Ravi rolled his eyes and puffed out his cheeks as if one part of his face was pursuing the other. 'Yes and no,' he said. 'Yes, on certain conditions, like. No, if not.'

'And the conditions?'

'Well, you're wanting to move on, I gavver. Get on the road.'

'Yes. I'm anxious to leave.'

'Don't blame yer. Bumhole of a country, this is. East or west are you going?'

George truly did not know. In the end he said: 'East. Towards Australia.'

'Good for you, mate. Great country. Well, I'll tell you what I'll do. I'll buy the stamps at my own price, which won't be yours. But I'll throw in an air ticket to 'ong Kong which is on your way, more or less.'

'And what do I have to do for you there?' Assignments took him less by surprise now.

'Just take the stamps, what I've just bought off you, and some others which a dealer mate of mine has been waiting to ship, to a bloke in 'ong Kong. That's all. Nothing not above board.'

'Why doesn't your dealer mate send them by post?'

The Indian sniffed disparagingly. 'Don't trust it,' he said. 'Funny 'ow fings just disappear in the post. The minute they're insured, somebody is in the know, see. By 'and is safer.'

'How do you know you can trust me?' inquired George. Hong Kong was sounding like gong in his mind.

'Aw, come on. You're a Brit.'

'So was the woman who stole the stamps at Jeli.'

Ravi shook his head largely. 'Welsh,' he corrected. 'You're English. Different altogevver.' He half turned so that his coast-like profile was once more presented against the window. 'Anway, we'll 'ave you watched, don't you worry. We'll see you get on the plane and we'll have you watched the uvver end. It's nonstop so if you ain't got a bleedin' parachute you ain't getting off. If you get the stamps to the dealer in 'ong Kong a bit

245

sharpish I'd be obliged, because these geezers what do the surveillance is expensive and it comes by the hour.'

'What price are you offering?'

'Five thousand two hundred rupees.'

'That's only half what they're worth.'

'And a ticket to 'ong Kong.'

'To sell them again for you.'

'Them's the rules, mate. You don't 'ave to play the game. What d'you say?'

XII

Hong Kong has one of the world's more tentative airports. Kai Tak's runway juts like an extended tongue out into the busy harbour so that the effect on the incoming traveller is that of landing on the flight deck of an aircraft carrier. The landward approach has the double anxiety of the plane almost crawling through rifts in the mountains, over roofs and hanging Chinese washing and children playing in the yard of a school. Several streets have to be negotiated *en route* to landing.

'I thought we were going to stop for the traffic lights,' said George conversationally to the stamp dealer in the small and smelly room behind his Kowloon shop. The dealer was half Portuguese, half Chinese, from Macao.

'Soon,' he murmured looking closely at the contents of the envelope George had delivered, 'more room. We take over China.'

Within the longer packet there were two smaller envelopes. The man opened the first, glancing up minutely at George, as if to check what he was doing, and revealed the page of Canadian provinces that George had sold to Ravi Mackintosh. The dealer made approving noises and George was acutely aware that he had sold them cheaply.

'You know about stamp?' asked the dealer idly.

Taken aback, George almost retorted that the items lying before them were from his own prize collection, but the man continued: 'You try learn about stamp. Good deal business.'

'I'll try it some time,' muttered George. He hesitated. 'Do you need me to stay any longer? I came straight here from the plane.'

The man from Macao, without lifting his eyes, said ominously: 'I know.' He began opening the second envelope. 'Stay, I must check everything okay.'

George watched the man open the second envelope and unfold the protective covering. The stamps were spread on the table. Contrasting expressions rolled across their faces. The dealer's was one of satisfaction. He began to grunt. George felt his own mouth drop, close up and drop again. The stamps had once been his own. The last he had seen of them was at Jeli when he had sold them to the magistrate who wanted them for his son who owned three cars, a video business and also, temporarily, Myfanwy.

He trudged out into the hot, hilly city, tired with his journey, not merely the miles he had just flown but with *all* of it, the entire damned odyssey. It seemed to stretch back through all his life. He was flagging; the spectacular spread of the harbour, the packing case buildings, the iron background of mountains, the people and the traffic passing about and below him as he walked down the steep slope were all wasted on a jaded eye. The sight of his former stamps had shaken him. He did not know where he was going. Glancing at the smoggy sun the thought came to him that if he could only turn his back on it, open his arms and somehow fly in the opposite direction, sooner or later he would arrive back where he had started, at Shillington. On the other hand if he persisted on his present course he would, in time, reach the same place. There was one advantage of a round world; it gave you a choice. He decided to compromise with a bath and a shave.

He had five thousand three hundred rupees, and five hundred Hong Kong dollars, a total, he had calculated on the plane, of about three hundred and fifty pounds sterling. It was, he thought, time to regroup. He was halfway round the world and it was the moment to make plans, to consider the situation. He would also buy a suitcase. His carrier bag days were over. People found it difficult to treat seriously a man with a carrier bag.

A large hotel loomed up at one junction and he considered it from the opposite curb while the Hong Kong tramcars banged by. It looked expensive by its very size. He wavered, then muttering sternly to himself he crossed the street. If he stayed only one night he would find somewhere more modest the next day. Perhaps he would even leave and omit to pay. The criminal thought came to him as he faltered at the pavement edge. He had never had ideas like that before. Between vagrancy and felony there was only a narrow alley. He went across the street.

They were either busy or accustomed to eccentric travellers, because no one at the reception desk even glanced at him as he checked in. The room charge was five hundred local dollars a day. He could afford at least one day there. A Chinese bellhop looked around for his luggage and scarcely arched an eyebrow when the plastic bag was indicated. He picked it up with some care and, despite George's protests, followed him to the elevator and escorted him to the room. 'Stay long Hong Kong?' was the only question asked.

'A week or so,' answered George.

The boy carried the carrier bag into the room, put it on the rack reserved for suitcases, and left. It was a reasonable room. George walked to the window and opened the light curtains. As he did so the amazing city opened out at his feet: the great round harbour with its choker of buildings, ships and boats creasing the water, the roofs below him like rafts, the sky pushed into odd corners between the mountains. He gazed at it for several minutes. Where did he go from here?

He chose the bathroom. He ran a bath and lay among the suds for half an hour, scarcely rippling the surface, staring at the tiled wall beyond his battered feet. Inspecting his feet even from that range made him recognise how threadbare they had become. They were not his usual feet. Here, in Hong Kong, he would rest them, restore them, perhaps even introduce them to a new pair of socks. Also he would here obtain a pair of scissors and a razor and cut his toenails and get rid of his beard. The beard, he confirmed in the mirror, made his eyes look mad.

Behind the door was a towelling dressing gown, bearing the monogram of the hotel. The shameful thought occurred to him that it could be the largest item in his new suitcase. He lifted it from its hook and discovered a bonus, a pair of blue and white swimming shorts. These did not belong to the hotel. He tried them on. They were too big round the waist although they would have fitted him tightly once. Regarding himself in the full-length mirror he saw what deep patterns the sun had imprinted upon his body. His forearms, face and neck were fried brown. A deep chevron of brown went down the front of his chest but the rest was toffee or white. It was like marquetry work. His legs were thick and hairy, pale at the top, mahogany at the knees below the striped drawers.

Outside the window the sun remained bright. He stood feeling it coming through the glass, staring out over the long view. Then he transferred his look downwards, directly above the mass of his beard, and observed, far below, that the hotel had a swimming pool. He decided to have a swim. It would be a pity to waste his new-found drawers. Afterwards he would order a pot of tea and chicken sandwiches, then shave off his beard, and come to a firm decision about the rest of his life.

There was a special lift to the pool from the end of the corridor, adjacent to his room. He put the dressing gown over the shorts, with some doubt pushed his newly-cleansed feet into his shattered shoes, and went down.

It was a small pool, fitted onto the roof of the third floor of the hotel which jutted out from the rest of the building. Dust and din rose from the traffic. Outside the glass door the sun struck him forcefully. There was only one other person there, a young woman of truly athletic beauty, tall-limbed, slender-armed, wearing a one-piece black swimsuit that dropped like an axe-cut between her exemplary breasts. Her neck was firm, her face splendid, her hair fair. Every inch of her body, as far as he could see, was conscientiously tanned. When she spoke it was with an Australian accent. 'Hello,' she smiled shiningly. 'I'm Charmaine Mangles.'

'I'm Oliver Loving,' he replied blindly.

Ron Mangles, her husband, excessive in a green shirt and plaid trousers, appeared noisily through the swing door while they were conversing. Behind him he dragged a leg like a dead albatross. He invited George to join them for a drink but quite absently as if he had something ponderous on his mind. They were up from Sydney on business. What was he doing? George said he had come to Hong Kong to have his beard shaved off and Charmaine laughed with a luxurious huskiness. No sooner had the drinks waiter come to the pool than there came a loudspeaker call for Mr Ron Mangles to go to the telephone.

'Shit,' the man grunted looking around suspiciously at the adjacent windows and roofs. 'They could hear that in the street.'

Charmaine ordered the drinks and she and George sat at a

table under the Oriental sun and drank pink gins. She was only twenty-four, she confided, and this was her first time outside Australia. It was in the nature of a part-business, part-honeymoon trip because she and Ron, who was twenty-five years older, had only been married two months. She had met him on the Queensland Gold Coast, where she had been on vacation, and had married him because she felt sorry for him being as lonely as he was and so rich.

'You have a wonderful name, Mr Loving,' she murmured. 'Oliver Loving. It's so beaut.'

George was already regretting the lie, for which he blamed the black swimsuit with its awesome plunge. But he would only need to sustain the charade for a while. He was a damned nuisance, Oliver Loving, an unsporting bastard, jumping up like that, pushing to introduce himself at the first inkling of a pair of exceptional breasts.

The husky laugh accompanied almost everything Charmaine did. She laughed as she stood, an art deco figure, and plunged exotically into the pool, thighs and calves abutting, toes thrust back, backside of black satin as bent as a boomerang. Watching her, waiting for her head, wet shoulders and slippery bosom to resurface, George spilt his gin. He walked unconfidently to the poolside and levered himself into the shallow end. He was not much of a swimmer. His beard floated like a door rug before his face as he dog-paddled towards the two-metre depth. Charmaine had already touched the far end and was ploughing back towards him like a corvette. She pulled up, face streaming, beaming brown shoulders and the naked half of the breasts clear of the surface.

'You look like that old bloke in the sea. Father Time, is it?' she laughed. Familiarly she tugged at his beard.

'King Neptune,' he corrected.

'Right!' she exploded as if he had won a general knowledge test. She began to finger the beard speculatively but pulled her hand away when her husband came through the glass door and onto the sun deck.

'Ron,' she called. 'Everything all right?'

'Come out and let's go and eat,' he called back, dragging his encumbering leg along the poolside. George continued to dog-paddle.

'Must go. Goodbye,' said Charmaine. She pushed out a slim

251

hand and they shook hands below the surface of the water. Her eyes were full of concern. 'Nice to meet you, Mr Loving,' she whispered with a kind of foreboding.

George remained in the pool, practising his dog-paddle, while she climbed out. His quick glance when she was finally on the side, water slipping down her smooth backside and flanks, was followed by a cautionary look towards Ron Mangle who remained hunched and staring towards China, as if bad news had come from that country.

The Australian put a robe round his wife's shoulders, still apparently without focusing on anything closer than several miles away. He continued to ignore George, beard-deep in the pool, and only Charmaine waved briefly as she was hurried away. For a further few minutes George remained there. At least Oliver Loving could now be put safely away; back where he belonged, in storage. George climbed out, dried himself, picked up his key from the table and went up in the lift to his room. The fatigue of the plane journey now dropped over him. He lay on the bed in the hotel dressing gown and went at once into sleep. When he awoke it was night outside the window with the lights of Hong Kong splashing on the clouds. His telephone was ringing. He picked it up. It was Charmaine.

'Mr Loving,' she said tremulously. 'I took the liberty of noting your key number. Could you please come to suite number seventeen, fourth floor. Ron is not at all well. In fact, he's dead.'

George sat quickly upright. 'Dead? Good God! Are you sure?'

'Positive,' she trembled. 'I've tried pinching him.'

'I'll come right away.'

'Oh, thank you. Thank you so much. I didn't know who else to call.'

He rolled from the bed and splashed water on his face from the bathroom basin. He put on his other shirt, trousers and shoes and hurried to the lift. Three spruce Japanese men occupied it and regarded him with mild interest. He caught sight of his wild exterior in the lift mirror and gave them a ghastly bearded smile. 'Emergency,' he explained. 'Somebody dead.'

'Ah so, somebody dead,' said the least short of the trio.

'Somebody dead,' repeated the others. All three performed a reverent bow still uncompleted when George left the lift at the

252

fourth floor. His right shoe was flapping like a dog's tongue as he loped along the corridor. At suite seventeen he knocked and the serious face of Charmaine appeared as it was opened. Her tan had paled.

'Mr Loving, thank God,' she whispered. 'I've never been alone with a corpse before.'

George went into the sitting room and then followed her to the bedroom. The suite was luxurious, its silks, brocades and veneers emphasising the commonplace form of the dead man lying in striped pyjamas on the bed. One of the pyjama legs hung empty as an airfield windsock. Ron's artificial leg, knee to foot, was standing in a corner.

'Did you call a doctor?' asked George studying the cadaver sideways.

'It looked too late for a doctor,' she answered, her hands flying about like butterflies. 'I didn't know what to do. You are the only person I know here.'

She was wearing an oyster satin robe, her hair pulled away from her face so that a rim of whiter skin was revealed. She looked more powerfully seductive than ever. Suddenly she flung herself at him, the unexpected force almost knocking him down. 'What a terrible thing to happen to me!' she wailed, her arms clutching him to her body.

'It isn't all that good for Ron either,' George tried to point out. The feel of her overwhelmed him. His hands had somehow found her silken waist. Guiltily he retrieved them. 'I think we had better call somebody.'

'I put his clean pyjamas on,' she said like a confession. 'I thought it was all right to move him. He was bare, you see. We were . . . we were just retiring . . . now he's gone for good.'

Charmaine began to cry copiously. George shushed her and led her into the sitting room. 'You have my sincere sympathy,' he said.

'I was just taking off his leg,' she shuddered. 'He liked me to do that.' Further sobs engulfed her.

George picked up the telephone and asked for the manager. The assured and quiet Chinese voice which replied faltered when he explained the circumstances. It seemed he scarcely put the instrument down when there was a brisk rapping at the door. No fewer than four dark-suited Chinese were there, each apparently lending the other moral support. 'Prease,' said one,

253

his eyelids blinking furiously. 'You have a probrem? Somebody dead.'

George let them in. Charmaine had retreated towards the window and was posed like a lovely statue by the drapes. The quartet followed him towards the bedroom but would not enter, confining themselves to peering round the door. They retreated as one, shuffling backwards. One crossed himself and said, 'Catholic Christian.'

'Are you person in charge of dead guest?' asked the leader of the Chinese.

'Not really. This is Mrs Mangles, the . . . widow.'

Charmaine gave a brief tragic nod. The Chinese men all bowed sombrely towards her. 'Please, Mr Loving,' she pleaded. 'Be in charge. I don't know what to do. I'm only twenty-four.'

'Ah, good. You in charge,' said the Chinese pointing at George with swift relief. 'We must have everything quietry. People in hotel not know. Guests not like dead bodies, especially Chinese people not enjoy. Bad for hotel.'

'It's not all that good for Mr Mangles,' pointed out George once more. Everyone seemed only to think how death affected *them*. 'I'll see he doesn't cause too much fuss.'

The irony was taken seriously and the main Chinese thanked him. 'We will arrange to have him carried,' he said. 'Our own mortician. Special rates for hotel guests. He goes down back rift to basement, out at night. Nobody offended.'

'All right,' sighed George. He glanced at Charmaine who had pushed her head through the divide in the curtains, giving her a decapitated aspect. The quartet left and Charmaine's face emerged. 'Would you like a drink, Charmaine?' asked George.

'Yes, please,' she said quite cheerfully. 'Scotch for me.' He poured two Scotches and added some water. They lifted their glasses. 'It's like a film, isn't it?' she said. 'Drinking like this with a body in the next room. Do you think we ought to have a toast to him?'

'Why not,' said George. He lifted the glass. 'To Ron Mangles.'

'To dear, dear, Ron,' said Charmaine reverently. Over the rim of her glass her eyes rose boldly. 'And to you, Mr Loving. For being such an angel.' She thought again. 'Wrong,' she amended herself, 'in the circumstances. But thank you anyway.'

Lifting his glass George said: 'I ought to tell you something.'
'What's that?'

'My name isn't Oliver Loving. It's just a name I use sometimes. My real name is George Goodnight.'

'I know that,' she answered affably. Each had the whisky just below the nose. The eyes remained meeting. 'Ron had you checked out just before he went like that. He always had people checked out. Come to think of it, it was just about the last thing he ever did.'

'Checked me out? Why was that?'

'He was in business. He had to be careful. The minute you appeared at the swimming pool he had you on his suspicious list.'

'He must have been in a touchy sort of business.'

'Oh, he was. Import and export.'

He said nothing. She finished the Scotch and held out the glass for a refill. 'Most of it unofficial,' she added quietly. 'That's what I'm afraid of. You won't leave me, will you?'

The hotel doctor arrived, a cheerful, small, cherry-cheeked Scot called Cathie who sniffed the whisky on the air as soon as he stalked into the room.

'That's a fine perfume you're wearing, madam. Would it be the Famous Grouse by any chance?'

'Water or without?' asked George moving towards the decanter.

'Without, certainly without,' said Cathie. 'We have to conserve water in Hong Kong. You are Mr . . . ?'

'George Goodnight,' answered George after a conscious hesitation. 'I'm a friend . . .'

'. . . of Mrs Mangles,' completed the doctor. His eyes turned silvery as he disposed of the Scotch with quiet relish.

'And the late Mr Mangles,' mentioned George sombrely.

'Ah,' said Cathie as if suddenly recalling why he was there. 'Indeed, *Mr* Mangles,' He wagged a finger. 'He is only late after I say so.'

Charmaine had been standing dumbly beside the decanter where George had placed it. 'If he's not late now he never will be,' she whispered. 'Even I can see that.'

'Mrs Mangles, my deep condolences,' returned Cathie. He drained his glass. 'Now let's see that they're in order.'

With a sprightly step, more like someone attending a birth, he went into the bedroom. George almost followed him, as if there might be need to make an introduction, but he paused outside the door. Cathie was going about his work with a thin, timeless whistle. 'There appears to be a leg absent,' he called back into the room.

Charmaine answered. 'It's in the corner, doctor.' She went to the bedroom door and pointed at the artificial leg.

'So it is,' said Cathie apparently pleased with the confirmation of a difficult diagnosis. He picked it up and took it over to the bed. 'And it fits.' He removed the appliance and emerged from the room, leaning the leg against the wall by the door. 'Dead,' he said. 'Quite surely dead. His heart.' He looked at Charmaine. 'How did he come to lose his leg?'

She shook her head. 'I don't know,' she confessed. 'He's always been like that – since I've known him – I didn't like to ask.' Her limp eyes rolled on Cathie. 'We had only been married two months.'

'Tragic, tragic,' said the doctor without emotion. 'Still, sometimes shorter marriages are better. I've been wed these thirty years, God help me. I'll have another wee drop before I go.'

George brought over the decanter and poured the Scotch into the glass.

'Will you be taking Mr Mangles home to . . . wherever it is?' inquired Cathie.

'Australia,' Charmaine told him. 'Oh yes. He'll have to go back. His family will . . .' She broke off with a start of realisation. 'I'll have to tell his family! I'd forgotten. I don't even know them.'

'I'm sure Mr Goodnight will help,' suggested the doctor adroitly but quietly. The glass went vacant again. 'Well, I'll issue the certificate. Heart attack. Natural causes. No post mortem necessary. Then you can ship him home.' He regarded them breezily. 'No further help needed, I take it? No sedatives required?'

George glanced at Charmaine who was already shaking her head. 'Will they come . . . tonight?' she asked. 'To see to . . . to take Mr Mangles away?'

'Bless you, yes. They're quick off the mark here. Lots of competition. They've probably got an appropriately sized coffin all ready in the basement even now. As soon as it's a bit quieter, when people have gone to bed, they'll have it up here and out again in no time. Then you can get a good night's sleep.'

He left briskly as he had arrived. They had scarcely closed the door on him, however, when his place was taken by an unusually tall Chinese in a light grey suit.

'Allow me to introduce,' he said with an elongated bow. 'I am Gregory Chan, the business partner of Mr Ron Mangles.'

'Come in,' said George. 'I take it you know he is dead.'

'I have a message,' said Chan with a brief nod.

Charmaine had poured herself another Scotch and now sat on the edge of a chair, bronzed hands clutching her glass like a prize specimen.

Chan walked into the suite. He turned, with ominous authority, into the bedroom and returned at once. 'Yes, dead,' he said indicating that he had cleared up any last doubt.

'This is Mrs Mangles,' said George. 'And I am George Goodnight, a friend.'

'Of Mrs Mangles,' said Chan. It was neither a question nor a statement.

'Of both Mr . . . the late Mr Mangles and Mrs Mangles.'

'Ah, yes. There is an old Chinese saying "A friend in need is a friend indeed".'

'How apt,' said George.

Chan had obviously come to a decision. 'There is no need for worry,' he said precisely, the tips of his tall fingers touching. 'We are not to get out of our prams, as the saying is. Everything will be done.'

'Everything?'

'I will . . . my associates will arrange all. The body must be returned to Australia. Does the family of Mr R. Mangles know about the sad news?'

'No,' whispered Charmaine. She was nervous of him. 'It's only all happened this evening.'

'We will take care of that.'

'Who,' asked George a trifle firmly, 'is "we"?'

Chan produced a large business card written in English and Chinese. It said "Chan and Chan. Imports and Exports". One of his long fingers came like a snake's head over the corner of the card. 'If there is anything you wish to know, this is the

257

number. We are well known in Hong Kong and throughout the East.'

George glanced at Charmaine who nodded in a frightened way. Her eyes seemed to have backed into her head.

'Well,' said George. 'As long as there are references. I mean I am a stranger here myself.'

'We know,' said Mr Chan. His eyes flicked up briefly. 'That is why you must not have responsibility.'

'I want Mr Goodnight to help,' Charmaine's voice vibrated.

'I am a lawyer,' put in George so quickly he surprised himself.

'We know,' reiterated Chan. He bowed. 'If Mrs Mangles wishes you to look after her . . . interests, then of course that is fine with us.' He looked towards the bedroom. 'We will look after Mr Mangles.'

Chan regarded them loftily, his fingers like a roof under his chin. 'Have a nice stay in Hong Kong,' he said. 'We will be in touch.' The fingertips tapped together.

He turned and left, the door closing without noise behind him. They looked at each other. Charmaine said: 'I feel a bit crook,' and began to sway. Hurriedly George stepped forward and held her arm. The skin on her elbow was warm. 'I think I'd better lie down for a bit,' she went on. 'It must have been the drink.'

She turned as if to make for the bedroom, remembered what was in there and veered abruptly towards the couch. Solicitously he guided her to a seat. She put her legs up, a fine fawn knee and straight shin breaking through the aperture of the dressing gown.

'Sit down,' she invited, patting the cushion at her feet. 'Please.' He saw to his concern that there were huge tears in her eyes.

'I was engaged to a lifeguard,' she sniffed. 'He was a beaut swimmer.' The tears overbalanced and dropped globularly down her cheeks. Her bosom heaved sorrowfully. Tentatively he held her hand.

'They often are,' he said inadequately.

'Eugene,' she wept. 'Bloody big bloke he was. Muscles. And now . . . now look where I am.' She swept her hand about the room, taking in the whole of Hong Kong with the gesture. 'In the middle of a million Chinks, with a dead bloody husband

258

. . . booh . . . boo . . .' Every undulation in her satin-clad body trembled with the sobs.

'I'm here,' George said without much assurance.

'Yes . . . you,' she sniffed. Sitting up on the couch she operatically threw her arms wide and hugged him to her. Pleasure roared through his body. 'You've been so bloody good, George.' Her top half was held sobbing against him. Grief, he thought guiltily, had its better moments. 'So bloody good.' Her voice had become a whisper.

With a snort she suddenly stiffened up, sat away from him and wiped the tears off her face with two or three urchin swipes of her hand. Skids were left across her cheeks. Her eyes were crystalline, her lips tightened, her expression hardened. She had apparently come to a decision. 'You've *got* to stay with me,' she informed him firmly. 'I'm going to need you. You are *really* a lawyer, are you? I mean a proper lawyer?'

'Yes, of course . . . but . . .' It was all happening again.

'No buts about it.' She gripped the top of his arm fiercely. 'George, I'm going to need *somebody*.'

'Well, anything I can do . . .'

'There's plenty.' She regarded him once more fiercely. Now she scarcely looked as if she needed help, certainly not protection. 'Listen, you saw that slant-eyed bastard, Chan. I mean, you wouldn't feel safe with him around, would you? I wouldn't. I need a man to look after my interests.' Her voice and expression dissolved. 'And me.' Pleadingly she turned the big eyes on him. 'I want to get home safely to Deewhy.'

'Deewhy?'

'That's where I live. Or my mum and dad do. You look a bit like my dad. Deewhy, north Sydney.' An additional thought occurred to her. 'You're not busy, are you?'

'Not at the moment.'

'You don't seem it. You'd have been slicker, for a start, if you'd been busy. And you wouldn't have that shaggy beard. You don't look as if you've got anything to do at all.'

He was conscious of feeling a little ashamed. 'No . . . well, that just about sums it up. I'm just travelling . . . to be honest I'm wandering.'

'You're a bit ancient for that,' she said softly but bluntly. 'Wandering.'

'Don't I know it,' he confessed.

259

She shifted sideways to make herself more comfortable, like a child anticipating a bedtime story. 'Why don't you get another couple of drinks,' she suggested, 'and tell me about it.'

'But what about . . . Ron?'

'Ron? Well, they're coming to pick up Ron. You heard what that tall Chink said. I don't think we need worry about Ron. They'll look after him. What I'm worried about is that they may look after *me* . . . *us* that is . . . as well.'

As George stood she patted his hand and smiled with her expansive teeth. He went to the decanter. It was almost empty and he distinctly recalled it being full. There was an unopened bottle of Johnnie Walker Black Label beside it on the tray. He broke the seal and turned the top.

'I'll pay you, of course,' she said from the couch. 'Your usual rate.'

'It's not that,' he said honestly. He poured two glasses of Scotch. 'But the fact is I've got very little money. I was going to have to move out of here tomorrow. You'll understand when I've told you the background.' He took the glasses and returned to the couch. She tucked up her satin knees to make room for him to return to his place.

'I have money,' she said briskly. Her eyes widened. 'And now I'll probably get some more, don't you think?' It had the innocence of an afterthought.

'I would have thought so. Mind, these are somewhat unusual circumstances.'

'Anyway, I need you to help me to get home to Australia. I don't see how even Charlie Chan, or whoever he is, could argue about that.'

They were sitting quite cosily now, at opposite ends of the couch, but with the side of his arm and his shoulder unavoidably touching her drawn-up leg.

'You have a story to tell me,' she reminded him.

'Ah yes. How I came to be here in the first place. Yes . . . I'd better fill you in.'

'Yes. I think you should,' she said purely. Her crammed eyes blinked.

'It's a long, long story.' he warned. He was aware that the whisky was slowing his words. He attempted to steady himself by taking another drink. 'Although I can truncate it.'

'Don't do that,' she said soothingly. 'But if it's a long one

260

we'd better have refills handy. Why don't you bring the bottle over?'

George looked at her doubtfully. He went to the cabinet but looked back. 'Are you sure? he said. 'They'll be coming for . . . for Ron.'

'So they come for Ron,' she said blatantly. 'As long as they don't want us to help carry the . . . the . . . Ron.'

'I don't think it's a good idea,' he said taking his hand from the bottle.

'Bring it,' she ordered firmly. He believed her eyes crossed briefly. 'I'm thirsty. I've had a bad shock.'

Uncertainly he picked up the bottle, walked over and put it on the low table beside them. She patted him encouragingly. 'It's necessary,' she said. 'We have to have some help. Now tell me what you were going to tell me before we started arguing.'

George smiled and sat beside her once more. Strangely he felt reassured too. He was no longer alone.

He related his tale, or most of it, leaving out things he felt were better omitted. She listened in silence apart from drawing in her breath and her chest at some of the revelations and making single-word comments at intervals. They both expressed surprise that their glasses needed replenishing at other intervals. When he had finished an hour had gone.

'What a story,' she sighed. 'How did you just keep going on?'

'Because there didn't seem to be any point in going back,' he said with rueful truthfulness. 'When you've gone so far round the world you might as well keep going on. It's all the same.'

'I want to lie down,' she announced sleepily. 'After a nightcap.'

He looked with astonishment at the bottle. It was half gone. She intercepted the look and put her hand towards it.

'I've still got the strength,' she said. 'Even if you don't.'

'I have,' he corrected. 'I'll manage.' He poured them a measure each. They weren't bothering with the water now. As a salve to his conscience he made the measures small but she caught his wrist with unsuspected strength and tipped the bottle again.

'We'll drink Ron's health as well,' she suggested.

He knew very well what was going to occur. It was disgraceful and, sober, he would have been able to resist it. In his floating state, however, and hers, there seemed to be little he could do to prevent it happening. She gripped his wrist again as she stood up. Towards the bedroom they rolled, knocking into things, he attempting to order his thoughts, she giggling and assuring him of the undoubted truth that Ron would not object.

As they stumbled across the room she fell to her knees and he had difficulty in lifting her. Her breasts lolled luxuriously. 'I might as well pray while I'm down here,' she sighed. 'You as well. We'll pray for Ron. I haven't since he passed away.' She looked up, her big eyes overloaded. 'Come down and help me.'

His vision swimming, George tumbled forward onto his knees.

'I'm going to pray like I did when I was a little girl,' Charmaine decided, getting the words together with care and eventually triumph. 'Just hold my glass, will you?'

He took the tumbler and she knelt upright, placed her hands together and let her lashes fall over her cheeks. The drunkenness went from her face, her eyes squeezed tighter but quivered open.

'I can't think of anything to pray,' she suddenly sobbed. 'Not a single bloody prayer.'

She was not inclined to try again. She wiped her eyes, the mascara trails like tribal marks. He helped her to her feet and she reclaimed her glass, emptying it in a continuing upward movement. Her robe had dropped open. Beneath it she had on a brief pink slip, the upper lace cushioning the fine brown breasts. She caught him looking.

'They're all I've got really, George,' she said.

As she spoke she eased down the top of the slip and let her splendid globes roll out. They trembled below his nose. 'Touch them if you feel like it,' she invited. 'I don't mind you touching them.'

As if of its own motivation his free hand went up. They descended again, both kneeling on the hotel room carpet. Putting his glass on the low table beside him George shuffled round on his knees so that he and Charmaine were face to face. His other hand came up to the other breast and he felt them with his palms.

They were thus engrossed when, after a brief knock, the door was unlocked from the outside and opened. Four Chinese came into the room bearing an oak casket. They took in the scene

262

with no display of surprise. 'Coffin for Mr Mangles,' said one man at the front.

George was speechless. Clumsily he attempted to shovel her bosom back into the top of the slip. By a swift, deep retraction of her diaphragm she accomplished it herself.

'Mr Mangles is in there,' she nodded sideways.

The two stood up. Her neck and her face were scarlet. George tried to pat her reassuringly but she was rising to her feet and moving away from him. Following her to the bedroom door George saw the men lift Ron Mangles in one practised movement and slot him deftly into his box. The leader of the quartet studied a piece of paper.

'There is one piece missing,' he said. His eyes ascended until they were almost round. 'Leg.'

Dizzily Charmaine looked at George and then back at the Chinese still studying the worksheet. 'He didn't have a leg, well not two,' she corrected herself defensively. 'He's not had two for years.'

The Chinese made an impatient sucking noise. 'There is toy leg,' he said.

Charmaine nodded towards the wall by the door. 'It's there,' she said sadly. 'I wanted it for a souvenir.'

'No keep it,' said the man assertively. 'Part of Mr Mangles. Must go.'

He strode past them, picked up the propped artificial limb, returned and unceremoniously clanged it into the coffin. Two of the other men closed the lid with a bang. They prepared to lift it to their shoulders.

'Half a minute,' George remonstrated despite his confused head. 'How do we know this is all right and above board? Doesn't Mrs Mangles get a receipt or something? You could be anybody.'

The Chinese regarded him with a narrow glint. 'This paper,' he said holding out the slip he had been studying. 'For Mrs Mangles.'

'Thank you,' sniffed Charmaine. She sat on the bed and morosely stroked the coffin. She accepted the chit.

'We take Mr Mangles,' added the man. 'Mr Chan in touch with you tomorrow. Okay?'

The final word was addressed to his colleagues who, at the signal, deftly lifted three corners of the coffin onto their shoulders. The leader inserted his shoulder under the vacant corner and they set off, adroitly navigating the doorway. George, and then Charmaine, followed them to the door of the suite and watched them march, casket aloft, down the long, carpeted and deserted corridor.

George turned towards Charmaine. Immediately she fell against him, pressing her bosom against his chest, hanging on to his beard with her fist. His eyes swivelled up and down the passage. No one was there. He eased himself and her back into the room. She still adhered tightly to him. 'Please . . . don't go,' she whispered beginning to cry voluptuously again. 'I couldn't bear to be all alone.' She rammed herself even closer. Their arms went round each other. 'I'm just a poor lonely widow,' she sobbed.

As the car, sent for them by Mr Chan, drove towards Kai Tak, George had a moment to reflect that his views of Hong Kong had been almost entirely through windows. Now he looked at the boxy scenery flickering by, the tramcars and traffic, and the crowding people, until the road reached the waterfront and the majestic outlook of the great harbour. Charmaine regarded it with dull eyes.

'I can always say I've been to Hong Kong,' she said moodily. 'Even if it didn't turn out the way Ron expected.' She remembered George and squeezed his arm, looking carefully towards the driver first. He was cut off by a window. 'But I met the kindest man alive.'

'Don't say "alive" like that,' he suggested. 'It sounds temporary.'

'Oh, it's not,' she said sincerely. 'I'm looking forward to showing you Deewhy.'

'You're sure?' he asked warningly. 'You *do* still need me? I'm not just on a free ride?'

'No way are you,' she retorted. Her voice descended hoarsely. 'Listen, this whole creepy bunch frighten the bloody life out of me. That Chan man. I don't like the way they *arrange* everything. They could arrange us.'

He pressed her wrist with more confidence than he felt. 'I don't think they want anything but to get us to Australia,' he said. 'The simpler the better. They don't want any trouble.'

The car turned into the conglomerated airport complex.

264

Planes landed and took off under their noses. Inside the departure gate Gregory Chan was waiting. He bowed.

'I hope everything was right, Mrs Mangles,' he said. 'Your take-off time will be in one hour . . .' he looked at his watch, '. . . seven minutes.' He regarded George carefully. 'Mr Mangles will be travelling with you. This way please.'

Yet another Chinese appeared alongside them and silently took over as escort. He conducted them along the busy concourse, pushing people and their baggage aside to make a path. Eventually they arrived at a door in a corner and this he unlocked with a key taken from a small velvet wallet. He motioned for them to go ahead and they walked up a stairway to another door which also needed unlocking. It opened into a small but heavily decorated lounge. The Chinese, still unspeaking, bowed and went out by an opposite door which he unlocked. They stood looking around. The sounds of planes were muffled to throbs. A further door faced them and Charmaine stepped decisively forward and opened it. She halted, frozen in her attitude, her back to George. He heard her gasp.

'George,' she said slowly. 'Ron's in there.'

Moving to her side and looking over her shoulder he could see the coffin side-on, lying on a trestle in the middle of the room.

'He looks so lonely,' she complained. Slowly she shut the door. 'Mind you, he usually was.'

They sat on two of the plush purple chairs in the lounge. The door to the corridor opened briskly, enough to startle them, and a young Chinese, reassuringly uniformed, came in.

'Mrs Mangles. Please come to Immigration.' Charmaine glanced at George but went out obediently. She looked back at him from the door. George moved forward but the young man firmly stopped him. 'You next, Mr Goodnight,' he said and closed the door.

George sat down again, then stood up and walked uneasily around the room. The windows were high and thickly glassed. He came to the door through which they had seen the coffin.

He put his hand on the handle and, hesitating only briefly, opened it. The coffin was there with its lid open.

George let out a startled choke and round the corner of the coffin poked a cheerfully creased face. 'Gud-dye,' said the man breezily. 'Just taking a look. Seeing who was at home.' He put the lid down and deftly turned the screws at the side of the coffin. His teeth, which he now turned on George in a jagged grin, were like cut-outs of soiled orange peel.

'*That* is Mr Ronald Mangles,' George protested. 'What business have . . .'

'I know it is,' returned the man affably. 'It says so on the side on this plate.'

'What are you doing here?' demanded George. 'Who are you?'

'Tommy Barton,' said the man. He moved forward, short, sparse-haired, round, ill-dressed, red-faced. 'From Adelaide.' The orange-peel teeth dropped once more.

George found himself involuntarily shaking hands. 'George Goodnight . . . Hertfordshire, England.'

'Well, I must be on my way,' said the man. He moved towards the far door, behind the coffin.

'But . . . wait a minute,' protested George.

In a surprising moment the door was opened and the man was gone. George took an interval to react. Then he went into the room, past the coffin, and opened the door. The man was at the end of the long corridor. He turned briefly and cheerfully waved 'Gud-dye', and clattered down the stairs. Thoughtfully George returned to the room, glared at the coffin, and then went into the lounge. Carefully he sat down and thought about it. Purely on the basis that Tommy Barton was an Australian and everyone else was Chinese he decided to say nothing about the incident. There were times when doing nothing seemed the right thing.

Charmaine returned, to his relief, accompanied by the Chinese in uniform. 'Mr Goodnight, please. This way for Immigration.'

Charmaine nodded to him reassuringly. He smiled at her and went out, down another flight of stairs, into a white office with a window over the airport apron.

'Passport, please,' said the Chinese seating himself behind the desk. George handed the document over. The official flicked through it. 'Australian visa, okay,' he said.

Looking from above, George was amazed to see the visa stamped on the page. He had never applied for an Australian visa in his life. He swallowed and looked away. The Chinese was stamping the pages.

266

'Okay, okay,' said the official. 'Sorry the man died. Good trip.' He caught sight of George's plastic carrier bag. 'That your hand luggage?'

'That's my luggage,' corrected George.

'Not much.'

'I haven't got much. I meant to buy a few things here, a suit and a suitcase for a start. But I haven't even had time to have a shave.'

'Take a long time shave that off,' said the Chinese nodding at his beard. 'But plenty of time on the plane.'

George thanked him for the idea. He walked from the office and up the stairs. Charmaine was in the lounge listening at the door to the other room.

'They just came to get him,' she said sombrely. 'I heard them grunting. It shouldn't be long before they call us now. I'll be glad to get home.'

She sat down heavily and it seemed possible she might again cry. 'It's all been too much,' she said. He sat down and put his arm round her comfortingly.

'Somehow an Australian visa has appeared in my passport,' he said. 'It must have been done while it was held at the reception in the hotel.'

'They said they arranged things,' she said. 'Mr Chan seems efficient even if he is creepy. He's been almost as useful as you.'

She laid her head on his shoulder and as if it had set off a timed device the door to the other room opened and Chan appeared. Charmaine straightened up.

'Mr Mangles is on board,' he said without reacting to their intimacy. 'Now we all join him.'

In the corridor was a Chinese stewardess who indicated that they should follow her. They walked straight from the building and out onto the tarmac. The Jumbo was standing only yards away. Chan had the tickets and boarding passes. George felt a flush of gratification as he and Charmaine were directed to First Class. Chan moved into the rear of the plane.

They sat down and George once more looked at Hong Kong through a window. They were the final passengers to board. Charmaine held his hand nervously as they taxied along the single finger of runway and rose above the boat-crammed harbour. The hills and the bays pulled away below the wings.

'Goodbye Hong Kong,' whispered Charmaine, like a child leaving the seaside. 'See you again one day.'

All the weariness seemed to overcome her. She lay back in the seat and her eyes closed; her hand slipped from his. George studied her. Her broad beautiful face was composed, her eyes apparently held down by the weight of the eyelashes, strung out like guy ropes on a tent. He eased back and was quickly asleep himself. After an hour he awoke. Charmaine still slept. Rising carefully from the seat he went down the aisle towards the toilet. On the way he asked an Australian stewardess for a pair of scissors which she produced. In the toilet he cut, trimmed and eventually shaved off the beard that had been accumulating since he landed in India weeks before. He pushed the hair down the chute marked 'Towels'. It took more than half an hour. When he had finished he scarcely recognised himself in the mirror. The top half of his face was mahogany, the bottom pale as soap. Outside the toilet he was confronted with the unforgettable appearance of the man with the soiled orange-peel teeth.

He took in George with no surprise and a jagged smile.

'Gud-dye,' he said.

XIII

The cemetery at Bollongonga, New South Wales, was not as George's vision of Australia had been. The bleak fingers of the great Port Kembler steel works poked into the sky behind the graves. It was a stifling day, overcast, which the arrival of lukewarm rain did nothing to assuage.

George stood with Charmaine at the graveside. She cried some large true tears below her big black hat. Her hand had dropped towards his, but with the Mangles family assembled, as in a gang, just opposite he thought it better that he should not join them together. At the top end of the grave, into which the coffin had just been lowered, appeared four men in sombre suits with large hats held across their stomachs.

'The police,' Charmaine whispered.

After the burial the rain stopped and the graveyard began to steam horribly. George stood back while Charmaine stepped uncertainly forward to bid her in-laws goodbye. They had met for the first time a few minutes before the funeral. She stood, long and beautiful in black, the seams of her stockings going straight up her legs, shaking hands and kissing her way through the assembly of dubious kin. The grave-diggers were already beginning to shovel the red earth. The drumming of the soil on top of the coffin lid quickly gave way to the softer sound of earth on earth. The clergyman who had mumbled a few last hopes hurried off and was now in the distance, his cassock like a piece of wind-blown paper.

One of the police, a short man in a black suit, trilby and proper tie, walked round the grave and stood, ominously waiting, at George's side. George grinned towards him and said: 'Caught them in the act, did you?'

'You're right,' said the policeman.

'What was it? Drug smuggling?'

'Drug smuggling, right,' repeated the officer. His eyes were on Charmaine's legs.

269

'In the coffin,' suggested George.

'In the coffin,' confirmed the man. His eyes remained in the same direction. 'You knew?'

'I guessed,' corrected George. 'I've seen it in the films. Not very original, I must say.'

The policeman said nothing more but did a tour round the grave, looking down throughout as if it were part of his duties to see that the job was properly done.

Charmaine had come to the end of the relatives and she now glanced around for George. He met her as she walked slowly away towards the gate and they went out together but without speaking. The suited policeman followed, studying ground still like someone following a spoor. George's unease was increasing. He helped Charmaine into the waiting car and followed her. The man boarded a car parked behind.

'I'm going,' Charmaine whispered. 'It's almost Christmas, you know.'

Both remarks took George by surprise. 'Is it?' he said to the second. 'I'd forgotten.'

'It's the twenty-third of December,' she said. She was holding his hand but looking straight ahead down the steaming road. 'I'm going up to the Gold Coast to see my fiancé, Eugene, my ex-fiancé that is.'

'To see if he'll have you back?'

'Yes, that's it,' she said stonily. 'I'm very grateful to you for what you've done.' She began to reach into her black handbag.

'And now you're going to settle with me,' he said sadly.

'I said I would. I said I was . . .'

'Hiring me.'

She looked straight at him. 'That's it,' she said, her voice hardened. 'Hiring you. Thanks very much.'

George felt hurt and deeply alone inside.

She had taken an envelope from the handbag and now she handed it to him. 'That should settle it,' she said. He took it. Then he leaned and kissed her on each cheek. She did not react. The car was slowing and he realised they were at a railway station. 'I get out here,' she said.

'All right,' he said. She turned and left the car, closing the door behind her. He sat haplessly. She did not look back.

While he was staring after her, watching her walk briskly towards the station entrance, the car door on the opposite side

270

was opened. The plainclothes policeman stood there. 'One door closes, another door opens,' he said.

'Or closes,' said George regarding him with increasing suspicion. The officer was again watching Charmaine. One of the other policemen was now walking with her towards the station. She still looked straight ahead as though he were not there.

The policeman who had opened the car door now got in. The driver had remained stationary, looking to the front. George found himself moving over and the newcomer sat down. He took off his trilby. His head was wet with perspiration. 'This is no season for hats,' he said. Leaning forward he tapped the glass partition. 'The station, Bill,' he said.

'This is the station,' pointed out George.

'The police station,' said the man. 'My name's Bert. Bert Crozier. I'm a detective sergeant.'

'And I'm innocent,' George informed him. 'If you think I'm mixed up with that lot, Mangles and those Chinese, then you're wrong.' He looked wildly out of the window. The nondescript streets of Bollongonga were going by. They stopped at a level crossing while a train went past. 'Charmaine will tell you. She knows the truth . . .'

'She doesn't often tell it,' sniffed Crozier. He leaned sideways confidingly. 'Don't worry too much,' he said with a certain sinisterness. 'It may be all right.'

'Oh good. I'm glad to hear that.'

'It all depends on a lot of other factors.'

'Like what?'

'That would be telling.'

'Look,' said George desperately. 'All I know is that Ron Mangles inconveniently snuffed it and I tried to help Charmaine. She called me first. I mean, I hardly knew them. I'd only met them once – by the swimming pool that day.'

'It will all be in your statement,' muttered Crozier. 'Surely you must have thought that the whole thing smelled a bit?'

'Well, odd-looking Chinese kept popping in and out,' conceded George. 'And at the airport in Hong Kong I saw this chap looking into the coffin.'

Slowly Crozier replaced his trilby and looked sideways at George from below his brim. 'You did?'

'Yes. He had the lid open. He was a little chap, red-faced with teeth all over the place, as if somebody had punched him.

He told me his name but I forget it now. And then he was on the plane.'

'You saw all that?'

'I've just said so.'

The car drew up outside a building frowning through dusty eucalyptus trees.

'The station,' confirmed Crozier. 'Did you have any plans for Christmas?'

'Christmas? I'd forgotten all about it.'

'Well, we've just fixed you up.'

Bollongonga Prison was an indifferent place to spend Christmas. George sat on his narrow bunk on Christmas Eve, staring up through the window bars at a single, gloating star, his thoughts far from the fabled stable of Bethlehem.

'I'll kill the bastards,' he muttered. 'I'll murder them.' He hesitated, hope melting. 'Whoever they are.'

'Better find out first,' suggested his cellmate, a man like a rabbit, called Bunn. 'No use murdering the wrong people. When I was off in the bush there was a bloke called Dan who was always wanting to murder somebody or other, mad as mad. He used to get rid of it by chasing Abos with a club. They always used to run like fuck but one day the Abo he was chasing turned round and grabbed the club and clubbed him. And that was the end of Dan.'

Bunn was there for stealing opals. As they sat in the cell the door rattled open and a clergyman wearing denims with his dog collar appeared, young and apprehensive, a protective warder hovering shadowly behind him. 'Happy Christmas, inmate!' the priest called to George, flinging a package in his direction. George caught it.

'Happy Christmas, inmate!' he called at Bunn and tossed a similar parcel which the little man fumbled and dropped. The door was replaced fiercely.

Bunn picked up his parcel and said to George, 'Did you hear that? He called me "mate".'

George did not correct him. Disconsolately he opened his parcel. Inside was a packet of biscuits, a container of butter and a miniature pot of meat paste. There was also a bag of boiled sweets, a packet of bent cigarettes, a Book of Common Prayer and a shoe-cleaning kit.

272

'Not bad, not fucking bad,' enthused Bunn eagerly exploring his gifts. He began to riffle through the prayer book pages. 'No pictures,' he said less happily.

'It's like they give you for breakfast on a plane,' grunted George. 'Apart from the book and the shoe stuff.' Randomly he opened the prayer book. 'The stranger that is within thy gates,' he read aloud. 'That's choice for a start.'

Bunn investigated the shoe-cleaning kit morosely but then brightened and said: 'I think I'll eat my tucker.'

George accepted the invitation to join him and they both crunched through their crackers having spread the meat paste and butter with their fingers.

'Happy Christmas,' said George raising his cream cracker.

'Same to you, mate,' replied Bunn raising a toast with his.

They munched meditatively for a few moments. 'How long do you think you'll get?' asked George.

'This time? Well, five years with two parole, I reckon,' said the Australian. He said it flatly as someone estimating the length of a contract. 'What about you, d'you think?'

George was shocked. 'But I haven't *done* anything,' he said haughtily. 'I'll be out of here in a couple of days. I'd better be.'

Bunn gave a philosophical grunt. 'I know lots of blokes doing ten years who was going to be out in a couple of days,' he commented. He examined George as if definitively summing him up. 'You're the sort of bloke who ought to get out to the opal fields,' he said. 'Might make your fortune. Blokes have.'

'I'm no miner,' said George. His cracker was finished and he felt curiously bereft. There was a morsel of meat paste left and he nibbled that from the end of his finger.

'Don't need to be,' shrugged Bunn. He had finished his gift also and now looked around as if wondering where it had gone. 'You can *scratch* for opals as well as mine them. They could be right there under your boots. In Coober Pedy they reckon that you can throw your hat down and maybe you'll find an opal where it drops. You can wear out a lot of hats that way as well.'

There was only a single bleak bulkhead light in the cell. Its shaft shone down on Bunn's meagre face. He leaned forward confidingly. 'I found the biggest opal in the world,' he said out of the edge of his mouth. 'Once.'

'You did?'

'Dropped it down the dunny. Biggest ever. Beaut. A pigeon's egg. And I dropped it down the dunny.' His neck seemed to elongate as he leaned and whispered. 'When you find an opal like that you don't tell a bugger. You keep your mouth shut and carry on like nothing has happened. Walk around whistling. Then one day, or night is better, you up and vanish. And you got to keep the stone on you all the time. Never let it out of your sight. Even on the dunny. I took it out of my pocket and I was gazing at it, sitting there crapping, a bit boozed, and I was kind of smiling at it, I suppose, turning it over. That's when I dropped the bastard. Right between my legs. I half caught it and I sort of grabbed at it, but it slipped then, out of my legs and down the hole. Last I saw of it.'

George studied the nipped face. 'Couldn't you . . . get it back . . . fish it out?' he asked.

'You ain't seen them Coober Pedy dunnies,' Bunn told him morosely. 'Old mine shafts and they go down for ever. And at the bottom there's all the shit and everything floating. I tried, 'course I did. I got a Greek who would do anything for money and I tried lowering him on a rope, but he kept passing out. Every time he came up he'd be unconscious. Then I got a pump but it was no good. That opal is still down there now.'

It looked as if Bunn was going to cry. 'All my fucking troubles started then,' he said disconsolately. 'That's why I'm here on Christmas Eve.'

'What about the opals you . . . they allege you stole?' asked George with care.

The spidery Australian looked sulky. 'I found them,' he said unconvincingly. 'I told you, you can just *find* them. You have to dig down sometimes but sometimes they're just there under your boots. And these bastards I found. Honest.'

'You must tell the court that,' suggested George watching Bunn blink with guilt.

'Well, there's another bloke who will say that he found them first.' Bunn's eyes dropped. 'And then I found them *after* he'd found them.' He crumpled and rolled back onto the bunk. 'And they won't believe me. I've found opals before.'

George said nothing more. The little man had closed his eyes and seemed already asleep, his knees brought up to his chest, his hands on his head. He looked like a chimpanzee. Sighing

274

bitterly, George stretched on his bed and looked at the bars. Beyond the window it continued to be Christmas Eve.

At Christmas dinner it was grandiosely announced that a Sydney radio station had, as a seasonal gesture, arranged for twenty-five prisoners to have free telephone calls to anywhere they chose. The man sitting next to George at the long table had been weeping throughout the meal and pounding at his tinned turkey and potatoes with a heavy spoon. Splashes of gravy and gobs of potato had been deposited over his neighbours who had protested without making him either cease weeping or stop pounding. The pronouncement from a rostrum at the end of the room, the beginning of which he missed because of his sad activities, eventually stilled him. Slowly he lowered his spoon and turned with red and streaming eyes towards the chief duty warder who was revealing the good tidings. Everybody cheered but then a disgruntled voice topped the others: 'Only twenty-five?'

There were one hundred and fifty prisoners in the room and the realisation of odds hushed them.

'I want one,' sniffled George's neighbour. 'I've got to ring my wife.' He looked around, seeking to astonish the others. 'She thinks I'm *guilty*.'

They were all to draw numbers from a hat, the lowest twenty-five to be the lucky ones. They circulated the hat while the men were eating their Christmas pudding. George drew number seventeen. The weeping man opened his raffle ticket; everyone around watched narrowly. A sob convulsed his face.

'Twenty-six,' he blurted. 'Twenty-bloody six! Oh my God . . .'

'Here,' said George pushing his ticket roughly at the man. 'Don't start on again, for Christ's sake. You're soaking your pudding. Have this.' The man's face seemed to expand. He held out a tremulous hand for the ticket as if it were likely to be cruelly pulled away at the final moment. 'I don't have anybody to call,' shrugged George as the man claimed it. He thought his fellow-prisoner was going to kiss him. Backing away he threw up his hands for protection. 'Steady, steady. It's perfectly all right.'

'You're a Pommie,' the man said in a hushed way. He held up the pink ticket, rising to his feet so that everyone could see

275

it, and bawled, 'The Pommie bastard's given me his phone call!'

George walked back to the cell with Bunn after the dinner.

'Fancy doing that,' said the Australian half admonishing. 'You could have *sold* that ticket. You'll never make a prisoner, mate.'

'I hope I won't have to,' muttered George. They locked themselves in the cell and stretched out on the wooden bunks.

'If I'd have won, I'd have used the bastard,' Bunn still reflected. 'Even if there wasn't a single bugger to telephone, I would have thought of something or somebody.' He had a further idea. 'I could have rung the Governor of this place and told him to go and fuck himself.'

Outside the bars the sun shone generously over the warm world. Cars could be heard and sometimes a trace of voices.

'All off to the beach today, I suppose,' said George looking up at the grille. 'It's odd being in a country where everybody goes to the seaside on Christmas Day.'

'Christmas Day,' put in Bunn reflectively. 'Always went prospecting Christmas Day. Unofficially. The mines' inspector wasn't about then and you could do some digging in places where you weren't supposed to, like the cemetery. Nobody ever looked for opals in the cemetery.'

From outside the door came a key rattle and it was opened by a warder, apologetically, as if he was loath to intrude on them. With him was the weeping man, now re-weeping. He had the pink raffle ticket held out towards George. 'No answer,' he said. Silently George reclaimed the ticket.

'Lots of blokes had the same,' sobbed the man as though it were some comfort to him in distress. 'Makes you wonder where they all go, don't it?'

'Are you certain you don't want to try again later?' suggested George, holding out the ticket.

'No. It's all right, Pommie. She won't be there. It'll still be no answer.'

The warder was impatient and said: 'There's no more calls until tonight.' He closed the door. George retreated to his bunk and regarded his ticket. Glancing across to Bunn he said: 'Do you still want to telephone the Governor?'

'Naw, I ain't got the guts,' admitted the thin man staring at the ceiling. 'It was only boasting.'

'Is there anybody else?' inquired George.

'I could ring the mines' inspector, the interfering bastard. But that's no good either. He'll be giving evidence against me when I come up. It'll only make it worse.' He paused and half turned. 'You got nobody at all?' he asked.

'Not in Australia,' shrugged George. 'Come to think of it, not many elsewhere either.' He wondered where Charmaine was.

'They didn't say just *in* Australia,' pointed out Bunn. 'Nobody said that.'

Slowly George turned towards him. 'They wouldn't wear that, not overseas?'

'Why not? They said one call each. They didn't say where.'

'Hello, operator. This is the prison. Bollongonga. Can I make a call out of Australia under the radio station scheme?' George was jammed in a small aromatic cubicle.

'Well, it doesn't say you can't,' said a young man's voice. 'I could ask the radio station, but if I were you I'd just make it. I won't know. It's Christmas.'

'I just dial it out?'

'Right. Is it to the UK?'

'Yes.'

'Dial 0011–44 and the local code, minus the first nought, then the number. Station XVY Sydney can afford a couple of dollars.'

George thanked him, thought carefully about it, and dialled the codes and then his own number. Ten thousand miles away in his house at Shillington, in England, he heard the telephone begin to ring. It thrilled him in an odd way. He was conscious of his inward ediness. It sounded clearly; he could imagine it echoing around the rooms and furniture. It continued to echo. It was not picked up. He let it ring, a lump accumulating in his throat. There was nobody there to answer. Sadly he put down the receiver. The phone rang immediately. It was the operator.

'No luck?'

'No reply.'

'There's been a lot like that. Funny how people clear off when somebody's in the nick. Do you want to try another number?'

'Well . . . can I?'

'Why not? It's not busy now. I'm just handling these special calls for Station XVY. There's no special instructions. Try again.'

This time he dialled the Birchs' number. It was picked up almost immediately by Cynthia. At once he could tell she was distressed. He decided not to say who it was.

'Hello. Is Freddy there please?'

'No, he's *not* bloody well here!' she rasped and slammed the phone down with such force that he winced in Australia.

He stood staring at the receiver before slowly replacing it. It rang at once. 'No luck again?' asked the operator.

'They didn't want to speak,' George told him dismally. 'My friend wasn't there. I think he must have run away or something.'

'Christmas, New Year,' said the voice philosophically, 'is when people quarrel and run away. It happens everywhere. Want to try again? Somewhere else?'

'Well, I don't have . . .' He had an idea. 'You don't mind?'

'They promised you a call and you haven't had one yet.'

'Thanks. Right. It's a village called Somerbourne Magna, Wiltshire, in England again. I know the number but not the code.'

'Sounds a good place.'

'It is.'

'Hold on. Somerbourne Magna, is it? I'll be back.'

He returned quickly. 'It's 72227 locally,' he said. 'According to International Inquiries. They sounded drunk, but still . . .'

George thanked him sincerely. Carefully he dialled the separate codes once more and the call was quickly picked up. A voice came faintly over a tremendous wash of background noise. He thought it was the line until he heard someone laughing above the others. He called down the mouthpiece for Molly but the man couldn't hear him.

'It's George Goodnight!' he called.

'Can't 'ear. What you want?'

'It's George Goodnight. *GOODNIGHT.*'

'*Goodnight* to you!' bawled the voice. ''Tis only noon!'

The line went dead, as emphatically as the truncated call to Cynthia. He pursed his lips angrily. Half-plastered peasant! The phone rang.

'Not having much luck,' said the operator.

'Not a lot,' he agreed. 'But thanks anyway.'

278

'Try another,' the man encouraged. 'This is a challenge for me too. It's like a Christmas game.'

'Well, quite truthfully, there isn't anybody else. Not anyone I'd want to telephone or who would want to hear me.' The names ticked briefly through his mind as he said it. He realised he was almost friendless.

'Nobody?' said the operator. 'There must be *somebody*, for God's sake. Why don't you try ringing the Queen.'

George heard himself laugh dryly. 'I think she's probably busy,' he said. 'And we're not that close.' Then he said: 'I suppose I couldn't try a number in France, could I?'

'Too right, you can,' the response came. 'This is getting interesting.'

'I don't know the number,' George said awkwardly. 'It's a hotel at Cherbourg.'

'That shouldn't be too hard,' said the man. 'It'll keep International Inquiries off the bottle for a bit.'

'Right. Well, it's in Cherbourg. Hotel Bismarck. The proprietor is called Wolfgang Müller.'

'Cherbourg. Bismarck. Müller. It's a whole new world. I'll call you back.'

George put the telephone down and stood waiting. The cubicle reeked of disinfectant. There would have just been room to sit but there was nothing to sit on. Every now and then the warder who had escorted him from the cell materialised outside and hovered but appeared to be in no hurry, indicating with a wave of uniformed arm that he should continue. Now the man appeared again and George put his head round the folding door. 'Won't be long, officer,' he promised. 'Trouble getting through.'

'S'all right with me, mate,' shrugged the warder pleasantly. 'It's Christmas. I'm on double overtime.'

There was an urgent bell and the operator came back. 'I've got it,' he announced triumphantly. 'They're as pleased as hell at International Inquiries. They've really entered into the spirit. Anything else you want to know, they'll get it.'

George said: 'I don't think so, thanks very much. You've all been very kind.'

'It's Cherbourg, that's 0011–33–33 and the number is 48 73 03.'

'Splendid.'

'Is that okay?' The voice sounded reluctant to go away. 'I'll get it for you if you like.'

'Oh, well, if you can.'

'Sitting here,' the Australian voice said, 'it's a bit solitary. Everybody phoning all over the place and I'm just stuck here.'

'I'm not exactly mobile,' George assured him.

The youth laughed. 'I'll have to have your name,' he said. 'I want to remember all this. Mine's Ollie, Ollie Smith.'

'I'm George Goodnight,' he said.

'Goodnight? Oh, is that why they shouted "Goodnight" down the phone from England?' He paused guiltily. 'I couldn't help overhearing. I was checking you'd got the connection. Why are you in the chokey?'

'A misunderstanding, I hope,' George told him fervently. 'I'll be out in a couple of days.'

'I see. Well, I hope so. Bloody disgraceful spending Christmas in prison.'

'I wouldn't recommend it.'

'I'll get you this number.'

'Yes, thanks.'

'Won't take long.' George could hear him dialling. A distant but clear voice answered at once. George felt himself start with pleasure. It was Monsieur Julien.

'You're through,' said the operator. He sounded almost disappointed that it had been so easy.

'Thanks.' George raised his voice. 'Monsieur Julien,' he said succinctly. '*Monsieur*, it is George Goodnight.'

'*Alors! Monsieur*, where are you?'

George told him.

'Australia! *C'est impossible!*' He turned from the mouthpiece and gabbled in French, returning quickly. 'Very nice!' he exclaimed. 'A happy Noël . . . A happy Christmas to you, my friend.'

'And to you,' returned George. He felt a touch of emotion. 'You are there with Wolfgang and Marie?'

He could sense the awkwardness all the way from France. 'No, no, Monsieur Goodnight. Marie only.' His voice descended. 'Wolfgang is no longer. He was killed in the car with Mademoiselle Joby . . .'

'The car?' breathed George. The shock caused him to tremble.

'Yes . . . you did not know . . . ?'

'I knew about Janine. But I thought . . . I thought it was illness. The lawyer just said . . . she had . . . died.'

'It was accident,' the Frenchman told him hoarsely. 'At Valère, towards Paris. The old man was ill, so Wolfgang said he would drive Mademoiselle Joby . . . and this disaster happened. It was in the rain.'

'Oh God, what a terrible thing,' blurted George. He felt his shoulders crumple.

'I am sorry to tell you, my friend.'

'I am so shocked . . . Please tell Marie I am sorry. I cannot find the words. I will telephone or write to you a little later. In the New Year.'

'Yes please. I will await that.'

'Right. Thank you.'

'Marie is here with her father for the Christmas. With me also. The old sailor, you remember. With the no arm. They are back together now.'

'Oh, I see.' There seemed nothing more he could say. His fingers trembled on the receiver. 'Goodbye, *monsieur*.'

'Goodbye, Monsieur Goodnight. I am sorry it was so bad news.'

George replaced the phone. It rang and the operator asked if the line had been clear. He said it had been.

'Right. Well, I hope everything turns out for you.'

'Thanks, and you.'

Sombrely he put the phone down. The warder appeared at the door, this time looking at his watch. 'All finished?' he said. 'Good. It's my tea time.' They began to walk down the corridor, starting off side by side, but the warder, as if realising that this was too companionable, dropped back behind George so that George had to speak over his shoulder.

'Is there anywhere I can get an atlas? I need a map of France.'

'Prison library.' It was only a suggestion. 'May not be an atlas there, though. Gives people ideas about escaping, see. It's closed today anyway. Christmas.'

They returned to the cell. The warder opened the door and they were confronted with the terrible sight of Bunn hanging by the neck from a pipe projecting from the wall. The noose was made from oddments of string and rope and even as

281

George and the warder stood, fixed in the first shock of seeing him, it broke under the little man's mean weight. His face revolved to them almost pleadingly, like someone caught cheating at a game. The warder pushed George aside and charged into the cell just as the string gave way, depositing Bunn on the floor. He landed on his knees and remained in an attitude of prayer, rubbing his neck.

'Only practising,' he told the warder defensively. 'Wanted to see if it worked.'

'What the bloody hell!' shouted the warder. Roughly he pulled Bunn to his feet, but the little man fell down again. 'And at Christmas!' the guard bawled.

'Sorry,' said Bunn, apparently apologising to George and the warder at once.

'Come on,' said the warder, roughly lifting Bunn to his feet again. George tried to help steady him. The small prisoner began to cry.

'Stop that now,' cautioned the warder. 'It's all your own bloody fault.' It was like admonishing a child. Obediently Bunn wiped his eyes. The rims were red against his pallid face. The warder, muttering about the trouble he had been caused, ushered him brusquely out of the door. Both men glanced back at George, Bunn with a wispy and apologetic smile. The door closed like a hammer.

George sat on his bed, his head in his hands. 'And a Happy Christmas to you, too,' he muttered.

Valère, he discovered from the prison atlas, was the village adjacent to St Laurent l'Eglise, the place by the river where he and Janine had gone that day. He touched the map gently with his fingers, tracing the main Paris road, then the byroad, then the river, the small River Moenne which edged against the road at that point.

'Don't have many inmates asking for maps of France,' chatted the prison padre who was escorting him. The library was dim and gritty, the books in wire cages, prisoners themselves. The padre, in his confused way, had apologised to inmates all along the corridors for not having visited on Christmas Day. It was, he had explained to several who had clearly not missed him, his busy day of the year. 'Birth of the Christ Child, etcetera,' he said. He told George: 'They like studying local maps, New

South Wales, so that they can pick out their own homes. Nostalgia and that. Remembering familiar streets.' His expression fell. 'Or escape plans,' he added glumly. 'We have had our disappearances.'

George thanked him and after the padre had locked up the atlas they walked back towards the cell corridor. 'Not the best spot in Australia to spend Christmas,' mentioned George conversationally.

'Jesus spent Christmas in a stable,' the padre put in primly. 'And *He* hadn't done anything.'

'Neither have I,' pointed out George with bitterness.

'That's to be seen,' returned the clergyman, as if he did not believe in innocence. They had reached the cell and he was waiting, hands poised together in an attitude of airy prayer, for George to enter.

'The sooner the better,' said George going in.

The padre closed the cell door, intoning absently as he did so: 'I'll pray for you.'

'Stuff it,' muttered George when the door had clanged. Disconsolately he sat on his bunk. Bunn's had been stripped of its sheets and pillows. He lay back and looked at the ceiling, at the pipe from which poor little Bunn had tried to suspend himself. Valère. He saw that day again. A faded summer, a different country; the river, the old man with his cheese and the waving necks of the swans. The gentle Janine standing below the trees. All vanished now. If everything on his journeys over the past months had been merely one failure leading to the next, which it certainly seemed to have been, then he was glad of that one time and that one person. For that and for her it had been worth running away.

So deep was he in his melancholy that the metallic sound of the door startled him. A square of face examined him through the grille. The door clattered open. It was a warder he had not seen before. 'You've got a visitor . . .' The warder studied a scrap of paper. 'Goodnight, G. That's if you are Goodnight, G.'

'That's me,' said George sitting up. 'A visitor?'

'Somebody feels sorry for you,' said the man with a shrug of his face. 'They do at Christmas. Locked up.'

'Jesus spent Christmas in a stable,' George informed him as he went through the door. The man frowned as if trying to recall the name. 'You ask the padre,' added George. He went

283

along the corridor, the warder following. From one cell came the sound of an accordion being moodily played.

'I wouldn't mind being the padre,' reflected the warder as if unwilling to let the subject languish. 'All excepting he's a poofter,' he added thoughtfully. 'I don't reckon being one of them.' The corridor ended and the warder unlocked a door. George entered a long room with small sideways tables set along the wall. Each table was occupied by two people, a prisoner and a visitor, except the final one. Seated there was a fair-haired young man wearing a blue shirt. He did not look towards George but sat with his hands together on the table before him. George glanced back to the warder and nodded his head questioningly in that direction.

'That's him,' said the warder undiplomatically. 'Looks like he's blind.'

George studied the stranger at a distance and then began to walk towards him. The head was held in one position, not quite upright, the ear slightly angled to catch a sound. George emphasised his footsteps as he approached the table.

'Ah, George,' said the visitor. He stood up and held out a stiff hand. A white stick which had been lodged against the table fell noisily.

'Er, yes,' said George. He retrieved the stick and shook the hand. 'Pleased to meet you. Sit down. It was nice of you to come.'

'But who the hell am I?' laughed the young man. 'I mean, you're not likely to have forgotten meeting me, are you?'

'Well, I suppose not.'

'We have met but not face to face.' The voice was strong and confident. 'In fact it was only yesterday.'

George was astonished. Then he realised. 'Ah, yes. I recognise the voice now . . . you're the . . .'

'I'm the telephone operator. I'm Ollie Smith. I thought I'd just come and cheer you up if I could. I keep away from the crowds at holidays, on the beaches and everywhere. This must be one of the quietest places.'

George felt overcome. 'Well, thanks for coming,' he said uncertainly. 'I didn't expect any visitors. I don't know anybody.'

'Why did they stick you in here?' asked Ollie.

284

'It's all a damned nightmare,' sighed George. 'I hope to God it will be all over tomorrow. It bloody well better be.'

As though he had known the youth for years George described the events leading from the moment he walked down to the swimming pool at the Hong Kong hotel. Ollie kept whistling in short bursts through his teeth. He never interrupted with questions but let the adventure run on. In the end he enthused: 'Shitting hell, what a yarn.'

'It's not such fun when you're taking part.'

Ollie shook his head. 'They must have put you inside to keep you safe over Christmas,' he said decisively. 'Protective custody. If it's a big drugs case there's no knowing what could have happened to you. What was Christmas Day like? Apart from your free phone call.'

'It was hardly Ding-Dong Merrily on High,' George sighed bitterly. The young man looked sincerely sorry. 'They gave me a shoe-cleaning kit as a present,' George told him. 'And my cellmate tried to hang himself with bits of rope and string.' He paused then said firmly: 'When did you lose your sight?'

'How long have I been blind, you mean?' corrected Ollie. 'Five years next April. Motorbike accident. It hit me. I was just walking along the street.'

'That's terrible.'

'It wasn't all that good. I was hoping to qualify as an accountant. I never intended to be a phone operator.'

'Compensation?' asked George. 'I'm a lawyer, as it happens.'

'You're a lawyer?' grinned Ollie. His eyes were completely closed, the lids over them, sometimes slightly fluttering.

'I am. What happened about it?'

'Almost settled,' said Ollie. 'It's taking long enough but it's nearly done now. I'll be rich soon. Well, quite rich.'

The warder approached, tiptoeing, apparently anxious not to disturb any of the line of successive conversations. 'Half-hour is up,' he whispered. Strangely, the youth looked at the watch he was wearing. 'I always keep that on,' he explained to George. 'I like to hear it ticking. When I get my money I'm going to have a bleeper watch.' The warder had walked away to a decent distance but he kept his eyes moving sideways towards them. George rose from his chair. He held out his hand, realised that Ollie could not see it and moved it towards the youth's hand. Smiling, Ollie rose and they shook hands firmly.

'How old are you?' asked George.

'Twenty,' replied the visitor. 'How old are you?'

The blunt return surprised George. He had to think. 'I'm forty-three,' he said. 'God, I'd almost forgotten.'

They were standing over the table now and the warder was hovering near, taking brief tentative steps, almost the hops of a bird, towards them. 'Thirty-three minutes,' he muttered. 'Three minutes over.'

'Just coming,' said George affably. He began to lead Ollie towards the door. The stick tapped on the bare floor.

'When you get out, what will you do?' asked the young man.

Again the question took George by surprise. 'I don't know,' he said. 'Various things. One thing is to try and trace someone. It's a girl who went missing a long time ago. I promised her mother. I'll tell you about it sometime.'

Ollie said astutely: 'If it's a name you want to trace I can probably help. We've got millions of names.'

'There's a man called Stuart Vaughan,' said George. 'He was a stamp dealer.'

He had not realised how cool the prison had been until they took him out into the sun. Three mumbling brim-hatted, plainclothes policemen came to fetch him and the chief warder shook his hand strongly as if he had won something. Everything, it appeared, was going to be all right. The padre was entering through the outer office door as he was passing through.

'Ah, an inmate becomes an outmate,' giggled the clergyman. 'God be with you.'

'Have a word with Him for me,' suggested George.

With the policemen he went out into the overwhelming sun. They had a car waiting. He got into the back with one of the men and they drove towards Sydney. His escort was not inclined to conversation. 'Just imagine,' ventured George thoughtfully, 'being incarcerated in a prison and then being brought out into the sun to be hanged or shot.'

For several minutes there was no reaction from any of the men until the one next to the driver said: 'When they used to top them it was always inside, wasn't it, Wally?'

'Inside the prison,' confirmed Wally who was the driver. 'Topped them inside.'

George took in what he could see of Australia through his

286

hot window. Occasionally the route broke out into burned and scrubby country scattered with gum trees and once he saw a wallaby lying sprawled dead at the roadside but that was the only touch of nature. Small towns and eventually suburbs occurred, from his low viewpoint merely wooden walkways or pavements, shaded by random awnings or corrugated iron. Briefly clad people crowded them, pushing in and out of shop doorways carrying groceries and multiple tins of beer piled like ammunition for a siege. The heat was almost visibly rising from the ground, windows glared, people bent their heads against the sun as they would have done against a wind.

'It's strange,' essayed George eventually, 'to see Christmas in the summer.'

'Hottest for Christ knows how long,' offered the driver almost religiously.

'More than thirty years,' the man next to George informed him. He emitted a dried sigh. 'Thirty-two degrees and my fucking mother-in-law.' He glanced at George with genuine envy. 'Better off in the pokey,' he said.

'It was wonderful,' said George insincerely. 'They gave me a shoe-cleaning kit.'

They drove deeper into Sydney, the streets gradually becoming taller until they curtailed the sky and the sun. There was a lot of traffic. George looked out for the Harbour Bridge and the Opera House but did not see them.

The car rolled down a hill. Some of the buildings were old and solid, others glassy and high. They glimpsed a shining band of water between two lofty streets. A tramcar clattered beside them once they had reached the level.

The police driver was halted, grumbling, in traffic for several minutes before the car freed itself and descended another gradient into the yard of what was undoubtedly a police building. A blue van stood in the forecourt with a confection of blondes in the back. They waved provocatively as the four men climbed from the car. Modestly George waved back, making the women laugh.

He walked with the others through the door, arched with sooty masonry, into a widespread foyer. Hopeless-looking people were sitting on benches. A woman stood alone, crying into a piece of newspaper. A young constable filled in a form from answers supplied by a curled-up old man. Behind the

287

reception desk a sergeant greeted them briskly. 'He's waiting,' he said nodding sideways.

'Right on time,' said the man who had driven the car. His tone was defensive. He looked for confirmation towards the others. They both checked their watches. Walking along a soap-smelling corridor they turned into a panelled anteroom and the man at the front knocked on a door of opaque glass. George could see the silhouette of a man apparently scratching his head. He called for them to enter. He had been standing holding a telephone to his ear. He replaced it and came forward to shake George's hand energetically. 'Thanks for all your help,' he said.

George took an offered chair. His three escorts waved their hats in silent salute and went out.

'I'm Commander Dobby,' announced the man. 'Francis.' He sat on the edge of the desk. He was thin and tall but even so his suit was too tight. The cuffs had climbed up his forearms as if he had belatedly grown. 'Thanks,' he said again.

'For what?' demanded George. 'For going in the nick over Christmas?'

'That's part of it,' Dobby nodded amiably. 'It wasn't too bad, was it? Cooler than outside.'

'So everybody tells me,' replied George. 'But when I go into the cooler I generally like to know what it's all about.'

'Cooler, cooler!' Dobby stifled his laugh. 'That's quite good, that is. Have some coffee.' There was a pot on a tray with two cups. George said he would and the policeman poured them out. He levelled off the sugar on a spoon and put it in his own cup, then, indicating the extravagance by his smirk, he put two piled spoons into George's.

'It was one of the biggest catches we've ever hauled,' he breathed. 'Bags of it. Cocaine and heroin. All in the coffin with poor Ronnie Mangles.'

'You would have thought they could have thought up some-thing better than that, wouldn't you?' commented George once more. The coffee was not much of an improvement on the prison's; perhaps from the same supplier. 'I've seen half a dozen films where the loot, or whatever, is in the coffin. There was one where it was full of banknotes and it went to be cremated.'

Dobby looked pained. 'I haven't seen that one,' he said. He

lifted his cup and spied on George across its rim. 'Anyway that's where it was, in the coffin.' He put the cup on the desk, walked round it, and looked as though he was tempted to divulge a secret. 'We, the police that is, would be grateful if you would now forget the whole business. You won't be required as a witness. We've got the Chinese blokes all nicely tied up. They'll be coming up for trial in a couple of months.'

'What about Charmaine?' asked George.

'Ah, the Widow Mangles,' mused Dobby. 'Well, *she* knew what was going on. She knew it wasn't just a honeymoon. Charmaine is a tough lady, believe me. She's testifying, so we won't charge her.'

'I hope she marries someone less complicated next time,' answered George. He looked up. 'Your people took my passport, by the way.'

Dobby went to his desk and took out an envelope. 'It's in there,' he said. 'There's also a modest cheque. It's to cover your expenses . . .'

'I haven't had any. I've been in prison.'

'. . . and inconveniences. It's a gratuity from our special source.' He laughed shortly. 'It's officially our Informants' Deposit. We call it the Narks' Fund.'

'Thanks,' said George. 'I'll still accept it.' He took the envelope and stood up.

'Anything else we can do for you?' asked Dobby.

George thought and then said there was. Dobby looked surprised and disappointed. 'Oh, what's that?'

'There was a man called Stuart Vaughan living in Sydney. He's vanished now but he was here ten years ago. He was a stamp dealer and he got into some sort of trouble. He might be in your records.'

Dobby nodded: 'We can soon check him,' he said. 'Why did you want him?'

'Nothing very dramatic, don't worry.' He decided to lie. 'It's to do with some stamps. I am in the business myself, in a sort of part-time way. He has a collection I'd like to see.'

'And he's not in Sydney now?'

'I haven't had a lot of time to look. Not even in the telephone book. But I don't think so. He left after whatever the trouble was.'

Dobby made some notes on a pad. 'I'll get somebody to

screen him,' he said. 'Give me a call in a few days. What are your plans?'

'I don't have any yet,' said George. 'Only keeping out of prison.'

Dobby saw him to the door. They shook hands and he went out into the corridor. He walked through the soapy smell, wondering how much was in the envelope, resisting the temptation to open it in case they were watching. As he entered the main foyer, its small dramas still being enacted on its seats and around its walls, a policeman approached and said: 'Mr Goodnight?'

'I didn't do it,' said George.

'I never said you did, sir.' He glanced behind him. 'There's a young bloke turned up, wants to see you,' he said. 'He's blind by the look of him.'

Looking towards the benches George saw Ollie sitting in his upright position, his hands on his white stick. He grinned and stepped towards him. 'Hello, Ollie,' he said. 'They've let me out.'

'I knew,' nodded Ollie. 'We telephone people know everything. That's why I came up. The prison told me you were here and people helped me. Being blind has its kudos too.'

George sat beside him. The policeman moved away. 'I've got a reward,' said George quietly. 'For helping the course of justice and being deprived of my liberty over Christmas.'

'How much?'

'I don't know. I'm just opening the envelope.' He did so. He realised he was doing it noisily for the young man's benefit. He pushed aside the passport and took out a second envelope which he again audibly opened. 'There's a second envelope,' he said. 'Wheels within wheels.'

'Hurry up,' urged Ollie.

'Wait a minute. Ah, here we are . . . a thousand dollars.'

'Well, that's not bad.'

'Only adequate,' said George. 'For what I've suffered.' He put the cheque back in the envelope and put that in the larger envelope. 'I was going to buy some clothes,' he added. 'Before I was so rudely interrupted.'

'I've found out something about Vaughan,' said Ollie, his stare straight ahead. 'The man you wanted to find. The stamp bloke.'

290

'You have? Good God, how did you manage that?'

'I told you, telephone people know everything. It wasn't all that hard. We keep records of bad debts going back years. I got somebody to check and he turned up right away. Left without paying his bill.'

'You found his address?'

'Eighty-four, Chiswick Way, Paddington.'

'Marvellous, Ollie.'

'The trail's years old. That was in 1973.'

'It's a start. Thanks very much.'

'What are you going to do now? Right now, I mean. You've got to have somewhere to go from here.'

'Yes, I suppose I have. At one time that would have been my first consideration. But after all this sauntering around I don't think like that any longer. I tend to let things happen as they will. I mean, I'll probably walk out of here right into the arms of Elizabeth Taylor and it's ten to one she'll take me home and put me in her bath.'

Ollie laughed. 'Well, my old woman, my mother, isn't exactly Liz Taylor, although she might put you in the bath if you ask her. She says you can come and live with us if you like. Just somewhere until you decide what you're doing next.'

George found himself swallowing hard. 'She did? You're sure?'

'I heard her.'

'Sorry. I'm a bit overwhelmed that's all. She doesn't know me. I mean I might get drunk and wet the bed.'

'I warned her you might. She didn't seem bothered.'

'And you've got room?'

'Enough. You can have the old man's room. He's gone walkabout.'

'Well, thank you,' said George. 'What can I say?'

'Don't say anything. Just point me towards the door. This place niffs of soap.'

XIV

'It should never have happened to someone like him,' said Ollie's mother. George was drying the dishes while she washed. Evening air came through the perforations in the fly curtain. The kitchenette had a bare neon strip. She stopped and gazed down into the soapy water as if she had spotted something, leaning forwards on her hands, suds up to her elbows. 'He's a decent kid. Even now you can see he's not bitter. I'm the one who's bitter. You see these useless, pasty-faced little bastards hanging around. Druggies, bikeys, queers, hair all colours like bloody gala birds. You'd never think this was supposed to be an open-air country.'

George dried the last cup on the draining board and waited for her to continue with the washing. She did so with a start, emerging from her reverie. 'Ollie's never made a drama about it. And that ugly bugger, the bikey, he's still roaming around at a hundred miles an hour. Pretends he doesn't remember. I was waiting on the curb with Ollie one day last year and he had the nerve to toot his horn. I'd like to see him come off and crack his neck.'

She looked as if she might be going to cry. Almost savagely she pulled the plug from the sink and let the water gurgle down. George watched it disappear. Ollie's mother took the tea towel from him and wiped her eyes with it. 'Sorry,' she said, 'But there doesn't seem much justice in the world.'

'It's sadly lacking,' agreed George. They went back towards the small sitting room. The front door to the street was open with the perforated fly door closed. The evening was breathless. Shadows passed as people walked by. There was a bar up the street and they could hear a bottle rolling along the gutter. She was a tired-faced, oval woman, her eyes set in shadows, her hair pulled away behind her neck. Her face was pale and so were her arms. They were at the back of Sydney, a great many streets between them and the shore. 'I never go,' she had said.

'It's not like when we used to go to Southend in the old days, when we were young.'

She sat down in a small wooden fireside chair. There were still suds on her wrist. She wiped them off on her pinafore. Ollie was working at the telephone exchange. George sat in a chair opposite Ollie's mother. It was small and it felt frail. The fireplace was black and empty as a dead grin. Above it was a commonplace picture of an English hay-making scene. 'At least I thought he would get a decent bit of compensation,' she continued. 'But as time's gone on even that seems to have gone all wrong. It's shrunk and shrunk. They're now trying to shift some of the blame onto Ollie, would you believe, saying he walked into the road and the bikey was distracted.'

'Have you got any of the case papers?' asked George. 'Perhaps I could run my eye over them. If you like, that is.'

'I've got them,' she said rising from her low chair. Despite the warmth she was wearing woolly slippers. 'You're a lawyer. I'd forgotten.'

'It hasn't done me a lot of good,' George reminded her. 'I've just been in prison.'

There was a varnished bureau at the back of the room. She pulled the front down and took out a thick untidy file. 'Everything goes into this,' she said. 'I haven't got much order. My husband was the methodical one. Too methodical.' She sat down with the file on her lap and opened it. A photograph fell to the carpet. George picked it up. 'Ah,' she said with something close to a laugh. 'That was on the boat coming out when Ollie was three. Taken at sea.'

He looked at the dim photograph. Her hair had been long and blowing then. The indistinct man beside her waved and the small boy peeped tentatively through the rails. 'A new life we were going to have,' she said sadly. 'Ten pounds each. That's all you paid to get out here. Ten pounds. It was too cheap really.' She lifted some papers from the file. 'There,' she said handing them across. In contrast to the rest of the contents they were clipped firmly together.

George took them and read them through with care. She went out to put the kettle on, remaining out there while he read. 'What do you think of it?' she asked when she returned.

'Well, at least I know something about it now,' he said. 'But

293

I would need to know a great deal more before I could really raise your hopes. I see the settlement is imminent.'

'Next couple of weeks,' she said. 'I think we're going to be very disappointed, don't you?'

He handed the documents back to her. 'It's one of those cases where you might consider scrapping everything. Go right back to the beginning,' he told her. 'At the end you might come out with substantial damages – after all a young man has lost his sight. On the other hand, there would be another lot of waiting, months at least, a lot of aggravation, not to mention the expense – and there's no guarantee that you'd end up winning. Ollie's solicitors have gone about matters in a straightforward way but it's not very imaginative.'

She shook her head. 'I never thought they were any good,' she said. 'Too soft by half. But I can't see Ollie wanting to go back to the beginning. It's been too long. I certainly wouldn't want to go through that lot again.'

He nodded with understanding. 'The law is often more of a mule than the ass it's generally reckoned to be,' he said. 'It won't be moved, not easily or very quickly.'

'It won't buy him new eyes,' she sighed. 'No matter how much it is.'

'It should be enough to make life a little more comfortable for you both,' George pointed out. 'I should hope so anyway.'

'I'd like to go home,' she said firmly. 'To England.'

'How does Ollie feel about that?' he asked.

Bleakly she looked across at him. 'He wants to buy a motorbike,' she said.

'But why not?' protested Ollie. It was odd to see him exasperated. His eyelids fluttered and his arms revolved like paddles. 'Why not, for Christ's sake? I don't have to *drive* it. I can get on the back and somebody else can drive. *You* can.'

George looked at him unbelieving. '*Me?* You want *me* to drive it?' He looked towards the young man's mother. She shrugged helplessly.

'Why not?' repeated Ollie. They were in the park, standing in a group. Children were screaming as they jumped in a plunge pond. Traffic choked the road. There was so much noise nobody noticed them. 'You've driven a motorbike, haven't you?'

'Yes,' snorted George. 'But years ago. When I was your age.'

Ollie reached out with both hands and located his. 'Then it's all right, then, isn't it? You on the front and me on the back!'

A vagrant who had been asleep on a bench behind them looked up as if he wished they would move on. Then he changed his mind and asked them the time. Ollie held out his wrist so that he could see his watch. The man gave a grumbling thanks, stretched, left the seat and stumbled away apparently to some assignation. Ollie's mother shepherded them both towards the bench, shaking her head as though things were getting beyond her.

'Ollie,' said George reasonably, 'the logic doesn't fit. You can't buy a motorbike just so that I can drive you around Sydney. I'm not sure how long I'm likely to be here. And I haven't been on a bike for . . .'

'Not Sydney,' said Ollie quietly. They could see he had made up his mind. 'Not *just* Sydney. Australia.'

'Australia!' George shouted the solitary word.

'Don't be silly, son,' placated Ollie's mother. Patiently she patted his hand. 'George has got more to do than that.'

'What?' demanded Ollie. 'Go on. Tell me what's he got to do?'

'Well . . .' said George deflatedly. 'I've got to . . .'

Ollie blurted. 'You've got to do *nothing*. Honest, now.'

'I know, Ollie,' said George. 'But you can't be serious.'

The blind youth leaned forward, his face radiant in the park sunshine. 'Listen, I always wanted to see Australia. I've never been outside this state, hardly outside Sydney. I *can't* see it now. But if we go together *you* can see it *for* me. You can describe it for me – tell me about it. Once I get the money I'll quit my job, we buy the bike and away we go.'

George looked across at the boy's mother. Her eyes were wet. 'How far is it to Alice Springs?' he asked.

They opened a map on the living room table and measured the distances, calculating them with the approximate inch between the top of George's thumb and the knuckle. As they did so the immensity of the country made itself known to George. 'God, it goes on forever,' he said. 'There's yards of it. You don't realise.'

Ollie sat eagerly leaning across the map peering down from

295

beneath his eyelids as if he could see every road, every river, every contour.

'You're obscuring Perth and Fremantle with your chin and your elbow is on Darwin,' pointed out George mildly. He was one of the family now.

Ollie's mother sat back smiling a little. 'It's big, isn't it?' she sighed regretfully. 'We've never seen a thing, really.'

'Sydney to Alice Springs,' mused George. 'We'd better take an extra petrol can.'

His thumb rocked across the distances. Below Alice Springs, two half-thumbs away, was Coober Pedy. 'Throw your hat down and you might find an opal worth a million,' he recited. 'And here, up to the north-west, is Ayers Rock.'

Ollie leaned over as if trying to locate it. George took the boy's finger and put it on the place. 'There it is,' he grinned. 'Feel the bump.'

'I want to climb Ayers Rock,' said Ollie decisively.

'Thanks,' said George.

'No, I do. I always wanted to see from the top. Now I'll have to feel it.' He banged the back of George's hand with his. 'You can tell me what it's like.'

'As long as you don't have to carry me up there,' commented George. He glanced at the boy's mother and they exchanged smiles. He felt at home with them; the small humid house, the days of heat, the common street, the drunks leaving the midnight bar.

He had two thousand two hundred Australian dollars. During his stay in Hong Kong, the adventures with Charmaine Mangles and the late Ron, his flight and Christmas incarceration, he had scarcely had the opportunity to spend. Adventure could be surprisingly economical. The remaining Indian money and the reward he had received from the Australian police made up the majority of his funds. He was paying Ollie's mother sixty dollars a week for his board, her modest assessment from which she would not be moved, and now, at last, he had gone out and bought himself a suitcase and some clothes. Ollie's mother had laundered his Indian safari suit. 'Terrible stuff, but it would be from there,' she sniffed. It now hung, frail as old skin, on its hanger in his room.

Wearing his new, fawn lightweight suit and pale shoes, he had also gone to Paddington where Stuart Vaughan had lived.

296

The house in the leafy suburb was now occupied by a New Zealander and his family. The man was affable and invited George into a front room where the sun came in pieces through the shutters. George sat down and looked about him, aware that at some time Janine Joby's daughter had in all probability sat in that same room. The New Zealander had never heard the name Vaughan mentioned but he gave George the address of the house-letting agents.

As he left George saw a lopsided swing in the overgrown garden at the side. The uprights were rusty and the seat hung by one forlorn chain. 'My children are too old for swinging,' said the New Zealander as a sort of apology.

George said: 'That looks as if it's been here for a long time.'

'It was here when we arrived. It looked like that even then.'

George walked to a main thoroughfare and took a bus into the centre of Sydney. The letting agents' office was in a street leading down to the waterfront at the Circular Quay. 'We've only been handling that property about five years,' said the woman who came in answer to the receptionist's call. She went to the rear of the office and returned with a folder. 'There's no mention of the name Vaughan in our records.'

'Thanks, anyway,' said George. 'Perhaps you could tell me where I can find the oldest established stamp dealers in Sydney.'

The woman, a middle-aged, chesty person wearing a large lace blouse, said: 'Well, we know one stamp dealer, through the business. John Upney and Sons. Young Street. Do you know where it is?' she asked. 'Young Street?'

'Well, no . . .'

'I'll show you. I'm just going to lunch.' She turned to the girl at the reception desk and told her: 'I'm going to lunch.'

'Oh, all right, Miss Sowerby,' said the girl. There was a touch of the sardonic in her tone. 'I'll tell everybody.'

'I bet she will,' said Miss Sowerby as they went into the street.

'You shouldn't have troubled,' said George awkwardly. 'I'm sure I could find it.'

'I'm glad to get out,' she said. 'How long have you been here?'

'In Australia? Oh, just a couple of weeks.'

'Here for Christmas then. That must have been different for you. After England.'

'It certainly was,' agreed George. They had reached a street junction.

'It's right down there,' she said pointing one way. He thanked her and she turned and went in the opposite direction, her broad bottom swaying. George walked towards John Upney and Sons, Philatelic Dealers.

There was no display window, just a small showcase by the door. It contained a good selection of Australia state stamps from the 1930s, commemoratives from the visit of the Duke and Duchess of York, the future King and Queen. He pushed on the door.

Inside was an office with an ugly desk, and display cases around the walls. An elderly man sat at the desk bending close to a catalogue as if he were not sure it was true. He appeared unwilling to acknowledge George's entry until he had completed what he was doing. Eventually he looked up, a thin, grained face with raisin eyes peering above the rounds of his glasses. George said: 'I'm trying to trace someone in the Sydney stamp business, or who was some years ago, and I wondered if someone here might know of him.'

'I've been here longer than anybody,' boasted the old man briskly. 'I'm Fred Upney. My father started the firm. Died in forty-six.' His voice became conspiratorial: 'Now they're all waiting for me to join him.' He let out a cackly laugh and clutched his chest. 'Won't be long now, either,' he said. 'Who was it you're trying to find?'

'A man called Stuart Vaughan.'

'Wilf Vaughan,' said Mr Upney at once. 'Called himself Wilf. It was probably Wilf Stuart Vaughan or Stuart Wilf Vaughan.'

'He lived at Chiswick Way, Paddington.'

'Same bloke. What would your name be?'

'I'm sorry. It's George Goodnight. I'm from England.'

The old man shook hands sitting down. 'I can tell that,' he said. 'I knew you were a Pom the minute you came through the door. You sort of *crept* in. Poms never do anything straight-forward. They creep about.'

'Sorry,' said George. 'We think it's politeness.'

'Probably is,' acknowledged Mr Upney. He laughed gumm-ily. 'Why do you want to find Wilf Vaughan?' He pulled a

298

second chair towards his own and, as if George had not noticed, nodded at it. George sat down.

'It wasn't really him I was after,' he said. 'He had a daughter . . .'

'That's right,' said Mr Upney at once. 'She looked a bit like a dark mouse, dark under the eyes and skinny. Not healthy looking.' He blinked at George's expression.

George leaned towards him: 'Do you know what's happened to her?'

'God help me, I don't,' returned Mr Upney. 'Just gone, I suppose.'

'And you don't know where?'

'Not a clue, mate. It was years ago.'

'Ten years at least. He left in a hurry, didn't he?'

'Yes, he did, now you mention it. Some deal he did, not stamps, something else. He, you know, dabbled. It had a big niff about it. He up and vanished, never saw him again.'

George tightened his mouth. 'That's a pity,' he said. Mr Upney appeared to have lost interest. His eyes had returned to the catalogue on the desk. George stood up. 'Well, thanks anyway,' he said.

'It's not much,' shrugged Mr Upney looking up. 'I didn't know him that close. There's a dealer called Fewing, Harry Fewing, who knew him a lot better.' All at once he seemed to have decided to help. 'Hand me the phone book, will you.' George moved towards a rank of directories set like foundation stones in the bookcase.

'Brisbane,' said Upney. 'Third along. The effs.'

George selected the volume and handed it to him. Giving himself completely to the task the old man pushed his catalogue aside and replaced it with the directory. He had the touch of a stamp dealer, flicking swiftly, arriving at the right entry without hesitation. 'Fewing, he said. 'That's him.' He recited the number.

To George's further surprise he picked up the telephone and dialled. It was answered at once.

'Hello, Harry, is that you? Fred Upney here . . . yes . . . Long time . . . Will you be at the Congress? No, nor me. Don't know what half the silly buggers are talking about these days. Listen, you were a pal of Wilf Vaughan's . . . right . . . yes, he had a lot of trouble . . . Where did he go? . . . Right . . . Did he? . . . He had that girl . . . his daughter, pale looking . . . Oh, right . . . she went to . . . ? You don't know where . . . Why am I? Oh, there's this bloke from England asking about him . . . well, the girl . . . Okay, Harry . . . you don't . . . What about the wife, Wilf's . . . Darwin . . . Did she . . . ? Right, Harry. Keeping healthy? Great. I'm fine except I'm too bloody old . . . Ha! . . . Okay . . . Thanks!'

He replaced the telephone. 'You heard that,' he said. 'Says Wilf Vaughan went to America after whatever the trouble was. He thinks the girl went with the wife, she and Wilf separated, and she went up somewhere near Darwin, so he thinks.' He looked at George. 'It's useful, is it?' the old man said.

'It's something,' said George. 'She's at Darwin. If she's still there, that is.' He stood and held out his hand.

'Near Darwin,' corrected Mr Upney as he stood up to shake hands. 'Could be anywhere in five hundred miles.' He smiled anciently. 'You're not a bad bloke for a Pom,' he said. 'If you could stop yourself creeping around.'

'I'll bang the door when I go,' promised George with a grin. He turned to leave.

The old man said: 'Was that girl his? Wilf's? She didn't look like it.'

'No,' George said. 'He got her for a packet of stamps.'

In the courtroom Ollie sat between his mother and George. It was another Sydney summer day and the sun caused the row of round-topped windows in the chamber to blaze like furnaces. The ponderous routine of the case made Ollie's mother twitch with impatience and nervousness. Ollie kept his head almost unmoving, suspended, his face listening to the voices. Only once did the judge return the young man's attention; at the moment when he announced the award. He judged that there had been a proportion of blame attached to the victim because he stepped off the curb and had distracted the motorcyclist by waving to him. Damages were therefore on a lower scale than might have been. Oliver Smith would receive fifty thousand dollars.

'For a lifetime's blindness,' said the young man's mother bitterly as they walked down the steps of the court. 'And just because you waved.'

'An action of friendliness,' nodded George. 'I wonder how

300

often that's been taken into account in cases like this.' He shrugged. The sun was at midday and people were sitting eating their workday picnics in the shadows of the court building and under the trees of a small park. The girls looked brown and fresh in light dresses. Ollie walked straight by, only hearing their voices.

'You could appeal,' said George when they were on the bus going home. 'I think, properly handled, you could improve on the amount of damages considerably. But that would take a good length of time, another year perhaps, and it might not be successful.'

'We take the money and run,' said Ollie decisively. On the bus he appeared to be looking out of the window.

'It's disgraceful,' sniffed his mother.

'It's *my* blindness,' he answered with the first sharpness that George had ever heard in his voice.

A wretched look wrinkled his mother's face. George shook his head, a brief warning, towards her and she said nothing more until they were in the small house and she was pouring tea.

'When are you going to get this motorbike, then?' she asked quietly.

'As soon as possible,' Ollie told her. 'As soon as my money comes.'

'Ollie,' said George cautiously. 'There are a few things you ought to think about.'

The mother looked gratefully at him. Ollie, drinking his tea, said: 'What are they? I know what *I* want to do and you *promised.*'

'Yes, all right, I promised,' said George. 'But that money has got to last you the rest of your life. It's meant to make things a little easier for you, and, incidentally, for your mother. As you get older there are all sorts of things you may want. You may feel you need some special training for something or something to help you . . .'

'Like a guide dog,' put in the boy acidly. 'Or a new stick.'

George took a deep breath. 'All I'm trying to say is that I don't think you ought to be in too much of a hurry to blow it. I know it sounds a lot, fifty thousand dollars, but it's going to have to last a long time.' Abruptly it occurred to him that he had never spoken to anyone like this before, young, middle-aged, or old; giving advice. There had never been anyone who had asked, not even Tina.

'I want to go on the trip,' said Ollie determinedly. 'I always wanted to see Australia. This isn't Australia right here. Not this street. Not Sydney. There's bloody miles of it. I can't see it now, but at least I'll be able to *feel* it. And you can tell me what it's like.' Something oddly like a pout occupied his face. 'It's not much to ask,' he said.

His mother got up suddenly and fumbled with the teapot. She picked it up and took it towards the kitchen, cradled in both hands like a conspirator with a bomb.

'Where's she gone?' inquired Ollie in a whisper.

'To refill the teapot,' said George quietly.

'Listen, George. You've *got* to take me. I've done bugger all in my life, George, and now I can't even *see* what I'm doing. I've got to learn *things*, all sorts of things, and you've got to help me. I'll never do anything here.'

The expression was animated. George patted his hand. The whisper resumed: 'It's not just the house, or this street, it's *mum* as well. And my job.' His face was shining with desperation. 'Listen, if I don't do this now, with you to help me, I'll be stuck here, George, doing the same thing for the rest of my life. I can't do that. Christ, it's bad enough when you can't see anything but when there's nothing to look forward to either it's fucking disgraceful.'

Ollie's mother returned with the teapot and poured out another three cups. In the silence the tea sounded like a waterfall. The front door was open because of the heat and the afternoon shift of drunks from the corner bar paused outside the insect mesh and squinted in. 'What you doin' in there?' inquired one mischievously through the wire. 'What they up to, Jackie?' he asked his companion. The shape of a second inquiring head appeared at the mesh.

With both anger and accuracy, Ollie picked up his teacup and flung the contents at the door. 'Have some bloody tea!' he shouted. The liquid splattered through the holes in the wire and the pair shouted and staggered away with curses. Ollie's mother was shocked. She stood up and went to the door and closed it. The drunks came back and banged on the mesh and then on the low window of the room, but then they went away.

302

'It's time we moved from here anyway,' said Ollie. His shoulders were shaking.

'That's what I thought,' said his mother touching his arm. 'I thought now we could get somewhere.' She looked towards her son and by some instinct he returned the look.

'Listen,' interrupted George. 'I've got an idea. It depends on what you think of it.'

Both heads inclined to him hopefully. 'For a start,' he said, 'I don't think fifty thousand dollars is an adequate award for a lifetime's blindness. Acknowledging the fact that I've not been familiar with the case all through, I have, however, read the documents pretty thoroughly and I can't help thinking that it hasn't worked out as it should have done. You *did* wave, I suppose?'

Ollie said: 'Everybody said I did. In my evidence I said I *might* have. I don't remember. Nor stepping into the road.'

'I can't believe that was argued sufficiently,' said George. 'And even if you did, no one would ever wave to *anyone* if they thought of the dangers involved. And we would all stay safely anchored to the curb. How well did you know the youth on the bike?'

'Same school,' said Ollie.

'Is he someone you *would* wave at? A close friend? Someone you would greet?'

'He's not that. He never was. I said I don't remember waving.'

'What we are talking about in the end, in my view anyway,' said George, 'is a boy, aged fifteen, who never saw *anything* again.' Their interested faces warmed him. 'In my view,' he repeated.

'But an appeal might take ages,' put in Ollie. 'You said so yourself. We'll never get on that trip.'

'I've thought of that as well,' answered George. 'Say you did lodge an appeal and, I suggest, change your legal representatives, you – we, that is – could still go off on this exploration.' The young man leaned closer, his eyelids flickering.

'What on?' he said.

George grinned. 'A motorbike, if I can still ride one,' he said.

'I mean what *with*?' corrected Ollie. 'What do we use for money?'

'What do we use for money for the appeal?' put in his mother. 'The lawyer's costs?'

'One at a time, please,' laughed George. He half turned to the woman. 'We must use solicitors who will take a bit of a gamble,' he said. 'They will know that there's already fifty thousand dollars security anyway, in the kitty as it were — damages would never be *reduced* on appeal. If we lose, of course, the fifty thousand is going to be short by the amount of their fee.'

'Tell me about the trip?' asked Ollie anxiously.

'Well, I can get hold of some money, in a roundabout way, from home,' said George. 'That's partly how I've been keeping myself going anyway. It involves selling postage stamps I own. In any event I would not have let you finance the journey entirely. I would have paid my half. Now, all things being equal, I could put up the money for the trip. You won't be required, I shouldn't think, even by the solicitors, for consultations, for three months. They won't have sorted through the last batch of papers by then. Solicitors are slow people. A preliminary meeting with you ought to be enough to keep them going for a while.'

Neither son nor mother said anything. The woman's head merely nodded, the youth's face was glowing.

'So what we do,' said George in the absence of any comment, 'provided nobody in England has nicked my stamp collection, is to go on the trip with me putting up the money. Travelling around was, after all, my reason for coming here. One of the reasons anyway. Then, as and when you got your damages, you can pay me back for your half.'

George felt the youth's hand curl round the back of his neck. Ollie pulled their heads together. 'Jesus, George,' he said. 'You're better than a father.'

'A bloody sight better than *your* father,' said his mother.

'Good morning, Fisher, Brent and Raney. Can I help you?'

'Fisher? That *is* Brent and Raney?'

'Fisher, Brent and Raney.'

'Oh, yes. Oh, I see. Is Freddy Birch there, please? This is an overseas call. From Australia.'

'Austra . . . Oh, is that *you*, Mr Goodnight? We've all been wondering. We've got an office sweepstake on where you'll turn up next. There's a map on the wall and . . .'

'Yes, I heard. Can you put me through to Mr Bir . . .'

'Putting you through. Is it really *hot* there, Mr Goodnight? It's awful here. It's not stopped since Christmas. Ah . . . there he is . . . you're through . . .'

'Hello, Fred. It's George.'

'Hello, George. I was wondering when you'd turn up again.'

'I telephoned Christmas Day. But you weren't at home.'

'No. There was some trouble. You spoke to Cynthia?'

'Well, not exactly "spoke". It was the briefest conversation. I asked for you and she slammed the phone down.'

'I see. She never mentioned the trouble?'

'I didn't have time to tell her who it was. I was in prison at the time.'

'Prison! Christ, not again.'

'Penitentiary to penitentiary, that's me. This time it was in Australia.'

'That's where you are?'

'Don't worry. I'm paying for this call. What was the trouble, Fred?'

'Oh, you know. We've not been getting on too well.'

'Sorry about that. You've still got my stamps safe?'

'Your stamps? Oh, yes, they're all right. It's about all that is. You know what it's like at Christmas, George, everything seems to get on top of you – and out it came. I cleared off.'

'On Christmas Day?'

'Christmas Eve actually. I . . . I went to Leighton Buzzard.'

'You didn't!'

'I went to a small hotel and shut myself away all Christmas. I had sardines on toast for *my* Christmas dinner.'

'But Leighton Buzzard? It sounds like The Call of the Wild . . .'

'Very funny. I bet you wouldn't like ruddy sardines for Christmas dinner . . .'

'Where I was it would have been a treat.'

'There's someone I know at Leighton Buzzard. A girl. She was in her house with her parents. I was in the hotel down the road. I just wanted to be near her. I know it sounds odd.'

'It obviously sounded a bit fishy to Cynthia.'

'That situation isn't at all good. You *are* paying for this call, are you?'

'I am, Fred. Don't worry.'

'We got together for New Year, me and Cynthia. You know, made it up. But it was hopeless. We went to the Hopsons' party and Cynthia sobbed all the way through "Auld Lang Syne". Holding hands, charging in and out, you know, like they do at midnight, and booing her bloody eyes out. It's no better now. In a way, George, you've got a bit to do with it, quite a lot actually.'

'Me?'

'Well, going off like you did. How many men would like to do that? Dump the bloody lot. But they daren't. It unsettled me, I can tell you. Not right away but when I started thinking about it. I sit here, season in season out, staring through the same picture window. Sometimes there's leaves on the trees, sometimes there's not. But they're still the same trees. And you're gallivanting around the globe.'

'I wouldn't call being behind bars gallivanting.'

'Well, no, I suppose not. Sorry, George. I'm just envious of the freedom, that's all . . . Do you want some more stamps?'

'Yes. The lot.'

'The lot?'

'Yes, I've got an expensive time coming along.'

'Christ. What is it, a harem? No – don't tell me.'

'It's not a harem. It's a motorbike, among other things.'

'God, it's years since I was on a motorbike. I doubt if I could get my leg over one now.'

'Obviously you can still manage it elsewhere.'

'Stop, George. It's no joking matter. It's a terrible mess, George. This girl. Lucy . . . oh, it's a big story. This is a long call, George.'

'It's all right. I have friends in high places. The telephone exchange.'

'Oh, it's criminal is it?'

'It's surprising how quickly us hoboes slip into it. Like pinching bread or milk from people's doorsteps.'

'Well, her name is Lucy and she works, or at least she did, she's moved now so that we don't have to see each other . . . she worked on this same industrial estate. I saw her standing at the bus stop one evening last summer and I gave her a lift.

That's how it started. She's only been married a year. She's nineteen, George, not much older than my daughter. Imagine, a man of forty-eight and a girl of nineteen.'

'It's rarely the other way around, thank God.'

'It's made me so miserable. It's destroying me and Cynthia. It's upset Lizzie, and Lucy was in a hell of a state. She tried to creep out to see me during the Queen's Speech on Christmas Day. But her mother, who's a Tory councillor, stopped her. Made her listen to the speech. What a fucking fine time for patriotism. I think I may just run away like you.'

'It's a long road, Fred. As you say, there must be thousands of men would like to do it. Perhaps I ought to start an advisory service when I get back.'

'Big joke. It's very serious from where I am. I'll send the stamps.'

'Yes, Fred. I'll repay what I owe you for postage sometime.'

'All right, George. But you'll keep in touch, won't you? You won't stop phoning because there are no more stamps?'

'No. Of course I won't.'

'I may need your advice. Anyway, give me the address.'

'Fisher, Brent and Raney.'

'Mr Birch, please. It's George Goodnight.'

'Oh, Mr Goodnight. Quite a regular. Still in Australia? It's stopped raining here . . . You're through.'

'Hello, Birch here.'

'Fred, it's George. I got your cable. What's the trouble?'

'George. It's the stamps. Cynthia's given them back to Felicity.'

'Christ!'

'Exactly. Snooping around my things, playing bloody detective, and she found the stamps. Your name was on the albums. They went straight back to your missus.'

'Women!'

'There was a terrific row. I reckon those stamps have finally done for our marriage. I can't tell you what it's like at home. Anyway, Felicity's got them and there's nothing I can do about it.'

'What lousy luck. Damn it.'

'What will you do?'

'I think I'm going to have to ask for them back.'

'Hello, Tina. It's George.'
    'George! I've been worried! Oh, I've started crying.'
    'Don't cry, lovely. How are you?'
    'I'll be all right once I've dried my eyes. Oh, George, I miss you. We went to Torquay for Christmas. It was horrible. Where are you, George? When are you coming back?'
    'I'm in Australia.'
    'Wow! Is it hot?'
    'Humid today. But it has been. I telephoned home at Christmas but there was no reply.'
    'It was wet and miserable in Torquay. Mummy was really down in the dumps. I think she might have even been missing you.'
    'Christmas is like that,' he said.
    'Did you have a lovely time? Were you with lots of people?'
    'Well . . . yes, I was actually.'
    'Come back, George. When are you coming?'
    'I can't get any further away than this. Whichever way I go now I'll be heading towards home.'
    'George, you sound so different. You sound much braver now. Have you still got your fan-dancer, the one who was in the paper?'
    'No. It wasn't serious. We just shared a cell for a while.'
    'You're joking again. I miss you joking.'
    'How is school?'
    'Same as usual. We're not playing hockey because of the beastly weather. Sometimes I'm stuck in the classroom, looking out of the window and I see a plane going by and I think that maybe you're on it.'
    'One day.'
    'I think Mummy might even have you back, if you asked nicely. She's pretty fed up.'
    'I can't yet. I've got to do things I've promised to do here. It's just as difficult to run back as it is to run away. I'll tell you some tales one day.'
    ' "Tales marvellous tales, of ships and stars and isles where good men rest." It's a poem we're doing. It reminds me of you. It's by James Elroy Flecker.'
    'Why don't you write to me and write it all out.'

'Yes, of course. You've got an address now?'

'Yes. Have you got a pen?'

'I've got a lipstick pencil.'

'It's 104, Boundward Road, Chullora, Sydney.'

'Got it. I'll write today. I'll put the poem in.'

'I'm going to have to telephone your mother. It's just something that's come up. She's . . . she . . .'

'She'll be all right. She's feeling sorry for herself.'

'Felicity.'

'Yes. Who's that?'

'It's George.'

'George? . . . Oh, *George*. Good gracious, fancy you turning up.'

'Yes, it's me. I'm here.'

'Where? You're not thinking you're coming home, are you?'

'Not immediately. I'm in Australia. I rang before, on Christmas Day in fact, but there was no reply.'

'There wouldn't be. We were away, Tina and I. It was wonderful. We were guests of a friend of mine; a beautiful manor house in Surrey. A real old-fashioned Christmas. How did your Christmas go?'

'Oh, terrific. Usual thing down here. Beach picnic, nude bathing. That sort of occupation.'

'You liar, you were in prison.'

'Prison? Good God! Prison? . . . Fred Birch told you.'

'I don't speak to Fred Birch. Not after the way he's treated Cynthia. How would he know anyway? Oh, I suppose you call him on the sly.'

'Who told you then?'

'Your Mr Burtenshaw. From the *News*.'

'Burtenshaw? What's he up to? Who in hell told him?'

'He's a reporter, isn't he? He finds things out. Several times he's called me and twice he's turned up here. He's on your trail. Wants to write about your adventures.'

'He can bloody well forget that.'

'I don't think he will. He wrote one article about you. "The Man Who Got Away" I think it was called. It should have been "The Man Who *Ran* Away". That was when those damned pictures of you appeared here, roped up to that little tart in India. I can't tell you how humiliating that was for me.'

'It wasn't all that elevating for me.'

'How . . . how do you get into situations like that?'

'They come looking for me. How's the divorce coming along?'

'It's in hand, thank you. It takes two years' separation. So don't come back yet.'

'I wasn't intending to. But could I have my stamps, please?'

'Ah, you know about the stamps.'

'Yes, and I need them to finance me.'

'Ah, that's how you were doing it. Freddy was sending them. Now I've got it. There's more to you than I gave you credit for.'

'Perhaps I'm not so lazy now. I'd be grateful if you'd send them.'

'I can't see any reason why not. Give me an address.'

'Don't give it to Burtenshaw.'

'There's no worry I would do that. Every time you're made to look a fool it reflects on me.'

'How is Tina?'

'I was wondering when you would ask. She's fine. She's back at school, of course. Working hard. She's taken to poetry. I had a letter yesterday and she'd written a line she likes from a poem. What was it? About stars and islands.'

' "Tales marvellous tales, of ships and stars and isles where good men rest." James Elroy Flecker. A lovely poem, I've always thought.'

'Yes . . . yes, it is.'

'Well, I must ring off. You'll send the stamps? Have you got a pen?'

'Yes.'

'It's 104, Boundary Road, Chullora, Sydney.'

'It sounds heaven. How could you telephone me on Christmas Day if you were in prison? You're such a liar.'

'I escaped in Santa's toy sack. Goodbye, Felicity.'

'Goodbye, George. Ring again next year.'

XV

The last picnic table before the great central Australian desert was among a clutch of eucalyptus trees on a brown-domed hill. George turned the motorcycle and sidecar up the ragged track to the parking area. Two sunburned girls were sitting on one of the wooden picnic benches, one blonde, one ginger, wearing shorts and chequered blouses over big outdoor breasts and pack-carrying shoulders. They looked amazed at the arrivals.

'What d'you call that thing?' inquired the ginger girl. She pointed at the machine, and the blonde, who appeared to be subordinate even in her manner of sitting, also belatedly extended her finger. 'What d'you call that thing?' she demanded.

'It's a BSA 500 cc motorcycle combination,' replied George calmly. He had climbed from the front saddle, adjusted the 'L' plate, taken off his crash helmet and begun to guide Ollie by the elbow, so that he could leave his stick behind the sidecar. Ollie, dangling his helmet, was grinning in the vague direction of the girls.

'And you should see her move!' he shouted.

They regarded him oddly, at first because of his shout, and then his puckered eyes.

'Where are you heading?' the ginger girl asked, turning to George.

'West,' he told her pointing like an explorer to the interior. 'Until we reach the sea.'

The girls laughed, first one then the other like an echo.

'I'd like to see that too,' retorted Ginger.

'I'd like to see that,' confirmed the blonde.

George had released Ollie, but remained close enough for the boy to know he was there. He touched his elbow and they sat on the far side of the table to the girls. Ollie had four tins of beer and he set them down firmly, too loudly. His smile turned, searching the others out. 'Want a beer?' he asked.

The girls accepted and they went to the other side of the table and sat four in a line, facing the interior of Australia, drinking from the cans.

'We're going back towards Sydney,' said Ginger. 'We've had a gutful of the great Outback. Dirt and dust and creepies . . .'

'And crawlies,' put in the blonde.

'And stories,' sighed Ginger. 'We're tired of stories. Men telling yarns. Sometimes I think that's *all* there is out there,' she said with an odd bitterness. 'Legends and all that crap. The place is empty. I used to think the middle of Australia was wasted, now I know it's just a waste.'

She glanced at George. 'It's part of my thesis,' she explained with an honest shrug. ' "Outback – Legends and Realities" it's called. Does it sound all right?'

'Not bad at all,' he acknowledged. 'Is that what you're going back to do?'

'University of New South Wales,' she nodded.

'I work in a bank,' mentioned the blonde. 'But she's at university.'

They finished the beers and the girls stood, stretched their bare, formidable legs, said goodbye, and began walking, their packs bouncing over their backsides as they dropped down the slope to the road.

'We'd better go too,' said George when the girls had reached the road and turned towards the east. He picked up the beer tins and threw them in the rubbish bin.

'We'd better,' said Ollie with an odd grumpiness. He banged his crash helmet on the table. They walked down the incline to the motorbike.

'What did they look like?' asked Ollie eventually as if he had not wanted to ask.

'Nice,' answered George. 'Well, *I* thought they were all right. I don't know about you, you're a lot younger. You're not so particular when you're my age.'

'I'm not particular at all,' said Ollie.

'Oh, I see. Sorry. Well, one was ginger, the one who did all the talking, and the other fairish. And they were quite large, hefty, as you might imagine hitch-hikers.'

'Big tits,' suggested Ollie.

'Well, they didn't actually bare them,' replied George evenly. 'But they had something or other under there.'

312

Silently they sat on the motorcycle. Before George had a chance to kick it to life, Ollie said: 'That's the worst bit of it.'

'What is?' asked George over his shoulder.

'Women. Not being able to see what they're like.'

'You can hear them and you can feel them,' pointed out George. 'That's usually better. Feeling them is always the best of it.'

'Is it? Is that what you reckon?'

'I'll say it is. They don't all *look* beautiful, but they all *feel* beautiful, give or take a few.'

'I never thought of it like that. But even getting to feel them is going to be difficult for me. Unless you give me a hand . . . well, help me out, I mean.'

'Listen, we're heading into the wilderness not the wild life. I shouldn't think there's a lot of spare crumpet in the Simpson Desert.'

Now they both laughed. They donned their helmets. George prepared again to start the bike but once more Ollie checked him. 'I want to change my name,' he said bluntly. 'Ollie Smith sounds wrong. It's puny. It's a little kid's name. I think I'll call myself something else, George.'

'Try Oliver Smith,' suggested George. His foot was on the starter. He was about to kick it when it came to him. 'Or Oliver Loving,' he said over his shoulder. This time his foot came down and the machine broke into coughing life. Smoke and noise enveloped them. Dust flew up as they jolted forward.

'What?' bawled Ollie. 'What was it?'

'Oliver Loving!' bellowed George over his shoulder. He manoeuvred the machine onto the dusty road. He accelerated, heading west. Storms of red dust flew around.

'Loving!' shouted Ollie clinging on.

'That's it. D'you like it?' George had put his scarf round his mouth.

'I'll say I do! Loving! Oliver Loving! I'm Oliver Loving!'

The road ran straight as a rod to the burnt horizon. Around them the land was broken and brown, sometimes in the late day becoming vividly red. It remained generally low, almost cowering under the sun, with distant smudges of blue hills that looked cool and promising. The nights they spent at bare motels by the route until in the late afternoon of the fifth day

313

they reached Barraway, a settlement flattered by a mark on the map, so insignificant that if George had not braked they would have clattered past.

There was a store with a lone dust-hung petrol pump, three wooden houses and some lean-to shanties in front of which a group of Aborigines squatted desolately in the dirt. A brown child, its naked belly like a drum, hung onto a cur's tail, running behind it. Beyond the settlement was an acre of wrecked cars, piled in rusty pyramids as if they had raced towards the place from all directions of the compass and come together in momentous, simultaneous and multiple collision.

'That's called the driving school,' nodded the man at the petrol pump as George gazed towards the piled wreckage. Flies crowded the man's face like currants in a bun.

Flies landed and walked all over George also. He waved both hands in front of his eyes as if trying to break a spell. Ollie was doing the same. The Aborigines seemed to be taking a distant interest in the motorcycle but not enough to cause them to move from their squatting place.

'From Sydney?' asked the pump attendant. He had filled the tank and replenished the spare petrol cans in the sidecar. 'Not seen a rig like this in years,' he went on, not waiting for a reply to his inquiry. He kicked at the sidecar as if thinking it might cry out.

'We're on the trans-Australia race,' George told him, swinging his crash helmet. Ollie grinned through his cloud of flies. 'We're the leaders. There'll be hundreds along like this before long.'

'I won't be here,' said the man negligently. He was in his thirties with a neck like a root, long, red and sinewy. 'I go home at five.' He saw George searching the horizon. 'I live over there,' he said nodding at one of the shacks across the road. 'Along by the blacks.'

'We'll drive on for a couple of hours,' George said confidently. 'Then we'll stop somewhere for the night.'

'There's nowhere,' mentioned the man. 'Not till Bartley Creek. Three hundred and ten kays. Unless you want to doss on the road.'

'Nowhere?' queried George.

'There's a lot of nowhere on this route,' shrugged the man.

314

'If you're going to stay, it'll have to be here. Twenty dollars a night. That's with washing water. Eating is extra.'

They followed him across the baking road towards the shack. The flies, unable to believe their luck, followed them in gusts. The three men walked round the Aborigines who remained transfixed. The child with the extended belly and the dog now sat ten feet apart, moodily staring at each other in stalemate. George and Ollie stepped into the cowering wooden house.

The furniture was grubby red plastic. A nude girl demonstrated a carefree position in a calendar on the wall. The man saw George looking. 'Nineteen seventy-nine,' he said. 'We're getting engaged soon. This is the lodging.' They walked into the room.

Two iron bedsteads stood against the walls. The only other furniture was a bucket. 'World War Two beds,' said the man with a kind of pride. He kicked them as he had kicked the sidecar. 'From the hospital at Darwin. I'd want the money now.'

'Oh, you'd have to, wouldn't you?' sniffed George. 'You'd always have people sloping off without paying. And once they're out in this place they'd be out of sight after twenty or thirty miles.'

'I'd send the black fellas after them,' replied the man so flatly that George could not tell if it was a joke. Perhaps on a signal those dust-hung men with blank eyes would leap up and go hopping across the desert wielding boomerangs of vengeance.

The man said his name was Len, telling them as if it might come as a pleasant surprise.

'What's he called?' asked Len hoarsely, indicating Ollie. He had not asked George's name.

'I'm blind not deaf,' Ollie retorted. 'Ask *me*. It's Oliver.'

'You blind?' queried the man. 'And I reckoned it was just dust in your eyes.'

Ollie took it as a compliment and smiled.

'We got a dead man up the track,' mentioned Len. He led them back into the ragged living room. He filled a kettle from a bucket and wiped some dirt off the inside of the window before staring out and indicating with his head. 'About three hundred metres. Lived here years, Martin something, or maybe something Martin. Martin anyway. Prospector years ago, so he said. Didn't know he was dead till I wondered where all the flies had gone. You can still see them swarming up there now. Like smoke.'

'Is it upsetting the Abos?' asked Ollie. 'Dead man around?'

'Don't think so. They're always like that. I called the doctor from Frensham but there didn't seem no point in him rushing. He'll be over in a day or two with a hearse. Don't know where the money'll come from.'

He made them murky tea and while they drank it an Aborigine, naked except for what appeared to be the sole of an old boot at his crotch, appeared at the door and said something, nodding towards the visitors as he did so. Len shrugged and turned to them doubtfully. 'Want to hear the stories about the Dreamtime?' he asked. 'Ten dollars a throw.'

'I don't think so, not right now,' said George.

'Sometimes they're all right,' said Len. 'I like to listen myself because I don't have to pay and it passes the time. It's all about how they came here first. Some time ago.' He shook his head at the man who had attached his thin body to the door jamb like a creeper. The Aborigine turned his eyes sideways and muttered something else.

'He says the doctor and the undertaker are coming,' said Len. 'They're only ten kays away. Must have heard me talking.' He said something to the man who slithered away from the doorpost and vanished. 'You wouldn't have got any Dreamtime stories anyway,' he shrugged. 'They won't stay around if anybody is moving a dead body.'

They drank the tea after trawling flies from the surface and Len mentioned that the undertaker would probably bring some fresh meat from Frensham. He was right. As the encrusted hearse and the doctor's dust-coated four-wheel drive drew up outside, the undertaker, wearing shorts and a black shirt, brought in several parcels of groceries for which Len paid from a purse.

'Steaks, tins of this and that. Salad, lettuce and stuff,' said the undertaker. He took a long look at George. 'Looking for a job, are you, mate?' he asked bluntly.

'No, actually,' said George defensively, 'We're travelling.'

'A Pom,' said the man flatly. He nodded at Ollie. 'Is he blind?'

'Ask him.'

The man asked.

316

'I'm blind,' confirmed Ollie.

'I could use both of you,' the man said. 'Steady work.'

'Has Jack gone up?' asked Len who was pouring more of his malignant tea.

'That's right. I'll go up in a couple of minutes.'

'Old Martin will be missed,' added Len piously. 'The flies will miss him.'

'You'd look right in black,' confirmed the undertaker nodding at George. 'And a Pommie voice. The boy here looks right for it too. He's got a sad face.'

'Thanks, but no,' said George. 'I've been employed as the novelty figure before.'

The man, if he felt disappointment, denied it with a shrug. He gulped the tea. 'Better go up,' he said. 'There's only the two of us. He's got the aerosol.' He stood up with a half-wave of his hand and left.

Len opened the food parcel. 'The steaks look red,' he said dully.

Apparently unreceptive to George's expression as he examined the steaks, Len said: 'And salad. Don't get a lot of good fresh stuff here.' He regarded George and Ollie closely: 'You'll want a wash, I reckon,' he said.

'Frankly, I could do with a bath,' intimated George. 'I've got dust in every crack.'

'Bath? Well, let's see.' He began to search his memory. He took the bucket from which he had filled the kettle. 'That's all there is, mate,' he said peering into its limits. 'You could try spreading that over you. There's a shower over at the gas station but you can't trust it. Water's not steady. It comes from a tank on the roof. Rainwater.'

'How long since you had rain?'

'Oh, not too long. There was a good drop only three weeks ago.' He stood up decisively. 'It should be okay. Want to try?'

Ollie said: 'I will. This dust feels like a second skin.'

All three rose and Len led them out of the door. It was dropping towards evening, the sky russet, the heat declining by a few degrees. As they stood outside, the doctor's car closely pursued by the hearse came along the track. There was a coffin in the back of the hearse. The Aborigines had vanished. Only their cur watched. Both vehicles went by at a good pace.

317

'They won't stop,' said Len. 'They're racing the fucking flies.' He sighed. 'Now they'll all come back here.'

They crossed the road, George looking either way and cradling Ollie's arm. Observing the urban precaution, Len said: 'They got traffic lights at The Alice now. The world's getting busy.'

They passed the pump, asleep on its elbow, and went in through the door of the building. It was dim. They followed Len through a litter of old tyres and motor parts. 'Little ends from the driving school,' he said tapping various items as they passed. He opened another door. 'And there's the douche,' he announced. 'It's a bit dusty, but everywhere is.' Something pleased him in the dimness. 'There's soap. But,' he added, dropping his tone, 'there's no towels. How about newspaper? We've got newspaper. It's all been read.'

As the Australian went back across the reddened road for the newspaper, George surveyed the shower.

'What's it like?' asked Ollie.

'It's not a lot of use,' judged George. 'Except as a home for spiders. In theory, anyway, there ought to be some water in the tank.' He tugged at a corrupted chain hanging down the corrugated iron wall. A gurgle like a muttered threat, sounded above their heads. The showerhead vibrated and several spiders plummeted. Once again George pulled the chain. There was a deeper acknowledgement from overhead and jets of brown water squirted, dropping further spiders from their patient webs.

'Good on yer!' Len was at the door with the newspapers. 'Got it going. That'll see you right.' He lingered and then said: 'I 'spect you'll want to be private,' and went out.

'Sit down there,' said George to Ollie, guiding him to a wooden box. 'I'd better try it first.'

Ollie sat down, his face composed in the fatalistic mask he adopted when told to sit down and wait. George struggled out of his clothes. They were clogged with dust and sweat. 'I'll put these under after you've had a dip,' he said.

'What's "these"?' asked Ollie.

'Clothes,' said George knowing he knew.

Now naked, George looked untrustingly at the showerhead. After he tugged at the chain celestial rumbling resounded and rusty water ran. He kept the chain pulled. The flow increased and abruptly, as if the contraption had made up its mind to co-operate, the colour of the water cleared and it showered fiercely.

'Here goes,' muttered George.

'Good luck, mate,' said Ollie. He sat, eyes puckering, the unsure grin on his face. George strode into the shower. The lukewarm water struck his parched skin like a mountain storm.

'Wonderful!' he spluttered. 'Get your gear off, Ollie.'

Ollie stood and began to undress, folding everything carefully and laying the clothes on the box. George picked up the brick of crude soap and, stepping away from the shower's main flow, began an orgy of lathering. All over his head and body he soaped, under his armpits and into his crotch. Bubbles erupted and tongues of white froth rolled down his body. He had soaped everywhere and was about to step back under the shower when the water stopped. From the cocoon of soap his eyes bulged. 'No!' he gasped like a man issuing an order. 'Oh bloody no!' Frantically he tugged at the chain. An apologetic metallic clunk came from overhead like a coin dropping into a spent machine. No water appeared.

'The water's packed it in,' said Ollie. He stood naked, staring unseeingly towards George.

'I'll say it has!' bellowed George. 'And I'm up to my arse in carbolic.' Fiercely he tugged at the chain. 'Come on!' he shouted. 'Come on, you bastard!' The chain responded by breaking near the hole through which it entered the ceiling. It fell like a dead snake into George's hand. 'Oh God, that's really buggered it,' he howled.

Ollie began to laugh. Sitting on the box he cackled uncontrollably. George stared at him in anger through the soap he was trying to scrape from his body. 'Shut up, you little prat!' he bellowed. 'It might seem funny to you but it doesn't to me!' Scraping handfuls of soap from his chest he said: 'Go and get that dimwit from across the road. You can find the door, you walk straight across until you hit a wooden wall. That's the house.' He gazed down at his bubbling white torso. 'Jesus Christ,' he whispered to himself. 'I've got to get this stuff off.'

Ollie found his shirt and put it on. 'Nobody's going to see you,' George told him brusquely. 'Those Abos walk around starkers. Go on. This stuff is drying.'

Ollie began to smirk again. Wearing only his shirt, he detected the door. Len was standing on the other side of the empty track as if hesitating in the face of heavy traffic. 'Everything all right, son?' he called.

'The water's stopped!' Ollie called. 'George is all soapy.'

Abruptly George appeared in the aperture, beside Ollie, and the man on the far side of the track began to laugh. He doubled from the waist. 'Ho, ho . . . oh bloody 'ell! Oh, what a fucking sight! Ho . . . ho . . .'

'Stop it!' bellowed George. He shook his fist and a dollop of soap flew onto Ollie's shirt. 'Do something, you prize prat! Get some water!'

In the final light a clutch of Aborigines appeared round the corner of their shanty building across the track. Seeing George, they clung closer together and regarded him with expressions of mystification and respect. Still hanging together, eyes unbelieving, limbs sagging, they ventured a few paces. George took a step out towards the road and at a single silent signal the tribesmen turned and ran off into the swallowing dusk. Dogs came out, barked and backed away. Women and children began to cry within the ragged walls of the shanties.

'The black fellas think you're the spirit of the bloke who snuffed it up the track,' explained Len coming over the road. He was still trying not to laugh. 'Water ran out?' he said.

'Oh no. Not at all,' returned George savagely. 'I walk around like this from choice. Get me some water, for God's sake.'

'None available,' shrugged Len.

'It's drying on me,' said the anguished George. He began to scrape the lather away. 'I'm getting stiff.' Handfuls of soap came from his chest as he scraped with his hands.

'Never get it off that way,' offered Len. 'You'll be in a hell of a state once it really dries. And then, when the sun gets to you . . .' He decided to help. 'There's a waterhole ten kays to the west. It's a sacred place for the Abos . . .'

'I don't care. Let's get there.'

Still naked and caked he caught Len by the arm and pulled him towards the parked motorcycle.

'I'm coming,' said Ollie urgently. 'I'll get in the sidecar.'

They had unloaded the extra petrol cans and their baggage so there was room for him. He clambered in without help and Len climbed onto the pillion. Standing beside the machine, the soap like an ever-tightening skin, George said to Len: 'You drive.'

320

'Never learned one of these,' said Len.

'Christ Almighty!' bellowed George. There was nothing for it. He climbed on the front of the machine and kicked the starter with his naked foot. It hurt. 'Shoe!' he snarled at Len. 'Give me one of your shoes.'

'Don't get it soapy,' cautioned Len mildly. He removed his right shoe and handed it to George who rammed it on his foot. He kicked the machine again and this time it responded. He drove it out onto the track. Evening dust leapt from beneath the wheels. It flew up about them, adhering to George's sticky skin. His eyes were burning as he sent the bike roaring along the road.

It took them five minutes. Len directed them down a sidetrack to a place where some ghostly trees congregated. At their centre, just a glimmering, was a pool. Hardly waiting to stop the machine George jumped off and plunged straight into the tepid water. With utter gratefulness he felt it close over him. He surfaced and plunged again. His head broke the surface in time to see Ollie, now merely a shape in the darkening hour, jump into the pond also. A lonely-looking moon came up, surprisingly quickly, as if soliciting company. They swam in the pool while Len squatted on the bank where he was soon joined by an indistinct group of muttering Aborigines. Len called out: 'They're saying this is a sacred place, mate. They're going to report you to the Abo Affairs Officer on Monday.'

As they drove on the next day the land became ever more vacant. Even the bristly outcrops of scarred trees that had previously occurred did not grow. The sun was livid, toasting the desert, singeing the small areas of their faces that were exposed outside the goggles, the helmets and the bandit scarves about their mouths. Dust rose from the road like gunfire. Names on the map went by without any visible corresponding mark upon the scene. Everywhere looked the same. Burned and empty.

Weeowonga did materialise; two shacks with a weakly water tower, a pair of distraught trees and a fly-invested Aboriginal family who hunched in a shelter fashioned from beer crates. They regarded the arrivals with pebbled eyes, their faces unchanging and their lips unmoving. Eventually an old man with a grey beard like a garment rose from his squat and, when they had halted and dismounted, served them a beer, saying not a word, merely giving the cans to them and holding out his hand for the money. As they were about to depart, the natives now not even garnering the effort to study them, the old man made a visible rally and asked them to stay in order to listen to some stories of the Dreamtime. Here it was only five dollars.

George apologised for the lack of time to take advantage of the bargain. He mounted the machine and Ollie climbed up behind. The Aboriginal family now observed them go and, as though on a single swivel, revolved to see them swerve from the road after less than a hundred metres and fall into a red ravine.

The motorcycle bucked fiercely, slewed and slithered; its passengers shouted through their scarves as it took off like an inelegant flying machine and dived suicidally into the desert cleft. Its three wheels landed with fortuitous accord on the dropping slope and it bumped down the red incline, lumps of desert flying, engulfed by its own choking dust. At the bottom it shuddered to a standstill amid the spreadeagled wreckage of several other vehicles.

Both passengers remained stunned and rigid on their seats. After the final collision they hung on, George to the bike, Ollie to George. Ochre clouds billowed around them. As they subsided they remained fixed as two clay figures. Coughing out small, rusty explosions as he did so, George lifted his helmet and called over his shoulder, 'Are you all right?'

'I'm okay,' gasped Ollie. 'Where are we, George?'

'In the shit,' replied George. The hulks of the other vehicles surrounded them. A lizard slid slyly from a shattered car window.

Ollie began to laugh. George coughed, his laugh trapped inside by layers of dust. Eventually, amid the convulsions, it escaped and they sat on the broken motorcycle, deep in the ravine, both guffawing. The Aborigines had, with sinister confidence, crept along the track to view the accident. The others hung back while the old man with the scarf beard moved like a tracker to the edge of the depression and peeped over. He saw the two men, still adhered to the motorcycle, heaving and choking with outrageous laughter. He muttered a single-word

322

phrase which in their prehistoric tongue means 'madness' and backed slowly away from the scene, the others following.

The Aborigines returned to their depressed shacks but after only half an hour their spirits were a little lifted by another fist of dust from the east. As the vehicle neared they resumed resignation because it was the familiar truck of a man from Ootenawarra sixty kilometres' distant who had heard every variation of Dreamtime. Stoically they observed his arrival and departure without even a wave. It was often too hot for courtesies. They heard the truck pull up shortly past the settlement and knew, by their deep instinct, that the two white men had climbed out of the ravine.

George and Ollie sat with their personal packs on the side of the highway. The truck stopped and the lean, blue-eyed face that looked from the window broke into a toothless smile.

'Gud-dye,' he greeted them.

'Gud-dye,' responded George and Ollie together. 'Nice day,' added George.

'Christ, a Pom,' said the newcomer.

'I'm afraid so,' admitted George.

'Gone down the hole?' said the driver. He climbed from the truck and examined the ravine. 'Which one is yours?' he asked. 'Oh, the bike. I can see now.' He stepped back from the edge and regarded them incredulously. 'How far did you come on that?' he asked.

'Sydney,' said George a little proudly.

'How far did you think you were going to get?'

'Perth,' Ollie told him. 'At least.'

'Jesus. Only a mad bloody Pom would try that. You'll be wanting a lift, I s'pose.'

'It's either that or the Flying Doctor,' said George.

The man began to laugh. 'My Irish grandfather said that the only time he liked to see a Pom was when the Pom was in trouble. The only good Pom is a suffering Pom, he used to say.'

'He should be here,' shrugged George.

'Get in,' laughed the driver. 'There's room for three in the front.' He looked towards Ollie, and George, catching the glance, tapped his own eyelids. The Australian nodded. 'You all right, kid?' he said.

'I'm fine,' said Ollie. 'I was getting a sore arse on that bike anyway.'

They got into the front of the truck and started on the road again. 'I'm going to Ootenwarra,' he said. 'It's about sixty kays. But there's nothing there. There isn't even a way out. I look after the telegraph lines in this area and that's where the bastards put me. I could drop you at Marunga, there's a rail stop there.' He looked at his watch. 'There's a train Thursday,' he added, 'or Wednesday if you want to go back to Sydney.'

'We want to go on,' George told him. Ollie nodded.

'Then it'll be Thursday. She goes to The Alice. There's a shack of sorts at Marunga and some emergency tucker. It's not much of a place but you'll have to sit and wait there a couple of days.'

The fire had diminished to a red eye outside the door. Neither having had culinary or camping experience they had inexpertly cooked two tins of string-like stewing beef and now they stretched on two equally sagging canvas beds. Whistling sounded in the dark desert. A single wind fidgeted uncomfortably like someone hoping to be invited in.

'George,' said Ollie from his bed.

George was at the final breath before dropping to sleep. 'Yes . . . what d'you want? God, I was nearly gone then.'

'Sorry.'

'It's all right. Felicity, my wife, used to wait for that very moment before asking the last unimportant question of the day. Timed it to a second. What is it?'

'Well, what's it like? When that bloke picked us up today and said about his Irish grandfather hating the Poms, it made me wonder. That's where I come from after all – I'm a semi-Pom – and I don't know anything about the place. Except for London and that Princess and suchlike. Stuff you see on the television.'

George shifted. It was a dark night, so dark that he could not see the sky through the open door. Ollie had been concerned about dingoes but they could not sleep with the door closed.

'The man's grandfather didn't say he *hated* the English,' corrected George. 'He said that he liked to see them suffer. That's true of most people, particularly those we ruled in one way or another.'

Unsure that he had understood, Ollie said: 'It must be crowded like hell, though, England. All those people in that

324

little place. And it's an island, isn't it?' It sounded like a half-question.

'It was when I left,' agreed George. 'As for the population, well, it's sometimes necessary to stand on one leg to give the other chap a chance. But it's got its compensation. There's the odd green place. And the weather is splendid.'

'I always thought it was shitty,' ventured Ollie after a silence. 'Rain and fog and snow. No proper summers.'

George said irritably: 'We do, I admit, have rain and fog and snow but we don't mind. Honestly. We sit beside the fire toasting muffins.'

'Are you homesick, George?'

'I am now,' grunted George. 'You've started me off.'

'I can never understand why you just left like that. You had a house and a good job and a wife. That's what most people want. Like they aim for.'

George sniffed at the dark. The alien night continued with its bereft signs and grumbles. 'Sometimes I wonder myself. An act of courage, really. Desperate courage. In a way I'm a sort of hero, I am. An example to the faint-hearted.'

Ollie grunted from the other bed. 'Usually you don't think of heroes running away.'

'Have you finished for tonight?'

'Yes, sorry. Thanks for telling me about England.'

'Go to sleep.'

'All right, George. Goodnight.'

'Goodnight, Ollie.'

At three in the morning the Sydney-bound train rolled past, trembling the hut, but without waking the two wanderers.

In the glaring afternoon of Thursday the westbound express appeared on the horizon, shimmering like a veiled dancer. They stood by the track and waved their shirts as the engine took shape. It wheezed and shrieked to a halt apparently astonished that the pair should be waiting at the lineside.

Heads emerged from windows, the driver hung from the front of the train, which had overshot, and stared back at them. Eventually the face of a guard was thrust out above them and regarded them with deep distrust.

'What d'you want?' he inquired brusquely.

George looked at Ollie who fluttered his eyelids. 'We'd like

325

to get on the train,' George called up. 'If it's all the same to you.'

The man looked flustered. 'Get on? Well, yes. If that's what you want.' He stepped back and pushed open the door; a short flight of steps came down. George guided Ollie to the bottom of the ladder and followed him. The guard had still not recovered from his surprise. 'Haven't picked anybody up at Marunga for years,' he ruminated. 'Or dropped anybody down for that matter.' Suspicion returned to his face. 'You're going to The Alice I take it. All the way.'

'All the way,' George assured him. 'How long does it take?'

'We'll be there tonight,' said the guard. He led them along the corridor.

'We had some of the emergency food,' George told him. 'In the hut.'

'Ah, better put it back,' said the guard conscientiously. 'You never know.' He unlocked a compartment door. 'A few tins of meat and some Christmas pudding,' he suggested, picking up some packages. 'Keep for ever, this stuff. And some tinnies. That should be all right, mate. You can pay when you buy your ticket.' He glanced up on the thought. 'You've got money, have you?'

'We're loaded,' said George. He was about to take the food and beer and jump from the train again when the guard did it first. He was elderly-looking but he dropped lightly to the ground. He was quickly back, waving his flag and blowing his whistle from the short embankment. The long train began to groan, the engine heaved and wheezed. They began to move westwards across the desert.

'You even made your beds,' said the guard approvingly. He glanced at George. 'But you're a Pom. I s'pose you would.'

'We're trained,' said George.

The guard whispered. 'The kid's blind?'

George nodded.

'Here, I'll give you a good compartment for yourselves,' the man offered. 'He won't want people staring at him.'

George was becoming accustomed to the illogicalities of people's regard for blindness and he merely nodded as if grateful. The guard opened a polished wooden door and let them into a narrow two-seated compartment. The seats were facing each other.

326

'Tea's at five,' said the guard solicitously. 'We get to the Alice at nine thirty.'

He left, closing the door with deference.

'He changed his tune,' commented Ollie settling back. 'Was it because of me?'

'I showed him we had some money,' George said. 'At first he thought we were going to rob the train.'

'You're a lying Pom,' retorted Ollie but without heat. 'Being blind's got its advantages. I could even get in the pictures free.'

'You're not missing much here,' George told him looking from the window. 'It's like it's been nearly all day. Dried red mud most of it. Not a duckbilled platypus in sight.'

The train was only trundling, a velocity it scarcely exceeded throughout its journey.

'If this was England I s'pose it would all be green, would it?' said Ollie challengingly.

'Blazing green,' assented George. 'Woods and meadows and peaceful villages. Ah, it's bliss. Cows parked here and there. Milkmaids in smocks.'

'With big knockers?'

'Enormous. Developed by carrying the milk churns across their shoulders. And there's cricket on the village greens and the huntsmen in their red coats. It's like one big happy jigsaw puzzle.'

'Do you know any poems?' asked Ollie.

'Some,' said George. His surprise made him hesitate.

'Tell me one then.'

'What shall I tell you?' George recited. 'Oh, tales, marvellous tales, of ships and stars and isles where good men rest.'

'That's a good one.'

'It's "The Golden Road to Samarkand". It's by James Elroy Flecker.'

'A Pom?'

'One of the worst,' confirmed George. 'I forget what comes next but there's a bit about "The world's first huge, white-bearded Kings". My stepdaughter Tina sent it to me in a letter.'

'Where's Samarkand?'

'I'm not all that sure. Sort of Persia, I think. In Russia now, I expect. Quite a lot of places are. Flecker lived in Cheltenham.'

'That's in England, is it?'

'The very best of England. They have a famous girls' college there.'

Ollie blinked his lids. 'That reminds me,' he said cautiously.

'Of what?'

'When we get to The Alice do you think I might be able to . . . you know, George . . . have my first . . . serious woman?'

'We could send a message ahead and have them lined up on the platform,' said George.

'You're taking the piss. I'm twenty years old and I've not . . .'

'Sorry, but how do I know?'

'It's just that I think about her,' Ollie said grumpily. 'Like what she will be like.'

'I'm not sure what the crumpet situation is in Alice Springs,' said George. 'We should have gone to Las Vegas.'

'There's bound to be *someone*,' said Ollie.

George felt a rush of compassion for him. 'Listen, with your charm you'll be all right. If you find you've got too many to handle perhaps you might give your mate here a little thought. I could do with some carnal knowledge.'

'A naughty,' corrected Ollie. 'It's called a naughty.'

The guard came in and George paid him for the tickets and the food he had replaced in the shack.

'That old place,' the guard said, 'belonged to a missionary once. He went out there to convert the Abos, but they wouldn't be. So he just stayed there, for years and years, till one day the guard on this train found him dead by the side of the track. The dingoes had been chewing him. I always thought it was a waste of life. You got anywhere you're going to lodge in The Alice.'

Ollie shook his head and George also. 'It shouldn't be too difficult should it?' George said.

'Sometimes,' said the guard. 'The Alice is a great place for passing through. People coming and going.' He produced a card from his pocket. 'Todd Villa,' he said. 'My daughter's place. Very clean and all right it is too. She'll have rooms. She'll be at the station anyway. She always comes down to see me. They put some traffic lights in the Alice and her husband got himself knocked down and killed. Last June. So she's trying to make a living. You'll like it there.'

XVI

Her name was Clementine. There was a statue of a camel at the station at Alice Springs, commemorating the dauntless animals and their Afghan drivers who opened the routes through the dead deserts of Australia, and Clementine was half hiding behind it. Her father came from the train and they embraced.

'I brought you a couple of lodgers,' said the guard. 'This is them. I don't know what their names would be.'

'I'm George Goodnight,' said George. He realised Ollie was trying to contact him with his stick so he shuffled nearer. 'And this is Oliver Loving,' he said. A grateful tap came from the youth.

'Oliver Loving,' Ollie confirmed, saying his new name to a stranger for the first time. He smiled and his lids blinked. He thrust his hand out into the void before him and gently Clementine shook it. 'My friend is a Pom,' said Ollie nodding to the position which George had just vacated.

'So I hear,' laughed Clementine. 'If you really need some accommodation, I have room. My car's outside.'

Her father had duties with the train and left them. 'That's all I see of him,' said Clementine with a shrug. 'Once every couple of weeks.' She looked around. 'Have you got much baggage?' she asked. Ollie's rucksack and George's modest suitcase were on the floor.

'We travel light,' said George picking up his bag. Ollie found his pack unerringly. She watched him pick it up.

'The car's parked,' she said. 'I'll have to get it.' She walked away.

'What's she like?' asked Ollie eagerly.

'Too old for you,' George told him firmly. 'About thirty or so. Very nice. She's about five feet three, neat, brown hair and kind eyes.'

'What else?' asked Ollie.

'I'm not telling you.'

'I like to know, you know.'

'In this case I've told you enough.'

'I can't help it. All I've got is my imagination.'

'Stop moaning. Here she is.'

A dusty estate car drew up, the woman's bright face in the open window. 'It's no use cleaning it,' she apologised. 'It's just as bad in an hour. It's a gritty time of year.'

They put the bags in the back and both climbed into the rear seat. As they drove, the town went by, streets with wooden walkways, the sun fierce on the road.

'That's the new traffic lights,' she pointed out. 'Some people haven't got used to them yet.'

Her house was on the edge of the town beside what appeared to be the excavations for some future highway, a broad trench of sand and dust. 'The River Todd,' Clementine indicated. 'Most of the time there's no river to see. Then it rains and you'd think the Pacific Ocean was coming by your door. We had some black fellows washed away last year. They sleep on the riverbed because the gods protect them.'

The house was wooden, two-storeyed, painted grey with white edgings. The door was open and a brown dog lounged on the porch mat. 'There's a dog in the way,' mentioned George quietly to Ollie. He had now become accustomed to guiding him by a single touch on the elbow.

'There's no way of moving him,' said Clementine. 'I'm afraid you have to remember to step over.'

'I won't step on him,' said Ollie.

The woman glanced at George as if fearing she might have offended the youth but George reassured her with a small smile. They stepped inside. A song sounded from a radio.

'It's a nice house,' said Ollie at once. He looked around the hall unseeingly. 'It feels fresh, you know what I mean? Like you get some air through it.'

Clementine looked pleased. 'That's very difficult here,' she said. 'But we do get some cool from the trees at the back. It can get very cold in the winter. In the twenties in the day, but at night you need a fire.'

It was ordered and freshly-painted inside, all white boards, with dark wooden furniture, some old scenes in frames, a baby

330

grand piano and lace curtains briefly moving at the open windows.

'It's a good day for getting some air through,' said Clementine. 'Sometimes it's so hot you have to shut everything up and hope the fans work. But there's a sniff of breeze today.'

They went into the living room where a cat was stretched on the sill, its stripes interlaced with the stripes of light through the shutters. There were chairs with faded cushions and a long flowered sofa, used books in a case, and the radio still broadcasting the song, unfamiliar to George.

'I'll show you the rooms,' said Clementine. 'There's a big one, and a medium-sized one overlooking the garden.'

Hurriedly Ollie said: 'I'll take that.' He looked defiantly to where he believed George was standing. 'I can manage.'

George, who was on his other side again, moved silently round. 'I'm certain you can,' he said. 'I'll still be able to hear you snoring through the wall.'

She showed them into the smaller room first. Ollie turned his face in half a dozen directions, his nose extended. 'It's fine,' he said. 'It feels really good to me. Just leave me here, will you? Can I shut the door?'

'It's seventy-five dollars a week,' she said, 'each. Is that going to be suitable?'

'That will be fine,' said Ollie. 'Won't it, George?'

'Very good,' said George. He grinned at Clementine.

'I'll show you the other room,' she said hurriedly. They walked along the landing. 'How long will you be stopping, do you think?' She opened the door. The room was on the cool side of the house at that time of the day. There was a double bed, an electric fan, a dressing table and a double wardrobe. On the walls were some monochrome drawings of the Outback. The veil of lace curtain stirred at the window.

'What a pleasant room,' George said. He walked a pace or two inside as if to test it. She moved to the window and pulled a curtain a little aside.

'The river view,' she smiled.

'I don't really know how long we'll be here,' said George looking out at the arid watercourse. 'We don't have any fixed plans. We're just wandering about. Seeing things. Or I am.'

'How long has he been like that, poor lad?'

331

'Blind? Since he was fifteen. An accident. I'll tell you about it sometime.'

'You're like his father.'

'Acting father, I suppose. He's a very good kid.' He stood back from the window. 'If we take it a month at a time, is that all right? I feel like settling down for a while. I've been on the move for months.'

She said: 'You must tell me about that too. A month at a time is fine.'

'A month in advance, the rent?' he said.

'If that's all right with you. It's the usual arrangement. And . . . and it would be useful at the moment.'

They walked downstairs, tapping on Ollie's door as they went by. He called that he was going to take a shower when he had unpacked. They went into the living room and walked out into the garden. There was a wooden garden seat under an awning. Well-watered flowers crowded gratefully under the shade.

'Would you like a beer?' she asked. 'Or, being English, perhaps you'd like a cup of tea.'

'Being English, I would,' he replied.

She went back through the french doors. He sat down in the shade and stretched his legs out. The grey-striped cat appeared and after giving him a cursory examination jumped up and sat on the seat beside him.

Inside the house the faint music was still playing. He could hear the sound of teacups. A memory of Molly walking through the garden at Somerbourne Magna, tea on a tray, wearing the blue dress, came to him.

'Sugar?' Clementine called from the house.

'Yes please, two,' George called back.

A smug and enveloping feeling of safety, comfort, came over him. Sitting in the shade, the cat, the sound of teacups. He recognised it as domesticity.

On the second day they were returning to the house, nearing it, both sweating, tramping along the dusty riverbed, George telling Ollie what there was to see, when Ollie said: 'Somebody's playing a piano.'

It was several paces more before George could hear it.

'It's coming from our house,' Ollie said. He was always

332

pleased on such occasions and he cocked his ear like a red Indian detecting a distant drum.

They went into the garden, gum trees fanning out shade, and went towards the open window of the sitting room, standing outside the limp lace curtain. Clementine was playing hesitantly, some tune neither of them knew. She stopped and they heard her say, 'Hell.'

George began to applaud and Ollie joined him. She began to laugh in a slightly embarrassed way and called out: 'Don't spy.'

They went through the open door, stepping over the stretched dog. The hallstand, the photographs and the tiled floor gave George a sensation of familiarity, as though he had known them for a long time. Ollie went up to his room, confident on the stairs, also at home. George walked into the room where Clementine was sitting at the piano. 'What was that you were playing?' he asked.

'You probably didn't recognise it,' she laughed but he thought a touch wearily. 'It's an old thing. I used to play it years ago, when I played first.'

'When was that?' He sat on the fringe of an armchair. She was wearing a light brown dress, her hair rolling a short way over her neck.

'At school,' she replied. 'A long time ago. I didn't bother with it for years but last June, when Frank, my husband, died, I thought I would take it up again. Something to do.' She turned fully away from him as if studying the music on the stand. 'It was funny, if anything like that could be funny. The piano came in the day after the coffin went out. The Aborigines who live out here on the river thought it was another coffin coming *in*. They're as superstitious as hell, you know. They decamped, cleared out, and they haven't been back since.'

George said: 'It must have been a terrible experience for you.'

'It certainly was.'

'It was a road accident, wasn't it? Your father said something about it on the train.'

She played a few disjointed notes. 'Historic in its way,' she said. 'They put the traffic lights in at The Alice. They're the only lights between Darwin in the north and Port Augusta, which is not far off Adelaide – in other words, the entire length

333

of Australia. Nobody here knew what the hell to do about them. People were driving miles just to avoid them. There were crashes. But Frank was the first casualty. He walked across on the red.' She half turned and smiled seriously. 'I'm sorry. There's nothing more dreary than a sorrowing widow, is there? They say the first year is the worst.'

'Don't apologise. It must be very difficult.'

'Difficult, that's it. They say that after the first year, the anniversaries, Christmas, New Year, and what-have-you, it gets easier. After June seventeenth I'm going to be getting better.' She shifted right round on the seat. 'Would you like a beer?'

'Yes, thanks. I could do with one. We walked to the actual Alice Springs.'

She rose and he followed her into the kitchen. A miniature radio was relaying messages from remote places. Clementine turned it off and said: 'It's a long time since I've been to the springs. When you live in a place it always seems you don't bother about going. It's always there, so I suppose you always think you can go tomorrow.'

'It's very peaceful,' he said. She opened a can of beer and gave it to him, opening one for herself. They drank from the tins. 'The water and the trees and the old cable station.'

'That patch of water is sacred,' she smiled. 'It's the only wet thing we've got until it rains. Once that dries up The Alice is in trouble. Did Ollie enjoy it?'

'Ah yes. I told him everything I could see and he paddled in the water and had a sniff of the trees and felt some of the walls of the cable station. That's all he can do. Unfortunately.'

He had already told her how and why they were travelling. 'Accidents,' she sighed. 'Poor little chap.'

'He wants to climb Ayers Rock,' said George.

'Take a guide and you should be all right.'

'How far is it?'

'From here it's about three hundred and sixty kilometres. It's about four hours, a dead straight road. When are you thinking of going?'

'I don't know. He seemed to have temporarily forgotten it. When he's ready he'll say. It should be in the next few weeks.'

Clementine turned to him, the incongruous beer can held up

334

to her gentle lips. 'Let me know,' she said. 'Maybe I could come too. That's something else I always meant to do.'

Within a month George was unofficially employed by Sack and Sack, lawyers, in Erskine Street, Alice Springs, doing research with land and property matters, while Ollie was working at the Todd River Camel Farm.

There was a bar next to the white, wooden office of Sack and Sack, called Traces. The owner, Dimitri Papalangelos, had worked in the opal fields in South Australia, and he called his bar Traces because that was the term used when the first signs of an opal seam was discovered. 'Me,' he confided to George, 'I found the biggest opal ever found at Coober Pedy. That's the place where you don't say nothing if you find opal. They're all Greeks and Italians and Serbos and Croats down there. They live under the ground, you know that?'

George said he had heard.

Dimitri said: 'They live secret. Dig, dig, dig. Even in their houses they dig, through the walls, see? Sometimes into the house next door. Maybe when the lady is in the bath.'

'You found the biggest opal?' said George.

'Sure I did. Me. Dimitri Georgios Eric Papalangelos. I find it and, like everybody, I don't tell nobody. I just keep it, hug it to myself, you know. Take it everywhere. All secret.'

'Everywhere?' said George.

'Sure. That's how I lost it.'

'You *didn't* lose it? Not the biggest opal in the world?'

'Sure, I lost it. Like I'm telling you. You not heard this story about me?'

'No,' replied George truthfully. 'How did you lose it?'

'Down the dunny,' sighed Dimitri spreading his hands. 'Sitting there, looking at it, thinking about when I should get out. You say nothing, you just get out, see. And she slipped from my hands.'

'They're very slippery, opals,' agreed George.

'You been in Coober Pedy?'

'No, but I've heard about it.'

'It went down the hole.'

'No!'

'So it did so. Down the hole in the dunny. Splash! And those dunnies are the deepest holes in Coober Pedy.'

'Didn't you try to get it back?'

'Try? Sure, of course I try. Sent down a diver, everything, but nothing. It was lost.'

George drank his beer. It was evening and he usually called into Traces on his way home. Dimitri polished the bar, served other customers, and polished the bar again. His polishing brought him back to George. 'How is that boy of yours?' he asked. 'He's down at the camel farm, right?'

'Right,' acknowledged George. 'He's doing well. He likes the camels and they like him.'

'He takes people for rides?'

'The camels know the way,' George assured him. 'They always go the same route following the riverbed. The fact that he can't see where he's going doesn't make a lot of difference. And he helps out cleaning up.'

'Cleaning up camels? Phew!' grinned Dimitri. He polished harder. 'How long since he can't see?' he said.

'Since he was fifteen,' said George. He looked into the pond of his beer. He was in a cream shirt, brown shorts and long socks. His hair was cut. 'He's not my son, you know.'

'I was thinking he was. It seems like you're his father. He's a good kid. But it's tough.'

'He'd like a woman,' mentioned George. His eyes came up from his beer.

'So would I,' said Dimitri fervently. 'All I got is a wife.' He laughed roughly. Then he said: 'You mean, like a nice girlfriend?'

'I mean like a woman. He'll get a nice girlfriend at some other time.'

Dimitri nodded. 'I see it now. You mean he wants some *experience*. To give him confidence. To break his duck, like we say.'

'Exactly. I don't suppose there is much of that sort of thing around The Alice.'

'There's that sort of thing around everywhere,' said the Greek wisely. 'If you know where. In The Alice there's Kate, Caravan Kate that they call her. She's in that business line.'

'How do I find her?'

'Well, it's not always she's here. She travels, you know, with her caravan, that's why they call her that. Sometimes she's at the Alice, sometimes at Tennant Creek or even up to Darwin.

336

One day she was down at Onadatta. She goes where she feels like. When she's at The Alice she goes down by the river. You see her caravan there, out a bit, twenty miles or so. Where she's not too much to be seen. I'll let you know when she's here next. I can find out. She's okay too. About twenty-five. Years, I mean. Not dollars.'

'Jesus, George, I'm so nervous.'

'Do you want to go back?'

'No. God, we've got this far. If I went back now I'd never do it. But, I'm shaking.'

'Don't shake. Remember it's a caravan.'

'Stop making jokes. She's really nice, is she?'

'She's really nice,' George reassured him. 'I wouldn't tell you otherwise.'

'Not hard-bitten or anything?'

'Not hard-bitten or anything. You just go and let her do the rest. She's looking forward to it.'

'Why?'

'Oh Christ. Because you're a young chap and it's your first time.'

'I suppose there aren't that many blokes get to my age still being a virgin.'

'These days, you do have a certain rarity value.'

They were sitting in a car George had rented, below some gum trees, looking out over the desolate bed of the Todd River. On the other bank a white caravan stood below another clutch of trees. The day was late and becoming dim. Ollie was staring through the windscreen as if he could see.

'Are you ready to go?' asked George looking at his watch.

'Yes. Yes ... but ... George, just tell me again. Tell me what she's like.'

'All right. She's twenty-five. About five foot three. Nice-looking figure. Not too big, but everything where it ought to be.'

Ollie braced himself. 'Right, then. I'm ready for it.'

He opened the door of the car, got out and stood helplessly. George regarded him with pity. He left the driving seat and took Ollie's elbow, only a touch to show him the direction. Ollie had his stick. 'We're going across the riverbed,' he instructed. 'So we have to go down the bank here. It's sort of shale.'

He helped the boy down the three-foot bank and they walked together across the wide and sandy shape of the dried watercourse. It was uneven but easy. Quickly they were at the other bank. As they reached it the door of the caravan opened and out stepped Kate. She had put on her best clothes and her jewellery. Her face was flushed in the dusk.

'Let me help you up the bloody bank,' she shouted cheerfully. Ollie had reacted at the sound of the metal door opening and now he tightly held George's hand. Kate regarded the boy and looked at George. 'Come on up,' she called after a moment. 'That's the best place. By the stones.' George manoeuvred Ollie to the place she indicated and she reached down and held his free hand. He allowed her to guide him up the bank. George remained in the riverbed. Kate took Ollie to the caravan and returned to George. She handed down Ollie's white stick.

'I'll go back to the car,' he said looking up at her. His face was on the level with her exposed knees. 'How will I know when to fetch him?'

'I'll flash a light,' she said. She hesitated. 'I'll look after him,' she promised. 'I feel quite honoured.' She turned and walked with a brisk sway back to the open door of the caravan. George watched her go anxiously.

Retracing his route across the dried shoals of the river he climbed the opposite bank and turned to look at the caravan once more. Pink curtains had been decorously drawn across the lit windows. The sky was becoming very dark. He returned pensively to the car and sat down to wait.

Even after all the years, he had no difficulty in remembering his first time. It was just before he had gone to university, 1960, when general copulation was just becoming fashionable. After years of meaningless mutterings and hopeless post-dance manipulations on doorsteps it had happened to him easily and abruptly and to his considerable astonishment. Adele Verity, a pear-faced full-bodied girl, whom he had taken out several times without much accruing, had without warning plunged her hand down the front of his trousers.

'I can't find it,' she complained in a whisper. She began to rummage around.

338

'It's in there somewhere,' he recalled replying hoarsely. God, he hoped to God it was not going to let him down. Not now.

It turned out that she had just started on the Pill and was anxious to see if it really worked. He was a test case. Her parents were upstairs asleep in the semi-detached house. It was summer and he could hear her father snoring through an open window. Temporarily leaving the mysteries of George's trousers, and with a conjurer's smile, she produced a key and held it up. It opened the laundry room, a place isolated behind the kitchen. They had crept in there and had spread a whole binful of damp un-ironed clothes on the floor and there made love. Even now George recalled the odour of Oxydol.

His remote reverie was disturbed by something striking the roof of the car. At first he imagined that a fragment had fallen from the tattered trees below which he had parked. But the firm tap was soon followed by another and then several and, within a minute, the mightiest rain he had ever known was pounding like a hundred drummers.

So fiercely was it dropping that he felt certain the car would be dented. Outside the windows the water was like a metal curtain. The din was thunderous. He crouched lower in the driving seat and thought of Ollie in the caravan.

There was nothing he could do, only sit and wait for the end of the engulfing deluge. Thickly it fell for another half-hour. When it had eased to the intensity of a normal storm he caught a flick of light in the driving mirror. He grunted and stretched from his crouch. Grumbling, he decided to wait, perhaps the rain would stop entirely. It did not and after ten further minutes there came another flashing signal from the bank of the riverbed.

He picked up Ollie's white stick and with no cover or protection at hand he left the car and ran through the downpour towards the near bank. He was soaked before reaching it. The lamp, like a light buoy swaying out at sea, signalled again and he cursed. 'All right, I'm coming, I'm coming.'

It was very dark on his side and he slithered down the decline into six inches of swift-moving water. It filled his shoes and ran gurgling around his ankles. The river was thickening. Apprehensively he took one stride forward. His shoe came off in the mud. Bending and cursing he located it, pulled it out of the water and then took the other off also. He threw them back onto the bank, turned, strode and stumbled forward. To his relief the water became no deeper and shoals and islands were still clear of the surface, but everywhere was cloying sand or sticking mud. Increasingly swearing, he forged on through the ooze below and the rain all around until he reached the distant bank. He could see the caravan door ajar now and that the lamp was being poked through the aperture.

Ollie's face in the doorway greeted him rapturously. 'Great, George! Thanks, George! You came to get me.'

Standing, puffing and soaked, his hair plastered like a skull cap, George snorted: 'No, I'm just practising swimming the bloody Channel.'

Caravan Kate's face appeared in the cosy, lit interior behind Ollie. 'Oh, he's been a gentleman,' she enthused.

'I'm pleased,' said George sourly. 'Why didn't he stay the night then?'

'There was no way of letting you know,' said Ollie. His face was shining. He was still within the van. 'We didn't know morse code, did we, Kate? Anyway, I want to come back now.'

Water was running down the inside of George's trousers. 'I'm getting pneumonia,' he complained.

'Oh, come on, George,' admonished Kate. 'Don't spoil it now.'

He looked at her speechlessly. Eventually, level-voiced, he said to Ollie. 'We'll have to go now, before the river is over our necks.'

'That won't be for hours,' said Kate helpfully. 'Little shower like this won't do anything.'

'Oh good,' breathed George. 'Are you ready, Romeo?'

'Ready,' grinned Ollie. 'I don't care if I do get wet. Goodbye, Kate. Thanks for everything.'

'It's all right, darling. Thanks too. You're a lovely boy.'

She leaned over his shoulder, he turned his head and they kissed fully. He jumped from the caravan with a resounding splash.

'Oh, it *is* raining, isn't it,' he said mildly.

'Of course it's bloody raining!' retorted George pulling him towards the bank. 'Come on, for God's sake.' Ollie turned and waved back towards the caravan.

They got to the dark and slippery bank and slithered down it, George still muttering and cursing. Ollie kept laughing.

340

They staggered through the mud, sand and swiftly running water, sometimes up to their knees.

'George, she was a good sort! It was bonza, George!'

'Yes, yes. Let's get across before we're drowned.'

'We won't, George. Kate says it's just a shower.'

They splashed and splattered on, Ollie flailing with his stick, George grasping his other hand or sometimes clutching him round the waist to stop him falling. Twice he himself fell onto his hands and knees in the slime. Frightened, Ollie called out: 'Where are you, George? Where have you gone?'

'I'm here,' sighed George wetly as he rose. 'I'm still with you.'

The rain was thickening again, drumming down on them as they fell and faltered through the morass and the darkness. Ollie gabbled on about the wonders of Caravan Kate, and at the very centre of the slippery river, where it was darkest and with the downpour descending ferociously, he stopped, grabbed at George for support with one hand, threw his white stick up into the storm and raised his freed hand in a salute of triumph.

'Ya! Yoo-hoo-hoo!' He shouted. 'I'm a man!'

'I couldn't hear a word, George, and she couldn't hear me.'

'Like being inside a drum.'

'Deafening. I was dead scared, I can tell you, what with one thing and another. I mean I was nervous enough to start with but with all that racket banging on the tin roof . . . well.'

Ollie was sitting in his bed, chest naked, eyes batting, hair shining. George, wearing his pyjamas and robe, sat on the edge.

'Now you're *sure* you want to tell me?'

'Of *course* I want to! I've *got* to tell you! Christ, George, I've got to tell *somebody*, haven't I?'

'Yes, I see. Some things are like that.'

'Are you going to listen? Or do I have to go and tell Clemmie?'

'No, no don't. I think it had better be me.'

'So do I.'

'All right. I'm listening.'

'Good. Well, it was belting down on the roof. It was scary but she . . . Kate . . . shouted in my ear that there was nothing to worry about. It had rained plenty of times before. The only trouble was that we had to keep bawling at each other, at the tops of our voices because you just couldn't hear a thing. It was hard going, I can tell you.'

'And not all that romantic.'

'It was, though, in a funny way. I think she honestly enjoyed it.'

'It must have been a change from whispering sweet nothings.'

'That's just what she said. I mean she was bloody hoarse in the end, but it *was* different, there's no getting out of that. Especially for me, it was.' Ollie paused. Because there was nothing in his eyes it was difficult to judge his expression. George stood up.

'Don't go yet, George,' said the young man.

'Oh, sorry. I thought that was it.'

'There's a lot more. I just have to be careful how I tell it. I don't want it spoiled.'

'You're certain you don't want to keep it to yourself.'

The young man turned his bright face, quickly, and said, 'No, hang about a bit. I'm only going to tell it to *you*.' George sat on the side of the bed again. 'She was really nice to me,' continued Ollie. 'I could feel she was coming towards me. She put her arms round my middle and her chest . . . you know . . . her chest . . . pushed up against me. Honestly, I didn't really know what to do. I just sort of dropped my chin on it. It was like a pillow. Two pillows. And then . . . are you still listening?'

'Of course I'm still listening.'

'Good. Thanks, George. Well, then she caught hold of my hands, which were sort of spare, and guided them up so I could feel her blouse. She put them on the buttons and I unbuttoned them. It was a lace sort of blouse. I remember my mum had one once, when I was a little kid, and I always liked it. I even put it on once when she was out but it looked ridiculous. But now this was great. I undid the buttons, six altogether, right down, and opened the edges of the blouse. She kept telling me things but I could hardly hear her because of the racket the rain was making. We had to keep shouting at each other. It's a wonder you didn't hear me from across the river.'

'It was raining on the car roof,' George pointed out.

'So it was. Sorry. But then it all . . . took place . . . George. It was better than I'd ever thought. It was beaut, George, it was beaut.'

342

'You seem to have enjoyed it,' mentioned George mildly.

'I'll say. It was different . . . better . . . than I could believe. Thanks for taking me, George.'

'That's all right. I would like to say the pleasure was all mine, but it obviously wasn't.'

'You should try it, George. With Kate, I mean.'

'Yes. It would bring back a few memories.'

The youth laughed. 'I'm telling you like you didn't know it existed.'

'Don't worry about that. I'm not sure I did.'

'Get away.' Ollie suddenly dropped back on the pillow. 'It's tiring, though. I'm shagged out.'

George rose. 'You'd better get some sleep then,' he said. 'I'm glad it was all right.'

'It was, that's for sure.' The boy settled back on the pillow. 'You know what's next, George?'

'Ayers Rock,' guessed George.

'That's it. I want to climb Ayers Rock.' He paused and seemed as though he had suddenly gone to sleep. 'At night,' he added.

George was working late at the office with papers appertaining to some land rights in the Never-Never. The sun had dropped into the iron hills and the earth began to breathe once more. He went for a beer at the bar next door to the office and then drove out to the camel farm. Ollie usually finished about seven, after the last of the day's tourists had gone, and was driven home by a young girl with a station wagon. The same girl, slight and brown, her fair hair pulled back into an uncompromising pigtail, was standing in the yard of the farm when he drove in. He had heard Ollie refer to her as Linda. She waved as he got from the car.

'You come to pick him up?' she said. She climbed over the wooden bars of the corral fence. She was wearing jeans and an open shirt showing her slight brown neck.

'I was late at the office so I thought I might as well,' said George. 'That's if it's all right.'

'It's all right,' she said. She was watching for something in the evening distance. 'You're George, I know. He's told me about you.'

'And you're Linda,' said George. He looked in the same direction. 'He's really taken to the camels.'

'They've taken to him,' she replied. 'You can't fool a camel, you know. You can't bully them either. We had a man here who thought he could. He struck a match on the camel's arse. The camel kicked him and then sat on him.' She nodded towards the horizon. A small dust smudge, like a bush, had appeared. 'Here they come now. He's got some Americans. Do you want a beer, George?'

'Thanks,' he answered. He was getting accustomed to the unending tinnies and stubbies now. Distances were measured by how many tins of beer it took to drink on the way, roughly a tinnie every two miles. She went into the wooden office. George sat on the fence, his knees thrust forward out of his shorts like pieces of brown rounded wood. Linda came back and tossed a tin to him while she opened another herself. The camels had become small moving bumps; the dust cloud grew.

'He's got a natural feeling for it,' said Linda. 'A real aptitude. Because he's blind, I suppose. Above all, you've got to have *feel* with a camel. The camel can do the seeing. He knows where he's going.' She was a very small girl. Her face was neat and her top teeth projected a little. She half turned to him and asked: 'How long do you reckon on staying at The Alice?'

For some reason the question surprised him. 'I don't really know,' he admitted. 'We've not talked about it.'

She appeared relieved. 'You seem to have sort of settled in. Look at you, you've got a job and everything. And Clementine makes you comfortable.'

'We seem to have settled in, as you say,' George agreed. 'The job is strictly unofficial. I don't even have a work permit, but nobody seems to mind out here, and I thought I might as well be occupied. It's only temporary.'

'You like it, though?'

'Oh yes. There's nothing like negotiating land rights in the Never-Never.'

'Clementine told me what you were doing, travelling around. I think you've been great for Ollie.'

The camels were clear now, trudging along the dry riverbed, strung out in their own skirt of dust. George finished his beer.

'He's been very good for me,' he told her. 'He's been a companion. More like a son.'

344

'He's beaut,' she added simply. She climbed down from the fence and threw the beer tin accurately into an empty oil drum they used for rubbish. As she began to walk towards the nearing camels George threw his tin at the drum and missed. Linda grinned at him. There were five camels. Ollie was on the back of the leader, swaying easily with the movement of the animal.

'See,' said the girl. 'He was made for it. Gan-Gan knows it too. That's the camel.'

The short caravan turned slowly into the yard. The Americans, two middle-aged couples, were voluble. Linda went forward and helped them down as the beasts folded their legs. 'George is here,' she called to Ollie.

Ollie shouted to George and then slid down over the leading camel's neck as it knelt. It turned its great soft and sleepy head and made to nuzzle him. He patted its flank and it obediently and ungracefully rose and strutted away towards the compound.

'If your mother could see you now,' said George seriously.

'I sent her some pictures,' Ollie said. 'But they're beautiful. I wish I could see them as well.'

George agreed. The beasts were noble-faced and softly coated, walking away towards the compound and their evening meal with a remote grace.

'There are more camels in Australia than any country in the world,' said Ollie with a sort of pride. 'They've sent some from here back to the Arabs for breeding. They're that good.'

Linda was waving to the Americans departing in their car. She walked towards Ollie and George. 'Was everything okay?'

'Fine,' said Ollie. 'We went as far as the old watermill. They didn't work me out. I'm just like everybody else when I'm up there.' He turned towards George and pushed out his hand to make sure he was still in the same position. 'I've got some more to do,' he said. 'They've got to be fed and groomed, so I'll be some time.'

Linda began to smile. 'I'll give him a lift,' she said. 'It's on my way.'

'Yes,' said Ollie. 'It's on her way.'

George left them and walked towards his car. He had rented it for a month and then another. The third month was approaching. He drove through the chasm through which the road and the railway reached Alice Springs, the gateway through which the pioneers, laying the telegraph cable across

Australia, had entered the bowl of countryside and found fresh water. The town was low and white with few buildings rising above the others. He knew some people now and several waved to him as he pulled up in the traffic. It was a good time of day, shadows slung like hammocks across the streets. On the outskirts of the town the houses supported piles of logs, for the nights of winter that turned cold. He turned the car off the main highway and drove alongside the arid river once more. The house came into view and he felt a pleasure in seeing it. It had become home.

Clementine was sitting watching television. She seemed introspective. George said he would wait for Ollie to return before eating.

'Do you want a beer?' she asked.

'Could I have a cup of tea?'

'The beer not good enough?' She smiled amiably at him. As she went towards the kitchen she brushed by him, the folds of her light dress against his bare knees.

'Do you mind?' he called after her. He sat on the settee and looked at the television commercials. 'Making tea?'

'Not at all. The tinnies get a habit, that's all. I'll have tea myself.'

When she had made it she returned and unselfconsciously sat beside him. He sipped from the cup.

'Excellent,' he said. 'Good texture.'

'As good as your wife made?'

'Yes. Quite as good.' He took another sip. The piano lid was closed.

'I haven't heard "Where the Wattle Grows" recently,' he commented.

'I got fed up with The Wattle,' she said. 'Whether it grew or not. Playing the piano is too damned solitary.'

'Tennis.' He suggested. 'Try tennis.' He suddenly realised that England was on the television. A green farmland scene, chalk cliffs and a massive sea running onto shingle. Clementine glanced sideways at him as they sat beside each other on the settee, the teacups held before them.

'Homesick?' she asked.

'Suddenly, yes,' he nodded pensively. 'Yes, oddly enough, I am.'

An English voice began to describe the geological formation

346

of the Channel coast. 'Alice Springs must be in a fever,' he commented.

'They put all sorts of things on. It's a wonder it's not about China,' she said.

'Then the Chinese get homesick,' he said. He leaned closer to the set. Fields and short hills and lanes were appearing. A dog ran across a green slope rounding up puffballs of sheep. 'It's odd,' he said. 'I didn't realise I'd been so long away.'

She stood up and took his cup. 'Sometimes I think I'd like to live in a green country,' she said as she went towards the kitchen.

'You have to put up with the rain,' he called after her. 'Not rain like here, a downpour then out comes the sun. England is a grey country.'

He watched the rest of the programme while she prepared the evening meal in the kitchen.

'Was it like that where you lived?' she asked coming back and looking at the fields on the screen.

'In between the houses,' he said. 'The trouble is you don't notice it. Appreciate it, I suppose. There was a man who used to fish in a small river. Every night I used to see him from the train. I swear he used to stand there just to make me livid. That was the nearest I ever got to everyday nature. I used to watch it on the box, just like this.'

A station wagon pulled up outside and they heard Ollie tapping his stick quickly along the path. When he came into the house he said: 'Linda's friends are having a barbecue. Is it all right if I go?'

Clemmie was standing at the kitchen door and George was sitting in front of the television. It was as though they were a family. George said: 'Clemmie's made dinner now.'

'It's all right,' Clemmie said. 'It can go in the freezer.' The boy thanked her and went back outside. He tapped his way back to the vehicle.

'That was odd, wasn't it?' said Clemmie remaining at the door.

'I know what you mean,' agreed George.

'Just like he was . . . a son,' she added going back into the kitchen.

They had spent only a little time together in the weeks he had been in Alice Springs. Ollie was usually there in the evenings, listening to music through earphones. George would read the newspaper or watch television. Occasionally he and Ollie had gone as guests to the ex-servicemen's club. Clemmie often went out to see friends or brought them to the house. Tonight they were in together.

George was suddenly aware of the odd domesticity of the situation when they sat down to dinner at the kitchen table.

'Quite like old times,' he joked awkwardly.

'For me too,' she said.

They managed to converse through the meal. He helped her to wash up and they returned to the sitting room together. She went to the piano and opened the keyboard lid. For twenty minutes she played while he sat in the easy chair.

'That's all I can do,' she said eventually. 'The full repertoire.'

'Play it all again,' he suggested with a grin.

To his surprise she said, 'All right, I will,' and began to play once more.

'Does it sound any better?' she asked over her shoulder.

'Wonderfully so,' he lied.

He had never seen a picture of her husband in the house, which he thought was strange. Now, leaning over to the bookshelf he took out a photograph album and he saw at once that it was full of them. He had been a lean man, and careless-looking; his shirt was torn in the first picture and he had failed to shave in several others. He had an Australian nose, sharp and thin, and strong eyes which may have been laughing and may have not.

'That's Frank,' she said as she half turned.

'Yes. I can see. Do you mind?'

'Not at all. There's a whole lot in there taken at the regatta last year.'

George looked up. 'Regatta? You have a regatta?'

She left the stool. 'I'll say we do. It's famous.' She walked over to him and sat on the arm of the chair.

'What do you do for water?' he asked.

'We do without it.' She took the album from him and turned a few pages. 'There. See. That's how it's done.' Her voice had dropped. George could see that Frank was in most of the pictures. 'It's called Henley-on-Todd. Big day of the year in the Alice.'

He laughed when he saw how they did it. The races were

348

held on the dried-up riverbed, the competitors encased in wood and cardboard boats through which their legs projected.

'It was great,' she said sadly. 'That's Frank in the middle of that crew. And that's him in the doubles and the mixed crew.'

'Where are you?' he asked. 'I don't see you anywhere.'

'Oh, I took the pictures,' she said.

She stood up and, handing the picture album back to him, went towards the kitchen. 'Beer or tea?' she called back.

'Tea, if you don't mind,' he said.

'You're breaking me of the habits of a lifetime,' she said with studied cheerfulness. 'Right, tea for two it is.'

George bent over the photographs. Frank, laughing, shouting, stripped to the waist, wearing a swaggering cowboy hat; face burned, eyes alive. In two of the cardboard boats he was partnered by a dark girl, a pretty face, hair hanging free; breasts prominent beneath her dress, short-skirted, legs brown.

When she brought the tea into the room Clemmie said: 'They were the last pictures of him. A few hours later he was dead. It was that day.'

George closed the book too quickly. 'I'm so sorry,' he said. 'I didn't realise that.'

'It's all right,' Clemmie said quietly. 'I take it out and go through it myself sometimes. It gives me the excuse for a bit of a cry. But I don't have Frank's picture around the house. I found that too painful.'

They sat, a few feet apart, drinking the tea. 'Was he from Alice Springs?'

'No, South Australia. Near Port Augusta. He always said he was just passing through, you know. Most people are doing that. He'd tried most things, prospecting and that sort of occupation, and he had a go at various business schemes but nothing much worked. When I first met him, just after I came here from Melbourne, he was cleaned out. Didn't have a cent.'

She stood up, firmly, went to the window, and stared out into the warm darkness. From there only a few lights of the town were visible. 'It's a real breaker of dreams this place is, you know,' she said. 'The Alice is famous for it. You should go to the museum and see the aeroplanes that have crashed in the Outback, and they haven't been found for years. One pilot wrote his will on the side of the plane. And there's cars they've found way out beyond civilization and no sign of the people. It's a hell of a big country for getting lost.'

She turned and walked back into the room. 'Do you want to see the news?' she asked. 'It's ten.'

George turned on the television.

'In the cemetery there's the grave of Lassiter,' she said. 'Funniest-looking tombstone you ever saw.'

'I've seen it,' said George. 'You can see it from the road. Red stone.'

'That's it. It's supposed to be Lassiter himself. He looks like a dwarf hunchback. And he's clutching a pan or a sieve or something.'

'Ah yes. He spent all his life looking for a lost gold seam,' said George. 'But he didn't find it.'

'Never did,' she agreed. 'He saw it once, so he said, but when he went back he couldn't find it again. Probably plastered. All his life he wandered about looking. Then he vanished and they didn't find his bones for years. Frank is buried in that cemetery.'

She said she was going to wash her hair before going to bed. George remained watching the news and the sports programme which followed. The telephone rang. It was Ollie to say he was spending the night at the house of Linda's friends.

A feeling of solitude came over George, a melancholy, a mild sensation of wanting to be part of something again. He went to his room and put on his pyjamas. He had brought a book up from the sitting room and he put it beside the bed.

He went out onto the landing intending to go to the bathroom. Clemmie had left her room at the same moment, in her dressing gown and slippers, her hair in a towel. They turned a corner of the landing at right angles, all but colliding and both letting out exclamations. Then they both laughed before stopping at the same instant and looking at each other.

Suddenly her face fell against his chest. 'I won't keep you,' she whispered as if that aspect had been on her mind for some time. 'I won't stop you going.' She pulled the towel away and her damp hair fell down at the front and the back. George laid his cheek against it. He could hear one of their hearts thudding against her breasts.

'We'll be company for each other,' she whispered.

XVII

During the half an hour that it takes the sun to set, the great mound of Ayers Rock changes colours many times. They watched it from the car, Clementine dictating the shades to Ollie as they occurred. 'Lilac, blue . . . pink . . . rose . . . what would you call that, George?'

'Heart attack puce,' suggested George who was driving. Ollie leaned over from the back.

'It's a real show,' said Clementine. 'And it's good because there's nothing else to see.'

'Wild camels live around here,' said Ollie looking about with his blank eyes. 'Watch where you drive, George.'

'If I hit one with this thing he won't be wild, he'll be furious,' George said. 'God, now look at it. What's this called, Clemmie?'

'Blushing rose,' decided Clementine. 'And there's the reception committee.'

Three large, old cars were drawn up at the side of the track. The men grouped around them were Aborigines. Even at a distance and in the deepening dusk their stooping postures identified them. George brought the car to a halt and they all got out. There were eight men and two boys. The leader was the biggest, a wide, shaggy-bearded man wearing a tartan jacket over baggy trousers.

'You want to climb the Rock?' said the leader with some aggression.

'That's it,' said George. He wondered whether Aborigines shook hands. No one offered. 'My name is George Goodnight . . .'

The man gave him no time to introduce Clementine or Ollie. 'Great Big Charlie, I am,' he said fiercely. 'These others got names but they don't matter.'

George regarded the man with surprise and Clementine and Ollie grinned.

'We can see in the dark, you know,' offered Great Big Charlie.

'That's why we need your help,' said George like some explorer who has chance upon natives of uncertain demeanour. 'We want to go up at night.'

'Without us you don't go up,' said the Aborigine. 'It's two hundred dollars.'

'I understand,' said George. 'You want it now?'

'Yes, now. You might not come down.'

The three whites laughed but not the tribesmen. George took the money from his wallet and handed it over. Great Big Charlie counted it pedantically and then indicated that they should follow him. George turned to lock the car but the Aboriginal leader shook his head. 'Nobody steal that,' he said. He narrowed his eyes and looked through the car windows. 'Nobody,' he confirmed.

They began to walk towards the glowering rock, the three visitors with Great Big Charlie, the other natives slouching behind. 'Ayers Rock,' announced Charlie unnecessarily pointing towards it. 'About one million and a few years old. Sixteen people have died on the rock in the last century. Seven from falling, the rest from heart attacks.' They were adjacent to the first shoulders of the mountain now. Charlie slapped it like an affectionate keeper might slap an elephant. 'Here we got the memorials of the dead people I just told you about.' On the rock were some bronze plaques. Charlie produced a pocket torch and ran its beam over the nameplates. 'This one died on his birthday,' he said. 'It was his life's ambition, it says.'

As they continued to walk round the indented base Charlie leaned towards George and said confidingly: 'I bet you're surprised.'

'Well, not actually *surprised*. I've seen pictures of it,' said George uneasily.

'Not the *rock*,' said Charlie in a hurt way. 'Me. By the way I talk, eh? I bet you thought we all talk like "Fella belonga Missus Queen across the Wuk-Wuk. All yellow inside like Missus Queen". That sort of crap.'

'I hadn't thought much about it.'

'No? Well, I got a degree in Pidgin English from Queensland University so I speak it better than anybody. But it's dropping out of use. The boy's blind, I see.'

'You saw right,' replied George acidly. Great Big Charlie felt in his pocket and took a fifty dollar note from the money that George had given him. 'Reduction for him,' he said. 'Blind man in the dark.' Nonplussed, George accepted the returned note.

The party paused at the mouth of a long defile. 'That's the way up,' said the Aboriginal leader pointing like a visionary. 'You be back here at three thirty in the morning and make a start then.' He glanced at George. 'Don't worry about your money. It's safe. We're licensed. No point starting now. You'll be at the top in the dark and it can blow chilly up there. The idea is to see the dawn. We got to go back anyway. We got a rehearsal tonight. They're having a *Son et Lumière* at Darwin next week. About the Dreamtime and the Never-Never and we've got to get our act together. Crocodiles and everything.'

'What are we going to do until three thirty?' inquired George. 'Spin yarns and watch our billy boil?'

'There's a pub a few miles back down the road. New place. Quite good. Go there and get back here at three thirty.'

George sensed there was something else that Great Big Charlie wanted to say. As they turned to walk back to the cars he kept opening his mouth then closing it again. George thought he might even be catching flies. They had reached the vehicles and the tribesmen had pointed out the way to the pub when George said: 'Which of your chaps is going to be our guide?'

'I was going to talk to you about that,' said the Aborigine defensively. 'We're a bit short-staffed. We've got a lot of ceremonies on. All over the place. So we can't get you a first-class man. In fact, we didn't get you a man at all. Alf!'

Alf was one of the young boys. He disengaged himself shyly from the others and shambled forward.

'Alf,' repeated Charlie pointing by way of introduction. 'He's just a kid.'

'Does he know his way up the rock in the dark, that's the point?' said George.

'Oh, he knows,' Great Big Charlie assured them. 'He's one of our people, so he knows.' George realised that something detrimental to Alf was about to be exposed because Charlie took out the money and began to peel off a further fifty dollar note. Silently he handed it to George. 'He's got one drawback,' he said looking at the ground as if he had detected tracks.

'And that is?'
'He's scared. He's shit scared.'

At three-thirty they arrived at the rendezvous, thoroughly frightening the boy Alf who had dozed off under a blanket using Ayers Rock as a pillow. He jumped a foot into the dark air when George called to him and was a dozen yards into his run before he realised his error.

'Lots, big ghosts around here,' he excused himself as he shuffled back. 'Bigger ghosts up top. It's okay for Great Big Charlie home in bed.'

The lad was wearing the blanket like a poncho about his neck. Below, he was clad in dangling shorts and a pair of gaping army boots. George shone the torch over him.

'You send me back,' suggested Alf hopefully. 'Say you don't want to go up.'

'We want to go up,' George told him firmly. 'I think we'd better make a start or we'll miss the sunrise.'

'Rain tomorrow,' said Alf dolefully. 'The forecast is big rain.'

'Let's go,' urged George. Responding to the Englishman's push Alf set off along the base of the rock until they came to the incised defile. The Aborigine looked about him as though hoping some final postponement might present itself. When it did not he shrugged and began the gradual ascent.

At the luxurious Sheraton Hotel at Yulara that evening, the pub to which they had been directed, they had planned their order of climbing while listening to a string quartet play Vivaldi. Roped together, Clementine was to be first following the guide, with Ollie after her and George at the rear in case anybody fell.

It was only moderately steep after the first few minutes and a roving moon appeared, sidling around the mass of the rock as though seeking them out and anxious to light their way.

After twenty minutes they gained a shelf of rock and the guide sat down heavily and indicated that they should unloop the rope and do likewise. From below his blanket he produced a cigarette and a box of matches. He lit it and smoked sullenly.

George said to Ollie: 'There's not much to see so far. Except the moon's put in an appearance.'

Clementine shifted along the ledge towards George. She leaned near. 'He keeps letting off,' she reported in a whisper.

354

'Who? Alf?'

'Who else? I'm right behind him too and it's not very pleasant. I think it's because he's scared.'

'He *keeps* doing it?'

'Yes. He's done it six or seven times. I haven't counted.'

'Perhaps Ollie had better go up the front,' suggested George.

'Thanks a million,' said Ollie. 'You know my senses are hyperactive.'

'I'll go then,' sighed George. 'If he starts with me I'll mention it.'

He turned to Clementine. 'Will you be all right at the back?'

'Better than the front,' she said.

Alf said: 'Okay. One more up.'

They rose, put the ropes round them, and George took his place behind Alf, who made no comment on the change. After ascending a further twenty feet the boy emitted a little squeal of wind. George recoiled but he continued to climb. There came no further farts, however, before the narrow rock funnel opened and they could see the moonlit sky above them. They reached a second ledge and Alf turned to that. They took off the rope. The guide squatted and lit another cigarette.

'How are you getting on up front?' asked Clementine.

'He seems to have called a truce,' reported George.

Once more they formed up, donned the rope, and began to climb; over them now were open spaces in the rock. The sky expanded visibly around them, the moon dipped. Alf let off again. But they were almost at the flat summit. There remained another crevice, steep but well-used and not difficult. The Aborigine slowed as he was about to clamber out of the cleft and emerge at the top. The ragged army boots were on a level with George's forehead. They took a few more stuttering steps and then disappeared from view as their owner stepped out into the starlight. As George was about to make the final ascent there came from above them a long cry, a howl of shimmering terror. The rope slackened, and suddenly came writhing back like a snake. The three climbers solidified in the crevice.

'God, what's he seen?' demanded Ollie from behind.

'Hamlet's ghost, I think,' George answered. He climbed the remaining six feet. As his head rose above the summit level he saw Alf's boots standing untenanted on the moonlit rock, roughly aligned, the toecaps pointing out. There was no sign of Alf.

Ahead, however, was a darkened figure crouched close to the surface, appearing to drag itself forward.

'Okay, mate,' came a voice. 'Come on over. I've done my leg.'

'There's somebody up here,' George informed the others below. 'He's hurt. Alf's run away.' He clambered clear and turned to give his hand first to Ollie and then the heavily-breathing Clementine.

'I'm not sorry that's over,' she said. She stared ahead at the low moving form. 'No wonder he took off.'

They walked forwards towards the figure. He was a white man, crouched like a crab. His skinny face accentuated his brittle eyes in the moonlight. 'I've done my leg,' he said again. 'Fell on the way up.' Almost as an afterthought he added: 'There's another bloke. He's fallen down. On a ledge down there. Probably broke his neck.'

George took half a dozen paces to the edge. The moon glowed across the Outback landscape far below. At first he saw nothing but then, half turning right, he made out a figure lying on a shelf twenty feet down. The precipice did not seem unduly steep. 'There's somebody down here,' he called back to Clementine and Ollie. 'I think I'd better go and take a look at him.'

'Careful,' warned Clementine. She came over to stand by him and held his hand. 'It'll be daylight soon.'

George said: 'I'd better go down. It's not too steep.'

He lowered himself over the lip of rock and cautiously felt his footholds on the way down. It was not difficult although the drop was sobering. He reached the ledge and made his way along it. The head of the prone figure was lifted as he approached. 'Hello, Goodnight, old man,' said the man cheerfully.

It was Burtenshaw.

Burtenshaw was lying in the Flynn (Flying Doctor) Ward, his legs embarrassingly hauled up in traction, his left arm stiff across his chest like some sort of fixed political salute.

'Don't laugh,' he pleaded when George walked in. 'I can't bear it when people laugh.'

356

'It's a temptation,' admitted George. 'How are you feeling?'

Burtenshaw grimaced. 'Like I look,' he grumbled. 'Trussed up.'

'Trust Burtenshaw,' recalled George. 'That's what they used to say at the paper. Trust Burtenshaw.'

'Don't bloody gloat, please,' said the reporter. 'I've also missed the story, you realise that. First time in years I've failed to deliver.'

George said: 'I sent them a cable, unsigned, by me that is – I put Great Big Charlie's name on it. After all, he was responsible for the whole thing. By now your nearest and dearest will know you have survived.' He felt sorry for Burtenshaw; suddenly, as he said it.

Burtenshaw confirmed his pity. 'There's nobody near or dear enough to care, old chap. Only the boys in the Bailiff Club. They send their regards by the way.'

'Oh thanks.'

'Great Big Charlie is not an inappropriate signature, come to think of it. What a way to screw up a story.'

'Even the helicopter crew complained about your language,' said George.

The man in the bed sighed so deeply that his legs swung like twin booms and the bed creaked. 'It was all so well planned. I was going to give you the shock of your life, Goodnight.'

'You came close.'

The man in the next bed began to groan. They looked towards him and Burtenshaw said: 'There's enough stories in this place to fill a paper. He's had a tumble with a crocodile.'

'Saltwater or fresh?' asked George.

'What's the difference?'

'Whether it eats you or not. The saltwater variety are fond of humans. And they're a protected species now. The trouble is they know it.'

The pinioned Burtenshaw was regarding him with some envy. 'I would hardly have recognised you, George,' he said. 'You've changed . . . You look ten years younger and . . . well, you weren't the most interesting character around.'

'This sounds like the opening of an interview,' said George.

'If it is it's not going to do me much good,' the reporter grumbled. 'Christ, I can't move a finger. I even have to have someone help me pee . . . oh, and by the way, do me a favour.

Ask the sister if I can have the young nurse to assist me. They keep sending an old bag.'

'I just can't get over you following me up Ayers Rock,' George said. 'All the way from London.'

'I can't get over me falling at the last fence,' moaned the reporter. 'It was that potty Ocker's fault. Pissed when we started out. One slip too many and pushed me over the side.'

'According to the newspapers, he's a hero,' pointed out George. 'Crawling to get help.'

'That's the bloody press for you,' grumbled the journalist.

George said: 'But . . . I can't understand the whole business. Am I of that much importance?'

'Not importance, old son, *interest*. You're of great public interest. Successful lawyer, job, family, home, all the rest of it, takes off, goes walkabout. You did what thousands, no *millions*, of men would like to do – run away. And women too. It's romance and adventure. What happens next? See tomorrow's issue.'

George regarded him narrowly. Burtenshaw coughed and his encased legs began to sway about, causing a further onset of creaking from the bed. The man who had tangled with the crocodile turned towards them, a manoeuvre which clearly caused him anxiety. His face was a railway junction of stitches. The man closed his eyes in a groan.

'I'm not allowed to tell him jokes,' nodded Burtenshaw. 'They've just sewn his ears back.'

'How much did you dig up about me?' resumed George.

Burtenshaw peered in a pleased way through his dressings. 'Quite a lot, to tell the truth, old man. I'd got quite a dossier. The more I found out the better it looked. The editor was worried about doing a series because of your connection with the paper, but when I told him some of the choicer bits he could hardly refuse. I was on the next plane to Sydney.'

George said: 'You went to see Felicity, didn't you.'

'A couple of times. That's how I knew your address in Sydney because she'd sent you the stamps. That was a bonus really because I'd already got a whole lot of stuff from the Australian CID through a contact at Interpol. I'd have found out anyway. I went to the lad's house, Ollie's – God, travelling across the Outback with a blind kid, I couldn't *make up* a story like that. Ollie's mother told me you were in Alice Springs and it was easy – I followed you to Ayers Rock. I was going to get a picture of you as you reached the top of the rock, with the blind lad and the lady, and then I was going to interview you up there, whether you liked it or not.'

'And if I'd said "no comment"?'

'Oh, I'd have made it up. I didn't come all this way to lose. I've got enough background stuff anyway, from Somerbourne Magna onwards. All that was needed was a few deathless quotes.'

George put his head in his hands. 'And you're still going to do this series or whatever?'

'As soon as I can get a tape recorder.'

'That's honest, anyway.'

'It's the best way.'

After hesitating, George said: 'And how was Felicity?'

'I wondered when you'd ask. Bloody lonely and bloody unhappy.'

'Oh dear.'

'What did you think she'd be, Toast of the Town?'

'She didn't need me. I was an encumbrance.'

Burtenshaw said: 'I'm not saying she wants you back. Far from it, mate. That is a very bitter lady. They found your car, by the way.'

George looked up hurriedly. 'The car? Good God, I'd forgotten. Where?'

'Burned out in a wood, everything gone. Gypsies, they reckoned. And Molly's still got your suit at Somerbourne Magna.'

'Jesus wept, you *have* been busy.'

'Well, that bit was easy. Just followed up the car incident. And Felicity told me she'd telephoned you at the Red Cow, anyway.'

'Yes, she did.'

'And the lawyer Wintle and his wife saw you there.'

'Bloody hell!'

'I got that lead from Felicity too, I'm afraid.'

'She certainly spilled the beans.'

'The asparagus more like it. The expenses were heavy.'

'Oh, I see.'

'After Somerbourne Magna I lost you for a bit. In fact your

story jumped way ahead and I had to fill in the Cherbourg episode later.'

'And how did you discover that? Even later?'

'Stamps again. Your friend Freddy Birch. He didn't see any reason not to tell me because Felicity had the stamps back by then. He was also in a domestic corner, his wife . . . Cecily, is it? No, Cynthia. She had him by the short and curlies – divorce, money, all the bad news and he wanted to keep clear of all that.'

'So he shopped me?'

'It was all old stuff by then. Just in-filling. In fact I only went to Cherbourg a short time before coming to Australia. I went to see Monsieur Julien, he's the only stamp dealer in town, and although he admitted that he had met you he would not let on.'

'I'm glad somebody can keep their mouth shut.'

'Yes, that was a closed door. Mind you, I'm sure I could prise it open. I didn't have time.'

'Good. Where do we go next?'

'Rome. That's a peach of a story.'

'Who told you that?'

'Well, quite honestly, that was a gap too. I mean, at the start, I'd lost you between Somerbourne Magna and India. Your picture roped up to that dishy dancer was a godsend. In fact that was the thing that really spurred me on the trail. I thought: "What else has quiet, grumpy old George Goodnight been up to?"'

'What about Rome?'

The young nurse approached. 'Would you like tea?' she asked Burtenshaw.

'I'd like you to do the bedpan,' suggested Burtenshaw.

'Not while we're serving tea.'

'All right I'll have tea then.'

The girl glanced at George. 'Will you help him drink it?' she asked.

George said he would. She did not offer him a cup for himself. He picked up Burtenshaw's cup and, at the nurse's prompting, tasted it to make sure it was not too hot, and then lifted it to the reporter's lips.

'Rome?' he prompted.

'Ah yes, Rome. Well, when the pictures and the story from

360

India appeared – "English Lawyer in Indian Court Drama", you know, "Tied to Girl Dancer". It was marvellous stuff. We had a big spread, so did most of the others.'

'I'm not proud of it,' grumbled George.

'No, no. I'm only speaking professionally. Now where were we . . . you?'

'Rome,' repeated George.

'Ah yes. Well, when the Indian story appeared we had a call from a chap called Lowndes who said he had known you in Rome and had a story he wanted to sell us.'

'Lowndes would sell his mother,' grunted George.

'We didn't want his mother. He came down to the office – he's in some sort of high-powered Government security.'

'God help them.'

'Possibly. But he had this great tale to tell of the Arab sheik, how you saved his life in Rome and he took you back to the Gulf. It's a terrific drama, old boy. I actually went through Verdi's door at the Grand Opera Hotel, just like you did.'

A sort of hostile admiration was dawning over George. Burtenshaw detected it quickly. 'It's a great yarn, isn't it?' he said. 'It's "Round the World in Four Hundred Days".'

'Yes, it is,' agreed George. He wanted to leave now, to get out.

'Don't go,' said Burtenshaw. 'There's not that much more.'

'I know,' said George dully.

'Somehow I lost you in India. You vanished. The next sighting I got was when my pal at Scotland Yard tipped me off about this Interpol report of your trouble in Hong Kong and Sydney. He recognised your name.'

'I should have been called Smith.'

'That's the lad's name, isn't it?' said Burtenshaw. 'Oliver Smith. But he calls himself Oliver Loving. What's all that about?'

George said, 'He can't spell Smith.'

'You're getting fed up.'

'I am. Very.' He lifted the cup to the reporter's mouth again and Burtenshaw drew in a mouthful of tea.

'Thanks,' he said. 'They brew good tea here. I wonder if they do cake?'

'I'm not feeding you cake.'

'Why don't you just feed me the story?' His legs began to

swing again and the creaking started. He managed to still them. 'Tell the lot – you write it. Chistmas in prison and everything. Only *you* know the whole tale. The paper would pay you very, very well, you know.'

George stood up. 'I think you know the best bits,' he said. He regarded Burtenshaw strapped in the bed. 'At least you won't follow me now. Cheers, old man.'

He turned and went towards the door. The man in the bed called after him through the bandages! 'I'll find you, Goodnight. Don't worry. Read it in our next.'

George drove home grimly. Ollie was at the camel farm. He went into the house and found Clementine in the kitchen moodily peeling vegetables.

'I'm going to have to go,' he said sadly.

'I thought you might,' she said.

The road that runs straight and north from Alice Springs to Darwin, one thousand three hundred kilometres, is laconically called 'The Track'. It travels through some of the world's most gutted landscape, often made beautiful by patterns of sky, sunrise and sunset, and broken at places by green gorges with rivers. On the way also are small towns, staging posts, established in the vicinity of water by nineteenth-century pioneers playing out the first message cable across Australia to link with a sea-line from Singapore. When the junction was finally made, Sydney and London were in telegraph contact for the first time.

'She's a good lady, that Clemmie,' said the driver of the road-train. The casual compliment came after almost one hundred unerring miles. Straight and empty before them the road pointed. The great truck tugged three heavy trailers.

'She's very nice,' agreed George. The cab was air-conditioned. As the truck grunted along the highway the radio played; pop music, and people calling from remote outposts requesting more pop music. George had tried to sleep and the driver had turned down the volume. He scarcely needed to drive. Sometimes he switched the automatic gear into 'cruise' and rested his sandalled feet on the wheel.

'She seemed upset to see you go,' continued the man. He had a surfy's hair, dyed blond above his brown face. 'And the blind kid. I didn't know blind people could cry.'

'They can if they try,' said George.

'How long you been at the Alice?'

'Four and a half months.'

Something on the direct but dusty road seemed to demand the attention of the driver, although George could see no hazards or change in the vacant landscape, for he fell silent. They stopped at Tennants Creek and George went to the lavatory at the service area. As he sat there he could not remember leaving anywhere with so much regret as he had left Alice Springs. But a time came to go from anywhere. He was tempted to telephone Clemmie from the cafeteria but after getting change at the counter, he put the coins away. He was glad for Ollie. The previous evening he had been walking along the bank of the dusty Todd River, as naturally as a man in England might have strolled beside a reflective stream, when he saw a camel coming from the opposite direction. Linda was on its back.

'I thought you'd be out here,' she called down. 'It's the sort of place people come to do their thinking.' She looked around at the dried mudbanks.

'You wanted to talk,' he suggested craning his neck to speak to her. 'About Ollie.'

'Yes. He's just told me.'

'About leaving.'

'No. I know that. He's told me his name's not Oliver Loving, it's Ollie Smith.'

'Do you want to come down, or shall I come up there?' asked George, still looking up awkwardly. The camel's head, soft and strong, came round like a crane to give him an amiable nudge.

Linda spoke to the beast, which knelt awkwardly, its legs seeming to collapse one by one. She dismounted and patted its flank. It trundled off along the riverbed. 'Ba-Ba wants to do his business anyway,' she said. 'It's best to let him wander off. Camels can be shy.'

The sun had finally set after an agreeably moderate day: the Outback seasons were changing. Rain would come in a week or so. At the side of the riverbed was a group of ashen gum trees and George and the girl sat on the tough grass below.

'Are you disappointed?' asked George. 'About his name. My fault, I'm afraid.'

363

'Relieved,' she corrected. 'He's in a state now, you know. He wants to go with you but he wants to stay as well.'

George looked across the arid watercourse. Evening was turning on its regular show of colours. 'I think he's got to remain,' he said quietly and regretfully. 'I don't think he could ever be so happy as he is here.'

Her eyes became indistinct. 'Thanks,' she said touching his arm. 'You're a very good man.' Her small, brown puckered smile came back.

'Are your intentions honourable?' he grinned.

'Very,' she replied simply. 'I think he's the most remarkable boy I've ever met.' She paused then said: 'I've begun to love him very much, George. But there is a problem. I know he feels deeply for me too, but it's his blindness keeps getting between us. I want to marry him but he won't *ask* me.'

'These days,' said George raising his eyebrows, 'I didn't think ladies felt it necessary to be asked.'

She smiled. 'Equality hasn't travelled this far yet. But it's not that. I *would* ask him. I think so much of him I wouldn't back off doing that. But he's told me that he's likely to get a big financial settlement because of his accident. I don't want him to think I'm pushing him because of that.'

'Linda,' said George flatly. 'You ask him to marry you.' He opted for a large lie. 'His settlement is going to be minimal. I know because I've been getting the correspondence about it. I was the one who allowed him, encouraged him, to appeal against the fifty thousand damages he was originally awarded. I'm afraid it's turned out to be rotten advice. The whole thing has backfired. The only reason I haven't told Ollie is that I keep hoping things back in Sydney will take a turn for the better. Unfortunately they do not seem to be doing so. His lawyers are pessimistic. Very soon I was going to have to own up to him.'

Her face livened with hope. She said: 'Fifty thousand dollars is not very much these days, is it? And he has to think of his mother.'

'Exactly. There are also the substantial costs of the appeal. Frankly if he gets out with half that amount he's going to be lucky.'

She wiped her mouth with the back of her hand, like a child. 'I'm so glad,' she said. 'I mean, that's peanuts, isn't it?'

364

'It'll hardly pay for the honeymoon,' smiled George.

'And you don't mind?' she asked.

'He's not mine,' George told her. 'I just borrowed him.'

She looked as if she were going to cry. Instead she said: 'Ah, here's Ba-Ba. Look at the grin on his mug. You can always tell when a camel's had a satisfactory crap.'

'That Frank, the bloke Clemmie married,' said the road-train driver. They had travelled a further hundred miles since he had last mentioned the subject. 'He was no good to her. No bloody good at all.'

George was amazed. 'No good? I thought they had been happy. They hadn't been married long.'

'Too long for Frank,' he said. His eyes were steady on the straight, sunlit and empty road. He even had both hands on the wheel. 'Frank was a loose sort of bloke. He got himself engaged one night, on a promise at a barbecue, to Doll Henderson. Then Clemmie arrived and he turned around and married her, just like that. A month later he was back sniffing around Doll again, and others, allowing for the shortage of sheilas in this part of the world. In broad daylight too,' he muttered. 'Right out in the open. Showing off about it.'

'I see,' said George unhappily.

'You *should* have seen. Humiliation, I can tell you. The day of the last regatta he spent all his fucking time with the other girl, Doll, leaving Clemmie on the side. I even saw Clemmie taking pictures of them.'

'I saw them,' agreed George. 'But I didn't realise the circumstances.'

'Oh, there were plenty of circumstances, mate. It was after the regatta he got hit by the car.'

'So I understand.'

'Do you know what time it was?'

'No.'

'Four in the morning. At The Alice traffic lights. He was going home from Doll's place, drunk as a dingo. He went across on the red and just about the only moving car for fifty miles hit him.'

They drove while the day settled around them. The long straight road turned to bronze, the bordering wilderness dark-ened. They veered into another stopping place, a staging post, where several road-trains were parked, the bulky containers making a separate village of their own. The driver was getting off and a relief man taking over. He shook hands with George and wished him a good journey back to England.

England. George had known it all the time, but it was the first time he had fully acknowledged to himself, or anyone else, that he was going now in the general direction of north and home. The Alice had been the end place, the turning point. He sat in the cafeteria and thought of Ollie and Clementine. The lamb and chips and salad he had ordered arrived cold as stone and he grumpily sent it back. 'The Pom's whingeing about the grub,' he heard someone shout from the kitchen. It came back very hot; the lettuce sizzling, the tomatoes grilled, the cucumber charred.

Morosely he ate it. He was tempted then to go out and board the first Alice bus or hitch a lift on a south-going road-train. But he knew that was no answer. At some time in the future he would have to get out. It was not only the threat of Burtenshaw. In the end he had to go home.

He began to think, as he often did when lonely and low, of Janine. From his pocket he took a folded slip of paper with the name Mrs Joan Vaughan, Old Pump, Koora, Northern Territories. He had found the address in the Darwin telephone directory. He had telephoned from Clementine's house but the number had been discontinued.

The relief driver came up to the table and sat down. He was an older man, a squat Italian, almost black with the sun. He wore shorts and a sweatshirt with the simple word 'Roma' on it.

In the excruciating half-Austalian, half-Italian of those who had emigrated to the new land too late to change, the driver told him that he had once found the biggest opal in the world at Coober Pedy. George listened indulgently. They rose, as the tragedy was retold, and went to the waiting road-train. They climbed up each side of the high driving cab and were in their seats and on their journey before the Italian came to relate how he dropped the opal down the dunny.

'Do you know a place called Koora?' George asked the driver. 'It's on this road.'

'Sure, Koora,' answered the driver. 'You know somebody?'

George took out the slip of paper with Mrs Vaughan's

address and the Italian, putting on the interior light, took both hands off the wheel and both eyes off the road to read it. 'Vowgan,' he recited. 'I tell you the place. I know Koora. The Pump, she is still there.'

'How far from here?'

'Maybe four, four-half hours. You sleep, mate, I wake you.'

George uncomfortably slept, gripped by disturbing dreams. Myfanwy had stolen an opal and was being pursued by a posse of familiar people: Molly and Lance Onions, dead Wolfgang, the man with the orange-peel teeth from Hong Kong, and even old Fearnley-Banks who was running well, coughing but keeping up. As she passed him in the dream he was aware of Myfanwy's bounding breasts. She was a good distance ahead of the field and even had leisure to pause and confide to the dreamer that she had stolen the opal from her mother's gas meter.

When he woke the first inkling of dawn was on the edges of the earth. He felt wretched and aching.

'You didn't forget Koora, did you?' asked George.

'Twenty minute more. Maybe half-hour,' the driver said. 'I no forget. I no forget anything alonga da Track. Not many places to forget.' He sighed: 'Thata opal. How I came to lose it? Jesus, thata opal.' The tale had altered amazingly little.

'Koora coming up now,' said the Italian eventually. 'The Pump about two kilometres.' In the broad headlights of the great truck the name sign 'KOORA' showed up against the early hour dimness.

'You wanna stop?' asked the driver.

'For a couple of minutes.'

'Sure. Bit of a funny time to go visiting.'

'I just want to take a look. If I have to stay longer, you carry on and I'll get a ride later. I'll pay you the full amount to Darwin.'

The Italian in the dimness looked mildly insulted. 'You stoppa here, you only paya to here,' he said conclusively. 'Go take a look, see.' He began to brake. The long and ponderous trailers had to be slowed expertly and it took time. They came to a final stop at the side of the road where a single wan light peeped through the void. 'Somebody home,' commented the driver. 'I wait.'

George jumped to the ground. The driver opened his window

and said: 'Maybe you break your neck. Take some light.' He handed down a torch. George took it gratefully. Its beam immediately illuminated brown and broken ground ahead and he crossed it with caution. His eyes became used to the darkness and he saw the hunched form of a building where the solitary lamp was burning. As he neared he found a made path and beside it the wreckage of what had been a windmill water pump. The torchlight picked out the struts of the tower and the broken vanes of the wheel. It looked like a crashed aeroplane.

His feeling of uncertainty was replaced by one of excitement. The unreasonableness of waking strangers in the early hours, in an isolated place, was overcome by the breathless thought that in the shack ahead, now revealed with its covering roof against the night-time sky, might *just* be sleeping the lost daughter of Janine Joby. He looked back once more to the massive form of the road-train, its hazard lights blinking, then walked the last few yards to the wooden house. A roused dog began to bark inside.

It was a shabby place. The paint on the wooden door was flaking and as he touched it it came away in a great shard in his hand. The light that he had seen from the road came from a glistening oil lamp on the porch. There was a white plastic bell on the door, like a medal on a grimy old coat. Tentatively he rang and was astonished to hear surburban chimes sounding within. There were movements and voices and the dog increased its warnings. A woman was telling it to shut up.

The door did not open but a window did. A sash was pulled down with a crash that suggested some considerable force was needed to dislodge it. 'Who's out there? What d'ya want?'

Moving to one side, George saw the indistinct shape of a face behind the insect screen that covered the window. It was soon joined by a satellite face.

'It's early hours,' said the woman.

'Yes, I'm sorry,' said George. 'I know it's inconvenient but . . .' then inadequately: 'I was just passing . . .'

'Well, keep passing,' answered the man.

'He's a Pommie,' said the woman sideways. 'A Pommie coming here.'

George took advantage of her interruption. 'I'm going right away,' he assured them swiftly. 'But I'm looking for a Mrs Joan Vaughan. She lived here.'

368

'She's gone,' answered the man.

'Where? Do you have any idea where she went?'

'She's dead,' said the man with finality and relish.

'Oh, dead. Oh dear.'

'Years ago. Six or seven,' said the man.

'And her daughter? She had a daughter . . .'

'Went to America,' said the woman. 'The girl. Don't know where.'

'Is that all?' asked the man. 'We can't tell you any more.'

'No. Well, thank you. I'm sorry to have bothered you. There's no one else in Darwin, perhaps, who . . . ?'

They had gone. The window was pushed up with a thud that sent debris of wood, paint and dirt, scattering down. 'Thanks,' muttered George as he turned and went back towards the truck. He was almost there when the door of the shack was opened and he turned to see a ghost-white shape.

'Pom,' shouted the man croakily. 'Try Los Angeles.' The door was slammed heavily and the dog started howling again.

George climbed up into the cab.

'No good?' said the Italian.

'I've got to try Los Angeles,' grunted George.

'We no going that far,' said the Italian starting the big growling engine.

'You may not be,' answered George closing his eyes and lolling back in the copious seat, 'but I am. It's more or less on my way home.'

Once more he dozed, this time with no remembered dreams, and woke with the bumping change of direction as they turned into another staging area the same as the others, with parked train trailers dwarfing a low-roofed cafeteria. It was daylight. His face sore, his body aching, his spirit low, his cupboard bare, he trudged into the early morning atmosphere of greasy food and hissing steam. Rubbing his eyes he sat down. The driver had gone to the lavatory. When he returned George stood up and went towards the door marked 'Blokes'. There was a double line of urinals in the centre of the room. As he stood at the grim trough another man arrived and stood at the position opposite so that they were facing each other, looking at each other over the curved top of the vitreous enamel. The newcomer was rough-faced and stocky, with a shag of unkempt grey hair chopped off at the neck and short on top, ravaged

369

eyes and a notable nose. 'Only place with decent china along the Track,' the man told George. 'Tin or plastic everywhere else. This stuff came from Stoke, England, just after the war, just after they built the road. I heard you talking to Musso. You're English. So am I.'

'How d'you do,' said George. 'My name's George Goodnight.'

'Blanco Stern,' said the stranger. Oddly, they shook hands across the top of the urinals.

'You called him Musso,' said George. 'The driver.'

'Eytie,' sniffed Stern. 'I call them all Mussolini.'

'Are you travelling towards Darwin?' asked George. He had finished and zipped and was now, out of politeness, waiting for the other man.

'I am,' said Stern. He finished with what appeared to be a flourish and pulled up the fly of his creased white trousers. 'My ship's there. I'm a sea captain. Between Darwin and the islands.'

XVIII

The South Daja Islands, Tanimbar, Selami, the Ewabs and Misool, lie between the Equator and the northernmost capes of Australia. Darwin was far gone, the Gulf of Van Diemen and Melville Island had been navigated, and now they were sailing through the tail of the Indonesian archipelago, northwards into the Pacific.

'Know them like the back of this hand,' mentioned Captain Stern, holding up his hand to show George. He scowled from the wheelhouse window as if challenging any of the palm-treed isles or reefs to shift its position. The back of his hand, the veins, scars and callouses, was itself like a chart. 'Been down here so many years I could swim it blindfold. One day, with this bucket being what she is and the owners broke, I'll probably have to.' The wheelsman, a fat man from Sarawak, nodded in agreement. George could hear the plates of the hull grating and groaning at every rise and every fall of the moderate sea. They were three days out, making a steady six knots.

'Do you have many storms?' he inquired as casually as he could.

'All the time,' muttered Stern. The steersman nodded again dolefully. 'Anytime of the year. They hang around the islands; I think the buggers hide, lie in wait for us, sometimes, and then whoosh, they're on us.' He patted the brass binnacle with belated affection. 'But the old *Outcast* has come through every time. So far.'

'How,' inquired George, 'did she come to be called *Outcast?*'

'*An Outcast of the Islands*,' the captain said, 'That's her full name. But the paint needs doing on the bow. Most of the words have fallen off somewhere. There's not much to be seen on the stern either. You can just about make it out if there's not too much junk, ropes, tarpaulins, crew's washing, and so-bloody-on hanging over. She's registered in Zamboanga on Mindanao. Everybody calls her *Outcast* anyway. Five thousand, three hundred tons of rust.' He gave the Sarawak man a dig in his ample ribs and said: 'We're going to have a drink, Bertram, don't hit anything.'

It was clearly a familiar joke but Bertram laughed anyway. Stern motioned George out of the wheelhouse and down the ladder to the deck. Islands lay low and green off the starboard bow. 'Watu Bela,' said the captain. It was evening.

'All her sister ships were called after books,' said Stern. 'Ten years ago some Americans bought the whole fleet, if you could call it that, and gave them these names. It was a change from *Philippine Star* and that sort of thing.' They went into his cabin. Despite the general decay of the vessel it was lined with fine, deep-coloured wooden panels, it had a beautiful nautical desk, a velvet armchair and chintz sofa. There was a lamp which swung serenely from a chain – and a bookcase of used books. There was also an ancient gramophone with a winding handle. Stern opened a mahogany drinks locker and, without asking George what he wanted, poured out two generous glasses of Scotch. He nodded towards the chair and George sat down. On one wall were framed photographs of other ships.

'That's the fleet,' said Stern after they had raised their glasses. He stood up and studied the pictures as if he had not for a long time looked closely at them. '*Tropic of Cancer*,' he recited. '*The Moon and Sixpence*, *Land Below the Wind* and *Lord Jim*, by Conrad, like this one. She was called *The Nigger and the Narcissus* but the niggers didn't like it when all this equality business came into fashion, so they renamed her.' Each of the vessels looked the same and even the distance at which the photographs were taken could not disguise their deficiencies; they were small, battered and down at the hull. 'They had three more but they were lost,' said Stern.

'Lost?' asked George. 'Oh, I see.'

'Sunk,' confirmed Stern gloomily drinking his Scotch. 'But lost, really, because never a trace of them was ever found. Not a boat, not a man. The Pacific is a big ocean.' Without being asked he poured George another steady whisky, as if it were his due ration. 'How long since you've been home?' he asked and then, as though to avoid confusion, added: 'In England.'

'More than a year now,' said George.

'You'll be back in another,' forecast Stern a little enviously. 'I've been out here so long it's too late for me now. If you don't go within a certain time, ten years at the outside, home is just another foreign port.'

He stood up, a man going to fat, whose hair was falling out. 'This is England for me,' he said. He rose and reached behind the desk like someone revealing a secret niche. 'It's the only place there's room to keep it,' he explained. He brought out a broad, cardboard-covered folio, dull red and worn, the covers buffed, the front lettering faint. 'It's all I've got. I sit some nights, as far away from England as you can be, just about, stuck in this ocean, and have a few Scotches. And I look at it.' He laughed grittily. 'The crew think I'm perving with dirty pictures.'

The wide volume he handed to George was the *Ordnance Survey of Great Britain 1935*. The title page made the announcement in important letters.

'It's not all there,' explained Stern. 'It was half missing when I bought it in Honolulu but all the maps are England. I'm not worried about Scotland or Wales or the Irish, so it didn't matter they were missing.'

George turned the large pages. 'It's altered a good deal since this was published,' he commented. 'The last fifty years have been like two hundred and fifty.'

'Show me where you live,' suggested Stern leaning forward eagerly. He seemed relieved that George had not laughed at him. His eyes were aslant with interest and whisky. 'Try and fix the exact place.'

The ship gave a minor heave, like a sigh of patience, and plodded on through the warm, dark sea. Night had come down with tropical haste. The scent of curry drifted into the cabin. 'We'll eat soon,' said Stern still watching the pages turn in George's hand. 'Can you find it?'

'This is the page,' said George. 'Shillington, see. Between Watford and Hertford.' His finger touched his village. 'It's just a hamlet here, in those days. A church . . .'

'With a steeple,' said Stern leaning over eagerly to translate the signs. 'And there's an inn . . .'

'That's still there. And I suppose this is the main street, but it's more like a suburb now, a dormitory. All this area here, fields and these woods, are built over. My house is about here . . . there . . .' His voice became a little heightened. 'That's the general area. They built an estate called Uplands Valley, although the logic of that escapes me. About this spot.'

His finger, slowly, almost sadly now, found the railway line and he traced the journey he had made so many times: Shillington to London, London to Shillington. He could see himself again in the first class compartment, heavier, suited and waistcoated, pale-jowled, wondering whether to make the effort to read his newspaper and abandoning all pretence of doing so once the other man had grunted from the train at Hartsbourne. And there . . . there was the river, a wriggling blue line. There was the very place where it almost touched the railway. That was where the fisherman stood, that nameless loiterer who unknowingly was the trigger of these distant adventures. George looked closer and in surprise he saw that the river had a name, something he had never considered before. On the old map it said 'R. Dess'. Quite poetic really.

'That's the River Dess,' he said to Captain Stern. 'Very good trout fishing. A chap I know used to fish there all the time.'

'Where else do you know?' asked Stern. There was a knock on the door and a Malay, wearing ragged shorts and a yellowed steward's coat, appeared and said: 'Makan, Captain.'

'All right, all right, Rodney,' said Captain Stern. 'Keep it hot, will you?'

To George's slight surprise the man, seeing what they were about, stepped over the high threshold and studied the atlas also. 'Where Negri Sembelan?' he asked.

'It's not in this book, Rodney,' said the captain patiently. His voice became mock-colonial: 'This is big country, over sea.'

'It says Watford,' said Rodney pointing at the page.

He appeared satisfied with his discovery and went out, his feet padding on the deck.

'Eager to learn, these Kanakas,' said Stern. 'It stands them in good stead when they go home. He'll tell everybody in the village he's been to Watford.' He peered intently again. 'What else can you show me?'

'Here,' said George turning another ponderous page. 'North-west Wiltshire.' There, among the faded contours, was Somerbourne Magna. 'I know this place.'

The map showed how it had been long before the motorway; the London to Bath road straggling across the top, the lanes and the fields clearly outlined. He felt a pang as he picked out

374

the village inn. 'The Red Cow,' he said slowly. 'I stayed there once.' He could feel the deepness of the bed and see the generous and ghostly Molly at his door.

In the hot ship's cabin, far off in the southern tropics, he smelled again the English freshness of her hair and remembered the lushness of her bosom. 'It's a pretty place,' he said to Stern. The hamlet looked much as he had known it, the Somerbourne brook, the church, the piggling cottages. He could even pick out Lance Onions' house beside the footpath going up Somerbourne Hill.

'You can see Salisbury Cathedral from on top of this hill,' said George confidently. 'Beautiful view on a clear day.'

The sea captain, with the habit of a navigator's life, turned the page and then another. 'How tall?'

'Salisbury spire? Oh, I don't know. The highest in England.'

'I'll look,' he said. He appeared urgently concerned, as if checking the navigation of some nearing reef instead of a steeple the remote side of the world. He took a thick paperback from his shelf. Its cover was well handled. '*Facts About England*,' he recited. 'Bound to be in here. Ah, right. Here it is. Salisbury Cathedral spire – 404 feet.'

'That's it,' said George a little puzzled by his intensity. 'That's why you can see it so far away.'

'But you *can't*,' said the captain triumphantly. He refilled both the glasses with enthusiasm, relishing the moment like a chess player about to make the winning move. 'Look,' he said. 'Look at the chart . . . the map.' Busily he flipped the pages. 'See, here you have Somerbourne Hill. Marked 271 feet. Salisbury spire 404 feet. But . . . but look, *between* them we have this . . . Barleydown Top it's called: 480 feet. It says there.' He banged the page with his thumb.' 'Ordnance Survey 1935. And it can't have got any smaller. And it's right between the two! *Between* Somerbourne Hill and the spire. How *could* they see it?'

Deflated, George looked at the three separate pages of the atlas and saw what Stern had said was true. 'Well, well,' he sighed. 'I didn't actually see it myself.'

They had dinner and more whisky and later the captain played some Richard Tauber records on his gramophone. They sat silently and listened.

'Best singer in the world,' said Stern when they had heard them all. 'Was.'

That night the sea rolled long and heavy. George, loaded with rice and whisky, rolled with it. He dreamed deeply that he was once more in the hold of the dhow but that Cecil Meredith and his wellingtoned wife, from the *Sally-by-the-Shore*, were in command and sailing with a crew of Kanakas. He awoke, grunted, and lay in the narrow darkness. He had paid three hundred Australian dollars for his passage. Paulu Batu harbour on the island of Sakang in the Celebes was the first port of call. After that, even the captain did not know where they would sail. It depended on the cargo they could pick up.

George lay and smiled at the thought of Stern and his outdated England; his maps that no longer fitted, only rivers embedded and hills unmovable. 'What can you show me?' he had asked. What had Tina recited? 'What can I tell you? Tales, marvellous tales. Of ships and stars and isles where good men rest.'

He slept again and when he awoke it was bright day, the sun coming like an arm through the porthole when he pushed up the deadlight. He went onto the deck and smelled at once the mixture of spice and motor oil that tells the Pacific voyager he is approaching an island.

They were, in fact, close inshore, the land lying on the opposite side of the labouring vessel. He climbed across some boxes of tinned fruit that formed part of the deck cargo and stepped to the rusty rail on the port side. They were close to a palm-hung beach where a rush of small boys played football on the sand. A man in shorts and a flowered top was the referee. George watched closely to see if the boy with the ball would score a goal. He did and from the deck George joined in the general applause. There was no one to observe his suburban Saturday afternoon enthusiasm for the captain and crew were occupied in coaxing the *Outcast* into the shallow harbour and alongside the jetty.

Eventually the telegraph clanged in a dull way, like a bell with a bent clapper, and the ship lost way, nudging the wood and coral jetty. Ropes were thrown and some languid natives on shore made them fast. Shouts and greetings were exchanged between ship and land and a brown-skinned woman, holding a new baby, waited tapping her high-heeled shoe at the end of the jetty. Two of the natives in the crew began to laugh and shout taunts at another crewman who was standing at the rail, staring with miserable certainty towards the girl.

When the vessel was stilled and tied, Captain Stern left the bridge and came down to where George was standing. 'Paulu Batu, Sakang Island,' he said with a sweep of his arm like a formal introduction. 'If you fancy a good woman, this is the place.'

The Savoy (Air-Conditioned) Bar and Skittles Club was constructed of corrugated iron, threadbare coconuts, and thatch, and was the only place to go in Paulu Batu. As the extravagant Pacific sunset drained over the horizon Captain Stern appeared, arranged, to George's surprise, in an ironed white shirt and blameless shorts. He wore a braided cap, the last light of the sun reflecting on its gold.

'Have to keep up appearances,' he mumbled and then, more fiercely: 'Never let these Kanakas get the upper hand. That's what's been going wrong in the world. Letting the Kanakas get the upper hand.'

George had put on his fawn trousers and a white shirt but he was conscious of his bare feet, almost native brown, encaged in his sandals. Walking along the jetty he felt that Captain Stern had outsmarted him. Although he was a good deal taller and certainly slimmer, the skipper's sudden sharpness, his uniform and his authoritative stride, brought back to him the not unfamiliar sensation of being taken into custody.

As they left the jetty boards and walked on the caked earth of the main street, Stern acknowledged, and occasionally saluted, passers-by and inhabitants squatting in the porches of houses. It was not much of a place. The few shops had desolate windows, having been awaiting the godsend of replenishments from the ship. There was a place with a 'Guinness' sign, which nevertheless seemed to be a dusty chemist's shop. There was a bottled gas depot in an open compound and near it a hill of rusty cans. 'They eat a lot of tinned fruit and stuff in these islands,' said Stern nodding at the pile like a tourist guide. 'It's kept my owners going for years.'

'I thought they climbed for coconuts and fished with spears in the lagoon,' mentioned George.

'Not if they can help it,' the captain corrected. 'You can't live on coconuts, the ground is useless for growing vegetables

377

and they're too idle to do much fishing. So they eat pineapple chunks from Australia. When they need money they stir themselves and get together enough nuts to make a cargo of copra. That more or less keeps them going.'

A huge man in a type of skirt, bare-chested and wearing a cap approached them. George realised he was a policeman because he was leading two unhappy men in chains. He greeted the captain cheerfully and shook hands with George. Then, oddly, he introduced the prisoners, reciting their names and what sounded to be their addresses. The men's demeanour remained sullen but they shook hands and mumbled a native greeting.

'Most powerful man on this island, native anyway,' said Stern as they moved on. 'Rules the place. They chose him because he's the biggest.'

In a few minutes they had toured the town. There were only two motor vehicles, said Stern: the police car and a truck used to unload his ship. Neither of these were in use because the island had run out of petrol and there would be none until the drums had been unloaded from the *Outcast*. 'They'll leave them till last because they're the heaviest,' prophesied the captain. 'Nobody's worked out that if they got them ashore first the truck would work and the rest of the unloading would be easier. I suggested it once but no one acted on it. They don't like making decisions.'

On the outskirts of the town, at the edge of a lagoon separated from the harbour by a coral backwater and butting onto the Paulu Batu public library and unisex conveniences, was the Savoy. Its sign, neon but long doused, proclaimed that it was air-conditioned and that equipment for skittles was available. They paused to view the unpromising façade. Inside the wide doorway several pairs of eyes, eager and young, protruded. 'Skittles used to be very big here,' mentioned Stern laconically. 'National sport. But they lost the last ball two years ago.'

He led George into the obscure interior. An abrupt and heavy clanking began as soon as they entered. 'Turn it off, Sulky, for God's sake,' bawled Stern above the mechanical din. 'You don't have to impress us.' They walked towards the bar which was made from piled and bonded coconut husks. 'That was the air-conditioning,' said the captain as the clanking ceased. 'He only starts it to show off.'

378

There were a number of shadowy girls in the bar. As soon as the two men sat on their stools some of these became palpable and affectionate local greetings were exchanged. 'Knew some of their mothers,' remarked Stern. 'In a couple of cases their grannies. What will you drink?'

They both had whisky which had just been brought ashore from the ship. The bottles were broken out of a case. 'Japanese,' said Stern. 'Nobody knows the difference here.' The barman he had called Sulky laughed.

'We ran into a typhoon coming up through the islands a couple of years ago,' related Stern. 'She nearly went down with all hands. It made us a week late. They had no gasoline and no alcohol here and only a few tins of beans and spaghetti left. They were all along the harbour, crying their eyes out, when we docked.'

'Nearly had to go fishing,' nodded Sulky. Two of the girls, who had retreated after the native greetings, now approached and modestly requested pineapple juice which was poured from a tin. They were young, big-fronted, with coarse hair and broad noses. One put her arm through George's elbow and he smiled at her out of politeness. The return smile was brilliant, white teeth gleaming from dark skin.

'How are the teeth?' Captain Stern asked his girl. The girl pushed her fingers in her mouth and pulled out the entire set. George's attendant did likewise, standing youthfully before him, gums gaping, holding her grimacing teeth in the brown palm of her hand.

'Brought in a whole crateful last trip,' said Stern as the girls replaced the dentures and embedded them with a few practice yaws. 'They almost started a war. Everybody fighting over them.'

'What happens to their own?' asked George, studying the girls, now smiling resolutely again.

'They topple out,' shrugged Stern. 'It's endemic. Lack of calcium. No fresh food. It's gone on over years. Their hair's apt to fall out too. There's many a bride goes to her husband toothless and bald. But they make up for it in other ways. They call these islands the TNT archipelago – Tits No Teeth.'

George drank his whisky. Outside, a lagoon breeze riffled through the palms, an early moon was peering. Someone put a Rosemary Clooney record on a turntable. The girl pressed his arm again and said shyly that he seemed to be very strong. George sighed deeply. He seemed far, further than ever, away from everything he knew, and wished that he were not.

After an hour the record player broke down and the girls in the bar became furtive. They appeared relieved when from outside, across the scented night, came more music, now of a profound nature. It rose like a breeze over the palms gilded by early moonlight.

'Eldon,' explained Stern. 'Lives along the lagoon. American.'

'What's he doing here?'

'Nothing. That's what he came to do – nothing. And that's what he does. Want to see him?' Stern finished his drink. 'I've got some stuff for him on board, tobacco and mail. He won't even stir himself to go down and pick it up. I'll take you over there.'

They paid the barman and went out. The girls chorused their disappointment like starlings. There were no other customers. Some had settled for doing each other's hair. Stern promised to return and the girl who had first produced her dentures trotted to him and pressed his hand. When they were out in the night, on the sand, below the palms, they heard them laughing from the bar.

'They don't mean it,' said Captain Stern. 'They laugh at anything. Except jokes. They don't understand jokes.'

Through the fronds, along the curved beach, they could already discern lights. The music came towards them, and soon they could see widely lit windows. Going through the final screen of trunks they came to a tiled terrace, bowered with luxuriant flowers. The house was low and palm-thatched with french windows spread along its length. Sitting on a striped hammock was a brown, bald man in a South Sea shirt, smoking a large pipe. 'Wondered when you'd get here, Stern,' he called to them as they neared the trees. 'I'm fresh out of tobacco.'

The British captain called back: 'It's still aboard. Can you last tonight?' They advanced and shook hands. Stern introduced George. 'This is Bannington C. Eldon,' he said to George. 'From America.'

'Robinson Z. Crusoe,' amended Eldon shaking hands without rising. His shining head made him look older than he was. George now saw that he was no more than mid-fifties.

380

'What's the music?' he asked. 'I don't recognise it.'

'Mahler,' said Eldon looking over his shoulder at the hi-fi unit which took up the lower half of one wall. 'It's called "The Wanderer".' Another wall was occupied by the coloured spines of a thousand books. 'I play Mahler a lot. At least once a day. What will you drink?' As he asked his pipe finally died. 'Drat it, look at that,' he said peering into the large bowl accusingly. 'I could have sworn I'd last the night.' He looked expectantly at Stern.

'All right,' said Stern rising. 'Make mine a double bourbon. But don't pour it yet. You'll see me coming back.'

'Send one of the girls, or one of the crew,' suggested Eldon unconvincingly. 'Why go yourself?'

'Your mail is in my cabin,' said Stern. 'God knows where the crew are now, although I could take a guess. Don't worry. You're the customer.'

He walked away from the terrace, back through the palms, with the sea silver ahead of him.

'Shouldn't be hawking around the islands in his state,' said Eldon. 'Bourbon for you, sir?'

George thanked him.

Eldon sighed: '"The Wanderer" is as near as I get to wandering these days.' He tapped a gong beside the hammock and a girl, small as a child, beautiful and wearing a flowered sarong, appeared. 'Let's have two bourbons,' said the American. The girl bowed and served them silently. Her face remained grave and she only smiled as she backed away. 'All her own teeth,' said Eldon seeing George's expression. 'How come you're in these parts?'

'Wandering,' replied George with a wry smile. 'Back in the general direction of home at the moment.'

'Keep moving,' Eldon advised with unexpected vehemence. He pointed and shook his empty pipe like a gun. 'Don't get bogged down. That was my mistake, staying here.'

'It's a beautiful place,' ventured George.

'Despond Island,' returned Eldon. He drank his whisky fiercely and looked at the glass with a sort of surprise that the contents had diminished. 'Every goddamn day's the same. The sun comes up, the sun goes down, the moon comes up, the moon goes down. When we get a typhoon it's light relief. At least everybody gets scared.'

'How come you settled here?'

'Lassitude,' said the American. 'No energy to move on. Now it's too late. I've got nowhere to go now, not to call home.'

'I know how you feel. It's the penalty for running away.'

'Sure. Running scared. I got the hell out of it. I had a son, the good one, killed in a crash, and the other, the no-good one, disappeared even though I loved him. I didn't love my wife and she didn't love me, so I just quit. This is as far as I got. Twelve years I've been here, for God's sake.' He touched the gong again and George felt pleased when the little girl came back. She gravely poured two more drinks. George realised Eldon was watching his expression as he watched the girl.

'When Gauguin went to Tahiti he rode around the island on a donkey looking for wife. When he found her she was thirteen years old.' Eldon shrugged. 'You don't have to go on a donkey here.'

Stern was coming back through the trees and Eldon struck the small gong again. The girl appeared and Eldon instructed her to pour another bourbon. Stern reached the terrace and the American took the bundle of letters and the box of tobacco. 'I was telling Mr Goodnight about the boredom here,' continued Eldon. 'The goddamn sameness of it. Even the flowers are the same. That young lady,' he pointed to the girl handing the drink to Stern a few feet away. 'She can make three flower arrangements. Three only. I've told her but she never does a different one. The first on Monday, the second Tuesday, the third Wednesday, and then we start again with Monday's on Thursday. It drives me crazy.'

With a little bow and the leading edge of a smile the girl backed away and went out. Eldon picked up the bundle of mail. There were several newspapers and he opened one. '*New York Times*,' he said. 'Three months old. The news don't matter by the time it reaches here. It's finished, history. There could be an atomic war and it would only be a rumour.'

'There's something called fall-out,' said Stern.

'Who'd notice? Their teeth and their hair drop out anyway.'

'Do you think you'll ever leave?' said George. He felt embarrassed that he did not care for Eldon, probably because of the girl.

'I'm going every goddamn time there's a boat in but then I
382

get a new package of books to read or some new records to play, and I don't go.'

The music had stopped. and now the girl appeared and, to George's astonishment, without speaking replaced Mahler with a raucous rock-and-roll record. It blared out over the trees.

'She likes this stuff,' explained Eldon inadequately. The girl was behind them, standing within the house, sagging one way then the other to the insistent beat, her eyes opaque; the three middle-aged men watching her as voyeurs might have watched. Eldon covered his ears but did nothing more.

Stern rose. 'I think we'll be going,' he said. 'See you next trip.'

'If I'm still here,' said Eldon. He shook George's hand without feeling.

They walked away from the house, towards the mirrored lagoon again. The blaring music followed them.

'How extraordinary,' said George, shaking his head.

Stern grunted enigmatically. 'It's called slavery,' he said.

It took another day to unload the *Outcast* and reload with a cargo of poor quality copra. At dawn on the third day the scraping of the anchor chain awoke George and he went on deck to see they were leaving the lagoon under an opal sky. The land was still dark with the tops of the palms silhouetted like hands. They had left the jetty and anchored offshore late at night to save the island people having to get up early to help cast off and wave goodbye.

'I learned that lesson years ago,' said Stern when George went up to the wheelhouse. 'If you have to wait while the last drink is drunk and the last song is sung and the last man of the crew has been prised out of some bed then you've missed the tide and you can't get through the reef. Better get it all done the night before.'

Bertram, the steersman, aimed the old ship carefully for the part of the reef where the green-black water was untroubled by the teeth of the coral. The messman brought George a mug of sweet tea. The captain gave orders quietly like a man reciting a well-remembered poem. It was rapidly becoming light; long birds flew low over the water's surface and the island was turning green. On the bridge, however, George recognised the few moments of tension as the vessel went through the gap.

383

The deck crew all loitered in the vicinity of the lifeboat. 'I don't know why they do it,' said Stern out of the corner of his mouth, still watching the bow. 'That thing is rusted in.'

George thought how broad the vessel was and how narrow the passage. She went cleanly through the gap and the men cheered as she wallowed out into the sun-coloured sea of the new day.

Swift sunrise had lit the world. It made George feel suddenly glad he was there for it brought to him a convenient remembrance of winter mornings in England: trudging with the low-headed platoons to Shillington station; the steamy railway compartment and the soaked land visible when you wiped across the windows. Captain Stern set a course and Bertram began to sing a soft unmelodious song. George breathed deeply the early air and played with the thought that perhaps, after all, it would not be so bad to live among the warm islands. Like Eldon, perhaps, and his little, beautiful girl.

'He came out here because he thought he was dying,' said Stern when they were talking later. The *Outcast* was far out to sea and no land was visible. 'He thought he would be like Robert Louis Stevenson, you know, but then he blew the game because he didn't die. Whatever it was he thought was killing him went away. He'd be lost if he ever tried to go back to America now, or anywhere else, even Honiara or Manila or somewhere. He's better where he is, being aggravated by that girl.'

They were eating a curried lunch under a worn awning on the deck, sitting in two canvas chairs with a plastic table between them. The sea and the sky rolled by. There were no birds now, nothing but flurries of flying fish. Stern had produced a bottle of French white wine and when they had finished that they had another. It came, the captain told him, from Tahiti.

'*That's* where Stevenson wanted to die. In Tahiti,' Stern went on. 'He sailed there, you know, with his whole family. Wife, even his mother-in-law. He used to wander around Papeete in his pyjamas. But it was off the shipping lanes so instead he went to die in Samoa, which was on the England-Australia run, so he could get his money regularly and send his work to England.'

Stern went to lie down after lunch and George went to sleep in the shade of his cabin. Late in the afternoon it was Bertram

384

who roused him. The man's big face was creased. 'Capt'n Stern told me to tell you he's dying, sir,' he announced. 'You want to go an' see him before he dies?'

Hurriedly George pulled on his trousers, getting the wrong leg in the wrong hole. He changed legs. Stern had been at his evening whisky early, he thought, knocking back a few more after their companionable lunch. But as he padded along the deck he saw the natives of the deck crew grouped around the captain's door.

'Excuse me, chaps,' he said going between them to get in. Stern was lying in his bunk looking cornered.

'Something's gone,' said the captain. His expression was as if he hoped George might be able to repair him. 'One of my pieces has fallen down inside me somewhere. It's happened before. They took me off in one of those helicopters once.' A pale grin slid across his face. 'There's not one flying about outside, is there?'

'Afraid not,' said George. He realised it was really happening and a deep sadness moved into him because the man had been his friend for a short time. 'Just lie back and take it easy,' he advised inadequately. 'We'll get to somewhere as quickly as we can.'

'Somewhere,' smiled Stern again. 'Always going somewhere, we are. Me, and you too, if you're not careful. The world is full of Flying Dutchmen.'

He closed his eyes and George tried to think logically of what to do. He went out of the cabin and told the natives that there was nothing to worry about, the captain would be better tomorrow. They dispersed unconvinced. 'Tonight we got a stiff captain,' one said.

Insisting he would be all right, George went to the bridge where Bertram was on the wheel.

'Is he dead yet?' asked Bertram.

'No. God help us, perhaps he won't. Do you know anything about what to do? How far is the nearest port?'

Bertram answered the questions in order. 'We got a medicine box,' he said. 'But it's a mess. And just stuff for bruises and people getting cuts. Cedunna City on Baker Island is about a hundred miles east from here – where we're heading anyway. Sixteen hours' sailing.'

'Can't she go faster?'

'She can't go faster.'

'Do your best. Is there a hospital at this place?'

'Cedunna City? A mission hospital. They kill you off there.'

'We can radio ahead, I take it?'

'I already told them the skipper is dying,' said Bertram in the same flat, reporting voice. 'I told the ship's agent, Manot.'

'There doesn't seem much else we can do,' said George unhappily. 'No ships in the vicinity that might have a doctor?'

'I tried,' said Betram. George could see he was near to tears. 'I don't want him dying,' he said. 'I known him a long time.' Oddly he muttered an instruction to himself and turned the wheel in obedience to it.

George went back to Stern's cabin. The captain had his eyes closed but was still breathing. Pulling a wicker chair up to the bunk George sat down. He had no idea what to do. His idea of emergency treatment was opening somebody's collar. He sat for half an hour and then went to his cabin and poured himself a drink. Melancholy settled on him. To break it he made himself go out onto the deck. It had turned night without his noticing. Pendant stars were low against the sea. Phosphorescent blades cut across the waves from the ship's bow. Then he heard Stern calling him. It was a firm call and his hopes rose. He went into the captain's cabin.

'Where have you been?' asked Stern. He seemed to have gone lower in the bed. The face was grey.

'On deck,' said George, surprised by the question. 'On the bridge talking to Bertram. There didn't seem much else to do.'

'You're right,' sighed the captain. 'It's no ocean liner. Well, a burial at sea is always a novelty. Canvas coffin, last stitch through the nose, few words of prayer, committed to the deep, over he goes, amen. Rum all round.'

George regarded him defensively. 'You seem better to me,' he pointed out. 'You haven't stopped talking.'

'I've always talked. Silent skippers are bad skippers. Mad skippers too. But I'm on my way. I know it too well.'

The man's hand came from beneath the rough sheet and, hardly realising he was doing it, George took it and held it in his. Stern's eyes had dropped but he opened them and said: 'It's a pity we didn't meet earlier.'

'Yes,' said George sincerely. 'It is.'

'Thanks for your company, anyway, especially just now.'

386

'Look,' said George leaning down. 'We'll be in Cedunna City in a few hours. You're in no hurry to go, are you?'

'Not me,' answered Stern. 'But whoever organises these things is. I've wet myself.' He laughed, almost a cackle. 'The Stern is sinking,' he said.

George had never seen anyone die before and he was surprised to realise how ordinary it was. It was like a door closing, the distance between one breath and the next. Stern died as soon as he had said his little last joke. 'The Stern is sinking.' Because they had been talking that day, under the awning and drinking the wine, of Stevenson, George now, with a self-conscious mutter, recited: 'Home is the sailor, home from the sea,' half expecting Stern to look up and complete the epitaph.

George walked to the door, turned back and covered Stern's face, then went out again, closing the door behind him. The ocean was slapping and soughing against the old hull. The stars had climbed to their places and a fat moon was rising. He went to the bridge.

'Six hours to Cedunna City,' said Bertram. He had only slept for two hours.

'He's gone,' said George. 'He just died.'

'Nine hours then,' amended the steersman. George said he would go and get some coffee. There was no messman to be seen, the deck crew had shut themselves away, so he made it himself. He took the mugs to the bridge and gave one to Bertram. The man's brown face was damp. 'Years I sailed with him,' he said.

George went to his cabin but before getting into his bunk he went back to the captain's quarters, almost to check, to see that he was as he had left him. He uncovered the face and saw that the sailor still had the fixed smile of his final sentence.

George slept uneasily; it was a still night but he kept imagining he heard someone walking about the deck. At dawn they were off Cedunna City, in the southern Philippines, the now familiar line of palms against the pale sky, the water breaking on the coral reef, the unstirring town and harbour just distinguishable. Behind the settlement were some hills, smudges at this hour, which concealed the uprising sun. Because the sun rose late, people slept late.

George stood on the rail and watched the bow nudge through

the gap in the reef. The *Outcast*, like an elderly swimmer, flopped into the lagoon beyond. He drank a mug of coffee and went up to the bridge. Bertram was blinking his eyes to keep them open.

'The agent takes over here,' he said almost sullenly.

'Did he want to be buried at sea?' asked George. 'He talked about it.'

The big islander shrugged. 'He don't have no say in it now. It's the agent.'

The harbour town was becoming distinct. There were signs of slow activity ashore and presently a small boat left the jetty and came white-nosed out towards the ship. 'The agent,' muttered Bertram. 'Mr Manot.'

As the launch came alongside, a stubby, dark man in a white shirt stood in the bow, a despatch case below his arm. He casually timed the moment and leapt to the ladder trailing down the hull of the *Outcast*. 'Mr Manot,' repeated Bertram. 'The agent.'

Manot had the same half-Oriental half-Oceanic features, the eyes, the nose and the skin texture as Benny's wife's son at Somerbourne Magna. He looked about him as soon as he reached the deck, as if seeking someone in charge. Bertram remained at the wheel; now, as the ship lost way, leaning against it. George was standing at the top of the ladder to the bridge.

'Mr Goodnight? The passenger?' Manot said.

'Yes.'

'Ah, where is Captain Stern?'

'He's . . . he's dead. I thought you knew.'

'Yes, I do. But where is he?'

The manner was impatient. The agent's face was aloof as if he were busy that day and a death was inconvenient.

'He's in his cabin,' said George who decided he did not like Manot. 'At least, he was when I last saw him.'

Unhurriedly he came down the ladder. Manot jabbed out his hand and George automatically shook it. The newcomer patted his arm familiarly. 'Sorry you had to go through all this,' he said unconvincingly, adding as an afterthought, 'old boy.'

'That's perfectly all right, old boy,' returned George evenly. 'Do you want to see him?'

388

'I had better.' He looked around as if hoping somebody else might go instead. 'I don't like dead people,' he said.

'It's some of the live ones I don't care for,' said George moving towards the cabin. He opened the door softly. Manot followed and backed away a little as the Englishman took the sheet from his compatriot's moribund face. The smile, he was sorry to see, had frozen to a grimace.

'That's him,' said Manot curiously. 'Yes, Captain Stern. Dead.' He turned swiftly, saying as he did, 'If I remember, you paid three hundred dollars.'

For a moment George's surprise prevented his answer. He replaced the sheet over Stern's face. Manot was already at the door but apparently wanting to settle the matter before he went out. 'Three hundred?' he repeated.

'For the passage? Yes,' replied George, restraining himself. 'At Darwin. We arranged that it would be adjusted depending on how far I went with the ship. If she had a cargo going back towards Australia there would be no point. I'd be retracing my steps.'

'Right. So. Cedunna City would be another three hundred . . .' He held up a pale, flabby hand. 'But, in the circumstances, that will be void.'

'You are very generous,' said George evenly.

'You will be moving on?' suggested Manot. 'Where are you exactly heading?' They had stepped out onto the deck. The sun had cleared the hills and was rising like a balloon across the island.

'I'm not *exactly* heading anywhere,' George corrected. 'I'm going in the general direction of Los Angeles.'

'Ah . . . yes. That is good.'

'But I want to be at Captain Stern's funeral.'

'Of course. So you will. Funerals do not take long here.'

George was surprised to see the crew already going ashore. Another boat had come alongside and the dozen natives, each carrying a suitcase or a kitbag, were descending the ladder to it. Bertram was the last to go. He shook hands solemnly with George, but ignored Manot. 'Don't forget to lock up,' he said.

'I'll see you at the funeral, won't I?' said George.

'That won't be too long,' returned Bertram. He went over the side, threw his canvas bag into the boat below and dropped after it. He did not look up but sat with his head in his hands.

'I suppose I'd better get my belongings,' said George.

'Please hurry, Mr Goodnight,' said Manot. 'We must go ashore now.'

George went to his cabin and gathered his few belongings. Unhappily he packed them into the canvas bag that had once belonged to Clementine at Alice Springs. Manot was waiting on deck, walking a few yards each way with precise, impatient, steps. The boat with the crew was already halfway across the lagoon, heading for the town. After a moment's uncertainty, George went to Stern's cabin, opened the door, looked in and quietly closed the door again. As if to justify the action he said to Manot: 'He was a very good man.'

'Very good,' echoed the agent. He was already indicating the ladder. With difficulty George climbed down. Manot followed him and sat down facing him in the small boat. The crewmen started the engine and they pulled away from the *Outcast*.

'It is usual to just leave the ship like that, and with a dead man aboard?'

'Not unusual,' Manot assured him. 'Not in these parts. There is no doctor here today. There is suspected smallpox on one of the other islands. When he gets back he'll go out to the ship. There's no way this crew would stay aboard anyway. They're superstitious as hell.'

'I would have stayed,' said George doggedly. He turned in the launch to look at the ship. A clear spiral of smoke was rising from amidships.

'There's a fire!' he said hoarsely. 'It's burning!'

'So it is,' said Manot. 'The stove in the galley, you bet.'

'But . . . what ? What about . . . ? We ought to go back . . .'

'This man,' he said indicating the man at the tiller. 'Won't go back. No way. Not to a ship on fire. When we get ashore we tell the fire brigade.' He squinted towards the ship. George swivelled again. There was a deep glow on the deck and the smoke had thickened. As they watched, there came a dulled explosion and the glow widened like an opening flower with a red cloud rising to join the rolling smoke. 'Maybe they noticed it already,' said Manot.

He regarded George as if hoping for understanding. 'It is a great funeral for a seaman,' he said patting him on the knee. 'Lots of tribes send their chiefs out in burning boats. Better than the fishes eating you. Or the worms.'

390

They had reached the harbourside. It was a poor place, shabby boats and shabby buildings. People had gathered on the quay to watch the ship burning in the lagoon, although their faces seemed scarcely interested. The crew of the *Outcast* was grouped to one side but George could not see Bertram. Two grinning policemen were at the top of the stone steps, one limply holding a hand fire extinguisher.

'Where's the fire brigade?' asked George without much hope.

'No fire brigade today,' said one of the policemen, 'The man's sick.'

Disconsolately George looked seawards again. The old ship was burning fiercely now, a great welt of smoke above her. Sounds like grunts, as if she were complaining, came across the water.

'Insured, I imagine,' mentioned George.

'Sure, sure,' said Manot, his thick eyebrows rising slightly. 'Ship and cargo.' He sighed. 'But not the captain.'

XIX

Cedunna City was hardly more than a street along the harbour, with wooden houses and other buildings hanging their heads over the water. Other habitations were built on the early slope of the hill behind the town, but where the incline became difficult the buildings stopped and the green jungle began.

George, carrying his bag, trudged towards a sign proclaiming 'Imperial Hotel'. The street was red, wet earth and water-filled holes. It was like walking across a map, with craters of differing dimensions, some several feet across, with isthmuses, capes, headlands and reefs of mud and stones. He took a course between puddles and ponds. Brown boys on bicycles cut through the water but he guessed it was no novelty. The air was clammy and the first clouds of another downpour were swollen on the sea. He turned to see if any sign of the *Outcast* remained but she was gone for ever; the lagoon had smoothed, and only a thinning feather of smoke marked the place where Captain Stern had gone, in fire and water, to his grave.

There were mud-caked cars and trucks in the rankling street, few of them moving, some looking as though they had not moved in a long time. They were parked, noses down like animals, along the line of unadorned shops, fetid bars and asbestos offices. Men hung about the bars and women gathered with no animation outside the shops. There were neon strips visible through grubby office windows. Even the boys on the bicycles soon abandoned their riding games and were grouped around a muddy crater, increasing the volume of its water. Cedunna City was no paradise.

A bus bumped along the street, its colours scarcely revealed through the mud. Above the driver, however, was a bold sign saying: 'Servicio 1A-Cuaidad' and for a moment George saw again the bus from Somerbourne Magna with its banner proclaiming 'Warminster', splashing darkly along a faraway English road.

Behind 'Servicio 1A' came the abrupt honking of a klaxon. Dilatory men looked out of bars, women turned without hurry from their languorous gossip and the boys stemmed their urinating. As soon as 'Servicio 1A' had passed, he could see that a sort of fire engine was bouncing behind it; an open truck with buckets clanking along its flanks, a ladder pointing up like an artillery piece, and a coiled hose, the nozzle of which bounced along the road. Its crew consisted of one, the driver, who drove devilishly, in and out of craters, skidding around other moving vehicles, a wild-eyed man wearing pyjamas and a fire helmet.

Great gobs of rain began to drop. Dark sky had pulled over like a lid. The sea frowned and the reef growled. Fortunately George was almost at the Imperial Hotel. Along its front it had a greenish wooden veranda, below which were rundown bamboo tables and chairs, split and ill used, some overturned. It was occupied by one creased man, wearing a straw hat from below which he watched as the rain began to dribble from the overhang of the roof, a few runnels at first, becoming a veil and, before long, a cascade. He studied the water as if he were deeply interested. Even when George wished him 'good morning' he returned the greeting only from the edge of his mouth and without taking his eyes from the rain.

George walked into the hotel. The foyer was an indoors version of the veranda, infirm tables and chairs, standing lopsided in the dimness, with a scratched desk upon which rested an impressive but unburnished handbell. A flight of naked stairs went up on his right, turning a bend, and up there, heard above the drumming of the rain, a girl was singing tunelessly. George picked up the heavy bell and clanged it several times, having to use both hands. The singing went on unstilled but eventually the man came in from the terrace and said: 'You was ringing?'

'It's a nice big bell,' said George looking at its tarnished flanks.

'All we got left,' said the man mysteriously. He had a slow American accent. 'You want a room? There's a good room.'

George indicated he did.

'How long? How many nights and days?' The man had gone round the desk and, with difficulty, lifted a lectern Bible from somewhere below the desk. He was still wearing his hat and in the general dimness his face was indistinct.

'This is a Bible,' he said opening the pages. 'We write in the margins. Someone started doing it years ago, and we've just kept on, never stopped. We're up to the Psalms of David now.' He leaned closer. 'Can't see in this light. Psalm one hundred and three, I make it. There's not a Bible like this in the world. Sign here, please.'

'I bet there isn't,' said George, signing. He swivelled the bulky book back towards the man. 'Nor a more useful one.'

'You don't know how long?'

'Not yet. I've just come off the ship. The *Outcast*.'

'She sank this time, I hear,' said the man. 'Thought she would. Blanco Stern went down with her.'

'He died at sea,' George told him.

'A good man, as far as these parts go. You'll be on your way, I guess, as soon as you can get out. The bus is tomorrow.'

'I'll probably aim for that.'

'Room's thirty dollars a night. And my name's Copeland. Teddy. Have you got that sort of money?'

George reassured him.

'I should hold on to it,' warned Copeland. 'It goes easy here. When you're not looking.' He pushed the brim of his hat back for the first time. He was not as old as his movements and speech made him appear. His eyes were small. 'This ain't much of a place,' he said. 'The room's right at the top of the stairs.'

'Thanks,' said George. He picked up his bag. 'You wouldn't like some money in advance, would you?'

'Nope. That's okay,' said Copeland. His demeanour indicated that a deposit might involve him in additional work. 'You can't get out of Cedunna City till tomorrow. You ain't going to run away anywhere.'

The rain abruptly ceased as George was going up the stairs, and he could hear his own footsteps. The girl was still singing flatly at the far end of the upswept corridor. There was a key in the door of the first room on the right. Tentatively he went in and was gratified to see a sturdy wooden bed with brass-handled lockers beneath the frame. There was a substantial black chest, also brass-bound, in the room, a flowered basin and jug and a chamberpot with an eye painted on the bottom within. He thought the furniture must have come from a ship.

394

The door had closed behind him but now, with the briefest knock, it was opened and the girl who had been singing so badly came into the room. She had a mischievous face, pale brown skin, and her black hair in a long pigtail. There was a wild cast in one eye. Without speaking she picked up the chamberpot and began polishing it.

'You hear me singing?' she said. 'Pretty good, hah?'

'Very good,' said George.

She was rubbing the inside of the receptacle. 'See that,' she pointed at the eye. A devilish grin flitted on her face. 'He look up, see you when you pee.' She laughed. 'Pretty good, hah?'

'Very good,' repeated George.

'Everything okay, this room?'

'Yes, it's fine, thank you.'

'You American?'

'No, English.'

She whistled. 'English gringo. Hah, pretty good.' She went out as quickly as she had entered. He heard her go down the stairs and, after a while, begin to sing again.

He poured some water from the jug to the basin and washed his face. He still felt sad about Stern and thought of him lying in his bunk on the floor of the lagoon; another face, another voice, another person in the long procession which began so far back in his travels. One day he would write their names in a book.

He felt he needed a drink and some food and, after counting his money, he went down the barren stairs and out onto the wooden veranda at the front.

Rain was dripping like a bead curtain from the overhanging roof, each bead glittering in the renewed rays of the sun. Steam rose from the muddy street outside, people appearing and vanishing through it like spectres. One of these shapes solidified and, as it reached the wooden steps of the Imperial, George saw it was Manot the shipping agent.

'Every day now it rains like this,' he said. 'Sit down, have a drink.'

'I was just about to,' muttered George.

'Good, great. I join you.' He waved towards the interior of the hotel, dark as a cave beyond the door. 'I like to have a talk anyway.'

Copeland shuffled out.

'Two whisky,' ordered Manot and then added: 'How's that girl?'

Copeland shuffled back inside without replying.

Manot turned to George. 'You like whisky, I guess,' he said.

'It will do,' said George cautiously.

'She's a good girl,' said Manot. 'But she sings, all the goddamn time she sings.' He regarded George's sombre expression and slapped him lightly on the back. 'You keeping the old stiff upper jaw, hah?'

'Lip,' corrected George. 'Stiff upper lip.'

Manot laughed. 'One day I will know this language,' he said. The whisky arrived and the agent lifted his glass. 'To the stiff upper lip, eh?' he smiled. George raised his silently.

'You still don' feel so good about Captain Stern,' said Manot.

'No. I liked him.'

'Good man, good captain. But he was dying anyway. This trip, next trip, the trip after. He didn't have too long. Heart, liver, kidneys, everything. You should see the doctor's report from Darwin. Even toenails growing in. What d'you call it?'

'Ingrowing toenails,' suggested George.

'Right. You hit it right on the head. Bad ears. Everything wrong from toes to ears. We only keep him because we know he didn't have too long.'

'Neither did the ship,' pointed out George. The drippings from the roof had diminished now. He watched them hang and drop like jewels. The level of the vapour was lower in the street.

'Too bad the ship burned,' agreed Manot. 'Important cargo.'

'So you said. The insurance company will be pleased.'

'No, they not,' answered the agent seriously. 'Fuckin' angry, I would tell you. I don' know why. That's business. We have other ships and plenty of cargoes that don' go on fire. It's just too bad.' He finished his whisky, asked George to have another on him and called for the drinks. Copeland brought them out.

'Too bad she went down,' said the hotel keeper. 'And Captain Stern.'

'Buried at sea,' said Manot, correcting a technical point. He waited until Copeland had gone and then said solicitously, 'But I feel a little bad, you know, bad, about you, Señor Goodnight. How much money you got?'

'You want the rest of the fare?'

396

'No, forget it. I told you forget it.' He shuffled his chair closer. There were no other drinkers on the veranda. 'You going to tell me how much? How you going to get out of this place?'

'By the bus, I suppose,' shrugged George. 'It's the only way, isn't it?'

'Bus or car,' said Manot. 'And the road gets very bad for a car. The bus gets to Tenopulca, about twelve, thirteen hours, so-so, all depending on the holes in the road. Lots of rain, lots of holes. But from Tenopulca you can fly – to Manila and all the world.'

'The world sounds very attractive just now,' said George.

'You travelling a long time?'

'Long enough,' said George.

'It's dangerous. It gets hard to stop. No place is just right. Look at me – *here* in this goddamn place. And I come from Mindanao.' Both of his hands went round the glass and, as if it lent him security and sincerity, he tapped it lightly on the table. 'I been thinking about you. Your situation. And I had a talk on the phone with my bosses in Manila.'

George regarded him suspiciously.

The agent went on: 'I think that we maybe help you. We got you here, we get you out. Responsi . . . respons . . .'

George helped him. 'Responsibility?'

'Sure. Out of here and on your way home.' He had not returned George's look but stared over his tapping glass towards the street. 'Home,' he repeated. 'I mean, for God's sake, I think you entitled. If you think all about it, you a goddamned shipwrecked mariner.' He now looked towards George, his black eyes intense with sincerity. 'We going to give you the bus fare.'

'Thanks,' said George.

'And from Tenopulca the air ticket to Manila.'

'I see.'

Manot carried a small briefcase which he now opened fussily. He produced two tickets. 'The bus,' he said handing the first over. 'Take a bottle of drinking water. And the plane.' He handed over the other ticket. 'That's some help, eh?'

Not without hesitation George accepted the tickets. 'You're not trying to get rid of me, are you?' he suggested.

Manot appeared shocked. He stood ready to go. 'Rid of you?

You mean pushing you out of Cedunna City. No way.' He had picked up his briefcase and now he used it like a pointer. 'Where is there for you in Cedunna City? You must not stay. You belong to the world.'

He shook George's hand with a grip like wet wood. George watched him go into the diminishing mist of the street. The mist was now much lower and Manot looked to be walking with no legs. He turned and waved eerily. George looked at the tickets. The bus ticket was stamped *'Primera Clase.'*

'First class,' said Copeland who had arrived with a menu and was looking over his shoulder. 'That's good. Take water with you.'

'The bus is tomorrow,' said George.

'That's okay,' said the hotel man. He handed George the plastic-covered menu. 'We got a call for the best room anyway. That's your room. Some guy coming in on the bus tonight. The bus take you back tomorrow.'

The menu said starkly: 'Breakfast' 'Lunch' and 'Dinner' at three separate levels. There was nothing more written. 'You want lunch?' asked Copeland taking the card back. 'It's fish and potatoes and papaya.'

'My favourite,' said George. 'Haven't got any wine, have you? I want to celebrate going away.'

'Only beer,' Copeland told him seriously. 'Philippine beer.'

'All right. Fish, potatoes, papaya and Philippine beer, it is.'

'Thanks,' said Copeland. 'You made up your mind quick.'

He went into the hotel and within a moment the tuneless girl emerged smiling with a tray of food and the beer. She put the used whisky glasses on the next table and whisked some raindrops away with her small hand. Then she set the food on the clothless table in front of him.

'You go on the bus tomorrow?' she said.

'I am. I'm taking some water.'

'I was going to tell you. Also you don't let nobody steal the water. Second class passengers and those people. They will try.'

'I'll take two bottles,' he said. The fish looked appetising baked almost brown but the potatoes were mushy and the papaya provided a promenade for flies.

'Tonight,' she said before she went away, 'there is good time

398

at the Salon de Thé, just down the street. Good dancing. Spot prizes. You will come?'

He said he thought he would. He began to eat his lunch. The fish was good. He left the vegetables and drank his beer. Copeland came out and said there was bread and cream cheese or red jello. He chose the bread and cheese.

Now the sun had become fierce and between the overhang of the veranda and the low tops of the buildings across the street was a path of heavy blue sky. Most of the water that had fallen on the muddy road had been steamed off leaving a rimed surface. Since it was the middle of the day there were few people to be seen and only an occasional vehicle went by. He remained the only lunch-eater on the veranda, a shadow among shadows.

The girl came out to clear the dishes. To his surprise she merely moved them to the next table and sat down confidingly. 'Maybe,' she suggested, her odd eyes taking him in, 'this afternoon you like to rest with me?'

He was still capable of astonishment.

'My work, it is finish,' she added as if he might be worried about that aspect. 'I just take these dishes and wash them, then I come to your room and we rest.'

'All right,' said George looking at her. She winked with her straight eye.

He waited a few minutes before he left the table and walked into the dim hotel, guiltily glancing about him. Copeland rose from somewhere below the desk and smiled wolfishly. 'You going to rest?' he called blithely as George neared the top of the stairs.

'Yes, I thought I might,' answered George looking back.

'That Pepita, she gives a great rest,' shouted Copeland.

George opened his mouth but could frame no words. He half waved his hand at the hotel keeper, a gesture that could have meant anything. He attempted to unlock his room door but discovered that the key did not work and the door opened anyway at a touch. Pepita was already there, pulling back the calico coverlet of the sturdy bed. She gave him a brief, chambermaid's smile, so brief that he wondered if he had misconstrued her suggestion. But a moment later she took a large pillow from one of the brass-handled drawers below the bed and placed it longways on the mattress. She plumped it up with a few butcher-like blows of her small brown hand.

'That for me,' she informed him. 'This bed fuckin' hard.'

She continued to be busy. She pulled over the opaque curtains and then, as if reverting to her everyday work, she dusted out the one-eyed chamberpot with the end of one of the curtains. George laughed.

'Funny, hah?' said Pepita in a pleased way. She pointed at the eye. 'He see you when you pee. Good joke, hah?' She looked at him quizzically. 'You want to rest now?'

'Yes,' said George. Firmly he pushed his guilt behind him. It was all part of the day to her and he needed the company. Worse, less honest, things had happened in Shillington. She began to undress, and went through the sequence quickly and practically, without attempted seductiveness. When she was naked he had only completed unbuttoning his shirt. She had scarcely any shape. Her body was straight, chocolate-cream skin, with breasts smaller, it seemed, than her eyes which were now turned on him, asking approval, the odd one as beguiling as the other. Her stomach was oval resting on a small cornet of black hair. 'Pretty good, hah?' she said.

She lay on the elongated pillow and appeared to forget he was there. While he completed taking his clothes off she examined her nails.

'Would you like me to pay now?' he asked her.

'No problem,' she said airily, still looking at her nails. 'It go on your bill. Copeland, he fix it.'

Naked he lay down beside her, putting his hand on her stomach. She looked towards him sleepily. 'In England, they rest like this?' she asked.

'Occasional Sunday afternoons,' he said.

'After mass,' she nodded understandingly.

Her hand, as if it moved without her, slid towards him and began to stroke his thigh without interest. 'You been away long?' she asked.

'I have,' he said.

'I want to be away. I want to go Manila. Los Angeles maybe. No good here. Cedunna City go mad when the bus comes. Not like England, hah?'

'Some places in England,' he corrected. A further intrusive

400

memory of the Somerbourne Magna-Warminster bus was interrupted by her hands. He turned half towards her and she kissed him, her slim face pressing hard and unmeaningly against his jaw. He stroked the small bosom, each breast fitting comfortably into one hand.

'I can't go Manila because my mama,' she mentioned. 'But maybe she dead next year.'

She encouraged him to move above her but then, sizing him up, she said, 'Maybe I ride you.'

'That's what I was thinking,' he said.

'You big guy. Maybe I want to breathe.'

She slid off the pillow and indicated that he should take her place by giving it a further professional plumping. He stretched out and looked at her kneeling between his legs. Her eye wandered but her smile was sure and she crept up his body with practised and feline ease. When she lowered herself to him her weight was only just noticeable, the crown of her head came just below his chin and when she began to move it collided with his jaw like a playful and repeated punch. She began to sing.

She sang in Spanish, tonelessly, the song continuing until they had finished.

'Pretty good, hah?' she said rolling to the side and turning her face to his.

'Pretty good,' he agreed, 'Pepita.'

'Another man coming this room tonight,' she told him conversationally. 'He come from the bus.'

'But I'm still here tonight,' he said.

'Sure. But this best room. This man say he want best room.'

'I'm being moved out?'

'No. You stay. All rooms have reservations. People come on the bus. You have this man with you. It is a bed for two.'

'I'll see Copeland about that,' he promised.

'He tell you same thing,' she said confidently. She fumbled at the side of the bed, opened one of the brass-bound drawers and produced a cigarette and matches from a private cache. Lying naked she lit the cigarette and began to smoke. 'You don' smoke?' she said, the thought occurring late. 'I not see you smoke.'

'No, I don't,' he said.

'Me, I smoke. Most times I smoke.' She smiled beguilingly. 'Only bad thing I do,' she said.

Easing herself from the mattress she took the chamberpot and unselfconsciously squatted across it. A tinkling echoed from within. 'Him looking up at me pee,' she said looking down between her legs. When she had done she stood and poured some water from the pitcher into the bowl. He watched her from the bed wondering about her life. She began to wash her thighs and she looked up and smiled. 'You now,' she beckoned. He walked over, declined her invitation to use the pot, then stood while she washed him. The hand of guilt touched him but he thought she would have been unable to understand it. It was done now anyway.

'I'd like to give you something extra,' he said.

She smiled. 'Sure. A tip for the chambermaid. Twenty dollars.'

'Are you sure that is all right?'

'Maybe thirty dollars?'

He gave her the money and she thanked him with a brief kiss on the cheek. She dressed as casually as she had stripped. She pushed him gently back towards the bed and he sat on it and then, as she made a sleeping mime with her hands against his face, he lay back. She took the extra pillow, examined it, brushed it down with her hand, and replaced it in the bed-drawer.

'Pretty good rest, hah?' she said moving towards the door.

'Very good,' he said. 'Thank you.'

'No problem,' she answered. She picked up the chamberpot and the wash basin, emptied the latter into the former and went out. He could hear her begin to sing on the landing. He closed his eyes and began, not for the first time, to think of the strange lives of people in this world.

He awoke in the late afternoon, got up and found a shower cubicle at the end of the corridor. He showered, dressed and walked out into the humid street. The siesta time was finished and the shopkeepers were reluctantly opening their premises. He went to buy toothpaste, a new razor, and a clean shirt and some light trousers. Trousers seemed to last less time than shirts. As he walked from the shops to the jetty he counted the various trousers that he had obtained, worn through, and variously abandoned in his long journey. From the first pair he purchased from Patel at the motorway service area he made it eight pairs, including shorts.

The harbour was desultory, a few small sailing craft, a handful of half-hearted fishing boats, and a litter of dinghies. A few boys sat fishing from the jetty and another group played games about the elephant legs of the palm trees. The water was squalid and cluttered.

A large palm had dropped on its side and an old man, clothed in tatters, stretched out along one end of it, his knee like a knuckle, a thin snore wheezing from his open mouth. George sat on the other end of the trunk and took stock of his personal situation and finances.

No more stamps would be forthcoming. The last of the collection had been sold to old Fred Upney in Sydney. Now he found himself with approximately twelve hundred Australian dollars plus a bus pass to Tenopulca, and a plane ticket to Manila. It was not much; enough to keep travelling on.

For half an hour he sat looking out into the lagoon as the day diminished. It was the best time. The sea began to make its own shadows. Early lamps were showing in the town. The ragged old man who had been asleep on the other end of the trunk stirred and looked at his wristwatch. George asked him the time and the man told him it was almost six. 'The bus is in Cedunna City,' he said proudly. 'It is here now, in the street. Tomorrow you go on the bus.'

George agreed that he had planned to do so.

'Take water,' muttered the man. 'Good water.'

Thanking him, George walked back towards the street. The bus had indeed arrived, mud up the windows, boys and bent old men carrying the passengers' baggage and an assortment of cargo to various destinations in the town. He began to quicken his step towards the hotel, thinking about another man having his room that night.

There was baggage lying about in the wooden foyer but no people. He went up to his room and opened the door. A man was sitting on the bed, facing away from him; short and sparsely ginger-haired. He turned round quickly. The orange-peel teeth were unmistakable. So was the greeting. 'Gud-dye,' he said.

Astounded, George went crabwise round the room.

403

'We're sharing,' said the man benignly. 'I'll be near the window, if it's all right with you.'

'Hong Kong,' breathed George. 'You were the one . . . opening the coffin at the airport . . .'

'Now let's think,' said the arrival, standing up and rubbing his ginger jaw. 'Who would I have been then? Barry Thompson from Perth, Craig Brown from Townsville or Tommy Barton from Adelaide?'

'Tommy Barton from Adelaide,' George decided for him. 'I remember your name even if you don't.'

'Too right you do!' exclaimed the man holding out his hand. Doubtfully George shook it. The orange-peel teeth hung out in a smile. Letting go of George's hand he became quickly serious. 'For the moment, however, pal, I'm Adrian A'Dare from Sydney.'

'You *are* a policeman, I imagine,' said George. 'I mean, all that business after Ron Mangles died . . .'

'You imagine right,' said the Australian. 'You ought to be one yourself. You sail close enough to trouble.'

'It sails close enough to me, more like it,' grumbled George. 'It's the *Outcast*, is it?'

'You're great. What deduction.'

'It's about the only suspicious thing that's happened around here for years,' said George. 'You don't need to be Sherlock Holmes.'

The man smiled again and sat down on the side of the bed. 'And here *you* are,' he said smugly. 'What about that. The minute I saw your name on the passenger list, your name *was* the passenger list come to think of it, I thought: "Well, hell, there's good old George Goodnight again. I must go and see how he's doing."'

George sat on the room's only chair. The chamberpot had been restored to its corner. 'I had nothing to do with the Mangles business, for which, incidentally, I spent Christmas inside.'

'Best place,' said the Australian. 'Best place until everybody had been sorted out. You were safe in the chokey. And I didn't reckon you had anything to do with the *Outcast* either, except as a witness, which will do me a treat. No, George, it happens to you blokes who wander about. Trouble finds you, you don't

404

have to look for it. In Aussie it's always the same old hoboes who end up in situations.'

'Thanks,' said George. 'Never thought of myself as a tramp before. I suppose I've become one. What's the story with the ship. Insurance?'

'You'd be *very* good,' approved the detective again. 'Captain dies, ship burns and sinks, and all of a sudden it's got an expensive cargo. She's insured in Sydney, that's how I came in. I work for myself, see, I'm not official police, I'm irregular. Like I told you, the minute your name came up I was on the case, on the plane, on the amphibian, on the bus and here I am. What do you know about Manot?'

'He's become very solicitous for my welfare,' said George. 'He's given me not only a bus ticket to Tenopulca tomorrow but a plane ticket . . .'

'Amphibian,' corrected the other man. 'God, it makes you spew.'

'I thought he was being a trifle generous.'

'Generous. Nothing. I reckon we can do better than that.'

'What do I have to do this time?'

'No big deal. I think I can get your evidence in affidavit. Between us, I don't think there'll be too much official bother over this one. I've come to frighten them, the owners, that's all. So the claim gets a bit more reasonable. I talk to Manot then go back to Manila to have a few words with the big bosses, and everybody, I hope, is happy.'

'Was it you who put the cocaine or heroin, or whatever it was, in Ron Mangles' coffin at Hong Kong airport?' asked George. 'Just out of interest.'

The teeth came out like flags. 'You're getting better all the time, George. You think I slipped in phoney evidence?' He backed away from the waist and his gingery eyelids crinkled up. 'Now would I tell you something like that? We can take it that I was just making sure that Ron Mangles was comfortable. After all, that's a hell of a long way to travel in a box.'

The Salon de Thé at Cedunna City had been opened and named by a Frenchman from New Caledonia some years before, and had passed from him into a succession of owner-ships, each one at least as hopeless as the one before. Only its misnomer had remained unchanged.

405

George and the Australian, who was now Adrian A'Dare, walked along the hot dark street after a drunken dinner. One of the luxuries of his occupation, A'Dare revealed at inebriated length, was to become anyone he wished. He even carried a miniature printing outfit that enabled him to produce visiting cards, headed notepaper and even convincing letters of introduction. He could go to his room and emerge having acquired a novel persona, even though it was possible to do little about his appearance. His height, his hair and his teeth were beyond disguise.

'I have to confess,' said George indistinctly as they sat at the bar of the Salon de Thé, drinking their several whiskies of the evening for there had been no wine available at dinner, 'I must say I didn't care for you a lot in Hong Kong. It's difficult to take to somebody you first see prying into a coffin.'

'Shush,' warned A'Dare loudly. His teeth hung out as he grinned. 'In my game you've got to be careful of big ears.'

'It's not your ears I'd worry about,' said George eyeing the teeth with an inebriate's lack of tact.

'Here's the band,' said A'Dare swivelling on his stool. A straggle of sweaty-looking musicians were dragging drums and other equipment onto a platform at one end of the room. The sides of the place were open to the night with the fringes of the fronded roof projecting like rude tongues. Outside a brief breeze stirred the vegetation but it had not enough energy to penetrate the building. There were some miscellaneous girls at one end of the bar, coyly giggling to each other; men had come in and were drinking moodily.

'That little sheila at the hotel,' mentioned A'Dare mischievously. 'That Pepita. I've cracked it, I think.'

George managed surprise. 'You're a quick worker,' he said. The Australian bought two more whiskies. It was Japanese and tasted of tin.

'Mate, I'm not an investigator for nothing. Just by instinct I can tell you it's *there* if you go about it, I just know it is. It's there.'

'*What* is there?' asked George.

'You know . . . oh God, the bloody Poms. A bunk-up is there. Nooky . . . a naughty . . . you get me?'

'Oh, that. What makes you think so?'

'A lifetime's experience, brother.' He glanced up and his

demeanour changed. 'Ah, here's our friend Manot, alias Franchino, alias Raphael Persimmons of Eton and Oxford, alias God-knows-how-many-others. I went to see him for a quiet hour tonight before dinner. We had a long talk about this and that. About your affidavit. About ships and insurance. Cabbages and kings. I have a feeling he's going to be nice to us tonight. Ah, good evening, Señor Manot.'

'*Buenos días*, my good friend,' answered Manot. He came slinking along the bar. He would have looked more at home in a country where he could hide behind an upturned collar. He pretended to be surprised by George's presence. 'And Señor Goodnight, it is you. And you are *together*.'

'Bonds of Empire,' said A'Dare. 'Strong as ever. Have a wet.'

'I will take a little water,' replied Manot uneasily.

'A little water for Señor Manot,' A'Dare told the barman. He turned solicitously. 'Have a large one?'

'No. *Muchas gracias*,' said Manot seriously. He handed an envelope to George. 'After discussion with my owners,' he said, 'I have to give you this ticket, business class, Manila to Los Angeles.'

'Your owners did right,' nodded A'Dare seriously. 'How long have they owned you, by the way?'

Manot got the joke and looked sullen. 'They own the ships,' he said. A'Dare was about to hand him a glass of water. 'Want ice?' he asked and pushed his squat, haired fingers into the bartop ice container and dropped two grey cubes into the water. A third missed the glass but he caught it between his legs. He retrieved it and put it in Manot's drink. 'Up yours,' he said cheerfully raising his whisky.

George lifted his glass and Manot made the toast with the water. 'Up yours,' he echoed sombrely.

Pepita came into the place and at once levered herself onto a stool which had the look of having been awaiting her. The barman brought her a drink without being asked. The other girls sniggered close about her and knowingly looked up the counter towards George who felt uncomfortable.

'See,' said A'Dare in a large whisper. 'See, she's perving me. Who told you it was there? I did.'

'That girl,' said Manot as if it were a doleful duty, 'is not good. She has many full houses.'

George swallowed so fiercely he almost fell from the stool. 'What . . . d'you mean . . . full . . . houses?'

'Pox,' A'Dare told him. 'Or poxes.'

Manot said: 'I know well. You must please now drink with me.'

'Whiskies, thanks,' said the Australian swiftly. 'Doubles.'

'Always I buy doubles,' said Manot in a hurt way. He gave the barman the order.

'Go on, have a double water,' suggested A'Dare. Manot smiled tightly. The band had begun to play lamely as if it needed winding up.

Pepita slid from the stool and advanced brazenly on the men.

A'Dare muttered: 'Didn't I tell you, mate?'

His face fell like a cracked wall when she touched George's arm and smilingly asked him to dance. 'Shit,' he said banging down his whisky. 'Shit,' he repeated to Manot. 'The bloody Pom.'

'The bloody Pom,' nodded Manot.

On the dance floor Pepita pushed herself close to George's stomach. 'That man I don' like,' she complained in a whisper.

'Manot?'

'No. I not like Manot for a long time. He always want to screw me but I don' let. But other man, your friend, I don' like him now, just today. He follow me around.'

George squeezed her hand and her good eye turned on him with the other straining to follow it. 'But you I like, okay,' she said. 'Tonight you in bed with me not him.'

As they danced George felt the Japanese whisky swilling around against his inside walls. They whirled and it whirled with them. He was beginning to feel indistinct. The other girls brought men onto the dance floor and it seemed that time passed quickly. Everyone danced close. On occasions he found himself back at the bar with A'Dare making less sense all the time. Manot had gone. The Japanese whisky was potent but George managed to stay on his feet, although swaying. He and A'Dare drank a number of toasts relating to their countries and the unshakable bonds between. Appropriately, during one of these sessions of inebriated chauvinism, the band, in George's honour, although he did not realise it, struck up a ragged version of 'God Save the Queen'.

408

'Attention!' ordered George bumptiously. 'Our National Anthem.'

'Stuff your national anthem,' said A'Dare abruptly aggressive, 'What about *ours*?'

'This *is* yours,' insisted George. He was rocking at attention. Others were trying to dance to the unfamiliar tune.

'S'not,' argued A'Dare like a truculent boy. 'We don't want your fucking national anthem. Go and save your Queen yourself.' He remained grimly on his stool.

'You will not speak of the Sovereign like that, in those terms,' said George, adding without confidence, 'It's *lèse majesté*.' To his own surprise he found himself pulling A'Dare off the stool. The Australian's face became suffused.

'Pommie bastard!' he shouted. He gave George a clumsy push which sent him staggering along the bar, knocking the drinks and drinkers sideways. There were howls and protests and at once, as if they had only been awaiting the signal, everyone in the place began fighting.

Stools, and the people sitting on them, toppled, each against the next. Fallen customers lay in an entangled line like a collapsed rowing crew. The men struggled up and began punching at the most conveniently placed neighbour. The girls emitted scheduled screams. They knew the emergency drill and crawled and wriggled away to safer corners although some began fighting between themselves, skirmishes that eventually spilled into the main battle which was now consuming the whole place.

It seemed to George that he was striking out in the middle of a colourful and revolving fairground roundabout; he could clearly hear the clamorous music. He realised vaguely that this was the effort of the staunchly-playing band, only terminated by the backward collapse of the dais on which they sat. There was a crack, heard clearly above the general mayhem, and the musicians slid rearwards as if jettisoned over the side of a capsising vessel.

Although the contest had begun as a personal confrontation with A'Dare, the little Australian was swiftly swallowed up in the general fray, and the next time George saw him was as their crawling courses converged on the way to gain the safety of the main exit.

'This way, mate,' confided the Australian. 'Time to piss off.'

409

They went like reptiles on their bellies to the door and slid into the street. As if it had been only waiting for them the rain began again. It dropped rather than fell, dull, separate bullets at first, quickly thickening to a bombardment. Before they were halfway across the street they were soaked. George fell down in the mud and A'Dare had to pull him upright. Then A'Dare toppled to hands and knees, and began walking on all fours, howling like a dingo. 'Get up, you boozed bastard!' swore George trying to tug him to his feet. Unsteadily the small man became upright, his legs spread apart in the mud. His fists began to flail uselessly trying to make contact with George who was out of range. Eventually the Australian over-balanced and fell forward again. In the violent rain George dropped on his knees beside him. 'Ollie!' he shouted. 'Come on, Ollie lad!'

They were found, still crouching in the slimy street, by three of the girls from the Salon de Thé who emerged after the rain had ceased, and who helped them towards the Imperial Hotel, deftly picking their pockets as they did so. They were encouraged, dripping, to their room by the girls and by Copeland who was behind the desk when the company arrived. The mud-caked pair were pushed through the door and the girls departed laughing to count their loot. The fracas at the Salon de Thé continued for some time and later several injuries were sustained from police batons.

Stiff with mud, George and A'Dare remained on the bed until seven o'clock when Pepita came into the room with a pot of hot, harsh, coffee. She began to sing, horribly and threw open the shutters to admit the dank morning air. Like survivors from some lost swamp age they stirred, groaned and creaked. Pieces of dried mud fell from them. George felt the lumps drop from his lids as he opened his eyes. 'Oh God,' he said holding his head. 'Oh God.'

'The bus, she goes at eight o'clock,' said Pepita cheerfully. Once A'Dare was awake and they were both, still like half-reclaimed mummies, sitting up, side by side, in the bed, shakily drinking coffee, the girl produced their stolen money, tickets and other documents. They realised what had happened and thanked her sincerely. 'Girls big thieves,' she assured them, pocketing the rewards they had offered. 'I only learning.'

A'Dare, although he made several sporting attempts, found it impossible to leave the bed. George forced himself, groaning,

410

to do so. He went to the end of the corridor and stood in the shower still wearing his clothes. The mud went down the drain and blocked it. Brown water swilled around his ankles.

He returned to the room and, unable to make the effort of speech, dressed himself in his meagre spare clothes. Pepita was sitting on the bed picking pieces of mud from A'Dare's chest. The Australian sat up with his eyes closed, his orange-peel teeth hanging negligently outside his mouth. The girl interrupted her task to kiss George an emotional goodbye.

''Bye 'bye,' said A'Dare from the bed with a weak wave. His eyes remained closed. His stomach stuck out like a Buddha's. ''Bye 'bye,' he repeated.

George put his wet clothes in yet another plastic bag, picked up the holdall that had been Clemmie's and, having paid the philosophical Copeland over the desk, he walked out on another chapter of his travels and his life. He boarded the bus to Tenopulca and it pulled out of Cedunna City at 8.50. He forgot to take a bottle of water.

XX

The bus to Tenopulca took fourteen and a half hours with stops at many vapid villages along the route; places called MacArthur, Eisenhowertown and Roosevelt City where it was rumoured that a hundred Japanese soldiers died one wartime evening. They were bathing, unguarded in the river, and were caught naked by an army of Filipino guerrillas who machine-gunned them before they could run out of the water. The man who told George the story was half-Japanese himself. His father had been one of the occupying army. 'Innocent, unarmed men,' he lamented.

They were the only occupants of the '*Primera Clase*' section of the bus, a roped-off area at the rear of the vehicle of half a dozen seats and a brass spittoon. The front section was a rabid free-for-all: people, produce, chickens. At Eisenhowertown a man pushed a goat aboard and it bleated for seventy miles. As the sun climbed so the interior heated, like a lidded pot on a stove. George sat melting, cursing his omission of the water bottle. The bus bounced over holes in the ragged road and tore through long channels of brown water. The Filipino-Japanese chewed a succession of small leaves that seemed to salve his thirst. He left the bus at the settlement after Roosevelt City, a place simply called Tojo, and here George purchased a bottle of water for an exorbitant price although he was given a reduction on a half-bottle of Japanese Scotch.

He returned to the sole occupancy of '*Primera Clase*' but now the other man had left there was a shift in the attitude of the people swaying at the front. George, perspiring, bruised by the bus's bounce and with a hot thirst, sat drinking whisky and water in alternating mouthfuls. A sly-looking man with a small boy of villainous appearance pushed through the bouncing passengers, luggage and livestock, and both approached with smiles that were at once ingratiating and evil. It was the boy

412

who was spokesman. '*Señor*, mister, my father he needs your water.'

'I need my water myself,' replied George with childish truculence. 'I get thirsty.'

'My father,' said the boy patiently, 'also he gets thirsty. My father he is an old man.'

George stalled. 'How old?'

He appeared to have scored a point because the child's expression became uncertain. He turned to his father and questioned him in Spanish. The man shrugged his shoulders and the boy turned his crafty eyes back on George. The bus bounced and groaned. 'My father he says he is old,' shrugged the boy. 'But he does not know how much.'

'I'm old,' said George huffily. 'Older than your father.'

'You gringo,' argued the lad. 'You not old.'

George picked up the Japanese Scotch bottle, took a swig of whisky and followed it with a mouthful of limp water. Then he handed the water silently to the boy whose face softened immediately to that of someone of his own age. He said '*Muchas gracias*,' and took the bottle, half-full, with both hands. The man's face too lost its wickedness and his beak-like mouth opened like that of an expectant nestling. His need went unanswered because the boy ignored him, took a personal draught from the bottle and at once backed away into the moving mayhem at the front of the bus where he began industriously to sell mouthfuls of water to the eager passengers. His hands were soon full of coins. The father's tiny black eyes followed him and turned distraughtly back to George.

'Kids can be a disappointment,' said George.

The man did not understand but he recognised the tone. '*Si, si*,' he agreed hopelessly. The lines in his face had lost their wickedness and were now merely old. Hopefully, trading on the sound of George's single sympathetic sentence, he nodded towards the whisky bottle.

'Shit, all right,' sighed George. To the man's overwhelming happiness he took a final swig and handed it across. It was not thirst-quenching without the water anyway. He wondered how far the next stop was. The Filipino grasped the gift, looked with ungrateful doubt at the giver, and elaborately wiped the mouth of the bottle before taking a deep gulp. There was only time for one because his evil son, wriggling through the bodies at the

413

front of the bus, reached him like a snake and snatched the bottle. The Englishman and the Filipino exchanged hurt expressions but that was all. A shrug was all that was left. The deprived man turned and went, bent, back to his place. When he reached it George saw him talking angrily to his neighbours and glancing with hatred towards the end of the bus.

There was, however, no further intrusion. The 'Primera Clase' rope was a demarcation respected by the remainder of the peasant mob. They argued, fought, spat, stole and jostled, all to the cackling of the caged hens and the poignant bleating of the goat, but they made no effort to break the barrier. The bus stopped only once more, at a place where the passengers, observing some time-marked ritual, lined up on each side of the road, males one side, females the other, and squatted over two opposite ditches. The squatters modestly faced away from each other so that the spectator was treated to two parallel lines of oval posteriors edging the road. There was no village here, just a petrol pump and a man selling cakes and sticky yellow and pink drinks. Most of the passengers, having completed their toilette, purchased something from the vendor. George remained in the bus with the caged chickens and the goat.

By now it was evening and the heat was diminishing. Mountains and trees enveloped the sun and eventually the daylight; the roughshod bus barged on, its headlights swaying along the road. During the final three-hour stretch to Tenopulca, down through the sightless hills and to the coast once more, many of the passengers went to sleep, lolling and rolling against each other like shapeless bags. Even the animals quietened. George remained resolutely open-eyed, hanging on to the seat in front, wondering how long the driver – unchanged since they began the journey – would keep awake. Several times they struck soft earthbanks on the corners as they descended to the plain, and, viewing from his rear position, George came to the conclusion that it was only these buffets which jerked the man in charge of the bus from his doze.

Eventually, however, they dipped down into flat country, lights began to appear, odd points that spread out into a skein of illuminations marking their destination. Exactly fourteen and a half hours after leaving Cedunna City, two hundred and ninety miles away, the bus ran through the main thoroughfare of Tenopulca, a long street of noise and raucous lights.

414

The local passengers fell off with their bundles and baggage, many into the arms of emotional relatives. George alighted last, behind the goat which appeared demoralised and muted by the journey, and stood surveying the scene of welcome. A feeling of solitariness came upon him. Everyone was greeting, embracing, kissing someone. There were tears for old people and carryings for children. George saw the boy who had purloined his water and Japanese whisky being hugged by a fat lady festooned with beads and shells. The boy's father stood by, apparently abashed, holding both empty bottles as if they were trophies. George knew again the feeling he had experienced on the station at Warminster, more than a year before, when a grandmother had been welcomed by a child and had said: 'Let's be going home.' Here was he, still alone; still with nowhere to go. He had chosen to dispose of welcomes.

Away from the excited crowd by the flank of the bus he walked with Clemmie's canvas bag on his shoulder and his still-damp clothes from his muddy shower in Cedunna City. Last night seemed an age ago.

Tenopulca was a honky-tonk town, neon signs flashing above the hovels with holes for doors, each one a bar or a brothel. Ten variations of loud music blasted into the street, cars blared their klaxons, and somewhere a number of women were screaming. It did not seem a likely place for a night's rest.

His bones ached so much after the jogging journey and the depravities of the previous night, however, that he fell asleep the moment he stretched out on a bed in a hotel at the very heart of the cacophony. He had not eaten since the night before and he had intended to go out and find something but sleep caught him before he could attend even to that. When he awoke it was early daylight. Outside his window the town had upon it a dissipated silence. The only sounds were the creaking of the hotel signboard in the early sea breeze and the hollow hammering of surf upon sand.

Now he was very hungry. Quickly he washed and shaved and walked down to the lobby. It was like a burial vault, ornately decorated and draped with prostrate bodies stretched out on every available horizontal surface, including the top of the reception desk. There was a bell, the type to be struck with the hand, standing almost against the hair-hung ear of the man sprawled on the desk. George hit the bell resoundingly but the sleeper scarcely paused in his snoring. To George's surprise, however, a moustached man with complaining eyebrows answered the summons. 'It's very late, *señor*,' he said.

'Not for me,' George told him. The man revealed that they had some hamburgers left and chipped potatoes and sweetcorn and George agreed to have them. He also asked for some coffee.

George walked out to the front of the hotel where a man lay among some wrecked tables and chairs apparently in the position he had fallen during the night. Nearer the street the furniture was still in place and he sat down and waited. The sun had just risen, the Pacific rolled into shore, its surf as white and regular as perfect teeth; the small breeze pushed the palms and the street was dirty and deserted. The waiter brought the baleful food, and the coffee which was fresh so George did not complain.

There was a desolute peace pervading the town. There were bottles and other trash in the street, one of the neon signs still flashed the message 'Drinks, Girls', pale against the day sky, dogs patrolled and somewhere a child cried. The air was already warm. George took out the air ticket that Manot had given him and checked, what he already knew, that the day's flight to Manila was at noon.

As if this were some signal to which they were responding, aircraft engines grated in the sky. The plane had topped the mountains and now appeared low over the lagoon. The amphibian was ancient and ugly, double-winged, an engine perched over the fusilage like a large hat on an old woman. It coughed horribly as it lowered itself towards the green water. For a moment it hesitated over the surface as if it feared getting wet then, duck-like, flopped, rose, and flopped again, sending up a plume of spray and blue smoke. It pulled up quite sharply then turned its snub nose towards the shore and, with jaunty pride, chugged in.

'She made it,' said an American voice behind George. 'She made it again.'

Turning, George said: 'Surprised?'

'Surprised?' said the man. He was middle-aged, portly, wearing a white shirt and black trousers. 'Sir, I'm fucking amazed.' He had a pleasant tanned face and anxious blue eyes. 'My name's Westerwood and I tell you why I'm amazed,' he continued. 'Because I fly her. Every time she comes down in

416

one piece, without breaking up, I feel two ways – I feel glad for the guy who's just brought off a miracle and scared for myself because the next miracle has to be mine. I'm flying her out today.'

'They used to call this plane a sea-cow,' said Westerwood with a cautious fondness. 'Built in 1950 fifty and then mothballed. This outfit bought three in fifty-six at San Diego.'

They were leaving the shore in a launch with the co-pilot, a nervous man from Honolulu, and the flight engineer who ominously carried a hammer. The flying boat nested on the midday lagoon, both ugly and beautiful, a graceful hull, swan-nosed, topped by the ungainly rigging of her wings and heavy-looking engines.

'She looks all right,' ventured George. 'For her age.'

Westerwood laughed wryly. 'The other two sank,' he mentioned. 'From twenty thousand feet.' The moon-faced Hawaiian glanced at him as if he wished the remark had gone unsaid. The flight engineer minutely examined the head of the hammer. Behind the launch, at the jetty, another boat was taking on passengers for Manila. Ahead, cargo was being loaded into the aircraft's hull from a barge so low in the water that even the easy waves obscured it.

'This trip, continued Westerwood, 'is my last but five. Six more and my contract is up. I take my pay-off and run.'

'It *is* safe, is it?' asked George.

'Sure. Safe as a flying house. I always get jittery. Maybe that's not such a bad thing.'

'Keeps you on your toes,' said the Hawaiian as if finishing a well-recognised sentence.

'It certainly does. Right on them.'

They were approaching the white plane now. It lolled in the olive water, tethered like a large melancholy animal. The boatman took the launch round to the opposite side of the hull, away from the loading barge. On the tail, on that side only, was painted a blue swordfish, and along the hull 'Historic Airlines Inc'. George was wondering if it was too late to go back.

There was a gangway like that of a ship lying sideways against the plane's body. The launch eased in and the flight engineer was first aboard, disappearing quickly into the fusilage.

As the rest embarked, the sound of heavy hammering came from within. George carried the canvas holdall. He had dried his Cedunna City clothes in the early sun and had abandoned yet another plastic carrier. It was now hot August. His plan, as he went towards the east and into the coming winter, was to buy a pullover and later a coat.

Inside the flying boat it was spacious and scruffy. The co-pilot took a broom and began sweeping industriously between the seats. 'Nobody ever thinks of doing this job,' he complained with his face void of expression. 'Me, I have to do it all.'

Westerwood had gone forward to the flight deck. He returned, more positive and cheerful now that he was aboard, and suggested that George should sit in the jump seat next to the flight engineer while they flew. 'Back here,' he said indicating the passenger cabin, 'so many people get sick.'

George's gratitude for the warning was tempered by the size of the space he was required to occupy on the flight deck. The midget seat was tucked into one corner of the crew's glass pod. He swallowed his misgivings, however, and sat, jammed into the place like a cork in a bottle. The noon sun was fierce through the window but he found a cord and, pulling it, discovered that a small dirty blind was released. It kept the magnified rays from his face. The Hawaiian came in, head bent, and looked up through the glass at the sky. 'Those guys,' he grumbled, 'they tell you one thing. Then you get everything else they don't say. See what I mean?'

Although he was not at all sure, George agreed.

'I guess they have to say something. So they just make it up,' said the man ducking out again.

From the rear came the sounds of passengers boarding. One was wailing and had to be threatened before he eventually quietened. George continued sitting, wedged and apprehensive. The flight engineer, still clutching his hammer, now came forward and, ignoring George at first, began rummaging without patience in a pull-out pocket stuffed with charts and papers. Eventually he discovered what he needed in a second drawer, a forlorn manual, its spine broken, into which he delved hurriedly.

'Nothing ever gets explained,' he eventually complained to George. 'This thing is a goddamn puzzle.' He digested the information he sought and then went out again. There came the sound of renewed hammer blows.

Westerwood eventually came forward and sat in the pilot's seat. 'Our luck is lousy,' he said staring out of the window at the land in the manner of one considering swimming. 'Now we've got a priest on board. A Holy Joe.'

'That's bad, is it?' said George. 'A priest?'

'Terrible. Even fishermen won't take a priest out. It's asking for trouble. But he won't leave. I asked him and he won't go. Says his mother needs him in Manila. A go-go girl more like it.' He sat disconsolately and fingered the controls. 'Okay,' he said, mostly to himself. 'Let's see if this thing works.'

The Hawaiian reappeared and took his seat beside Westerwood. He watched the pilot's actions with the attention of a first-day novice. George was torn between reassurance and panic. The flight engineer came in, closing the door behind him. They were now enclosed in the hot glass cabin. 'I think maybe it'll last for a few hours more,' the flight engineer muttered. Neither of the other men replied. Putting the hammer into the documents pocket the engineer turned to George and said with a shrug. 'Talk to yourself.'

Westerwood began throwing switches, turning knobs and staring at the pattern of the dials. He wiped one with his sleeve. Apparently satisfied he pulled positively at a knob and with a spluttering roar one of the engines fired. He looked surprised and pleased. The cabin began to vibrate. A pair of earphones were hooked alongside George's seat. He picked them up and put them on. Violent pop music blasted his ears. He took them off again. He could see the co-pilot was listening to the same wavelength because he was making little dancing movements in his seat. Westerwood started the second engine. The flying boat wanted to go forward. She jogged a little to one side, started to chug over the water and then lost the power from the starboard engine. The plane began to describe a sedate but alarming circle in the lagoon. Westerwood said 'Shit' and restarted the engine. Having done so he glanced over his shoulder towards the flight engineer who returned the look with a shrug.

Now the craft seemed to have decided to obey and, having revved the engines further, the pilot let her move slowly through the water. He turned conversationally to George. 'No luxury spared,' he shouted with his destroying smile. 'No coffee, no stewardesses, no announcements. Nobody would hear them

419

with this racket and the walls are thin. We print the "Welcome aboard" message on the vomit bags.'

Smiling weakly George waved his acknowledgement of the information. He pulled at his seat belt, testing it, and it came away at one corner and hung uselessly around his body. No one else on the flight deck was wearing one so he said nothing.

'I think they're cooked enough,' shouted Westerwood to the Hawaiian. He gave the engines further verve. 'Let's get this show on the road.' All at once, George was gratified to see, he straightened his back and took a firm hold of the central column. For the first time he appeared to be quite sure of what he was doing. The co-pilot and the flight engineer stiffened expectantly also. All three stared attentively ahead, like men watching a race in which they have a high stake. The American increased the throttle and the ungainly machine began to skid across the big green lagoon. Fingers of spray came up and smeared the screen. The town and the island were going by like a swiftly-running frieze. The hull began to bounce uncomfortably. Westerwood eased back the stick mouthing encouragement as he did so. Slowly, achingly, the flying boat pulled off the sea and dragged itself into the air, it seemed to George only just in time for directly they were airborne, trees and the huts of the village passed slowly below them, the upturned faces of the apprehensive inhabitants clearly to be seen.

The flight engineer nodded approvingly and George saw him uncross his fingers. In a minute more they were clear of sea and land, up in the hot Pacific sky and setting a course north. As the machine climbed so the engines settled to a disgruntled roar. At cruising height Westerwood turned from the controls to George as if he owed him an apology. 'The outfit's got no money,' he said loudly. 'Not a damned dime. You saw we only had one side painted? The Swordfish?'

George nodded.

'They can't afford to keep this ship out of the sky long enough to paint the other side,' Westerwood continued. He produced a bottle of Jim Beam and began to open it. 'There's no in-flight service for the passengers,' he grinned. 'Only the crew.'

Acknowledging the ritual, the Hawaiian produced four metal containers and a measure of the bourbon was poured into each and passed round. They toasted each other and as they did so

420

the aircraft gave a slight bump. At once Westerwood's eye went to the starboard side horizon. 'That goddamn storm's coming up,' he said in a hurt way. He glanced at the co-pilot. 'I thought they said it would miss.'

The Hawaiian squeezed his moonface into a shrug. 'That's what they said,' he confirmed. 'Going south, they said.'

'Bastards,' grunted Westerwood.

'D'you wanna go back?' said the co-pilot. It was a suggestion.

Westerwood made a face. 'D'you wanna break the company?' he asked.

'Rather break the company than my neck,' put in the flight engineer, 'They can always get another company.'

'Ask them,' said Westerwood to the man beside him. 'The weather station. Maybe it's veering.'

The co-pilot turned a dial and spoke close into his mouthpiece. George could see the storm, like a bruise, thickening to the east. The Hawaiian said to Westerwood, 'It's on course.'

'Fuck it,' said Westerwood. He turned, again as though he felt obliged to explain to George. 'This thing can't get above it,' he said. 'And she can't crawl under it. And she can't speed up, or slow down.'

'So we are flying right into it,' said George.

'You should be an airman,' grunted the pilot. He turned to the front. The way ahead was still bright but below them the sea was churning. 'I knew that Holy Joe would bring bad luck,' he said. 'They always do. Let's hope he's got some real good prayers.'

'Right now he's taking confessions,' said the flight engineer looking through the door behind him. 'They must have seen the storm coming.'

'Maybe he should start in here,' suggested Westerwood.

The Hawaiian started to get up. 'I'd like to confess,' he said seriously. 'I'm a Catholic.'

The pilot pushed him back. 'You sit right there,' he said stonily. 'I'm interested in the future not the past. Whatever you've done can't be so bad as to deserve what's creeping up on us right now.'

For a while George had thought that they might be doing it for his benefit, as a cruel joke, but now he could see the real anxiety in their actions. He was sorry his seat belt did not work. 'My seat belt is broken,' he said confidingly to the flight engineer.

The man seemed surprised that the subject had been raised at all. He leaned into a locker at his side and trawled out a piece of cord which he handed silently to George who thanked him with an uncertain smile and tied the loose end of the useless belt to the seat fitting.

Now the arms of the storm were beginning to enclose them. Ahead a long peninsula of purple cloud raced across their course. The sun blinked, the waves below frothed and darkened. The flying boat bridled like a disquieted donkey. The door to the passenger cabin opened and the anguished priest, a Filipino in robes, staggered in. He was a conscientious man and while the plane bucked increasingly he steadied himself with one hand, made the sign of the Cross with the other, and blessed them copiously in Latin. From the passenger section came the sound of prayers and religious responses. It was a cheap airline and the travellers knew of its disastrous history.

'Get him out of here,' snarled Westerwood at the co-pilot.

The Hawaiian looked at the priest as he might have looked at St Peter. 'But . . . but . . . we . . .'

'Get him *out!*' ordered the pilot. He decided to take the action himself. Putting the dithering co-pilot's hand on the central column, he half rose and said to the priest, 'Thanks a lot, Father. Now blow.'

The Hawaiian watched with the growing terror of someone who does not believe in tampering with fringe powers. Westerwood pushed the priest firmly back into the passenger cabin and slammed the door. As he did so, and as if in riposte, the first of the big storm clouds hit the plane like a fist, sending it slewing and vibrating through all its parts. The engines squawked. Westerwood thumped the co-pilot on the shoulder but before the bemused man could turn to the front he had jumped into his own seat and taken the controls himself.

'Radio our position – up shithouse creek,' he ordered brusquely. 'Make sure they get it right. They'll have a rescue ship out here in a day or two.' The sky was black all around now. Gobs of rain were hitting the glass. The aircraft rolled and groaned. Westerwood appeared suddenly concerned that he was ignoring George. He half turned, laughed extravagantly, and bawled: 'At least we never get trouble with hijackers!'

422

Thoroughly frightened, George was hanging on to his seat with both hands. He tried closing his eyes but a spasm of lightning made him open them. It was like being photographed by a great camera. Rigid-faced he sat while the three crew members were thrown about by the convulsions of the air. It was impossible to see anything. The rain now fell on them like a waterfall. George could hear the co-pilot repeating their position to someone sitting in a chair on the ground. Westerwood, fighting with the two halves of the central column like a man holding the horns of a bull, began, suddenly and madly, to sing:

> Mairsey doats and dozey doats
> And little lambs eat ivy,
> A kiddleativy too
> Wouldn't you?

How long it went on George only knew after it was over. It was probably no more than half an hour. At one moment they seemed to be clipping the fingertips of the ocean waves and at the next they were bouncing among the nightmare clouds. No one on the flight deck thought the plane would survive. The Hawaiian prayed, the same prayer over and over again, the flight engineer had taken up the hammer again and was gripping it like a charm, Westerwood continued to sing raucously, and George sat as still as he was able and as frightened as he had ever been. Once he thought he heard the wings folding.

But then, so unexpectedly it was like a miracle, they ran into a brief valley of sunshine. The three airmen cheered madly and George joined in. There was immediate blackness as if to silence their assumptions, further buffeting and more violent rain. But now they knew they were going to win. Another lead of sun with some blue sky appeared. The revealed ocean below was almost white with anger but with an exultant bellow from its engines, the ugly, staunch flying boat burst into a great field of blue with upright clouds like loitering angels.

'She made it,' sighed Westerwood. 'I always knew she would. What a beauty.'

The priest made another entry, blessing them with one moving hand and muttering a thanksgiving to which all four men appended a heartfelt amen. 'Many people have been throwing up back here,' reported the priest. 'It's not been a good ride.'

As he retired, Westerwood nodded below. Blue sky and the vertical white clouds now occupied the visible world and these were joined by a wriggle of land and, a little further, buildings standing like dice.

'Manila Bay,' announced Westerwood with something of the pride of ownership, adding, as if someone might doubt his navigation, 'In the Philippine Islands.'

'I can see my mother,' shouted the co-pilot pointing five thousand feet below. 'See, she is waving to her favourite son.'

'Which one is that?' laughed the flight engineer. He asked for the string back and George unknotted it from his seat belt and handed it to him.

Now the storm had vanished behind them like an assailant running away. The engines purred like cats. They swung easily over the boats in the bay and Westerwood landed her elegantly in a long creamy seam across the green water.

'How d'you feel?' he asked George.

'Relieved,' said George.

'You are going on to Los Angeles?'

'That's the idea.'

'I'd go now. The first plane you can get. If you don't you maybe won't ever find the courage to fly again.'

'I think you're right,' said George.

The Hawaiian co-pilot had pushed the earphones close to his head with both fat hands. 'Captain,' he said slowly. 'There's tanks in the streets. There's shooting going on.'

The election which deposed the long-misruling President Marcos in the Philippines was, as elections in such places go, almost bloodless. There were a few deaths and some people were injured, one of whom fell from a first-floor window at Manila airport and landed on George Goodnight. George lay on the ground winded and with a hurt back. The youth who had fallen suffered a broken leg. The authorities at the airport, having had a total lack of battle casualties, were anxious to make the most of the occasion. George found himself being borne in the second of two ambulances which drove with screeching sirens and a police escort through the Manila streets. He lay on the stretcher within, his holdall at his feet, forbidden to move by two eagerly conscientious attendants. His back was painful.

At the shining white hospital he was astonished to see a half-moon of doctors and nurses, twenty at least, standing as a beaming reception committee. The youth who had fallen from the window was carried as swiftly into the casualty department as any stricken first-line soldier. George, still prostrate on the stretcher, held down in fact by the firm hand of one of the orderlies, was borne up the steps and the nurses, so starched they crackled as they moved, leaned towards him all smiles and unconcealed readiness.

Two doctors examined him after three nurses had squabbled to take off his clothes. They put him into a suit of striped pyjamas, stiff with newness, and put him into bed in a small room, the door of which they locked.

There followed four days of x-rays and tests, all conducted in glimmering rooms and with ethereal equipment that looked brand new. Relays of doctors came to see him and the nurses rubbed lotions into his back and buttocks. He began to enjoy himself. The food was superb and his injury went away. On the fifth day a new person came, a man in a long, pale suit, grey-haired and with serious spectacles. 'And how are you feeling?' It was a question asked from the height of authority, as if this person could act on information. George said he was much better, thanks to everyone, and he felt it was truly time to continue on his journey to Los Angeles.

'Ah, it was Los Angeles you were going to. I see. There was a big crowd at the airport, wasn't there? It is all the enthusiasm after the revolution. That is why the young man fell from the window. Over-excitement followed by overbalancing. For some the election and its aftermath has been a disappointment, you know. They were hoping for more shooting. The tanks were out and the troops ready. But nothing much happened. Marcos went and it was all over.'

The man sat on the end of the bed. 'I am Dr Raphael Spinoza,' he said holding out his hand. 'And know you are George Goodnight, an English lawyer, because I have studied your passport. My first information was that you were also a doctor, which would have been perfect.'

Perfect? The not unfamiliar, uncomfortable feeling settled on George, like a door opening and a finger beckoning.

'You have no idea how the people here in Manila feel,' said Spinoza.

'Very relieved, I suppose,' replied George with caution.

'Yes, of course they are, but you cannot understand the burden which has been lifted from them. They expect life to be very different now, and *quickly*. This hospital, for example, has hardly ever been used. While we have children dying of tuberculosis, three or four in a bed in poor hospitals, this place, which is full of modern equipment, has been all but empty. It was for people who could pay only.'

'I see.'

'Indeed. And this is only one thing. There are many.'

'It is very interesting,' said George. 'And you have my best wishes for the future.'

'You could help us with it,' said Spinoza suddenly. He smiled behind his lenses as though offering a great blessing and spread his hands. 'You arrived – as if you had been sent from Heaven. Word came to me and I am here to ask you.'

'Me? What could I do? I'm on my way to Los Angeles.' He knew he was fencing off the inevitable. Here he was; available again.

'Of course, you may go at once.' The man looked deeply disappointed. 'But there is no flight to Los Angeles until tomorrow. Perhaps, in this case, you could spare a few minutes to listen to what I have to say.'

George drew in a full breath. 'Please,' he invited without enthusiasm.

The reflective smile returned. The man patted George's knee. 'I knew you would,' he said. 'You are an Englishman. It is fair play.' He pursed his lips. 'Now I will tell you.'

'Please do.'

'The people expect very much from what has happened in the past few days,' said Spinoza. 'And it is right they should. Too long they have suffered. But they will expect it too quickly, everything changed in a *flash*, you know. And that is not always possible, especially in the Philippines. I have been given a high responsibility by the new government. I must get the medical services reorganised – in a big hurry. There are still many people who die in this country who would not die in other places. The people expect much. And not just in Manila but other places. If they do not get changes quickly they will be

426

disappointed, they will think what we have told them is lies, just like the past régime.'

He drew a deep breath and George said: 'I am still listening.'

'Good, because this is the important part. About you. I need at once, today, a man like you to take charge of a hospital in a distant part of the country.'

George felt his mouth dry. 'Me? In charge of a . . . why me?'

'One reason is that you are English – and you look exactly right. The people in that region have seen enough of local officials and they do not believe or trust them any more. They will be impressed by you. And they will trust you.'

'But . . . Jesus Christ . . . I don't know the first thing about . . .'

'You will not have to operate,' smiled Spinoza. 'Do not worry. There will be doctors. All you would have to do is to administer. Organise. The hospital is funded by the World Health Authority, the United Nations. They sent a team to inspect it last year. Now it needs someone whom the local people will trust. Someone from outside their experience. Someone from *England*. When I saw you, and I understood you were a doctor, I thought my prayers had been answered. The pay is five thousand US dollars a month.'

XXI

The Santa Bernardina Leper Colony was on an island in the Rio Santos in the northernmost province of the Philippines. The small aeroplane lurched and swung above the packed jungle as if it had lost its way, the pilot apparently content to let the machine find the landing strip by its own trial and error. Turbulence tossed them about and George was grateful when both the plane and its pilot came to the same conclusion and they set course for an indistinct airstrip alongside a few huts crouched within one akimbo arm of the big river.

The man who had come to meet them, Señor José Campos, had forgotten to bring the wind sock, an important aid in a country of irregular terrain and air currents. The pilot roared low over the strip, gesticulating until Señor Campos, realising the error, took off his shirt and hung it on a tree. With a final bank of the wings and a short study of the lolling shirt the pilot landed the aircraft on the soft strip. He said he would have to leave again quickly before his plane sank too deeply into the soft green ground.

'It is not a good thing that you come here,' were the first words Campos spoke to George. He was a squat young man with a track of baldness up the centre of his head, lank black hair suspended down the sides like bead curtains.

'Why is that?' asked George. They were walking from the plane towards a jeep parked on a track alongside the landing stretch. Campos had reclaimed his shirt and was putting it on over his hairy body as they walked. The pilot had said that he would need the shirt to judge the wind for take-off but Campos ignored the request.

He said to George, 'There will be much trouble.'

'I don't see why,' argued George. 'Dr Spinoza is anxious about the hospital now that the previous controller has gone with the new régime. He has asked me to take over for three months until a new permanent head can be appointed. The new government is anxious that the people here should know that they are not forgotten, that *something* is being done. I am that something.' He thought it sounded pompous; here, however, he thought it might be an advantage, even a necessity. 'The United Nations, through the World Health Authority, finances this project,' he continued, 'and they have to be assured that their money is being properly spent. Otherwise they might not pay up.'

He saw Campos's stomach contract in a thick sigh as he climbed behind the wheel of the jeep. 'Is that all your luggage?' asked the Filipino nodding at Clemmie's holdall. He started the engine.

'That's all I'll need,' boasted George. 'I've been most of the way round the world with less.'

The jeep began to spring down the track. 'You can't talk about the people,' said Campos, 'in these parts. There's no people in these parts – not for many miles.' He nodded about him at the unrelieved green growth. 'It's mostly stuff like this.' He swivelled his eyes towards George, the whites almost yellow. 'You know it's lepers,' he said.

'I know, I know,' answered George impatiently. 'Dr Spinoza gave me all the unpleasant details. I've had to read it all up because I'm not a doctor. But I understand I won't be in any danger of catching it.'

The man drove for another mile along the track. It eventually emerged where the powerful river pulled itself along like a thickly patterned snake.

'So you're not a doctor?' said Campos, his curiosity surfacing.

'Exactly,' said George. 'I'm a lawyer. From England. Dr Spinoza thought I was right for the job which I gather is mainly organisational.'

'A lawyer might be better,' said the driver agreeably. 'I never met an Englishman before. Plenty of Americans. Gringos we call them.'

They rounded a bend in the river and came to a landing stage with an untidy motorboat tied up. A man, brown as earth, was crouching on the planks of the stage. He stood up and rubbed his legs as if crouching made them ache.

'Santa Bernardina,' said Campos nodding to some white buildings on what appeared to be the far bank of the river. 'Now you will see.'

A lump of misgiving rose in George's stomach. He had only a vague notion of what a leper looked like. 'Let's go across,' he said.

He sat in the stern of the boat with Campos on the cross seat in front alongside the driver. The man started the popping engine and they set out carefully into the wide stream.

'The election go pretty good, eh?' suggested Campos without turning round.

'Everybody seems very pleased,' answered George neutrally. 'I was a bit late for it. They were letting people out of prison by the time I arrived.'

'Ah,' nodded the other man. 'It is good they let people from the prisons. It makes more room for people going in.'

'What makes you think they will?' asked George with some sharpness.

'Why not? That is what prisons are for.'

Deciding not to pursue the topic, George studied the white buildings as they neared. He could see now that they were set on an island with the river swooping round on either bank.

'Is the medical director ashore?' he asked.

'No,' said Campos. 'He is here in this boat.'

'You! Good gracious, I am sorry,' said George. 'I didn't hear you say.'

'I didn't,' said the Filipino. 'It's no big deal.'

'How many patients do you have?' asked George. 'Dr Spinoza thought about a hundred and fifty.'

'Two,' answered Campos flatly. 'Just two.'

'Two!' George burst into a jokey laugh. 'Very good.'

'You'll see,' said the other man flatly. 'You can count them.'

The boat nudged a wooden jetty. There was no one on shore to help. The buildings on the island looked spectral even in the humid sun and among the bright emerald. There was a big crucifix a few yards from the island jetty, a marooned Jesus. His eyes drooped dolefully as if He might be wondering if it had all been worth it.

'Come, I show you the patients,' said Campos. 'Also the staff.'

A nervous nurse, middle-aged and none too spotless, was standing in the shade of a covered way between two of the buildings.

430

'The staff,' introduced the Filipino. 'Maria. Would you like some coffee? Or some beer? I would recommend the beer.'

George said he would accept the recommendation.

Campos said: '*Dos beers*,' to the nurse and she went away, apparently gladly. 'Now,' said Campos, 'the patients.'

Still hardly able to believe him, George followed along void corridors. It sounded as if they were wearing clogs. Damp was rife and a green dust or mould had accumulated in corners. Windows were broken, holed in the middle like perpetual screams; there was a deep air of decrepitude.

'The patients,' said the medical superintendent pausing outside a door, 'are in separate parts of the building.'

'Different sexes?' asked George. 'Or different stages of the disease?'

'They just hate each other,' corrected Campos. 'Deeply. They are man and wife.'

He opened the door and a figure, upright but hunched in a chair at the far end of the hut-like building, raised a head as bare and slow as a tortoise. He had been staring into the screen of an old television set.

'Patient one,' Campos told George.

The long ward was lined with iron beds, some with stained rolled-up mattresses, others with rusting springs. The nurse had followed them with the beers which she carried on a tray bearing a single glass and a bottle opener. She said something to the medical superintendent in Spanish and went away.

'Maria says she's going to clean this ward next week,' he said without emphasis. 'But she said it also last week.' He looked at the single glass. 'That's for you,' he said. 'But I drink it straight from the bottle. It is for hygiene, you know.'

He opened the bottles and handed one to George. The superintendent drank his tipped up, like a Spaniard drinking wine from a goatskin, pouring it in without the bottle touching his mouth. George tried it and choked. 'It is only practice,' said Campos. 'Let us see our patient.' He made to walk then paused warningly. 'Don't mention his wife,' he said. 'It makes him mad. He speaks okay. His father was an American soldier. He's a war baby.'

The man looked shrunken and sore. His eyes turned up towards them slowly as if the hinges were stiff. They dropped

431

again towards the television screen and did not lift until Campos spoke to him. 'How are we today?'

'*We* maybe are okay,' replied the man dully. 'Me, not so good. Bits come off.'

Sadly George regarded him, a particle of the world's ills. The leprosy had dug deeply into him and would go on digging.

'This is Mr Goodnight,' said Campos. He put his hand firmly on George's wrist to prevent him shaking hands. 'He's English.'

'From England,' said the man. He seemed at once to realise that George was there in an official capacity. 'This place,' he said waving his right hand about the ward, 'used to be more fun when there was more people.' There were no fingers on the hand. 'Now it's no fun.'

'How long,' asked George, 'have you been here?'

'Years,' said the man. 'Goddamn years. But not much longer.' His deep hurt eyes turned to Campos. 'Is *she* still alive?' he asked.

'Your wife? Sure she is.'

'She ought to be dead by now.'

'Don't you want to see her? She's only along the corridor.'

'No, I don' wanna see her. She gave me this pox.'

His eyelids descended with a mechanical finality to the cartoon film on the set, Yogi Bear. Campos nodded sideways. They got up and walked towards the door.

'It's no fun any more!' shouted the man savagely up the empty ward.

'That's dreadful,' said George shaking his head as he reached the corridor. 'You don't realise.'

'Leprosy is not what it used to be,' said Campos. 'It does not occur now. Not like it did. Lepers are a dying breed.'

They walked along the resounding wood. 'The others all died?' said George.

'Not the ones he was talking about. He had the fun he remembers when they were brought in to make up the numbers.' He paused and sat on an unsafe-looking table, wiping the dust away from an area before he did so. 'This you ought to know,' he said bluntly.

'It sounds as though I should,' said George. Campos was still holding his beer bottle and he tipped it up in the Spanish way once more. He wiped his lips with his hand.

432

'Dr Spinoza told you about there being a hundred and fifty leprosy patients here, right?'

'Yes, he did.'

'I tell you, like you see, he was a hundred and forty-eight wrong. There's never been that many here. Fifty maybe, years ago, but leprosy is not a disease of today. People don't get it. It's been cut out. But the man in charge of this area, this territory, a Señor Miguel shall we call him – you can see his full name on the wanted posters – he gave the phoney figures so the United Nations paid up the subsidy every year.' He wafted his hand around. 'You can figure how much was spent on the hospital.'

George looked at him narrowly. 'And you were here? You knew about it?'

'Sure I was. But things always worked like that. When Marcos was President anyway. Maybe they will now. Who knows? You can't change everything in a couple of minutes. It's the *nature* of things. Somebody will always be after lining their pockets. I didn't steal anything. I just took my salary, when I got it. I have two other real hospitals to deal with in this state.'

Nodding, George said: 'I apologise, I wasn't suggesting it was you.'

'Thanks. And anyway, even though this place is like it is, it *is* keeping two cases of leprosy. It is necessary as long as there is even *one*. If this closed, where would these two people go? They can't support themselves and they can't live among other people – they'd be stoned to death.'

'How did you get your imitation patients to come here?'

'Ten dollars each. We didn't tell them it was a leper colony. We brought them upriver from the coast with doctors and nurses from other hospitals. *They* got fifty dollars. All for the benefit of the United Nations visitors. The UN team, they flew in, went at a run round the wards where we'd painted the phoney patients, and got the hell out of it. Straight back to Manila where they could have fun. Everybody got their money and back home they went. Old Hank was pretty upset when he was all alone again. He'd thought the good old days were back.'

'How long will he, Hank, hang on?' asked George.

'Only his wife keeps him alive,' answered Campos,

433

unemotional as he had been throughout. 'He's not going to die before her. Also, it is the same with her. She won't give up until he's gone. Strictly from a medical view I would put the bet on her.'

He slipped from the table and led the way along the corridor. In parts the virulent greenery from outside had pushed through the wooden walls and up through the floorboards. 'Little fingers,' commented Campos pulling one tendril away. 'Soon it will be all the hands.'

They went into a room at the end of the corridor where a scarred woman sat alone apathetically watching a television. The room was more private, more homely than the long ward in which the man had sat similarly staring. Across her knees she had an extended piece of linen, like a tablecloth, which she had been embroidering.

'What is this?' asked George kindly. He touched the edge of the material.

'She doesn't know,' said Campos. 'I have asked her many times. It is just embroidery, she says. For something to do. I think it is her shroud.'

After an initial glance the woman took no further heed of George. Her face was heavily marked by the disease and so was one of her hands. The other, he noticed, was untouched. She had beautiful hair. Her eyes peered through tunnels in her face. They stared fiercely at the black and white image on the television. George moved round and saw that a woman was giving a cookery lesson.

Campos was already wandering out as if he had become too familiar with the scene. 'And that,' he said as they returned down the corridor, 'is the Colony of Santa Bernardina.'

'How long since they saw each other?' asked George.

'More than one year,' Campos shrugged as he walked. 'They started to fight. A real fight, you know.' He demonstrated with his fists. 'Lepers fighting is a bad sight.'

He led the way across a compound to a frowning bungalow. It had once been painted white but now its skin was so cracked the wood beneath was exposed, dark with damp. One of the treads in the stairs that led to the veranda was missing and Campos pointed silent warning. 'This house,' he said, 'is like our patients, falling into ruin.'

It did not take long to view the inside. There was one large

434

room open on all sides, a kitchen in which squatted a rusting kettle, a humid bedroom, a shower cubicle, and two other small bedrooms. In the main room were some bamboo chairs, a table, a cupboard and a polished desk, so fine as to be incongruous. On the boards were some faded Indian rugs. 'I will get Maria to air the sheets and the tablecloth,' said Campos. They went out onto the veranda. The Filipino said he had to go down-river about twenty miles to a village surgery he ran. He would be back the following day. 'It will be necessary that you make a first report to Manila,' he said.

'I'm afraid so,' confirmed George. 'God only knows what I'll say.'

'Maybe He will tell you,' said Campos. 'Maria will bring your food.'

George thanked him and watched him go across the compound and turn towards the landing where the boat was waiting. He went back inside and walked around the decrepit bungalow once more. He would have liked a cup of tea and he eyed the rusty kettle with dislike. He went into the first bedroom, took his sweaty clothes off, and stood in the tin shower. As he pulled the release chain a jet of foul water shot from the pipe and struck him in the stomach. He kept pulling the chain and eventually water, cleaner now, came out in several lukewarm streams, although only a smattering escaped from the showerhead. He dried himself on a towel the size of a handkerchief. Maria came across the compound with six bottles of beer standing like skittles on a tray. Later she brought some unrelished fish and rice.

It was dark by nine. Insects droned through the hot night, coming into the bungalow and dancing in formations around the light. Their droning became so intrusive that George turned out the lamp and sat in the dark. The blue aura from two separate television sets glowered across the compound. He pulled the top of the last of the six bottles of beer and eased himself back into the bamboo chair. With an apologetic crack one of the legs collapsed and he found himself sloping to the floor at the left hand, back corner. He struggled for a moment but then realised he was not uncomfortable so he remained lolling sideways. 'Welcome, George Goodnight,' he recited, 'to Santa Bernardina.'

*

435

'Tell me about your queen,' asked Hank. 'Do you know her real well?'

George admitted that he did not. 'I've only seen her once,' he confessed. 'Apart from on television.'

'I see her on television,' said the leper. He nodded at the set. 'Right on there.' He appeared to be searching for another question. 'Do you have ice cubes in England yet?' he asked.

'Oh, we've got ice cubes,' George told him. 'In winter the streets are full of them.'

'Winter,' said the man almost longingly. 'Is hard to know about winter. Here it just rains or it don't rain. I've seen winter on the television.' He nodded at the set again as if anxious it should not be left out. 'Right on there.'

George sat alongside him. A basketball match was being played on the screen.

'I know who wins,' Hank said. 'I just keep it on for company.'

They had been talking for half an hour.

'What sort of houses do you guys have?' asked the man. He had a hole in his neck through which a whistling sound was emitted when he spoke.

'Houses? Well, they're usually brick, red brick, with tiles on the roofs, or slates.'

'Don't they have that grass on the roof?'

'Grass? Oh, thatch. Well, sometimes. Those houses are very old.'

'I've seen them,' said Hank pointing at the screen. 'Right there.'

He appeared to have an idea which pleased him. 'Why don't you draw a picture of your house,' he suggested. 'So that I can get the idea.'

George, taken by surprise, said: 'Yes . . . all right, I'm not much good at drawing but I'll show you. If I can remember.'

'You been away a while,' said Hank. It was a statement not a question.

'Quite a while.' There was a book lying on the locker at the end of the ward, Hemingway's *Across the River and Into the Trees* layered with dust. He took it and blew the dust away. Then he drew within the covers. 'Inside or outside first?' he asked.

'Do outside,' decided the man. He leaned forward in interest. 'It'll give me more idea.'

It was apparent that Hank had not talked to anyone at

436

length for a long time. George began to draw the exterior of his house at Shillington. The walls and windows, the bays downstairs, the chimney to one side. Hank liked the chimney. 'That's so Santa Claus can get in,' grinned George.

The ugly man laughed and struck George's shoulder with a blow like a feather. 'Get away, you're kidding,' he said.

'Summer or winter?' asked George. 'For the trees.'

'Winter,' said Hank. 'I can see plenty of goddamn summer from here. All the time.'

'Like this,' George told him. He surprised himself with both his memory and his drawing. The bare branches of the beech in the garden were etched against the paper sky.

'Great, great,' murmured Hank. 'What happens to the leaves? Where do they go?'

'All over the lawn,' answered George. 'They make a hell of a mess.'

'I know how the tree feels,' said Hank. 'Pieces falling off. What's that?'

'That's the sunroom,' George told him. 'You sit in there when its sunny.'

'It shades you?'

'No, it gets the sun on you. The sun is different there.' When he had finished the drawing George looked at it reflectively.

'Put some people in,' said Hank. 'You have some people you can put in?'

'Yes, of course. Look, here's Fred my neighbour.' He drew a figure looking over the fence. 'That's if he's still there. He's got woman trouble. He may have gone to Leighton Buzzard.'

'You don't say. Most men have woman trouble.'

George was drawing another picture, quickly as if his memory had been aroused. 'This is the inside,' he said. 'The sitting room.'

'What are those you're drawing?'

'Lamps. We had some good lamps.' He drew Felicity sitting in a chair.

'Your wife,' guessed Hank. He glanced at George. 'Trouble?'

'I'm afraid so. That's why I'm not sitting in the other chair.'

'Women and trouble, they're the same thing. Mine gave me this pox.'

'I've been talking to her,' said George.

'Has her goddamn eye fallen out yet?'

'Not that I noticed. She misses you.'

'She'd miss her eye more. Last time I saw it, it looked like it was coming out any time.'

'Well, it's still in place. She's got beautiful hair.'

'Her hair. Sure, that was always okay. Kinda long.' He nodded at the television set. 'I got this now. I like the ball games.'

Casually George said: 'It's a pity you can only get the one channel and it's not in colour.'

'Nothing's right in this life,' complained Hank. 'It would need a goddamn great antenna up above the trees.'

George left and walked along the corridor after Hank became fidgety and said the talking made him tired because he was unaccustomed to it. Almost before George was out of the ward he had begun to doze. He was only in his forties but he looked frail and old.

Contact was more difficult with Bella, Hank's wife. She was in the same attitude as he had left her the day before, the burrowed eyes fixed to the meaningless screen, the linen still over her knees, the needle held in her untouched hand poised to perform a stitch. It was only when he arrived that she began to embroider again, guiltily as if he might be there to monitor her progress.

He sat down patiently and pretended to be interested in the television programme. The reception was flickering and grained. It was an elderly comedy film which re-introduced him to Will Hay. Big Ben and the Houses of Parliament stood in the background. George began to laugh. Bella half looked at him and scowled: 'No goddamn good.'

He felt he had made contact.

He sat with her for half an hour; he said little, she said nothing. Eventually complimenting her on the embroidery, he left and walked across to the bungalow. He had a beer and a shower and waited for Campos to return.

The boat appeared faithfully upriver, almost floating on the early evening mist. It was the best hour of the day, between the heat and the insect-hung night, a sweet-rotten smell coming from the trees, the undergrowth and the green river.

'I've been organising,' said George. He liked Campos and they walked from the jetty and sat in bamboo chairs on the veranda. Campos had brought some whisky with him.

438

'Your mission is to organise and administer,' agreed the Filipino. 'The first must come first. What have you been organising?'

'Hank and his wife,' said George. 'I want to get them together again.'

'Have you told them?'

'Not directly. I've put out a few feelers. If they had a colour television with more channels I think that would be a help.'

Campos raised his eyebrows and smiled appreciatively. 'It is nice. But they would fight over the channels. Besides, it is not possible here. You would need a hundred-foot antenna.'

'In that case we get one. The United Nations might as well pay for some genuine improvements.'

The medical director nodded. 'We could fly one in,' he agreed. 'It wouldn't take long. Which room would you place the set? They're both too proud to move.'

'I think the new television would be a big inducement,' replied George. 'But in any case I think we ought to move them out of that ghastly hospital and into here.'

'This house?'

'Why not?'

Campos shrugged. 'This is some organising,' he said. 'Okay, why not. There is a phone link tomorrow. We'll tell them.'

It took only three days for the new television set and its aerial to arrive from Manila. George and Campos were at the landing strip as the plane circled the trees and came to ground. Two men in green overalls immediately began unloading the cargo. 'New governments are always so quick,' observed Campos with his customary dryness. 'If you want things to get done, have an election.'

On the island the two engineers, as silent as any men George had ever known, worked swiftly. They looked at the bungalow, surveyed the trees, and, as if communicating by some unspoken connection of minds, decided on the most advantageous place for the lofty aerial and proceeded to erect it, locking one piece into the next until its square head peered out over the jungle in the general direction of the capital city. They paused only to drink a beer each and then they connected the set, with its thirty-inch screen, crouching, coaxing and connecting, all anxiety in case it failed them. It did not. At the first attempt, while they all grouped expectantly, and Maria, the nurse, loitered at the door, a flickering shape materialised and a crackling signal sounded. Maria applauded singly. One of the silent green men ducked behind the set and knelt there for two minutes. The telepathy was still working. The second man, at the mentally given moment, turned on the power and an ocean liner appeared sailing coolly among the Norwegian fjords. They all exclaimed and applauded as if no one had ever before witnessed the miracle. The green overalled two stood at each side of the set, like a stage magic duo with their cabinet, bowed, packed their tools and returned to the aeroplane for take-off before nightfall.

George had rarely so much enjoyed an evening's television. Maria brought some hastily-prepared food and joined the two men in front of the set. For most of the time the Englishman could not understand what was being said on the screen, although Campos loosely translated the news and a few jokes in a comedy programme, but there was an American film with Doris Day which he enjoyed although he thought he had seen it before. They all stayed up to watch the late movie, a gangland war story set in Los Angeles, the shouts and bursts of gunfire echoing across the tropic river and through the entwined trees.

'I heard the shooting,' Hank mentioned sulkily the next day. 'I figured the revolution had gotten here.'

'Come over and watch if you like,' said George casually.

Hank held up his bitten hand. 'No, no,' he said. 'No, I like this one fine.'

George made a pretence of trying to tune the old set before tutting his way from the ward.

'It's all these beds,' called Hank after him. 'All these metal beds.' He waved his hand at the empty rows. 'They screw up the picture.'

Along the corridor George found Bella surprisingly more accommodating. She nodded vigorously to his invitation to view the new television. He found Maria and between them they helped the poor woman over to the bungalow because she could scarcely put feet to ground. As they made the short journey she cried out because of the sudden heat of the sun for it was a year since she had felt it.

Once she was settled before the new set, however, her embroidery on her knees, she watched it intently and made little humming noises. George sat with her and so did the

440

nurse. After about an hour there came a stealthy sound outside and Hank stumbled in through the bungalow door. He had managed to cross the open space unaided but now toppled onto his hands and knees and had to be helped up while his wife cackled cruelly.

He said nothing to her and, after finishing laughing, she returned her attention to the television programme which was about wheat-growing in Canada. George put him in a chair and he too settled down sedately, every half an hour stealing a quick sideways look at Bella.

'She's still got the eye on this side,' observed Hank in a loud whisper. 'You sure the other one is still in?'

George assured him it was. Maria went away and came back with a brush. She began to brush Bella's hair, making it shine. The woman shifted with pleasure. Thirty minutes later, during the commercials, both George and the nurse left and when George returned with Campos an hour later the couple were still sitting hushed, having apparently not quarrelled.

In the evening both Hank and Bella returned to the main hospital building, Bella asking George and Campos, who were holding her up, to pause so she could enjoy the moonlight. When they settled her in her room she thanked them both, first in Spanish and then, for George's benefit, in her English. 'Good kind,' she said.

Hank put his television on but said it was not the same and turned it off disconsolately and went to sleep in his chair. Two days later George suggested that he might like to move into the bungalow and, after first refusing, he said he would consider it. That night he wanted to watch a late cowboy film and he announced that he would give the bungalow a trial.

Bella said she was finding the journey to the new television set was becoming difficult and she agreed to occupy the third of the bungalow's bedrooms on condition that she was not obliged to speak to her husband or even look at him. Her terms agreed, she also moved in.

Ten evenings later Hank died so quietly during a war film that no one noticed until it finished at midnight. They brought a disgruntled-looking priest upriver and buried Hank in the plot at the end of the island where lepers had been buried in previous years when the colony had been at its most populated. At the last moment, as they were carrying the body from the house, Bella donated her embroidery as a shroud. Maria cried and crossed herself before putting the linen on Hank in his coffin, the last but one kept in a store on the island. Before it was put in the earth, she retrieved and hid it.

Two days later Bella also died, in the course of a Spanish song recital. Campos was not surprised for he knew that each had only remained living to spite the other. The priest, now thoroughly ill-humoured, was summoned upriver once again and after the service asked pointedly if anyone else felt unwell. The final coffin was brought out. Maria produced the shroud and laid it on Bella, admiring the needlework as she did so.

The plane called two days after Bella was buried and George took it back to Manila. It was exactly one month since he had arrived at Santa Bernardina and as he walked across the airstrip he realised he was sorry to leave. There was now nothing to keep him there but in many ways he wished there had been, for he had grown fond of the peace, the place and its few inhabitants. Campos and Maria came to the strip and waved as the small aircraft took off. He looked down on them as the pilot climbed into a full circle, two white figures on an emerald floor. As they set course they banked over the green sliding river, above the island and its now pointless white buildings. They were low enough to see the small segment of land with its ranks of crosses where Hank and Bella now lay. He gave them a little salute. They had put something into his life.

During the flight the small plane bucked and bumped, movements which, he was sure from his seat behind, jolted the pilot's attention from a comic paper he was reading. Eventually they were above the city by its reflecting bay. 'All stopped now,' shouted the pilot over his shoulder. 'No more election until next time.'

They landed like a moth among all the heavy planes of the world airlines. George regarded them from the cockpit as a minor space adventurer might view the vehicles of a different, distant world. As he left the airport he passed the point where the Filipino had fallen on him. A girl was sitting in the sun on the same windowsill.

He took a taxi to the Avenida Malabon where Spinoza had

442

established his office and was shown at once to the room. The tall man looked tired but peered warmly through his glasses.

'You are back,' he said. 'I was expecting you.'

'The hospital ceased to exist,' shrugged George. 'The patients died.'

'This I hear.' He looked uncomfortable. 'My apologies. I send you on a wild-fowl chase.'

'Not at all. It was very rewarding. It's a pity the way it turned out.'

Spinoza sighed. 'We did not know. Many things we did not know. Only now we find out. Funds were sent month after each month for the running of a hospital for a hundred and fifty. I myself went with a United Nations team. The place was full. Of course, we did not stop long. Leper colonies are not favourite places. But now we know it was a great trick, a fraud, an act. The district governor – who we have just arrested at Mindanao – was pocketing the money.' He increased his sigh. 'I suppose we shall have to give some of it back to the UN,' he said regretfully. A new complication struck him. 'And who knows how many other Santa Bernardinas are in this country of ours.'

George said: 'I wouldn't offer to give too much of the money back. After all there *were* two patients and they had to be kept in a hospital. A hospital is a hospital.'

Spinoza regarded him gratefully. 'I will have to consider that point of view,' he nodded. 'We must not be too hurried. I am glad anyway that you found it was good for you.' He turned some papers on his desk. 'You are, of course,' he said doubtfully, 'entitled to the full salary for the three months, fifteen thousand dollars.'

'It's a temptation,' George smiled. 'But I feel that I would be taking advantage. It was not exactly arduous. Señor Campos is a good man, we got on splendidly, and the nurse Maria was very kind.'

'Nurse?' queried Spinoza. 'There was only one nurse?'

George nodded. 'Just one, Maria,' he said. 'She is to go to one of the other hospitals downriver with Señor Campos.'

'On paper there was a staff of eighty-five,' said Spinoza distraughtly. 'What a cheat it is! The UN inspection team saw doctors and nurses when we were there. We *saw* them with our eyes.'

'Brought upriver for the day,' George told him. 'Like the patients.'

Spinoza said: 'This country has had bad men and bad communications. The first feeds on the second. Nobody can know how they are cheating – and in the days of Marcos nobody cared to ask. They were too busy. Everybody cheating for themselves.' He looked hopefully across the desk. 'For how much will you settle?' he asked.

'One month, five thousand dollars,' answered George. 'If the exchequer can stand it.'

'It will,' smiled Spinoza. 'It is very generous of you, Señor Goodnight.'

'I will sit down and write a full report before I go,' said George. 'I'll put in everything I can remember. What you do with it is up to you. At least it will be in black and white.'

'That also is most generous. Then you will be on your way, which is a pity. The Philippines needs people of integrity, even Englishmen.' He looked embarrassed. 'I did not mean it to sound like that,' he said.

'I understand,' grinned George. 'But I must be on my way.'

'To Los Angeles?'

'It's the next stop.'

'In the south,' said Spinoza attempting to sound casual, 'there have been many problems with the running of the district clinics. What has been going on is a bigger disgrace than Santa Bernardina.'

He looked up with innocent hope, the lights of the room reflected in his glasses. George was already on his feet. 'I will write my report tomorrow,' he said holding out his hand. 'Then I must be away. I have a lunch appointment in Los Angeles on Friday. An old friend of my wife's.'

XXII

'Fisher, Brent and Raney.'

'Good morning. Could I speak to Freddy Birch, please.'

'Mr Birch is no longer with Fisher, Brent and Raney.'

'Good heavens, I thought he was there for ever.'

'So did we. I have a number for him. It's 0525 74128.'

George took the pad from the nightstand at the side of the bed. The Californian sun was vivid between the shutters. He could hear the constant cars on the freeway outside the window. He asked the girl to repeat the number and wrote it down. He put the telephone down, studied the four digits of the code and shrugged. Then he dialled again.

'Hello, Birch Associates.'

'Freddy? Is that you? It's George. George Goodnight.'

'George! Good gracious, you've found me. Are you back?'

'No, I'm in LA.'

'I'm in LB – Leighton Buzzard.'

'Ah, it's all becoming clear.'

'I wish it were to me. George, I'm having a terrible time.'

'What's happened?'

'In a nutshell, I left Cynthia, or she threw me out, take which you like, and I came here to live with the girl I knew . . . you remember?'

'Yes, of course.'

'It only lasted a month. She went off with a greaser from the local garage who serviced her car. Now I'm stuck here.'

'That's terrible, Fred. But Birch Associates doesn't sound too bad. You've struck out on your own.'

'My associates are woodlice and spiders, George. I can't even get anybody to clean this sodding room. This in a country of three million unemployed. And business is terrible.'

'I'm sorry to hear it all, Fred. Is it definitely all off with Cynthia?'

'Definitely, mate. Women will forgive some things, but not

pissing off with somebody half their age. It's insult to injury. I should have done what you did, taken to the road.'

'Why don't you? It doesn't sound as if you've got much to lose. In a year or so you'll probably have caught up with me.'

'Oh leave it out, George, will you! I've hardly got a bean and I'm a different type. I'm scared to move. I've done it once, and look where I am. In one fucking room with a load of fucking woodlice in fucking Leighton Buzzard. I could cry, George. I should have stayed behind my lawnmower where I belonged.'

'Seen anything of Felicity?'

'Well, obviously not since I left. I didn't see much of her before. She didn't approve of me from last Christmas onwards. She seems to spend a lot of time in London.'

'Oh?'

'I believe she was getting some job up there. Personal assistant or something.'

'Oh, was she?'

'But my own problems, you know, have been taking up all my time. I don't know what the position is there.'

'What about Tina?'

'Oh yes, Tina. She was home in the August holidays. You ought to have seen her, George. Sunbathing in the garden. You know . . . she's . . . well, growing up.'

'She's not sixteen yet.'

'Oh, don't get me wrong, please. Don't *you* start. I was just saying how . . . *well* she looked . . . healthy. I'm glad you're the one paying for this call, by the way. This could be the one that made them finally cut off the phone. And that would be the end for me.'

'Don't worry, Fred, I'm paying.'

'What are you doing in Los Angeles?'

'Nothing at the moment. Just got here. I've been in the South Seas, in the Philippines, all sorts of places.'

'I'm really envious. It's amazing how you've just kept going. What happened about the stamps?'

'Oh, it was all right. Felicity sent them to me in Australia.'

'That was very sporting, I must say. Cynthia would have had a bonfire.'

'Wives tend to calm down after a while. And, after all, they are my personal property, or, rather, *were*. I've sold them all now.'

446

'But you've managed to keep going. This call must be costing a fortune.'

'I've managed. Being British, English, helps.'

'In what way?'

'There's a rumour still circulating in the world that we've got integrity. We *look* as if we can be trusted.'

'When are you coming home?'

'I could come now, today, Fred, and it's a temptation. I'm afraid I'll forget my way before long. But I haven't got a lot to come back to, have I?'

'Even less reason than I've got to stay here. George, have you ever seen a woodlouse copulating? There's a couple at it now. At least I think so. Incredibly awkward.'

'You should see camels.'

'That must be amazing. So you're not coming home?'

'Yes, I am. But slowly. I've been coming home from the day I left really, Fred. Even a wanderer has to have an object.'

'Let me know when you're really coming back, won't you?'

'Yes, of course.'

'I'll show you around Leighton Buzzard.'

'Hello, Clemmie? Is that you, Clemmie? It's George.'

'George! Oh beaut! George, how are you?'

'I'm fine. I'm in America. Los Angeles.'

'Oh darling, I was worried. We've all been worried. Why didn't you write?'

'Sorry. The places I've been the mail was a bit unreliable. I thought I'd wait until I got here before phoning. How is Ollie?'

'He's great, George. He and Linda are getting married next month. I am too.'

'You are!'

'Yes, George. You know the driver who took you away from The Alice that day. Him. He's very nice and kind.'

'Yes, I remember. He talked a lot about you.'

'I thought it was the best thing. I can't waste my life waiting for Mr Perfect to turn up. Not in The Alice.'

'No. Of course not . . . I wish you every happiness.'

'Thanks, George. I'm afraid you can't speak to Ollie. He took Linda to Sydney. He's waiting for his case to come to Court.'

'I'll keep my fingers crossed.'

'He's coming back and bringing his mother with him. He seems to think she'll appreciate the camel farm. You . . . you're not thinking of coming back in this direction are you . . . by any chance?'

'No . . . Not at the moment, Clemmie.'

'I was sad as hell when you went.'

'So was I.'

'But it was right. I know that, George.'

'Thanks for saying it.'

'Burtenshaw went home. He's still on your trail. He's a determined cuss. Where have you been?'

'Up through the Pacific. I ended up in the Philippines.'

'I knew it. I wondered who started that upheaval. You seem to have the knack of changing people's lives.'

'Not guilty this time. It was all over the day I arrived.'

'What are you going to do now?'

'I'm not sure. I'll give it a few days.'

'We had some rain this week. It came down for five hours yesterday.'

'The river must be quite damp.'

'It's softening up. Ring me again some time, will you, George?'

'Is it a double wedding?'

'Yes. October sixth. Don't send me a message, or anything, please. Just to Ollie and Linda.'

'All right, Clemmie. But I'll think about you on that day.'

'And I'll think about you. Goodbye, George, love.'

'Goodbye, Clemmie.'

'Tina, this is George.'

'Oh, George, it's you . . . Oh, I'm crying, George. I thought you'd gone for ever.'

'You know I wouldn't do that.'

'Where are you? Are you home?'

'I'm in Los Angeles. I'm coming back by easy stages.'

'You're not scared to come back, are you?'

'A little. How are you? How is school?'

'I'm fine. School's boring. I can't wait to finish. I want to be a trade union leader.'

'Jesus.'

'I mean it. Women can, you know. We've got to stand up

448

and be counted. I may also be a Labour MP. It's very fashionable.'

'Really. Times change, don't they.'

'Where have you been, George? Please tell me.'

'Let me see . . . what can I tell you?'

'Tales, marvellous tales, of ships and stars and isles where good men rest! Or is it stars and ships?'

'I've seen some ships, a lot of stars, and, strangely, isles where good men rest.'

'You say it so beautifully, George. Better than Flossie Smirthwaite, who takes us for English. What's Los Angeles like? Are you going to be a film star?'

'I doubt it. How is your mother?'

'She's all right. We fight sometimes. More than we used to. She says it's because I'm growing up and I want to do things.'

'You haven't been getting into trouble, have you?'

'Nothing terrible or exciting. I only wish I were old enough, that's all. It's a long time coming.'

'It'll come, Tina. Don't rush it. Listen to your mother.'

'You didn't.'

'That's different. What is she doing?'

'Oh, she has this job. Personal assistant, whatever. The man is nice but he's happily married. Mother has a new hairstyle and a new car. She's in London a lot.'

'Does she seem happy?'

'I don't know. She's always busy. Even in the holidays. I spent most of the time at Bournemouth with Barbara John's family. It was great, though. They have trade union conferences there, you know, at Bournemouth, although it's a really reactionary town.'

'What sort of business is your mother working in?'

'Well, business business. It's something to do with promotion, publicity that is. I think it's all sorts of things. When will you come back, George? I'm dying to see you. Are you brown all over?'

'I can't remember. I'd like to see you too, Tina. I'll be back quite soon. In a few months. By Christmas perhaps.'

'That would be just *ace*, George. I'll wait for you.'

'I'll telephone again in a while. I'll keep in touch. Now behave. And work hard. Even trade union leaders have to work hard.'

'Especially.'
'Goodbye, Tina.'
'Goodbye, George. It's made me happy. Keep safe.'
'And you.'

All through his travels George had found himself projected onwards, made to move, pushed and propelled by circumstances which were often none of his making. Now, in California in the fall, he found himself in a pleasant and relieving vacuum. Nothing violent or eccentric occurred to him. The countless inhabitants of the coast and the endless city of Los Angeles were too occupied with their own frenetic lives to provide George Goodnight with adventures. Events moved around him as swiftly and as inconclusively as the speeding cars on the figured freeways, but none of it involved him.

He began quietly and modestly to enjoy himself. He had six and a half thousand United States dollars and he saw in this justification for a pause in his journeys, a time to regroup, to rest, a time to think about the past and the future. For the first three days he stayed in a middle-range motel on Santa Monica Boulevard, believing there was a touch of home in the seashore with its sand and shingle, and cold autumn water. There was the patched-up Santa Monica pier with its closed stalls and sideshows, the clairvoyant's boarded booth, its fishing deck.

Two blocks along the street were some service apartments which were available for rent by the month. They were small and shabby, two roughly furnished rooms with a cubby kitchen and a bath, but the off-season rent was low so he took one for a month and settled down to a comforting solo domesticity. He sat on the pier in the balmy sun and talked with the anglers who seemed to be no great threat to the Pacific fish. Now he had time he fell to wondering how much that river fisherman in England, the man who had in many ways triggered his travels, had actually caught. Perhaps he had misjudged him. Perhaps he never hooked anything but was merely a prey to loneliness and wet.

As soon as he was settled he attempted, without much hope, to discover some trace of Stuart Vaughan, once of Sydney, Australia. He went to all the leading stamp dealers in Los Angeles and to meetings of three philatelic societies, at one of which he gave an impromptu talk on British Possessions, but without arousing a single memory of Vaughan. He seemed to have vanished for ever and with him any clue to his acquired daughter. George did not even know Janine's daughter's name. She was no more than a shadow.

Each day, also, George walked along the crunching beach, at times doffing his shoes and socks to paddle in the chill water. There were few people about for it was now October. He became on nodding terms with a variety of joggers and had conversations with elderly people walking their dogs, but otherwise he was solitary.

He purchased groceries from a crammed, cheerful store where he became on bantering terms with the owner, a Pole, who had emigrated from New Jersey. He cooked his own meals in the tight kitchen and found, to his surprise, that by taking time and surveying instructions he could produce palatable results. Even on his long and varied journey there had often been an adjacent someone who could cook. One evening he made a list of all the people he had met on his odyssey whose names he could recall, beginning with Benny the manager of the English motorway service station and ending with Dr Spinoza in Manila. It was a long catalogue.

From Los Angeles there were bus excursions to various parts of the coast and inland to Palm Springs and Lake Tahoe and Las Vegas. He took them all, usually finding himself travelling with groups of silvery Americans looking over their own country. In Las Vegas he stayed two days and won one hundred and fifty dollars at roulette, which he then spent seeing a magic show and eating an indigestible Italian meal. Even there he spoke to few people. He began to relish his solitariness.

The apartment downstairs from his own was occupied by a Hungarian with a cough who said that there were interesting boat excursions from Long Beach out to Santa Catalina island. The Hungarian had always wanted to go but had never done so because he had no one to go with. It was better to be with a companion when coughing. He and George set out early one Californian morning and took the two-hour voyage across the sea to the tall island and had lunch in the misty harbour town of Avalon. The Hungarian, who did not cough at sea, said it reminded him of somewhere on the Danube and George thought it was a little like the Isle of Wight.

George bought his newspapers each morning from the same

451

stand. Nothing seemed to be reported from Britain. He bought a few novels and a book on card tricks, which he practised in the privacy of his home but with little finesse. He decided his hands were too big. He rented a television and often sat in the evening watching everything it offered. He had slipped into a life of singular indolence. The cost of doing nothing, however, surprised him and at the end of the month, when he had renewed his rent for a second month, he counted his capital and found it had halved. He would have to find some work.

Hollywood Big Time Agency was located on the Avenue of the Stars in three rooms, one of which was occupied, when George entered, by a small hopeless-looking man caring for a chimpanzee. It was difficult to tell one from the other.

'There ain't the work any more,' he complained to George. 'In the old days, Goldwyn, Zanuck, in those days they had spectaculars, not the little asshole movies they have now.' He nodded at the chimp who was studying its fingernails. 'He was never out of work then.'

From the inner office came a girl so blonde, shapely and shining, she might have been finished on a machine. She wore a trembling ice-blue blouse. 'Nothing today, Mr Stanocki,' she said.

It was the chimpanzee's jaw which seemed to drop. 'Nothing?' said the man only half incredulously. 'But what about the commercial? He said there'd be the commercial.'

'It's been put back,' she told him with a brusque smile. 'Indefinitely. Please keep in touch.'

The small man eased himself off the chair and touchingly helped the chimp down. 'I'm going to have to sell him soon,' he told George. His eyes were damp. 'He's got to eat.' The chimp's paw went up to meet that of the man and they went out holding hands.

'That creature is full of bugs,' said the girl. She took in George with a quick professional survey. He told her his name and she smiled. 'Goodnight,' she repeated, writing it on her pad. 'Now I've heard each and every one. Goodnight.'

'Mr Mullinski told me to call,' said George. 'When I was passing.'

'I guess he'll see you now,' she glittered. 'I'll check.' She turned and walked back to the inner office. He was staring blatantly at her legs when she turned as if on a spring and caught him at it. 'One moment,' she said. 'I'll be right back.'

On her swift return he resolutely kept his face neutral and his eyes above the level of her ice-blue shoulders. Her eyes glowed as if she were the bearer of celestial news. 'Mr Mullinski will see you now, Mr Goodnight,' she smiled.

Tamely George thanked her and walked by her as he entered the office. A man in blue check trousers and a red check shirt was sitting with his feet on the desk, knocking the toes of his shoes together. He opened them in a V shape and viewed George between the cleft. He had a ragged moustache. 'Good morning, Goodnight!' he exclaimed. 'Not bad, eh?'

'I've heard it before,' said George.

'I bet. There's nothing new. There's nothing old either. It's a good thing to remember that. There's nothing new and there's nothing old. If you quote it I'd be grateful if you'd attribute it to me.'

'On each occasion,' George assured him.

'I compose them all the time. I was a scriptwriter once. Before I got wise. Better wake up in spring than winter, I say.'

'I'm sure that's true,' said George. 'I was wondering if I might get some employment as a film extra.'

'No hope,' said Mullinski with hardly a pause. 'They don't make that sort of film any more. You're too regular. That voice used to be a novelty. Like in Aubrey C. Smith's day, but not now. What's gone is here and there, I say.'

'Oh, that's a pity.'

Mullinski had a massive book at the side of his desk. He opened it halfway down and let the pages roll back from his fingers. 'All these people are in the same line, waiting for work,' he said. He stopped a page at random. 'Look, here's a guy got his *own* bicycle – and his own *tuxedo*. And *he* can't get work. What chance do you have?'

George began to rise. 'I'm sorry to have taken up your time,' he said.

'Hold it, hold it,' said the agent waving him down. 'Nothing is gained by a premature sunset.'

Dumbly George sat down again. Mullinski pushed the big book aside. 'But that's showbiz. Never mind, there are other possibilities.'

'Such as?'

The agent folded his red-check arms across his blue-check trousers, making a mad pattern. 'Well, it's acting,' he said. 'In a way.'

'What sort of way? Not pornographic pictures?'

'Skin flicks! God, no. That's passé. There's nothing so far gone as the day before yesterday. Or yesterday.' He thought about the thought. 'The past is passé.'

'What then?'

'Well, there's a good, expanding business right here in California for people like you. Limey butlers.'

'Butlers! But I've never . . .'

'So you've never! You're English so you're halfway there. And you look the part. Half the part is looking the part. People think it's chic, you know, crème de menthe, to have an English guy in a funeral outfit standing about while they eat dinner. They pay good.'

'How much?'

'A hundred and fifty dollars a night.'

'It's by the night?'

'Sure. They just rent you. Next night you're a butler somewhere else. You have to buy your own costume. But then it's yours. You don't need nothing else. A butler's costume is a joy forever.'

He regarded George, measuring him up mentally. 'You'd better change your name. Goodnight, for a butler, sounds too much like a joke.'

'How about Loving. It's a name I sometimes use, Oliver Loving. He was a cowboy.'

'You don't say? As long as you're not.' He wrote it down. 'PKA that's Professionally Known As . . . Oliver Loving.'

He selected another folder. 'We already got people working all over the state,' he said shuffling through papers and photographs. 'But they don't look like you. They don't sound like you. We have to pass some of them off. We got a Mex here for Chrissake who calls himself Sir Robin Hood. And another guy who's supposed to be a Lord something. He looks like the goddamn Hunchback of Notre-Dame.'

'When do I start?' asked George. 'I've been a maitre d' in Simla . . . in India.'

'That's even better. You could start tomorrow night.' Mullinski took a card from a packed tray with the flourish of a sleight

454

of hand expert. 'Mr and Mrs Ralph Dooney, Eagles Crag, Beverly Hills. He's in waste disposal. There's big money in shit, believe me. Dinner party, forty guests, and they need a butler.'

'A hundred and fifty dollars?'

'You got it.'

'I'll try it. I'll go out and buy the clothes.'

'Rent them.' Mullinski stood behind the desk and shook hands fiercely. 'Great. I knew you'd be the one,' he enthused. 'Opportunities are rarely overcome before a swallow dies.'

George went into the lemon autumn sunshine. Two blocks along the street was a theatrical costumiers and he found he could hire a tailed coat, trousers and shirt by the day. It seemed the logical thing. He went back to his small apartment on Santa Monica Boulevard and put it on. It fitted well and he practised bowing and scraping in front of the mirror.

They sent a car for him at 4.30. The chauffeur, a Puerto Rican, looked at him in his black clothes and said: 'No shit.' George sat in the back seat of the chrome vehicle and was taken through the streets and up into the suburban heights of Beverly Hills. The house was large and ugly. There were loud pictures, graceless ornaments and gilt and gold everywhere; drapes and tassles and ponderous wallpaper loaded the walls. The carpets bowed under the lightest footstep. The dinner table, now being arranged by a multitude of small brown people, gleamed and sparkled. Chandeliers floated. It was going to be an ostentatious evening.

He realised he was going to enjoy himself. He could be pompous again. The other staff were Mexican, California's servants, damed by an overwhelming black housekeeper. She and the black cook were the only stable household employees and she treated her minions with gigantic authority. She said that George looked so fine in his suit.

He stood tall and grave and cranked forward only an inch or so when he handled the evening coats of the arriving guests, intoning the few words of greeting and guidance with his deepest English resonance. As they walked into the main house he heard them whispering about him. He thought of Bollins in faraway Shillington.

He supervised the pouring of the wines throughout dinner and dispensed the port himself, moving regally around the guests. They observed him with sideways curiosity and he could see that the host, the garbage-grading Mr Dooney, and his simpering young wife were pleased with the impression he was creating. Someone made a mild joke at his expense and he returned, at just above a mutter: 'Indeed sir, indeed.'

If they were watching him he had ample opportunity to return the observation. The men were mostly elderly and the women young to early middle age, the latter wearing extra jewellery and defensive looks. There was one wife who was a beauty. Her features were notable; engrossing eyes, lofty cheekbones, and a neck fine and pale that curved to exposed and spotless shoulders. Her dress, pale blue and soft, opened decorously to display the upper reaches of her bosom. She smiled perfectly. In the kitchen was a table plan pinned to the cork notice board. He saw that she was Mrs Sidney Lennard. Mr Lennard, who was three places down the table, was the oldest guest present. George had to give him a delicate nudge to rouse him for the soufflé.

As the guests departed, gushing compliments, and as he was stepping towards her with her mink wrap, the beautiful young woman asked quietly: 'And what is your name?'

'Loving, madam,' George replied.

'You're very good, Loving,' she whispered. 'And tall.'

As the cars crunched from the gravel forecourt and George shut the door, Mr and Mrs Dooney embraced each other happily.

'It was so wonderful!' said the young Mrs Dooney. 'I wish I'd been a guest!' They were nice people and they assembled all the staff and thanked them for making the evening so much of a success. Everyone went away and Mr Dooney drew George aside. 'You were terrific, Mr Loving,' he said. 'We must use you again. We're throwing a big party next month to celebrate the opening of the new sewer outfall. We've got to have you here that night.'

George promised he would do his utmost. He was driven to Santa Monica by the Puerto Rican chauffeur who now also seemed impressed and opened and shut the car door for him. He dozed in the back seat and thought idly of rich elderly Mr Lennard with his young and desirable wife.

Three weeks later, after George had donned his butler's costume on numerous nights, Mullinski called him to the office.

456

'I been getting such good reports of your butlering,' he said. 'Terrific stuff. I never knew people pay up so quick. Money follows mouths, I say. Now somebody wants you permanent. And I get a cut.'

'Who,' asked George with mixed feelings, 'might that be?'

'I'll tell you who it is, not who it might be,' said Mullinski. 'Somebody saw you that first job you did, at the garbage man's house, Dooney.' He glanced at a slip of paper. 'Lennard. People called Lennard.'

Closing his eyes briefly, George saw again that glance, that smile, those shoulders, that neck, that modestly promised bosom. 'I remember the gentleman,' he said.

'Two thousand a month and they keep you. Clover comes to those who can chew. They live in some place near Fort Worth. What d'ya think?'

Comanche Mansion was a house of magnificent proportions and excessive luxury located ten miles from the edge of Fort Worth, touching the Texas desert on one side and its own fashioned grounds on the other. It was a red single-storeyed home, with deep roofs, widespread windows, including one depicting 'The Last Indian' in stained glass; and cooling trees which, like its lawns, were heavily watered.

The housekeeper, Annie, another black lady, greeted him and handed him on to a manservant who showed him to his accommodation, a comfortably shaded apartment, on the far end of the building. There was a view of the staff swimming pool from his window.

'Mr and Mrs Lennard is away till the end of the week,' said the man, a limpid-eyed black. 'I been here six months and it's nice, man, it's real nice.'

They shook hands. 'There's a Loving County in Texas,' said the man who's name was Clifton. 'And a town called Loving down in New Mexico. Named after some cowboy.'

'I know,' George told him. 'I've looked up the family history. I'm no connection as far as I can see. Do you know a place called Bartholdy in Texas?'

'Sure, little town other side of Austin. You know it?'

'No, only someone there. He's the editor of the local newspaper.'

'It ain't too far. You could get there on your day off, maybe. See your friend.'

He went and George once more unpacked his belongings. He had acquired another suitcase in Los Angeles and bought clothes and shoes. Now he hung them in the closet where his butler's tailed coat looked like a perched crow. He had a shower and lay on the bed with a towel round him.

During the first week there was little for him to do except familiarise himself with the house and the staff. He spent a day in Fort Worth, looking in the extravagant shop windows, found a stand selling foreign newspapers. He bought *The Times* and the *Daily Mail* and took them back to the house. He spent an hour reading them and he thought how strange it would be to go back there.

From Los Angeles he had written separately to Ollie and Clemmie so that the letters would arrive before their joint wedding day. He had told them not to write back at once because he thought he might be moving on. Now he had the time, and a set address, he composed a long letter to each of them. He wrote at length also to Tina at school, so that it would arrive before the Christmas holidays, ten pages describing the places he had seen and a selection of his experiences. He wrote to Fearnley-Banks in India and to Monsieur Julien at Cherbourg. He had much to tell. To Molly at Somerbourne Magna he sent a picture postcard.

When Sidney Lennard and his wife returned to the house it was in two cars. They travelled across the red country throwing up dust like charging buffalo and turned into the iron and ornate gates. George was standing at the top of the portico steps with the members of the household. The Lennards were in the first car, the second being filled with luggage and packages from stores. The old man took his time leaving the car. 'He waits for the dust to settle down,' said Clifton to George while they waited. 'The dust hurts his cough.'

It was two minutes before Sidney Lennard thought it was safe to leave the car. He got out helped by the chauffeur. The chauffeur of the second car opened the other door for Francesca Lennard and an audible feeling, almost a thrill, went through the assembled staff as her egress was preceded by a long and lovely leg. She followed it none too hurriedly, stood on the sunlit drive, and waved. 'Hi, everybody!' she called.

458

'Hi, Mrs Lennard!' responded the staff as one. George was taken unawares by the trained greeting and merely opened his mouth and flattened it to an awkward smile. The old man mouthed soundlessly. George thought he looked even more elderly in the sunlight than he had done indoors. The chauffeur accompanied him to the steps and George, undecided where his presence should be, moved towards him.

Sidney Lennard only saw him when he was six feet away. The leather-faced old man stopped on the bottom of the wide arch of steps and eyed him as if trying to recall where they had met. Then he realised. Half turning to his wife, further along the step, he called shakily: 'Oh, so you got him.'

'Good afternoon, sir,' said George hurriedly. 'Welcome home.'

George thought he heard the old man reply 'Asshole' but it so shocked him that he was sure he had misheard. Francesca was smiling like the afternoon sun. 'Good afternoon, ma'am,' said George. 'Welcome home.'

'I'm so glad you could get here,' she said thrillingly. She watched her husband's slow progress up the steps. 'I was afraid you might have other commitments.'

'No, madam, I was glad to come. Thank you for the compliment. I hope I will fit in.'

'I'm sure you will,' she replied. 'Perfectly.'

Four men were already hosing down the cars. The others were bearing in the luggage, with the maids taking charge of the shopping packages, squealing quietly among themselves as they examined the store labels. Francesca followed her husband into the shadows of the house. At the top of the steps she was greeted by the housekeeper. 'We will be dining alone tonight, Annie,' she said. 'Then retiring early.'

There seemed little for George to do except appear tall. Inside the white columned hall he hovered, making odd unheeded suggestions to men carrying the cases. Francesca Lennard watched her husband stagger towards the nearest lavatory, waited a moment, then stepped with a light and guilty step towards him. 'I'm really so glad you could be here,' she said. 'I'm sorry my husband called you an asshole like that.'

'It's . . . it's perfectly all right, madam.'

'Like you see, he's old and he's not too well. Being unkind to people who can't answer back is his only recreation.'

'I quite understand, madam.'

'You're quite a find,' she confided. 'There are only a few English butlers around. Did you learn the profession in London?'

'No, madam, in Los Angeles,' he said truthfully.

'But the rest of you is all English?'

'I'm afraid so, madam.'

She leaned a little closer. 'I'd be grateful if you would economise on the "madam",' she said. 'I find it overpowering. Perhaps only every three or four sentences.'

'Of course,' he replied. 'It makes matters easier for me also.'

She half turned. The housekeeper was watching and waiting. 'Anyway,' she said still confidingly. 'Welcome, Loving.'

For a month he continued with his duties at Comanche Mansion, trying to keep his eyes from Francesca Lennard. In all his life he had never desired anyone before, not like this, utter desire with no alleviating circumstances. It seemed that she avoided him scrupulously, their ways scarcely intersecting, their gazes never touching. When he saw her in the distance, within the house, he turned and made a diversion through some corridor or room because he felt he could hardly trust himself. At night, in his quarters, making himself read, listen to the radio or watch television, he imagined her in her luxurious bed only a few steps away cross the lawns if you avoided the security guard and her doberman.

'That dog,' said Clifton as he polished the silver in the kitchen, 'is a mean thing. He's called James, and that's after Jesse James, man, because he's a killer. And he sleeps at the bottom of Mrs Lennard's bed.'

Each night the young wife retired at the same time as her husband and the house quietened. They did no entertaining at first and there were few duties for George to perform. He began to wonder why he was there.

'Old Mr Lennard,' said Clifton, 'he don't like that dog and that dog don't like him. One night, maybe he was feeling a little frisky, Mr Lennard I mean, and he crept into Mrs Lennard's suite and into her bedroom, and the dog jumped on him real bad. Pinned him to the carpet. He ain't never been there since.'

460

The late Texas weather was burnished days and rosy evenings, with the nights sharp, starlit and cold. On most days Francesca would go riding, sometimes with neighbours, sometimes alone. One morning at the end of his first month the cook called George and told him that Mrs Lennard had left instructions that he was to take the jeep and meet her in the desert at midday, carrying with him her lunch.

'The place,' said the cook, 'is called Goodnight River Bend. It's a straight road.'

He drove across the gritty land, the wheels of the jeep throwing up red clouds. There were dawdling hawks in an unclouded sky. An unreasonable sense of excitement was building up within him. He drove fast to keep his mind on the road. The Goodnight River Bend was signposted. Charles, that old cowboy, had marked places too. It took George half an hour. He stopped the jeep and waited and then saw her riding across the coloured country a mile away, coming towards him wreathed in dust, and alone.

He climbed from the jeep and placed the small picnic hamper on the seat. His eyes went back to her. As she neared he saw that her hair was flying and she was laughing. How beautifully she laughed. She turned the horse in a half-circle on the bank of the almost dry river and pulled it up. Shakily he walked to her and helped her down, the first time they had touched since their handshake.

'Well met, Loving,' she smiled. The tone was artless. 'I'm glad you found it. I hope you brought something good. I'm hungry.'

Her breasts nosed against her silk shirt. With difficulty he took his eyes from her and went to the jeep, picking up the hamper from the seat.

'Did they put some champagne in? Just a half bottle?' He produced it and she smiled directly at him. 'Two glasses, I hope,' she added. 'You need a drink after driving in this dust.'

'Thank you, madam,' he said. He opened the bottle, poured her a glass, and handed it to her. He glanced up and she said: 'Go ahead, please.' He poured a glass for himself. 'It's not wise to drink too much of this when you're riding,' she went on, viewing him over the horizon of the glass. 'The horse gets to know. He figures there's a weakness somewhere.'

'Horses and I have so far studiously avoided each other,'

461

George said formally. He was wearing a white shirt and black trousers, now coated red. There was perspiration along his hairline and a rigid knot in his chest.

'You've done a lot of things, been in a lot of countries though, so I hear,' she said casually.

He asked her if she would like a canvas seat from the car but she said she would prefer to stand.

'I have visited a few places in the last couple of years,' he said. 'But never on horseback. And I've never been at the Goodnight River Bend before.'

'It could be named after you,' she said, her eyes laughing and examining him at the same time. 'Goodnight.'

'You know, madam?'

'Of course. I had you investigated before you came here.'

'Goodnight, my real name, sounded inappropriate for a butler,' he admitted. 'I spoke to the man at the agency, Mr Mullinski, about it and he agreed. I am familiar with the Goodnight and Loving story so I opted for the second partner.'

'How did you know that?' she asked. 'Is it a story known in England? In Texas, yes, but in England?'

They were standing several feet apart. The sun flickered on the champagne glasses.

'A newspaper editor from Bartholdy near Austin – I met him in London – he told me. I intend to pay him a visit soon.'

She looked concerned. 'What was his name? Not Honeystone?'

'Yes,' he said surprised at her tone. 'John C. Honeystone.'

'He committed suicide last year,' she said gravely. 'Shot himself the good old Texas way. He was ill and he had other troubles.'

George saw himself sitting with Honeystone at the Dorchester and Honeystone saying: 'This town is sure some place for girls.'

'That's terrible,' he said quietly. 'He was a nice man.'

'I'm sorry to be the one to tell you,' said Francesca.

'I did not know him well. I only met him once but he had a strange effect upon my life.'

'How was that?'

'I was living a very steady existence at home, deadly boring in fact, and it was the Goodnight and Loving story, or partly anyway, which started me travelling. I saw a sign in England saying "To the West" and I've been almost round the world since then. Going east actually.'

She smiled gently at him. 'And now you are here,' she said.

Then she turned quickly and went towards the horse which was drinking from the depleted river.

'I'll get your lunch prepared,' said George.

'Don't worry,' she answered looking back over her shoulder. 'I can fix it.'

'Yes, of course. Would there be anything else, madam?'

'No, not for the present, thank you, Loving. We're having a dinner party for my husband's business associates soon.' She made a face. 'I'm sorry to say. I'll discuss that with you sometime.'

'Yes, madam. I'll be on my way back, then.'

'You know the route?'

'It's a straight road. But thank you.'

He climbed into the jeep and started the engine. His heart was full. He had driven only a few yards and had just turned to wave goodbye to her, when she called loudly, 'Loving!' He slowed the vehicle.

'Madam?'

'Thank you for bringing my lunch.' She was standing in the sun, so beautiful he could do nothing but the thing he did. He stopped the jeep, backed it up on the track and slowly got out. Fixing her eyes, fixed upon him, he walked towards her, then began to hurry before his courage failed. As they came face to face, her breasts pointing at his shirt, he folded his arms blatantly about her. To his overwhelming pleasure and relief her answering arms came up round his back. They kissed deeply. Once, twice and then again.

'You're not a butler really, are you, Loving?' she said.

'No, madam, I'm a lawyer.'

'I'm so glad. That will make this relationship so much more socially acceptable.'

She had suggested midnight, the natural hour for this sort of thing. And by that time, she promised, the doberman would be asleep.

George waited, counting each minute, in his room, attempting to read, trying to watch television, changing his clothes three times. This was a factor, he realised, which must not be overlooked or even underestimated. The logical clothes for making the excursion across the lawns to the french window of her suite would be his butler's coat and trousers since, if apprehended, he could at least plead that he was about his duties, that he had detected noises from that part of the house and had, naturally, gone to investigate. It sounded thin but, corroborated by Francesca, it would be better than nothing. On the other hand it hardly seemed in keeping with his role as midnight lover to arrive with romantic stealth in the uniform of a servant. That would not do.

He considered pyjamas and dressing gown but, posing at his mirror, practising looking attractive, he came to the conclusion that these were equally unsuitable. They were more comfortable but the aspect, he had to concede, was suburban. Lovers did not appear from the Texas night in wide-striped pyjamas and paisley dressing gowns.

Sports clothes, check trousers, a golfing sweater and a raffish open-necked shirt appealed to him, but there the mood was one of out of doors not between the sheets. Eventually he chose a black tracksuit which, he knew, could result in his being taken for a burglar, but was supple for moving in the dark and had a certain dash about it. He was anxious, more than anxious, that everything should look right. For the first time in his life he wished to look desirable. He wanted her avidly. 'You Flash Harry,' he told himself sombrely in the mirror.

At last it was time. The late television news had faded and he tremblingly turned off the set. He squinted from the window. It was one minute past twelve. The routine security patrol was late. He knelt, like someone at devotions, and kept his eye to the crack between the curtains. Ah, there it was, a brief slice of torchlight beyond the neighbouring wing of the house, gradually nearing to become a conscientious searchlight probing every bush, every bank, every garden seat and summerhouse, and finally covering the walls of the main mansion, curling like a slow white firework. George watched as it touched and circled over the wing where Francesca was waiting. He blinked and backed away as it picked out his french door with what seemed uncanny and accusative accuracy. But in a few moments it had flicked away and was gone. His breath was tight, but he was ready to go.

With his fingertips he pushed the door. The night was pointed with stars and the air was as sharp. His training shoes, black with white chevrons, touched the grass. He crept a few creeps and looked guiltily behind, bending low, to see if he was

464

leaving footprints in the dew. He was and he realised that on his return journey the error could only be compounded. Cowardly worries shot through his guilty mind. Out there, under the chill starlight, his confidence and even his lambent desire were dimmed. He almost went back. Then he saw the merest light ahead, at her window, the tremor of a lone candle, and without another hesitation he went across the grass with the fast, high-stepping, shadowy movements of a villain. His breath seemed to fly from his lungs and not return. Panting, he reached her french window. The pale outline of her face appeared near to the glass and he heard her opening the latch. Desire and excitement ran through him.

She was, by contrast, excessively calm. She beckoned him in like a business caller as soon as the glass door was open and closed it in a cool and efficient way behind him, testing the latch and pulling the curtains across. The candle stood, doused, at her bedside.

'Where,' asked George as he made to embrace and kiss her, 'is the dog?'

First she kissed him, full of urgency and passion, her slim body clamping itself to him. For all his engulfing enjoyment, he still swivelled his eyes to pick out the doberman.

'He's okay,' she whispered, pulling him round to face her again. 'He's immobilised. I hope you're not.'

She was wearing a pale blue silken robe and below that a nightdress of deft lace. 'You look adventurous,' she said standing a pace back. 'Have you been for a run?'

'Only across the lawn,' he said. His hands were caressing her ribs, the luxury of the silk, the web of the lace, the thumbs against the undersides of her delicious breasts. 'I think I've left some footprints.'

'Is this going to be a love assignation or a secret society?' she asked with some impatience. 'Security won't be around for another two hours. Footprints will have gone by then. Come.'

Reassured and ashamed of his anxiety he put his hand in hers and she led him round the huge bed. The doberman was prostrate on the carpet. 'I gave him a sleeping draught,' Francesca explained. 'He's been having some bad nights.' She slipped the silk robe to the floor.

Now they were at the edge of the bed and he had calmed himself, he took in the nightdressed loveliness of her. The mystic eyes, the prominence of the cheekbones, the open lips and the finely tanned skin. From her bosom her body seemed to slide away down to her feet. They kissed again, with greedy passion this time, crushed to each other. He kissed her lips, her neck and her nose. She summarily pulled down the trousers of his tracksuit. 'Loving,' she said, 'is a good name.'

Getting out of his clothes had always been an awkward business for George. He was not unclumsy and garments often became wedged; zips would grit their teeth and buttons refuse to yield. He also always felt foolish standing naked except for his socks. This time, the flexibility of the tracksuit meant he accomplished everything easily. She sat on the fringe of the bed, coated only by the ephemeral nightdress, and surveyed him. 'Loving,' she said sincerely, putting her slender hands out to him. 'You're the best and biggest butler we've ever had at Comanche Mansion.'

He eased her onto the sheet and clambered up onto the bed, his left knee between her legs, almost astride her.

'You're like that guy who holds up the world,' she said.

'Atlas?'

'That's him. You're like an older Atlas.'

This, he knew, was how real lovers went about it. He was vastly enjoying himself. He slipped his thumb into the strap of the nightdress and worked it over her shoulder and down her delicate arm. Another inch and the lace was pulled away from the pale breast. The nipple regarded him like a woken eye. He bent and kissed it. She shivered and spread her thighs. At that moment his head turned. She felt his start.

'Your dog,' he whispered, 'is staring at me.'

'Jesus, so he is,' she confirmed having looked from beneath him. 'It couldn't have been enough. He's still dopey, though. Let's go on, darling, let's go on.' She kissed him with encouraging passion. George continued to regard the dog. It had not moved its prone position but its eye was like amber. Francesca had another glance. 'Perhaps we had better hurry,' she suggested.

After all the promise and the anticipation it was not the perfect performance. Both lovers were aware that at each moment the doberman was rousing a little more. By resolute concentration they gave to each other to the best of their ability at that difficult moment. At the climax a shadow was cast over

466

the whole romance by the feel of a small, pointed, wet nose on George's buttock. 'Good dog,' he whispered unconvincingly.

'Oh, my God,' she moaned. She stretched to look. 'I don't want him to bite you.'

'Nor do I,' agreed George fervently. 'Do you think he'll let me get to the window?'

She had an idea. 'I'll give him some chocolates,' she decided. 'He loves marzipan and those whirly ones, but not the nuts because they get in his teeth.'

'Better that than me,' said George. 'Get the chocolates.'

She slipped from below him and went gracefully naked to the dressing table. She took a golden box with a red ribbon from a drawer, opened it and placed a chocolate in her mouth, closing her eyes for a moment with the taste. George eyed her with impatience. He could feel the dog's wet nose beginning to explore his exposed backside. Francesca went round the bed and passed a piece of marzipan in front of the doberman's nose. 'James, James,' she enticed. 'It's candy time.'

The dog was still half-drugged and only his amber eyes vaguely followed the pendulum movement of the bribe in her fingers. She set it on the sheet directly before his nostrils which now moved slowly from George's rump. George shifted fractionally across the bed, an inch, a pause, then another inch, then six inches, a foot, and finally, relieved, slid over the other side. He began to climb into his tracksuit, anxiously because rumbling growls were issuing from the doberman like an actor gradually remembering his lines. The dog became conscious enough to take the chocolate from the sheet, treating the hurriedly dressing George to a view of serried and saw-like teeth. The marzipan was taken at one gulp. George edged towards the window. He blew Francesca a kiss.

'Goodnight Loving, darling,' she whispered. She had put her robe about her but it hung open all the way to her toes. He was tempted to return for a last feel and embrace but the dog groaned again. George went out of the french window into the starry Texas night.

The trouble with Francesca – George believed at first anyway – was that she was twenty-four years of age and sexually needy, even, he began to think, greedy. Every night he was summoned to step like a shadow across the damp grass to her suite where

467

she would be awaiting him exquisitely in her big bed, the doberman on the carpet poleaxed now by drugged chocolates. By the day the dog stumbled half-slumbering around the house and grounds and George felt a slice of sympathy, for he was experiencing like symptoms.

There were, however, after their first passionate encounter, nights when, to his relief, she only wanted to talk. They would sit in the bed, like a well-married couple, discussing the household and its exigencies, even putting together the menus for the morrow, while wedged naked between the silk sheets. 'This is what I need,' she told him pushing the nubs of her breasts into his ribs as he sat with his arm decently circling her. 'I need an ordinary relationship. That's why this is so good, George. After sex you need to talk.'

Not only did her old husband never have sex with her, nor even play out preliminaries, he only rarely conversed with her, and then in short bitter barks so like the sound of a doberman that several times even the doped dog had lifted its black and copper head in response. 'Sidney only wanted me like a toy, a nice-looking toy,' she complained to George when she was cutting his toenails late one night. 'He bought me just like something you buy from Neiman Marcus.'

'You must have known that,' George pointed out reasonably. 'Steady with the big toe, will you . . . You must have known he had only money to spend. It could hardly be passion.'

'I knew, I knew all the time,' she sighed. 'You're going to have to watch this toe. The nail curls in a little.' She was wearing a nightdress and, as she knelt, the tunnel between her breasts opened like a lair. She saw him looking and met his eyes. With soft pleasure she crawled up his body until she lay above him. He carefully removed the scissors from her fingers. They made a little love before continuing with the conversation. 'You're the sort of man I should have married, Loving,' she sighed.

'My wife couldn't get rid of me quickly enough,' George said. They had decided that she would continue to call him by his butler's name to prevent any verbal slips during everyday conversation within the house.

'We could have a sweet house by the sea,' she said, her eyes going up towards the vision. 'Somewhere warm but where the sea gets rough. Like southern California. And you could work

468

in a lawyer's office in San Diego and come home to me and I could learn to cook and cut your toenails.'

He leaned back smugly. 'You do it jolly well,' he said examining his feet.

'You're making jokes. I love the way you say things like "jolly well". It would be wonderful. If we only had a lot of money we could run away together and do it.'

'I've got precisely three thousand and seventy-five dollars,' said George.

'Is that all?' she asked sharply. 'What do you do with your salary? I mean, you don't have to spend a lot here, do you?'

'I support a convent in the hills,' he said. 'It's none of your business.'

She looked unhappy, her face dropping and even managing to form a small double chin. 'I haven't got a personal cent,' she complained. 'I could raise ten thousand dollars if I robbed the household account. Sidney doesn't let me have anything of my own. I can buy what I like but I mustn't have any money. I think it's stingy.'

'Very stingy,' he agreed. 'It stops you running away with somebody else.'

'Stop it,' she sulked. Her eyes revolved, blue and concerned, towards him. He kissed her mouth. 'I know I got myself into this,' she said. 'I was greedy for it all. But now it's nothing. I'd be happier with you in a little beach house.' She glanced up cautiously. 'Not *too* little though.'

'Exactly,' he said. He put an avuncular arm about her shoulders. 'I'd never be able to support you, not *you*. You're used to having too much.'

She backed away. 'Oh, but I'm not. I could economise. I wouldn't have *Harper's* or *Vogue*, I promise.' Her optimism collapsed quickly. 'We'd need money,' she agreed, low-voiced. 'Quite a lot.'

In a sort of vexation she wriggled down under the bedclothes until only her head was visible. She was lightly frowning. He leaned back against the bedhead and looked at his watch. The doberman snored. 'We *could* get it,' she said suddenly. 'We really *could*!' She sat abruptly upright in her bed, her trembling breasts pushing like twin faces from beneath the blankets.

'We're not robbing your husband,' he said firmly.

'Not robbing,' she corrected. 'Just *using*. Listen, you know

469

the dinner next week, Saturday, when all those old bores come along. His business friends. It's a kind of pre-Christmas affair. Every year they come here, all of them tycoons, millionaires and that sort of person. They come to play a game, a dirty game, I always think. They sit around and decide who they are going to *ruin* next year. They can do it, manipulate money around like Monopoly. They buy this and sell that and squeeze here and ease off there. And they just do it for the hell of it.'

'An odd pastime for Christmas,' he said.

'It's awful. I have to sit there. I'm always the only woman. He likes to show me off to them. And I'm not even allowed to speak. Not that I understand much of it. It's when they're drinking the brandy, the liqueurs, and they've got all these papers spread across the table and they start this – playing. They are *so* evil. You should just see their evil faces. They all come up with ideas and put forward figures and that stuff. Then they make a plan, a game plan, and they work it out then and there. It's sick to watch because they laugh and roll about like devils, all over some poor bastard they're going to send to the wall.'

'At home it's called beat-your-neighbour-out-of-doors.'

'Is it? Well, hush. The point is, Loving, they have to build some people up to knock the others down. So they push money into companies, millions of dollars, and force them right up the ladder. They let them stay there for a while, maybe even until next Christmas when they meet again, but then they knock them down. It's just a cruel sort of fun.'

'And your idea is to make use of the information,' he guessed.

'Why not? I've got ears and though Sidney thinks I'm dumb, I'm not dumb. I just note the names of the companies they're going to boost and we take our money, all we've got, say twelve thousand dollars, and we get in *early*. If we get out at the right time we could make a million. I know a guy who's a broker in Dallas. He helped me when my car wouldn't start once. We could use him to do it.'

George leaned back against the headboard. 'It's not bad, Francesca,' he admitted. 'It's not even illegal.'

She leaned against him, stroking his arm with her bosom, her face against his jaw. 'Oh, just think, we could hit the trail. Just like Goodnight and Loving.'

'Bonnie and Clyde,' smiled George.

Twenty-five rich men in twenty-six long, sinister cars came to the dinner at Comanche Mansion. Alder B. Sutterfield, certainly the wealthiest of all, liked to arrive in one car and go home in another.

The cars, all black, were fanned out in front of the house, patrolled by security men and each occupied by its unmoving chauffeur, set as a shadow, throughout the evening while their masters were at the table.

Very few of the rich men enjoyed their food; some had ulcers and other disorders which curtailed their eating, others had no desire for what was on the table apart from the financial data which they had met to ponder. 'Every year,' moaned the cook as the waiters returned with yet another mauled but uneaten course. 'Every year it's the same. Work, work, work for a week, get the dinner all perfect, and then they send it back like it was poison. Every year I say "this lady quitting today".'

'But you're still here,' pointed out George, watching another convoy of trays borne aloft to the dining room.

She regarded him with the scorn only found in a black woman's eyes. 'So they got no taste,' she said. 'The money's good.'

The guests, old, sombrely dressed men, with not a smile between twenty-five faces nor a single softness in the eyes, crowded around the dark oblong table, muttering between themselves, pawing the food and eyeing the glasses with unconcealed suspicion. As he went in and out of the room about his duties George kept his glance away from Francesca. She looked perfect in an emerald gown, modestly sexual, unspeaking and unspoken to, at her husband's flank. The men made comments in grunts across the table usually to the detriment of some distant business rival or about some venture whose doom they were fashioning.

This convocation of the avaricious brought out the brooding worst in Sidney Lennard. He sat spooning his food, pushing it from one part of the plate to another and then onto another plate entirely, like someone shifting commodities. He locked his blue-skinned lips and eyed his guests evilly like a concealed sniper. Francesca sat miserably, also playing at eating. George observed her husband pour her half a glass of claret and then refuse to replenish it. The old man's eyes went to the water jug and she was obliged to continue with that. 'It's not to your benefit,' he whispered gratingly.

After he had served the first round of liqueurs George left the room. The millionaires were preparing for their business game, eyes glistening, hands clenching and unclenching, tongues licking lips in their eagerness to start. Francesca lounged back in her chair, a sulk of disinterest on her face. Sidney Lennard made the opening gambit, the first manoeuvre. George knew little of it for he was only passing to and from the room, softly shutting the door each time.

By ten o'clock the dinner and the game were over. None of the men were staying for they shared a universal fear of shedding their business clothes on alien territory, of even being caught in their pyjamas, perhaps minus their teeth. That would make them vulnerable.

George supervised the helping on of coats as the visitors departed for their purring cars. Alder B. Sutterfield pressed a dollar note into George's hand.

'That's how the bastard got rich,' said Francesca when he slipped to her suite at midnight. 'Generosity is a weakness to those guys.'

'How did you manage?' he asked. They were sitting on her bed, unusually fully clothed. With a touch of sly triumph she took from the sleeve of her dress a slip of paper with a list of names, written in black and all, except three, crossed through in red. 'I even managed to hijack the racecard,' she said. 'The ones cancelled out are the companies which are to be what they refer to as "blitzed". They'll be bombarded, put under so much financial pressure that they'll collapse. The other three are the lucky ones, until next year, because they're going to get the boost.' She read the names slowly: 'Forrester Industries, Penmobiles, Johnson Burt.'

'Do you know anything about them?' he asked.

'Not a thing. I don't understand half of what those people say. And I didn't want to look too interested this time, because I've never shown any interest before. I did what I normally do, look bored, and I got up and left the room a couple of times too. They didn't even notice I'd gone. As far as they're concerned I have the same status as the mustard pot.'

472

George gently took her hands and cupped them in his. 'You want to go on with this, don't you, Francesca?' he said.

Her husky eyes unrolled to his. 'Sure, I do,' she said low-voiced. 'It's a risk, but I don't think it's too much of a risk. Not the way those guys work. Didn't you see how they went away rubbing their dirty hands? They don't lose so there's no reason we should.'

'I'm not even talking about the money, so much,' he said. 'It's the whole thing. You'll be running off with a man twice your age.'

'I'm married to one three times my age,' she pointed out.

'Who's bound to want revenge,' he said. 'He'll be humiliated and he'll be after us.'

She leaned forward and kissed him on the mouth. 'If it's okay with you,' she breathed, 'it's okay with me. I know what I want. You and a million dollars.'

He had already withdrawn his three thousand and seventy five dollars from the bank in Fort Worth, the teller handing it back disdainfully as if it had proved an embarrassment to them. Francesca left for a shopping trip in Dallas, momentarily catching his eye as he escorted her to the car. She returned in the late afternoon and that midnight she told him that it had all gone to their plan. 'The broker, my friend,' she said, 'was not too impressed with the three selections. But I explained that I expected them to do better in the near future. He got the message because he asked me if I would mind him putting a little wager on them as well. I said it was okay by me. Now, dear Loving, all we have to do is wait.'

The wait was not prolonged. Within a week, Forrester Industries, Pen-mobiles and Johnson Burt had gone resoundingly to the wall. None had been in robust health previously but their ends arrived with swift and simultaneous drama, leaving many people without work just before Christmas and Mr Burt, of Johnson Burt, lying spreadeagled on the concrete thirty-one floors below his open office window.

'We,' said George as he realised, 'have been stuffed.'

Francesca was weeping. 'How could it happen?'

'They *made* it happen,' shrugged George. 'Your husband and his cronies. You said they could make anything happen and they did.'

'And I picked up the bait,' she nodded miserably.

'*We* did,' he said. They were meeting in the desert, at Goodnight River Bend, for fear of being observed elsewhere.

'They knew all the time,' she sniffled, putting her face against him. She looked up in alarm. 'Perhaps my room is bugged.'

'Someone like your husband always has means of knowing what is going on,' he said patting her head. 'I bet it's given him his first laugh in years.'

'You'll have to go, Loving,' she whispered decisively. 'I'm sorry about your money.'

'And you will have to stay,' he said flatly.

'I haven't got anywhere else to go,' she said. 'And I can't live without money. I need quite a lot of money to live. I got this for you, by the way. It's all I could get.'

She handed him a ticket and a hundred dollar bill. It was wet from her tears.

'The bus goes at midnight.'

'It's a bus ticket?' He looked at it.

'Trailways to New York,' she confirmed. 'I think the quicker you get your things together and leave Comanche Mansion the better. I'll be sorry to see you go, darling, but there's nothing else left.'

'Will he . . . take it out on you?'

'No. Never. I'll have to juggle the housekeeping account, but he'll still want me around. He'd be afraid I would abandon my principles and leave even without money. I'll just lie low for a while. Maybe I'll cut his toenails for him. I'll be okay.'

'Can we keep in touch?'

'I'll write to you. At the Hilton in New York.'

'I doubt if I'll be there.' He held up the hundred dollar note.

'You can still collect your mail. They won't know.'

It was the last time they ever saw each other. They kissed and then went separate ways. He found that Clifton had already packed most of his belongings for him and that one of the cars was waiting to transport him to Fort Worth. Clifton carried his suitcase down the steps and put it with a shrug in the back of the car. There was a trace of a smirk in the chauffeur's profile. Clifton shook George's hand and said: 'Well, man, you lasted longer than any butler we ever had.'

George got into the car. As it was about to drive away Sidney Lennard staggered to the top of the steps. He motioned for the

474

chauffeur to lower the rear window. When this was done the old, wicked man regarded George and said: 'Asshole.'

As they drove away from Comanche Mansion, George never to return, he remarked to the chauffeur: 'Mr Lennard only ever said two words to me. One when I arrived and one when I left. Both the same word.'

XXIII

From Fort Worth to New York City is a forty-hour journey by bus. George sat towards the back, next to the lavatory: there were many passengers travelling immediately before Christmas. He sat hunched and unhappy, depressed at the thought of not seeing Francesca again and with the realisation that, after all the time and all the miles, he was heading for the last stage of his circumnavigation of the world with only one hundred dollars in his pocket. He had also begun to feel ill.

Fitfully he dozed and watched through the window the dun winter landscape, the bleak eye of water lying on mud, wind tearing at trees; the only comfort the Christmas lights of the towns through which they passed.

At one of these, a brief place the name of which he did not catch, a woman carrying two giant teddy bears, one pink, one green, boarded the bus followed by two thin, fretful children. They sat towards the front, the teddy bears occupying a double seat. When the bus became full there were altercations about the removal of the bears to make way for human passengers. Twice the bus driver was called to intervene, the woman in a crude voice arguing that the children would scream if they were removed. The bears were removed. The children screamed. The bears were replaced. George closed his eyes painfully. He could feel his throat throbbing and he began to shiver.

Every few hours the bus stopped to refresh the passengers and replace the driver. At the first two stops George bought himself coffee and a hamburger in the bus terminal café. After that he did not feel well enough to eat. When late at night the neon sign 'Terminal' showed through the window he was fevered enough to believe it held a double meaning. With a great effort he disembarked to get some coffee, and smiled at the mother and children as he passed, merely a token of comradeship, the acknowledgement that he and they had been aboard longer than any of the other passengers; they were the bus's oldest inhabitants.

'My kids are hungry,' said the woman. Her face, though young, was as coarse as her voice. Her eyes glittered with challenge. Thinking it could only be a conversational remark, in fact unsure in his bemused state that he had heard it right, George smiled politely and went on down the aisle. He was standing in the line at the coffee counter when the two small children crept up to him and pulled at his jacket.

'Mommy says to tell you we're hungry,' said one.

George looked down at the narrow, pallid, tear-wiped faces. Their hair was in knots, their eyes gummy. He could not tell whether they were boys or girls.

George had his only hundred dollar note in his hand. A woman with an ant-eater nose looked at the children and looked at the note. She turned to a shuffling priest who was her neighbour in the line. 'Tell him to buy his kids some food,' she ordered. 'You tell him.'

'They need some food,' said the priest to George. 'Get them something to eat.'

The children regarded George with evil triumph. George, eyeing the long-nostriled woman and the priest balefully, bent and asked the children what they would like. They each had giant hamburgers and french fries, and were only prevented from re-ordering by the call for the coach to depart. George helped the infants aboard. The priest said: 'Suffer little children.'

The mother was still sitting with the two teddy bears. She saw the ketchup smearing on her offsprings' faces and said to George: 'The kids were hungry.'

He felt too feverish to comment. He stumbled back to his dark seat as the bus moved away from the late and empty town. There, mercifully alone, he curled up and dropped into a sleep full of sweat and nightmares. When he awoke the bus was hissing through a rainy dawn across a cold countryside.

He ached everywhere. The sweat had dried inside his clothes. His raw throat throbbed, his chest heaved, his eyes streamed, his temperature towered. He desperately needed a drink. An hour later they ran into a small grey town, a dejected Christmas tree, its illuminations pale, standing in the bus terminal. The day was scarcely light.

477

As he went along the aisle, people stirring, coughing and groaning on either side, the two children raised their bereft faces to him and chorused: 'We're hungry.'

George made a feeble protest to the mother who merely confirmed: 'The kids are hungry.' The nose woman and the priest were regarding him as if they would report his meanness to the authorities.

Leaning towards the woman, shaking from his ague, George said thickly: 'Listen, I haven't got very much money.'

'You had a hundred bucks,' she returned in a low rasp. 'They saw it.'

'But . . . why don't *you* buy them something?'

'That's easy,' she returned. 'Because I haven't got a nickel.'

'Nothing?'

'Nothing till we get home. And then I don't know.'

People were alighting from the bus. 'All right,' sighed George. The children were quickly to the cue and began pushing down the aisle.

The woman looked with a sort of wan defiance at George. 'I'll have some coffee and egg and hash browns,' she said. 'Egg sunny side up. I'll be right over. I have to go to the powder room.'

Stumbling on aching legs from the bus, George swayed to the line at the counter. He bought the children hot dogs and milkshakes, the sight of which made him queasy. He carried his coffee and her egg and hash browns to a table where she was already seated expectantly with the teddy bears.

'Would the bears like something?' asked George.

'Stoopid, they're stuffed,' said one of the children whom he now believed was a girl.

'I know how they feel,' said George to the mother. He put his head in his hands. 'God, I feel terrible. I've got flu or tonsilitis or pneumonia or something.'

The woman was outraged. 'Don't you pass that to my children!' she ordered. 'Why don't you move away?'

Had he felt the least well George would have retorted rudely but he had no strength. He picked up his coffee and drained it. 'They must have cost twenty or thirty dollars,' he said nodding at the toy bears.

'Forty each,' the woman said with grim pride. She straightened the ribbons at the bears' throats.

478

'Couldn't you have bought *one* and saved some money for food?'

She looked amazed. 'But I have *two* little children,' she snarled. 'Don't you know *anything* about little children?'

He gave up and staggered back towards the coach. He crouched in his seat and closed his eyes, squeezing his whole face down inside his collar. At least the inside of the bus was warm. He had perfected a low agonised groan now, which he sounded if anyone showed signs of claiming the seat next to him. At this early hour, however, the bus was only half full. He dropped into another fevered sleep. Three hours later he had another cup of coffee and some aspirin. The children had pizza and ice cream and the mother a plate of prawn balls. Two more hours of driving went by and they stopped again. Apprehensively he opened his eyes. The two children were beside him, holding the green teddy bear between them. For a panicky moment he thought the mother had disembarked, leaving them with him. But she was standing up a few rows forward collecting her belongings.

'Mom says we're leaving now,' said the child he was now almost certain was a girl. Candles were hanging from both their noses. Their eyes were glutinous.

'We hate the people in this bus,' offered the other.

'This,' added the first one, 'we're leaving with you.' She handed him the huge green bear.

'We hate the colour,' said the second.

He had no energy to refuse the gift. The woman did not even glance back but mouthily ushered her children along the aisle, carrying the remaining bear under one arm. 'Let's get off this goddamn thing,' she bawled as they made for the door.

With nausea, pain and weakness oozing through him, George crouched dumbly as the bus continued on its way, the smiling green teddy occupying the entire seat beside him. By now he did not care.

At 7.30 on the black morning of Christmas Eve the bus finally turned into the city terminal in New York. Icy rain rattled the windows as it rolled through the deadened streets. George opened his glued eyes and saw that they had arrived. He felt aching and ill. Shivering uncontrollably he pulled his butler's tailed coat closer about him. His ribs hurt when he breathed.

479

Even the inside of the bus had turned cold in the night and he had taken the coat from his case for extra warmth for it was the nearest thing to an overcoat that he possessed.

He attempted to abandon the green teddy bear on the seat but the driver called as he was manoeuvring down the aisle: 'Hey, mister, you forgot your bear!'

Reluctantly returning, George picked up the huge smirking toy and staggered out of the bus. He felt terrible. Every fibre in him groaned, his head, his ears and his throat were throbbing. Once more he tried to dump the teddy, leaving him on a seat in the terminal only to have a puffing businessman follow him into the rainy street, shouting and hugging the bear. 'Don't forget this fellow,' panted the man. George paused blank-eyed, his shoulders drooping. The man looked at him strangely and said: 'If he goes missing somebody's Christmas is going to be spoiled.'

'Yes, yes, of course,' nodded George. He vaguely reclaimed the great green bear. Oddly its arms went round his neck.

The man, realising there was something amiss with George, backed away. 'Thanks,' he said incongruously. 'Merry Christmas.' He hurried off before George had recovered sufficiently to thank him, so George waved the bear's straw-stuffed paw in his direction. The man turned and saw the bear waving and began to run in a frightened way.

George stood under some shelter from the freezing rain. His legs were trembling. Somewhere he had to find a bed. He had counted his money in the bus. He now had seventy-three dollars. In the early, icy light, it was difficult to see far up the street. He walked a few yards, the rain soaking through his butler's coat, the bear tucked below one arm, his suitcase in the other. God, he felt ill. He felt so dreadful he wanted to drop down where he was and lie there; he would have done so if he had thought anyone might heed him. But the people in the street went past him heads down against the rain. He would probably just remain in the gutter.

The area was near the Port of New York and the streets leading up from the bus terminal contained several indistinct hotels, some with names, others with the single proclamation 'Rooms'. He went into one of these. Behind a desk an unprepossessing man in a thick jersey examined him. There was a

480

loaded cosh in the counter attached to one chain and a German shepherd dog growling in a corner attached to another.

'It's a hundred bucks in advance,' said the man before George could speak. He looked briefly at the teddy bear but made no comment. He had seen everything. 'On account of Christmas,' he added as if giving some sort of blessing.

'I don't have that much,' George told him in a whisper of desperation. 'But I'm ill. I've got pneumonia I think. I must get to bed. Will you take fifty?'

'As a rule it's fifty,' the man said like a consolation. 'But it's a hundred on account of Christmas, like I said.' He studied the teddy bear. 'Maybe you got something to sell.'

'Clothes,' said George. 'And a watch.' He hesitated. 'And this,' he added, nodding at the green encumbrance. 'The bear.'

'Across the street,' directed the man. 'That guy buys anything. It's a hundred bucks. Twenty dollars a day for the room. A hundred in advance. We don't take one-nighters or riff-raff.'

'On account of Christmas,' added George miserably. He dragged himself out into the rain again. The man who would buy anything had a sign above his premises which said: 'I Buy Anything'. Unfortunately, he did not open to buy anything until nine o'clock, so George went back to the bus terminal, found the cafeteria and bought a cardboard container of coffee. He sat with his hands round the container for half an hour and then, on the principle of being hung for a sheep, he bought another. The teddy sat upright in the seat next to him and people kept saying: 'Now look at that bear, will you? Did you ever see anything so cute as that bear?' George's eyes streamed and his whole frame shook. He began to wonder how long he could stay conscious.

At nine he went out into the rain again. It was thicker and icier. The man who bought anything was late that day and George had to wait under an awning like a waterfall, hoping to God that the man had not decided to take a holiday because of Christmas Eve. Eventually, to his huge relief, there came a rattling of bolts and chains from inside and the door swung open. The shop was hung with Christmas streamers but the proprietor's expression was lacking. 'Too late,' he said before George had a moment to speak. People in this area interrupted first. 'Maybe last week I'd have bought the bear, but it's too late. Come back next year.'

'I won't be alive next year,' forecast George confidently. The man examined his condition and apparently agreed. 'I've got a watch,' said George. He held out a shaking wrist.

'Take it off,' said the buying man brusquely.

George did so and handed it to him. 'You ain't got AIDS have you?' asked the man suspiciously, looking closely at his red and streaming eyes.

'No,' George assured him. 'I could just do with a little, that's all.'

'A little what?' asked the man absent-mindedly turning the watch over.

'Aid,' said George. He spread one hand. 'It was just a joke.'

'Yeah, I get it. The watch is worth ten dollars.'

'But I paid . . .'

'I told you what it's *worth*. What's that coat you're wearing?'

George put down the bear and got out of his coat. 'It's a butler's coat,' he said. 'I've got the trousers, the pants, too. And some shirts.'

'Let's see,' said the proprietor. He tested the material of the coat. Eagerly George opened his suitcase, causing half the clothes to tumble out. 'That's more like it,' said the man. 'Maybe we can do business.'

'How much for the lot?' challenged George, indicating the case's entire contents. 'I need a hundred dollars.'

The man lit a cigar and began turning over George's clothes, the sports sweater he had bought in Fort Worth, the tracksuit in which he had crept to seduce Francesca, his pyjamas and paisley dressing gown.

'Difficult size,' grumbled the man. 'Where's the butler's pants?'

George held them up. 'Two pairs,' he said.

'Only one coat?'

'Only one. They're expensive. I need a hundred dollars.'

'Sixty,' said the man. 'Best I can do.'

'This lot is worth hundreds,' muttered George. He did not want to upset the dealer. 'If I don't get a hundred I might as well have nothing. I need a bed.'

'I can sell you a bed,' said the man looking up.

'A hundred,' said George desperately ignoring the remark. 'All or nothing. I'll throw the teddy bear in as well.'

'It's a funny colour,' grumbled the man. 'Whoever heard of a

482

green bear.' He sighed as though the world was becoming too heavy for him. 'Okay, okay,' he said. 'Just because it's Christmas. A hundred.'

The money was in ten dollar notes. George trembled as he took them. All he wanted was a bed. He shivered so much he could hardly step into the road. His ribs felt as if they had been hammered. He heaved each time he breathed. Only the rain cooled him. As he crossed the road in the thick freezing downpour his eye was taken by a red neon sign that abruptly jumped to life. 'Liquor' it proclaimed simply. Forcing his steps to turn that way he went into the store and bought a bottle of bourbon and a bottle of aspirin.

The black man behind the counter eyed him dolefully. 'What you doin' for Christmas?' he asked. 'Goin' to kill yourself?'

George took the aspirin packet and the whisky. 'I think God's going to do it for me,' he said.

Throughout the rest of Christmas Eve, through Christmas Day and for three days after, George lay in the small and ugly room. At the window sagged black curtains, with a channel of dirty daylight down the centre.

There was a doorless closet, a frail chair, and the iron bed into which he so gratefully submerged himself. The bed jingled when he shivered and the room's only source of warmth, a single struggling radiator, sometimes rattled to accompany his cough.

When he had first opened the door and turned on the single dusty bulb the bed was before him, and, poor as it was, he regarded it hungrily. It was clothed with a few layers of rough blankets, two sheets hard as cardboard and a solitary pillow. Groaning he had taken off his top clothes, thrown them aside and burrowed below the covers wearing his shirt, socks and underwear. The blankets touched him like a blessing. He had taken three aspirins, a long swig from the bourbon bottle, and pulled the bedclothes over his head.

He lost all feeling of time. Sleep came and went, sweat oozed from his body; he had processions of nightmares. Several times he forced himself from the bed and went to the clanging lavatory along the corridor, drinking the water from a tap above a bucket as he had once done in Delhi. The bottle of bourbon lasted him two days for he slept long between drinks taken straight from the neck. Each time, the drink was preceded by two or three aspirins. Once, when he left the bed to visit the lavatory, he looked from his grim window on his return, sweeping a channel in the interior dust and looking through the gauze of the dirt outside to the coagulated lights of the city.

He was scarcely aware of a sound. It was as though this narrow room was severed from the world. Once someone stamped up the stairs almost outside his door and once he thought he had been wakened by a police siren from the street, but that was all he heard of Christmas.

On what he believed must be the third evening, he awoke feeling cooler but lightheaded. The bourbon bottle was empty as a blind eye and he did not relish taking the aspirins without. He swilled his face under the tap in the lavatory, peered down the dusty stairs and returned to his bed. The sheets were damp with his perspiration so he took them off and lay back between the coarse blankets which were sheltering more life than his own. He then fell back to sleep and did not awake until rain was beating on the window the following day.

Having been entirely overlooked during New York's seasonal celebrations George was amazed when a timid knock came on his door and a fat woman entered at his invitation. Her jaws worked incessantly as if they housed a small engine that provided her motive power. 'That guy across the street,' she began when she was just inside the door, standing at the bottom of the bed. He confronted her over the edge of the blankets. She held out something. 'That guy, he says he found this in the pocket of the coat you sold.' It was a dollar note.

Strangely George immediately realised what it was, remembered the day it was handed to him by the careful Alder B. Sutterfield as he left the infamous dinner at Comanche Mansion.

'Thank you,' he said hesitating but then leaning from the bed and taking it. She regarded him with curiosity and pity.

'Ain't much,' she said. 'But I never did hear of that man giving anything back before.'

'Christmas, I expect,' ventured George.

'You been in here all the time?' she asked. 'All through?'

'For four days,' he nodded. 'I've been feeling ill.'

'You look it,' she said. 'You want some chicken soup?'

'Oh, please,' whispered George. It seemed that her plump
484

grey dress and blue apron had been turned for a moment into the raiment of an angel. 'I've had nothing since I got here.'

'He would let you die, Balaskos,' she said nodding savagely over her shoulder in the direction of the stairs. 'As long as he got his money. Why should he care? He's gone off and I'm in charge here now. I'll get you some chicken soup.'

She went away, the jaw revving as if to provide extra power. George got up, went along the corridor to the lavatory and washed his face below the tap again. There was a mirror, a cobweb of cracks radiating from its centre. He took it out on the landing where the light was less dim and examined what he could see of himself in it. Between the breaks he saw fragments of a ghostly face, white flesh, black holes where he remembered his eyes. He returned shakily to his bed.

The lady appeared quickly with some lavish chicken soup and he ate it greedily. She was a Jewish woman whose family came from Holland. Her name was Vanderpump and she sat on the frail chair and observed him eating with manifest satisfaction. Unprovoked she began to tell him the story of her family. It went on interminably. It was the most uninteresting tale of any immigrant family that has ever been related. George leaned back on the pillow waiting for something to happen in the narrative. His eyes closed. He began to slide down into the bed.

'Look at you, you must be tired,' she acknowledged. 'I'll tell you what happened next . . . well, some more . . . later. You ought to rest now. I'll bring you some more chicken soup tonight.'

George dropped into a profound sleep once more, grateful for the bed's warmth, ragged though it was. His chest still ached when he breathed but the fever had abated. When early darkness came over the city he saw the lights brushing the window. Mrs Vanderpump returned with a further consignment of excellent soup, and sat down at his bedside to continue her family story.

Even she recognised that it had elements of monotony, because she kept promising more interesting episodes shortly. 'I have never said this much to anybody before,' she confided and George thought this was undoubtedly true. He was the perfect captive audience.

Long into the evening she continued. George feigned sleep in the hope that she would go away, but she continued, apparently content to hear the story herself. He opened his eyes and she was still in the thick of it, her sister in Detroit, her uncle who had almost been struck by a streetcar – one of the more exciting episodes – and how they had once lost little Ben on Jones Beach. 'But we found him again,' she said with a tinge of regret.

Not until it was late did she rise. She had pressed her wide posterior to the light chair for so long that it adhered to her as she stood up. She pulled it away like someone unsticking a stamp from a letter. 'Tomorrow,' she promised, 'I'll tell you about the Vanderpump hardware store in Elizabeth, New Jersey. And maybe I bring you some whisky. I know where Balaskos hides it. And the rest of the chicken soup.'

For two further days the situation continued. She brought the food and the drink but he was required to listen to more of her family's story. George thought it was impossible that *any* immigrant family could have lived through so many mundane experiences. There were no pogroms, no deportations, no suffering, no poverty, no riches. All her father remembered about Ellis Island was that they had met a nice family from the next Dutch village. She continued to victual him, incanting 'Wish you better' at every initial mouthful and she asked for no reward other than his attention to her tale.

'Hello, Felicity?'

'George. You've reversed the charges.'

'I know. I'm sorry, Felicity, but I *had* to ring you and I haven't got a bean. I've been desperately ill. All over Christmas, stuck in a crummy hotel. I thought I was going to die.'

'Oh dear.'

'I had pleurisy or pneumonia, I swear. I'm very weak now.'

'Something always seems to spoil your Christmas, George. If you're not in prison you're in bed.'

'Oh, please, not now. You must realise how difficult it is for me to do this, to ask you this. But I must have some money. I want to come home.'

'I'm not sure I ought to encourage you to do that.'

'I mean, home as in England, not Shillington. I promise I won't bother you, Felicity.'

'You do sound terrible. Is it cold there?'

486

'Freezing. I'm sorry about the collect call.'

'For God's sake stop cringing, George. If there's anything worse than you being drunk, bossy and abusive, it's you being apologetic. How much do you want?'

'Would five hundred pounds be all right?'

'Yes, I suppose so. But I want it in writing and I want a receipt. In a few months we have a divorce coming up, remember? We'll have to share out the spoils, such as they are, anyway. I don't mind you having an advance on your bit.'

'God, thanks, Felicity. You're a sport. I can't tell you how bad I've been. And in one filthy room. How is Tina? How was your Christmas?'

'Tina went to her schoolmate's house at Bournemouth and I went to Switzerland with a friend.'

'That must have been wonderful.'

'It was. Now is that everything, George? I'm paying for this call remember.'

'Yes, but one thing. I need the money quickly. I've got enough for three days, at a pinch. The lady is letting me owe for my room until the owner gets back.'

'There's always a lady who will help, isn't there?'

'It's not at all like that. I just have to listen to her family saga. It's like *A Thousand And One Nights* in reverse. If I listen she gives me soup. But will you send the money right away, please, Felicity? I'll send off a letter today asking for it but I'd be grateful if you didn't wait to receive that.'

'All right. Where shall I send it? To this hovel?'

'No, you'd better not. I don't trust Balaskos.'

'I wouldn't either.'

'No, Mrs Vanderpump is all right but not Balaskos. Send it . . . send it . . . where do I know? Ah, yes, send it to the New York Hilton, will you? I can pick it up from there.'

On New Year's Eve George walked unsteadily into the lavish lobby of the New York Hilton to be quickly intercepted by a security man. The greeting was peremptory: 'Where ya goin', bud?'

George looked down at his grimy appearance, his clothes twisted, his chin hung with whiskers (his razor had been in his hurriedly-sold suitcase). He tried to rearrange his matted hair.

487

Lamely smiling through untidy teeth, he said: 'I was just going to see if there were any letters for me.'

'The thing you just came through was a door,' said the man nodding in the appropriate direction. 'That's the way you go out.'

George regarded the man with truculence. 'You can't stop me . . .' he began. The man could. With an unseen twist of his hand he caught George's wrist and turned it behind him with such technique that George found he could not struggle and that his protest was reduced to a squeak which failed to raise a single eye in the busy lobby. Because of the restriction he had to move on the balls of his feet, slightly bent forward, so that it appeared that he was tiptoeing from the place. He was almost at the door when a voice he recognised before it had completed the sentence said: 'No need for that, old boy. I can vouch for this gentleman.'

Still holding George's wrist the security guard turned, making George totter round also, like a dainty horse learning a trick routine. They were confronted with Burtenshaw.

He was dressed in a heavy woolly overcoat with a flamboyant bow tie that lounged from the front. 'This is Mr George Goodnight, the eminent British lawyer,' he said. He thrust out his hand: 'How are you, George?'

The hand George tentatively projected was the one the security man had held in his spiteful pinch and there was no strength in it. The man now began saluting profusely, mumbling as he backed away. George regarded him unkindly.

'I never thought I'd have to be grateful to you for anything,' he said to Burtenshaw.

The journalist laughed without sound. 'You saved me once, old boy. Now we're all square. Come and have a drink.'

'Felicity told you,' muttered George as they walked towards the bar. No one else apparently noticed that George looked like a vagabond. The bar waiter, however, guided them to a hideaway seat normally reserved for lovers. George asked for a gin and tonic.

'You look terrible,' said Burtenshaw studying him. 'Ghastly.'

'Thanks. I'm a picture of health compared to last week. Felicity has sent the letter, I suppose. You wouldn't be lurking here for me to collect it otherwise.'

488

'I understand that she has done so,' acknowledged Burtenshaw. 'It is, in fact, waiting for you at the desk. I checked.'

'You've got my interests very close to your heart, haven't you?' said George. 'Still.'

The drinks arrived and Burtenshaw said: 'Cheers. Happy New Year, old man.'

George mumbled an indistinct wish. The gin and tonic was delicious. It ran cool and sharp down inside him like a mountain waterfall. He got through it quickly.

'I wouldn't mind another of those,' he said, eyeing Burtenshaw. 'It's all on expenses, I imagine.'

'Naturally.' Burtenshaw beckoned the waiter who looked at the vanished double gin with a touch of surprise. 'You can always charge for two. The way to make a profit, however, is to buy only one. But this is a special occasion.'

'You still want to write this story,' said George wearily. 'I've told you I'm not interested. What's happened to me is mine, it's private.'

'You look as if you could use the money,' suggested the journalist. 'I'm authorised to offer you twenty thousand pounds, five thousand now, five when I've finished the interviews, and ten on publication.'

'It's private,' repeated George. 'Nobody could understand it. It would look ridiculous, preposterous. These things only happen if you go halfway to meet them.'

'That's a wonderful line for a start,' enthused the reporter. 'You could tell a tale, George. Every job-stuck, home-stuck, wife-stuck, kids-stuck man would be jealous.'

'Half the working population might leave,' suggested George.

'It might solve unemployment,' said Burtenshaw.

The second drink arrived and George now sipped it. 'Listen, Burtenshaw,' he said. 'You're a good chap, you do your job as well as you've ever done it, but unfortunately I don't want you to do it with me. The answer is still no.'

The other Englishman's face tightened. 'You mean bastard,' he said grinding his teeth. 'I follow you, I help you out . . .'

'Wait a minute,' George cautioned. 'I didn't ask you to play the Christmas fairy, mate. I'm through the worst bit. And as for helping people out, you could be a pile of dingo-gnawed bones upon Ayers Rock if it hadn't been for me. Just remember that.'

'How far is five hundred quid going to get you?' demanded Burtenshaw. George had never seen him rattled before.

'As far as the next corner, perhaps,' said George. 'But what happens round that corner, who knows? Anyway, I'm going home.'

'To do what? You've poisoned yourself, Goodnight. Professionally and privately. Felicity doesn't want you. What woman or firm would want you now? You're hardly reliable and you're forty-five.'

George nodded agreeably. 'You're right, I've got rid of the old reliability. Frankly, I don't know what I'll do, or what I want to do. Maybe I'll keep moving, George Goodnight the Flying Dutchman, the Wanderer, Hoffman of the Tales.' The drink had made him feel a little lightheaded. He leaned forward: 'What shall I tell you, tales marvellous tales . . .' he recited.

Burtenshaw stared at him: 'We could call it that,' he said hoarsely. 'What a title! See, you've already provided the title . . . "The marvellous tales of George Goodnight."'

George finished the gin and stood up. 'And that's all I'm going to provide,' he said. 'Thanks for the drinks, old chap.'

'Damn you,' said Burtenshaw angrily. 'You're such an awkward bastard, Goodnight. Always were. It's just because you don't like me. It's personal, isn't it?'

'You've put your finger on it,' said George. 'I was always jealous of you, Burtenshaw. I'm not now.'

'I'll write it,' threatened the journalist. 'I'll write it anyway, without you. I've got enough stuff, believe me. Bags of it. And I can ferret the rest out. I'll make you a hero despite yourself.'

Softly George laughed. 'You do that,' he said. 'Let's see how much you can get right. Did you know I went looking for buried treasure in the Antarctic? Have a good time, pal, and watch the libels. Remember, I'm pretty hot on libel.'

He stood up, dodged the potted plant which had concealed them, and went across the main concourse of the lobby. At the reception desk he produced his passport and asked for his mail.

'Which room number, sir?' asked the clerk doubtfully eyeing him.

'I haven't checked in,' said George evenly. 'I intended to do so but I changed my plans.' He turned round. Burtenshaw was still standing by the potted plant. 'That gentleman over there, Mr Burtenshaw . . .'

490

'Oh, yes, Mr Burtenshaw, sir. We know him.'

'He can vouch for me.'

'Oh, that's correct, sir. He asked if you had any mail.' The man reached into a pigeon hole in the desk. 'Let's see. Mr George Goodnight.' He handed up the letter. 'And Mr George Goodnight.' He held up another.

George looked at the second letter. It was postmarked Fort Worth, Texas. He smiled wanly and opened the first. In it was a cheque for five hundred pounds with a simple message in pencil, 'U.O.ME £500.' For the first time in five years, he thought affectionately of Felicity. Then he opened the second letter. There was almost as brief a note from Francesca. 'I'm okay. Love you for ever. The enclosed came for you.' Also inside was a letter with an Australian stamp. It was from Ollie, written, he guessed, by Linda. There was also a cheque for thirty thousand Australian dollars.

'Dear George,' said the letter. 'Linda and I were married on October 6th, and we're very happy. Clemmie did not make it. She changed her mind. Charlie was upset but he's gone up to Darwin and got another job. My settlement was two hundred and fifty thousand dollars, thanks to you. My mum cried so loud in court they had to throw her out. I enclose a cheque for twenty-five thousand for your professional advice and services. The solicitor said that this was right and fair, so don't argue. The other five thousand is for my half of our trip and the motorbike . . .'

George found tears filling his eyes. There was a lot more of the letter but he thought he would save it until he got to his room. He looked up at the clerk. 'I think I'd like to check in now, if you please,' he smiled.

For a week he lay in the extravagant bed, his meals and drinks borne to him, the first snowflakes of the New York year rocking beautifully past his high window. Every few hours he got up and stood at the glass to see it filling up the city below. He enjoyed the indulgence of sending a message for a doctor who diagnosed that he had pleurisy but that the worst was over. 'You should have called me earlier,' he said as he fussed in his bag. He sniffed approvingly about him: 'It's just good that you got yourself somewhere cosy to be sick. This is not a bad place to suffer.'

George began to eat well again. He called Ollie in Alice Springs and spoke to Clemmie who sounded weepy. 'I ran away.' He could hear her sniffling from seven thousand miles away. 'I couldn't face it in the end. Poor Charlie was wrecked. He had a new suit too. My heart wasn't in it, that's all.'

Ollie was full of excitement. The camels were all fine and he hoped Linda would not try riding them when she was expecting their baby. His mother had arrived in The Alice but was now longing for her back street in Sydney, just as she had longed for a remote England from Australia. Homesickness was her vice. George thanked him for the cheque. 'You saved my life,' he said and told him briefly why.

'You saved mine, George,' said Ollie seriously. 'I owed you that.'

Each day George had the leisure to read the *New York Times* from the first word to the last. It was an item on the final page which caught his special notice. It was as brief as anything in the paper, a small boxed advertisement which said: 'Stamp Auction: The second auction of the Joby Stamp Collection from France will be held on January 15th, at Carrington Rooms, 2393, Third Avenue, New York. Jarrold Pike Inc., Auctioneers, 1876, Lexington Avenue, New York.'

He immediately telephoned. 'Oh yes, sir,' said the man. 'The first part of the collection was sold in October. We got some record prices, I'm proud to say. Would you like me to mail you a catalogue?'

George instructed him to send it by messenger and it arrived within an hour. He sat in the Hilton bed and turned the pages slowly. Pictures from the past were there before his reflective eyes. There were some of the stamps he had so carefully and with such quiet enjoyment catalogued at the Villa La Manche a year and a half before, when Janine was there and he was there with her. Page after page he turned. The Rose Victoria from the Gold Coast, the fine pair of British Columbia, the set of four Tasmania. His head dropped and he closed his eyes. That was the brief time when he had been happiest in his travels, in his life.

He telephoned the auctioneers again but a distancing voice informed him that no further information was available, only that the stamps were being sold on behalf of the Joby family. If he cared to reserve a place at the auction that could be done right away.

George said he would. He thought of telephoning Monsieur Benoit in Paris but decided against it. He spent the next week enjoying the luxury of New York in winter, not even leaving the hotel until the day before the auction when he walked with care along Sixth Avenue in the icy sunshine. After ten minutes, although he was wearing a new overcoat purchased on his behalf by the Hilton hall porter, he returned to his room, stretched out on a deep chair, poured himself a drink and agreeably turned to the excitements of afternoon television. He wondered whether he ought to afford himself the satisfaction of buying back his watch and his clothes, but he decided not.

The following day he took a taxi to the Carrington Auction Rooms on Third Avenue. The stamp sale was in a tall pale green and white room with oval windows. Outside it was snowing again. The chairs, lined facing the rostrum and on either side, were already mostly taken by people in heavy coats, bowing over catalogues, mumbling like monks. There were two opened doors leading into two aisles between the chairs. George took his catalogue and sat on one of the chairs set at the side. He had studied the numbered lots minutely during his days of inactivity, playing a guessing game as to how much each item might achieve.

He realised that he was out of touch and, in any case, the majority of the items in the catalogue were from the general, confused, part of the Joby collection which must have been collated after he had left Cherbourg. There were only a dozen lots taken from the fine collection of British Possessions which he had catalogued during his days at La Manche.

The room was just short of full when the auctioneer, a precise, short man in a morning jacket, arrived and with few preliminaries began the bidding. Bids were conducted almost in secret, it seemed, in a code of flicked eyebrows, crooked fingers and imperceptible scowls. George could see little of the business from his place, although the prices were affording the auctioneer some satisfaction. It occurred to him that perhaps Monsieur Benoit might have sent a representative, or perhaps even made the journey himself. It was possible, now he considered it, that one of the Joby family might even be present. He began to look carefully about him.

Then he saw her.

She had just come into the room. A man made space for her and she sat on the end of a row on the opposite wall. It was all apparent, the small profile, the profound face, the calm eyes, the slight frame. His breath caught. Janine Joby's lost daughter.

Immediately George wanted to get up and go across the room to her. The auctioneer's incantation went on. 'One hundred and fifty, one seventy, one hundred and eighty dollars . . . two hundred.' George, tingling inside, could not take his eyes from her. She was wearing a dark blue coat. There were still snowflakes on the shoulders. Around her head she had worn a silk scarf but now she took this off and shook her hair. The same hair. Her deep eyes were in the direction of the auctioneer.

Incapable of sitting immobile for a moment longer, George mumbled excuses to his neighbours and, bowed low, made for the back of the room. This was not easily done without some disturbance because of his size, his inherent clumsiness and the bulk of his overcoat. The auctioneer fussily stopped the bidding while George was on his way, saying in a thin voice, 'Now we may proceed,' once George had gone through one door. A moment later he appeared at the second door, still at a crouch, and proceeded to move in the opposite direction to that which had taken him up the complementary aisle. The impatient auctioneer stemmed the bidding again and said: 'We'll get going when the war games quit.'

Flushed and breathless George looked up. But now he was almost there. One of the people who had turned to look at him with curiosity was Janine's daughter. 'Miss Joby?' he asked.

'That's me,' she replied. She regarded the crouching man with a little amusement. He recognised the look.

'I am so sorry about this,' he said hoarsely. 'But I need to speak to you. Urgently. I knew your mother.'

The young woman's face straightened. She left her chair and George stood. He glanced apologetically at the purse-lipped auctioneer. He made way for the young woman and they left the room together. As they went out the auctioneer's nasal voice followed them: 'Now the introductions have been made, maybe we can proceed.'

In the corridor outside, George faced her. She examined him quizzically.

'You knew my mother?' she said.

494

'Very well,' he said. There was a long seat in the corridor below a painting. 'Let's sit down,' he said. 'Please. I recognised you the moment I looked at you. My name is George Goodnight.'

'How long ago?' she asked. Her voice was American. 'When did you know her?'

'Just before she died,' he said. 'I was . . . I was very close to her. I promised her I would try and find you.'

At once tears came to her eyes. 'She died,' she said, 'and she wanted to find me?'

'Very much,' he told her. 'I went to the house at Paddington in Sydney where you lived with the Vaughans.'

Astonishment crossed her face.

'I saw the swing you used to swing on,' he smiled. 'And I went to Koora near Darwin, the wooden house. And I've asked after you in many places. And now here you are. I was so overcome when I saw you.'

'Can we walk outside?' she said. 'It's stopped snowing, I think.'

He understood. They went out of the building. The snow had ceased but it was thick and soft underfoot. There was a small park, little more than a garden with a few skeletal New York trees, a frozen fountain and a snowy bench. 'She really wanted to find me,' she sighed.

'She had no idea what had happened to you. She . . . I . . . don't even know your name.'

'Christine,' she said her eyes on the snow as they walked. 'I still use the name Vaughan. It was only after my father . . . well, Stuart Vaughan, died that I came to find out that I was not his daughter. He would never have told me. Even then, and maybe this sounds crazy but it's what happened, even then I was not anxious, not over-anxious, to find out about my past. Maybe I was afraid of it. I didn't want it intruding. I have a life of my own now, I'm just about to be married.'

'I understand,' nodded George. 'But it mattered a great deal to your mother. She had tried to find you over the years. Her father, your grandfather . . .'

'He gave me away. I know that much from Stuart's papers. It was a shock to me, I can tell you. But when I came from Los Angeles to New York after he died, I guess it all faded and I didn't think it was too important. It happened a long time ago.'

'How did you come to be here today?' he asked. They stopped in the snow and he spontaneously held out his hands to her. Hers came slowly forward and took them.

'I knew my real name was Joby and that the family was French. But it's not an uncommon name in France. The man I thought of as my father, Stuart Vaughan, was always connected to the philately business. A friend who knew a man who knew Stuart Vaughan through the stamp business called me a few months ago and told me that a Joby collection of stamps was coming for auction in New York. That was the first part of the sale in October. I came and I sat and listened and I asked a few questions. But I didn't do anything. I guess I was still backing off. So I came today.'

George said: 'I would have recognised you anywhere.' They walked a few more paces. 'I think you must get in touch with the Joby lawyers. You come from quite a wealthy family, you know,' he said.

She smiled, Janine's quiet smile again. 'Thank you, Mr Goodnight,' she said. 'It was good of you. Very good. But I'm not after anything.'

'As for me,' he shrugged. 'I'm just glad I've found you.'

Air France Flight 070 from New York to Paris landed on time at Charles de Gaulle. The European mornings were growing a little lighter. Monsieur Benoit was waiting for George and his car was outside the airport.

'I cannot believe how you discovered her,' said the lawyer shaking his head as they drove along the autoroute to the city.

'I looked up and there she was,' said George.

'After all your journey.' He smiled at George. 'You look well, *monsieur*. You have had a good time in the world?'

'In parts,' said George. 'It has been varied, to say the least. Now, I don't know how to stop it.'

The Frenchman nodded. 'Ah, yes. I understand. It is like a runner. He must keep running.' He moved his eyes sideways. 'Are you prepared for another little assignment?'

George was startled. 'Now? I was on my way home.'

'But uncertain about arriving there,' pointed out Monsieur Benoit. 'Anxious.'

'Backing off,' said George. He remembered Christine had said that. 'I feel I won't know where to go, who to see, if

496

anybody. I don't have many friends. I was too lazy. I can't just walk the streets. There's a chap at Leighton Buzzard but apart from my stepdaughter I wouldn't think there'll be a lot of flags put out for me. The only certainty is my looming divorce.'

'Then what I am going to suggest will give you a pause, a little time to prepare yourself for your invasion of England,' said the lawyer smiling. 'And I think it is of interest to you. It concerns the Joby stamps.'

'I see. You want me to sort out the rest of the collection.'

'Exactly. Monsieur Julien can be of some help to you. He is too old to carry out such a performance and he would be overjoyed to see you. The family have decided to keep the house for the summers. How long the work would take I cannot tell. Only you would calculate that.'

'Two months, three months, if I remember the state of things,' said George doubtfully. 'And remember I only really have a good knowledge of British stamps and I'm a bit out of date with those. Who organised the stamps for the New York sale?'

'A Paris company,' said Benoit with a grimace. 'But it was very expensive and Monsieur Julien was not happy with the way they went around it.' He paused and then said: 'How do you think?'

'Where is Janine buried?' he asked.

'She was cremated. The family wish. Her ashes were scattered to the wind at La Manche.'

George nodded sadly. He knew how hard it would be. It would mean going to the house again, where he and Janine had been together. He saw himself with her, eating, talking, walking by the sea, and standing that day by the shaded river not far from the very place they were passing in Benoit's car at that moment.

'Yes,' he said slowly. 'I would be pleased to do it.'

XXIV

Above the January Channel stood the sturdy house, scudding clouds flinging brief shadows across it. There were a few minutes of sun. Monsieur Julien had suggested that George went there at first alone. George walked the hill and went into the courtyard. Everything was as it had been, except now it was winter and she was not there. Some small branches had been blown from the bent courtyard trees onto the gravel and he picked them up and removed them to the wall at the side. The door was opened by the ancient Henri who showed no recognition but merely bowed. In the shadows was the grumbling old woman servant. As if they had long rehearsed their parts they withdrew at once and he was alone.

Twigs of wintry sun came through the windows as he stood sadly, remembering the patterns of a summer's day. Everywhere was clean and echoing. The room where they lived together, happy in each other's company, the bedroom where they had lain embracing through the nights. He stood at the door, looking in at the bed, his heart full, and walked in and touched the counterpane. On the dressing table was a single photograph and he went to it; even at a distance it struck a memory. It was Janine and him standing by the Cherbourg quay, taken by Marie from the Hotel Bismarck. George picked it up, his throat full. She was smiling, the seashore wind disturbing her hair. They had been holding hands. Gently he kissed her.

He went downstairs again. The place was hollow, nothing touched, nothing moved, only winter sunrays moving like fingers over the floors. He stepped through the rooms and although they were furnished they seemed to echo. He went down to the annexe where the stamps were stored. Many of the drawers were still occupied with envelopes, packets and albums. He picked up a few at random and studied them in the dimness. Again the pale sun broke the shredded clouds outside and cut in at the window where he used to sit at his task. He went to

498

the place and stood in the cold beam, looking out over the curling grey waters of the Channel.

George knew that he would not be able to work there, not in that place of echoes. He went back to the hall, looked about him and, as Henri appeared, walked out. He strode purposefully over the courtyard and with the wind behind him almost ran down the hill towards the roofs of the town.

He had been staying at the Villa Bismarck and now he returned there thoughtfully. Coming back, he told himself, as he lay on his bed in the same room as he had occupied before, had been a mistake. It saddened him beyond anything he had ever known. The past, as Mr Mullinski had chaotically put it, was passé.

Monsieur Julien came to dinner that evening and George suggested having the stamps brought from the house to the town. Marie had plenty of spare room. They could work on them, a section at a time, in the parlour of the hotel, for it was the deserted time of the year.

With Benoit's agreement over the telephone the stamps were brought to the Villa Bismarck. The collation and cataloguing took almost three months, with George working at the parlour table six hours a day and Monsieur Julien helping sporadically.

When the task was finished George told the old Frenchman that he was going home to England the next day. He had to face it sometime. He sailed on the noon ferry from Cherbourg to Plymouth, for some fancy, a little more procrastination, had made him decide to retrace his early steps. There was no hurry. Nobody eagerly awaited him.

Marie had a few minutes' weep and her father, who still wandered the town cursing the occupying Boche, came to the harbour wall to wave with his absent arm. Monsieur Julien also walked to the ferry gangway and George sensed there was something the Frenchman had been wanting to tell him.

'Wolfgang, you understand,' Monsieur Julien said at the last moment, 'Wolfgang lived for three days after the motor accident. Marie and I went to see him in the hospital near to Paris. He told us that on that day Madamoiselle Joby had told him to drive to this place by the river that she liked to visit.'

'I remember it,' said George. 'I went there with her.'

'It was not a happy matter. Wolfgang had been there before, when he was a German soldier here. Twelve French men and women, of the Resistance, had been taken there and executed by shooting. And it was because of Janine's father that this happened. He was a traitor, you see, an informer for the Germans.'

Slowly George shook his head. 'And she believed it was a happy place. He was some father, her father. And Wolfgang told her this?'

'*Oui, monsieur.* In the hospital he told us that, of course, he had known for ever, for years, since the Occupation, what Monsieur Joby had done, but he had kept it secret. The war was over. Now, when they went back to this place, he was overcome for he remembered it very well. The women had been shot as well. And so he told her about her father. He was a good man, Wolfgang, and he would not intend to injure her. Perhaps he should have been silent. But he was not. When the motor accident happened, only a few minutes later, they both had their eyes full of tears. All for something so long ago.'

At eight that evening the ferry docked at Plymouth and he stepped ashore in England going at once to the boarding house kept by the stoker's widow. There was a new photograph on the wall, a different sailor with different biceps; the landlady had remarried while he had been away. The whole world was changing.

The notion of returning by the same route, retracing his steps, appealed to him for reasons of romanticism, acclimatisation, and indecision. If he had gone straight to Shillington, which he still imagined as home, his eventual but tentative objective, he would have undoubtedly been required to leave again after a fairly short interval. Where then would he go? To Fred Birch at Leighton Buzzard?

What he was planning was hardly brave, almost as hesitant and devious as his running away, which he preferred to think of now as his escape. Here he was, almost two years later, going back but slowly, prepared to give himself up if anyone would civilly accept his surrender. He tried to tell the landlady, after supper, of some of his travels but he was in the wrong house. She had scarcely been beyond Plymouth but, through her husbands, and various others it appeared, she had journeyed everywhere. There was no story of his that could not be matched and bettered by her Charlie or her Horace. George

500

lay in bed, again looking at the same ceiling, listening to the Plymouth Sound wind, and knowing that to return from an epic was often, and certainly in his case, to return to indifference. He thought of Cecil and Annie Meredith, deep in their wholesale groceries in Wolverhampton, and wondered where John, Joe and Donald were sailing that night.

The following day was Wednesday, a light spring morning, and he knew there would be a bus from Warminster to Somerbourne Magna, taking people home from the market. He caught the London train and got out at Warminster station. While awaiting the bus he bought the local newspaper. Plans for the carnival were again afoot and there were excitements over the diversity of the floats and proposed quality of the carnival queen. 'The experience of the past two carnivals,' the journal hoped ominously, 'will, it is trusted, not be repeated this year.' George wondered what he had missed the previous summer while he was in the leper colony in the Philippines. Melksham man had been found drunk again, although there were no additional circumstances mentioned. This time he had merely been found and had not been incapable, disorderly or indecent. There was also to be a sale of effects.

The bus drew up in the market square, 'Somerbourne Magna' displayed above the cab, and he was among the first to board it. Apparently the driver had keener eyes than the other occupants. "Ello there!' he exclaimed with West Country cheeriness as George paid for his ticket. "Aven't seen you around for a couple of weeks.'

Since his last journey they had renewed the plastic covering to the seats but enough time had elasped for it to split again. He sat at the back and listened to the talk of the village people; people who had never been to, perhaps never heard of, The Alice or Cedunna City, and who did not care. Eventually a ripe-faced woman with a woollen scarf gagging her ears turned, abruptly, as if it were his turn. 'You know that Molly, don't you?' she said. 'At the Red Cow?'

Slowly George admitted he did. Several neighbouring women now revolved in their squeaky seats, as much as their bodies, bulky coats and shopping baskets would permit, and studied him.

'Got married two weeks last Saturday,' said the first woman.

'Lance Onions?' asked George.

'Him,' she confirmed as though she were disappointed that he guessed correctly. 'And never before time either.'

''Cepting his name's not Lance,' put in another woman. ''Twas Cecil or something wa'n't it?'

'From Somerset,' said a third gossip accusatively.

'How is Bert?' asked George seeking to steer away from Molly.

'Gettin' smaller, I reckon,' said the middle woman. ''E can 'ardly look across the bar now.'

The others laughed with crass jollity.

''E got disappointed,' put in the first. 'When that whatser-name . . .'

'Mrs Thingy.'

''Er with that 'orse and trap, 'cept the 'orse died.'

'Ah, 'er. She went off and married the vicar. Just like that. They took a church hike up to Somerbourne 'ill and 'e proposed to 'er up there, so they reckon.'

'While they were looking at Salisbury Cathedral spire,' suggested George.

'That was supposed to be what it was for, the church hike. Wanted to see it with the sun going down behind, so they said.'

'It's the wrong direction,' said George a little sternly. 'The sun goes down in the west. Salisbury's south-east.'

The three women looked at each other as though he had mentioned the infallible. 'Is it now?' said the first woman, her face crammed with thought.

'They don' bother with things like that around these parts,' said her friend dismissively.

His pedantry seemed to have put him out of order as far as they were concerned because almost as one they turned away from him and began gossiping among themselves. From his window George watched the spring fields of Wessex, new pale corn, crops, poetic meadows, lying below the undecided sun. Red roofs lay between greening trees. Sheep and cattle and arched horses browsed the fields; the sky over them laden with bulky yellow clouds. George still felt like a stranger in a strange land.

His apprehension multiplied as they neared Somerbourne Magna. He was last off the bus at the churchyard, where there were two new graves piled with tulips and daffodils and one bright, unweathered tombstone. Rooks were noisily nesting in the elms. With his **single** suitcase he walked down the tight and twisting street towards the Red Cow.

It was now late afternoon and the inn door was locked. Familiarly he went round the side, through the garden gate. Molly's face was framed in the kitchen window where she was standing at the sink. She looked up from the soap suds and saw him looking in at her. She screamed vividly and rushed back out of sight.

'Molly, Molly,' he called moving to the kitchen door and calling at the crack. 'It's all right. It's me.'

He heard the bolts on the door being manoeuvred, he thought to open it. But when he tried it he realised it had been barred. A quarter of Molly's face appeared at the side window and stared at him in one-eyed horror. Then she vanished. He stood haplessly.

He could hear her shouting within the walls. Sitting on the garden seat he waited until the bolts were withdrawn again and Bert stood there. He was undoubtedly smaller. 'You come for your suit?' the innkeeper inquired. 'Molly's just gone to get it from where it's hid.'

'Thank you,' sniffed George, polite but offended.

'Can't be 'elped,' Bert told him with truthful sorrow. 'Lance wouldn't like you 'ere. Lance gets violent.'

'Still?' said George.

At that moment the aperture was widened and Molly stood behind her father, holding his original suit on a hanger. Even though she tried to conceal herself behind Bert he was slight enough for George to see she was enormously pregnant. Her face was puffed and her hair rankly dyed. ''Ere it is,' she said nervously handing the suit forward. 'Thought you was never coming for it. I 'ad to keep it 'id.'

'Thank you,' said George, again politely. He took the suit. 'Sorry to have troubled you. I was not worried about the suit. I came to see you.'

'Lance is upstairs, asleep,' she warned in a whisper. 'Driving off tonight.'

'Wick?' he inquired.

'Wick,' she confirmed.

'It's the furthest 'e ever goes, north,' put in Bert. They were patently anxious to shut the door. George sighed his disappointment and, thanking them again sadly, he turned away. Standing in the small village, holding a suitcase and a suit, he realised he was stranded and once more with nowhere to go. He looked up over the blossoming fruit trees in the tangled back garden. The roofs of the motorway service area were showing above the rim of the hill. With a shrug he began to go that way.

He was not altogether surprised to see the deckchair in which he had rested that far Sunday afternoon had not shifted its place. It had probably never been moved. The previous autumn's dead leaves were held in its lap. He tugged at the faded canvas and emptied them out. The stream kept up its unheeded conversation. It was fuller and almost covered the stepping stones. Balancing with his case and his suit he went carefully across.

The early evening was spread golden. The clouds stayed aloft but the sun had dropped beneath them and shone wide with gentle rays.

He walked up the long-flanked hill, through high spring grass and rampant flowers. The April breeze brushed his face and pushed at his hair. The roofs of the service area began to grow. He reached the top and turned to look down on the hamlet below, Somerbourne Magna, and the meadow that had been the first steps of his long journey through the world. Its roofs were aslant among fresh trees, the carpet of the flowered field tumbling down from below his feet. He could clearly hear the clatter of the brook. He sighed, turned again and went through the gate in the hedge towards the motorway.

He was relieved to see that Ben's vegetable garden had become a reality. Echelons of carrots, lettuces and peas were patterned out. There was a glass cold frame and compost heap steaming like a small Vesuvius. Something had worked.

Ben was on the forecourt, still hobbling, walking back towards the pay kiosk. George called to him and he looked up as if unable to remember. Then his face changed and he limped forward brightly. 'It's been months,' he said shaking George's eagerly offered hand. 'Where you been? Not in Westbury all this time?'

George laughed a trifle and said: 'A bit further. Don't tell me somebody's run over the toes again.'

'Same thing,' said Ben. 'Two years ago now, near enough.'

504

He remembered that clearly. 'Never get better now,' he said. 'The bones went wrong.'

George said he was sorry to hear it. 'Can I stay?' he asked. 'One night. I'll rent a car tomorrow and drive to London or wherever.'

'In the motel? Aye. There's plenty of room. My wife runs it now.'

George felt at last pleased. 'Ah, everything's all right there now is it?'

Ben looked puzzled, then alarmed. 'Oh, no, not *that* one. Not 'er. You've been gone longer than I reckoned. No, that one came off the back of the boy's motorbike. She was never happy though. I'm married again now. She's a bit on the plump side but she's kind. Go on over and she'll show you the room.'

Ben began to count some money in his hand as if its value might have diminished during the distraction. George turned moodily and walked towards the motel, his fears confirmed, his heart heavy. There was nobody for him to know; he was scarcely remembered and where he was remembered he was no longer welcome.

'Birch Associates, Leighton Buzzard.'

'Fred, it's George.'

'George? Oh, George. Good God, George, I'd forgotten all about you.'

'Most people have. I'm back in England.'

'Ah, the wanderer returns. Where are you? When are we going to see you?'

'I'm on the motorway. At the Somerbourne Magna service area. I'm staying here. In fact I was wondering if I could come and stay with you for a few days, Fred. It's not a matter of money but . . . well, I just don't seem to *know* anybody here. I can't think where to go.'

'Sorry, old boy, can't be done. I'm still living in the same place as my office. That's why I'm still here at this time of day. There's no room. And anyway the fiancée comes round every evening and . . .'

'The fiancée! Yours? Your divorce shot through quickly, Fred.'

'Well, it hasn't actually happened yet. This lady is my fiancée-to-be, as it were. Prospective.'

'Putative.'

'Yes, if you say so . . . She's very nice, George, and I'd like you to meet her once we've got a bigger place. She owns a boutique in Luton. A few years ago she was Miss Letchworth.'

'Well, you seem to have sorted out all your problems, Fred.'

'It certainly seems like it. Funny how things work out. I've joined the tennis club and everything.'

'You'll be having a lawn to mow next.'

'Oh yes, I expect so. Anyway, George, keep in touch. Let me know when you're settled in. We'll get together and have a laugh about old times.'

'Quite a few laughs. All right, Fred. See you then.'

'All right, George. Hope you get off the motorway.'

'Tina? Hello lovely, it's George.'

'Good gracious, George! Just a moment . . . I'll be one moment only . . . Right, here I am, back. I had to tell Fenella Walcot something. And here comes Debbie Danby . . . Hold on.'

'I'll ring back if you like. When you're not busy.'

'No. Hold on, George, will you. Be a dear . . . This won't take a moment . . . There now, I'm back. I'm organising the Hop you see and I'm fixing up partners, dates, with boys from Benson's School.'

'There's money in that sort of thing.'

'You're wicked, George. Where are you, by the way?'

'I *am* by the way, actually. By the motorway.'

'You're back! In England. How wonderful. Why are you by the motorway? Have you broken down?'

'No, but I'm getting fairly close to it. I'm staying at the service area motel. It's the only place that feels like home.'

'Poor George. Feeling sorry for yourself. You'll soon be sorted out, I expect. Are you going to see Mummy?'

'Yes, I thought I might go up to Shillington. Perhaps tomorrow. How is she?'

'Busy, busy, busy. She's got her hooks into her boss.'

'I thought he was happily married.'

'He was.'

'Oh, I see. Well, I hope she can spare me a few minutes. I'd like to come and see you, Tina. How about Saturday?'

'Darling, I can't. I've just told you, it's the Hop. It's frightfully important and I'm on the committee. And there's

506

this boy at Benson's. God, you should see him, George. He looks just like Sting. And he's got it for me. I'm drooly about him. George. I'd like to have his children.'

'Christ, steady on! You're not even sixteen yet!'

'Not long though. I could have a child this time next year.'

'Stop talking rubbish, Tina.'

'It's not rubbish, George. It's life. How would you know?'

'All right, Tina. I didn't telephone you to have our first quarrel.'

'Sorry, George. Some things are serious.'

'Of course they are. In different ways. How's the trade union movement?'

'I've had to give that the elbow. There wasn't room for it. It's passé anyway.'

'The past is. How about Sunday then? Or the following weekend?'

'Sunday is no good, George. The sixth-form girls are going to Benson's for tea. A sort of thank you for the Hop. And next weekend we're going to Wales on a field study. The boys will be coming too. We're going to sleep in tents. Separately of course.'

'You seem to be pretty full up until the end of the year.'

'Don't be cruel, George. I haven't heard a toot from you for months. Mummy said you were dying in New York but she thought you were over the worst of it. Then you turn up like this. If you'd given me some notice . . . oh, now I've started to snivel. My mascara is getting all gunged.'

'All right, Tina, I'm sorry. I should have realised. We'll arrange something soon.'

'Very soon, George. Keep in touch, won't you?'

'I will. Goodbye, Tina, love.'

'Goodbye, George.'

'Oh, hello, Felicity. It's George.'

'Ah, home safe and sound, are we?'

'Yes we are. You don't sound surprised.'

'Well, I knew you had to turn up sometime. Where exactly are you?'

'Somerbourne Magna . . .'

'Oh yes, the Red Cow, if I remember. How is she?'

'I'm at the motorway motel. I wondered if we could get

together. We'll have to talk about things. Perhaps I could take you out to dinner or something.'

'Not even the something, George, I'm afraid. I'm just off to Minorca. Tomorrow morning. On business.'

'With the boss?'

'Yes, as a matter of fact, Mr Gangler is coming too.'

'Has a lot of business in Minorca, does he? Promotion, exploitation, publicity. It must be very big there.'

'I don't like the tone of what you are saying. But, in any event, what you may think or say is of no concern of mine, George Goodnight. You wanted adventure, now enjoy it. Three months and the divorce will be through and we can have our share-out. Yours less five hundred pounds.'

'You got my receipt, I take it.'

'Yes, thank you. It's in the file.'

'I could drive up this evening. Perhaps we could just have a drink together.'

'I'm not thirsty, George. I'll be back in a week or so. Why don't you ring me then?'

'All right, Felicity. Have a good time. Love to Mr Dangler.'

'Gangler.'

On top of it all the cafeteria food had deteriorated. George ate a listless dinner of sausage, egg and chips. Even as he cut the sausage a glazed rigor mortis appeared on its skin. The bread had a curly brim, the butter was liquifying, and the tea cool and mysterious. The waitress was not. He finished, wiped his mouth temperamentally and walked out onto the service area forecourt. In the middle of the broad April evening, a cuckoo sounding with distant clarity and with only light traffic on the road, he found Benny in concerned conversation with the driver of a truck and trailer. Wearing orange overalls, the driver sat on the step of his cab. Even sitting down he was tall. His face was tall also, one of the longest George had ever seen, and featured a wild moustache.

George wished them a pleasant evening and Benny waylaid him. 'This is Walter Fanshawe, Mr Goodnight.'

The man stood in sections, like a hydraulic machine. When he shook hands his arm swung like a cable. 'Call me Fanny,' he invited lugubriously. 'Everybody else does. Fanny Fanshawe.'

'Walter's got a problem,' said Benny. 'He's carrying eels.'

508

For a moment George thought this might be some parasitic illness, like worms, and stared sympathetically at the tall skinny man. But Fanshawe patted the side of his vehicle and said: 'Millions and millions of them. Baby eels. Elvers they call them.'

'They come from the River Severn,' said Benny.

'Only at this time of the year,' put in Fanshawe.

'And Walter takes them abroad.'

'All over,' said Fanshawe spreading his enormously long arms. 'Moscow, Turkey, Rumania. Everywhere where they like eels. They puts them in tanks and feeds them up until they're huge . . .' His arms spread further. 'And then they eats them. This cargo's worth a fortune.'

'What's the problem?' asked George. 'Hijacking?'

Fanshawe emitted a little dry laugh, more like a cough, which mildly disturbed his overhung moustache.

'His mate's not turned up,' said Benny. 'He's ready to go across to the Continent and his mate hasn't come. He's rung the bloke's wife but she reckons he's gone up north to play snooker.'

'You can't depend on anybody today,' complained Fanshawe. ''arwich, 'ook of 'olland tonight, I've got to be on that ferry.' He patted the cargo again and listened as if he expected the baby eels to respond. 'Time is of the hessence.'

'You lose the eels?' suggested George.

'The bonus,' corrected Fanshawe. He appeared to be looking into the distance. ''Ave you got your passport with you?' he asked innocently.

'Me? Yes . . . but . . .' The familiar realisation came quickly. 'But I couldn't drive one of these. I'd need a licence . . .'

Benny said impatiently, 'You don't need to drive it. You just have to sit with him.'

'I fall asleep by myself,' confessed Fanshawe. 'I didn't used to, but I do now. I'm all right if there's somebody with me to talk to me. My boss will fly somebody out to Germany or somewhere to take over from you. But I can't get 'old of 'im now on the phone. I've tried. You can come back then, if you want. But I've got to get on the move tonight. My boss will make it worth your while.'

Slowly, George turned towards Benny.

'It's easy,' said Benny. 'You reckoned you wanted to travel.

Hanging around Westbury and Devizes isn't travelling, is it? Now's your chance. Sit and talk, that's all you've got to do. Tell him a few tales.'

'Tales, marvellous tales,' muttered George. He felt inside his jacket. His passport was there. 'Where's the final destination?'

The long man in the orange overalls looked at him hopefully. 'Istanbul,' he said.